THE BLACKGUARD'S BOND

THE BLACKGUARD'S BOND

Book II of The Bard's Heresy

Justin D. Bello

ISBN 13 (Print): 979-8-9900597-4-0
ISBN 13 (Digital): 979-8-9900597-5-7

The following work of fiction is set in a fantastic, but quasi-historical world, and contains graphic violence that is intended for mature audiences. Readers should be advised that much of the mature content is based upon realistic situations that were part of an extremely violent period of human history. Potentially disturbing scenes include vivid descriptions of battle, blood and gore, murder, torture, implied sexual assault, and violence involving animals.

To all those fighting to hold back the darkness
without hope of recognition or reward.

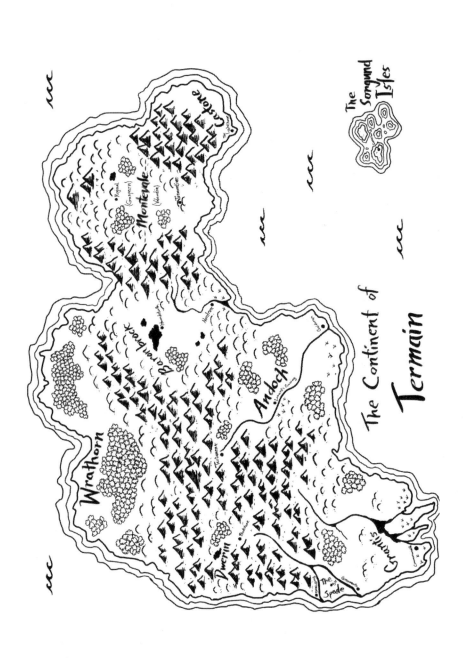

The Continent of Termain

The Songund Isles

TABLE OF CONTENTS

PROLOGUE

Dandon Rood was troubled. It had been eight months and more since the Council of Five had convened, and in that time, not only had one of the councilors been replaced, but somehow their number had grown by two. There were seven now that sat around the table of the council chamber, and three of them were not even men of the Order.

King Kredor II still held symbolic command of the meeting from his seat at the head of the table, and on his left sat the three traditional councilors, Rordan Baird the Chancellor, Hagan Shawn the Hierophant, and Rood himself, the Warlord. However, opposite them, to the King's right, Natharis Tainne formally occupied the role of the Loremaster, and he was now joined by Alvin Bemis, "Speaker of the Council of Lords and Commander of the Lords' Private Levies," as well as Lord Marcel Pryce newly dubbed "Viceroy of Grantis in the name of the Guardian-King" (though what he and his son were still doing in Andoch was beyond understanding to Warlord Rood). Not one of them could claim actual membership in the Order of the Guardians, yet somehow they would now have a controlling voice in the Order's mission and affairs.

Behind each councilor stood a chosen steward who was often considered the "spiritual successor" to his master, and in many cases, at least among the Guardians, the boy to stand as steward would one day fill the council seat, anointed under the title of his former master. The Warlord smiled inwardly thinking of the great stir it caused when Hobart, the Wrathorn Foundling, was chosen to attend the old Loremaster rather than some foppish lad of noble birth. The Chancellor could hardly look at him for fear, and the Hierophant, even when sober, seemed unable to remember the big man's name. It gave the pair of them some small consolation at least to know that since Hob was already anointed under one title, he would be unable to ever to assume the role of councilor. *No more than would this bastard Tainne,* Rood thought as he drained his goblet, *Thank the Brethren.*

"Warlord Rood," King Kredor said suddenly, "Do you have anything else to add?"

The Warlord sat up straighter in his chair and cleared his throat, "In regards to what, your majesty?" He no longer had patience for polite talk around a table, especially when he knew very well it was all simply an elaborate farce. Kredor would do what he wanted and bugger anyone who disagreed with him. If only he had not been such a coward; if only he had stood with Rastis when he had the chance.

"Remind him, Paddock," Kredor smiled.

To Rood's left, a small man dressed in red and white motley sat at the foot of the table. Kredor had found him as a replacement for the sons of dead Lord Vendik, his former wards. The one was lost during the King's hunt last autumn, gored to death by a boar. The other simply disappeared—the same day, coincidentally, as the Loremaster's former steward. *The weasel-faced boy. The one who replaced Hob.* The Warlord pushed those memories away.

With an elaborate flourish, the small man hopped up upon his stool. "Despite the surrender of the senate, Grantis teems with unrest," he piped, gesticulating passionately as he spoke, "Viceroy Pryce suggested that the kingsmen stationed there remain behind under his command to keep the peace while the armies of Dwerin withdraw to the Spade."

"Very good, Paddock," the King said with amusement, "At least *you* were listening."

Dandon Rood ignored the slight, "I see no problem with this, sire. Would you have me recall my commanders from their commissions then?"

2

Kredor looked to the viceroy, "Marcel?"

Lord Pryce smiled with false benevolence and the Warlord marveled at the resemblance between father and son. Ever since Rood relieved the former partisan of his stewardship, he had been expecting some redress from the powerful noble family, especially after Pryce the elder was named Viceroy with Pryce the younger to serve as his steward. Only then did the Warlord realize that *this* was their redress, *this* was their retribution—that while Rood may have found the young Pryce's conduct unbecoming and unworthy, the family's influence and wealth was such that they could simply circumvent such inconvenient notions as honor and merit. Still, on the positive side of things, the viceroy did at least withdraw his son from the Order. *Another blessing!* Rood thought, *There are enough anointed scoundrels these days. No need for any more!*

"It was my hope," Pryce began while his son leered behind him, "That the officers could remain behind under *my* command to serve as captains for the guardsmen."

"My apologies, my lord," the Warlord said, "But these are men of rank, anointed with Guardian titles. They are justiciars and cavaliers—field commanders, elite soldiers. They command soldiers, not citizens. Besides, maintaining law and order is the jurisdiction of the Chancellor."

"My constables are all too busy hunting Rastis's Blackguards or trying to track down that thief of a steward who stole *The Book of Histories*," Rordan Baird said, "Surely your men can organize a duty roster or oversee a patrol?"

The Warlord sighed and rubbed unconsciously at the stubble already sprouting from his heavy jaw. This was a dirty job; for in the wake of the war, the bountiful harvests of Grantis had been taken as spoils to be gorged upon by the soldiers of Andoch and Dwerin while the conquered farmers were left to starve. Overseeing the unrest that resulted from such treatment was not work fit for honorable men. "Your majesty, these officers of mine are men of great honor and lineage," he said, "The Stone, The Hart, The Spur—they are men of legend. They're spoken of in song! I hardly think it fitting to place them in the roles of...politicians."

"I do not need them to debate the finer points of justice, my good Warlord," Pryce said, "I merely need them to command the peace. I doubt your men are unfamiliar with the notion of martial law?"

Rood cast his glance around the table, but found himself alone and without support. Justice, he supposed, for his own silence months before.

King Kredor refilled his goblet with wine. "Come, come, good man," he said, "Don't look so sour. I'm sure your boys will be out of the city and back in the field soon enough." He took a sip from his glass, "What else, then? What's next on the docket, Paddock?"

The little man glanced down at the roll of parchment before him. "Word from King Dermont of Montevale!" the little man piped.

"Isn't he amusing?" Kredor grinned to the other Councilors, "He even reads!" He shook his head fondly at the jester, "So what is the word from Dermont? And since when is he king? I thought his father still lived?"

"Dermont celebrated his coronation on the first of Beartide during the Feast of the Awakening," the Chancellor said, "King Cedric abdicated, your majesty."

"Well, I'll abdicate Dermont if he thinks he can hold onto the title of king for very much longer. At least Marius had the good sense to call himself the 'regent.' I suppose this is the price we pay for betting on the wrong horse!"

The small man giggled with laughter and shook his arms vigorously to indicate to the others at the table that they should do the same.

The Warlord drank from his glass to avoid having to feign appreciation of the King's wit. The jester was a vulgarity and an even greater violation to the solemnity of the chamber than the new Councilors. How the little man could endure such demeaning treatment was beyond the old soldier. He shook his head and sighed. The news of Marcus Harding's death had stung Rood deeply. Harding was a good friend, a scholar, and a damn fine soldier—a rare combination, and one the Warlord himself could not claim. True, in spite of his age, Rood's skill with a blade had never rusted; however, outside of battle tactics and stratagems, he had no head for study so he had nothing but respect for those who did. He simply preferred to leave the learning to his friends, though it seemed he was lacking more and more in that regard as well.

The King sipped his goblet. "So, what does Dermont say?"

Rordan Baird touched the tips of his fingers together when he spoke, "Only that he prays there will be no ill feeling between Andoch and Montevale in the coming years. In fact, he hopes that—since it is his own brother who gallant Sir Harding Anointed as the new Tower—he hopes that we will count each other as friends. He also suggests that…if it should pass that your highness sees fit to seek consolidation of authority among the realms…"

"Please, man, speak plainly," Kredor sighed.

The Chancellor nodded, "He claims he will support your call for the Protectorate, as long as he be permitted to remain as your loyal governor in Montevale. As a show of good faith, he has sent a gift of twelve white destriers as well as…" Baird paused to clear his throat, "A rather exorbitant sum of gold…"

Kredor leaned forward onto his elbow, "Does he now?"

"Montevalen cavalry is second to none," Lord Tainne observed mildly, "They would make a grand addition to any army, and if clad in armor from the foundries of Dwerin…"

The king nodded slowly, "The horsemen share a border with the Broken as well, don't they?"

"They do," Tainne said, "Through the Nivanus Pass. Grantis failed to win a war on two fronts, should the Barons prove…disagreeable…" he allowed the rest of his words to remain unsaid.

"Your majesty," the Chancellor spoke up, "There is more. King— Prince—er…Lord Dermont has two requests."

"Ah, there's the rub," Kredor said, "What does the horse boy want?"

"Well," the Chancellor unrolled a parchment and read, "First, he asks that his brother, Beledain Tremont, now the Tower, be permitted to render his Oath of Fealty in writing rather than in person so that he may continue to aid in solidifying the peace in the reunited land. I have it here."

Kredor exchanged a glance with Lord Tainne. The acting Loremaster quickly perused the document and gave a nod.

"Fine. I suppose he can keep his brother," the King said, "Besides, if he betrays us, we can always claim he went Blackguard and take it as an excuse to ride on Montevale."

The Warlord stared into his goblet. *Will he not even attempt to mask his ambitions anymore, or does he care that little for honor?* A quick glance at the jester offered an answer.

"What's the second request?"

The Chancellor glanced at Hagan Shawn, sitting in silence with eyes closed at the King's left. "It appears that this matter might also concern you, my lord Hierophant," Baird said rather louder.

Hagan Shawn opened his eyes and reached for his goblet. "I am listening," he said.

Baird's eyes darted over the parchment. "It is the opinion of Lord Dermont," he said, "That in order to ensure that a lasting peace is secure and that the War of the Horses remains a thing of the past, he should take to wife the Princess Marina, sole surviving child of Marius, the White Horse."

"Ah!" Kredor said, "The one who declined our offer of a visit. As far as I'm concerned Kredor may have her as he likes," he eyed Lord Tainne muttering, "Saves me from having to smell her."

"As you wish, sire. However, your options grow few," Tainne returned.

"We achieve our ends, Tainney, and my options extend to every girl on the continent." Though every word of their publicly private conversation was heard, the king raised his voice to carry across the chamber, "A horse girl for a horse boy! They can raise a stable of foals and let them trot around their castle! The court could even call bets!"

Again, the little man set to giggling.

"Indeed, sire," the Chancellor said, "however, there is a…concern…"

Kredor pursed his lips. "Yes?"

"It seems that in brokering the peace, Marius granted custody of his daughter to the Tower, or at least, to the one who bears the title."

"I still fail to see how this concerns us?"

"The issue, my lord," the Chancellor continued, "Has to do with the rules established by the Church of the Kinship defining the legal requirements for marriage."

Alvin Bemis, Speaker for the Lords, nodded, "I believe the matter is one of consanguinity then."

"No, thankfully. Five generations have passed since the war began, and the girl is of age—I believe she's eighteen or nineteen or some such, enough to be a mother many times over. In any case, that is not the problem," Baird said, "No, the matter in this case is one of consent."

"The girl does not wish to marry him?" the Warlord asked.

"That's neither here nor there," Lord Bemis said, "It's Marius, I assume, who refuses to give consent."

"Yes," the Chancellor nodded, "He abjectly refuses, or he would if he were not...confined. However, some of his more loyal nobles during the war have raised complaints against any form of match without consent."

Kredor shook his head in confusion, "But you said that Marius gave over his rights to the Tower?"

"Yes, he and his daughter have become...wards, shall we say? In the custody of the Lord Beledain, and as the Tower is a member of the Order, Lord Dermont claims it is the Council who must offer consent."

"He cannot just have his brother do it?"

"Lord Dermont did not wish it to appear that he was trying to undermine either the rules of the Kinship or the chain of command among the Order. He begs a document avowing to our consent so as to appease any who might question the legality of the union," the Chancellor sighed, "For this he has also sent a *second* large sum of gold."

Kredor sat back in his chair and folded his arms. "I think I'm beginning to like this Dermont," he smirked, "What say you, Lord Hierophant?"

Hagan Shawn took a sip from his goblet and then reverently folded his hands upon the table. "I see no reason why not," he said, "I ask myself, would the Kinship do likewise? Does one Brother ask another Brother's permission? No, he asks the Father, and in like manner, so too does Prince Dermont ask permission of the Father of all Sovereigns—namely, the Guardian-King. Perhaps the Montevalens have learned their lessons after a century of war and are ready to return to the embrace of the Church? I see no reason to hinder them."

"You'll draft it yourself, then?" the King asked, "In religious matters, none would question the word of the Grand Hierophant."

Hagan Shawn nodded gravely, "I shall have one of my celebrants write something up and I will sign it with my own hand."

"Very good," Kredor said impatiently, "Anything else, Paddock, my little toad?"

"The Archduchess of Dwerin writes again to thank you for your hospitality during her visit and she prays that your royal highness will do her the honor of attending her wedding to Sheriff Beinn come Harvestide."

"Lady's teat!" the King sighed, "Why would I ever want to do that? We'll not be able to have the same fun with the bloody Sheriff around."

"I apologize, you majesty," Lord Tainne said, "But I have already accepted on your behalf."

"Why?" Kredor shrugged with annoyance, "I hardly have need for either of them anymore. Darren Beinn made such a mess of his own damned realm after his brothers died that Rordan had to send half his clerks to keep the mines in working order. Thank the Brethren that Padraig Reid's no fool. Had he not held the Spade long enough for Bemis's levies to arrive, things might have very easily gone a different way!"

"I believe it would be the political thing to do. Besides, Darren claims they were murdered by the same Blackguard that absconded with Josephine's daughter. They deserve our sympathy, not our criticism," Tainne sighed, "If Blackstone was to pull its support—"

"Then we'd either smash them like we did the Senate, or burn out the new fields we won them in the Spade and let them starve!"

Lord Tainne's pale blue eyes flashed, yet his voice remained as impassive as ever, "It will be hard to claim an empire with all your allies in revolt, and even harder to govern."

At length, Kredor sighed, "Very well. Send Josephine a note of thanks for her…note of thanks—and add something about it being a lovely time or some such," he snorted, "For there were a few of those, after all. The Archduchess is a practiced hand at pleasing…conversation."

"And the wedding?"

Kredor sighed, "Invite Josephine to hold the ceremony here. Hagan can preside over it himself and it will save us all the journey over the mountains. They can't bloody well refuse an offer like that, can they? To be wed by the Grand Hierophant himself?"

"I will write to the Archduchess at once, your majesty," Hagan Shawn said.

"Good," the King said, "Let them come to us. Bloody Dwerin. Hideous countryside. Nothing but forges, foundries, and fools."

Dandon Rood folded his hands upon his lap. *How far we have fallen without you, Rastis. How far indeed! I only hope whatever you were up to sets things right…*

"Anything else, Paddock?"

"That ends the agenda!" the little man sang.

"About time," the King said, "Then for the sake of the bloody Kinship, I call this meeting adjourned. Now, be off!"

With a sigh, the Warlord rose to his feet alongside the other Councilors and remained standing while the King and his jingling jester hurried away. Behind Rood, his new steward, Galen Pine, stood at attention, proudly carrying Duty, the Warlord's ancient great sword. Galen had been a partisan assigned as standard bearer to Richard Cormier, known as the Hart, but had been injured defending the King's standard when a Grantisi cohort breached the Andochan line. According to Sir Richard, the young man was but one of five left when the Hart himself finally arrived with more men to heal the breech. Even now, the young man's wounds still pained him and he would walk with a limp for the rest of his life. Yet, he had stood strong while the rest of the kingsmen around him had fled. That was courage, the Warlord reflected, that was honor, and that was what the Guardians were meant to stand for.

"Alright there, Galen?" the Warlord asked.

"Yes, sir."

"Quite a heavy blade, isn't it?"

"Not for me, sir," the young man said, "It's as light as a feather for the pride I feel every time I lift it, my lord."

"Good," Dandon Rood smiled kindly, "I feel the same."

CHAPTER 1: THE BROCK

Geoffrey made his way through the crowded streets of the Hounton Quarter, tired but content after another day of honest work. For nearly two weeks he had helped Cousin Delmar and Cousin Glenn, monks of the Monastery of St. Golan the Ram, prepare their stall for the influx of pilgrims that flocked to the city of Galadin every year for the Feast of St. Aiden on the 15th of Suntide. In the small courtyard below the Cathedral of St. Aiden, beneath the statue of the Brother Perindal, they had constructed a small pavilion where they might best serve the Kinship's faithful with their art: the thick, dark ale known by some as St. Golan's Feast and by others as The Ram's Reward.

Geoffrey first met the two men one morning when he was visiting the cathedral himself and spied them down the lane struggling beneath the weight of a great hogshead of ale. He rushed to help them and before long, he had unloaded their whole oxcart. Grateful for the farmer's strength, the monks offered him a wage for assisting them through the end of the festival season. It was not much, but it was work, and good work at that, helping the country cousins.

There wasn't much need for a farmhand in the city, so he took to hiring himself out as a strong pair of arms and a stronger back; however, among the rich merchants hiring day laborers at their warehouses around the city, Geoffrey knew that he stood out as a foreigner, an outsider. As a non-native to the Brock, his way of speaking and his appearance were more in line with the folk of Grantis, or even Kord, nations historically known to be at odds with Baronbrock's traditional allies in Andoch. It wasn't that people became unfriendly or unkind, but from time to time, Geoffrey sensed it gave them pause, made them hesitate. Of course, whether this was actually the case or the result of finding himself in a new land after four decades of living in the same small village, he was uncertain; however, he didn't like it, particularly since many of the merchants he sought employment from were foreigners themselves—from Andoch, to Dwerin, to Montevale.

Still, the vast majority of the native folk of Galadin, and the monks of St. Golan's in particular, knew no such prejudice or fear. Geoffrey liked them and liked working for them. It felt good to earn a living by his own two hands again. It returned his sense of pride, and it alleviated some of the guilt he felt every time they hocked another piece of Brigid's jewelry.

"You're home early," Annabel smiled as he walked in through the door of the small house they rented. She was sitting in the front room spinning wool into yarn, a service the landlord, a weaver called Faden, offered in exchange for a small reduction in their monthly tenement fees. "Is everything alright?"

Geoffrey smiled and kissed her on the brow. "Fine," he said, "So fine, the cousins fear they might run out. Delmar's gone back to the monastery to fetch another few barrels while Glenn sees to the stall and assists their abbot. Apparently, he's come to town on some business with the Baron. Either way, they won't much need me the next two, three days or so."

"So I'm to have you underfoot again, eh?"

"Looks like," Geoffrey smiled. He kissed her again and stretched his back, "Where are the children?"

"Upstairs," she said, "Anyway, I've got a stew on for supper, just so you know. It'll be ready soon enough."

"Why'd you make a stew on the first day of summer?" Geoffrey teased, "They call it Suntide for a reason. No wonder it's so hot in here."

"Go hungry then," Annabel returned, "Or better yet, seeing as you'll be home the next few days, you can do the cooking. I've got plenty of work to do here."

"Alright, alright," he grinned, "Hot stew in hot weather it is. You'll hear no more complaints from me."

Annabel raised an eyebrow, "I doubt that." She finished her spool and, with a sigh, stood up and crossed the room to return Geoffrey's kisses. "Come on, you," she said, "We'll eat as soon as Brigid returns."

Geoffrey's brow furrowed as he followed his wife up the stairs. "So she's gone out again, eh? Did she say where?"

Annabel sighed, "I shouldn't have said anything." She led the way into the hall to where Fredrick and Greta sat on the floor, and passed on into the kitchen. "You're father's home, children."

"Daddy!" Greta squealed, running over to him.

Geoffrey lifted her lightly in his arms and tossed her high into the air. "There's my little lady," he smiled, "What did you do today? Did you help your mother with her stew?"

"You'd best watch yourself, Geoffrey of Pyle," Annabel threatened from the kitchen.

"I've been playing with my new doll," Greta said, "Her name is Cora."

Geoffrey took the little rag doll from his daughter's hands and looked it over. "Where did you get this?" he asked, "I thought your doll got eaten by the neighbor's dog."

"It did," Greta said, "But Brigid got me this one."

"Brigid got you this one?" Geoffrey repeated. He looked down at the floor where his son lay stretched out over an old book about herbs and poultices that once belonged to Cousin Martin in Pyle. It was one of the few things salvaged after the chapel fire. "And what about you now?" Geoffrey remarked, "Too busy to say hello to your da?"

"Hello…" Fredrick muttered.

"Brigid said if he reads ten pages, she'll take him up to the guardhouse to watch the men spar," Greta told him.

"Oh she did, did she?"

"Geoffrey…" Annabel sighed.

Geoffrey sighed and set Greta back down on the floor. "Go play," he said, and made his way to the kitchen to where his wife was finishing the meal. He leaned up against the doorframe and folded his arms; Annabel eyed him closely.

"Go on. Let's hear it."

"I just think that it is unwise and unsafe for her to be wandering the city alone," he said, "That's all I'll say."

"Really?"

Geoffrey shrugged, "I guess I could also say that there are times where I wonder where she…acquires certain things—the doll and such—and I especially worry about her bothering the guards again."

"Geoffrey, with the money from those jewels and bangles and such, I really don't think you need to worry about her thieving," Annabel said, "And as for Freddy, he just wants to watch them. I don't see anything wrong with her taking him up there to watch that."

"There isn't, if that's all it is," Geoffrey said, "But all the while they're sparring and Freddy's watching, she's thinking away in that head of hers trying to find out how to sneak past them and get into the castle. She thinks if she does that, she'll be invited right in to talk to the baron to find out where this Marshal fellow is. Mark my words, if she keeps at it, she could end up getting hurt—or worse."

"Geoffrey, she's sixteen—seventeen come Stagtide," Annabel smiled, "There are girls her age getting married and having babies. If they can take care of themselves *and* their families, I'm sure she can take care of herself. She's almost a woman grown!"

"Aye, she is," Geoffrey said, "All the more reason to worry about her—especially with all these pilgrims about. They act all 'holier than thou,' but I see them. The pardoners at the cathedral are making a killing these days selling notes of clemency—G's for gambling, D's for drunkenness, L's for lechery, B's for brawling. I've seen some of the same men stopping by twice in the same week—one fellow twice in the same day! Another tried to use his D-Mark to pay for his ale from the cousins on credit! She thinks with those fancy knives on her belt she's invincible, but the way they glitter in the sun, they're more likely to draw thieves and other unsavory types."

"Kinship keep any suitors that come calling for Greta when she's of marrying age. You're liable to greet that the door with that club of yours."

"Aye, maybe I will."

Annabel shook her head in exacerbation, "What would you have me do, then? Lock Brigid upstairs in her room—a room in a house she owns more right to than we do?"

"I'm not saying that. I just wish you could convince her otherwise."

"Me? Convince her otherwise? The Daughter of Dwerin?"

That had been a rather unsettling revelation. They had gone to the marketplace to sell another piece of jewelry—a brooch enameled with the symbol of an anvil. Geoffrey assumed it was some soldier's pin, an officer, perhaps something left to the girl by whomever her father was. However, the merchant refused to buy it claiming it bore the personal crest of the Beinns, the Archdukes of Dwerin, and therefore must have been stolen. Only after they returned home did Brigid finally explain everything—about Blackstone, the sheriff, the archduchess, and Gareth the Blade (who she called the Falcon). She told him about Andoch and the Guardians, and something called a Blackguard. Regardless, the brooch now remained one of the few pieces left from her stash that they had not yet sold, and Geoffrey did not expect that they would find a buyer any time soon.

He sighed and Annabel went back to readying the meal. Six months had passed since that winter day in Dwermouth when Brigid had appeared like a ghost at the docks while Geoffrey stood in despair eyeing the merchant galleys bound for Baronbrock. But in that time, strangely, the girl had somehow inserted herself into the little peasant family, helping to heal the wound ripped open by the loss of their son, Karl, killed in the battle at the Ashfort. The children quickly came to see her as an elder sister, particularly Greta, who seemed to idolize her for her beauty and her kindness (and her willingness to play after having grown up among two brothers). In fact, the little girl flat out refused to allow her mother to plait her hair anymore, insisting she be allowed to let it fall loose because "that's how Brigid wears it."

Annabel too, quickly came to care for Brigid, though truth be told, when Geoffrey first appeared with the pretty young noblewoman in toe, she feared her husband had gone mad. Before long, however, Annabel seemed to look on Brigid as would a kind of aunt or even mother, and it was this instinct that Geoffrey could also not help but feel, for as maternal as Annabel's devotion became, such was the level of his paternal care for the girl as well.

She did not always make it easy though. For instance, one morning during the voyage to the Brock their ship was struck without warning by a terrible storm. Geoffrey, Annabel, and the children had been hiding in the hull frightened for their lives, when suddenly, the captain, furious, ordered the farmer on deck and demanded he take Brigid below. She was standing at the starboard rail laughing in the rain while great waves of surf washed over the ship and thick streaks of lightening lit the sky above. Apparently, some of the more superstitious sailors claimed she had called the storm on purpose and her abundant mirth was making it worse.

Thankfully, they reached the Brock in one piece, and from the port city of Nordren, it was only a few days journey to Galadin. Unfortunately, once they made their way to the castle, the Houndstooth, to present themselves to the baron as Gareth and Regnar had told them, the guards turned them away. For the baron, it was said, was unwell and would not see anyone. To Geoffrey, it was disappointing, particularly after such a long journey, but that was that. Until the man recovered, they would simply have to wait. This was not a sentiment that Brigid seemed to share. Ever since then, she had taken to simply disappearing at various points throughout the day.

Of all her doings, to Geoffrey, these were the most concerning. Where she went, she never said, though in fairness, he did not often ask. It still didn't stop him from worrying. *St. Aiden preserve us! That girl will be the death of me!*

For today, however, he could rest easy, as a moment later, he heard the sound of the door followed shortly thereafter by Greta's singsong greeting.

"Brigid!"

Annabel shot Geoffrey a look of quiet reproach and with a sigh, Geoffrey held up his hands in concession.

"Hello, Greta! How have you and Cora gotten on this afternoon?"

"Very good! She's much nicer than Mina who the dog ate!"

"And how about you Freddy? Did you read what I asked you?"

"Yes…"

"Oh don't sound so sullen!"

"I mean, yes, Brigid, I read it."

"Good. After dinner then we can sit and you can read to me."

"And me too!"

"Yes, and Greta too, and if you do well enough, tomorrow we'll go watch the guard. Alright?"

"I suppose…"

"I suppose…" Brigid repeated, imitating the dour octaves of the seven-year-old. Her lips spread wide revealing two rows of fine white teeth and her bright blue eyes shone with joy, "Annabel, I'm home!"

"Alright, dear, very good! We'll sup in a moment!" she called, "Geoffrey's home already too."

"Hello, Lady Brigid," Geoffrey said simply, and with a nod added, "Oi, son, go help your mother carry everything in."

Freddy breathed a sigh, folded the corner of his page, and with a muttered, "Fine..." went off to do as he was told.

"Hello, Geoffrey," Brigid said hesitantly, "I just...popped out for a bit."

Geoffrey nodded, but remained silent. Over her arm, he noticed that, in spite of the heat, she carried her old dark cloak and within its folds he caught a glimpse of a golden hilt.

"I'll just take this up to my room," she said.

Again, Geoffrey nodded and after she had gone, he washed his hands at the basin in the corner. Freddy set the table and Greta chatted away on the floor, lost in some private world with her new doll. The scene was one of domestic simplicity and it made Geoffrey sigh with contentment. Still, he knew very well that it was due in large part to the young noblewoman, and though he, himself, may remain distant, she had become a very important piece of the small peasant family—a family that already learned what it was to suffer a loss.

"Do you think Annabel needs any more help?" Brigid asked when she returned.

He shook his head, "She's fine. Freddy's helping her."

"I see," Brigid said, "His reading is really coming along now."

"Good."

"I only wish I could find a book that was more enjoyable—Bard's Tales or Sorgund Fish Stories or some such. Though I guess it can't hurt to know how to apply a poultice to a wound or mix a salve..."

"True enough, I suppose." Geoffrey sighed, deciding to make this one of his rare inquiries. "So, how are things at the castle?"

Brigid bit her lip. "Well..." she began hesitantly, "Not so well, I should think."

"Why do you say that?"

Brigid, as she always did, sat down at the foot of the table, yielding the seat of honor to Geoffrey. It was part of the awkward interplay of noble and peasant and yet another aspect of their acquaintance that the farmer found slightly distressing. For, as much as Geoffrey felt obligated to uphold the traditions necessitated by class, Brigid seemed determined to undermine them. Frankly, he was surprised she had missed the chance to correct him when he referred to her as *Lady* Brigid.

"Well," she began, once they were both seated, "Two more of the baron's knights have arrived from the fiefs. That's five now of the seven that make up Galadin. I wouldn't be surprised to find the others arriving to the city within a day or so."

"The Feast of St. Aiden draws near. I'd say that was a rather important holiday for those of the Saint's bloodline."

Brigid shook her head, "True, but I don't think it's a feast that they prepare for. It seems...rather more serious."

"What do you mean?"

"All the knights that have come have only been accompanied by a few soldiers—a small retinue to accompany them on the road. Not a single one has brought a woman—no wives, no daughters, no sisters—not a one. It can't be a feast without noblewomen."

Geoffrey folded his arms in thought. That made sense. Even in Pyle, a holiday feast was for everyone. Greta clambered over to Brigid and the young woman lifted the little girl and her doll into the chair beside her.

"Someone else arrived today too, but it wasn't a knight. It was another baron."

"The fish one again?"

"No, not Nordren—and it's usually just one of his men that comes delivering messages and such. He'll ride in, stay for but an hour or two, and ride out the very same day."

Geoffrey ignored the quick flare of anxiety he always felt when confronted with the level of detail that characterized Brigid's investigations. He remembered the first time when she had matter-of-factly remarked upon the times of the watch rotations and certain idiosyncrasies marking a few of the guards. *This one is easily distracted, that one falls asleep...*

"This was an actual baron himself, not just his men or one of his household. He came in a big carriage and his guard bore arms divided white and blue *per pale*—that is, vertically down the middle. The white side bore the emblem of a blue harp and the blue side bore a white tower," she paused, "I think it may have been the Lord-Baron. The round tower is the symbol of the Brock itself and only the Lord-Baron would be allowed to wear that. The harp, though, I don't recall."

Geoffrey nodded, though the talk of arms and emblems meant nothing to him in the least. The symbol of the red acorn on his shield, as Brigid told him, might very well symbolize a strong warrior with an ancient lineage; but to Geoffrey, it was just a picture on a fine shield. The function mattered, not the design—craftsmanship over artistry. Pretty things were reserved for the nobles, and they were welcome to them.

"Anyhow, they say that Baron Arcis has been ill for a long time," Brigid continued, "I wonder now if perhaps…he may have died. Without an heir, the Lord-Baron may be here to choose a successor from among the knights of the fiefdoms, unless he chooses to name one of his own. Then again, if the old baron named a successor himself, the Lord-Baron would have to acknowledge the new lord and the others renew their fealty," she sighed, "Regardless, I do not know what that means for us in finding the Marshal, but I'll try to learn what I can."

Geoffrey made a face, "Or perhaps you should…just let it be…"

"Geoffrey…" Brigid sighed.

"I'm only saying. Every lord gives public audience eventually—especially a lord supposed to be as great as Galadin. Just have patience."

"But what if Galadin is dead?"

"There's nothing that we could do about that now then, is there?"

"You know as well as I do that we need to see the baron," Brigid paused, "I'll be careful—believe me—and I know you worry, but…we've come so far. I need to know what we're to do from here. The Falc—Gareth said it was important."

Geoffrey sighed. "As you say," he said, "But remember there's other things come to be very important—maybe not in the castle, but to the folks in this house—and there's not one of us that could handle seeing a certain young lady come to any harm."

At that moment, Annabel returned from the kitchen carrying the pot of hot stew and Brigid's reply went unheard. Freddy followed behind his mother with a flagon of weak ale and took the empty seat at his father's right across from his mother.

"There we are," Annabel smirked, "Hot stew on a hot day. Geoffrey's favorite! Welcome summer!"

CHAPTER 2: AMBER SUNSET, GOLDEN DAWN

In the darkened chamber, Lughus sat in silence with his head bowed. From his chair in the rear corner, he watched as one by one, the knights in command of each of Galadin's seven fiefdoms made their way into the room, knelt at the foot of their lord's bed, and renewed their vows of fidelity and service. Some of them wept openly, others were quick to replace their helms to hide their faces, but in the end, each man among them spoke his oath with a voice as strong as on the day he first made it. Then, lying in repose upon the mattress, his body drawn and withered from the long, losing battle he waged with his disease, Baron Arcis Galadin offered each man his blessing and fought to control his fits of coughing so that he might leave his loyal retainers with a few personal, private words. Finally, before withdrawing, each knight offered up a small pouch of dirt collected from the grounds of his fiefdom to be scattered over the lord's remains within his tomb.

Beside Lughus on the floor, Fergus, the great hound, rested his head gently on the young man's knee, his sad, hazel eyes all the more forlorn. He remembered reading once in some obscure bestiary at the Loremaster's Tower that all dogs, though the Hounds of Perindal in particular, could see beyond the veil of the living, discerning the spirits of the dying and the recently departed as they awaited the call of the Kinship to guide them to the Realm of the Blessed. He breathed a heavy sigh and ruffled the thick golden fur between the hound's ears.

In the remaining corners of the room sat three other men who would bear witness to the baron's final moments. First, to the lord's right sat Sir Owain Rook, who from the time of Sir Wolfram of Parth's death, had served faithfully as Baron Arcis's seneschal. Rook was a large man with hair the color of a magpie and a thick, curling mustache. His eyes glowed red from grief, and as he sat in the full regalia of his heavy plate armor, his expression was one of utter numbness, like a river basin after all the water has gone dry.

On the baron's left, in the simple rough spun habit of a country Cousin sat Randal Woode, Abbot of the Monastery of St. Golan. Woode was a man in his late forties with dark eyes that seemed naturally squinting and thick brows. His head was shorn smooth, but for two small patches behind his ears and a short, dark beard. From what Lughus gathered watching him that morning, Woode was a man of great self-discipline and austerity, though he was not unkind. The abbot had been requested to oversee the quiet, private ceremony in place of Padeen Andresen, Provincial Hierophant of Baronbrock, High Cleric of the Cathedral of St. Aiden, and an anointed Guardian under the title of "the Breath." For although the ascetic cousins and their sister lay-preachers, the Handmaids of the Lady, may tend to the needs of the faithful, they were not directly under the command of the Order of the Guardians in Andoch. Choosing the abbot over the provincial was likely to cause an incident once it was discovered; however, in light of other potential complications, Andresen's wounded pride was of significantly little concern to the dying baron.

Finally, the last of the four to bear witness to Arcis Galadin's final moments was the man who sat directly across from Lughus in the chamber's other dark corner. He appeared like the others, solidly in middle age, with short, silvery hair that was even curlier than Lughus's mop of burnished gold. His light blue eyes were keenly marked by crow's feet and his smooth-shaven cheeks shone like apples, marking him as one who was no stranger to laughter. He was not armed or armored, but rather arrayed in finery befitting a statesman of great import. His tunic was of purest white cloth embroidered along its hems in dark blue thread with a crenellated pattern like that of a curtain wall or the top of a round tower. His surcoat of baronial blue was emblazoned on the front with the Tower of the Brock while on the back it bore the emblem of a harp, both of which were sewn in white. Upon his knee he carried his cap, a great puffy thing striped in the two-tone colors as the rest of his garb, and against the wall beside him, he carried a small walking stick carved of holy oak.

As Lughus watched in silence, the man caught his eye and offered him a sympathetic nod. As he returned the gesture, Lughus tried to imagine what the man might look like with a long length of gray beard, for he was none other than Perin Glendaro, Lord-Baron of the Brock and nephew to Lughus's beloved tutor, the Loremaster Rastis.

The memory of the old man brought a wistful smile to his lips, for it was less than a year ago that he wore the rough burgundy robes of a Loremaster's apprentice in the Order of the Guardians. There, he lived a simple life of reading, writing, and illuminating manuscripts. Now, however, he was clad in the outfit of a young nobleman—a fine mail hauberk beneath a surcoat of baronial blue embroidered with a golden hound rampant, soft leather boots, gloves of calfskin, and a golden cloak fastened at the shoulder with a brooch. He was still not certain he liked the change of clothing or the life that came with it; yet he also knew that there was no going back.

When the seven knights of the seven fiefdoms had all paid their final respects, the baron beckoned the four witnesses to his side. Lughus breathed a sigh and unconsciously patted the pommel of his sword, Sentinel, blade of the Marshal, resting comfortably in its scabbard on his baldric. He noticed that this simple gesture had become a habit of his over the past months whenever he was forced to face something that made him anxious, as if to remind himself of his duties, of his honor, and of the oath he had sworn to Crodane. The sight of his grandfather—a man he had only just come to know—lying shriveled and feverish in his final hours certainly qualified.

"So we come to it," the dying man observed, his voice no more than a whisper.

Sir Owain's eyes must have discovered some hidden reserves; for once again, thick tears welled and began tracing their way down his cheeks. Lughus felt his own throat tighten and he breathed another sigh. Death had followed him far too closely as of late. First Crodane, then word came that Rastis had fallen to some illness, and now, Baron Arcis. His eyes fell to his grandfather's hands—spindly thin, the luminous blue veins clearly visible beneath skin that seemed transparent. Still, it was an easier sight than to look the dying man in the face, to meet his eyes—green as a summer meadow—for they were too like the color of those that he saw in his dreams.

"So good of you to come, Perin," Arcis smiled weakly at the Lord-Baron, "I wanted to be here when you met, so that I might introduce you personally."

"I am honored you should call for me, Baron Galadin," Glendaro said, "Though it grieves me deeply."

"Even on my deathbed you refuse to do away with formalities," Arcis laughed, though the laughter soon became a terrible cough.

"I'm afraid, my lord, that to me, you shall always remain the noble lord you were forty years ago when I was but a child at Highboard. My father always said, he might have been the Lord-Baron by title, but it was an honor he could only hope to share with the great lord of Galadin."

"And as you can see, thanks to the efforts of your own uncle, my passing will not be the last, for the Galadins shall live on in my grandson, Lughus."

Perin Glendaro smiled, "He's the spitting image of the Saint himself."

"In more ways than in just appearance," Arcis said, though with some hesitation, "For like the Galadins of old, he also carries a title."

For a moment the Lord-Baron paused. "Ah, I see," he said at last, "I think I understand now the meaning behind the question your steward requested I look into for you."

Lughus's brow furrowed and he cast his eye upon his grandfather. This was news he was not aware of.

"From what I could tell, there was nothing prohibitory?" Arcis said, "The precedence had been set. A man with a Guardian title may also act as a baron, correct?"

"You are correct," Baron Glendaro said, "Though in truth, the precedents all occurred before the requirements of the Oath of Fealty. It is true that in Andoch a man might hold a title and also remain a lord; however, I am not certain of any rulings among the Guardians themselves in regards to their members holding lands in other realms. I know my uncle gave up his claims when he became the Loremaster, and more recently there's a Montevalen prince who was forced to forsake his rights when he swore his Oath. Yet, in your case, to gain a barony *afterwards*, I am just not certain. Though, I assume that regardless of my answer to your question, your intentions would remain the same?"

"They would," Arcis said, "And…Perin, I will tell you as well so that there will be no surprises further down the road, that he shall not be making the Oath of Fealty either."

The Lord-Baron's eyes went wide, "He shall not?" Lughus felt Glendaro's eyes upon him once again, "I understand now why Provincial Andresen is not to be joining us—no offense to you, of course, my good Abbot Woode."

"None taken, my Lord-Baron," the abbot said, "However, might I add, that even if the boy does bear a title, the blood of the Blessed Saint flows through him. What right does the Order hold to demand he bend the knee before them? I should think that perhaps it would be more appropriate for the Guardian-King to swear fealty to him."

"That makes much sense to me too," Sir Owain said quietly.

"You Galadins have always flaunted your disapproval of the Oath," Perin sighed, "Which I suppose is appropriate considering you were there at the beginning." He offered Lughus a wink, "My uncle is not the only one fond of history…"

"Yes," Baron Galadin said, "And it's a shame that so many of the most faithful servants of the Light should be branded with the deplorable label of 'Blackguard' while Kredor sits in Titanis hoping to set himself up as a new emperor. I only pray it does not take a second Warlock to put him in his place…"

"Kin keep us," the abbot said.

Lughus felt a shiver of anxiety run through him and again he touched the pommel of his sword.

"Considering the fate of the Grantisi Senate, I think perhaps we should avoid talk like that for the time being," Glendaro sighed, "At any rate, Lord Arcis, in regards to the matter at hand, you have put me in a rather…awkward position. You seek to acknowledge the boy as your heir, but the Guardians will claim him as theirs as well."

Lord Arcis smiled, "I know I have, Perin, and I am sorry for it. Things were not intended to develop this way, but such as they are, they must be. However, if you recall, it was I that, by your father's decree, occupied a particular spot of bother not too long ago—one that, as it would turn out, had dire, dire consequences."

The Lord-Baron avoided the dying man's eye, "I remember, my lord, as did my father—and to his dying day he regretted it."

Lughus reached down to pat Fergus on the head, ignoring the sudden memory of the eyes in his dream—eyes once soft and green turned vacant and cold in death.

"Then let your father rest easy," Arcis said, pointing a bony finger at his grandson, "Let this be the good to come out of that time of darkness. Acknowledge him as my rightful heir and the new Baron of Galadin so that no matter what mistakes were made in the past, we shall have a future."

A heavy silence fell over the room, and in the flickering light of the candles, dark shadows danced across the walls. As he watched them, Lughus remembered the words of the Marshal and his chest tightened at the reminder of his duties.

At length, the Lord-Baron spoke. "I will acknowledge the boy's claim," he said, "The Glendaros owe you that much and more. However, my word alone will not mean anything should the other barons find him unacceptable and contrive to put it to a vote, especially when they learn he is a Bla—a Guardian unsworn. Lords know what Roland Marthaine will think of it! And now *you* claim him as *your* heir? I can only wonder the earful I'm to receive considering the boy's been believed to be dead for the last...what? Fifteen? Sixteen years? Which, of course, raises the matter of his age..." he sighed and turned toward Lughus, "I hope you are ready, lad."

"He'll be just fine. I am certain," Arcis nodded toward Sir Owain and the seneschal began shuffling among the objects on the baron's bedside table, "And as far as his age, he's seventeen, Perin, as of the ninth of Salmontide."

"And I can only assume my dear uncle was a part of this business from the start?"

"You might call him the author. For, in truth, I begged his aide and he wrote the rest."

The Lord-Baron sighed wearily, "Regardless, Andoch is certain to take issue."

"Perin," Arcis said, "Considering the rumors we hear regarding your noble uncle, are you certain that the Guardian-King is as loyal a friend to the Brock as one would think?"

"I suppose not..." the Lord-Baron said, "And for a man on his deathbed, you seem extremely well informed."

Arcis laughed again, which of course brought another bout of coughing. Abbot Woode offered the dying baron a cloth and held up a small brass bowl as the old man choked into it, spitting out great red globs of blood and sputum. When he recovered, Sir Owain held out a roll of fine parchment and took a moment to ready a quill and a stick of hot wax.

"Here is the formal will that I had my steward draw up," Arcis said, "By this, my signature, and my seal, I name Lughus, son to my daughter Luinelen, heir to the Barony of Galadin and all my rights and holdings." Quickly, he signed his name and with Sir Owain's help pressed his signet ring onto the drips of hot wax.

"I am to sign as primary witness, then?" Perin asked, perusing the document, "And Sir Owain and Abbot Woode as secondary?"

Arcis nodded and lay back on the mattress in exhaustion. Woode took another cloth from beside the bed, wet it in a basin of water, and applied it to the dying man's forehead. The Lord-Baron signed his name, affixed his seal, and passed the document to Sir Owain so that he and the abbot could apply their monikers as well. Finally, the seneschal addressed Lughus for the first time.

"You must sign too, my lord."

Lughus looked up in surprise. He had yet to get used to being referred to as "my lord" and each time he heard the title uttered, he felt the urge to look around him to see what nobleman had suddenly arrived.

Carefully, he signed his name, and from around his neck, he drew his mother's signet ring and used it to affix a seal of his own. When he finished, Sir Owain took the document and held it up for Baron Galadin to approve.

"Then it is done," Arcis said, "Thus, I may die in peace." He coughed again into his cloth and spit into the jug. The four witnesses stood idly in silence. "If you do not mind, then" Arcis finally said, "I would like to speak alone with my grandson."

The remaining three witnesses nodded gravely. "I will be just outside the door should you need anything, my lord," Sir Owain whispered to his lord.

"Thank you, Owain."

Gently, Abbot Woode touched his finger to the old lord's brow and quietly whispered a prayer. Once more, Lughus felt his eyes begin to burn. He looked away, only to meet the steady gaze of the Lord-Baron himself.

"The summer assembly of the barons meets at the midpoint of Stagtide," he said quietly, "Rest assured that I will stand by my acknowledgement of you—for the sake of both your grandfather, as well as my uncle. You may consider me your friend."

Lughus nodded, "Thank you."

"Your grandfather was a great man and your mother was a marvelous woman, so forgive me if I am expecting you to follow in their footsteps," he smiled, "Though from what my uncle said of you when he wrote to me last year, you are already on the path."

When the abbot finished, Baron Glendaro returned his attention to Lughus's grandfather, "Goodbye, Hound of Galadin. May you lie forever in the embrace of the Lady of Light!"

"Goodbye Perin," Arcis said, "May the Brethren keep you and all the Brock free from Darkness."

The Lord-Baron nodded, turned stiffly, and left the chamber followed by Sir Owain and the abbot.

When they had gone and the door of the chamber shut behind them, Baron Arcis breathed a great, gasping sigh of exhaustion and sank deeper into his mattress. His eyes grew red and moist and there were traces of blood on his teeth and lips. "Sit, my boy," he whispered, "Please, sit."

Lughus retrieved a chair from the corner and placed it at his grandfather's bedside.

"I'm sorry we have not had much time to know one another," the old man said, "And for keeping you cooped up like a rabbit in this castle for so many months, but I'd rather keep you secret and keep you safe should Kredor have sent his men after you. Once I'm gone and you have been declared publicly as my heir, however, you will be free to follow your own path."

"I don't mind it," Lughus said quietly, and in truth, in his life as an apprentice, there were times when a whole week might pass in study at the Loremaster's Tower without him ever setting foot outside. The world of books offered nearly endless escape from the confines of the Keystone, let alone the dusty study rooms of the library. Plus, there was a great part of him that worried that should he explore the city below the castle ridge, he might stumble upon other strange visions like he had with Theo Nordren at the ruined tower. His sleep these months offered enough upsetting apparitions; he had no wish to add more when awake.

"Sending you to Rastis was at once the greatest and worst decision of my life."

Lughus nodded his head, but he could think of no words to say. Again, his hand touched Sentinel's pommel.

From the moment of his arrival at the Houndstooth last autumn, it was as if he had somehow walked through a doorway into another person's life. For as long as he could remember, he had believed himself a penniless orphan who somehow had the good fortune to be taken on as ward to the great Loremaster, and though the journey northward to the Brock had changed much of that, it had not prepared him for the sudden and drastic transition to the life of a young nobleman, a life he was still not sure that he wanted.

Still, much of him had remained the same, in spite of the apparent change in fortunes. He had the same thoughts, the same feelings, and the same interests as he did among the books and among his fellow apprentices, his brothers. Now, however, he stood to become the master of a castle, a baron with knights and fiefdoms of his own, and the heir to a powerful lord in the bloodline of the greatest of saints. In no way did he feel prepared for this level of responsibility.

But he had sworn an oath, and no matter his own cavalcade of fears or doubts, he would not see it broken.

The baron tried to smile and it made Lughus want to weep. Arcis had received him with such genuine affection and unmitigated joy these past months that he could not help but feel ashamed, unbefitting of such positive regard. Never had he encountered such a thing, for even Crodane treated him with quiet reserve upon their first meeting. However, in spite of the many years of separation, the old man seemed determined to love him as his mother's son.

"Sir Owain tells me that you have bested all men in the guard with your sword," he said, "He will not admit as much to you, but he believes that you are more than a match for him as well."

Lughus gave a wan smile, "I lack his experience, though."

"Still, Crodane must have taught you well indeed!"

"I hope so."

"He was a good man," Arcis observed.

"He was."

"Though I suspect he never forgave himself for what happened to your mother."

A lump formed in Lughus's throat. "No," he said, "He did not."

"At least he can be with her now, and soon so will I."

Lughus gave a nod and Fergus rested his head on the young man's knee.

"It will be good to see her and your grandmother once again," Arcis continued, "Wolfram too. It's funny that we should so fear death when it seems to carry with it the promise of so many happy reunions."

Lughus sighed. He had had enough talk of death for one day, and as the old man waned, there would only be more. "What did you mean about Rastis?" he asked, trying to change the subject, "When you asked the Lord-Baron why he should fear upsetting King Kredor?"

Arcis gasped at air and stifled a cough. "No one has heard from Rastis in some time," he said, "Not since word reached us that he had fallen ill."

"And you...you fear the worst?"

"Sending you to me required that Rastis play a very dangerous game, for he knew Kredor would try to use you as leverage in his unlawful bid for the Protectorate. Once you were gone, the King would be displeased, and with a hothead like Kredor, he did not discount the possibility that he might be charged with treason."

"Treason?" Lughus's gray eyes flashed like a thunderstorm, "It's treason to prevent the King from willingly committing an injustice?"

"I'm afraid it is often considered treason to prevent the King from doing anything."

Lughus sighed and settled back into his chair, gripping the hilt of his sword in despair. How many more could he stand to lose? A mother, a father, a mentor, a master, a grandfather...and the Brethren alone knew what had befallen Royne and Thom. "Do you think Rastis is in danger?" he asked.

Arcis was silent for a moment, and suddenly erupted into another fit of choking coughs. Lughus went to help him, but the old man waved him back for fear he would come too near and rolled away onto his side. When he finally recovered, he lay for a moment in exhaustion before attempting to speak.

"If he is, then Rastis was prepared," Arcis said, "He is after all, the Loremaster. One who carries such a title should not be taken lightly.

Besides, even if he is in trouble, you cannot help him now. Your duties are to wait here for Regnar and Gareth."

Lughus felt a cold chill at both the prospect of Rastis being in danger and the sight of his grandfather's final suffering; however, even though he had been waiting six month and more for the remaining two of the Three to arrive in Galadin, he would not disagree, for somehow he sensed the old man would not last the hour and he had no wish to upset him any further.

The baron wiped the blood from the corner of his mouth. "Once they arrive, they will help you."

"Grandfather," Lughus said softly, "I don't understand. What are they to help me with? What should I do?"

"It is the duty of the Galadins to protect the people—not just of the Brock, but of all Termain, as it was with St. Aiden before us. As the Marshal now, as well, I'm afraid your responsibilities increase tenfold," he paused suddenly as another bout of coughing overtook him, "You cannot...you cannot let the Brock support Kredor in the Protectorate—even if it means war! If Kredor succeeds in naming himself emperor of all Termain, his tyranny will know no end. Every man, woman, and child from Dwerin to Castone will suffer. Yet, that is only the beginning..."

"What do you mean?"

Slowly, the old baron closed his eyes. After a long moment of intense effort, he moved his lips as if to speak, but no words came. Again, he was seized with fits of bloody coughing, and, as before he gasped for air. This time, however, the desperate bouts would not subside. Again, fear clutched at Lughus's heart as he watched helplessly as his grandfather thrashed about like man drowning on dry land. He frantically shouted for help and like a mad beast, Fergus ran laps around the chamber, barking feverishly at the door. In a flash, Sir Owain and the Abbot burst in and rushed to the old man's side; however, it was too late. The coughing ceased and the old man lay still.

Arcis, Baron of Galadin, was dead.

CHAPTER 3: COMMONWEALTH

The city of Commonwealth, or Alendis as it was known before the formation of the Grantisi Republic, was believed by scholars to be the oldest city in all Termain. Built in the early days of Old Calendral, it had preceded Floraine as the capitol of the empire and the seat of the emperor's power; yet, although its walls and palaces were ancient and bore the marring of thousands of years of wind, rain, and storm, to say nothing of war, they still stood tall and strong.

Royne and his young steward Conor had arrived only two weeks earlier, smuggled through the encampments of soldiers from Andoch, Dwerin, and Grantis by the nomadic trading caravans of the Wayfolk. The journey had taken significantly longer than he would have liked as the Wayfolk often stopped from town to town and camp to camp to barter and entertain the various soldiers with music, dancing, and displays of legerdemain. Still, he understood that in doing so, the nomads bought themselves enough goodwill to continue their seemingly aimless journey south a few leagues more. Truly, Rastis had chosen wisely in his selection of guides—not that Royne would expect anything less from the Old Loremaster—and though the long months hiding out within the shelter of the Wayfolk's covered wagons was almost as maddening as the slow, lumbering pace of their oxen, he was safely away from Titanis and the clutches of King Kredor and Natharis Tainne.

Or so he thought.

Grantis, long respected for its disciplined infantry and professional soldier class had not been able to mount the type of concerted defense that most would have expected, and though he could scarcely believe it, the Republic saw its armies brushed aside with exactly the same ease that the Guardian-King had foreseen. It was disappointing, not simply because it proved Kredor right and Royne wrong, but because the young Loremaster had always held the ideas of the republic in such high regard. For, although Grantis was not a nation without flaws or its own internal problems, the senate, elections, and abolishment of the hereditary noble class seemed to him a step in the right direction toward the establishment of a free and enlightened society. He had not expected, however, that those very same ideals would also play a part in the republic's downfall. For, whether senator or lord, commoner or noble, men were still men, and subject to the same virtues and vices.

The Grantisi senate had consisted of one hundred senators elected from the various cities, towns, and villages across the republic. When the war broke out, however, rather than stand together as one to defend the entire nation, many of the senators fled the capitol city for their country estates, demanding in many instances that entire battalions of legionnaires be dispatched to accompany them. Thus, the mighty legions were soon cannibalized to serve as little more than household guards for the wealthiest of the republic's politicians, and when the armies of the Guardian-King and his Dwerin allies marched to war, they met only isolated pockets of resistance rather than a single, unified resistance force.

That being said, there were some noteworthy attempts at defending the Grantisi heartland. The remnants of both the Second and Seventh Grantisi Legions, whose commanding officers, after the loss of their first battalions, refused to sacrifice any more of their soldiers to the senators, had mounted a respectable, if doomed, defense of the floodplain outside of the city of Lindonwood; and the Fifth Legion had succeeded in harassing the Dwerin Lord Padraig Reid's armies in the Spade for months before reinforcements arrived from Andoch. However, in the end, the results were the same, for when the few senators remaining in the capitol became overcome with fear and doubt, they gathered together one final time to issue a formal proclamation of surrender. Any of their fellows whose signatures had not graced the document were branded with the name of brigand and declared subject to imprisonment and execution.

Still, little enough of that mattered to Royne, at least in a practical sense. For, it was not to fight a war that he had come to Grantis, but rather to learn. According to Hob, it was Rastis's intention that he make his way to Commonwealth so as to meet a man known as Salasco the Wall. Salasco was a Blackguard, an Anointed Guardian who upon receiving his title refused to swear an Oath of Fealty to the Guardian-King. A year earlier, Royne would have considered such a man to be little more than an outlaw and a scoundrel; however, since learning first hand of Kredor's true intentions, he was certain now that the real villain was the one who sat upon the throne.

And of course, the fact that he, himself, was now a Blackguard precluded further judgment in that regard. Instead, what drew Royne's ire was the fact that, since arriving in the city, he had been unable to locate the man. For two weeks now, they had searched in vain for any sign of a man named Salasco, even going so far as to enlist the help of the Wayfolk caravan master, Niccolo Ducant, whose jugglers, dancers, and bards regularly plied their trade among the occupied city's inns and taverns. Still, they came up with nothing. Salasco was a ghost, and the Wall merely a legend. Now, even worse, was the fact that it would not be long before the Wayfolk would be moving on, continuing their meandering trek across the continent, and although they offered to take the boys with them, Royne refused. For, though he was no knight, nor did he consider himself a man of any great honor, his time as an apprentice had bequeathed him with a sense of duty, and until his duty to Rastis was fulfilled, he could not venture on—be it with the Wayfolk or to Baronbrock and his best friend—his brother—Lughus.

In any case, Royne knew that if they did not find Salasco soon, Conor and he would be all alone in a city where they were not only strangers, but hunted men.

Royne considered this now, sitting within the shadow of one of the ancient stone guildhalls that lined the perimeter of the Grantisi Forum. It was the first day of the Month of the Sun, the first day of summer, and although Royne had traditionally been one to avoid the out-of-doors, with the oppressive humidity of the southern heat, he found the open air slightly less deplorable than the stuffy interiors of the Wayfolk's wagons or the dank, malodorous confines of the Grantisi alehouses. The Forum at least offered the chance of an occasional breeze gusting in off of the river.

As the center of life in Commonwealth, the Forum also offered an excellent view of current affairs within the city, the realm, and beyond. At various intervals throughout the day, town criers would shout the latest news concerning not only trade, but the latest decrees set down by the occupying Andochan forces. Most importantly, however, it was a place so thickly packed with people that it allowed Royne to fade into anonymity, to hide in plain sight of the regular patrols of Kingsmen. For he had, after all, stolen one of the most sacred relics of the Order of the Guardians, and though it was his by right of being anointed under the title of the Loremaster, it was also that which King Kredor and Lord Tainne most desired.

Fat lot of good it would do them anyhow, Royne smirked, drawing *The Book of Histories* forth from the burlap satchel in which he kept it, *For, only the true Loremaster can read it!*

Carefully, he opened its blank pages, placed his finger on an imaginary line of text and began to read. Somehow, though he could not explain it, in his mind's eye he discerned words upon the page, words he somehow *remembered* writing. However, the hand scrawling upon the crackling parchment was not his own, but rather someone else's, another past bearer of the title—just as it had that day in the Groundlings when he had last seen Hob. It was amazing, unfathomable, madness. The whole thing defied logic, defied rationality, and if anything, Royne was a logical, rational young man. He did not believe in superstitious mumbo jumbo any more than he believed in such nonsense as magic. However, reading the book seemed to threaten all of that. So, he decided long ago to deal with it in the same manner that the peasants and the men of the Hierophant's Tower dealt with logic, reason, and factual truth: by simply ignoring them.

Regardless, there was a certain comfort in the whole thing, for in spite of his loneliness and his isolation from his friends, the words of his predecessors made him feel slightly less alone. Especially once he realized that the more he read and the closer he came to the present, he would eventually come upon the familiar, spindly penmanship of Loremaster Rastis. How he longed to skip ahead to the pages Rastis wrote, as if by simply reading the man's words, he could again hear the voice of his beloved mentor. Perhaps more importantly, he might also gain a better grasp of this Key of Salvation business and why Natharis Tainne was putting so much effort into such an absurd flight of fancy. Of course, by its very nature, History was linear—past to present, cause to effect, and the book seemed to operate by the same principles. For when he tried to flip ahead, the pages remained mostly blank but for a few fragmented sentences that quickly faded to nothing. Thus, he would just have keep reading and wait.

Still, there were certain flashes of insight that by some preternatural sense struck him, at times, as relevant. For instance, there were many references in the early days to a Guardian anointed under the title of the Bard. This alone was not surprising, for although the Bard was considered to have authored the majority of the folktales and legends recounting the deeds of the Order's heroes and knights-errant in the days before the Siege of Three and the Oath of Fealty, Royne knew from earlier research that the Bard by most accounts probably did exist; in fact, many considered him to have been one of the most influential members of the Order, a contemporary even to the Council of Five. Over the years, the majority of his life had simply been exaggerated and many absurd fairy stories and local legends somehow attributed to his authorship. Unfortunately, like many others, his title appeared to have disappeared sometime in the second century after the Warlock's fall.

Another thing that stood out to him as he read the book were the occasional accounts of political crises that from time to time embroiled the Order itself—from both without and within. From the beginning, the Guardians were in some sense a group fundamentally divided by the varying nature of their leaders. Aiden Galadin and Halford Drude were hardly the best of friends that the Hierophants would have the common folk assume. In fact, the book confirmed Royne's hypothesis that they did not seem to interact much at all. For, Galadin was a peasant and Drude was a noble. St. Aiden's men fought along the roads and forests, freeing villages or helping poor folk oppressed by Wrogan's Dibhorites to escape, whereas Drude was the traditional knight of the field and his followers were often his fellow exiled lords and retainers fighting to regain castles and lost fiefdoms. As a result, the alliance and the founding of the Order itself seemed mostly built upon a matter of convenience. It was no small wonder, then, that after Wrogan was defeated, many of Aiden's men returned home to their families while Drude and his followers should set themselves to establishing their own sovereign realm in Andoch.

So it was, then, that the Order was often embroiled in conflict related to these opposing ideologies. Aiden's men saw the role of the Guardians as guides and servants, while Drude's retainers believed that the Order should instead command and protect. Unfortunately, or so the old Loremasters seemed to believe, neither side could see the necessity of the other—and never would, for the Siege of Three and the Oath of Fealty brought an abrupt end to the debate.

Royne sighed and shut the book. He had just finished reading the account of another Blackguard—Redondo the Knave. According to the Oath, a man who gained a title had a year and a day to present himself in Andoch to swear fealty to the Guardian King. How they could determine whether or not he was late, however, was rather unclear, and Royne sincerely doubted there really was any accurate means to it all. Regardless, poor Redondo, by his own admission appeared too late. He claimed his wife was ill and dying and rather than leave her, he chose to stay by her side until the end. Much to the disgust of the Loremaster at that time (a Bernard Delany, also known to Royne for authoring a rather in-depth guide to various pigments used in metalworking), Redondo was executed anyway, despite what seemed a completely legitimate reason for his tardiness.

So much for honesty, Royne muttered bitterly, *So much for telling the truth...*

The sudden patter of footsteps caused him to start and his heart leapt up into his throat. Hurriedly, he slipped the ancient tome back into his satchel and drew forth the hood of his habit, no longer the familiar maroon of a scribe, but faded now to the coarse brown shade of a country cousin.

"Sir! Sir!" piped a young boy's voice, "Sir! Come quickly."

"Aiden's Flame, Conor! Calm down!" Royne said tersely, "You scared me half to death." In the past few months, the boy had proven himself a competent and disciplined steward, though his sprightly cheer could at times wear on the young Loremaster's patience.

"I'm sorry, sir," Conor said, "But you said to find you immediately if I heard anything so when I did, I come running as fast as I could."

Royne breathed a sigh, "What are you blathering about?" Out across the forum, a patrol of red-cloaked soldiers marched past in a double rank led by one of the Warlord's partisans. Royne shouldered his satchel and subconsciously pulled his cowl even lower to shield his face.

"I was by the stables at the west gate watching them feed the horses," the boy said, falling in at his master's side, "When all of a sudden these men came in to board their mounts…"

"And…?"

"And I heard them talking…"

"Yes, yes," Royne waved a hand and with the young boy in toe, passed inconspicuously out into the bustling throngs of merchants, burghers, and other assorted townsfolk. There were cloth-dyers selling fine linens, tanners selling leather, and grocer upon grocer selling olives, fresh vegetables, dried fruit, large wheels of cheese, and sacks of grain, to say nothing of the innumerable wine merchants. There were at least half a dozen vintages for every fief. "So are you going to tell me what they were talking about," Royne asked after a moment, trying to ignore a sudden craving for a thin slice of hard cheese and a cup of Candleford Dry Red, "Or do you expect me to guess?"

"Well," the boy said, hustling after taking two strides to one of Royne's, "At first they were complaining about the kingsmen and the sentries posted at the gates and along the roadways."

"Were they Grantisi?"

"They were."

"Nothing unusual about that. People don't take too kindly to enemy soldiers telling them what to do in their own homes."

"I expect not, sir, but…" Conor paused to leap over a dung pile left in the center of the square by a passing carthorse, "These men seemed different."

"Different? Different how?" the young Loremaster scoffed, "Please, Conor speak sense, or at the very least speak plainly." He paused, suddenly aware of the fact that he was walking in the wrong direction. After spending most of his life within the confines of a single stone tower, the vast expanse of the great southern city was like attempting to navigate a bloody labyrinth, to say nothing of the journey from Titanis with the Wayfolk. On more than one occasion he had gotten lost in the woods along the roadside while answering nature's call and the caravan master had been forced to send folk to find him. *Bloody cheese, is what it is—and the wine. They fill the air with the aroma so as to confuse folk, make them walk around in circles until they give in and buy it!* With a sigh, he paused, "Which way back to the Wayfolk camp?"

"That way," Conor pointed, "Back past the inn with the cockerel sign."

"Then why in the Abyss did you let me walk all this way past it?"

The boy shrugged, "I thought you wanted to go this way."

"So these men?" the young Loremaster continued, after correcting his course.

"Aye, sir?"

"You said they were different?"

"Yes."

"How?"

"Oh!" the boy said, "They were armed."

"Armed?" Royne stopped suddenly and pursed his lips, "You're certain."

The boy shook his head. "They were trying to keep them hidden beneath their cloaks, sir, but I saw them all the same. Short swords, like the ones the legionnaires used to carry."

"Well, I suppose that is different..." Royne folded his arms and scratched his chin as a drover passed driving a trio of goats to market. Under the terms of the Grantisi surrender and subsequent occupation, arms were forbidden within the walls of the city. Any travelers were to check their weapons with the Kingsmen at the gates for the duration of the visit. Of course, that was not to say that men did not find ways to smuggle them in nor was it that unusual to imagine there were men of the legions still fighting the war. In fact, just last week the crier claimed that the kingsmen had routed a band of highwaymen comprised entirely of men from half a dozen legions who had refused to lay down arms. *But were they really highwaymen, or were they organized? Surely not all of the generals have surrendered...*

At length, the drover passed and Royne and Conor continued on their way. "Interesting, Conor. Well done," he said, "I'll have to think on that. Though, of course, it still doesn't help us much in finding the Wall."

"But that's just it, sir," Conor said, "The men—I heard them talking. They were looking for the Wall too."

"What?!" Royne cried. He stopped short and spun on his heel only to step in a pile of refuse dumped among the gutter. "Black Abyss and Red Death!" he cried, scraping the gunk off his boot. A pair of housewives clucked their tongues at him as they passed in a mixture of amusement and reproach, mistaking him once again for a wandering cousin.

"At first I thought they meant the city walls," the boy prattled on, "But sure enough, they meant Salasco, and as soon as I heard them say his name, sir, I come running for you."

The young Loremaster ignored the two women and scuffed his boot on the street to clear off the last bit of gunk. Finally, after weeks of searching they finally had a lead. Soon enough he could talk to Salasco, find out what Rastis wanted, and begin making plans to reach Lughus in Galadin. With any luck, by year's end they could rally the Brock to arms and march on Kredor, Tainne, and any of the other bloody Guardians who cared to stand in their way. *Then all will be settled,* he thought bitterly, *Then they will know justice.* Rastis would be free, a tyrant deposed, and a Golden Age of Wisdom and Enlightenment would spread like wildfire from Dwerin to Castone! For the first time in a long time, Royne's lips spread into a smile—a smile free of cynicism, free of irony. "Tell me, Conor," he said suddenly, "These men, where were they going?"

"I'm sorry, sir?"

"The men with the swords. The legionnaires. Where were they going?"

"Oh," Conor gave a nod and paused, screwing up his face in thought. "I'm afraid I don't rightly know, sir," he finally said.

"You don't know?"

"I'm sorry, sir."

"Warlock's bullocks, Conor! You didn't think to find out where they were going?"

"No, sir. I'm afraid not, sir."

Royne breathed a heavy sigh, "Aiden's Flame, Conor! That's our only lead."

"I'm very sorry, sir."

Royne's spare shoulders slumped in dejection as a thought suddenly occurred to him. *Armed men enter the city in secret looking for Salasco the Wall...*

"Holy gods, Conor, he could be in danger!"

"I'm sorry, sir."

"You're certain they didn't say where they were going?"

"No, sir, they just went on through the inner gate into the slums and I lost sight of them."

Royne's jaw clenched in sudden irritation, "The slums?"

"Aye, sir. They went through the archway to the Ruined Quarter and I lost sight of them when I ran off to find you."

The Ruined Quarter, Royne thought, *Of course.*

Despite the Grantisi values pertaining to equality and democracy, Commonwealth's poor section was one of the worst in all Termain. Just because a man had the potential to raise himself up to the level of a great lord through hard work and diligence, not all did, and whereas the bondsmen sworn to a nobleman of another realm was entitled to some (albeit limited) rights of protection from their lord, the freemen of Grantisi were on their own. Thus, the Ruined Quarter was a place of squalor, crime, and wretchedness. It was a place no man walked alone, even in the light of day, and should he find himself inclined to pay it a visit, it was never, ever by choice. It was exactly the type of place in which a fugitive, an outlaw, a Blackguard could disappear.

Suddenly Royne felt very stupid; however, his frustration with himself loosed itself on the young steward. "Conor, you bloody fool!" he cried, "You just said you didn't know where they went!"

"Apologies, sir," the boy muttered, bowing his head, "But they never *said* where they were going…"

"Just shut up," Royne said tersely, "And stay close. The Ruined Quarter is not a place to get lost."

Conor's eyes went wide, "You want to go there now?"

"We've little choice in the matter, I should think," Royne said, feigning confidence to mask his own anxiety, "Who knows what those men were at? I just hope we find Salasco before they do, else who knows what we'll find."

"I'm very sorry, sir," the young boy said again, "I should have thought."

"Well, it's alright now," Royne said with a heavy sigh, "Let's go."

Together, the pair made their way through the forum to the archway that separated the main city thoroughfares from the slums. There the cobblestones slowly disappeared in place of uneven dirt tracks riddled with furrows and gullies from where the poor folk had dug out bits of clay to build or repair the walls of their earthen hovels. The scent of dung and garbage weighed heavily on the air and along the edges of the pathways, piles of feces and rotting food swarmed with flies. Rats scurried about in the open, fearless of the shambling figures of the district's inhabitants who shuffled by stinking of filth and mildew. A few regarded the two of them with smiles teeming with wickedness and although he had neither skill nor training, Royne suddenly felt incredibly vulnerable without any sort of weapon.

Regardless, they continued onward, deeper into the destitute mishmash of huts and shanties. At the sound of a grunt, Conor went white and Royne, to his own surprise, stepped before him. His fists clenched as his body went tense in alarm; however, it was only a feral pig snuffling through a pile of trash. For a long moment, Royne watched it trying to discern just what it was that the creature was eating, until he chanced to glance over at his young steward. Conor's eyes brimmed with tears and his lip quivered in horror. *He's remembering the boar,* Royne realized, *He's remembering his brother.*

"Come on, Conor," Royne said gently, patting the boy on the shoulder, "Let's go."

Without a word, the boy began to move again and they continued on.

At length, the dirt path opened up into a broader space, a type of square, where it seemed that generations of dung collectors had taken their old, worn-out carts to die. Broken wheels, harnesses, and beds were strewn about here and there, packed together with dried feces, mud, and other assorted garbage. The odor was so strong that Royne was forced to shield his face with his sleeve and Conor's complexion was beginning to transition now from pallid white to noxious green. Yet beyond the shattered carts and piles of filth stood another earthen hovel, and inscribed upon the coarse leather flap that served as a door were nine crude rectangles arranged in an off-centered pattern of three by three.

"Those look like bricks," Conor said, pinching his nose against the smell.

The young Loremaster nodded, "The Wall."

Without a word, Royne led the way past the broken carts to the leather flap. There were no windows, but along the edge of the doorway, he could make out the soft light of a candle or some other light source. With an awkward flick of his wrist, he knocked on the flap and cleared his throat. "Salasco?" he called, "I say, Salasco the Wall?"

A heavy silence hung upon the air, though inside, Royne could hear a soft sound of movement. Conor looked up at him questioningly, but Royne ignored him and knocked again. "Please, Salasco," he said again, "We must speak with you. Please, I assure you, we come as friends."

"Is that so?" said a voice. At once, the flap drew back and a pair of men strode forth, their short swords drawn and ready before them.

"Aiden's Flame!" Royne cried. Dragging Conor with him, he leapt away from the hovel just as two more men appeared from among the broken carts.

"Who are you?" one of the men demanded, the same it would seem who had spoken before. He drew back his hood to reveal a set of angular features and dark brown hair, close-cropped along his scalp. Beneath the shadow of his rough-spun cloak, a cuirass of boiled leather adorned with brass rivets covered a close-fitting mail habergeon.

Royne did his best to swallow his fear. "I might ask you the same question," he said, "Your blades and your armor mark you for Wolves, though it appears you had the good sense to trade your green cloaks for something more inconspicuous."

"I have no time to waste on fools," the man sneered, "I have come to fetch Salasco the Blackguard who men call 'the Wall.'"

Royne's heart beat like a hammer against his sternum and he folded his arms to keep them from shaking. "Why?" he wagered, "Do you intend him harm?"

"I do not," the soldier said, "Though if you do not tell me what you know of him, I cannot say the same for you."

Royne's mind raced as he tried to think, though with the sunlight glimmering on the soldiers' swords, he found it nearly impossible to focus. *What an end for the Loremaster!* he thought, *To die among shit heaps!* He could sense the color draining from his face. "I do not know where he is, nor have I ever met him," Royne said at last, "But if you seek a Blackguard, then perhaps I can help you, for I am one too."

"You?" the soldier scoffed.

Royne took a deep breath and nodded, "Me, though only recently. Why else would I be here among the filth and shit of a thousand beggars if not to hide from the bloody red-cloaks? Blackguards are hunted men. I came here seeking Salasco's help."

"Well, the Wall is not at home."

"So I see. However..." Royne paused. *This is madness, you fool!* he thought, *But what other choice is there?* He sighed, "However, if you are indeed Wolves, then it appears we share the same enemies, and as you need a Blackguard, here I am. Perhaps we can help each other."

Something in the young man's tone seemed to give the soldier pause. He continued to eye Royne with a measure of skepticism, but need, if not belief, appeared to move him. With a heavy sigh, the soldier nodded and exchanged a look with his fellows. "Very well," he said at last, "You're coming with us."

CHAPTER 4: FATHERHOOD

Prince Beledain Tremont stood atop Corlindus the Colt, the southern great tower of Tremontane Castle, and looked down over the courtyard of the place that had once been his home, but had now become his prison. Atop the battlements where Bel's father, in his infirmity was wont to pace, armored sentries now stood watch. No longer were they clad in white tabards bearing the symbol of the Black Horse, the emblem of King Cedric's household guard. Now they wore gray tabards marked with a bloody red handprint, the arms of Wilmar Danelis, the Sundering Hand, Warden of Tremontane Castle in the name of Bel's brother, Dermont, king of the now united Montevale.

United in name, Bel thought, *Though in little else…*

Since the Month of the Horse, Valendia and Gasparn, the southern and northern regions of Montevale, had been united once again after a century of fratricidal conflict. Bel himself was there on the day that King Marius the White Horse, his daughter Marina, and his Lord General, Sir Marcus Harding, a Cavalier of the Order of the Guardians known as the Tower, were trapped with only a small force of retainers in an abandoned mountain keep while the forces of the then Prince Dermont closed in. Though he was the youngest son of the Valendian King, Bel conspired with Sir Harding to end the war and ensure the survival and fair treatment of the Gasparn royals and their soldiers. However, in doing so the Guardian gave his life, anointing Beledain as the new Tower and naming the Valendian Prince his successor as Lord General of Gasparn.

In the end, Dermont claimed his victory and named himself the sovereign of the united Montevale; but his success was limited, for Marius still lived, Marina was unwed, and Bel had finally recognized and stood opposed to his brother's megalomaniacal ambitions.

The Silent Prince breathed a sigh and shut his eyes against the breeze. The night air was cool atop the tower, a refreshing change from the warmth of the daytime sun. He was clad in the garb of a nobleman, though his clothing no longer bore any mark or insignia—Valendian, Gasparn, or Montevalen, for Dermont had claimed that as a member of the Andochan Guardians, it was inappropriate for him to wear the arms of his birth or station. Bel acquiesced, though he recalled making no oath to the Guardians or their King Kredor, nor would he ever—even if it meant becoming a Blackguard. His loyalties were to the people of Montevale. He swore to Sir Harding that he would end the War of the Horses, and though in some sense he had done so, a war could never truly be over without the assurance of a lasting peace.

Bel touched his side, just below his right arm, where the Tower had struck what should have been his fatal blow. He still had difficulty understanding what had happened, and how, in an instant, Harding had healed his body and transferred the wounds to his own. Afterwards, Jarvy had told him there were stories about the Guardians and St. Aiden being able to perform miracles of a sort; however, such things were the stuff of Bard's tales and fairy stories meant for children, surely not reality.

Yet somehow, it had happened and Bel bore the scar to prove it.

There were other things too. He had strange dreams, sometimes nightmares, about battles he had not fought and about castles he had never seen. There were times where he remembered things—bits of history for instance—that he had never taken the time to learn about, and whereas he once trained under his father's seneschal Sir Emory Knott to ensure proficiency with all knightly arms, he found himself more often favoring the lance or the spear, even on foot. Not that there had been much opportunity for testing his skills mounted, for in accordance with his agreement with

Dermont, he was to remain at Tremontane under the eye of Lord Wilmar so as not to insight any trouble, and the courtyard, though spacious, provided little opportunity to put Igno, Bel's beloved chestnut stallion, through the paces. Besides, even if he were allowed to venture forth on a longer ride, he did not trust his brother or his brother's friend enough to leave those he cared for unprotected—his father, Sir Emory, Marius, Marina, and especially Lilia.

Again, Bel sighed and rubbed at his eyes, wondering impatiently how she fared in their private chambers below. As soon as the midwives arrived, he had been banished so as not to interfere. From the moment she woke him, lying beside her in bed, he felt the needles of anxiety pricking him all over and his heart was a wild horse galloping across the plain. He must have looked quite a sight, stricken with anxiety, for in spite of the first pains of her labor, she laughed.

After the battle at the Nivanus keep, Dermont forced Marius, Marina and Bel to travel north to Reginal in order to announce to the Gasparn nobles that the war was over and to encourage them to show fealty to the new Montevalen king. Dermont remained with most of his army in control of the former Gasparn capitol, and Lord Wilmar was sent south with his "charges" to take command of Castle Tremontane. Thus, it was midway through the spring when Bel finally returned to Lilia and she was already heavy with child.

She wept when she saw him, and when he told her everything that had passed in the north, she called him a fool for not marrying the Gasparn princess. However, when he held her that night while they lay together, his hand gently resting upon the curve of her belly, she told him once again how much she loved him.

In truth, there were times where Bel found himself oddly glad for his confinement since it allowed him time to be with her, to attempt to make up for his long absence over the last few months, and to aid her in the challenges she faced as a result of her condition. She was forced to don a peasant woman's frock in place of the boiled leathers of a skirmisher, she grew steadily less lithe and agile, and she no longer felt comfortable sitting a horse—all things that, of course, she found extremely frustrating. Bel did his best to aid her in whatever way he could, and in spite of her frustrations with herself, he found her no less brave or beautiful than the day he departed for Gasparn. Her passion for life, already incomparable, seemed only to have grown, as did her delight in battle, albeit vicariously, and where once Bel thought of her as a lioness of the mountain steppe, he discerned a new softness to her, as well as a heightened ferocity at the prospect of her impending cub.

Of all of the surprises Bel discovered upon his return, however, perhaps the most interesting was the strange amity that had developed between Lilia and his father, King Cedric. According to Sir Emory, they would often sit together or walk the walls in deep conversation while, without them, the war went on. Whenever Bel asked her what they spoke of, she would only smile and say that it was private. Still, it made him happy, and there were few enough causes for that these days.

From the top of the opposite tower (Rowena the Mare as it was known), a new light appeared, fainter than the great braziers along the castle battlements. With it, a figure shuffled out clad all in white. At once Bel knew it for King Marius and he was glad for the way his drab, gray clothing concealed him against the darkness of the night sky. Though the White Horse and his daughter, the Winter Rose, were under Bel's protection, it was often Sir Emory or his few remaining men who kept watch over them daily. For Bel no longer held any command—in either the Tower's Guard or the Valendian light company—and he avoided interacting with the Gasparn royals personally, fearful that his presence and his role in the reversal of their fortunes might exacerbate their confinement. He did ensure, however, that they received every comfort, demanding that the entire tower be given over to them and those few servants brought with them from Reginal. It was far more space than they needed, but perhaps the overindulgence would allow them to feel some measure of respect, some return of dignity.

The whole situation was misery and made Bel's skin crawl with guilt. He turned his back on the castle and crossed the walkway to peer over the edge of the walls at the city below. There, he spied the Cathedral of the Sires, vacant for nearly seventy years after the Grand Hierophant withdrew his officials in a show of public disapproval of the ongoing War of the Horses. Now, it had been restored to its former glory. It amazed Bel to think that Dermont had so easily secured a peace with Andoch after the war and Sir Harding's death, considering how opposed he was to any suggestion of doing the same with Marius and Gasparn. Then again, very little of what Dermont thought or did made any sense to Bel anymore.

The sight of the Cathedral, however, brought his thoughts back again to Lilia, and he wondered how she fared. A great part of him wanted to push past the old midwives so that he could see her. For although he knew Lilia was tough, childbirth was dangerous, probably more dangerous than war, and he had already lost loved ones, directly and indirectly, as a result. When Larius, King Cedric's eldest son and heir, lost his wife and son in childbirth, the grief had driven him to suicide and hastened their father's madness. Although Bel tried not to think on such things, he could not keep the thoughts out of his mind altogether. Should the worst happen, what would he do? Would he do the same? Perhaps that was why over the course of their relationship Lilia had often attempted, albeit unsuccessfully, to engineer a certain distance between them. Until he left for Gasparn, she refused any talk of love, suggesting that their time together could never last. Then, once he returned, and in spite of her condition, she encouraged him to leave her for the Princess of Gasparn, and though she admitted now that she loved him, she refused to become his wife claiming that his role in the larger scope of the realm was too important for him to be bonded to a simple peasant. When she said things like that, it was usually his turn to get angry.

A gasp of alarm woke Bel from his reverie. "Prince Beledain?" said a voice, "Strange to find you wandering the walls at this hour?"

"Good evening, King Marius," Bel said, regretting his forgetfulness regarding the wandering king, "I'm sorry if I startled you."

"It is quite alright," Marius said, "For I am just as guilty of the charges I would brand upon you." He covered the flame of his candle from the wind; however, nature prevailed and the light went out. "Damn," he whispered, "Oh well, no matter."

"Tomorrow I'll have Sir Emory find you an oil lantern," Bel said, "My father used to walk these paths long into the night as well. If you have a mind to pace it'll keep the flame secure."

"Thank you, but no. I would rather not make a habit of such wandering and having the means to do so may simply encourage it."

"As you wish."

King Marius sighed and leaned against the crenellated battlement. Bel was amazed at how much the man had aged in so short a time. The silver had overcome the sable in his hair and beard and his shoulders seemed perpetually slumped. *A king without a country—what hope for the future does he have now?* Bel thought.

"So what is it that keeps you from bed tonight?" Marius asked, "It's a sorry thing to see a young man bearing an expression far more appropriate for the old."

Bel smiled weakly, "I've been banished."

"What?" Marius looked stricken and inwardly Bel cursed his poor choice of words.

"From my chambers," he said hurriedly, "Lilia, my..." he paused, "My...wife is lying-in, and the midwives forced me out."

"Ah," Marius nodded, "I see. Then, let me be the first to wish you joy."

"Thank you."

"You thank me, but you do not yet know what is to come," the old king grinned, "Hence forth, every waking moment of every day from now until you die will be riddled with fear and anxiety over your child, and the best you can ever hope for is to bury that fear long enough to get a good night's sleep."

Bel smiled, but remained silent.

"You think I'm joking," Marius laughed, "You'll see."

"I do not doubt you," Bel said, "Though it seems strange that people would go on having children if it brought nothing but fear."

"Of course not. It just seems that men most often see the worst before the best. In a sense, though, I suppose it's rather wise. We are knocked down by the ill for the good to raise us up again." Marius sighed, "In truth, you will have fear—that much is certain—but the joy your children bring you will outmatch anything else you can ever hope to know."

"Well," Bel sighed, "To be honest, I feel I already know the fear—for both the child and the mother."

The old king nodded, "Marina's mother died of childbed fever. Annalisa, my queen."

"I'm sorry."

Marius sighed, "A mother pays with her life to bring a child into the world, and when he's grown, a lord or a king steals him away to die in a ridiculous war. How fair is that, I ask you?"

"You sound like my father."

"Perhaps it's because, at our age, your father and I have become lost souls, wandering ghosts simply awaiting our graves. The world has passed us by, yet still we linger. I suppose you could say such a thing grants perspective."

Bel breathed a heavy sigh and gazed beyond the city below to the plains. In the east, he could already see the sky lightening. "I'm sorry things are as they are," he said at last.

"You did what you could, which was not insignificant," Marius said, "My daughter lives, and thanks to you, is not the thrall of your accursed brother."

"Though it seems we are all his prisoners."

"It is better than the alternative. You tried your best and against such a hard thing as life often is, what more can a man do but that?" the old king sighed, "I do not hold you responsible for what has happened any more than I blame Sir Marcus. The Tower was ordered to end the war as expediently as possible. He made a gamble taking the path of the Nivanus, and it failed. We all simply—"

The appearance of another light from within the Tower of the Colt moved Marius to silence. Tentatively, the servant carrying the light addressed them. "Pardon me, my lords," he said, "But Prince Beledain, they've called for you."

Bel's head felt light and his hands tingled. The old king grinned and patted him on the back. "Go to them," he said.

Bel nodded silently, and before he even knew what he was doing, he was through the door to the tower and on his way to his chambers, the servant hurrying after him with the light. With every step upon the stairs, his breath grew quicker and a dull, nagging ache radiated from the depths of his chest. He was excited and terrified all at once. However, when he reached the door to the chambers where Lilia lay, a stout, weary-looking midwife blocked his passage any further.

"Is it over?" Bel asked quickly, "Are they alright?"

"Calm yourself, my lord, please," the midwife said sternly.

"Why?" he asked, "What's wrong?"

"Hush, my lord, calm."

"Why?" Bel asked anxiously, "Why do I need to calm down? What's happened?" His hands trembled and he bit his lip, "Speak or let me pass."

The midwife suppressed a sudden flash of irritation and held up a stern hand. "You have a son," she said, "And healthy at that."

"A son?" Bel repeated. His lips spread wide into a smile, "A son?" She was right. Lilia said it would be a boy. His heart leapt and his knees grew weak. "A son, you say, and healthy?"

"That's what I said, my lord."

"Aiden's Flame," his whole body trembled, "And Lilia? How is she? Is she fine? Can I see them?"

The midwife held up her hand again to calm him. "Please, my lord..."

Bel fought to control his rising anxiety. "Speak! Tell me!" he begged her.

"She lost a great deal of blood—more than was to be expected, but we seem to have it managed. Still, she is very weak and needs rest. Barring any infection, however, she should recover."

Bel rubbed his eyes; he felt a pain in his stomach like he had just been kicked by a horse, "She'll recover? You're certain."

"My lord, there are no certainties when it comes to these matters."

"None?"

"Please calm down, my lord."

Bloody harpy! How can I be calm when you won't let me pass?! he thought. All around him, the world seemed to be moving incredibly slowly while his every thought or action was consumed with the need for haste. His chest felt light and heavy all at once, and part of him felt like he was about to vomit. He waved his hands in exacerbation, "For the love of the Father Alantir, can I see them or what!?"

The midwife narrowed her gaze, and for a moment, Bel eyed her like an opponent in battle, wondering how difficult it would be to knock her aside. Luckily, before it came to that, she gave a terse click of her tongue. "You may pass, my lord," she said, "But you had best calm down. As I said, she's weak and needs rest, and the baby will need sleep as well."

"I understand," he said, struggling to suppress his agitation. *Give her a pike and a shield and no cavalry charge would ever break that line!* he thought as she finally, finally let him pass.

Inside, more midwives wandered about here and there, but Bel hardly saw them, for his eye beheld only Lilia lying pale and languorously in their bed. When she saw him, she smiled wanly and raised the tightly wrapped bundle of linen in her arms.

"Your son," she whispered triumphantly.

Struck dumb with emotion, Bel ran to her side and kissed her deeply. Her mouth was dry, he thought, perhaps absurdly, and he meant to call for water; however, a moment later, when she gently passed the baby into his arms, his mind went blank.

"Our son," he said.

He was so small and so pink, bundled up so tightly that only his little face was visible, framed by tufts of black hair along his crown. He gave a little yawn and for a moment, Bel's vision blurred and he feared he would faint.

It wasn't until he heard Lilia's quiet laughter that he was able to think straight again. She wiped away the tears as they began slowly trailing down her cheeks. "You should see your face," she grinned.

"You should see yours," he smiled.

"Shut it. You know I hate to cry in front of you."

Bel shook his head. "Not that," he said, bending to kiss her again, "You're beautiful."

Lilia rolled her eyes. "Such nonsense," she said, breathing a weary sigh.

One of the midwives pushed a chair over to the bedside so that he might sit, and Bel, remembering, asked her to bring water. He looked from his child to the young mother beside him. Her skin was pale and her eyes drooped shut.

"He's very handsome," Lilia observed with another sigh, "Like his father."

Bel watched her, and his stomach tied in knots, "How do you feel?"

"Weary," she breathed, "But happy."

Bel hugged his son close, the baby's skin soft against his cheek. He could not get over how seemingly fragile and delicate the baby was. For a moment, he feared that simply by holding his son, he might somehow break him. A great lump formed in his throat and he recalled King Marius's words.

He felt Lilia's hand touch his arm. "Marcus…" she said.

"What?" Bel repeated.

"You can name him Marcus," Lilia repeated.

"I thought you didn't like that name?"

"No," she said, "I just thought it a bit odd that you'd want to name your son after a man meant to be your enemy."

"Aye, but he was also my friend," Bel said, "And he saved my life."

"I remember," Lilia breathed a heavy sigh and reached out to take his hand.

The midwife returned with water and offered it to Bel. "I'll take the child, my lord," she told him, "He needs his cradle so as to let the humors settle properly."

Bel shook his head in confusion, "Of…course."

51

"Give him here," Lilia said, "Just a moment."

The midwife took the boy from Bel and held him alongside his mother's cheek. "Goodnight, Marcus, my little colt," she whispered and kissed him lightly on the head, "I love you."

"It's near dawn," Bel said as the midwife placed his son in his crib and gently set it rocking from side to side, "The sun will rise soon on the first day of summer. A son with the sun."

Lilia nodded, "I'm so weary." She breathed another sigh, "Lie here with me?"

Bel smiled, and seating himself along the edge of the bed, he offered her water to drink. She emptied the cup and he set it on the floor beside them before lying back at her side.

"Don't go," she whispered, letting her head roll to rest on his shoulder, "Even if they try to make you, don't."

"I won't," he said, and kissed her brow, "I love you."

"I used to get *so* angry at you for saying that," she told him.

"Believe me, I remember," he said, kissing her again.

"I'm sorry," she said, "I was just...I was just...afraid."

"Why? What were you afraid of?"

She swallowed slowly, and again, tears traced down her cheeks. When she spoke, her voice was thick, "I always thought you would have to leave me, and I knew the more you said it, the more I felt it, the harder it would be."

"Oh Lilia," he whispered, and suddenly the tears welling in his eyes, "I told you; I love you. I would never leave you."

"I know," she breathed, "Believe me. I know. But I think..." she paused, "I think I might have to leave you..."

"What do you mean?"

Bel watched as her hand slowly drifted along the inside of her leg and the white linen sheet turned sopping wet in a steadily widening lake of crimson. "Lady's Grace!" he cried as panic gripped him, tearing at his heart, and turning his blood to ice. "She's bleeding!" he shouted at a passing midwife as he felt Lilia going limp in his arms. In his cradle, the baby suddenly began to cry. In an instant, the world seemed to collapse and Bel felt more helpless than he had ever felt in his life. The women rushed to Lilia's aid, and before Bel knew it, the woman from the hallway was pulling at his arm, saying some madness about him waiting in the hall. "No!" he screamed in abject terror, his cries echoing those of his newborn son, "Help her! In the name of the Brethren! Help her! *Help her!* She's bleeding!"

CHAPTER 5: THE SEA DRAGON

Regardless of the hour, from dawn to dusk and back again, the Sea Dragon was a lively and ribald tavern. Beneath the wooden signboard, two wide double doors stood perpetually open in sun and storm to entice any sailor with two coins to rub together into spending them within. The common room had been built beneath the overturned hull of an old longship and where once men sat at oars preparing themselves to raid and pillage the coastal villages of Termain, Kord, Tulondis and even further, great iron braziers burning seal oil hung on thick chains above a dozen round wooden tables. From the common room, the starboard side opened into a series of small rooms for dice and gambling, and to port, a hallway opened into another area that served as both an inn and a brothel. Across the Sorgund Isles, the Sea Dragon remained one of the most beloved, most revered attractions, perhaps even more than the Mermaid, the Shipyard, or even the brothel at Pearl's Rift, and it seemed an exceptionally busy evening on the night when Thom and Magnus passed through that open doorway.

As always, the sight of the enormous, red-bearded Wrathorn and the chubby, freckled boy with hair like a great gingery mushroom drew an awkward blend of grimaces and jeers, though never, ever, within the big man's range of hearing. Magnus Bloodbeard, of course, was well known by reputation and had been for a number of years. It was not that he commanded respect, per se, but was rather known for his ferocity and his short temper. The boy, however, draped in his odd burgundy robes, stained now along the edges by the salt of the sea, was somewhat of a curiosity. He turned up with Magnus sometime in the early winter not long after rumor had spread that the Wrathorn warrior had finally met his end. Then, one day out of the blue, here comes Magnus, boy in tow with quill in hand to scribble down the seemingly random misadventures of the self-described Wrathorn King.

There will be plenty to write about today... Thom thought miserably, pinching his nose against the stench of spilled grog, pipe smoke, and tavern strumpets that wafted out over the tavern floor like an early morning fog. His face had already turned pale, for after months and months of wandering the Isles from ship to ship and port to port, Magnus had finally caught word that one of his old shipmates had returned to the unofficial Sorgund capitol city of Coverland. And when a man came to Coverland, sooner or later, he would make his way to the Sea Dragon.

Meekly, Thom followed in Magnus's wake as the big man crossed the floor of the common room, traversing the inverted longship all the way from bow to stern where a large mob of mariners sat laughing and drinking around two round tables pushed clumsily together. A pair of painted whores flitted about from man to man giggling and flashing occasional peeks at their bare breasts. Thom had met many of their kind over his travels with Magnus, and though he no longer feared them as he once did, they always made him feel rather sad. When they spied Magnus coming, they subtly tried to get away. Clearly, they could sense that there was about to be trouble; however, heedless of the danger that was Magnus, the drunken sailors held them fast upon their laps.

Thom muttered a quick prayer to the Brethren that they would not be counted among the dead.

"Look who it is, boys!" one of the sailors grinned, "It's King Magnus, back from the dead!" Of all the men, he seemed to be the one in charge, dressed gaudily in bright red silks and pantaloons sewn from cloth of gold. A heavy falchion hung from a thick leather baldric running from his shoulder to his hip and his few remaining teeth shone with gold against the nut-brown shade of his sunburned skin, "What can we do for you tonight, your majesty?"

"You can fucking die, Pavlos!"

In a flash, the big Wrathorn drew his great bearded axe, Death, and swung it with all his might in a wide arc in front of him. One man fell dead, his chest split open in a mess of gore while a second lost half his arm. The rest of the crew leapt to their feet and drew their weapons, jostling the tables and knocking the two prostitutes to the floor.

Thom dove for cover behind another table, overturned as the tavern's other patrons scattered to escape. One of the girls had fallen nearby and he was able to help her crawl to cover beside him. He shut his eyes and stopped his ears against the sounds of battle, his nose burning from the sickeningly sweet odor of the whore's perfume, and tried to think on happy times long ago in the Loremaster's Tower. A moment later, however, something heavy knocked into the table and the girl beside him shrieked in fright. Thankfully, when Thom chanced to open his eyes, it was only a headless corpse sent flying by Magnus's frenzied wrath. He rarely threw up at the sight of such things anymore, though the same could not be said for the girl at his side.

A few minutes later, the sound of the fighting seemed to die down, and while the poor prostitute beside him huddled close to him, digging her fingernails into his arm in an effort not to be sick again, Thom peeked around the table's edge to see if Magnus had finally finished up yet.

Apart from the Wrathorn Blackguard, only three men remained—a sailor with a spiked club, a sailor with one eye, and the man with the falchion, Pavlos—the man Magnus had come to kill. Apart from them, the floor was strewn with blood and dead bodies, though thankfully, Thom noticed, the other woman had not been harmed either. She cowered in the corner behind the remains of a broken chair, spidery lines of makeup streaming down her cheeks with her tears.

The three sailors opposing Magnus eyed each other carefully and began sidestepping around to try to flank him. Magnus took a step back, his beard and his leather brigantine splattered with crimson. "You sold me to the bloody Guardians, you bastard," he growled.

"So we did!" Pavlos spat, "Call it fair exchange for the fucking gold you cost us!"

"I call it mutiny and betrayal!"

"Aye, and so did we!"

The man with one eye lunged at Magnus with a longsword, but the barbarian easily dodged the blow, and in one swift motion, grabbed the man around the shoulder, threw him to the floor, and separated his head from his neck.

"Where are Slink and Rodolf the Churl?"

Pavlos spit on the ground and raised his falchion, "Fuck you and fuck them too!"

Magnus advanced on the sailor with the club and swung his axe. The man tried to parry the blow, but Death snapped the wood like kindling and tore into the man's belly. Thom looked away so he wouldn't have to see the man's intestines spill to the floor and plugged his ears against the screaming. Beside him, the whore fainted.

When Thom looked back around the table, he could see that now only Magnus and Pavlos remaining. He unplugged his ears and listened.

"I'm going to kill you, Pavlos!" Magnus hissed, "I'm going to kill you and piss on your corpse!"

"You're welcome to try, you filthy Wrathorn pig-fucker!" the pirate swore, "Come now! Do your worst!"

"Where are they?!"

"If I knew that, I'd have killed them myself! The bastards took off without me to sell the bloody thing!"

"What?!" Magnus shouted, "To who?"

"Fuck you!"

With a cry of fury, Magnus charged and brought his axe down with a ground-shattering blow only to miss when Pavlos turned tail and ran for the door at an all-out sprint. Without a second thought, Magnus dropped his axe, and chased after him, tackling him to the floor. The two rolled about in a mad frenzy of snarling and savage clawing, until finally, Magnus emerged the victor and squeezed the sailor's throat between his hands. He did not ease his grip until long after Pavlos's body fell still and stopped flopping about like a fish on dry land.

At length, an eerie silence fell over the tavern and Thom patted the prostitute on the cheek until she finally awoke with a start.

"Sweet Lady's Grace, Magnus!" a man snapped, rising from cover behind the bar, "How about a little warning the next time you feel like destroying the place, you bearded, fucking clam! Give us a little more time to clear out."

Magnus glanced around him at the ruins of the empty barroom. In addition to the bodies and the blood, at least three of the tables and half a dozen stools lie broken on the floor with an assortment of crockery.

"It's not that bad," he said, "Besides, you're the one sent word he was here."

"I knew you were going to kill him, but not trash the fucking bar," the bartender sighed, shook his head, and poured two tin cups of grog. "Helma, find Yoren and Fink and tell them to clean this shit up."

The whore at Thom's side nodded, ran a quivering hand through her hair, and scurried off to do as she was told. Thom wandered over to where Magnus knelt down looting Pavlos's body. "You better hurry and count this lot before they started tossing them out," the Wrathorn said. He slipped the dead man's baldric and scabbard free from his shoulder and tightened it around his own waist. "Remember—the ones where the head came clean off count as two."

Thom sighed, "Sorry, I'm still not quite clear on exactly why they should count as two. It's still only one man."

Magnus found Pavlos's falchion and returned it to the sheath. "They count as two because it's harder!" he said, "It *should* count for more. Ask anyone. You ever cut a man's head clean from his body in one swipe?"

"You know very well that I have not."

"Well, there you have it then, eh?" Magnus sighed, lifted Pavlos's purse and tossed it to the bartender, "Here you go, Ivo, there's a start. I'm sure the others got more you're welcome to."

"They'd better," Ivo muttered. He drained his cup and filled it again. "Now hurry up and drink this with me. I'm already one ahead of you."

Magnus went off to join Ivo, and Thom went off to record the tally. He learned it was easiest to count by way of the torsos and the heads, for once the arms and legs started lopping off it was hard to tell what part belonged to what man. It was grim work, but he was less afraid of the dead than he was of Ivo, the Sea Dragon's owner. Luckily, Ivo seemed to have a liking for Magnus and usually only spoke to him. In fact, only once had the bartender ever actually even looked at him, but that alone nearly made Thom soil himself. Ivo's eyes were as cold and hard as flint.

"May your enemies flee before you and Death follow in your wake," Magnus said, raising his grog.

In the corner, the other whore was still sobbing with fear and Thom wondered if she was new. He was about to go try to calm her, when Ivo shouted at her from the bar. "Enough already with the fucking tears, Meera! Go get the other girls. We're not closing!"

Thom offered the woman a sympathetic shrug, but remained silent, and soon enough she hurried off to relay the message. Before long, the gaggle of prostitutes was back out front leaning suggestively in the doorway, and Ivo's men got to work dragging the bodies of the dead sailors out through the back door to toss over the pier. Little by little, men trickled back in to drink, gamble, and whore, and soon enough, the Sea Dragon was just as lively as it had been before Magnus's rowdy arrival.

When the last of the bodies had been picked clean and dragged out back, Thom found his way to Magnus at the bar. "That's nineteen," he said.

"Including the headless ones?"

"Yes."

"And you're counting them as two?"

"Yes, yes. I told you I would."

"Good," the Wrathorn grinned, "Though I think Pavlos should count for five, on account he's one of the big fish."

"Five?" Thom asked, "Why should that be?"

Ivo refilled Magnus's cup and tossed him a dirty rag. "Don't get blood on my bar," he snapped.

For the first time, Magnus noticed a gash on his shoulder. He wiped at it absentmindedly before turning back to Thom.

"Pavlos counts as five. Same for Slink and Rodolf when we find them," he said, "Make a note of it."

"Alright, alright," Thom sighed.

Since they took ship with the smugglers in Galdoran, Thom followed Magnus around the Isles in his personal quest for vengeance. Little by little, he was able to piece together the odd bits of the story that resulted in the Wrathorn Blackguard's capture at the Sandstone. From what he could tell, Magnus and three of his old shipmates had some sort of disagreement. What it was, the Wrathorn warrior would never speak of, even when Thom tried to convince him that it was necessary for writing the story. Regardless, Magnus was determined to repay their treachery with blood, and Thom was to record the adventure so that the tale could be spread far and wide as a testament to the true ways of the Wrathorn.

Magnus grinned and gave Thom a hard shove. "Two more to go!" he laughed, "Now that's nice, right? Won't be long that we're done and you're free to go back to Andoch or wherever it is you were wanting."

"Titanis."

"Aye, the city of Guardian tits. You're free to go back there and read and scribble all you want, and tell them the tale of Magnus the Great."

Again, Thom sighed and attempted to clamber up onto a barstool, but thought better of it with Ivo so near. He remained standing. "It took us near a year to find Pavlos. How long before we find the other two?"

"As long as it takes," Magnus said, "Now have a drink."

"No, thanks."

"Do it—Ivo, over here."

"Magnus…"

"Drink up! It might put some hair on that chest of yours."

"I don't like grog."

"Drink it!"

"Fine," Thom said, and with a shudder, he drank the foul, bitter liquid.

"Alright, Thom Crusher, there we are," Magnus laughed as the boy sputtered, "I'd say that now's about when you need a girl, but we all know how that went last time."

Thom's brow furrowed with indignation and he could feel his cheeks growing hot. Ivo's grog was strong. "Last time they were all very nice," he said.

Magnus laughed and with a nod to Ivo, helped himself to a jug of grog from behind the bar. "You do know what a whore is for, don't you?" he asked Thom.

"I know what *you* think they're for."

"Right. Well, I can tell you that they're certainly *not* for telling stories to, or for sitting around with whilst you pluck about on a lyre singing like a lark."

"They liked my singing. They told me I have a fine voice."

Magnus shook his head in exacerbation, "How have you not died yet?"

Thom folded his arms, "Well, what *am* I supposed to do while you're off…doing what you do?"

"*You* could be doing what I do!" Magnus laughed, "You should be, in fact. How old are you? Old enough, I'd say, to at least show an interest."

"I just don't think it's right," he said with a shrug, "It seems to me that many—if not most of them—never had a choice in their professions. They were bought and sold like cattle, and they're forced into a lifestyle that seems more like slavery than service."

"Great Bear's Bollocks! Listen to you."

"I just don't think it's right to take advantage of people due to poverty."

"What thoughts you think in that fat head of yours. It's the way of the world, matey."

"Aye," Thom said, "So it is with the nobles and the kings, but don't you hate all of them precisely for that reason?"

"One of the reasons, I suppose, but—" Magnus drained his cup, "Oh you know what? No! Just shut up. You have to ruin everything, don't you?"

The chubby apprentice shrugged, "It's just my opinion."

"Well, best to keep it to yourself whilst we conclude our business here, eh?"

"Fine."

A short while later, Ivo appeared and leaned in toward Magnus. As always, Thom pretended not to be listening. "They say *The Gander* came in from raiding the Grantisi coast, but neither of the other two was with him nor has anyone seen them."

Magnus pursed his lips. "Pavlos was a piece of shit and a hard man to stay around for too long. First ship they took that was seaworthy Slink and Rodolf would have gone off—so long as they could spare the crew," he paused, "Speaking of...*The Gander*'s cargo is yours so long as you help me find enough lads to man her."

"Planning a voyage?" Ivo crooned.

"So it seems."

"Any place nice?"

The Wrathorn warrior narrowed his gaze and stared into the depths of his drink, "Grantis."

"What?" Thom piped as his heart caught in his throat. A pair of cold stares silenced him further.

At length, Ivo chewed his lip, "You think after they left Pavlos, Rodolf and Slink might still be haunting the coasts?"

"No," Magnus shrugged, "But once I get to Grantis, I'll know for certain where they've gone." He paused to spit a great wad on the floor, "So, as far as a crew…?"

"Might be I could help with that," Ivo said, "With the war and all, goods out of Grantis have been scarce. Depending on what Pavlos and his men have sitting idle in *The Gander's* hold, I might be able to send some hands your way."

"They'd have to be solid lads now," Magnus said, "I don't want no craven milksops on this ship."

"Magnus," Ivo grinned, "You insult me. I might employ whores and halfwit potboys, but I still keep better company than you."

Once more, Thom felt Ivo's eyes upon him, but he pretended not to notice.

"The boy's got his uses," Magnus muttered.

"I don't ask," Ivo smirked, "And I don't judge."

"Fuck off," Magnus grunted, "So you'll help me, eh?"

"I'll ask around," Ivo said, "In the meantime, I assume you and your…what-have-you will be needing rooms? Maybe some company as well?"

"Grog and some food would be fine for now, and the rooms. We'll see about the company once the jug here is empty," the Wrathorn shrugged. "None for him, though," he added with a glance at Thom, "He don't think it's right."

"What times we live in?" Ivo laughed and pounded his hand on the bar top. "Do as you wish," he declared, "Or who, rather. Pavlos paid your way."

CHAPTER 6: ST. ELISA'S GROTTO

The moon shone high as Brigid passed like a shadow through the cobblestone streets of Hounton. The night air was cool, a pleasant break from the warmth that had come to mark the days, and for the first time in a while, she did not feel uncomfortable beneath the cover of her dark cloak. No, this time, her unrest came from a different source, or perhaps, sources. For, she knew very well that Geoffrey ardently disapproved of her solitary wanderings around the city, particularly at night, and though he never once offered her any direct word of reproach, she could not help but feel guilty for contravening his wishes. She knew he meant well, and it was only out of concern for her wellbeing that he objected; however, while he was content to sit patiently awaiting an audience with the Baron, Brigid was not. As the Falcon told her, there were many mice running about the woodpiles of the world. She was but one, Geoffrey was another, and from the moment she first spied the Houndstooth on the ridge, she wondered how many more mice might be hiding in a woodpile of that size.

But the guards had turned them away claiming the baron was not receiving. They refused to believe anything either she or Geoffrey told them about Regnar the Vanguard or Gareth the Blade. Even when she showed them Whisper and Shade and Geoffrey showed them Oakheart and Acorn, they did nothing apart from speculate that the arms were stolen, for they were far too fine for the likes of two peasants. As a last resort, Brigid even told them who she really was—the daughter of the Archduke of Dwerin, but the men only laughed and reminded them once again that they would just have to wait.

To Geoffrey, this seemed reasonable. With rumors circulating that the baron was ill, he thought it prudent to wait rather than thrust themselves upon him at such a trying time.

However, while Brigid admired the farmer's patience, she simply would not give up, and if anything, felt an even greater sense of urgency. The drastic changes in her life since departing Dwerin had given her a taste for adventure, for making the impossible possible, and she could not just sit idly by and wait. She was, after all, the Blade, and if the Falcon had been able to find his way into Blackstone, then perhaps she might find a way into Houndstooth. Surely, no castle was impregnable—whatever the stories might say.

From Hounton, she passed through the archway into the Trade Quarter noticing a marked change in the condition of the buildings and the clothing of the few folk still out wandering the streets so late at night. Hounton, or "Dog Town" as it was sometimes called, generally housed the laborers and the other peasant folk, while the Trade Quarter was home to merchants, shopkeepers, and journeymen of the Weavers' Guild. In Hounton, Geoffrey, Annabel, Brigid, and the children were lucky enough from the judicious sale of her old jewelry to afford to keep a house of their own. Most buildings, however, hosted a number of families divided by floor. In the Trade Quarter, though not the fine houses of the wealthy Guild Masters and Rich Burghers of the Golden Quarter, the homes were often painted or had windows made of real glass. Some even had small gardens. It was here too, that most of the pilgrims visiting the cathedral for the Feast of St. Aiden found lodgings among the many inns, and it was they who were responsible for the majority of the raucous merrymaking that Brigid could hear floating upon the wind out of the taverns.

For a moment, she paused and watched them through a window—singing, laughing, dancing—and she could not help but remember her last days at Blackstone with her mother's betrothal upon the Feast of the Lady. It made her shudder and she pressed her hand to the space along her back, just above the baldric, slightly on the left-hand side. It was the place where Alan had stabbed her with her own blade. The wound had healed instantly when the Falcon traded his life for hers; however, she still bore the scars, internal and external. For, her chest grew tight whenever she remembered his death, and her blue eyes sparkled with tears.

But now was not the time. She shook her head, drew up her cowl, and hurried on her way in the direction of the cathedral in Saints Quarter. From this point on, she knew she had to be extra careful, for it was from here that the other day she felt the cold tremor of fear emanating from the direction of the provincial's manor. It was a strange type of awareness, similar in some ways to the feeling she had when she first saw Geoffrey at the docks in Dwermouth; however, whereas then she had felt a sense of familiarity, even friendship, this feeling was one of alarm, even dread.

Keeping to the shadows, she scurried along the streets and past the great cathedral to where even now pilgrims knelt in the courtyard deep in prayer before an enormous bronze statue of the great saint. Others walked barefoot around the perimeter of the building, pausing at each of its five sides to utter orisons of adoration or contrition. The great carven doors of the cathedral itself, though, were shut up and locked for the night for fear of thieves and other unsavory folk; however, inside a brazier was kept burning at all times, illuminating the stained-glass windows to guide those outside in their acts of devotion.

In Dwerin, few people had much use for religion beyond its ceremonial function as a means to mark a feast, and although she had not attended the services like Geoffrey and his family, Brigid did find there was something about the idea of the religion that she could appreciate. Perhaps it was the notion of the Kinship as a family, a loving family—something she had never known herself. Living alongside Geoffrey and Annabel had offered some insight, watching how they interacted with each other, or with Greta and Freddy. In many ways, truth be told, over the course of the past few months, she had come to regard the little family with a deep, almost familial affection as well; however, as much as she might care for them and they cared for her, she knew that it was still not her own. Her real mother had only hate in heart for her, and her father had been dead now six years. Brigid was alone.

Behind the cathedral, a small path led past the handmaids' priory, Our Lady of the Brock, to the Gardens of St. Elisa, St. Aiden's wife. In the rear of the gardens, below the rocky crags of the ridge upon which the Houndstooth stood, was a small grotto with a natural spring. At night, while the daytime blossoms slept, moonflowers bloomed in great swaths and the small, marble stature of St. Elisa glowed in the light of the summer moon. The sight alone was often enough to cure Brigid of her restlessness, and when she discovered this midway through the Month of the Stone, it quickly became her favorite site in Galadin.

However, it gained another level of significance to her last week; for it was here that she saw the hound.

It was enormous. A great, golden creature with a long snout and floppy ears, it appeared from out of nowhere on the far side of the grotto's pool. For a moment, she was frightened, believing it to be a wolf or a bear or some other creature let loose upon her for trespassing in the gardens at night. However, rather than bark or growl or chase her, it simply sat down with its head held regally alert and watched her with its sad, green eyes. She could not tell how long she had stood there beneath its gaze before it finally turned and disappeared up along the ridge, yet she was certain now that it was a spirit hound—the symbol of Galadin—and the only place it could possibly have come from was the castle.

But how? Surely such a thing crossing through the town would have caused a stir, for the only way to reach the castle gate was by way of the Golden Quarter, and to reach the grotto from there, the hound would have had to cross both the Trade and Saint's Quarters as well. There must be another way then. Perhaps a secret path? One that lead up from the grotto along the ridge to the castle?

She was determined to find out.

A sudden sound from the direction of the path awoke Brigid from her quiet contemplation. On instinct, she dropped low to the ground and held very still. In the moonlight, she could discern two figures ambling slowly toward the grotto, and from the way they moved, they appeared to be men weighed down at the shoulders by chain hauberks. *The bloody watchmen!* she thought, *Aiden's Flame!* Thankfully, her dark cloak had kept her hidden from sight and she was able to dart behind the cover of a large peony bush. With any luck, they would make their rounds and be on their way, though she made a mental note to remember this new patrol route. Perhaps one of the handmaids in the priory had also seen the hound and complained to the guards about a golden monster stalking the gardens at night?

As the men drew nearer, however, Brigid could see that, although both were armed with swords and wore chainmail byrnies, neither was clad in the telltale tabard of the Galadin watch—baronial blue with a golden hound rampant. No, they were certainly not guards, and from the concealment of the peony bush, she watched as they wandered along the path toward the pool, straining her ears to hear whatever it was they were saying.

"Do you see anything?"

"Of course not. It's dark, you twit."

"That nun said there was a stair or some such hidden along the wall—a way for the clergy to sneak the relics to the castle in case of a siege."

In the shadows, Brigid's lips spread into a sly smile. She was right; there *was* a secret path. But, who were these men, and why were they so interested in getting into the castle?

"I still don't see it," the first man said, "Do you?"

"I can't see for shit, mate."

"Look, the order comes straight from Harlow. If we go back without finding out for sure, he's going to be right pissed at us both."

"I'll show you pissed," the second man snorted. He drew nearer to the edge of the pool and a moment later there came the sound of trickling water. Brigid's blood burned with indignation and her hands found Whisper and Shade.

"Oi! You can't do that!" the first man snapped in a harsh whisper, "That's sacrilege!"

"What do I give a shit about some Broken tart's pool?" he laughed, finished his business, and sighed with relief, "Wouldn't it be funny if the nuns bathe in here? Wouldn't it be funny to see their shriveled old lady teats?"

"You're one sick bastard. I've half a mind to tell the Hammer what you've done."

"Bugger the Hammer! I'm sick of his shit as it is. At least a dozen men we lost chasing this damned Marshal all those months back, to say nothing of the bastard's own hand, and still he carries on north into the Brock? I'll not die for that. Harlow can eat his bloody hammer for all I care."

Brigid's eyed flashed. The Marshal! They were after the Marshal! He *was* in the castle. Before she knew what she was doing, she leapt out of the shadows and drew her blades. Both men cried out in fear and the man who had just finished soiling the fountain nearly fell back into the water in surprise.

"What did you say about the Marshal?" she demanded.

"Warlock's balls!" said the man by the pool, "Who are you?"

Brigid was glad for the shade of her hood so that they could not see her blushing. She really had not thought this through. *What would the Falcon say?* she wondered, *What would he do?*

"I'm the one who's going to cut out your tongue if I get tired of waiting for it to speak," she said coldly.

The first man held out a hand in supplication though Brigid could see the other slowly moving toward his hilt. *What to do? What to do?* she thought.

"What do you want to know?" he asked.

Brigid felt her heart beating faster and faster in her chest. *Oh how foolish! Just like at Blackstone! Far too reckless!* "First, I want you to take your hand off of your sword," she said.

"No," he said simply.

The second man answered by drawing his blade.

"I'm warning you," Brigid said, "I'll kill you if you insist on fighting. All I want to know is what you said about the Marshal?"

The first man narrowed his gaze and drew his sword too, "You drew on us first."

"Aye, darling, I'd say that's hardly friendly," said the second, "Now how about you drop those knives on the ground and take down that cowl so we can have a proper look at you?"

Foolish! So foolish! Her mind raced as she tried to decide on a course of action—to fight or to run? Fight and they might kill her. Run and they might catch her. She steeled herself for the former; the last time she tried to run she was stabbed in the back. Better to face Death with a smile. There was always the chance it might frighten him away.

"Come on, lass, put down the knives. *Now!*"

Brigid raised her blades, "No."

The first man took a step forward and waved his sword, clearly expecting her to falter, but instead, Brigid stepped to the side and Shade knocked the blade away while Whisper countered, slashing at the man's sword arm. As he cried out in pain, she leapt back out of his reach. "You bitch!" he shouted clutching the gash across his arm, "Kill her!"

The second man grunted and charged, but she simply sidestepped out of his way, slashing at the back of his byrnie with Whisper as he passed. The blade could not sever the steel links, but it was enough of a surprise to give the man pause as she regained her footing.

Once more Brigid stepped back away from the pair, and realized suddenly that—to her surprise—she appeared to be winning. Her breath quickened with her pulse, and the smile returned to her lips. "All I ask is that you tell me what I want to know," she said, her blue eyes aglow in the moonlight, "Or, if you'd like, you can keep fighting and I can cleanse the pool you soiled with your blood."

The man with the wounded arm ground his teeth against the pain and transferred his sword to his other hand while the second man raised his blade and prepared again for another charge.

"You little shit!" he snapped, "I'll piss on your corpse next and leave you floating in the—"

The rest of his words were lost in a flood of growling and screaming. From somewhere among the moonflowers and the peonies, the golden hound appeared and wasted no time leaping into the fray.

The first man shrieked in abject terror. He lunged in panicked fury as the great beast tore at his comrade's throat, but before his sword could make contact, Brigid was upon him, thrusting both her blades between the tiny rings of his byrnie to the soft flesh underneath. At once, his body shuddered and went limp, but the sheer weight of the man nearly dragged her down to the ground beneath him.

With both men dead, Brigid leaned forward onto her knees to catch her breath. She threw back her cowl and her brow was moist with sweat. A great swath of her dress was streaked with blood, though thankfully none of it was her own. Carefully, she drew the daggers free from the corpse, wiped them clean along his britches, and turned to face the hound. Somehow, she did not believe he was a threat, but it was better to be cautious. To her surprise, however, she found him sitting again, just as he had that first time she had seen him beside the pool. His long red tongue lolled out of the side of his bloodstained jaws and Brigid had the distinct feeling that he was smiling. She returned her daggers to their sheaths.

"Um..." she began, feeling suddenly very strange about talking to a dog, "Thank you...I suppose..."

The hound gave a snort, ran to her side, and sniffed her. For a moment, Brigid drew back in fright, but when her hand grazed the hound's ear, she was surprised at its softness. Hesitantly, she patted the great creature on the head and a shudder of excitement ran through her. A spirit hound! She recalled the hours spent daydreaming to escape the confines of Blackstone and her wretched mother and cousin. How often had a spirit hound of Perindal made an appearance in those visions! Yet here he was now—in the flesh! Was it true that they could understand speech? That they were truly as intelligent as any man?

Before she had the presence of mind to ask, however, the hound gave her one last nuzzle, snorted, and ran off, disappearing along the rocky ridge.

"W-wait!" she called after him, straining her vision in hopes that she might spy the hidden path, "Come back!"

More than anything, she wanted to follow the hound, but in light of the two corpses, she knew it was more important now that she flee. Dead men had a way of attracting attention, particularly in the gardens of a priory. Quickly, she checked the bodies for any sign of who the men were or what they were doing—anything that might in some way bring her closer to the Marshal. It was not a pretty sight, particularly the man taken by the hound, but she ignored the churning of her stomach as she searched them.

Apart from their mail and their swords, there was nothing noteworthy about them. They could easily have passed for mercenaries or caravan guards. Both wore simple, nondescript traveler's garb that bore no mark, emblem, or insignia; however, when turning out their purses, mixed in among the small pile of copper pennies, both carried cloak pins fashioned in the likeness of a silver key.

Andoch, she thought, *Soldiers of the Guardian King! But what were they doing here? What were they after?*

And suddenly she remembered. They were Blackguards—her, Geoffrey, probably the Marshal too, and she recalled what it was Alan had said on that day long ago when she first met the Falcon. Blackguards were deserters, turncoats, hunted men. She sighed. Whoever this Hammer was, she had the feeling that he was not a friend.

At length, Brigid looked up at the stars shining behind the silhouette of the Houndstooth, and lifted her hood. Geoffrey would not be pleased when she told him what had happened, but he still needed to know. Quickly, she pocketed one of the brooches, and as swift as a shadow, ran for home.

CHAPTER 7: THE FIGHTING FIFTH

For two days, Royne and Conor were carried along behind the Grantisi soldiers as they rode with all haste westward across the fertile fields and planes of the fallen republic. The men spoke very little and rested even less—only as much as was necessary for the sake of the horses. Some grave errand drove them, one that turned their bronze complexions ashen with care.

As Royne had surmised, the men were soldiers attached to one of the few remaining legions that had refused to lay down arms after the larger Grantisi surrender (which would account for the clandestine nature of their visit to the capitol). Royne had never been one for military history or tactics, martial matters belonging more to Lughus's interests than his own; however, based purely on geography, he knew that by traveling westward, the men were nearing the region known as the Spade, which for years had been the source of border disputes and full-scale war between Dwerin and the republic. Thus, if the town criers were to be believed, the legionnaires operating in that area would have been attached to the "Fighting Fifth," as it was known, under the command of General Cornelius Navarro, the Gray Wolf, a seasoned field commander and a hero of the republic. Why such a man would have need of a Blackguard, Royne did not know; however, he figured there were few better places for a fugitive like himself to hide than among such a renegade force of fighting men.

Of course, at no point in their journey had the soldiers shown him the least bit of friendliness or courtesy, but as far as the young Loremaster was concerned, those were simply details. *The enemy of my enemy and all that,* he thought, *Surely even soldier-brutes can understand the logic there...*

On the afternoon of the second day, the riders halted at the edge of a streambed where cedar trees sprouted in small clusters against the backdrop of a clear, blue sky. Royne's legs ached from being forced to ride bareback behind the saddle of one of the legionnaires; however, as stiff and sore as he was, the soldiers had no intention of resting. Rather, they took their mounts by the bridle and lead them up through the stony creek into the thickening woodlands. Just over the crest of an embankment lined with brambles and elderberry bushes, the tops of a dozen or more pavilions crowned with the green pennant of the Republic flickered in the breeze. Almost at once, a cry rang out from some unseen sentry.

"Captain Velius returns!"

Royne followed quietly behind the other soldiers into the camp. Short stretches of palisade formed a tight barrier around the pavilions, though the camp itself extended much further into the woods where most of the soldiers had constructed rickety lean-tos or simply arranged their bedrolls in circles around their campfires and slept in the open air. Most of the men were clad in the green cloaks of the legion; however, beyond that single signifying mark, their equipment was as diverse as a common mercenary outfit—hardly befitting men attached to such a distinguished band of warriors as the Fifth Legion. Their boots and shoes were cracked and falling to pieces, their leather armors gone to mildew, and their chainmail hauberks marred with spots of rust. Their patchy whiskers and bleary eyes betrayed the signs of weariness and hunger, and many had turned up their trousers in the name of some gastric disease. Yet, as difficult as it might be to believe it, there upon their pennants beneath the emblem of the black wolf, were the five white bars that identified them as the "Fighting Fifth."

"Filthy Fifth" might be more appropriate now, Royne thought bitterly, doing his best to avert his eyes from the questioning stares of the beleaguered soldiers. At length, the captain led Royne and Conor into the center of the camp and the longest of the green pavilions. Outside of its entry, two men

stood guard outfitted in the full regalia of heavy legionnaires. At the sight of the captain, they snapped to attention and offered a rigid salute, placing their right fists over the center of their breastplates. The captain, Velius, returned the gesture with a curt nod and turning to Royne, narrowed his gaze.

"You and I will enter alone," he said, "You will not speak unless spoken to and you will do as you are commanded at once and without hesitation. Do you understand?"

Royne glanced around him at the other soldiers, trying his best to repress the sudden flare of resentment he felt at the captain's tone; however, he knew that he was in no position to reprimand the man for his discourtesy. "My steward," he asked, after a moment, "What of him?"

"He will wait here."

"What if I have need of him?"

"Is he deaf?"

"He is not."

"Then he should hear if you call, should he not?"

Royne felt his forehead flush with annoyance, but he remained silent.

"Enter," the captain said.

The interior of the tent was sparsely furnished with little more than a large wooden chest, a long wooden table, and a trio of canvas chairs. The table was littered with various accoutrements of battle, though of a considerably finer make than those of the other soldiers. There was a chain hauberk adorned at the shoulders with onyxes and pearls, a skirt of steel scales with green enameling, a breastplate traced with gold leaf, and a fine open-faced helmet fashioned in the shape of a wolf's mouth and plumed with horsehair dyed a deep green. Beyond these items, however, on the far side of the room were the pavilion's sole occupants. The first was a younger man dressed in a fashion similar to the captain, though by his salute, clearly of a lower rank. The other, reclining in a low cot covered in linen and animal skins, was an elder man perhaps in his later forties. His leathery complexion was dappled with beads of perspiration and his eyes were closed. Were it not for the occasional shudder or twitch, Royne might have thought he was already dead, for clearly he was in the process of becoming so.

"How is he?" the captain asked the younger man.

"The fits of shouting stopped at about midday yesterday, sir, though I'm not sure if that's a good sign or a bad one."

As he followed behind Captain Velius to the side of the cot, Royne caught the scent of some sickeningly sweet odor that brought his hand to his nose, and for the first time, he spied the bloody mass of bandages that littered the ground.

"This is General Cornelius Navarro, commander of the Fifth Legion, and the greatest leader in all of Grantis," the captain said, "You are going to heal him."

Royne started and his blood ran cold, "What?"

"Heal him."

Royne shook his head incredulously. "I know of your general, in fact, I imagine that there are very few across all the continent who do not. But, I'm sorry," he said, "I'm no physician. There is nothing I can do for him."

"No," the captain said venomously, "But you claim to be a Blackguard—a Guardian. Is that not so?"

"It is, or so I was told."

"So you were told?" the captain repeated, grinding his teeth.

"I was anointed by Loremaster Rastis Glendaro and was forced to flee Titanis to escape the Guardian-King."

"I do not care what absurd title you name yourself with any more than I care about your absurd trouble. However, if you are indeed a Blackguard as you claim, then you had best stop stalling and heal him."

Royne's spine tingled with anxiety, "I'm not quite certain I understand…"

"If the legends are to be believed, the Guardians are gifted with the power to heal," he said, "So heal."

"Look…" the young Loremaster sighed, anxiously glancing away from the wounded man, "There are many stories of the Guardians being able to do all sorts of things—healing wounds, charming beasts, defeating whole armies single-handedly—but trust me, they're all just that: stories. There's no truth to them at all. You need a physician, not a Blackguard."

"A physician cannot heal him," the younger officer said.

"Why ever not?"

"The wound has already gone to fester," the young man explained, "He left it untended for too long as we retreated from the last skirmish with the Kingsmen."

"I'm sorry," Royne sighed, "But if it's gone to festering, then there's certainly nothing I can do. Your best chance still lies in the hands of a physician."

"The only true physicians outside of the Order are the alchemists of the Sign of Four, but since the Guardians succeeded in taking the city, they've walled themselves up inside their compound. Any others are little more than mountebanks and quacksalvers."

"So you thought to try a Blackguard," Royne nodded, "I see."

"Blood and fire!" the captain shouted, "Enough stalling!" He shoved the younger officer aside and roughly grasped Royne's habit by the collar, "You will heal him now, damn you!"

"I'm telling you!" Royne said, struggling to keep his voice level. His heartbeat quickened like the beat of a military drum, "I cannot do it!"

"Then you had best learn!" the captain said, drawing his short sword, "Because if he dies then so do you!"

"I simply cannot do as you ask! I'm sorry! I would if I could, but I cannot!" Royne shouted, "Believe me! I am not your enemy!"

"Friend or enemy, I care not. You will heal him or you will die!"

"It is impossible! You're mad!"

"The stories say it's true!"

"Stories say a lot of things!"

"Aye, but there's always some grain of truth, isn't there? Guardians heal. Blackguards are Guardians. You are a Blackguard. *You can heal him!*"

"And what would you have me do next, eh?" Royne snapped, "Turn lead into gold? Conjure up a pack of strumpets from the ether to see to your bloody men? Perhaps I'll turn into a dragon and—"

A blow from the pommel of the captain's blade brought an abrupt end to Royne's protests. "You will heal him, or you will die!" he shouted, "Now! Do it!"

"You're not listening! I cannot do as you ask!"

"Then you will die!" the captain pressed the edge of the blade harder against Royne's throat, the knuckles of his hand gripping the hilt were white with wrath. Royne's eyes darted across the interior of the tent from the young officer to the dying general to the blank canvas walls, anywhere but the maddened eyes of the enraged captain. *Bloody soldiers!* he thought bitterly, *Beasts and brutes, all of them!* He cursed himself for joining them, and he cursed Salasco's absence. *Wretched Blackguards! Wretched Guardians! To the Abyss with them all!*

"This is your last chance," the captain seethed, "Do it. Now!"

At last, with a shuddering sigh, Royne tensed his jaw and shook his head. "Fine!" he said, fighting the urge to cry, "Fine!" The captain relaxed his grip and abruptly, Royne pulled away from the man's hold. He cast an arm furtively across his eyes and scowled. The soldiers might very well kill him, but he would not weep. He would not shame himself or his end with tears.

Slowly, Royne edged closer to the general's cot and examined the man closer. His forehead glistened with large beads of sweat and his breath came in short, staggering draws. Fever for certain. A large herbal poultice had been applied to the man's side, a typical soldier's cure, but completely ineffective at this stage of infection. He paused a moment to identify the herbs, consider their properties, and the relative appearance of the skin around the wound, the bits of dead flesh, the odor of putrescence. As he claimed, Royne was no doctor. He had never actually treated a real wound before; however, that did not mean that he was entirely without knowledge. He had read plenty of studies on anatomy and physiology and had more than once dissected dead rats and birds he had discovered in the Tower. True, a man was an entirely different and significantly more complicated creature, but in principle, it was the same.

"What has his urine been like?" Royne asked, "Cloudy? Clear? Any discoloration?"

The two soldiers exchanged an uncertain glance. "We did not think to look," the younger man said.

"I don't see why it should matter," the captain growled, "Bloody physicians. Piss-drinking fools and liars, all. You had better hurry!"

Royne ignored the man's muttering and returned his attention to the wound. *What am I doing? What am I doing?* he asked himself, *For the love of the Lady, what can I possibly do for this man? Think. Think. Think.* He tried to think back over the volumes upon volumes he had read over a lifetime in the Tower, but still he could not discover anything helpful. Even *The Book of Histories* offered little more than vague musings regarding the so-called "Gifts of the Guardians" and the alleged miracles of St. Aiden. *Bloody magic,* he cursed, *Soldiers, bastards, and fools!* He could feel his stomach tightening into knots as he once more noticed the captain's rising irritation at his back. *There's no such thing as magic! There's no such thing!*

Still, he realized with a sigh, something certainly had happened that day in the Judge's Tower, something that defied any logical explanation, for even now there was *The Book of Histories* to prove it. *The pages are blank and yet I read the words...*

"I grow weary of waiting," the captain threatened.

"I'm trying," Royne snapped, "For the love of the Brethren, I'm trying."

"You had best try harder then, and faster..."

Bastard! Royne took another deep breath. *Holy Lady, help me!* He shut his eyes, and in futility and desperation, touched his hands to the man's side.

All at once he was overwhelmed with a strange sensation. To his great amazement, he felt an unnatural surge of energy in the palms of his hands that traveled down through his fingertips to the general's wounded side. *Aiden's Flame!* A moment later, a quick, searing pain suddenly tore into the flesh of his own body and he nearly cried out aloud in agony as a slow, burning ache kindled in the depths of his insides.

What madness is this?

Stricken with terror, he tried to pull his hands away from the wound, but found that he could not. It was as if some unseen force kept him frozen in place. His heart pounded against his breastbone like a blacksmith's hammer and his vision faded to black.

There's no such thing as magic! he cursed, slipping into the oblivion of unconsciousness. *There's   no   such   thing!*

CHAPTER 8: SORROW & GRIEF

Northwest of the Sires, the three hills upon which Castle Tremontane stood, a small, stony brook ran along the edge of a moor. It was here that as a child, Bel had often ridden alongside his brother Larius—exploring the woodlands, sparring, or just taking the air. It was here too that he had ridden alone with Lilia the night before he departed with Jarvy on Dermont's errand of treachery in Gasparn. And it was here too that beneath the shade of an alder tree, they had last lain together and in all likelihood conceived their son. Thus, for Bel, it was a private place, a sacred place, and so it was here too where he chose to bury Lilia now.

He insisted upon digging her gave himself, though why, he was not quite certain. Perhaps it was to be one final intimate moment, something he alone would do for her, his final and personal farewell. He was unsure; however, when he quietly refused Sir Emory's offer of aid, the old knight did not press him and simply stood solemnly alongside King Cedric and the wet nurse, Elsa, who somberly carried the baby in her arms. Lilia's body, he had wrapped in fine linen and affixed to a litter drawn by Banshee—one final journey for horse and rider—while he rode ahead upon Igno, leading the way.

As he dug the grave, his vision was clouded by the haze of memories and weeping, and his eyes burned brighter than the chestnut stallion's coat. He thought of their first meeting on the bloody battlefield beneath the overturned wagon, of raids and skirmishes, of their defeat of the Snow Bear at the White Wood, and the time before the battle when they'd painted each other and made love beneath the shadows of the trees. Most of all, however, he thought of her holding their child, whispering sweetly that she loved him just before the midwife put the boy in his crib to sleep. It broke his heart to think that neither father nor son would ever hear that voice again.

When Larius lost his wife and child, he took his own life, and in the wake of Lilia's death Bel fully understood why. It was as if his arm had been cut off and left to bleed. There was no way to staunch the flow, nor would the blood ever run out. The wound would simply remain, gaping for the rest of his days, and more than once, he had thought about following his brother's example.

Yet, Larius had lost both wife and child whereas Marcus still lived. He was the piece of Lilia that still remained, the piece of the two of them together, and Bel knew that he could not take his own life and leave the child alone, no matter how much he might wish to join her in her grave.

Every few hours, the nursemaid fed, bathed, and changed the baby's swaddling, and in the interim, Bel sat alone cradling his son in his arms beside the vacant delivery bed. He found he had little need for sleep, nor for food, nor drink, though Sir Emory appealed to him to at least take some water lest he fall faint or his unbalanced humors somehow affect the baby's health or disposition. Still, the green shade of his eyes grew vacant and glassy, his skin pallid, and he no longer bothered to shave (Why would he? She was no longer there to complain of the roughness when he kissed her).

The sun had reached its zenith by the time he finished digging. When he climbed out of the hole covered in dirt and grime and sweat, he imagined he looked more like some revenant of the Warlock's conjuring than a mortal man. Dark clouds were rolling in from the Nivanus Mountains to the west and threatened to unload their grief in a torrent of weeping. Gently, Bel lifted Lilia's body from the litter, and laid her in the grave with the same soft touch as he had held her the other night. His whole body shook as he struggled just to breathe, and though he had thought himself over-parched for weeping, from somewhere within a new spring flowed forth.

Perhaps my blood has turned to water, he thought, *To nurture the seed of the Blood Blossom I plant…*

He gazed at her lying in the ground, and were it not for the shroud she might have passed for sleeping. It was the only time she was ever at rest, the only time she ever stopped moving. He glanced down to where her hands were folded across her chest and choked a sob at the sight of her fingernails bitten to the quick.

"Goodbye, Lilia," he whispered, "You were right. It hurts worse having said it, but I love you still," with an effort, he swallowed the lump in his throat and kissed her cold brow, "I promise to raise Marcus well. He'll know how much you love him, and he'll know you'll always be watching."

As soon as the final spade of dirt had been placed upon the grave, a light rain began to fall. Bel stood for another long moment staring at the ground. Above where Lilia's head lay buried, he placed two horseshoes—one from Banshee and one from Igno, bound together with a piece of steel.

A light touch fell upon his shoulder, but he could hardly feel it. "Larius…"

"It's Bel, father."

"Oh yes. I'm so sorry," King Cedric said in a forlorn whisper.

"What is it?"

"The rain and damp are not good for the child."

"I know."

"If you would like to stay, we can return alone."

Bel shook his head and turned away. They had been gone for hours; if they did not return soon the Warden may grow restless, may send men after them, may take liberties with those still held at the castle…

"We'll go back together."

King Cedric tightened his grip in sympathy, but remained as silent as his son. Sir Emory helped the old king and the nursemaid to their small carriage while Bel climbed up into Igno's saddle and took Banshee by the reins. He glanced back at Lilia's grave as the first crack of thunder broke overhead, and far off in the distance, he had a fleeting vision of a gray horse running across the plane, its mane and tail whipping along in the wind.

Goodbye, my Blood Blossom. I love you.

By the time they returned to the city, the rain was falling heavy and hard. The lightning flashed and the thunder grew louder and beside Igno, Banshee screamed at the sound and pulled at the tether attached to her bridle. Bel tried to keep her calm as they rode, but he knew the black mare could sense that something was wrong. *The horse and the rider are one...*

At the Gate of Levantis, the huge gatehouse entryway to Castle Tremontane, the soldiers of Lord Wilmar received them briskly, annoyed to be standing out in the rain. Tavik, Lord Wilmar's steward, awaited them in the gatehouse with news that the Sundering Hand wished to offer his condolences and speak with Bel. It was at that moment, the last thing Bel wanted to do in all the world; yet he had no choice. Sir Emory promised to see to King Cedric, the baby, and the horses, while Bel, stained with rain and grave dirt, followed the steward across the courtyard to the stairs leading up into the Tower of Derevain, the Stallion.

Lightning flashed, and at the accompanying thunder, Bel recalled standing upon those very steps with Dermont following the first disastrous battle with the Tower. Rage flared briefly in his breast when he remembered his brother's words. *Is that your common girl?* His breathing grew staggered and heavy. He stopped and called after the warden's steward.

"Do we really need to do this now?" he snapped.

Tavik inclined his head, "My lord insisted. He bid me tell you that he would be brief."

Bel's jaw tightened like a vice. *Leave a trail of bastards from here to Dwerin...* His chest ached and his fists clenched. "He had better be," Bel said aloud.

Wilmar Danelis, the Sundering Hand, Warden of Tremontane Castle, sat at the head of the table in what had once been the solar of the King of Montevale, long before the days of the War of the Horses. Danelis was a man of an age with Dermont with blond hair and fine teeth. Even as a boy, he had always exuded a certain self-assuredness that conveyed to those around him that where the young man walked, there was the limit of success, and like the Plague King's other boon companions, he had often tormented the Silent Prince in his youth.

"Beledain," the warden said, "I grieve with you."

Bel nodded stiffly. There were other people in the room, but he did not recognize any of them. Were they knights, retainers, wealthy townsfolk? He did not know, nor did he care, for it did not matter. Whoever they were, though, they seemed caught off guard by the Silent Prince's macabre appearance, annoyed by his lack of decorum. It made Bel angry, their resentment. It was they who summoned him, who intruded upon his privacy, who had invaded his home. *They have no right.* Tavik ushered Bel to a seat and then moved to stand just behind and to the right of his lord.

Lord Wilmar breathed a heavy sigh, "I'm sorry to call upon you now, but there are urgent matters King Dermont would have me see to, matters that concern you, I'm afraid."

Bel remained silent and a few of the unknowns at the table exchanged awkward glances at his impropriety. *What do they expect? My thanks? Polite words promising service? They can rot in the Abyss for all I care.* He knew better than to believe in the compassion of a man like Wilmar Danelis. The Sundering Hand earned his name when he razed the keep at Windfall to the ground. It was a very old building, built in the closing years of Old Calendral, and the masonry cracked and crumbled beneath the first barrage of trebuchet fire. After the battle, those members of the keep's retinue that did not die in the collapse were pressed to death beneath the very same stones that had comprised their home.

"What would you have of me?" Bel asked, his voice dry and gritty.

Lord Wilmar reached for his goblet and, seeing that it was dry, Tavik stepped forward to refill it. "Well," the lord said, after he had taken a dainty sip, "Good news." He lifted a piece of parchment from the tabletop, "Your brother successfully appealed to King Kredor for you to remain in Montevale rather than have to return Andoch and the Council to swear your Oath. Now you can continue to serve as the Tower and remain home in your brother's care."

As his prisoner, Bel thought. He remembered Lilia's warnings, all proven true. *He hates you. He hates you because he fears you…*

The lord cleared his throat and Bel wondered briefly if Danelis had been expecting his thanks. When the prince remained silent, however, he continued, "He also sends word of other news; integrations of nobles, reinstatements of those Gasparns proven loyal. Lord Talondaire has returned to his castle, Giles Pronet has been named Lord of the White Wood, Jarrett Harren is to be Lord of the Nivanus…ah yes! Here we are. Your Uncle Leon is well, as is your cousin Valerie."

Bel breathed a heavy sigh and felt a great tremor pass through his body, though whether out of grief, anger, or despair was impossible to discern. Val.

He had yet to send word to her about Lilia, about Marcus. Where was she now, he wondered, still with the light cavalry? Dermont would be a fool to displace her, and Uncle Leon—Bel had not seen him since well before his capture at the hands of the Tower when Dermont had refused to pay his uncle's ransom. Had Lilia ever met Leon? Certainly she had heard stories of him from Val. Leon the Black Lion—she would have liked him, for he believed women were no less valorous than men when it came to war, hence why Val was so formidable.

Bel rubbed his eyes and his fist clenched. *Why must I sit here listening to this?* Breathing became an effort and his heart felt weak. "For pity's sake, Wilmar," he pleaded, "Must we do this now?"

"Would that we could wait," the lord said, "But who am I to delay the words of a king?"

"Then could you please make your point."

"I'm getting to it."

Bel shut his eyes and felt a tear trace down his cheek, and suddenly his memory took him back to his boyhood. He was eleven years old and his mother had been dead a year. Her carriage had thrown a wheel while returning home from spending the Feast of the Lady at Roanshead with Val's mother. While waiting for her attendants to fix it, she caught a chill from the cold and died before the end of winter. Bel was heartbroken. He remembered very little of the seasons that followed, and when the next winter arrived, he was afraid to leave the castle for fear that he might catch his mother's cold. Dermont, as he often did, took it upon himself to "help" his little brother over his fears, so with his friend Wilmar, they forced Bel to walk the walls with them after a heavy snow—in only his underclothes—while they reminisced about his mother's funeral. When he began to cry, they pelted him with snowballs.

"You wretched scum," Bel said aloud, his voice as cold and bitter as the wind had been those many years ago, "Make your point now and be done with it."

Lord Wilmar's gaze narrowed and Bel opened his eyes to meet it unflinching. "I'll assume it's the death of your...woman that has put you in such a foul mood. Your brother told me how protective of her you were. And to die in childbirth like that, perhaps when the rain stops you might wish to walk the walls and clear your head."

"Perhaps you'd like to join me?" Bel replied.

Wilmar's lips twisted into a leer, "Perhaps, for old time's sake, but first let's hear what else Dermont has to say." He glanced over the parchment again and feigned surprise. "Aiden's Flame, look at that!" he said, "It seems that come Harvestide, we're to welcome a new queen! And what's more, Beledain, you already know her!"

Bel's jaw clenched, "What do you mean?"

"It seems the Grand Hierophant in Andoch has consented to your brother's request to marry Princess Marina."

Bel's blood turned to fire. "They cannot do that," he said, "It's against the rules of the Church itself. Marius and the princess both are in the custody of the Tower—"

"And the Tower is a Guardian of Andoch and a member of the Order. Hagan Shawn is on the Council of Five. He is your superior and his word supersedes yours."

"I swore no Oath of Fealty!"

"Were you not listening? I just told you. King Dermont took the liberty of seeing to that already on your behalf. Really, you should thank him from sparing you such a long journey."

"An Oath cannot be sworn by proxy."

"Apparently it can. How else could you remain in Montevale under your brother's care?"

"His tyranny more like."

"Call it what you will," Wilmar sneered, "You're lucky to be alive for the unrest you've sown among the people while your poor brother struggles to maintain peace. You promised to end the war with your absurd duel against Marcus Harding, but all you've done is exchange one horse for another. North and south, brigands roam the countryside in your name!"

"If I'm inciting a rebellion from within these walls, then Dermont chose a poor nursemaid when he decided on you."

The warden shook his head in condescension, "Were I your brother, I'd have thrown you off the walls months ago—you, your dead whore, and your bastard child!"

Without warning, Bel lunged from his chair at Lord Wilmar, knocking another man to the floor in his pursuit. Danelis backed away and a squad of guards rushed in to restrain the Silent Prince. Bel punched one of them in the face and split his knuckle on the nasal bar of the man's helm. His whole body seethed with an anger as he'd never known, not even in the heat of battle. It was blind, savage fury that gripped him now, and had they not beat him down with clubs, he would have killed them all with his bare hands.

"You wretched traitor!" Wilmar spat as two guardsmen knelt on Bel's prone form and bound his hands with a strip of cloth torn from a tabard, "I can't kill you without your brother's consent, but by the Brethren I will make you suffer!"

The prince's eyes seemed to shine with an eerie light. Blood ran down the side of his face from a gash on his brow, but in spite of the guards and the pain, he fought to knock the men from his back and rise to his feet. "Do your worst," he growled and threw himself bodily at the lord. Again, they beat him; this time with their fists for fear the clubs would fracture his skull or snap his ribs and kill him. Finally, swollen, bloody, and blinded by rage and pain, he fell limply to the floor.

"Take him to the courtyard!" Danelis cried, "And fetch those two fools captured in the town! It's time for another lesson!"

A loud thunderclap sounded as the guards dragged Bel out through the doors of Daravain and down the stairs to the cobblestones of the courtyard below. The rain fell thick and heavy, and though but the middle of the afternoon, it seemed the dead of night for the darkness of the skies. Lord Wilmar was shouting, but Bel could not hear it over the sound of the storm and the cries of frightened horses in the stables.

The lord's men drove Bel forward through the yard and forced him to his knees before the Gates of Levantis where two soldiers of Danelis's guard tied two nooses and set to threading the ropes through the bars of the portcullis.

Once more, Bel fought to his feet and like a maddened beast rushed at the lord, but again, they knocked him down to the cobbles. His blood mingled with the rain, pooling upon the wet stones of the castle that had been his home.

On either side of the gatehouse were a series of oubliettes, long held vacant in the years since the barracks had been built in the city over half a century ago. With the nooses tied and readied, the guards threw open the hatch covers and roughly pulled two men from out of the cells.

Lord Wilmar leaned over where Bel lay. "Recognize them, Silent Prince?" he hissed.

Bel blinked his eyes hard and shook his head to clear his vision. One of the men was old and wiry like a gray fox. The other, a younger man, was broad-shouldered with a noble bearing. He had not seen them since they stood beside him at Clearpoint on the day he became the new Tower; however, there was no mistaking them now. "NO!" He tried to stand, but he was too bloody, too beaten.

The two prisoners looked at one another and at Bel's broken form.

"Prince Bel!" Jarvy shouted.

Sir Linton Traver shook his head in disbelief, "Lord Tower!"

"We caught them in the city trying to find a way to reach their old commander," the lord leered down at the prince, "Now they've found you, and you get to watch them die. Bring horses! *His* horses!"

From the stables, another group of guards fought to control Igno and Banshee, dragging them by the bridle and stabbing at them with pikes to herd them forth.

"No!" Bel crawled along the cobbles. The rain had loosened the strip of cloth around his wrists and he slipped a hand free to weakly grab at Wilmar's boot, but the lord kicked him in the face and shouted a command. At once, Jarvy and Sir Linton were fitted with the nooses while the other ends of the ropes were tied to Igno and Banshee.

"No!" Bel grimaced as he heard the sound of the portcullis slowly rising, "You can't do this!"

Another thunderclap sounded and Banshee lashed out with fear, but was brought to bay with a jab of a pike. Igno shook his head in fury, but he too felt the blade of a polearm and Bel saw rain wash red blood down their flanks. He would have wept, but even if any tears remained within him left to flow, the intensity of his anger would have held them back.

"No farewells?" the Warden taunted him as he lie broken in the pouring rain, "Prefer to simply suffer in silence?"

Jarvy and Sir Linton stood straight with their heads held high. As much as he wanted to look away, Bel knew that he could not. He owed it to his men to look them in the eye and be with them all the way to the end.

"Down with the Plague King!" Sir Linton shouted.

"And long live the Silent Prince!" Jarvy joined in.

"Now!" the lord cried.

Already terrified into a frenzy from the storm, the soldiers slapped the pair of horses on the flanks and at once, they took off running. In a flash, the bodies of Bel's old comrades flew up into the air until they caught against the bars of the portcullis. Their necks snapped with a sickening *crack!*

"No!" Bel cried again, "NO!"

From somewhere deep within, he conjured one last burst of strength. With a monumental effort, he pushed himself up to his feet and dove for the warden one final time. Danelis attempted to step back out of reach, his eyes alight with amusement, but somehow Bel's hand caught the edge of the lord's surcoat and dragged him down with him as he fell upon the rain-slicked ground.

Meanwhile, wild and free, but still tethered to the portcullis by the hanging corpses, Igno and Banshee ran the length their ropes would allow, kicking and stomping at the guards, ignoring the red stab wounds as the pikemen attempted to get them under control.

Empowered by rage and anguish, Bel wrestled savagely with the warden like some mad beast brought forth from the Abyss. Lord Wilmar shouted to his men for help, but the enraged horses prevented them from getting near. At last, in his wrath, Bel's hands—beyond control—seized hold of the nobleman's head and pounded it against the cobblestones of the courtyard, again and again and again and again, long after the body had ceased spasming and fell still.

Bel's shoulders heaved with his staggered breathing, but he forced himself to his feet and armed himself with a pike from one of the dead lord's fallen guards. The pair of horses had knocked at least three men down with their hooves, but they were bleeding profusely from innumerable gaping wounds and Igno swayed listlessly where he stood. Again, Bel's chest shuddered with anguish. He hurried to the stallion's side and spitted the nearest soldier on the shaft of his pike as the red horse lowered himself to his knees and rolled over onto his side. Bel left the pike buried in the dying soldier and knelt down, cradling Igno's head in his arms as the light flickered and went out in his eyes.

Everyone I care for is dead.

A bolt of lightning flashed overhead and thunder shook the castle walls. Suddenly, the doors to the Tower of Corlindus the Colt opened and Sir Emory and the few remaining men of King Cedric's household guard followed him out into the courtyard. Wilmar's soldiers backed away, dragging the corpse of their lord with them up the stairs to the doors of Derevain. Banshee gave chase, snorting and stomping the ground in her madness.

"Prince Bel!" Sir Emory shouted, "Get up! Get up *now!*"

Bel ignored him and stroked the wet fur of Igno's nose.

"Aiden's Flame!" the seneschal roared and grabbed Bel by the shoulder, "On your feet now!" Thunder struck overhead again and the rain fell faster. Harder.

"They're all dead," Bel said without emotion, "They're all dead."

Sir Emory winced at the sight of grief, but eyed Bel sternly. "Not *all* of them!" he said against the sound of the wind and rain, "Not you and *not your son!*"

"My son…"

"Now *get up!*"

Bel's eyes flashed and with the old knight's aid he staggered to his feet, "We need to get out of here before the guards regroup."

"I agree," Emory said, bracing the young man's arm over his shoulder. He turned toward the four men bearing the mark of the Black Horse. Like the seneschal, they were old and gray, but they were loyal, and what they lacked in youth they made up for in experience. "Kelvin, ready the carriage and some horses. Denalt, fetch King Cedric and Elsa with the baby. Halm and Wrennen, stay with the Prince and see if you can raise the gate."

"Aye, sir!"

"Can you stand on your own?" he asked Bel.

"I think so," Bel said, steadying himself. He glanced up at the Tower of Rowena the Mare, "Marius and Marina. We can't leave them."

"I shall fetch them personally," Sir Emory said.

CHAPTER 9: SIGRUNA

After a few days of wanton debauchery at the Sea Dragon, Ivo sent word to Magnus that *The Gander*, sitting significantly shallower in the water without its cargo, was clear and ready for her new captain to take command. Apparently, Pavlos had decided to forego the sale of his illicit spoils until after he and has men had indulged in an evening of celebratory shore leave and as the beneficiary of the Kordish captain's misfortune, the Sea Dragon's hostler made a significant profit—plenty enough to refit the ship and see to the employment of a suitable, if motley, crew.

Clad in Pavlos's baldric and a studded leather brigandine, Magnus swaggered along the quarterdeck of the cog while all around him, the sailors readied the ship to make sail. Leaning against the rail, struggling desperately to master his fear, Thom's lips worked feverishly, muttering prayers to the Brother Galdorn.

"Oh Brother Galdorn, Lord of the Sea,
Safeguard our souls upon this journey.
May the weather be clear, and the seas remain calm,
Bring us fair winds and protect us from harm…"

Thom paused in his devotions and glanced across the deck at the salt-stained faces of the crew. *At least there's no need to worry about being attacked by pirates,* he thought, *They're already on board...*

"Oi, Thom Crusher!" Magnus called, "What do you call that bloody great bird over there?"

"What?"

The Wrathorn warrior chewed off a hunk of some odd root and spit a great wad over the railing into the sea. "The bird perched on the masthead," he said, "What's it called?"

Thom breathed a great sigh and wiped the sweat of his palms on his habit. "I'm not precisely certain what a masthead is..."

Magnus shook his head in disbelief. "The masthead," he said, pointing upwards, "The *head* of the bloody *mast.*"

"Oh," Thom muttered. He squinted up into the sunlight, "Some manner of duck perhaps?"

"A duck?"

"Or a goose? I can't quite make it out with all the ropes and such."

"The rigging."

"What?"

The Wrathorn shook his head and spit. "In all the time we've been in the Isles, how have you not learned this yet?" he sighed, "I swear sometimes you must be simple."

Thom pursed his lips, "At least *I* can read."

"Aye, and a lot of good that'll do you at sea," Magnus said, "You're just lucky you write as well, else I'd have never rescued you from that prison."

"Sorry," Thom said, "But how exactly does forcing me to follow you around like this count as a rescue?"

"Great Bear's Bollocks!" Magnus snorted, "All I wanted was to know the name of the fucking bird." He shook his head, "Just forget it. It's gone and flown off now anyhow."

Thom breathed a sigh and glanced out across the harbor. "Oh," he said, "It was an albatross."

"A what now?"

"The bird."

"Oh shut up," Magnus grunted, "In any case, were I you, I'd see all your things are stowed away safe in the cabin—the inks and feathers and all that other shite you made me buy for you."

"I can't very well write your story without ink, can I?"

"Just see that it's stowed because as soon as Ivo arrives to see us off, we make sail."

With a loud huff, Thom climbed down the stairs from the quarterdeck, careful to avoid getting in the way of any of the other sailors, busy as they were at any number of activities he could only guess at. *Boats, Blackguards, and blood!* he thought miserably, passing through the doors to the cabin. The majority of the room had been given over to Magnus, including the few amenities that the ship's original owner had added to ease the bothers of travel by sea—a canvas chair lined with pelts, a small private toilet, and a proper bed complete with a feather mattress. To Thom, this was the most enviable of all, for not only was it certain to be comfortable and warm, but lashed to the bulkhead as it was, the bed was not likely to swing about as much as a hammock, nor would it spill its occupant out onto the floor as easily as a cot when the seas turned rough. Still, Magnus had been generous enough to allow Thom space to hang a hammock in the cabin's corner as well as a small locker in which to store his few belongings and the accoutrements of his craft. It may not have been much, but when compared to the horrors of the voyage from Galdoran in the smugglers' vessel—the constant damp, the stench of mold and bilge below decks—it made a world of difference.

By the time Ivo arrived to see the vessel off, the sun was sinking low beneath the western horizon and one by one the stars kindled to life in the darkening sky above. That, Thom had to concede, was at least one aspect of life at sea that he could appreciate, for it reminded him of his days spent studying the maps and star charts with his friends in the Loremaster's Tower, and although he was in no way as skilled at such things as Royne was, tracking the movements of the constellations was some comfort, a beacon of intellect amidst all the barbarity.

"Alright, Magnus," Ivo called from the pier, "Let's get this over with." In his wake followed a servant carrying a large pot of wine and a prostitute in a white frock carrying a brass bell.

At the sound of the hostler's hail, the full complement of the crew, a dozen men all told, assembled on deck and bowed their heads. From the cabin, Magnus strode forth to welcome the visitors at the gangplank. "By the gods of land, and sea, and air, I welcome you aboard this ship," he declared.

Ivo gave an impatient nod of thanks and with a wave of his hand, ushered his followers along with him to take their places at the end of the line of crewmen. After this, Magnus accepted the pot of wine from the servant, removed the lid, and after a deep drink himself, passed it from man to man. When all had taken a drink and the jug made its way back to him, Magnus raised it to the sky, and pouring out the remaining liquid over the deck, continued his incantation.

"May the gods bless this vessel, guide her safely, and grant her fair winds. May her enemies flee before her, may her crew be always strong, and may her timbers remain as steadfast as the oak that bore them!"

"May it be so!" the sailors mumbled together.

From his place on the quarterdeck, Thom attempted as best as he was able to record the strange proceedings with as much linguistic decorum as he was able; however, as much as he had tried to follow along, he could not help but find the whole ceremony rather confusing, and, at least to a certain degree, somewhat comical, like children at play pretending to hold a wedding.

With dramatic ceremony, Magnus handed the empty jug back to the servant and motioned to the whore. "As I told you..." he whispered, "*Sigruna.*"

With a certain salaciousness that surely no man of the Hierophant's Tower would approve of, the prostitute raised the bell above her head and traversed the ship from bow to stern, from starboard to larboard. At the furthest point in each direction, she paused to give the bell a hearty ring and cried out, "May the gods grant you favor, *Sigruna!*" When this was complete, the woman returned to her place in the procession and Magnus continued on.

"By the gods of land, and sea, and air grant this ship, *Sigruna*, safe passage and fair winds, now and forever!" he shouted.

"Now and forever!" the crew responded.

Magnus remained piously solemn for a long moment afterwards, silently encouraging the others with him to do the same. At length, he breathed a heavy sigh and muttered, "Alright, that's it."

"Good," Ivo said. He waved the whore and the servant in the direction of the gangplank. "Take care, Magnus," he called, before following after them, "Don't get yourself killed, eh?"

"Same to you, Ivo," the Wrathorn warrior called, "Careful how much you water down your grog."

With a laugh, the hostler offered Magnus a final wave and said no more.

"Alright, you slobs," the Wrathorn shouted, whirling upon his crew, "Make sail!"

At once, the sailors spurred into action, running here and there across the deck and leaping like monkeys into the rigging. In a matter of minutes, the single great sail was unfurled and with a slow lurch, *The Gander*, or rather *The Sigruna* as she was now officially known, was underway drifting away from the harbor out into the open sea.

Magnus folded his great arms across his chest and with a piratical grin, turned to the young Apprentice. "You get all that, Thom Crusher?" he asked.

"I did," Thom said.

"Good. 'Cause you'll never see the like again this far south."

At least not outside of a theater, Thom thought, *And not without jugglers and a dancing bear.* He breathed a heavy sigh to mask his smile. "How long do you think it will take to reach Grantis?" he asked.

"Perhaps a week."

"A week?" Thom whined, "It took a week to reach the Isles from Galdoran."

"So it did," Magnus said, "But that was the stormy season. Summer's only just begun."

"I don't see what that should have to do with it."

"Everything."

Thom breathed a heavy sigh, "I just don't understand any of this."

"Which is why you sat up here instead of standing down there during the ceremony."

"I thought it was so I could record what happened."

"Both."

Thom shook his head. "Well, if that's how you want to be," he said, "I'm going to the cabin." With exaggerated effrontery, he stuffed his journal beneath a pudgy arm and began gathering together his quills and inkpot. As he made to scurry off, Magnus stepped in front of him, blocking his path.

"Why haven't you asked about the name yet?" he asked.

"What name?"

"*Sigruna.* Why haven't you asked me why I named her that?"

"The ship?"

"Aye, don't you think that would be worth writing down?"

Thom breathed a heavy sigh. "Fine," he said, "Why did you name the ship *Sigruna?*"

Magnus cast a quick, furtive glance around the ship to see that the other sailors were at their business. Then, with awkward nonchalance, he leaned over the rail as if inspecting the side of the ship. "It was my mother's name," he muttered.

"Your...your mother?" Thom repeated, and before he could stop himself, uttered a sharp chuckle.

"Oi! Fat fuck!" the Wrathorn snapped, "You better not be laughing!"

"Of course not," the apprentice squealed, biting the insides of his cheeks, "I wouldn't."

"You'd better not!"

Thom bit his lip and took a deep breath through his nose to suppress the urge to continue giggling. When he was able, he glanced over the rail at the horizon and turned toward the Blackguard. "I think it's very nice that you named the ship after your mother," he said.

"Yeah," Magnus grunted, "It is."

"It is."

"Of course it is. I just said that."

"I know you did. I'm simply agreeing with you."

"Oh shut up."

CHAPTER 10: THE MASTER OF HOUNDSTOOTH

From atop the great keep of Houndstooth Castle, Lughus watched as the sun gently kissed the surface of Lake Bartund to the west, setting the horizon ablaze with color. A falcon or perhaps a kite flew about in wide circles over the surface of the water before landing upon the jagged limb of an old tree on one of the tiny islands near the lake's center. He wondered what it would be like to sit alone on that island, listening to the gentle lapping of the waves upon the stony shore. Perhaps he would try it someday. It would be a nice place to sit and think, or perhaps read...

"I believe they're all set, my lord."

Lughus breathed a sigh. Behind him, Sir Owain and his grandfather's steward, Horus Denier, a spare, courteous old man with a thin white mustache, stood beside the large dovecote in the keep's northeast corner. Two servants had just finished tying notices announcing the old baron's death to the last of the carrier pigeons. All around them, the birds cooed in gentle, soothing tones.

"Set them free."

"Yes, my lord."

Following the baron's death, his remains were interred in the catacombs beneath the Houndstooth in a small, private ceremony, presided over by Abbot Woode. However, it had been the suggestion of the seneschal and the steward that they wait until St. Aiden's Day to make the formal announcement of Arcis's passing and Lughus's ascension. Now that it was the eve of the festival, with any luck, the birds would reach the nearest of their destinations by tomorrow morning. Lughus watched as the birds flew forth in one massive flock before slowly branching out to go their separate ways. *So it's done*, he thought, *What do I do now?*

Below the castle, the city of Galadin was teeming with activity in celebration of the holiday. Lughus thought back to the days of feasting that marked Kredor's coronation so long ago and had to smile at the memory of Royne's snide criticism of the new King's speech. He wondered if he would he be expected to speak tomorrow. If he was to be the new baron, it seemed inevitable that he would have to at least say something—but what, and when? They still had yet to inform the Provincial Hierophant of both Arcis's death and Lughus's arrival, opting instead to simply spring it on him at the mass for the adoration of St. Aiden at the cathedral. He wondered if Andresen would know him for a Blackguard as soon as he saw him, or if he had already sensed his presence, as it had been with Crodane and Willum Harlow.

Madness. He touched the pommel of his sword and ran a hand through his thick, bushy mop of hair.

Horus cleared his throat. "Ah, my lord…" he said softly, "If you should like, I can have a meal prepared for you."

Lughus felt his cheeks turn red. He forgot about the four other men standing nearby waiting on him. "I'm sorry," he said quickly, "I'm not very hungry, Horus, but thank you. Thank all of you."

The steward nodded and motioned quickly to dismiss the two servants. However, both he and the seneschal remained. When Sir Owain cleared his throat and exchanged a glance with the steward, Lughus turned toward them and leaned back against the crenellations. "Speak freely," he said, "Clearly, I am not used to…all of this."

Horus smiled kindly and inclined his head, "That is precisely what we wished to speak to you about, my lord."

Sir Owain nodded, "Aye, sir, it is."

"You see, my lord," the steward continued, "Though you may not yet feel that you know us well, we want you to know that we intend to serve you as loyally as we served your grandfather these many years and more."

"Aye," Sir Owain smiled sheepishly, "I do not speak as prettily as Horus, my lord, but I served your grandfather for all my life, and I remember Sir Wolfram, Crodane, and your mother, and I consider it the highest honor to serve you too."

Lughus breathed a heavy sigh. "Thank you," he said, "Thank you both, and if I'm being honest, I have no idea whatsoever about what I'm to do."

"It will all come to you in time," Horus smiled, "It is in your blood."

Sir Owain nodded in agreement, "Aye, and we'll be here to do as we can."

"Whether peasant, burgher, or noble, the people of Galadin loved your grandparents and your mother. They'll be quite happy to know that the line continues through you. Many feared that without an heir, the Marthaines may press a claim and attempt to install one of their relations or some other puppet lord. Thus, many will surely see you as a savior."

Lughus gave a smile and nodded, though Horus's assurances did not do much to put him any more at ease. "Will I need to give a speech tomorrow?"

"It might do to say a few words after the mass at the Cathedral. Owain or I will inform the Provincial before the service if you choose to do so."

"I suppose it would be for the best then."

"Given the notes you so prettily wrote for the pigeons," Sir Owain smiled, "I'm sure you should have no problem giving a speech."

Lughus nodded his golden head, but remained silent.

"Well, then," Horus said after another moment, "We shall leave you in peace. By tomorrow I will have the baron's private quarters prepared for you to assume as your own. Before he returned to the monastery, Abbot Woode oversaw the cleansing so as to prevent any fears concerning your grandfather's disease; however, if what they say about those with the Gift of the Guardians is true, you would be in no danger anywise."

That gave Lughus pause, for true enough, he could not remember falling ill even once since becoming the Marshal. Perhaps there was more truth to the legends than he knew. He would have to add that to the long list of things he needed to speak to Gareth and Regnar about whenever they arrived...if ever they did.

"Regardless," Horus continued, "Please, do let us know if you need anything, especially if you desire something to eat. The Abbot left us a fine gift of the Ram's Reward—your grandfather was always so very fond of it. Perhaps with a nice leg of mutton?"

"Not right now, thank you," Lughus said kindly, "I think I'd like to stay up here for a while, but the two of you are welcome to it, if you'd like."

Sir Owain laughed, "Aye, you'll make a fine baron indeed with generosity such as that!"

Horus nodded, "Good evening, my lord."

Once they had gone, Lughus returned to his rooftop vigil. Sir Owain and Horus had both been invaluable these past days handling any of the final matters that Baron Arcis had not preemptively seen to himself in the weeks leading up to his death. They alleviated some of the intense pressure and feelings of bewilderment, though Lughus still often felt much like a lost child wandering aimlessly in a crowded marketplace. Regardless, he was glad for both men and their guidance.

As seneschal, Sir Owain would serve as Lughus's right hand in overseeing the defense of the castle, the city, and the seven fiefdoms, and would also act as Lughus's sworn protector. Directly beneath him were Houndstooth's master-at-arms, Denan Flann, and the captain of the Galadin city watch, Walder Ross. Flann lived on the upper floor of the barracks in the middle ward. Ross, however, maintained lodgings in the garrison between the Market House and the Weaver's Guild Hall in the Trade Quarter. As a result, he was rarely seen at the castle.

Gazing out over the city, Lughus noted the location of each of the buildings. He would need to become just as familiar with the streets and buildings of Galadin as with the men. However, learning men's names was a start. Rastis, he remembered, knew the names of every man among every division of the Order, from the lowliest acolyte under the Hierophant to the most noble of the Warlord's Justiciars. Marcus Harding had been the same way, come to think of it. He seemed to know the name of every kingsman on watch at the castle. Names, therefore, were important. To call a man by his name was to assure him that he was more to you than a mere servant or slave. He laughed now recalling how Royne used to give false names to the Hierophant Hagan Shawn each time they saw him, for never once did the old man ever take the time to remember meeting them before (despite the fact that they lived in the bloody castle!).

Beneath Flann and Ross, there were the sergeants followed by the men-at-arms and watchmen. He would make sure to learn their names as soon as possible, as well as the names of all of the servants under Horus. Though not trained as warriors, the steward and his officers commanded a formidable army of their own. Horus handled the day to day running of the household, the accounts, and any other matters relating to stores, supplies, and coin—all things, thankfully, that Lughus not only knew nothing about, but also did not want to know. Beneath him, Brennan was the butler, Kelan was the pantler, Jergan was master of the wardrobe, and Boyce was the chief of cooks. Then began the long list of servants, maids, stable hands, pot-boys and scullions...

Lughus sighed. The Brethren only knew how he would ever keep them all straight, but he had to try. He swore that he would do so, and again, he reminded himself, he had no other choice. These were his people. He owed it to them.

While he stood musing atop the keep, the sun sank halfway down below the surface of the lake, its reflection now joining at the horizon to form a single fiery orb. Soon it would be dark and he would have to try once more to sleep. Thankfully, his grandfather had kept a number of books and he could read until he grew tired. Of course, he knew very well that weariness was not the problem, for he could easily have fallen asleep where he stood from exhaustion. No, to sleep would be to invite the dreams again—the visions he had come to realize were like memories. Not his own, but rather, those belonging to Crodane.

He knew right away that the woman he had seen with the golden hair and the soft green eyes was his mother, and at first, though it made him very sad, to have at least have had the chance to have seen her filled him with great joy. For the first few weeks after he had become the Marshal, he saw her often enough in his visions, and she was everything Crodane has said. She was kind, beautiful, clever, and very witty, and though she loved nothing more than to tease the poor swordsman sworn to protect her, it was clear that she cared for him a great deal.

However, slowly his dreams changed, and just as he had seen his mother, he also saw his father. Gaston Marthaine was a handsome man, tall and lean with the noble bearing of a hero and a warrior. His face was sharp and chiseled as of stone, and although Lughus was said to favor his mother in looks, there was more of his father in his appearance than Crodane had suggested, particularly to his nose. His mouth was no stranger to smiling or laughter, though when he did either, it seemed vacant of true mirth. His hair was dark and thick and his gray eyes peered out from beneath a severe, pensive brow. It was those eyes that stuck Lughus the most, however, for although in shape his own were derived from his Galadin blood, in color they were the same fulgent thunderstorms of his father.

In his dreams, Lughus saw his parents marry, saw through the façade of happiness in his mother's eyes, and wondered at the light of ambition in his father's. He saw them as they took up residence in Houndstooth castle beside a younger Arcis, his father claiming he chose it as their home for his mother's sake. He saw them at feasts, he saw them at festivals, and he saw them when his mother was heavy with child.

And then, he saw them die.

First, it was his father, defeated in a duel just below the keep in the inner ward, run through upon Crodane's sword. Lughus felt the surge of grief and anger that set the blood coursing through Crodane's veins on fire. He watched as his father doubled over in pain, blood running free from the gaping wound left when his mother's protector withdrew his sword. The lightning flashed one final time in his father's eyes and then went out.

The first night Lughus had this dream, it filled his heart with anguish and dread, and he sat awake and miserable until morning. Yet it paled in comparison to the visions of the next night when he witnessed the death of his mother.

She lay face down on the floor of her chamber clad in a bright yellow summer gown. The thick golden locks of her hair shimmered in the light of the afternoon sun as it streamed in through the windows. At once, Crodane ran to her, his throat thick and his vision muddled. He raised her in his arms and her head lolled flaccidly to one side revealing the bright purple bruising Gaston's strong fingers had left behind. "No!" he screamed, "NO!"

Confronted with such horrifying imagery, Lughus tried to wake, but found that he could not, and thus, he was forced to watch as Crodane cradled her corpse, unable to look away from the empty stare of her lifeless eyes. It left him shattered and broken, and while it was a vicarious experience,

Lughus understood now the depth of the former Marshal's grief having seen the worst moment of his life through the man's own eyes. Standing now atop the Houndstooth, it still made him shudder with dread and weighed him down with sorrow, for since that first night, it had appeared to him again and again any time he attempted to sleep preventing him from achieving any true sense of rest.

A sudden movement from below broke in on his solitary thoughts and he peered down to see a golden flash running circles around the grounds of the inner ward like a fallen star. It was Fergus, and from the rare sound of his barking, he was clearly agitated, perhaps even alarmed. Without further hesitation, Lughus ran back inside and down the five flights of stairs through the interior of the keep to where the great hound awaited him in the yard.

"Holy Brethren!" one of the guardsmen shouted as Fergus paced back and forth in agitation. His teeth were bared and he snarled and snapped as he loped about in circles flicking bits of slaver from his jaws.

"What is it?" Lughus asked the guard.

"I don't know, my lord!" the man said, raising his shield, "He just run in from the middle bailey raging about like that! I've never seen anything like it!"

"Fergus! Calm down!" Lughus said, "What is it?"

But the great hound would not settle. Instead, he ran up and gripped the scabbard of Lughus's sword firmly in his teeth in an attempt to pull the young baron along.

"Blood and fire!" The guard leapt back beside his partner in fright.

"Alright, Fergus, alright!" Lughus told the rampant hound, "You want to show me something, right? Fine, fine. You lead and I'll follow."

With what seemed a most human-like nod, the dog let go of the scabbard and charged off toward the gate to the middle ward. Clearly, Fergus was in great haste. Such urgency from as generally mild-mannered a hound as he was certainly did not bode well.

"What are your names, men?" Lughus asked.

"Naden, sir," the guard said, "And this here's Pike."

"Naden, can you fetch some men and follow me? And Pike, please tell Sir Owain we've gone."

"Aye, my lord."

102

As the guardsmen hurried to do as he commanded, Lughus ran after Fergus through the baileys and down to the curtain wall that ran parallel to the edge of the ridge overlooking the town. Soon, Naden and three other men caught up with them as they stood outside of an ivy-clad section of wall. There, a heavy, iron-bound door stood half-concealed by thick vines and greenery. A small rupture in the stones beside the frame allowed for a small space where the great hound could crawl through on his belly to the other side of the door.

"Where does that door lead?" Lughus asked the guardsmen.

"The postern?" Naden said, "I don't know, sir. I've never been through. Some say there used to be a hidden path that leads down the ridge to the Saints Quarter. It could be that?"

On the other side, Fergus continued to bark impatiently, urging the men to follow.

Lughus breathed a pensive sigh. He had never known the hound to be wrong. "Unbar the door," he said at last, and drew his sword.

CHAPTER 11: THE HAMMER STRIKES

Geoffrey was not at all pleased when Brigid told him of what had happened at the grotto, and even less by the blood staining her dress. For the first time in the months of their acquaintance, whether out of anger, fear, or exasperation, he lost his temper.

"What in the name of St. Aiden were you thinking?!"

"I'm sorry."

"By the Brethren, girl! You could have been killed!" he pounded his fist upon the tabletop and it wobbled precariously back and forth.

Annabel cast him a glance, "Geoffrey…"

Brigid lowered her eyes. "I know," she said, "It was foolish, and I'm sorry."

Freddy and Greta ran in, their eyes wide in alarm. "What happened?" Freddy asked.

Geoffrey waved a hand at them, "Go upstairs."

"Mama, what's wrong?" Greta whispered, "What happened to Brigid's dress?"

"Go upstairs!" Geoffrey roared.

Annabel's brow furrowed menacingly, but when she spoke, her voice was calm. "Freddy, take your sister upstairs."

Freddy pulled a face, "Fine."

"The guards are going to be looking for you..." Geoffrey muttered when the children had gone, "What are we to tell them?"

Brigid looked up and her blue eyes flashed. "The truth," she said.

"What? That you drew on them?"

"They're soldiers of Andoch trying to sneak into the castle. I heard them," Brigid said, "A friend walks through the front door; he doesn't steal in through the back. Think on Grantis. They say half the Senate was butchered at the hands of the kingsmen, many of whom had already surrendered. If they're sneaking about like this, it probably means the Brock is next."

"And what about you?" Geoffrey asked, "Weren't you looking to find a way in to the castle too? How would you explain that?"

Brigid sighed, "I think the Marshal is there—no, I *know* it."

"A lot of good that does."

"The hound knows me now too. Why would he help if he thought I was a danger?"

Geoffrey threw up his hands in frustration, "Oh yes, the hound. The bloody hound!"

Brigid's jaw went rigid and her eyes flashed, "It's real. I know what I saw."

"You saw a dog—a stray most like."

"I know what I saw."

"You don't know nothing."

"I know that you had better watch how you speak to me."

Geoffrey bowed his head in mockery, "Pardon me, my lady. I'm only a simple dullard of a peasant."

"Aiden's Flame, Geoffrey. You know I didn't mean it like that!"

Suddenly, Annabel waved her arms and shouted, "Stop it! Both of you!"

There was the scurrying sound of footsteps as Freddy and Greta ran to the edge of the stairs.

"Mama..." Greta called.

"One moment, love," Annabel said. She lowered her voice and glared from Geoffrey to Brigid and back again. "Stop acting like children," she snapped, "What's done is done. If we're in danger—from the guards or this Hammer fellow or whomever—fighting with each other is only going to hasten us to ruin."

Geoffrey breathed a heavy sigh and Brigid wiped a stray hair from her face. "I'm sorry," she said again.

Annabel eyed each of them again in reproach. "I'm going to see to the children," she said, "Brigid, I'll set out a new frock for you upstairs."

Geoffrey lowered his head to his hands and took a long, deep breath. He was still angry, though in truth, it was not so much at the young noblewoman, but at Regnar and himself. In fact, he was relieved that Brigid was safe, and if this golden hound did exist, then he owed it a haunch of venison for delivering her from harm.

Ever since this whole business began with Oakheart and Acorn, with Regnar the Vanguard, he knew that it would only come to misery. Already he'd lost a son and been forced to flee his lands, dragging his family across the continent on some fool's errand. Now, he learns he's an outlaw, a Blackguard, to be hunted down by the holy knights of Andoch and their king. Why, he did not know exactly, nor did he really know much about the Guardians beyond the church stories of St. Aiden and Dibhor's Fall. When Regnar, the old man-at-arms, offered to save him, it would have been nice if he'd also told him about that business first.

Not that it would have changed anything, truth be told...

"What do you think we should do?" Brigid asked.

Again, Geoffrey sighed. "I don't know," he said quietly.

Brigid rubbed at her eyes, and he could tell that she was straining to hold her voice steady. "You know that I would never intentionally do anything to bring harm upon any of you," she said, "Especially your children."

"I know."

For a long time they were silent. Until at last, Geoffrey stood up from the table. "For now, I say we do nothing," he declared, "We'll wait and we'll think. The cousins out of St. Golan's said their abbot was at the castle until a few days past seeing to the baron, but he planned to return again for St. Aiden's Feast. Perhaps he might be willing to send word to the baron, especially if that cloak pin is what you say it is."

"I think that's a good idea," Brigid said, "They can't sit idle if there are enemy soldiers in the city going about armed after dark."

"Alright then," Geoffrey said, "And...I'm sorry for yelling at you and for losing my temper. I just...this family's lost one before. We don't want to see another come to harm." He cleared his throat, "In any case, I'm sorry."

Brigid smiled weakly. "You've a right to be angry," she said, "I was reckless. I *am* sometimes reckless…and foolish, and more than once it's nearly gotten me killed."

"Forget it now," Geoffrey said, "At least you're safe. Just…" he sighed, "Promise me you won't go out alone again until we see what the abbot has to say? Alright?"

She nodded, "I promise, Geoffrey. I mean it."

"Good," he said, "Now, you'd best get rid of that bloody thing."

For the next few days, Geoffrey kept a sharp eye and a sharp ear regarding any news about bodies, grottos, or giant hounds, but to his surprise, heard nothing out of the ordinary. Like all cities, Galadin had its share of crime, corruption, and other dangers, for even if the baron might be descended from a saint, his people were no more or less virtuous than any others. The Weavers' Guild was particularly powerful in light of the great flocks and wool industries across the Brock, and many of the wealthiest masters soon found that their gold enabled them to buy up territory across the city to set up private, urban fiefdoms of their own. Thankfully, Faden, who owned Geoffrey's house and most of the others on their street, was a decent sort, if somewhat shrewd. He could have been much, much worse besides. Adolfo the Madder, for instance, owned half the western end of Hounton, three streets of shops in the Trade Quarter, and the majority of the warehouses along the lakeside docks. His rents were known to be high, his contract durations very long and binding, and it was said that, as a moneylender, to make a deal with him was like making a deal with the Lord of Darkness himself. He kept his own band of mercenary guards and owned an estate in the Golden Quarter, and though gambling and prostitution were illegal in Galadin on accounts of the cathedral and the many shrines, Adolfo was said to dabble in both.

With the Feast of the Saint so near and the pilgrim hordes packed in and about the city, even the unusual was passing for ordinary. Normally, bodies were often found floating in the lake at a rate of about one or two per fortnight, yet this week alone there had been four. Two drowned, one with his throat cut, and the last with a noose around his neck—but whether it was misadventure, foul play, or suicide that did each of them in was hard to tell.

As for the grotto, Galadin was home to numerous small shrines dedicated to the storied heroes of the past, from great men of the Order, all the way down to obscure, local saints. They were always busy during the daytime, packed with pilgrims, pardoners, and peddlers selling false relics and souvenirs. Even the gardens of the Priory were open to the public during the daylight hours and had anyone discovered the bodies of two unknown men, one of which was said to have been mauled by a dog, surely it would have been big news.

Strangely, however, it seemed the one subject relating to Brigid's story that Geoffrey found the most absurd was the one that most townsfolk seemed to accept—at least as far as rumor can be counted upon for truth. It seemed that nearly everyone had either seen or knew someone else who had seen a giant golden hound running about at night, and Geoffrey wondered how in the months that he and his family had come to live in Galadin, they had never heard of it before. Some said it was the Lord Perindal himself taking the shape of one his hounds to hunt the wicked, others said it was the Galadin Baron's ability to change shape, but most claimed it was a punishment loosed on naughty children for disobeying their parents.

Regardless, when Geoffrey approached the cousins about speaking to their abbot, they were at first very confused, mostly due to the reticent and intentionally vague account Geoffrey gave of his life in Pyle and his eventual journey to Galadin. However, in the end, they agreed to mention Geoffrey to Abbot Woode when he arrived, and if time allowed, they were certain he would be willing to meet with a man who had served them so well throughout the festival. He could then explain his story to the abbot himself.

Brigid meanwhile remained in and around the direct vicinity of their small house in Hounton. She made good on her promise not to wander, and when he returned from work each day, Geoffrey often found her sitting in the hall with Freddy and Greta reading or playing. Inwardly, the gift of reading was to both Geoffrey and Annabel, more valuable than all the coin from all the jewelry that Brigid had shared with them. For, although Geoffrey could read, it was something that simply came to him after he became the Vanguard, and as a result, he regarded his own ability with a certain degree of apprehension. Since Brigid had learned as a child in Blackstone, it was completely natural, and furthermore, she knew from her own experience how to teach others. Away from the farmlands, education meant opportunity, and when on the voyage over from Dwerin, Brigid discovered Cousin Martin's old book and offered to teach the children, Geoffrey and Annabel were overjoyed. Reading meant that their children could have a future beyond simply farming or spinning a wheel—not that there was anything wrong with those pursuits; however, to be able to read was like waking up in the middle of the night only to discover that as dark as it was, you could still see just fine.

And so it went as summer waxed and St. Aiden's Feast (and the meeting with the abbot) drew nearer, until finally it was the eve of the festival. Geoffrey had only just returned home from helping the cousins and sat in comfortable silence at the table, watching contentedly as his son read more of Martin's book. Greta was with Brigid in her room and Annabel was finishing her day's work at the wheel on the first floor below.

"You know, half those herbs used to grow wild around Pyle," Geoffrey told his son, "When I cut my leg once on the plow, Martin mixed a paste together out of what we took for weeds and it fixed it right up."

Freddy looked up, "What do you think Axel and Nicky are doing? You said they went on to become soldiers with that captain?"

Geoffrey sighed, "So they planned."

"Do you think they learned how to fight?"

"I'd expect as much. Captain Barrow was a good man. He'd not want them marching off to war just to get themselves killed." Geoffrey paused as a plethora of unhappy thoughts appeared like a shadow at the edge of his mind. He sighed, "Why do you ask?"

Freddy sat back in his chair and closed his book with a quiet gravity. "When do you think I can have a sword?" he said.

"What?"

"Or a mace or something."

Geoffrey smiled and shook his head, "I don't think that's something you need, son."

"Well, Brigid has her knives and she's a girl."

Geoffrey sighed, "Firstly, being a girl has nothing to do with it, and second, you don't need a weapon, son."

"Why not?"

"Why not? Well, look at me! When was the last time you saw me going about armed?"

"Then if you don't want them, how about you give me Acorn and Oakheart?"

Geoffrey shook his head, "Son, why do you want a weapon?"

Freddy raised an eyebrow, "I'm not stupid. I know that was blood on Brigid's dress."

Geoffrey sighed, "Maybe it was a mistake, letting you learn to read. You're getting too smart too quickly."

"If I'm so smart, than I must be responsible too. So...maybe a sword?"

Geoffrey shook his head and smiled in spite of himself. "How about I make a deal with you—" All of a sudden, he stopped. A strange feeling shook his breast and his breath caught in his throat. Freddy's eyes went wide.

"Dad, what is it?"

There was a clatter of footsteps on the stairs and Brigid appeared, her face ashen with alarm. "You felt it too?" she asked.

Geoffrey nodded.

Carefully, Brigid edged closer to the window and turned the shutter to peer out into the street.

"What is it?" Geoffrey asked.

"We need to go," she whispered.

Geoffrey's heart began to work faster and faster.

"Why?" Freddy asked, "What is it?"

"Freddy," Geoffrey said quietly, "I need you to go fetch your sister and bring me Oakheart and Acorn. I know you know where I keep them, and that you look at them when you're not supposed to."

"But I—"

"It's okay. Just, please, do it."

"Yes, Da."

"There are men by the well and they keep going off in pairs to knock on doors," Brigid whispered when Freddy had gone, "They're armed."

"They're not guardsmen, I warrant?"

"No."

"Do you think...?"

"Yes. There's a man leading them and he's only got one arm," she whispered, her voice unsteady with fear, "The men at the grotto said something about that—Lady's Grace, Geoffrey, we need to go!"

"Alright, alright," Geoffrey said calmly, "We're going. Run down to Annabel. I'll wait for the children and we'll leave out the backdoor through the alleyway."

"We should go to the grotto," Brigid said, "Maybe the hound—"

110

"The cousins are that way too. We could ask them for help, or at the cathedral."

"Not the cathedral. I had much the same feeling there as I do now by the provincial's manor," she shook her head, "Aiden's Flame, let's just go. We'll decide on the way."

When Geoffrey met Brigid and Annabel by the back door of the house, Annabel's face was stricken with fear. She hugged the children to her and was about to wrap her head with a shawl when Brigid stayed her. "We'll want to look as natural as possible," she said, "The more we cover up, the more attention we'll draw to ourselves."

"What's the matter?" Greta asked.

"We're going for a walk," Freddy told her.

Geoffrey mussed his hair. He had donned his shield, which in months passed he had covered with a strip of hide to conceal the emblem of the red acorn, and slipped the wrist strap of the cudgel loosely around his belt so that it might hang free, but could be drawn at a moment's notice. It still amazed him that he somehow knew how to do these things without ever having to pause to think about them. "You lead them from the front," he told Brigid, "And I'll hang back at the rear."

Brigid nodded. She had wrapped her cloak around her shoulders to conceal the hilts of her daggers, but left the cowl down. "To the Saints Quarter then—" she stopped. There was a knock at the front door.

"Go," Geoffrey whispered.

Together, the family stepped into the alley and followed it out into the main cobbled streets of Hounton. Peddlers hocked foodstuffs and other daily wares, hoping to make a few final sales to the wives of the working men as they readied their evening meals. There was a mood of celebration in the air, for the holiday meant an extra day of rest from one's labors and time to enjoy the summer sun free of toil. A neighbor waved at Geoffrey, and asked merrily if the cousins of the monastery paid him in coin or ale, and if it was the latter, whether he'd mind sharing. Geoffrey smiled and answered politely, but hurried on, hoping to avoid drawing the attention of any of the armed men at the well.

However, as the family turned the corner to head toward the Trade Quarter, he chanced a casual glance back and sensed at once that they were being followed. He cleared his throat with a loud cough, and Brigid nodded in agreement. Whatever it was, she had sensed it too. She quickened her pace, ushering Annabel and the children along past the shops and the street vendors.

The archway to Saints Quarter was in sight when once more Geoffrey felt the strange sensation of impending danger wash over him like freezing rain. Suddenly a man emerged from the crowd and shouted at them with the voice of doom.

"Hold, Blackguards! Stop in the name of the Guardian-King!"

Geoffrey drew his club, "Run!"

Annabel swept Greta up in her arms and with Freddy at her side ran after Brigid in the direction of the Saints Quarter. Geoffrey hurried behind them, his shield raised for cover. His heart raced like a stampede, and for the first time since Ashfort, he felt the battle rage stir in his blood. Behind them, the armed men drew their weapons and gave chase as merchants, pilgrims, and burghers scurried to get out of the way.

Past the cathedral they ran, to where the stall from St. Golan's stood at the base of the statue of Perindal; but the cousins of the monastery were nowhere in sight—gone, Geoffrey thought, to prepare for their Abbot's arrival. A Galadin watchman standing nearby eyed the family and their pursuers with confusion, but by the time he had the presence of mind to call out to them, Brigid had already led the way past him toward the priory and the Grotto of St. Elisa. Geoffrey shot a quick glance up at the statue of the Divine Brother. *If ever there was a time to release your hounds, Lord Perindal, it's now!*

As they reached the handmaids' gardens, a crossbow quarrel whistled past Geoffrey's ear and knocked three fingers off of one of the garden statues. A small cluster of nuns shrieked in terror and scurried away to cower before the fleeing family and their pursuers. The appearance of the marksman brought Geoffrey's heart to his throat at the new threat posed to his family. He had already lost one child to a stray arrow; he would not lose another. As they reached the garden path that continued onward to the Grotto, he stopped running and turned.

"Keep going!" he heard Brigid shouting behind him, "Don't stop! Don't stop for anything!" A moment later, she was at his side, daggers drawn, the dusk light dancing upon the blades. Her blue eyes shone like the heart of a flame.

"What are you doing?! Geoffrey shouted, "Go with them! Get somewhere safe!"

"It's us they want!" Brigid told him, "If we stay, they can all get to safety!"

Geoffrey's grimaced, "I'll not see you come to harm either! Go!"

"You can't face them all yourself!"

The spark of battle kindled in the farmer's chest. "You don't know what I can do!"

The first of the Andoch men were upon them. Geoffrey rushed forth to meet them, roaring a battle cry. With a quick jab, he knocked the first man to the ground with his shield before shattering the second man's face with Oakheart. In a flash, Brigid leapt upon the fallen soldier and opened his throat with Whisper.

Another quarrel flew through the air, but this time, Geoffrey swatted it aside with the targe. The broadhead tip tore through the hide covering and the bright red acorn insignia was laid bare. "It *is* them!" he heard a gruff voice shout, though he couldn't resist a sudden flush of eagerness—grim delight even—at the recognition of the Acorn. For, the emblem was known to his enemies, and it gave them pause.

Three more men charged. Brigid ducked a slice from a sword, sidestepped, and in the blink of an eye, drove Shade to the hilt in the vulnerable space beneath the attacker's arm. Geoffrey tore into the other two, whirling his club with fury and bashing with his shield. The holy oak club shattered the head of one man's mace, and the sigil of the acorn was the last the other saw before the edge of the shield crushed his throat.

Another crossbow quarrel flew dangerously close, piercing Brigid's cloak just to the right of her hip. In a flash, she ran ahead to dispatch the crossbowman as he struggled with his winch to reload. As he lie prone, choking out his final, bloody breaths, she made sure to sever the string of his offending weapon so that it could not cause further harm.

With the first wave of enemies lying dead or dying, the Blade and the Vanguard hurried to regroup before the next assault was upon them. Sweat poured from Geoffrey's brow, stinging his eyes and soaking his tunic. Beside him, Brigid's fair face was redder than he'd ever seen as she gulped down great draughts of air. There was no time for rest, however, as the one-armed man and his soldiers came for them, joined now by four heavily armored soldiers of the provincial hierophant's personal guard.

Brigid bit her lip.

"I'll hold them off," Geoffrey told her, "You get away. Find the path up the ridge and get somewhere safe."

"You're mad if you think I'm going to flee."

"Foolish girl! GO!"

"NO!"

The kingsmen were upon them. Geoffrey turned aside a blow with Acorn, and Oakheart shattered the man's arm. Brigid leaped back and forth, dodging another man's sword, and striking back with quick slashes of her daggers on her attacker's unarmored wrists and legs. Yet, with each vanquished foe, another stepped forth ready to take his place, and they knew that it would not be long before they would be overwhelmed.

Behind the Andochan soldiers, the man with one arm paced slowly nearer and nearer, his face alight with wicked glee. With each of the man's steps, Geoffrey felt his seething anger burn hotter and hotter, and while he had never seen the man before today, somehow he felt that he knew him, had always known him, and that the intensity of this rage was the product of centuries.

"The Hammer," Geoffrey declared.

Brigid's eyes grew wide with fear as the man's presence alone seemed to somehow affect her. As she dispatched another enemy, she glanced back to check his progress and suddenly misstepped. As the dead weight of her vanquished foe fell against her, she fell to one knee and before she could right herself, another soldier engaged and slashed her along the outside of her thigh. At once, Geoffrey was upon him and Oakheart transformed the man's face into putty.

Acting on instinct, Geoffrey took Brigid's arm and ushered her back toward the grotto's pool, covering them both with the acorn shield. There was no sign of Annabel or his children. He only prayed that they were safe and far enough away that they would be unable to witness his fall. The Hammer barked another order and still his men pressed on, forming ranks behind the armored guards of the provincial, their plate mail ablaze with righteous glory.

"I'm sorry, Geoffrey," Brigid whispered.

"Don't be," the farmer said, "I may have lost a son before I accepted the title of the Vanguard, but I'm thankful to have gained a daughter."

Brigid smiled wistfully, "It's nice to have finally known a father."

"Bring me their heads!" the Hammer shouted, "Death to the enemies of the Order!"

And then, when all seemed lost, Geoffrey's prayer was answered and Brother Perindal released his hounds.

A golden flash leapt over the farmer's head and the nearest of the enemy soldiers was dragged to the ground. There was wrenching snarl and a scream as the spirit hound raised its head high in the red light of the setting sun and let loose a bone-shaking howl.

"I told you!" Brigid cried, "I told you it was real!"

And the hound was not alone, for behind him at the grotto, as if emerging out of the very pool of St. Elisa, a golden youth clad in shades of baronial blue strode forth raising his sword, a small squad of men-at-arms following behind him. His gray eyes flashed like lightening and his teeth clenched in wrath. He ran into the fray, his longsword glimmering in the light, and for a moment, the Andochan soldiers drew back in fright. At long last, the Marshal had come forth.

The man with one arm drew a sword from his baldric and held it awkwardly in his left hand. "I see you still live, Marshal," he said, "Though it seems you've traded one dog for another."

The young man ignored the taunt and assumed his stance beside Geoffrey and Brigid. "You're the Vanguard?" he asked, "And the Blade?"

"And you're the Marshal," Brigid said, "We've been looking for you."

"I'm sorry," he said, "Are you hurt?"

The young man's calm surprised Geoffrey, caught up as they were in the thick of battle. "I'm fine," he said, "But she is."

"It's only a scratch," Brigid protested, her eyes alight with renewed excitement, "We're both with you."

"Fergus," the youth said, "Heel." The great hound ceased tearing at the lifeless corpse and trod over to where Brigid knelt and lowered his head. His tongue lolled happily from the side of his crimson maw in an expression that to Geoffrey seemed a type of self-satisfied delight.

At a sharp command from the Hammer, the men of Andoch spread out, preparing to advance, while the Galadin men-at-arms who ran forth with the young swordsman raised their shields. "Lay down your arms," the young man said, "By order of the Baron of Galadin."

"You three are outlaws and villains," the Hammer said sternly, "Your word means nothing—Baron or Blackguard."

The enemies advanced a step forward and without hesitation, the young man leapt forward to meet them. Geoffrey watched as the youth parried a blow from above, sidestepped, and countered, slashing one man across the middle before whirling his blade around to strike from on high and slice a second man from shoulder to navel. It all happened so quickly that had the farmer blinked, he would have missed the entire display.

"*Stand down!*" the Marshal shouted. His men closed to his sides and the Andochans drew back a few paces away. With the great hound at her side, Brigid clambered to her feet and readied her blades. Geoffrey took a step forward to stand with the men of Galadin and added the Acorn to their shieldwall.

Again from behind them at the grotto, there was a flurry of footsteps and now an aging knight with a thick black mustache ran forward wielding a heavy two-handed sword. He planted his feet at Geoffrey's side as another half dozen men-at-arms dressed in the blue and gold of Galadin joined them. The Hammer's face twisted in anger.

"So the Brock would become an enemy of Andoch?" he said, "For any man who backs a Blackguard makes an enemy of the Guardian-King."

"Aye, but your King's a long ways off," the old knight remarked, "And you threaten the Baron of Galadin. I'll see you all hanged before the sun finishes setting."

"What?" Brigid whispered, "The Marshal is the *baron?*"

The golden youth narrowed his gaze, "If you insist on fighting, Harlow, you'll die and your title will die with you. No more Hammers will ever live to stalk Termain," he said, adding, "Though from the looks of things, you seem to have misplaced yours."

"Perhaps it's with the old Loremaster," Harlow sneered, "It seems no one's seen him for some time."

The Marshal's knuckles went white around the hilt of his sword, but he stayed his hand, "Leave, Harlow, before more blood is shed. This is your last chance."

A long moment passed in silence as the tension mounted. Great beads of sweat rolled down Geoffrey's back beneath the soft light of the setting sun and he wondered how much longer the other men in their chain hauberks and breastplates could remain so still. Finally, at last, the man with one-arm sheathed his sword.

"This is not over," he said, "I'll appeal to the other barons, to the Lord-Baron himself if I have to."

"You do that," the old knight scowled, "But for now I'd advise you to run!"

Slowly, the men of Andoch turned and fled while the Galadin men-at-arms watched on vigilantly. When the last of them had disappeared back the way they had come, the baron sheathed his sword and turned toward Brigid. "Where are you hurt?" he asked, though Geoffrey noticed that when the young man's gaze met hers, his eyes instantly grew wide in alarm, as if suddenly taken by surprise. Hurriedly, he looked away, blushing.

"Really, I'm fine," Brigid said, "But thank you."

The baron gave a silent nod. A moment later, the old knight approached and leaned upon his sword. "We can still catch him, if you'd like, my lord," he said, "He can't have gotten far."

The young man rubbed his eyes wearily and shook his head. "Harlow is chief constable of the Order of the Guardians," he said, "If we were to kill him, it'd be nothing short of an act of war, and I'd prefer to keep the provocation on their side of things."

"I suppose you're right, but he'll still be trouble."

"He killed Crodane. He's already trouble," the young man said, "And those armored men were provincial guards—templars. Harlow must have sought refuge with them."

"Then I'll speak to Andresen right now," the old knight said, "He may claim to be a man of the gods, but he's also a man of Andoch and the Order. I'll offer him a friendly reminder that this is the Brock."

The old knight hurried off taking the small squad of soldiers with him and leaving Geoffrey and Brigid alone with the great golden hound and the young baron of Galadin.

"You're not Regnar or Gareth?" the baron smiled wanly.

Brigid shook her head. "No," she said softly, "They both...fell."

"I'm sorry," he said, "The former Marshal did as well—at the hands of that man, Willum Harlow, called the Hammer."

"Was that Crodane?" she asked, "I feel I've heard his name somewhere before."

The young man nodded. "We met a woman with some children along the ridge," he said, changing the subject, "Was that your wife?"

Geoffrey's heart leapt to his throat, "Aye, my lord. Are they safe?"

"I left a man to guide them up to the castle," he nodded, "They should be there now."

"Thank you," Geoffrey said, breathing a great sigh of relief, "Thank you, my lord."

The young man made a face and ran a hand through his hair. "Please," he said, "My name is Lughus. Just Lughus. I've only been a baron a few days, and to be honest, I'm not sure I like it."

Brigid smiled. "I know the feeling," she said, "My father was Danford Beinn, the Archduke of Dwerin, but now I'm happily just Brigid."

"The daughter of the Archduke?" he said in surprise, "Crodane told me Gareth went to Dwerin, but…" he paused, "I'm sorry, my lady."

Brigid raised an eyebrow, "If you're to be Lughus, then I'm to be Brigid."

Lughus smiled, and again, Geoffrey watched his cheeks flush beneath the light of her blue eyes. He suddenly felt very old and very tired. Perhaps Annabel was right. Perhaps he was becoming a cranky old curmudgeon. The young man turned toward him to allow his color time to fade, "Your wife said your name was Geoffrey?"

"Aye, it is, my lor—Lughus."

"It's good to know you, Geoffrey," the baron, Lughus, said. He offered his arm and Geoffrey shook it. In spite of his skepticism, he could not deny the sincerity he felt when he met the young man's eye.

"And who's that?" Brigid smiled, "He and I met some days ago, but I never caught his name."

The great hound loped to the girl's side and nudged her with his muzzle, nearly knocking her off her feet, yet she only laughed and at once began scratching behind his ears.

"That's Fergus," Lughus said.

"Fergus?" Brigid repeated, ruffling the thick fur around the hound's neck. She scrunched up her nose and met the hound's green eyes with her own playful stare, "What a strong name, good Fergus!" she observed, "He saved my life, you know."

"He must like you," Lughus smiled, "It was him that led me down here to meet you."

"Is that so?" she grinned, "I told you, Geoffrey, didn't I?"

Geoffrey smiled politely, but could not escape an inward flash of anxiety at the dog's presence. He did, after all, just watch the beast tear out a man's throat.

Lughus breathed a sigh, "You should both come to the castle. I have yet to eat and if you're hungry, we could...we could dine together?" he nodded toward Geoffrey, "With your family of course."

Geoffrey gave a modest shrug, "I'll come to collect my family," he said, "But we had best get back home. I would not want to impose."

"Oh come on, Geoffrey," Brigid grinned, "We've been trying to get to the castle for months. Surely we can stay now?"

A shock of fear ran down Geoffrey's spine as he imagined himself sitting in the castle dining with the baron. *No, no, no,* he thought, *That is no place for a farmer!* However, the young baron interrupted his protest.

"Months?" Lughus said, "You've been here months? I've been waiting for you since the end of autumn."

Brigid stood up and Fergus ran back to Lughus's side. "It was midwinter when we arrived," she said, "But the guards turned us away at the gates."

Reluctantly, Geoffrey agreed.

"Midwinter!" Lughus shook his head. "I'm so sorry. My...grandfather, he was..." the young man paused, "There's too much. I will tell you later. For now, accept my apologies and my hospitality," he said, "Both of you. You must stay in the castle as my friends," he smiled wanly, "I insist. We are after all 'the Three.'"

"'The Three?'" Brigid asked.

"You don't know?" Lughus said, "Then you *have* to come to the castle. I have the book, but I can just as easily tell you the story myself. He added, "As we eat."

Brigid exchanged a glance with Geoffrey and the farmer could sense her latent curiosity beginning to boil over again. *If we don't go now, she'll just sneak off anyhow,* he thought. "Aye, my lord," Geoffrey said at last, "It would be an honor."

"Lughus," the young man corrected with a smile, "Please. Everyone else calls me 'my lord.' I'd really like the chance just to be me."

"Don't worry," Brigid smirked and offered Geoffrey a wink, "It may take a few months, but eventually he'll get the hang of it."

119

CHAPTER 12: THE GRAY WOLF

It was dark when Royne finally awoke, though from somewhere close by he could discern the shadowy illumination of candlelight. As he glanced around at his surroundings, he could see that he was still in the general's pavilion; however, somehow, he had assumed the place of the dying man on the cot. A cold shudder of disgust ran down his spine at the prospect of sharing a dead man's bed, and as he lurched upright to a sitting position, he glanced about the interior of the canvas room. For better or for worse, he was alone. Whether alive or dead, the general, the captain, and the young officer were all gone.

"The book!"

With a cry of dismay, Royne leapt from the cot to his feet. His eyes scanned the room from the tabletop with its fine arms and armor to the old wooden chest to the entry flap hanging flaccidly in the cool night air. He spied his satchel hanging from one of the pavilion support posts, and with great relief discovered *The Book of Histories* was still safe and sound inside.

Right, he thought, *Now to find Conor and get out of here! The Beast can take these wretched wolves and their damned general. Better to risk the bloody red-cloaks!* Carefully, he peered between the slackened flaps of the pavilion to the Grantisi camp, and at once, leapt back in surprise.

"Look who's awake!" Captain Velius grinned, forcing his way inside.

Royne hurried to seek refuge on the far side of the table. "It's not my fault he died!" he shouted, "I told you I'm no physician! I did my best—"

"Which, it appears, was good enough."

From behind the captain, the flap of the pavilion parted and the dying general entered looking very much alive. He was dressed in a simple green tunic gathered with a belt of thick black leather, and his complexion, which had previously assumed the drab pallor of a corpse, appeared now to have recovered its rich olive tone. Alongside him, carrying a small brass basin and a long, thin blade, was the young officer.

"What?" Royne gasped, his eyes wide with a blend of shock and fear, "You're alive!"

"You shouldn't look so surprised. Do you think for a moment that you would be if he were not?" the captain smirked, "And close your mouth before you swallow a fly."

Royne felt his pulse quicken and the palms of his hands grew damp. "I don't understand," he stammered, "It's impossible."

"Never underestimate the power of fear," the captain grinned, "It can often turn the impossible...well, possible."

"That's enough now, Denaron," the general told the captain. He wiped his face upon a small towel and tossed it to the young officer, "My thanks, Petran."

"You're welcome, sir," the young man said. Quickly, he hurried to the large chest and returned the basin, towel, and razor within, the sight of which suddenly brought to mind Royne's own valet.

"My steward, the boy Conor," he said, "Where is he?"

"Asleep, or so he was when last I saw him," the captain said, "It is the hour before dawn after all."

"The hour before dawn? But it was mid-afternoon when we arrived!"

"So it was. Mid-afternoon—yesterday," Velius smirked, "You've been out for more than a day."

Royne shook his head, "Impossible."

"There's that word again," the captain leered.

"Enough," the general stepped forward and leaned upon the table. His eyes narrowed curiously at the young Loremaster, like one attempting to decipher a familiar text written in an unknown language. "Leave me with this man," he said abruptly, "I would speak with him."

At once, the other soldiers stood, bowed their heads, and departed from the tent, leaving them alone, and although he felt a quiet relief at the departure of the mordant captain, the general's presence was not without a different form of intimidation. *Bloody soldiers*, he thought, *Brutes and animals all...*

"You'll have to excuse Captain Velius," General Navarro said once they were alone, "Diplomacy is hardly Denaron's strongest attribute. However, he's a solid man to have at your side in a fight and he's as loyal as they come."

Royne gave a hesitant nod, "As you say."

"Will you sit down?" the general asked, motioning toward the chairs, "I feel I should at least know something of the man to whom I owe my life."

For a moment, Royne eyed the general skeptically, though he detected no trace of irony or derision in his tone. At length, he sighed and accepted the seat. "Thank you," he muttered, "Sir."

Among the arms and armaments upon the tabletop was a pair of clay cups and a jug. "I'm afraid I can offer you very little in the way of food," he said, "But, as this is Grantis, even in times of struggle, we find a way to ensure that the wine still flows."

"Again, thank you."

With a nod, the general poured Royne a cup, and raising his own, took a long sip. Royne joined him, though as the thick, fragrant wine touched his lips, he remembered to pace himself, for without anything in his stomach, he would quickly become drunk, and should that happen, he would be utterly defenseless.

"So," Navarro began at last, "Captain Velius tells me that you came to Commonwealth out of Andoch in search of this Salasco the Wall?"

Royne nodded, "As you say."

"He also claimed that you identified yourself as 'The Loremaster'?"

Hesitantly, Royne shrugged, "Yes."

"I must admit that I find that rather odd," the general replied, "For, the only Loremaster I have heard of sits upon the Council of Five alongside the Guardian-King."

"Perhaps at one time," Royne said, "But..." he paused, uncertain as to how much he should say, for he feared that he had already been far too trusting in treating with the captain, nearly to his own ruin. Although, Denaron Velius appeared to be little more than a sword, hardly a thinking man. A general, however, and not just any general, but the Gray Wolf, Cornelius Navarro, himself? Surely he could not have survived this long as a simpleton.

"Perhaps at one time," he said again, "But we are not the same. That man's name is Natharis Tainne, an Andochan noble educated not by the Order, but at the Lighthouse in Castone. He is but the 'acting' Loremaster, put in place when my predecessor voiced his opposition to this absurd hostility."

"And your name?"

"Royne…Royne Glendaro."

"Glendaro?"

As an orphan ward of the Loremaster, Royne had been less than a peasant, and as such was granted neither the privilege of a family name or village of origin. As a member of the Guardians, he would once have been able to identify himself as Royne of the Order or Royne the scribe. For obvious reasons, such associations were no longer applicable. Still, he could not very well hope to be taken seriously by the great men of Grantis without the legitimacy awarded by a surname, regardless of their democratic values. "Yes," he said, "Royne Glendaro."

"I recall another Loremaster, a Rastis Glendaro," General Navarro said, "Uncle to the Lord-Baron of the Brock; though I believe he was a much older man."

"He was," Royne said, but stifling a cough and corrected himself, "He is."

"He is your father then? Or is it Grandfather?"

Royne felt his cheeks flush. He did not want to speak of Rastis; the memory of their parting was still too fresh and his uncertainty regarding the old man's fate was too much to bear. "Something like that," he said at last, "Suffice it to say that Rastis was my mentor and it was him who spoke against Kredor's war. He was once the Loremaster, but now that title has passed on to me."

The general paused and sipped at his wine, "You'll have to forgive me if I seem a bit confused. Though there is much about the Guardians that I find difficult to understand, least of all what it was you did to me or how it is that I still draw breath."

"I admit that I am…a bit uncertain of that myself," Royne said, "Though as the captain said, there are plenty of stories that claim the Guardians were gifted with the power to heal. Others speak of certain immunities to disease and to poison. To be honest, I had always believed them to be simply the stuff of fancy," he paused, "Until now."

"Yet you yourself claim to be a Guardian?"

"Even among the Order there is much that is kept a secret," Royne said, "And though I might bear a title, I am no longer welcome among the Guardians. On the contrary, my life is forfeit unless I swear myself in service to the Guardian-King," he paused, attempting in vain to divert a sudden flush of anger, "But I will swear no Oath of Fealty nor bind myself to any king as rotten and base as Kredor. For, like a book, I have read him, examining his pursuits and his aversions, and as such, I believe I have come to know his mind and to know what it is that drives him. He is a brute, a fool, a mere beast of a man, driven only by the pursuit of gain and the absurd notion of power. Dominion. Empire."

"Empire?" the general asked, "Kredor seeks an Empire?"

"Not in name, at least not openly," Royne told him, "Instead, he calls for authority beneath the guise of legitimacy. He expects the sovereigns of the other realms to bow to his will and request his dictatorship under the principles of the Protectorate."

Navarro's eyes narrowed, "The Protectorate?"

Royne nodded, "In the past, when under threat of invasion from a foreign army, the leaders of the civilized realms across Termain—Dwerin, Montevale, Baronbrock, Grantis, and Castone—have appealed to the Guardian-King to act as supreme commander of the allied forces."

"I did not know Tulondis or Kord presented much of a threat," Navarro said.

"Nor do they," Royne said, "Kredor's war is a war of illusions, a war of convenience. He claims that Termain is beset by dangerous ideologies, heresy, and corruption. As the sovereign leader of a theocratic monarchy his desires become more than mere megalomaniacal ambition, but the will of the Kinship itself."

The general gripped his chin in thought, but he remained silent, pensive, watching with rapt attention as the young man spoke, and with a sudden thrill, Royne was shocked to realize that not only did the great man seem to be taking him seriously, but that he appeared to believe him. Apart from Rastis and Hob, never had any adult ever treated him with such esteem, had made him feel like he was not merely some scribbling fool in a woolen habit, but a man of learning, of wisdom, a speaker of truth.

"Now," Royne continued, with renewed vigor, "Kredor might be a fool, but he is not entirely stupid. He knows that as powerful as Andoch might be with its standing army of kingsmen and its mighty Order, he cannot conquer Termain through military might alone. Though the Guardians are formidable warriors, they are not now as they once were at the time of St. Aiden, and after thirteen centuries, they have grown few. Of the original three thousand who followed Aiden to Deathsgate, but half that number survived the battle. Of those, less than five hundred remain. Subtract those who serve purely as statesmen, scholars, and men of the church, and you have even fewer. Thus, Kredor knows that he must have allies among the other realms, allies who will bend to his authority and his whim."

"Dwerin was an easy ally to gain," Royne continued, "Since without the Archduke, the Mountain Kingdom was left without a stable leader and the Beinns have a reputation for treachery and deceit that could rival that of Old Montevale. Offer them the Spade, and their support was all but absolute."

"In Grantis, of course, the dissolution of the monarchy and the senate's decision to dissolve the worship of the Kinship as the official state religion made you an easy enemy. What democracy could possibly sustain its credibility after bowing down to a king?" Royne paused, "No, Grantis would not do, as far as Kredor was concerned. You would have to be dealt with, and if doing so secured the support of Dwerin, so much the better."

"And the other realms?" General Navarro asked, "Montevale? The Brock?"

"When the War of the Horses ended with the Black Horse victorious, I thought it a stroke of luck, for the Guardians had thrown in their lot with the White. However..." Royne paused and pressed the tips of his fingers together, "From what the criers in Commonwealth claim, Montevale now rides with Andoch. I can only speculate, but after a century of fighting, I cannot imagine that King Dermont sits very easily upon his throne, and as he attempts to put his own house in order, I very much doubt he would welcome foreign armies knocking at his door. Thus, he bows down to the Guardian-King as a means of securing his own rule."

"From what I understand, there are a number of senators in Commonwealth who are of a similar disposition," the general said.

"Yes," Royne said, "Though you will be happy to know that the Andochans have not treated them with anywhere near the grace with which they entreated the Montevalen King. They may have their lives, but their treachery has lost them any love the Grantisi populace might have ever had for them. At least once a week a senator is found burning in effigy in the Forum and the doors of the senate building are continually defaced with profane murals."

"In any case," General Navarro said, "You say that Kredor has the support of Dwerin and Montevale. What of the Brock?"

Royne breathed a sigh. "I do not know," he said at last, "They have not thrown in their support for the Guardians, though they have not taken a stand against them either. However, I do know that much of Kredor's hope for subjugating the Brock was dependent upon forcing the Golden Hound of Galadin to heel—a matter in which I believe he has failed." *Or so I hope*, Royne thought. He continued, "Should Arcis Galadin convince the Brock to take a stand against the Protectorate, it would present Kredor with a problem of enormous magnitude, for not only is the Brock a formidable force militarily, but it could potentially create a rift in the Order to rival that of the Siege of Three. Furthermore, the faithful of the Kinship would be forced to choose between the Saint and the King, the Galadins or the Drudes, the common or the noble…"

Royne's eyes narrowed and he pursed his lips in thought. *No wonder Rastis suggested I go to Grantis*, he brooded, *Where better to gain allies than among those who have already succeeded in throwing off the burden of oppression, of tyranny?* Yet, what was this business with *The Book of Histories* and Natharis Tainne's search for 'the Lock'? Why search for 'the Lock' and not 'the Key'? *Damn it, Salasco, where in the Father's creation are you?*

Suddenly, Royne stirred from his musing and fixed his gaze upon the general. "I would like to propose an alliance," he said.

"An alliance?" Navarro repeated.

"Yes," Royne said, "You seek to fight the Guardians and so do I. Alone, neither one of us can hope to succeed; however, together, we might just have a chance."

The general pressed the palms of his hands together and eyed the young Loremaster curiously, "You are suggesting that we join together to fight the combined might of Andoch, Dwerin, and Montevale? The Order, the Ironmen, and the Horselords?"

"Madness, I know," Royne smirked, "And I could tell by the state of the camp that your men have fallen on hard times. But you cannot expect me to believe that even now the 'Fighting Fifth' has given up, or that the Grey Wolf himself has decided to bend the knee before the Guardian-King?" he motioned toward the arms and armor laid out upon the table, "Don't tell me your valet polishes these to such a shine simply to let them rust. For, I had always heard it said that the Grantisi legions were the finest infantry in all Termain, the most disciplined, the most steadfast. Yet, in a matter of months, the kingsmen reduced you to this! A pack of scavengers hiding in the hills with their tails between their legs? Is that the legacy you would hope to leave? The legacy of the Republic? To falter in the face of nobility? In the face of a corrupt king?" For a moment Royne's eyes met the general's and he fought to control a sudden stab of fear beneath the intensity of the Gray Wolf's gaze, staring at the brazen young Loremaster with eyes that smoldered like a blacksmith's forge. *Careful now,* he told himself, *He's still a soldier. He's still a sword...*

"With you, or without you, I intend to keep fighting," Royne said at last, "Perhaps not in the field, but in my own way. I would, however, welcome your help, and I think that perhaps you might benefit from mine."

For a long moment, the general remained silent, his jaw set in anger and his lips pressed together so tightly that a knife blade might not have been able to part them. *I'm a dead man,* Royne thought bitterly, *Would that the captain had already killed me. At least it would have been quick...*

After what seemed an eternity, General Navarro's expression changed and the overt anger slowly seemed to dissipate, burrowing beneath the surface of his skin from whence it had crawled forth. Once more, he took up his cup, and as he returned it to the table, Royne noticed that the corners of the general's lips were turned upward in the slightest show of amusement; however, that hint of a smile did little to put him at ease.

"You have some nerve, my young friend," General Navarro said, "Though I suppose that is good, if you truly intend to see this through. For, it was not simply for his skill as a healer that my men sought Salasco the Wall, but for his wisdom. In his absence, I suppose that—for the second time—you will have to do."

CHAPTER 13: TEMPEST

Bel awoke to the jeering call of a crow somewhere high above him and the pungent scent of burning wood wafting past his nose. His body ached with the bumps, bruises, cuts, and scrapes of his last battle, but sleeping in the open air brought its own kind of peace. He pulled the blanket tighter around his shoulders and breathed a sigh, wondering where Lilia had slipped off to, and if they would have time to lie together once more before rallying the rest of the cavalry for another day of patrolling the Bloodline.

A horse grunted nearby, but he knew from the tone that it was neither Igno nor Banshee. Jarvy's Piper, perhaps? Maybe Briden had come to fetch him with Maggie. He breathed a sigh. "What is it?" he asked.

"You're awake?" said a familiar voice, though for some reason, he could not remember who it belonged to, "How are you feeling?"

"No worse for the wear."

"I brought you some water."

"Thanks," Bel sighed, but when he opened his eyes, his heart nearly stopped. For where he had expected to see the light cavalry camped alongside him, their horses staked around their bedrolls and campfires, he instead saw but a single squad of riders in chainmail hauberks and a carriage drawn by a pair of black horses. His joints locked and he felt the color drain from his skin. Somewhere to his right he heard a baby crying and the sound caught his breath. He lurched upright, but winced and fell backwards again at a sudden flash of pain. All at once, the memory of the past few days came back to him. His body went limp and his eyes began to burn.

Lilia, Jarvy, Linton, Igno—all of them were gone. All of them were dead. Even poor Banshee, who was so punctured with pike wounds that in the end Sir Emory had to put her down before they fled. At least Igno would have someone to run beside him in the afterlife.

"Prince Beledain," the voice whispered, and he felt a gentle touch upon his brow, "Would you...would you like some water?"

Bel took a deep breath and swallowed hard, as he finally recognized the voice. Another stone to add to his mountain of shame and grief. "I'm sorry," he said, struggling to control himself, "I'm...I'm not...myself." His voice grew thick and his body shook like a leaf upon the wind.

Princess Marina hushed him. "Just drink." Gently, she helped him raise his head and tipped the cup to his lips.

"Thank you," he managed, then drew his arm up across his eyes in hopes that she would leave him alone in his misery. She did not.

"When you fell from your horse last night, we feared you were dead," she said.

Bel bit his lip, "I no longer have a horse."

He heard her sigh. "I'm sorry," she whispered, "The horse that you happened to be riding."

The prince took another deep breath. He remembered kneeling beside Igno in his final moments while Sir Emory and his men hurried to make ready for their flight, but anything that happened after that was a blur. He could feel the hot tears welling against his arm and wished again that the princess would leave him be. "It appears I'm still alive," he said, his voice unsteady with grief and shame, "So, I guess that's something."

"It is," the princess said simply as she refilled the cup and again helped him to drink.

Across the camp, Marcus ceased crying.

"Your son is beautiful," Marina observed.

"He has the look of his mother."

"I'm very sorry about..." she paused, "About Lady Lilia."

He gave a wan smile, "You never had the chance to meet her, did you?"

Marina's voice fell to a whisper, "I thought that...in light of what happened at Clearpoint...I thought it would be rude of me. I thought she would hate me...and justifiably so."

"You were wrong. She wanted to meet you," he said, "It was I who...stayed away."

"I'm sorry."

"Don't be. All fault lies with me." *For this, for that, and for everything.*

"Here comes Sir Emory," she said a moment later, "I'll leave you to him."

Bel gave a nod and cleared his throat. "Thank you for the water," he whispered.

"Thank you, my lord," she replied, "For our lives and our freedom."

Don't thank me yet, Bel thought miserably. He rubbed his eyes and took another deep breath before very slowly, he raised himself to sit. They were somewhere among the Valendian plains encamped within a small copse of birch trees. Already the sun was high overhead.

"Thank the Father, you're alive," Sir Emory said, kneeling down to pat him on the shoulder, "I say, those tales about the Guardians must be true, for never have I seen a man take a beating like you did last night and awaken fresh as a daisy the next morning!"

Bel smiled weakly, "I hardly feel like a daisy."

"Well, it's hardly morning either," the old knight said, and with a touch more gravity, added, "Still, you're alive."

"For better or for worse."

Emory shook his head, "Don't say that. Not around me."

"I'm sorry," Bel said, "Tell me, is Marcus alright? I heard him crying."

"He's fine. In fact, he's more than fine. He's just eaten, which is more than the rest of us can say. At least for now. We're but a few hours ride from Woodshire. It's small enough to escape notice and Sir Norton Wherling has always held you in high regard. My hope is that we'll be able to rest there and take stock of things. We'll need to send word to your uncles too. Perhaps they can help smooth things along with...your brother...before it all falls further out of hand."

"Unlikely. Dermont's had them both retired and placed in command of border keeps at either end of the Nivanus, if I recall rightly. Shoulderidge in the south for Leon and Hoarfrost all the way in the north for Talvert."

"What of Val or any of the Gasparns? Some of them have found Dermont's favor. Might they help us?"

"Val's been attached to the Reginal court, and any Gasparns close enough to have Dermont's ear won't risk losing it on account of us," Bel ran a hair through his hair and felt the rough whiskers upon his cheeks. "What have I done?" he whispered, "I am such a fool."

"I wouldn't say that, my prince."

"No?" he said bitterly, "I killed Wilmar Danelis and stole Father, Marius, and Princess Marina. At the very least, I have broken the peace with Dermont and given him cause to do as he wishes to any of us. In all likelihood I've probably provoked the Guardians too for refusing to comply with their wishes and swear an Oath of Fealty."

"You've got half a year yet as far as I know to swear your Oath," Sir Emory said, "Isn't that what the provincial claimed when he first arrived from Andoch? A year and a day?"

"Let it be tomorrow or ten years from now. I'll not do it," Bel grunted, "My duty is to Montevale."

"And as for the Sundering Hand, he killed your men, your friends, to say nothing of the fact that you're a prince and he threatened your person. I'd call self-defense cause enough to kill him."

"You forget that Dermont absolved my rights when I became the Tower."

"Well, you're still a prince to me, and I'm sure there's others as feel the same too. Your boys that Lord Wilmar hanged...I doubt they're the only men out there who await the command of their Silent Prince."

"Did you know about Jarvy and Sir Linton?" he asked, ignoring the implications of the old knight's statement.

"I wish I would have, but no. I remember your man Jarvy," he paused, "Lilia told me he was the one that went north with you. As for the other, Marius said he was a good man and one of the lead riders among the Tower's Guard."

Bel shook his head, "This is all my fault."

"No," Sir Emory said, "It's Dermont's, though that doesn't mean you can't set it right."

"The last war began with brother against brother. Would you have me do the same?"

132

The old knight screwed up his face in thought, the great scar down the side of his face twisting like a corkscrew, "Do you think the war ever really ended? Perhaps the gods think it only fitting that a war begun by brother against brother should end the same way."

"Both of those brothers sought to see themselves crowned," Bel said, "And as much a Dermont may covet his, I have no interest in such a thing whatsoever."

"Which only serves to make you more qualified."

"No, Emory. No."

Sir Emory sighed, "I've been your father's seneschal since before Larius was born. I watched the three of you grow up. I taught you to ride. I taught you to fight. I think that qualifies me enough to say that something—I'm not sure what, but *something*—went wrong with Dermont somewhere along the way. Your father might not have taken the field for many a year now; however, that does not mean he was ignorant to the war. There have been plenty of unpleasant tales about the 'Prince of Plague.' Unsavory stories of terrible crimes committed in your father's name. Thanks be that there were also tales told of the Silent Prince, else he'd likely have died for shame."

Bel rubbed his eyes. He knew well the depths of his brother's cruelty, his corruption, and dishonor. He could no longer choose to ignore it as he had once done. They had very nearly come to blows upon the highland steppe when Sir Marcus Harding fell before the gates of Clearpoint. However, to begin the war all over again in earnest? An uneasy peace might still be better than war.

But, was that even an option anymore? For, he had killed the Warden of Tremontane Castle and stolen Dermont's would-be bride. And he regretted none of it, was proud of it, would do it again, in fact. He glanced up at the branches of the birch trees and watched a murder of crows alight from their perches and fly off across the plain.

He hates you because he fears you...

War with Dermont would be a different sort of affair entirely, for it would no longer be as easy as north against south, Gasparn versus Valendia. It would be something altogether different.

And Dermont was no fool. He was cruel, he was covetous, and he was in many respects, a coward, but to men of a similar disposition, which sadly appeared to be rather common among the nobility of both Valendia and the

Gasparn, he was not without a certain level of appeal. At the Battle of the White Wood, Dermont had been only too willing to sacrifice nine thousand infantrymen, mostly peasant levees, mercenaries, and men-at-arms of common birth while he and over a thousand noblemen, knights, and their retainers retreated without even drawing their swords. Men like Jarren Harren, a fop politician with hands as smooth and soft as a baby's ass, would live to avoid fighting another day, and to once again demand their tenant farmers and local militias give up their crop of sons and daughters to serve as fodder in the ongoing war.

After the Battle of Clearpoint effectively ceased the hostilities and established the uneasy peace, Bel and Marius were forced to accompany the now King Dermont to take possession of the northern stronghold at Reginal. The Plague King (since he was prince no longer) was unusually magnanimous in his treatment of many of the wealthier Gasparn nobles, gifting them lands in the south and providing Valendian lords with lands in the north that he had seized from men who refused to bend their knee to him, effectively integrating the gentry of the formerly divided nation and purchasing the loyalty of those whose hearts and minds valued gold more than honor.

No, Dermont was certainly not a fool, and should the war begin again, the Bloodline would no longer divide the two sides by place of birth, but rather by the weight of one's coin purses.

"I want to see my son," Bel said suddenly, and slowly tried to rise to his feet. Sir Emory reached out to help him, but to Bel's surprise, he found that in spite of his bumps and bruises, his wounds were not nearly what they should have been. That was at least some solace. "If you wouldn't mind, Emory, could you see to the camp? I fear that in allowing me to rest, I have once again put you all in danger."

The old man waved Bel's words away. "You needed it and we need you. Besides, there's still room in the carriage," the old knight said, "It will be crowded, but it would also give you more time to rest, should you need it. You took one bloody bastard of a beating, my lord. Of course, I'll not stop you either if you'd prefer to ride?"

Sharing a carriage with two displaced kings on the edge of madness, a princess he had refused, and his motherless son would not allow for much rest, to say nothing of Elsa, the nursemaid, and Lourdes, Marina's handmaid, whom he hardly knew. However, he could not bring himself to ride a strange horse again. The horse and the rider are one, King Cedric used to say, and with Igno and Banshee gone, it would be a long time before he rode again.

Bel shook his head, "If it's possible, perhaps I can drive the carriage?"

"Of course, my prince."

Sir Emory followed him to where Elsa and Lourdes, sat cooing over the baby. Not far from them, Bel's father and King Marius stood smoking their pipes and chatting.

"That's...unexpected," Bel observed.

"I'm not so sure your father knows who Marius really is," the old knight said, "Though I'm not so sure I regret that either."

"He's taken to calling me 'Larius' these past weeks."

"So I heard. I'm sorry."

"I suppose it's better than the alternative," Bel said grimly. He turned toward the maids, "How is he?"

"Quite fine, my lord," Elsa said bowing her head, "Tender and mild."

Bel glanced down into his son's little face, the only part visible for all the swaddling, and felt his heart flutter with both joy and sorrow. The boy would never know his mother, but he would remain her living memory, for there was just as much of Lilia to the baby as there was of him. *This is all that matters*, he thought, *This is all that matters now*. He hugged the baby to his breast and breathed in his scent. *Forget the war, forget Dermont, take your people and run!*

With a nod, Sir Emory went off to break camp and Bel walked away from the maids to pace among trees. The afternoon sun played upon their branches and clear, narrow shafts of light stretched like arrows through their leaves. The ground was still soft from yesterday's torrential rains and great swaths of moss hung like beards upon the slender white trunks of the tall birches. He could not help but think again of Lilia and the White Wood on the morning of the battle.

"Your mother would be in her glory now," Bel whispered, his voice thick, "She loved nothing more than the smell of danger and the sound of battle— except for you, of course." *And me...*

The baby gave a little yawn and the prince felt his knees go weak. "At any rate, we've plenty enough of the other now, between your uncle and the Guardians and whatever else. The Brethren only know what's to come of you," he bit his lip and shook his head in bitter anguish, "Marcus, your father is such a fool!"

A sound from beyond the trees ahead made Beledain start. He held the baby tighter to him and dropped to a crouch as his eyes peered beyond the white birches in alarm. Someone or something was moving just ahead, that much was clear, but whether beast or man, he could not be certain. His hand went to his belt, and to his horror, he discovered that he was still unarmed.

Bel took a cautious step backward, hoping to escape the notice of whatever it was that lie ahead; however, to no avail. For, almost at once, the trees grew silent and all movement ceased. Farther off at the campsite, he could hear Sir Emory and the others stowing away gear and preparing the carriage for the journey ahead. Bel's heart pounded against the wall of his chest, and he prayed it would not wake Marcus or set him crying. He would have to flee, and should whatever might lie in wait beyond the trees give chase, he would use his last breaths to shield his son from harm beneath his own bloody corpse.

At a rustling in the undergrowth nearby, Bel steeled himself to spring. In his arms, Marcus squirmed and gave another great yawn; Bel held the baby tighter in his arms.

"Prince Bel?"

Beledain allowed himself to breathe. "Marina?" he asked, "Is that you?"

She stepped through the forest, her green eyes nearly as red as her hair from weeping.

"Fire and Blood," he said, "You gave me a fright."

"I'm sorry," she said, biting her lip.

Bel averted his gaze, glancing instead down at the grass, "I'm sorry to intrude."

She shook her head and quickly wiped her eyes. "No," she said, "I should be the one to apologize. It was foolish to wander like this. I'm glad to see you on your feet, though, and with little Marcus."

Bel gave a silent nod. "Are you…" he paused, "Are you alright?"

"I'm fine," she said hurriedly, "I was just…I was speaking to an old friend."

Alone among the trees? he thought, but remained silent. *Perhaps we've all gone mad?*

"You must think me horrid," she said.

"Why would you think that?"

"Because of Clearpoint," she said, "And because of what I asked you, and what you nearly did to protect me. How painful that must have been for Lady Lilia—to have me in the castle as a reminder of…of everything," she breathed a heavy sigh, and ground her teeth in anguish, "It was wrong and I'm…I'm so sorry."

Bel shook his head, "Marina, I told you…"

"What woman would allow another in her home who tried to steal her man?"

"It was not like that."

"Was it not?" she asked, "Every day I lived beneath your roof, I wished that you would come to me, and it was wrong. It was wrong and it was unkind, and now she's dead, and I can't help but feel…" she fell silent.

Bel breathed a heavy sigh. *Dermont may be the Prince of Plague, but I am the Prince of Ruin, for those I care for either meet their ends, or must drown in the wake of my decisions.*

Suddenly, Marcus began to fuss. Bel held him up and saw that the baby had opened his eyes—green eyes, Tremont eyes, like his and like the princess's. Slowly, Bel paced over to Marina's side. "Would you like to hold him?" he asked.

"I don't think I should."

"Nonsense," Bel said, "Here." Gently, he took her arm and passed the swaddled infant over to her, supporting her elbow while she secured her hold and held the child close to her.

"He's so little," she murmured.

"He is."

Slowly, her tears ceased as she rocked the baby in her arms. Bel fought to control his pangs of grief, as in his mind's eye, he envisioned Lilia in the princess's place. *Oh Lilia, my love, my Blood Blossom, I miss you…*

Princess Marina breathed a sigh and raised Marcus to her cheek. "My purpose for coming out here was not to sit here weeping and wailing 'woe is me' like some waifish damsel in a poet's song," she said, "I'll weep and grieve for others, but, though it might not seem like it, I prefer action to self-pity."

"When my mother died," Bel said, "My father told me that a man who cannot weep, is a man with a heart of stone, and a man with a heart of stone, is no man at all. There is no shame in weeping."

The princess sighed, "King Cedric is very kind. It seems that he and my father have become fast friends. To think of all the wasted years they spent hating each other."

Bel gave a nod. "You said you had another purpose for coming out here?"

"I did," she said, "It was because of something you said this morning. You said that you had no horse."

"Igno and Banshee fell fighting so that we could escape," he looked up into the trees, "A great rider and his horse must be one. They must know each other, trust each other, think and act together. I was eight years old when Igno was born. We grew up side by side, and it was his saddle that was adorned with the silent bells. Banshee was Lilia's horse, and the two of them were one and the same. To know Lilia was to know Banshee, so when I came north in disguise, Lilia made me take her horse. It will be a long time before I know another such as either of them."

"Igno was the red horse of the Silent Prince, Banshee was the horse of your love," Marina said, "But you are also now the Tower."

"So I am."

The princess gave a wan smile, and still holding Marcus in her arms, led Bel back through the trees where she had stood concealed. There, standing on the edge of the plane beside the last cluster of birch trees, stood Tempest, the great searoan stallion who had born Sir Marcus Harding throughout his campaign in the north. His blue-gray coat shone in the light of the sun, outlining the beautiful musculature of his chest. A light breeze played upon the wild, loose locks of his main and tail, and his luminous dark eyes told of an uncanny intelligence and an empathic regard beyond most human beings. Like the majority of Montevalen folk, Bel was not particularly religious, but the regality emanating from the searoan was like being in the presence of the divine.

"He returned to the wild after the battle at Clearpoint," Marina said, "But sometimes when I walked the walls at Tremontane with my father, I could see him far off in the distance, running like a bolt of lightning across the plain. The searoans of Galdorn are smart as a man, they say, just like the spirit hounds of Perindal. He knew where we were and how to find us. It was just a matter of time."

The great horse plodded closer to the princess and lowered his nose toward her, sniffing the air around the baby. Marina beckoned to Bel and, as he approached, Tempest continued to regard him with his soft, compassionate eyes.

"He remembers you," the princess said.

Bel's breath caught in his throat, so overwhelmed was he with awe. He remembered the vision he had seen yesterday at Lilia's grave when the rain had only just begun to fall. Perhaps it wasn't a vision at all. Before he even realized what he was doing, Bel bowed low before the great stallion, and to his surprise, Tempest mirrored the display of honor, dipping his head graciously.

"H-hello," Bel whispered tentatively, "I am happy to see you again and to know that you are well."

Tempest uttered a low snort and shook his head from side to side.

"If you are the Tower," Marina said, "Then you must have a horse, and as you say, it cannot be just any horse—for often the horses of the Towers past are just as famous as the Guardian himself—and as you have lost your beloved partner, so too has he. As such, I thought that perhaps the two of you might find a path forward together, leading the charge to wherever the future takes us, with that ancient spear King Cedric brought with us as well."

Bel's eyes went wide, "My father brought Spire?"

"He said you would have need of it," she nodded, "He said Lady Lilia told him that the Silent Prince was the only one who could truly end the war."

Bel's eyes fell again upon his son, upon the princess, and upon the great stallion. His breast still ached with grief, but his heart felt warm with the thought of his lost love. *Lilia…* He reached out a tentative hand to gently run his knuckle along the searoan's nose.

"I am Beledain Tremont," he said, and his words suddenly assumed a sense of formality, with a tone and a resonance appropriate for the swearing of oaths. He took a deep breath. "I am Beledain Tremont," he said again, "Known by some as the Silent Prince, to others, as the Prince of Bells, and now, I am to be known by the Guardian title of the Tower. I swore an oath to Marcus Harding that I would end the War of the Horses and bring true peace to Montevale. For the sake of my son, and for all the sons and daughters born and yet to be born from Valendia to Gasparn, I swear once more that I will see this through." With a great staggering breath, Bel dropped to one knee and bowed his head once more before the great searoan. "If you, Tempest, Lord of Horses, find me worthy and have a mind to create a better world, then join me. Let my heart beat with your heart, my strength be as your strength, and my life be forever joined with yours."

By way of an answer, the great horse stamped the ground and Bel felt Tempest's muzzle roughly brush his shoulder and sniff his hair. He returned to his feet and gently ran his hand along the horse's nose, marveling at his own reflection in the great stallion's soft eyes. Beside them, Marina's eyes brimmed with tears, and in her arms, baby Marcus breathed a quiet sigh.

"Thank you," Bel whispered, his voice thick with emotion, "Let's ride."

CHAPTER 14: GENTLEMEN OF FORTUNE

With her hull sitting low in the draft, *Sigruna* looked very much the innocent merchant vessel as she drifted past the assorted ships of the Dwerin navy—galleys, hulks, and cogs—into the harbor of the Grantisi port town of Granmouth. Dressed in the respectable tunic and surcoat of a successful trader, one of the elder crewmen, a Montevalen by the name of Kradoc, even offered the Ironmen a friendly wave, a dumb show of gratitude for keeping the high seas safe from Sorgund corsairs and Wrathorn pirates. Beside him, a reluctant accomplice in the ruse, Thom stood disguised as a merchant's attendant clerk uttering silent prayers to the Kinship that Magnus's foolish attempt at subterfuge would succeed. Only when the ship had been safely tied to the moorings at the docks and the tax to the port official successfully paid, did he finally breathe easy.

"Clear skies ahead, eh?" Magnus grinned from beneath the shadow of the cabin, "Good work, lads."

Thom wiped the sweat from his palms on the sides of his new woolen hose and shook his head. It astounded him that the gods of the Kinship continued to answer his prayers, particularly when doing so appeared to further the Blackguard's morally ambiguous ends. His only hope was that they recognized him as an unwilling accomplice—in Galdoran, in the Isles, and most recently when on the journey westward the Sorgunders decided to relieve a pair of trade cogs of their cargo, hence the heavier draft and new clothing.

Not that he particularly disliked Magnus; in fact, in spite of everything, Thom recognized in the big man a certain endearing sense of madness as well as a certain odd familiarity due in part to his vague resemblance to Rastis's steward, Hob. Of course, the fact that his very survival seemed to depend upon the Wrathorn's continued patronage left him little other choice in the matter. With any luck, it would not be long before Magnus tracked down his old shipmates, killed them, and Thom could return to Titanis and the creature comforts of the Loremaster's Tower.

A cry from across the deck stirred him from his private thoughts and he looked up to see Magnus standing at the edge of the gangplank leading down to the pier. "Look alive, Thom Crusher," the Wrathorn shouted, "You're with me."

Thom Crusher. He could not recall when exactly the Wrathorn warrior had begun calling him that; however, Magnus had made it clear early on that he would not abide Thom's former nickname. Still, Thom couldn't help but feel that the new name was a trifle misleading. His brow knit with concern, "You want me to follow you?"

"How else will you know what to write down?"

"But Magnus, Grantis is under occupation."

"Huh?"

"The kingsmen have taken it over."

"Aye, so?"

"So they're likely to be everywhere."

"Ironmen too most like," Magnus said, "What's that to us? Let's go!"

With a defeated sigh, Thom gave up his protest, and hurried to follow along.

From the pier, Thom followed Magnus past the plethora of merchants and dock laborers toward the large daub and wattle buildings that marked the town proper. Granmouth was a lively port, though even in the noonday sun, the shadow of the Andochan occupation touched all like a tea stain. The local Grantisi citizens appeared to carry on the business of the day as usual, though beneath every visage there resided a cold resentment and a simmering lust for vengeance. It frightened Thom, for he recalled the suddenness with which the markets of Galdoran had turned to rioting at the crier's declaration of war. For better or for worse, the kingsmen seemed to be aware of it as well, patrolling the town in groups of no less than three, their hands never far from the hilts of their weapons, their eyes darting here and there like hunting hawks.

Only Magnus seemed untouched by the great miasma of anxiety, strutting about bold as brass, his great bearded axe dangling in plain sight from the thick baldric that traversed his massive shoulders. Merchant, peasant, Grantisi, or kingsmen, all averted their gazes when he passed them by. As Thom hurried to keep up with the big man's long strides, he once more set to muttering orisons beneath his breath, for the life of a Blackguard was considered forfeit, and in light of the ordeal at the Sandstone with Constable Harlow, it was unlikely much mercy would be reserved for a Blackguard's associates, no matter how reluctant.

That last thought struck Thom with a threefold stab of anger, fear, and regret, and he muttered a quick prayer to the Lady that she might keep Lughus safe. Though it was true that they might not have parted on the best of terms, Old Goldimop was still his friend, his brother. He only hoped that the Hammer rescued him in time to prevent whatever evil that rascal Crodane had wrought. Any man who could fool the Loremaster was bound to be the worst of villains. With a sigh, Thom shook his head. Thoughts of the past only made the present worse.

When they reached the marketplace, Magnus paused and peered out over the crowd. "Red cock and bollocks," he muttered, "Where the fuck it is?"

Thom caught up to him just in time to see an old crone shake her head and click her tongue at the big man's speech. "Barbarian," she hissed.

Thom held his breath in anticipation of whatever was to come, but Magnus only laughed. "Sorry, mum," he said with a wink, "Would I had more time, we'd have some fun, but you're not the whore I'm looking for."

The old woman's face contorted in disgust and she scurried off in a huff. Thom raised a hand after her in a halfway attempt at an apology, but by then Magnus had walked on and he was forced to follow after.

"Magnus," Thom called after him, "What exactly are we doing here?"

"Looking for something."

"What?"

"A brothel."

"Another one?"

"Aye."

"We must have passed at least two or three by the pier."

"But none of them was the right one, was it?"

"How should I know?"

"Well, they weren't. She wouldn't be caught dead in one of those places."

"Who?"

"Just..." Magnus grunted in frustration, "Just shut up and let me think!"

Thom breathed a heavy sigh, but said no more.

For more than an hour longer, Magnus wandered the pathways of the marketplace and the adjacent side streets searching and searching again in vain for the missing brothel. Before long, Thom began to notice an undercurrent of tension emanating from the crowd and more than once he sensed the kingsmen on duty warily marking the behavior of the increasingly agitated Wrathorn. Thom's palms sweat like a spring snowmelt and great patches of wetness appeared under his arms, though, he was reluctant to press Magnus any further.

At length, the Wrathorn halted once more and with a grunt of frustration folded his arms across his chest. "Warlock's balls!" he growled, pausing to kick at a rotten cabbage lying in the middle of the path. A man passed pushing a cartload of grain and Magnus whirled on him. "Oi, mate, what happened to the bloody Nymph, eh?" he asked the terrified laborer, "I could have sworn it was in the market here, but now it's not."

The carter's eyes went wide with alarm. "I...I can't say I know, sir," he stammered.

"The Nymph!" Magnus cried, "The brothel, you know! The nice one— clean like. Not one of those sailors' fuck-holes at the docks. The one for the rich merchants and the senators and the like!" But the man merely shook his head in confusion again and Magnus roughly thrust him aside. "Cock!" he shouted.

At the corner of a nearby shop, a trio of kingsmen began whispering to one another, adjusting their baldrics. *Lady save us!* Thom winced, and hurrying over to the Wrathorn Blackguard's side, held out a hand in supplication. "Magnus, please," he whispered, "Remember the kingsmen..."

144

"Oh fuck the bloody kingsmen!"

"Magnus, *please!* If they arrest you, we'll never find this Nymph you seek or the woman who works there."

Once more, Thom wiped his hands upon his leggings and began to prepare for the worst. Yet to his surprise, the big man calmed down. "I suppose you're right," he said.

The scribe breathed a sigh of relief and together he and the Wrathorn warrior crossed to the other side of the marketplace while the red-cloaked soldiers lagged behind warily. For a few minutes longer, the kingsmen continued to linger close at hand until finally, satisfied that trouble was no longer eminent, continued their patrol.

When they had gone, Thom took a deep breath. "Please, Magnus," he pleaded, "If you'd only tell me what it is we're after, perhaps I can help you. Else you're just likely to grow more frustrated until you lose control and kill someone. Then where will we be? Even if we're lucky enough to make it back to the ship, the Dwerin fleet is likely to smash us before we leave the harbor."

For a moment, Magnus considered it. "Aye," he said, "That's probably true. I do have a bit of a temper sometimes, don't I?"

"Then tell me. What are we doing here? Why is it so important that we find this woman and how does finding her help you find Rodulf and Slink?"

With a sigh, Magnus scratched his head and sat down on a large wooden crate. For a moment, the merchant who owned it tensed with annoyance, but appeared to think better of trying to reprimand a Wrathorn.

"Have you ever heard of a place called the Lighthouse? Not *a* lighthouse, mind you. *The* Lighthouse?" Magnus asked, "A great bloody tower far to the east in Castone?"

"Of course I have," Thom said, "The men who live there are called the Keepers. They're scholars, like us men of the Loremaster."

"If you're a man of the Loremaster, then you lot have got about as much in common with those bastards at the Lighthouse as a bear has with a fish," he paused, "Though I suppose you do dress the same in those funny...hooded frock things."

Thom sighed, "In any case..."

"In any case," Magnus continued, "Two winters ago, the old lads and I returned to Coverland to sell off the spoils we took raiding the trade routes between Tulondis and Kord. You know, way down to the south in the Pelacore Ocean? It's a good time of year then—aside from the heat. The war galleys of each land only keep watch so far for fear of drawing the ire of the other so it makes for easy pickings down the middle." Magnus shook his head and grunted with laughter at the memory of deeds that Thom tried not to wonder at. Thankfully, the big man chose not to elucidate either and carried on.

"So, I was sitting at the Dragon with that rat-bastard Pavlos, probably trying to keep from breaking his goddamned face, when in walks Rodulf with this…Keeper or what-have-you looking to hire a ship for some job." Suddenly, the big man stopped, "Why are you not writing this down?"

Thom's eyes went wide. "Do you want me to?"

"You're writing the bloody tale, aren't you?"

Thom sighed and rummaged through his pack for his journal. "This really isn't the most opportune place for me to do this," he said, "And you could have told me all of this on the ship. The Brethren only know how many times I've asked you in the past…"

"I'm telling you now, aren't I? So just shut up and write it down."

"Fine."

"Anyhow," Magnus chewed his lip, "This Keeper fellow—Caprice was his name, Vanek Caprice—said he needed a ship to carry him out to an island just north of the Kordish coast, a place marked by a ruin out of the old world."

"The Old World?" Thom asked, "You mean Old Calendral?"

"I don't know. Something like that. What's it matter though? It was a ruin, and according to him, full of ancient wonders," Magnus said, "Now, I'd heard tales like that plenty of times before—buried treasure, shipwrecks full of gold, and all sorts of shite that makes landsmen bastards take to the sea thinking they're sailors. What's more, there was something about him that just…that just wasn't right. So I told him to go fuck himself. If he wanted to find the bloody island, he could try swimming."

Thom gave a nod, his pen scratching at the page. "I take it the others didn't like that?" he asked.

Magnus gave a mirthless chuckle. "Well…one thing about sailors, you know, is that money never lasts long. The more you have the quicker it goes, and even though we had just come in richer than Kordish sultans, Rodulf,

Slink, and half the crew were already as poor as paupers. They wanted the job. But when I told them they were welcome to go and be gone, they said the Keeper wouldn't go along unless I agreed to go with them."

"Why?" Thom asked.

"He didn't say, just offered more gold—upfront."

"So you went?"

"I had to. A man offers five hundred gold pieces and you refuse a job like that, people start to wonder at your nerve."

Thom's eyes went wide with wonder, "Did you say five hundred gold pieces!? Five hundred!?"

"I know, right? Enough that you can't say no," Magnus said, "But plenty enough to tell you that something's not quite right."

"But five hundred?!" Thom shook his head, "I've never had a single one of my own, let alone five hundred!"

Magnus shrugged his shoulders in what seemed an uncharacteristic show of discomfort. "Do you want to hear the rest or not?" he asked.

Thom gave a nod and dipped his quill, "Go on."

The Wrathorn warrior gave a perfunctory nod. "Like I said," he continued, "The whole business smelled rotten to me from the start, but in the end, I went along with it. After all, shipmates are shipmates and it weren't right to have the whole barky suffer and lose out on my account," he paused, "Then again, given what happened in Galdoran, I should have let those bastards go to their deaths and be done with them."

"In any case..." Magnus shrugged, "This island of the Keeper's—it took time, but eventually we found it. Just like he said, it was a small place marked with the ruins of some bloody great watchtower, though now the place was little more than a rotted out old shell keep—not the sort of place like to be filled with riches of the sort he promised. Yet, the rest of the crew went along with it, mad with the love of gold as they were."

"It was near sundown when we arrived so we couldn't go wandering until the next day, but all that night, the whole business seemed to grow darker and darker. Clouds came in overhead and blocked out the stars, as if the gods themselves wanted no part in any of it," the Wrathorn warrior shook his head, "Something just wasn't bloody right with the place. All night, strange feelings pricked at my skin like a fucking jellyfish. It was...unusual, but also somehow...familiar. Meanwhile, this Caprice bastard just sat gazing out in the dark, reading his books of nonsense and smiling to himself. I don't think the man slept the whole time we were at sea. Just sat alone on the quarterdeck or in the bow staring blankly into nothing, staring with those strange eyes—blue like ice, so pale they almost seemed white. Every time he looked at you, you just wanted to break his fucking face."

"Anyway," Magnus shrugged, "The next day we went out to explore the ruin. Rodulf, Slink, and half the crew carrying spades and picks and such like a pack of bloody children. I followed after, keeping my eyes on the Keeper, but the nearer we got to the broken keep, the worse the whole business felt...odd."

"Odd how?" Thom asked.

"Just...odd," Magnus said, "What other kind is there? Odd—like not right. Like setting sail with a storm brewing or fucking a whore you think might have the pox. Bloody odd."

Thom breathed a sigh and made a note.

"In any case, in the center of the ruins, we found a campfire. Fresh. Warm. At that, the Keeper got all excited, grinning like a fox and rubbing his hands together like a bloody miser. Spread out, he tells us, anything we find is ours to keep, except for the big bloody key. That was his. But whoever found it and brought it to him would get an extra fifty gold pieces as a reward."

"Wait. A big key?"

"Aye, a big key."

"Did you find it?"

"Just wait. I'm getting to it."

Thom's brow furrowed. The key was the symbol of the Order and the Guardian-King. What would a Keeper want with a key? And why would a Keeper have need of a bunch of pirates? Surely their relationship with the Andochan nobility could secure more reputable folk to their employ. He breathed a heavy sigh and chewed at the nib of his quill, listening as Magnus continued.

"So," Magnus said, "The men did as this Caprice fellow said, but by midday after digging around in the ruins for hours only to come up with nothing, they were finally starting to grow angry. Pavlos started grumbling about gutting the bastard and hanging him from the top of the broken keep, or burying him up to his neck for the tide..." he paused, "And then we found the bloody hermit."

"The hermit?"

"He was a big man and strong, not young, but not old either, dressed in roughspun robes like...well, like you."

"Like me?" Thom repeated, "You mean like my habit?"

"Aye," Magnus said, "Though the color weren't exact. His was more brown."

"Like a cousin?"

"Eh?"

"Like a monk?"

Magnus shrugged, "I suppose. I didn't pay it much mind. I was too busy looking at his shield and the bloody great key that hung from his belt."

For some reason, Thom felt a touch of sickness in the pit of his stomach. "What did the key look like?" he asked.

"Big as a man's arm, it was, and shining like polished silver. Same as the ones on the flags of the bloody Guardians, same as on the hermit's shield."

"On the hermit's shield?"

"Aye," Magnus said, "A heater shield, enameled red with two crossed keys in the center."

Thom's heart gave a flutter, "You mean, he was another Guardian?"

"I don't know," Magnus said, "I suppose so, but not like that Hammer bastard in Galdoran. This fellow—*the* Shield, he called himself—he was different. Stronger."

Thom's face went white and his palms began to sweat again. "The Shield!" he said, "Magnus, the Shield is one of the most famous men of all the Order, but he's been dead for centuries. Are you certain?"

"That's what I said, didn't I?"

Thom shook his head. "This is too much..." he rubbed his eyes and made a note, "The Order must know he still lives! Lughus will be thrilled!"

"I'm afraid it's a bit late for that now."

"What do you mean?"

"He's dead."

"What?"

Magnus's face grew dark. "I killed him," he said.

"What!?"

The Wrathorn warrior's eyes fell. "He was the strongest man I ever fought," he said, "Had he fought with a weapon, he'd have won. But all he used was that bloody shield, bashing, blocking, and slashing with the edge." Magnus shook his head, "He was a true warrior."

"And so you killed him?" Thom wailed, "Oh Magnus, how could you?"

"I didn't have much choice," the big man growled, "And besides, it was proper-like. A duel for the blasted key—It was him that proposed it, not me!"

"And you won."

"Aye, I won," Magnus said, "I won and the bloody Keeper got his fucking prize." The warrior's lips twisted into a wry grin, "Aye, he got his prize alright…"

Thom's eyes widened, "What do you mean?"

Magnus's jaw set and he leapt from his seat on the crate to his feet. "When the Shield lay dying…" he shook his head, "Before the light went out of his eyes, he looked at me—not in fear or anger like most do. Nor was he…pathetic or weak. No crying or blubbering. He just…looked at me and held out the key. 'The burden passes to you,' he says," Magnus's brow furrowed, "Normally, a dying man says some shit like that, I ignore it. Chock it up to blathering and nonsense. But, with the hermit, well…it was different. And I knew right then I couldn't let the Keeper have it."

"So," he continued after a moment, "After we left the ruin, there was a storm—thunder, lightning, the whole mess—and while Rodulf and Pavlos and the others were busy keeping the barky steady, I slit the bastard's throat and threw his body in the drink."

"The Keeper?"

"Aye," Magnus said, "The Keeper."

Thom scratched out a note. "And what," he asked, "Did you do with the key?"

"Well, that's why we're here, isn't in?" Magnus said, "After the storm, the ship was right fucked so we pulled in to port here and whilst the others made the repairs, I hid it with the whores in the Nymph."

"You hid the Key of Salvation in a whorehouse?" Thom nearly shouted, "Magnus! That's perhaps the holiest relic in all the Order!"

"It was just for safe keeping. I knew I'd be back for it eventually," he said, "And what's this Key-of-Whatnot business?"

Thom shook his head. "Magnus, that's not just some trinket! It's the scepter of the Guardian-King!"

"Really?" Magnus gave a nod, "How 'bout that? I knew there was something special about it."

Thom gave a sigh. "We need to find that key!" he said.

"What the fuck do you think we're doing here, eh?"

"I just hope those women haven't sold it."

"They wouldn't," Magnus said, "Not Scarlet, in any case. However, if Rodulf and Slink got to her first then…"

"They know it's here?"

"Why do you think they sold me to the bloody kingsmen?"

"They figured out what you did?"

"I *told* them what I did," he said, "I told them they can keep their five hundred gold pieces and fuck themselves too."

"Oh Magnus!" Thom wailed, "How could you?"

"Oh shut up," Magnus said, "Now let's find the bloody Nymph before we waste any more time."

Thom put away his quill and shuffled to his feet. "If you knew this was where they were headed, why did we spend nearly a year wandering around the Isles?" he asked, "We could have just sailed back here, picked up the Key, and been on our way."

"Like you said, Grantis was at war with the Guardian-King," the warrior said. He hopped to his feet to resume the search, "No ship was making it in or out of any of these bloody ports without being boarded, sunk, or scuttled. Why else do you think Pavlos was busy raiding the coast? When Ivo sent word he turned up at the Dragon, I knew right away the blockade was over and in all likelihood, they had gone back for the Key."

"I see," Thom nodded, "Well, it's nice to know that we're trying to do something good for a change. Recovering the Key of Salvation for the Guardian-King could very well clear your name." *And mine…* the chubby boy thought.

"Ha!" Magnus laughed, "Hang the bloody key. I'm only after Rodulf and Slink. If the Key's still here then rest assured so too will they be. If it's gone, it'll mean they've already got it and set sail for Castone. Other than that, I don't give a shit about the wretched thing. It's already been more trouble than it's worth."

"Magnus! That key was fashioned by the Lady of Light herself!"

"Well, good for her," he snorted, "I'll tell you what, assuming we ever find it, the bloody thing's yours. Consider it your share of the spoils."

"Very well," Thom said, and, quivering with resentment, held out his hand. "Let's shake on it," he said, "Make it proper."

The Wrathorn raised an eyebrow at the apprentice. "Alright, Thom Crusher," he said, taking the boy's hand, "So long as you still finish my song, we'll call it a deal. Now all we have to do is find the damned Nymph."

"Are you sure this is the right town?"

"Of course, I'm sure. It's just..." he shook his head, "Things are much more confusing ashore...and when you're sober."

Thom breathed a heavy sigh.

"Gods, what's wrong with your bloody hands?" Magnus asked, "They're all bloody wet and clammy."

"My hands just get that way sometimes," Thom said, "Mostly when I'm nervous."

The big man wiped his hands upon his tunic in disgust. "What is wrong with you?"

"Well, at least my hands are clean."

"What's that supposed to mean?"

"I wash them."

"Aye, like a noble lady."

"Keeps me from getting ill. Look at how often the men aboard ship are sick. I bet if they washed their hands, it wouldn't happen near as often."

"I don't wash my hands and I haven't been sick my whole life."

"Yeah, well, you're a Blackguard. It's also why your wounds heal quicker."

"No, it's because I'm strong.".

"That's not under dispute."

"Then why are you arguing with me?" Magnus growled.

"I'm not arguing with you," Thom said, "I'm just saying."

"Great Bear's Cock!" Magnus grunted and with a swift kick, caved in the side of a merchant's crate. All at once, the townsfolk froze in alarm and the wine-seller raised his voice in indignation, wagging his finger in the Wrathorn's face. *Oh no!* Thom gasped and watched with horror as Magnus grasped the merchant by the scruff of the neck and sent him tumbling headlong into the remaining assortment of his stock.

Thom shut his eyes and took a deep breath of resignation. He could hear the sound of the kingsmen's boots upon the cobblestones, the clinking of their mail, and the sound of their blades being drawn. When he opened his eyes again, he was not at all surprised to find that they were surrounded. He cast Magnus a glare, but the Wrathorn simply shrugged.

"Lay down you weapons, barbarian!" the lead red-cloak called out, "We'll not have you disturb the peace any further!"

"Oh fuck off," Magnus said, loosing his axe, "I came here peaceful like, but if you really want me to disturb the peace, then we'd best get to it, eh?"

Thom breathed another sigh as the sergeant's eyes went wide with fury. *Here we go again...*

"Pardon me, my dear sergeant!" a feminine voice called out, "But I believe I know this man!"

Magnus's lips spread wide in a show of elfin glee. "Scarlet!" he cried.

Thom glanced out over the crowd in the direction of the speaker, but to his great surprise, it was not some wanton strumpet that had spoken, but a woman clad in the finery befitting the wife of a wealthy merchant or a minor knight.

"Lady Agrond," the sergeant muttered, "You...you *know* this man?"

Magnus raised an eyebrow at the sergeant's choice of words and the lady rolled her eyes. "Yes," she finally said, "He is an...old friend."

"Well..." the kingsmen eyed one another in discomfort, "It seems he was disturbing the peace."

"I have no doubt of it," Lady Agrond said, "Though surely there is no need to arrest him. Whatever mayhem he has caused thus far, Sir Agrond and I shall be happy to pay for."

"Yes, my lady," the sergeant said.

"Good day to you, gentlemen," she said, "You can return to your duties now."

For a moment the men hesitated, uncertain as to whether returning to their duties would actually be to ignore them. In the end, though, the sergeant sheathed his sword and with a slight bow to the lady, led his men away.

"Lady Agrond?" Magnus smirked once the soldiers had gone and commerce had resumed.

"It seems you're not the only one who Fortune favors," the lady said.

"Fortune favor me?" Magnus scoffed, "Can't say there's much cause to believe in that."

"You're not dead," she said, "Which seems an improvement from what I last heard—hanged by the kingsmen in Galdoran."

"And let me guess who it was told you that."

The lady sighed and slowly began to walk. Magnus strode along at her side while Thom, once more forgotten scurried after. The sweet scent of cloves and orange blossoms seemed to hang upon the air in her wake. Thom could not help but find it intoxicating.

"They arrived not long after the ports opened up again. Perhaps a month ago, no more."

"And the...what-have-you?"

"They asked about it. Offered a hundred gold for it."

"Could have made five."

The lady breathed another sigh, "I'm sorry, Magnus. They said you were dead—even had a braid from your beard to prove it. I think I might still have it somewhere."

"Hold onto it then. Might be worth something," he grinned, "The kingsmen shaved the rest."

"So they *did* catch you?"

"Bought me more like. It were the other three bastards as sold me out."

"Dibhor take their eyes!"

"Aye, so long as he lets me have the rest of them," Magnus said grimly, "In any case, I've already seen to Pavlos. All I need now is the other two."

"From what I gathered, once they left me, they were sailing east, or so they said, to sell it. Said if they got a good enough price, they'd be back. I told them to go fuck themselves," she sighed, "Magnus, I'm so sorry."

The Wrathorn warrior only shrugged. "No worries, darling," he said kindly, "There's no accounting for war and mutiny. Truth be told, I'm glad to see you're not dead either, let alone thriving as a noble lady!"

"With the money from your old mates, I sold the Nymph and...started over, you could say. Sir Agrond was one of the foreign knights left to command the town. Wasn't long after before he and I, well…" she smiled, "I wonder sometimes if more men have fallen by your hand or mine…"

"Ha!" Magnus laughed, "Yours surely! Though it's been some time since I've had a rival." He shook his head and breathed a heavy sigh. "In any case, love, I had best move on before I cause you more trouble."

"Can't say I ever much minded being troubled by you," Lady Agrond grinned, "But must you really go? Sir Agrond's often away on patrol—rebels in the hills and all. I would love some company…"

"Would that I could, darling," Magnus said, "But wind and tide…" He shrugged, "Perhaps after Rodulf and Slink are taken care of, I'll return."

"I'll look forward to it," the lady said, "You can repay me for the merchant's wine."

CHAPTER 15: THE MARSHAL & THE BLADE

"You must understand, my lord, that I had no idea Constable Harlow intended you harm—though in fairness to the constable, he *was* simply doing his duty."

Lughus sat unmoved at the head of the small table in his grandfather's solar—*his* solar, as he kept needing to be reminded—and watched the provincial hierophant closely. Padeen Andresen was a small man, old and wiry, with thin gray hair and a smoothly shaven face that shone with sweat in the light of the sconces. He was clad in the luxurious, white robes reserved for the most auspicious of ceremonies, and around his shoulders, a light cloth-of-gold mantle glimmered in rivalry of the rings on his fingers and the heavy gilded medallion around his neck. On either side of him, two young, fresh-faced acolytes stood somberly with folded hands and bowed heads. Andresen was the quintessential man of the Hierophant's Tower as Lughus remembered it: old, gold, and complacent.

"Furthermore," the provincial went on, "I must admit that I cannot help but feel slighted by the fact that I was not made privy to the late baron's final hours, nor was I informed until the very last minute of the—shall we say—

rather *complicated* nature of your ascension. Had I known, I could have written to the Grand Hierophant and perhaps he could have offered a solution. He may have even appealed to King Kredor himself. Even now, perhaps, it may not be too late. I could draft a letter, and so long as you agree to take the Oath, the King could offer you pardon. You could return to the order as a Foundling…as opposed to a…a…"

"Blackguard?" Brigid finished. She stood in the corner behind Lughus, idly tracing her finger along the spines of the books stacked upon a small shelf. "That's the word you were looking for, wasn't it? A Blackguard?"

The provincial ignored her, though his fingers twitched with suppressed irritation. At Lughus's right, Sir Owain's eyes betrayed a slight gleam of amusement, but to his left, Abbot Woode's face remained stern.

"What right does King Kredor have to interfere with the politics of a foreign land?" the abbot asked, "It seems that, as the King of Andoch, the affairs of Baronbrock are not of his concern."

The provincial forced a smile. "Had you remained a true member of the Order, Lord Abbot, you would know that we are not limited by such divisions. The Grand Hierophant leads the Church of the Kinship, and the Guardian-King leads the Council of Five, and while it is true that the Chancellor and the Warlord—generally speaking—remain officers of the Andochan realm alone, the men of the Loremaster and the Hierophant offer aid to all in need. As they say. knowledge and faith know no bounds, and wherever you find either, you shall find the Guardians!"

"So long as they swear allegiance to the King," Brigid muttered. She selected a book from the shelf and began gently flipping through the illuminated pages.

Andresen's face turned red and his eyes flashed. Lughus met his gaze unflinchingly. He knew that the old man was attempting to goad him into anger, into rashness, to make him seem little more than a child meddling in the affairs of greater men. Yet, while he might still be finding his feet as both the baron and the Marshal, he would not allow himself to be manipulated. His masters over the years—from Rastis to Crodane to his grandfather Arcis, had spent far too much time instilling in him the dangers of rashness and the virtues of patience. He would not betray them, or himself, for the sake of some weak old man's impotent taunts.

And in the meantime, he would enjoy watching as the Blade neatly turned aside the old man's rude daggers and threw them right back in his face. It was clear that as angry as the provincial might be at having to explain himself before the new baron, he was furious at being brought to task by the young woman.

"If I might ask, my lord," Andresen asked without bothering to mask his contempt, "Who is this young woman and why is she here? I must admit that her presence does not seem at all...appropriate."

"This is Lady Brigid Beinn," Sir Owain said, his eyes twinkling, "Daughter of the late Archduke of Dwerin. She is our honored guest."

"And another Blackguard," Brigid smiled.

Lughus felt a flush of heat at the flash of her impish grin. The provincial was not the only one who felt somewhat uncomfortable in her presence, though for quite different reasons.

The old man's mouth opened in surprise and his brow furrowed in confusion. "My apologies, my lady," he said at last, "And let me tell you how relieved I am to find you alive. You were believed to have been kidnapped by the same scoundrel that murdered your noble uncles! It is a such a...joy to find you safe."

"Yes," Brigid said blithely, "Thankfully, my dear Uncle Darren did not have the opportunity to kidnap me with everything else going on." She smiled again, "I had the honor of doing that myself."

Sir Owain's mustache curled with glee as he exchanged a glance with Abbot Woode, but while the creases softened upon the abbot's brow, Woode turned his taciturn gaze to Lughus, encouraging him to move on with the meeting. Beneath the table, Lughus touched the pommel of his sword and steeled himself to speak. This would not be pretty; however, it must be done. He would not allow any friend of Willum Harlow the freedom to cause any more trouble.

"Provincial Andresen," he said at last, "I realize that, as you claim, you were ignorant to certain factors relating to Constable Harlow and his actions in Galadin."

"Thank you, my lord."

"However, the fact remains that you not only offered protection to an enemy of the barony, but also to soldiers of a foreign land who, while in my city, threatened the lives of my people and my friends—the Lady Brigid included," he paused, wondering briefly if he had yet earned the right to call her 'friend.' He pressed on, "They entered the city under false pretenses, committed unlawful searches of private homes, and we have at least one report of them committing a gross act of sacrilege."

"Sacrilege?" the Hierophant gasped, "Preposterous!"

"What would you call a man pissing in the pool of St. Elisa?" Brigid asked.

The old man glared at her with unmasked contempt and Lughus felt his own anger flare. "If that were not enough," he continued, "You also provided Constable Harlow the assistance of your templars, who joined him in the battle upon the sacred grounds of the grotto, disrupting the prayers of the faithful, and profaning the holy site with blood."

"I assure you," the Provincial said, his face pale with repressed rage, "Those men—mine and those of Constable Harlow—did not intend on bloodshed, and many of them lost their lives in pursuit of their duty. Any violence committed was clearly in self-defense, and I'll not have their conduct questioned! Furthermore, Constable Harlow, or should I say *Chief* Constable Harlow, is an Anointed man of the Order honored with rank and title, and as a former apprentice to the Loremaster, I should think that you would understand that and offer him the respect he is due!"

A vision of Crodane's grave passed before Lughus's mind and his knuckles turned white as he gripped the arm of his chair. "While it is regrettable that men died, Willum Harlow exceeded the bounds of his authority and those that fell did so under his orders. Had Harlow kept to the limits of his authority, it never would have come to violence, though considering the Hammer and his men pursued folk throughout my city, I find the notion of self-defense extremely hard to believe."

"Listen here—" Andresen began, but the young baron cut him off.

"I am not finished!" Lughus seethed, struggling to keep his voice level, "As you yourself just claimed, the power of the Chancellor, like that of the Warlord, ends at the borders of Andoch, unless specifically contracted by the sovereign lord of a foreign land. Neither the Lord-Baron, my grandfather, nor myself requested any such assistance from the Hammer. If anything, he should be branded an outlaw for violating the limits established throughout the history of the Order," his gray eyes flashed, with his mounting fury, "If you'd like, I can cite several instances from the past that support this. I would challenge you to find but one to the contrary. Since the days of St. Aiden and the Fall of the Warlock, the sanctity of the other realms as independent entities had been paramount—though from what I hear of Grantis and King Kredor's unlawful pursuit of the Protectorate, the Order cares very little for history these days!"

"How dare you!" The old man thrust out his lip like a petulant child. "Perhaps the Loremaster was remiss in his duties, trafficking as he was with outlaws. Hopefully, Lord Tainne can help put things to rights again."

Lughus's blood grew hot with wrath, but he knew that he had to maintain his control. Again, he thought of Crodane, and he knew that although there were no blades drawn, this was no less a duel that the battle with Stokes at Lenard's Crossing. He took a deep breath, and when he spoke, his voice was calm and cold. "You forget yourself, Lord Provincial, when you speak ill of the Loremaster. Perhaps you should listen to your own words, for you chasten me with one breath and commit the same sin with the next!" he paused to breathe, "You and your men are to leave Galadin by dawn."

"What?"

"You will leave the city by dawn and leave the barony by week's end," Lughus commanded, "You and your men are banished."

The old man laughed, "You cannot be serious. I am the High Cleric of the Cathedral of St. Aiden, an Anointed Guardian under the title of the Breath, I am—"

"You *were* the High Cleric," Lughus cut him off, "Now you are a just an old man, and I suggest you *save* your breath. Now be gone, and if you try to steal any of the relics of the Saint when you depart, I'll have you hanged like a common thief!"

The room fell silent. The provincial's acolytes glanced around in uncertainty as their master struggled to speak. Even Sir Owain and the Abbot, though in agreement, seemed somewhat taken aback by the young man's sudden show of command.

"You grieve me, baron," the old man said at last. His lip curled into a sneer, "Though perhaps I should expect as much from one of Rastis's whelps and a bloody Blackguard to boot!"

Sir Owain and the Abbot leapt to their feet. "Come now, Padeen!" the abbot exclaimed.

"Silence, Mad Woode!" The provincial sneered. He snarled at Lughus, "Shame on you, boy! Shame on the House of Galadin! You are all heretics and Blackguards!"

Sir Owain signaled and two men-at-arms stepped forth from where they stood guard at the door. "By your leave, my lord," the seneschal growled, ushering the old man out of the room, "My men and I will see these fools to the gates."

"As you like, Sir Owain," Lughus said.

"Oh believe me, sir, it will be my pleasure."

"Shame!" the old man shouted once more as he was ushered out, "Shame on the house of Galadin! Shame!"

Abbot Woode hurried after them and shut the solar door. "My apologies, my lord," the abbot said, "It's the ravings of a wounded pride. Ignore it. You've naught to be ashamed of, quite the contrary."

Lughus rubbed his eyes and sat back in his chair. "No matter," he said, "I did not expect this to end pleasantly."

Brigid assumed Sir Owain's seat at the table carrying a small stack of books. "Still," she said kindly, "Well done. I especially liked the bit about history."

Lughus blushed. The nearness of her suddenly made Lughus feel both glad and anxious. "It's all true," he shrugged.

"I don't doubt you," she grinned, "As apprentice and ward to the Loremaster, I'm sure you've forgotten more than he ever knew."

Abbot Woode resumed his seat. "The Hierophants are fond of writing their own history—almost as fond as they are of crying heresy when anyone disagrees," he shook his head, "Meanwhile the old fool calls down curses on the Galadins the very night of the Saint's Feast. What dark days we live in!"

Lughus's eye traveled over the spines of Brigid's stack of books. *Journeys of the Kite, The Wake of the Wave, The Flame in the Darkness, Visions of the Eye*—all books he had read at the Tower. Apparently he and his grandfather shared more than simply Aiden's blood. *And now she has them*, he thought, *Does she want to read them too?* His chest felt funny—light—and he cleared his throat against the odd sensation. For the first time in a while, he was glad that Royne was an entire kingdom away; he knew his old friend would see right through the cool façade he was attempting to maintain in the presence of the Archduke's daughter. He turned suddenly to the abbot, "I did not know you were a member of the Order too."

"For a time," Woode shrugged, "Though I too never received the Rite of Initiation. In fact, I never passed beyond the rank of Acolyte before I was—shall we say—encouraged to seek a different path."

"What did you do?" Lughus asked.

"A bit of this and that," he said, "I too have had my share of adventures, though eventually, I made my way north to the Brock and St. Golan's. The rest, I suppose you could say, is history," he sighed and the hard edge returned to his features, "Yet if my experiences with the hierophants have taught me anything, it is that you should be prepared for the worst. Twice now in as many days you have drawn the ire of the Order. There will be trouble, you can rest assured, especially now that you have banished the Guardians from the tomb of their founder. In all likelihood they will call you a heretic in addition to a Blackguard and an outlaw."

"A heretic?" Brigid said, "He's a Galadin! How could they possibly call him a heretic?"

"Truth often matters very little in politics or religion, my lady," Woode said, "You offer a fine example yourself. As the provincial said, it was believed that you were kidnapped. Clearly, that is not the case."

Brigid bit her lip and her brow furrowed. A thin strand of hair fell down in front of her eye and Lughus watched her furtively for as long as he dared. Her expression was the same as when he first saw her yesterday—jaw set, eyes alight with determination, daggers gleaming in the dusk light. Even though she had fallen, she had not given up the fight. He'd never seen anything remotely like her. So bold and so beautiful, yet so, so deadly.

"To be honest, I'm somewhat surprised that they noticed I had gone," she said with a wry grin, "Most of the time, they seemed to hardly even notice that I existed."

"I have a hard time believing that," Lughus said, and immediately felt self-conscious. *What an idiot I must seem. What an absolute fool.* He shook his head, but again, his gaze found hers. *Her eyes are so incredibly blue...*

"Honestly, were it not for the fact that my departure came at a rather convenient moment for my uncle, I'm sure they'd be more than happy to just claim I'm dead," she sighed, "Not that it matters much. If my mother has another child, I'm sure to lose my rights anyway. Memories are rather short at Blackstone. It will be relatively easy for them to say I was never born in the first place."

"It does often seem that if enough men believe a falsehood, it has a way of becoming true," the abbot told her, "Your false death, my lady, would not be the first. You have some experience with that as well, my lord."

Based on the slight curl of amusement at the corners of the abbot's lips, Woode must have caught him staring. *Aiden's Flame, I'm an idiot.* He roused himself from his embarrassment and thought of something—anything—to contribute to the conversation. "So..." he began, "You're saying that even if we were to circulate a public statement about Lady Brigid—

"Brigid."

"Yes, I'm sorry," he said, "About Brigid's whereabouts and the like, no matter what we say, they'll just make something up? They'll call us liars and such?"

"Most likely," Woode shrugged, "They may even go so far as to connect you and your grandfather and the old Loremaster to the deaths of the other Beinn brothers, perhaps claiming that after murdering the Brothers Beinn, the Blade absconded with the heir to the throne at Arcis's behest. They could decry him as a heretic and a blood traitor with no respect for the Order or his great ancestor."

"But surely no one would believe that?" Lughus said.

Woode shrugged. "The most believable lies are born from a grain of truth," he said, "It's not...beyond the realm of possibilities to believe that the Galadins still hold ties to the Three, particularly that you now openly bear the title of the Marshal. Furthermore, you can rest assured that the Hammer and the Provincial will see to it that the events of today are twisted and manipulated to tell the story as they wish it to be as opposed to the story as it actually is."

"So when you control the story, you control the truth," Brigid observed.

Lughus nodded, "Rastis—the Loremaster—used to say something very similar regarding history."

Abbot Woode nodded, "Such is the case, it would seem."

"So if banishing the provincial provides Andoch with the grain of truth that they need to tell their false story," the young baron asked, "Why did you and Sir Owain not protest when I made the suggestion?"

"Because, my lord, we agreed with you, and still do," he said, "As does Horus, and so I believe, would your grandfather. Remember, after all, his decision not to include the provincial in any of the matters regarding his final days. Arcis did not like or trust Andresen, but he lacked sufficient reason to expel him. You, however, had that reason, and it needed to be done," the Abbot said, "They left you little choice."

"Then what do we do now?"

"That is for you to determine, my baron," Woode said, "However, I would advise that you be cautious and prepared. When he left here, they say Harlow claimed he would ride directly for Highboard to the seat of the Lord-Baron and I would not be surprised if the provincial does the same. You may rest assured that they will attempt to cause trouble when next the barons convene in the Month of the Stag. After an absence of fifteen years, there are some who will doubt you are who you are. The Hammer and the Breath will seek to exploit that."

Lughus's brow furrowed and his fist clenched.

"We stand very near the fire now and I fear we may easily be burned," the abbot continued, "Though, again, I say 'we.' For, I am, as I have been since your grandfather's passing, on your side. I would advise that you ensure the loyalty of your other allies as well—Nordren, Brabant, Derindale—the barons who traditionally back Galadin—as well as your knights. They may have renewed their allegiance to your grandfather at his death, but I am certain they anxiously await a chance to take the measure of their new lord. With the excitement of the day, you may not be aware that Sir Balric, Sir Gosbert, and Sir Herbrand arrived in the city this very morning. At the feast, that was they seated at the first table below yours. It may be wise to meet with them before you retire."

Lughus breathed a heavy sigh and rubbed his eyes. *How did I not recognize them?* There were too many new people, too many faces, too many names. "I had no idea," he said wearily, "I will call upon them when Sir Owain returns. I do not wish them to feel slighted, particularly if it should come to war. Though I ardently hope it does not."

There was a pawing sound at the door. The abbot rose from the table and opened it to reveal not a man, but Fergus. With a huff, the great hound sauntered in from the hallway and lay down beside the baron to gnaw on a the remains of a large bone. The abbot watched the massive hound for a moment and then smiled. "Still," he said, "Regardless of what the future holds, remember that you are not without formidable friends."

As if on cue, the great hound caught the bones between his front paws and closed his jaws around it with a loud snap.

"Now," Woode said, "I think I shall return to the feast. Shall I inform Horus that you intend to appear?"

Between Harlow, the holiday, and the provincial hierophant—coupled with his continued nightmares and anxiety over his responsibilities as baron—Lughus was exhausted. Thankfully, Sir Owain and Horus had seen to the needs of Houndstooth's new guests. It had been many years since lady's maids were needed at the castle and Jergan, master of the wardrobe, nearly had a fit trying to find suitable clothing for the farmer's family and the young lady, especially considering the fact that she was the daughter of a foreign head of state.

"If it's not too unseemly," Lughus said, "I think I will sit here for a moment longer."

"Very well," the abbot nodded, "Lady Brigid?"

"Brigid."

"Yes. Brigid then?"

She sighed, "I think I would rather stay here as well."

Lughus's eyes examined the tabletop.

Abbot Woode gave a nod, "Then I suppose I will leave the two of you with Fergus."

Brigid smiled at the abbot and flipped open the cover of one of the tomes. Lughus risked a glance and saw again how the light of the braziers caught her blue eyes, her white teeth, and the sheen of her long, dark hair. The lightness in his chest now settled into a dull ache, and for no reason he could discern, he again felt like a complete fool. Once the abbot was gone, they would be alone, and that thought made him both excited and terrified. "When Sir Owain returns," he said suddenly, "Can you send him? And if you don't mind, mention to the knights..." he paused to remember, "Balric, Gosbert, and Herbrand—that I would like to speak to them as well?"

"Of course," Woode bowed and withdrew.

For some time, Lughus and Brigid sat in silence. He glanced around the room, struggling to come up with something to say. At the Loremaster's Tower, he, Royne, and Thom had never had much exposure to women, particularly those of an age with them, but when they did, it was often with disastrous results. The nobles treated them like clowns for their habits—if they acknowledged them at all, and the few maids or female servants they met around the grounds of the castle often regarded them with resentment, seeing them as an accessible means of venting their contempt for their noble lords.

Not that Lughus had ever really wanted to spend time with either group anyway. The noble girls were snooty and self-absorbed, while the peasant girls were often course and cruel. In either case, the amount of time the boys spent reading and writing seemed to make them even more contemptible in the eyes of the girls—both rich or poor.

Still, as close as he was with Thom and Royne and Rastis and Hob, he had always been conscious of a certain absence, particularly after reading the adventures and romances. A great knight always fought for the one to whom they had given their heart—even St. Aiden fought for his wife, Elisa. The philosophers too had much to say on the subject—that every person alone was but half a soul and only when joined with another could either find peace. Royne, as always, made some rude comment or another about the word "joining," but Lughus knew it meant something more than such baseness. A soul was not a body; it transcended such things. But from the moment he read of this, he could no longer ignore the void in his soul. It was like an itch or a loose tooth; the more he tried to ignore it, the worse it grew. It made him feel alone, even in the company of his friends.

Besides, though it was true that Aiden and many of the other early Guardians in the old stories married and had children of their own, as time went by, the Council and the Church came to discourage such practices among the Order. Even in the days of Old Calendral, the hierophants and other members of the clergy were required by their position to remain chaste, for in a church where all men and women were family, the officials of the church were symbolic siblings to all. Marriage, therefore, would be seen as spiritually incestuous. Of course, Lughus and Royne had long believed that it had more to do with politics and the rights of inheritance than with any true philosophical belief. Regardless, it was rare that any man among the Guardians apart from the King and those of noble lineage like Pryce would ever marry and pass on their names and titles.

Orphan wards of the Loremaster, for example, were not afforded such a choice. Theirs was to be a life of service. Thus, they were not to hold to worldly things unless those things were directly connected to the carrying out of their duties, like the heirlooms of the Anointed or the other accoutrements associated with their various roles. A Loremaster's sage may collect books, but only in so far as they made him more knowledgeable, and thus, better equipped to serve the people. A Warlord's cavalier maintained his arms and armor so that he might better protect the people. And so on and so forth. By some of the more fundamentalist members of the Order, particularly among the members of the Hierophant's Tower, it was even argued that friends, family, and acquaintances were to be viewed by the same functional measures.

Loremaster Rastis, though himself the furthest thing from a materialist, held to much more liberal views in this regard (as in so many others). To Rastis, a Guardian's duty was indeed to serve humanity, but in doing so, he could not also deny that he too was human. So it was that Lughus, Thom, and Royne were able to grow together as brothers, with the old man himself as a sort of surrogate father, and Hob as a type of burly, boisterous uncle. And while it may not have been the most traditional of homes, Lughus knew that from it he learned the true value of friendship, of family, of affection born not from duty but from genuine concern.

Yet now, he was a noble too, and no longer a member of the Order anyway. And while his various titles carried with them a new set of duties and obligations, he was perhaps freer to be himself than he had ever been in his life.

And here was Brigid. Before he had even seen her and Geoffrey at the grotto yesterday (or the Hammer for that matter), he knew somehow that they were there—just as Crodane had sensed Harlow on the road from Galdoran so long ago. It was true that as the Blade, the Marshal would be predisposed to know her; however, there was something…more, something personal and unrelated to their Guardian titles. Whenever she spoke to him, for example, it was in a way that was…*normal*, for lack of a better term, more normal even than Sir Owain, or the abbot, or even Crodane. She spoke to him almost like Thom and Royne, like an equal or a friend, but still…different, unique. There was a truth to her, a lack of pretense. It made him want to ask her questions and tell her things. He didn't know exactly what, but…*things*, his thoughts, his fears, his hope, and he wanted to know hers too. He wanted to be her friend.

However, he found it hard to meet her gaze, to catch her eye without feeling his cheeks burning. For, she was pretty—no, not just pretty, but beautiful, like something out of a story or a song. She was like the stars or the moon, something that he just wanted to be near and to appreciate. Yet, he struggled to think of things to say to her, and once he finally did, he would find suddenly that his voice had gone away or that his head turned suddenly into a dense block of wood. He could not understand why exactly, but her mere presence had elicited some overwhelming effect on him, and he had known her less than a day.

Lughus shook his head and shut his eyes. He had to keep his mind from wandering, else he would say something stupid and she would turn away from him. She would think him strange, ridiculous, a scribbler masquerading as a baron. That was, after all, the truth. He had no idea what he was doing. He had no idea how to lead a barony. *What am I doing? What am I doing? Fool! Stupid fool!* He breathed a heavy sigh and without realizing it, leaned forward until his head fell against the tabletop with a solid *thunk!*

"Are you...alright?"

Aiden's Flame! What am I doing?! His stomach felt sick, "I'm sorry?"

"Lughus?"

He opened his eyes. "I...hello..." the young baron finally said, "I just..."

Beside him, Brigid had fixed him with her bright blue eyes—eyes like stars, like sapphires—and she was smiling, though not with ridicule. "Are you alright?" she said kindly.

Cautiously, he sat up straight and returned her smile. "I'm sorry," he said, "I'm...I'm very tired."

"Would you rather me leave you alone?"

"No, no," he said hurriedly, and again felt foolish, "I mean, unless you want to, but you're also more than welcome to stay too...if you like." *Shut up, you blathering idiot!* he told himself. "What...what would you like to do?"

Her smile became a grin and another stray hair drooped down across her brow. "I do not recall a time," she said, "In all the years I lived at Blackstone, when anyone ever asked me that."

"Really?" Lughus asked.

"Not once," she laughed.

"But you're the daughter of the Archduke."

"That actually means very little to me," she shrugged, "I was expected to simply do as I was told—by my mother, her maid, even my wretched cousin and his friends. I envy you your Loremaster. When you spoke of him yesterday, he seemed like a good man."

Lughus nodded. It was over dinner the previous evening when he, Brigid, and Geoffrey had briefly given abbreviated accounts of their adventures, their journeys to Galadin, and the fates of the previous Three—Regnar, Gareth, and Crodane.

"I never knew my mother or father," he said, "But I had Rastis, and my friends, Thom and Royne. Our friend Hob too."

Brigid closed her book and rested her hands on the tabletop. "My father only rarely came home, and I remember very little of him before he died," she paused and sighed, "As for my mother..." she shook her head, "She hates me...and though I know it's wrong, I...do not care much for her either."

Again, Lughus wondered at the color of her eyes. "How could she possibly hate you?" he asked, but hurriedly followed up with, "I'm sorry. That's not my business."

"I don't mind. It's no secret," she shrugged, "It's always just been that way. I suppose it's because...because I'm not like her, and I don't want to be."

"What do you mean?"

"It's like..." Brigid sighed, "Imagine a game like dice or chess or anything. Chess, we can say. My mother is very, very good at chess, so good that as far as she's concerned, it's the only game there is. She knows all the rules, all the right moves, all the ways to mislead an opponent, knows how to cheat and not get caught, and she's so good that people are in awe of her for her skill."

"Okay," Lughus nodded, "But you don't like chess?"

"No," she smiled, "Well, in the example. Actually, I do like chess, though I don't know if I'm very good. And to be honest, I highly doubt my mother has any idea how to play. She would see such things as boring or improper. It was considered a game only for men at Blackstone, but I would have to sit and watch my cousin and his friends play for hours. It was dreadful. They always let him win." She stopped, and this time it was her turn to blush, "What was I saying?"

"To be honest," he said bashfully, "I'm not exactly sure. It started with your mother and went to chess. But I think I know what you mean."

"Well, it's good you do, because it completely escaped me."

They shared a laugh, and Lughus suddenly found himself less nervous. "I'm very glad you're here," he told her.

"So am I," she said, "I'm not used to having friends—not that...I don't mean Geoffrey and Annabel are not my friends, but..." she paused, "They're more like I imagine a real aunt and uncle to be, a real family, if that makes any sense..."

"I know," he said, "Owain and Horus are similar, though it's hard when they insist on calling you 'my lord.' I just want to be Lughus again."

"Well," she smiled, "As long as you make sure to call me Brigid, you'll always be Lughus to me. No titles between friends."

"Agreed," Lughus said, though internally, his mind reeled. *Friend!* he thought, *Friend twice over!* He could not help by smile. "Brigid," he said, "If you'd like, tomorrow I could ask Horus about finding a chessboard?"

"Or we could go take a walk and buy one ourselves?" she said, "I'm sure the market in the Trade Quarter will have them somewhere. I have money enough I think."

"I...I don't know. I have not yet been around the town. Last night in the grotto was the first time I've gone out past the walls in months. I'd never even seen the inside of the cathedral until today. I had to come up with a speech for people I barely know anything about."

"What?" she laughed, "How can you be the baron if you don't know the people?"

Lughus shrugged, "My grandfather wanted me to stay here for fear of men like Harlow. But, you're right. You can't lead a people you do not know. I was amazed at the world, of Andoch, once outside of Titanis. From Lenard's Crossing to Galdoran to the lands bordering the Brock with all of their absent lords—it is important to see life for what it is for so many. A leader who is ignorant to the ways of his people leads nothing."

"Then it's settled," Brigid grinned, "Tomorrow we'll go. We can walk the town a bit and meet some of the people. I know a few from living in Hounton, though not well. Geoffrey thought we should lie low and not draw too much attention to ourselves. Still, after such a fine speech today, they'll all want to see you up close. We can take Fergus too. I'm sure he'd love to get out."

"Fergus? Are you sure people won't...be upset at the sight of him," Lughus said, ignoring her compliment.

From the floor, the great hound raised his head.

"I'm sorry, brother, but it's true," Lughus shrugged.

"Oh how could you say that?" Brigid smiled, "He's the symbol of your house and blessed by the Brother Perindal himself! The people see his image on every flag and every guardsman's shield. What's to be afraid of?"

Fergus gave a snort, stood up, and sauntered over to Brigid's side.

"And he's a big sweetheart too," she grinned, ruffling the dog's ears, "Nothing at all to fear."

"I suppose not..."

At that moment, Sir Owain returned. As he strode into the solar, his lips curled into a wide grin to match his thick black mustache. "The provincial has been set upon his way," he declared, "Though not happily. I've left a squad of guards at the cathedral just in case he decides to test you. Still, Andresen's a coward and an old fool. Not what I'd expect from one of those 'Anointed' or what-have-you. Your grandfather and he were cordial, though they had never been friends, least not since he presided at your mother's wedding."

"Thanks, Owain," Lughus said, hurrying past the subject of his mother, "I'm glad he's out of our hair for now, though the abbot believes we've not heard the last from him. Between the Hammer and the Breath, I'm sure to have called down Kredor's ire now," he sighed.

"Well," Brigid smiled, "Like the abbot *also* said, you've got formidable friends."

"Speaking of which..." Lughus sighed. *Friend! Again she said it!* "I should call Sir Balric, Sir Gosbert, and Sir Herbrand. Owain, will you introduce me?"

"Of course," the old knight said, "And trust me, you'll have naught to fear from them. Their families have supported yours for generations and they've brought gifts as well," he grinned, "I'll fetch them, the Abbot too, and perhaps some of the ale he brought?"

"Whatever you like" Lughus said.

"Good idea," Brigid said, "It'll help put them at ease."

Lughus nodded and turned back to Sir Owain, "As she said."

"As you wish, my lord," the seneschal said merrily, "I'll be back soon enough with the lads in tow."

"Why'd they bring gifts?" he sighed once Owain had gone, "I wish they wouldn't have done that."

"It's what they do," Brigid said, "Don't fret over it. It's more important for them than it is for you anyhow so just smile and act appreciative—even if you're not. They only want to show you that they're willing to respect you, and that's good." She stood up from the table, "At any rate, I'll leave you to it."

Lughus's eyes widened. "You're not staying?" he asked.

"They want to meet *you*, not me. I would simply be an intrusion. They'll not want me here."

But I do, he thought, "You stayed for the provincial. I'm sure it's fine if you stay for this too."

"It wasn't," she grinned, "But I admit I wanted the provincial to feel uncomfortable. Still, I should have asked you first instead of just inviting myself along. For that part, I'm sorry."

"I was glad you were there. I enjoyed the way you made the old man sweat," Lughus smiled, "You really won't stay now, though?"

"I'll see you again tomorrow," she said, "You won't forget will you? A walk through the city? The chessboard?"

"I won't. I promise," he said, "I'll think of nothing else." *Brethren help me sleep soundly now. If not the nightmares, then the nerves...*

"Good. It's best if we go early," she lifted her stack of books, "If it's alright with you, could I possibly borrow these as well?"

"Of course," he said, "You're my guest. What's mine is yours."

"Oh really?" Brigid grinned, "In that case then perhaps I'll take Fergus too. I thought I might read a bit and perhaps he can keep me company—as long as it's alright with him?"

The golden hound gave a great yawn, stretched, and lazily ambled to her side. His shoulder came up past her hip and when he gently nudged her with his nose, she rocked back on her heels. "I'd say that's a yes," she smiled.

"Just so you know," Lughus grinned, "He snores."

"Til tomorrow, then," she laughed, "Goodnight, Lughus."

He caught her gaze and held it for as long as he dared. Blue eyes like stars. If only those were the eyes he saw in his dreams. *I might never want to wake up.* "Goodnight, Brigid."

CHAPTER 16: BLIND SPOTS

If Royne believed that gaining the general's acceptance would somehow ingratiate him with Captain Velius and the rest of the Fifth Legion, he was sorely mistaken. Although it was apparent at once that the men loved the Gray Wolf and were prepared to follow him into the depths of the Abyss if need be, they were otherwise in a sorry state, and certainly in no mood to bother themselves with a bumbling scribbler from an enemy land. One look at the Young Loremaster with his lanky build and awkward posture proved he was no warrior. He lacked the strength to carry a legionnaire's shield, let alone to hold a position in a shield wall, making him the subject of derisive jeering and disapproving sighs whenever he passed.

For the most part, Royne ignored them, confining himself to the little tent he shared with Conor, safely protected beneath the shadow of the general's authority. He cared little for soldiers anyway. True, General Navarro had been kind enough to him, and of course, he would never have been able to escape the Keystone were it not for Dandon Rood. However, the average soldier was little more than an animal. Lughus could cling to his foolish ideals of nobility and chivalry and such, but Royne knew better. Epic tales of famous battles and heroic duels might sound thrilling when recorded in the pages of an old book rife with lofty language and hyperbole, but men still died—in every battle and in every siege whether commoner or noble. Villages were burned, women dishonored, and children put to the sword. It was the madness and the horror of war, and though Royne had never experienced it firsthand, he was not a fool. It was only natural. Allow men to act like bloodthirsty beasts, and they shall. More than once had he and Lughus had this argument back at the Loremaster's Tower, and although Old Goldimop conceded that war made most men into savages, he refused to believe that just because a man might be skilled in the arts of war that his conscience somehow became unclean. It was usually at that point in the argument when Thom would start whining in a sorry attempt to smooth things over, and to shut him up, they would simply agree to disagree.

Shut up, Thom Fatty!

Sitting alone in his tent, Royne smiled briefly before forcing those thoughts from his mind, for thoughts of his friends only highlighted the misery and loneliness that seemed to grow steadily worse by the day. *St. Aiden protect Lughus from the bloody Hammer!* he thought, *And Lady protect Thom from the Guardian-King!*

A slight twinge of guilt stuck him like a pin in the back of his mind. It was, after all, Lughus's idealism, his principles of honor and all that, that Royne believed would make him a good leader—the rare noble noble. *As long as it doesn't get him killed,* he thought bitterly, *Brethren protect him without a wretched bastard like me to watch his back…*

With a sigh, Royne shook his head and took up *The Book of Histories.* Losing himself in the affairs of the past made it easier to avoid the worries of the present and the uncertainty of the future. He had made great strides in the last few days, and now when he read the book, the words appeared before his mind's eye much faster, as if recalling an absent thought or a latent memory rather than forging them anew.

He had only this morning reached the year 963 after the Fall of Dibhor and the writings of a Loremaster by the name of Sabrun, and although Sabrun's records were, at first, rather dry—filled with descriptions of the construction of Mabolin Castle and a few entries regarding a blight that devastated a year's worth of wheat—963 turned out to be an incredibly important year and one that began yet another period of great controversy. For the first time, it marked the appearance a woman Guardian.

Her name, according to the record, was Amarthia, and when she appeared at the court of the Guardian-King to swear her Oath of Fealty, it seemed from Sabrun's description as if the very foundations of Castle Testament shook in the face of such effrontery. Even in St. Aiden's time, the Guardians had always been men, warriors mostly, who fought against Kalius Wrogan. Then, after the war was over, the majority of the Guardians, particularly those who remained in Andoch, became military officers, statesmen, or members of the clergy. For a woman to bear a title was, to the more rigid and fundamentalist among the Order's ranks, unthinkable. The Grand Hierophant in particular took her Anointing as a great sacrilege and a personal insult intended by her predecessor: the Bard.

By this time, or so it seemed, the Bards had all but disappeared into the legends and folktales that still exist to the present day. Most assumed that they all died out, for the Bard, like all who lay claim to that profession, was noted for his wanderings, and the last man to wear his title had not been seen nor heard of in Titanis or elsewhere since before the Siege of Three. When the strange and (according to Sabrun) enchantingly beautiful Amarthia arrived with news that she was not only anointed, but anointed as "the Bard," the Order was in an uproar.

The Grand Hierophant claimed that a woman Guardian was an affront against the Lady of Light herself. Among the Kinship there were many men—the Father and the Brothers—but only the single woman. In like manner, even in the days of the Old Empire, the clergy of the Kinship consisted entirely of men. Women could still serve as handmaids, nuns devoted to the service of the Lady, but could not preach or preside over the official sacraments of the church. Aiden's wife, Elisa, had been deemed a lesser saint (along with a few other women—famous prioresses or martyrs), but she was not a Guardian engaged in warfare with Kalius Wrogan. Therefore, the Grand Hierophant proposed that Amarthia be forced to take the vows of a handmaid and devote herself to prayer until such time as she could pass on her title to a man.

Loremaster Sabrun, however, did not see much sense or much proof in the Grand Hierophant's arguments against women nor in his proposed solution. To essentially imprison a fellow of the Order—in particular one so seminal as the Bard—simply for being born a woman, was, in his view, utterly preposterous.

Neither the Chancellor nor the Warlord held any strong opinions one way or the other, so in the end, it was the Guardian-King who decided the issue—Erolan Drude III. In spite of the Hierophant's laments, he not only allowed Amarthia to remain free, but also recognized her as a member of the Order. He did add the provision to the annals of the Order that a man may—with no other options—anoint a woman in order to save his title from being lost; however, at the end of her days, the anointed woman *must* return her title to a man, or else let it be lost forever. Loremaster Sabrun (who in certain ways regards reminded Royne of his own predecessor Rastis) had a great deal to say about the King's provision and the absurdity of such gender inequalities, but in the end, he was forced to follow the King's decree.

How curious... Royne thought, pausing in his reading. Obviously he had never known a woman Guardian, and though he had on a very rare occasion read of one or two, he had never really thought to find out why there were so few. He simply assumed it was but another example of the nonsensical gender bias that so often infected history. What was even more unusual, however, was the fact that he had never heard, *specifically*, of Amarthia the Bard, let alone any aspect of her story. Clearly it was a rather important moment in the Order's history. How had such a thing escaped his study, he wondered, and why had Rastis not spoken of it either? He would have to keep reading—but later, as Conor's sudden return broke in upon his thoughtful musings.

"What is it?" Royne muttered, closing the book's ancient pages.

Conor stood up straight and made a vaguely Grantisi salute, "The general asked to see you, sir."

Royne sighed and slipped *The Book of Histories* safely back inside its satchel. "Did he say why?"

"No, sir, but the others are with him."

"Others?"

"Captain Velius and Lieutenant Gigas."

"Wonderful," the young Loremaster muttered, rising to his feet. Gigas, the general's valet, was a decent enough sort—quiet, if a bit bland, but Captain Velius—not only was he the standard brute of a soldier, but he seemed to take a particular joy in mocking Royne.

"Well, I suppose I had better see what they want," he said at last, "Let's go."

Royne's tent had been set slightly apart from the main body of men, a situation he was rather glad for. As he approached the rest of the camp he was surprised to see the soldiers busy at a multitude of tasks: cooking over campfires, oiling arms and armor, tending to pack animals and chariots, and all sorts of other "martial things" that Royne knew little enough about and cared even less to learn. A large group of men were arranged into teams engaged in some manner of business along the edge of the forest, knocking down trees and lashing bits together in an effort to build something. As he approached the general's tent, he was forced to stop and wait while a group of soldiers passed by leading an ox dragging an enormous log. Clearly they found his impatience amusing, exchanging unsubtle glances at one another at his overt annoyance as he waited for them to get out of his way. When at last they had gone, the guards on duty outside of the general's tent ushered him in.

"About time you turned up," the captain said as Royne entered. Both he and the lieutenant were clad in the full regalia of war: chain hauberk, leather cuirass, vambraces, greaves, and high crested helm. The green cloaks of the legion hung from their shoulders, clasped along one side with pins fashioned in the shape of a wolf's head. Together they stood around the table flanking the general as he bent over a series of maps and rolled pieces of parchment. Like his officers, Navarro too was outfitted for battle in the fine accoutrements Royne recalled previously occupying the space on the tabletop while the Gray Wolf made his recovery.

Royne ignored the captain's comment and addressed the general. "You sent for me, sir?"

With a thoughtful sigh, Navarro lifted his eyes from the maps and raised an eyebrow. "Ah yes," he said, "Soon enough it seems you shall have your wish."

Royne's brow knit in confusion, "My wish, sir?"

"When first we spoke, you told me about your great desire to fight against the tyranny of Andoch and the kingsmen," he said, "It appears that very soon you will have that chance."

A cold flash of anxiety set Royne's heart fluttering. "Oh," he said, "Well...yes..."

Captain Velius's lips twisted into a sardonic smirk though he remained silent and allowed the general to continue.

"Tell me, Loremaster, "the Gray Wolf mused, "What do you know of the Guardian known as 'The Plow'?"

"The Plow?" Royne repeated, "Not much, I'm afraid."

"Then what use are you?" the captain muttered.

"He's a Cavalier of the Warlord's Tower," Royne replied, "I did not see him much around the castle."

"But you do know something of him?" the general asked.

"In a sense," he shrugged, "As a cavalier, he is one of the senior officers under the command of the Warlord. Only a justiciar is higher in rank, though a justiciar is usually tasked with leading an entire army. Cavaliers are most often placed in command of battalions of kingsmen or elite squads of warriors. Occasionally, they might be sent to aid other realms if a foreign noblemen successfully appeals to the Council of Five. This was the case most recently in Montevale. The Gasparn king appealed to the Council for assistance in ending the War of the Horses so the Guardians sent a man named Marcus Harding to provide assistance. Other times they can be tasked with directing mercenary soldiers hired to supplement the kingsmen should such a group prove too large or unruly for a gallant, the next rank. From what I understand, however, such a job is seen as beneath them and they do not like it."

"And this...Plow?"

Royne stroked his chin in thought. "The current Plow is Sir Lornis Ulban," he said, "I believe he was once attached to the court of a Lord Bemis, the Earl of Dunfathom, but I'm not sure. Once war was declared and the armies began to muster, the Guardians would have been recalled from such mundane posts as seneschals or border guards or the like in order to lead the Andochan armies."

"So you know nothing of value then," Velius snorted.

"I did not say that," Royne said tersely, "I just..." Suddenly, he paused, and in his mind, a multitude of thoughts and memories began to formulate all at once. Some were his own, but others soon surfaced that, strangely, seemed to belong to someone else. *Curious...*

"I don't know Sir Lornis personally," he said, "But there are stories of other men to bear his title. The first was—appropriately enough—a farmer out of eastern Andoch; however, after the defeat of Kalius Wrogan, he remained in Titanis with Halford Drude to aid him in rebuilding the city and driving the remaining Dibhorites out of Termain. When he died, the title was passed on to a lesser noble loyal to Drude, and for the most part that practice has continued ever since with the title making its way among many of the more landed families of Andoch. In fact, Ulban and Bemis are kin, which would account for the Plow's placement as seneschal since Dunfathom is one of the largest collections of holdings in Andoch. The Plows were particularly effective in subduing the Peasant's Rebellion in 314 following the great plague of that year, as well as in defending against the great Sorgund raids of 763. Some have suggested that the Plow will one day be elevated to the rank of Justiciar should its subsequent bearers continue to distinguish themselves since so many of the other titles seem to be weakening. Without knowing Sir Lornis personally, however, I can offer no opinion. However, it seems that in general, the Plows tend to be very serious men, skilled in the managing of an estate, and effective in garnering maximum yield from both their tenant farmers and their lands. They are disciplined leaders, knowledgeable of when to offer reward as well as when to resort to the rod, and quick to establish their authority when placed in command."

Tentatively, Royne ceased speaking and his brow furrowed sharply. *Very curious,* he thought, *Not sure how it is I knew all that…*

For a long moment, General Navarro remained silent in thought until at last, he folded his arms across his chest and regarded the young Loremaster standing across from him. "I'm not quite certain I understood everything that you said, for the ways of the Order are strange to us in the south. However, I believe I understand why this Sir Lornis was granted his current command."

"What do you mean?" Royne asked.

"Here," the General said mildly, motioning to one of the maps unrolled upon the table before him, "These were once the lands of a rather unfortunate senator by the name of Bruton. I say unfortunate because, after gutting half of the First Legion to protect his own lands, his resolve faltered after only the first assault upon his castle. Unwilling to endure a prolonged Andochan siege, he surrendered the following morn."

"At least the kingsmen had the courtesy to relieve him of his head anyway," Captain Velius added, "Saves us the trouble of having to tarnish our swords with the coward's blood."

"In any case," the general continued, "It seems that his castle and his lands have now been entrusted to this Plow fellow who, it appears, set the captured men of the First Legion to work in his fields."

Slowly, Royne nodded. "I see," he said, "You wish to kill two birds with one stone. You can bolster your ranks with his liberated soldiers, and use the fruits of the Bruton harvest to feed your own."

"Precisely."

Royne pursed his lips and glanced at the map before him. "What is it exactly that you wish from me?" he asked.

"This is a map of Villa Bruton and the surrounding farmlands," General Navarro said, "What I would like to know is this. Were you to lead an attack, how might you go about it?"

"What?" Royne asked, stifling an involuntary chuckle at the absurdity of such a request, "You are the soldiers, not I. My experience with military strategy does not extend beyond the chessboard."

"Then indulge me," the Gray Wolf said, "I do not doubt the strength and the skill of my men, but it now seems that the conditions that define the war have changed. My legion is but a shadow of its former numbers, and with the senate's surrender it seems we must live like brigands in our own homeland. We have no forts in which to seek shelter and no allies to come to our aid. We have barely enough supplies to last us through the week, yet to begin raiding and robbing caravans would be to steal from the very people we seek to liberate—our own countrymen." Navarro paused and when he spoke again, his voice was stern, "No, this war is no longer simply a war of soldier against soldier, of strength and steel. It is a war of wits, and for that, we must learn a new way of thinking."

"Alright then," Royne said at last, "Let me have a better look at the map."

Lieutenant Gigas stepped around the table to allow him a better view, and with a touch of nervousness, Royne carefully scanned the scrawled map of the late Senator Bruton's lands. In the center was a small village watched over from the northwest by a small stone castle set upon the edge of an area of woodlands. *Private hunting grounds, no doubt*, he thought, *My, for hating the aristocracy, these senators certainly know how to emulate them.*

"Where are the imprisoned soldiers housed?" he asked.

"There," the general pointed.

"And these marks over here are the granaries?"

"Yes."

Royne pursed his lips and brooded over the map in silence for a few minutes. While they waited, General Navarro nodded toward his young valet, and the lieutenant retrieved a jug of wine and a set of cups. As time wore on, however, Captain Velius seemed to grow more and more impatient with the young Loremaster.

"Blood and fire!" he cursed, "The obvious course of action is to attack the castle from the wood after dark. We use the tree line as cover from their archers until we can breech the walls with fire from the mangonels."

"If it the obvious course of action, then you can be certain that the Plow will have already taken steps to anticipate it," Royne said.

"Then what do you suggest, if you're so wise?"

Royne paused and stroked his chin again in quiet contemplation. "The castle is an irrelevancy in so far as our plans are concerned," he brooded, "Yet to the Plow, it will remain—as it was to you, Captain—the focal point. Tell me, how many men do we have exactly?"

"Less than eight hundred," said Gigas the valet.

"And how many of them ride amount?"

"Perhaps sixty. Light horse. Scouts. Skirmishers."

Royne scanned the map once more, chewing his lip. *They're not men*, he said to himself, *They're just pieces on the chessboard...*

"I agree with the captain," he finally said, "Assault the forest from the tree line with your mangonels and station a handful of men with each of the crews to guard them in the event of a counterassault."

"I thought the castle was an 'irrelevancy'?" the captain smirked.

"It still is. Just as much as the bloody mangonels your men are busy knocking together out there. I have simply given them the *appearance* of a purpose so as to fool the Plow into believing that they have one," he smirked, "At the first sign of us, he and his men will rally to the castle to mount a proper defense and those that do not will be driven there by our horsemen. Yet as much as it will prove their refuge, it will also prove their pen, locking them all up together like sheep in a fold whilst we liberate the prisoners and make off with the grain. The riders will call off their assault and the crews commanding the mangonels can simply abandon them and flee by way of the trees."

When Royne finally finished, the other men remained silent for a moment considering his plan. He cast a furtive glance across the table at the general, but found he had difficulty reading the man's expression. Still, he sensed a hint of something, but could not discern whether it was amusement or mockery.

"Tell me," Royne asked, "When were you planning on attacking?"

"It will take two days' march to reach Villa Bruton," the general said, "I had hoped to depart in a day or so once preparations are complete."

"Well," the young Loremaster said, "If I could convince you to wait a few days longer, I believe it might work considerably to our advantage."

"The men are at half-rations as it is," Velius scoffed, "Cut them any further and we're likely to speed the rate of desertion."

"Perhaps," Royne said, "But the fifteenth of Suntide is the Feast of St. Aiden. To men of the Order, there is no greater holiday. Hold off the attack until then and any resistance you meet is likely to be fat, drunk, and complacent from celebration."

"Though our own men could be weakened by hunger," the general observed.

"True, but perhaps the promise of a hearty meal might encourage the men to fight harder. A starving dog will fight off a bear if it stands in the way of its next meal."

"I suppose I wouldn't mind making off with a few tons of wine while we're at it with the grain," Velius admitted with a shrug, "Be a nice reward for the men, and a show of welcome to those liberated. Besides, who knows what else is to be looted about the village."

"No," General Navarro said, suddenly stern, "There's to be no looting beyond the grain. We may fight the Kingsmen, but the folk of the surrounding village are Grantisi. I will not abide the pillaging of our own people."

"As you say, sir."

"However," Navarro conceded, "If we should happen across any wine…I suppose we do not have to let it go to waste. It might also ease the pangs of hunger by offering a pleasant incentive while we wait the extra days." At length, the general stood and clasped his hands behind his back. "Very good, Master Royne," he said, "For one who claims no experience of warfare and tactics, your stratagem seems sound."

"Thank you, sir," Royne nodded.

"Save your thanks for the Feast of St. Aiden," the general said, "And should we succeed in our attack on Villa Bruton, then for the second time, it shall be I who is thanking you."

CHAPTER 17: REBELLION

It was nearly a week before riders arrived in Woodshire bearing the banner of the Sundering Hand, dispatched from Castle Tremontane by whatever nobleman had prevailed upon his peers to assume command in the wake of Lord Wilmar's death. For whoever it was, it was a precarious position. On the one hand, should the fugitives be apprehended and the Warden avenged, there was the promise of great honor and greater reward; however, should the Silent Prince be allowed to escape, there was no telling how King Dermont might unleash his fury on those he deemed responsible.

Upon arrival in Woodshire, the soldiers of the late warden made their way through the stony paths and peasant cottages to the small tower house from which Sir Norton Wherling, the Standing Stone, commanded the village on behalf of Tremontane's lord.

"News from the castle?" Sir Norton asked the men when he received them in the dining room that doubled as the house's hall, "I hope all is well with Lord Wilmar?"

The leader of the four men, a sergeant, removed his nasal helm and held it to his hip. "Sadly, Lord Wilmar is dead," he said.

"No!" Sir Norton gasped, "Lord Wilmar dead?"

"Murdered by the Silent Prince as he escaped with King Dermont's bride-to-be."

"I had not yet heard the king was to be married."

"To the Princess Marina, daughter of King Marius of Gasparn."

"I see," said Sir Norton with a sigh, "How dreadful."

"Indeed," said the sergeant, "Sir Eldar sends you this missive."

"And who is Sir Eldar?"

"Sir Eldar commands the castle in Lord Wilmar's seat whilst we await word from the king. He has asked all knights serving beneath the banner of the Warden of Tremontane to scour the countryside in search of the traitorous prince and those that aid him."

Sir Norton's brow furrowed. "Well," he said, motioning with the messenger's scroll, "I assume you've just saved me from reading this."

The sergeant remained stoic.

"You may tell Sir Eldar," Sir Norton said after a moment, "That I am his to command. I will dispatch my men-at-arms at once to scour the countryside for any trace of this Silent Prince. You have my word."

"Thank you, sir."

"Now, sergeant," Sir Norton said, "Will you and your men stop to eat, or do you have other messages to deliver?"

"Regrettably, my lord, we must away. Sir Eldar is in great haste to find the fugitives."

"I can only imagine. Perhaps another time."

The sergeant returned his helmet and with a nod led his men from the room. As soon as the heavy oaken door shut behind them, Sir Norton turned to the man dressed as a servant at his side, "I'd say three days is a rather liberal definition of 'great haste,' my prince."

Beledain sighed. "At least we have some idea of how long it will be until word reaches Dermont," he said, "Even at full gallop, it will take a rider another week or so to reach Reginal."

"That gives us at least some time to prepare for what's to come."

"You've been more than accommodating already, Sir Norton. There's no need for you to involve yourself any further."

"As I told you on the road after the Battle of White Wood," the elder knight said, "I'm your man, my lord. Even if all it earns me is a noose by your side. It'll still be my honor."

"Let's hope it doesn't come to that," Bel said, shaking his head, "I've had enough nooses these past few days to last me a lifetime."

"Aye, and they say it only takes one."

Bel gave a nod and pushed the thoughts of Jarvy and Sir Linton from his mind. There was too much to concern himself with at the present to dwell any further on his grief. Woodshire might provide refuge for now, but once Dermont learned of what happened, there would be few places left where they might find safety or rest. Bel remembered his brother's master of spies, a loathsome little man called Canton, whose men seemed to infest the far reaches of Montevale like rats in a plague. *Appropriate...*

"Sir Norton, please find me as soon as Sir Emory or his men return," Bel said, "Hopefully then we'll have a clearer picture of what to do next."

"As you wish, my lord."

From the hall, Bel made his way through the rear of the tower house to a small courtyard where the peasant folk gathered each morning to draw water from the well. Woodshire was a small village. Its inhabitants were mostly farmers or swineherds with a few tradesmen as might be necessary for daily life—a blacksmith, an herbalist, and a tanner. Sir Norton's guard, which numbered but eight men, took shifts patrolling the perimeter of the village, while their off hours were spent seeing to the other less auspicious duties of the household such as tending to the stables or serving at the master's table. The Wherlings were not a wealthy line, and neither Sir Norton nor his father had ever been able to afford the cost of the heavy armor of a cavalryman, let alone the funding to equip their men with anything more than boiled leather breastplates. However, they were good men and true, and if required, many of the peasants were capable archers as well. More than once over the course of the war had they been required to turn to hunting after their crops had been seized or burned.

By now, the menfolk had already gone off to the fields and the women had withdrawn to their cottages to see to the many thankless domestic duties necessary simply for survival. Bel did not envy the common folk their lot in life, and he doubted very strongly that were he born a peasant, he would have lived to become a man. He watched one woman milking her goat while nearby her children searched among their chickens, groping with dirty fingers for eggs. Each one wore the same vacant expression, carrying out their work in the same unconscious manner. Clad in the garb of a commoner, they paid

Bel little mind (if they even noticed him at all), and as he watched them at their work, it made him sad to realize that in all likelihood every person born in this village would die and be buried here with scarcely any change to their daily routines at all. They were born, they would work hard, and they would die.

Not that he was naïve enough to believe for a moment that every man among the peasantry was kind or honest or true. Ignorance and want were more than enough to turn many a man to vice, and there were plenty of bawdy songs and stories told among the soldiers about wanton wives and cuckolds, drunkards, scoundrels, and rogues. While roaming the villages along the Bloodline with the light cavalry, he'd seen plenty enough to turn his stomach with disgust—a woman with a crooked nose from being beaten by her husband, a man who made his living whoring out his two young daughters, a woman who accused half a dozen different soldiers of getting her with child in hopes of conning them out of coin. However, where they wicked because they were poor, or were they poor because they were wicked? There was no simple answer. For surely, there were rich men and poor men who were kind and good just as there were both rich men and poor men who were cruel and evil. Who was he to judge? He was not responsible for the actions of every man.

But then again, what was a leader for? To lead yes, but what did it *mean* to lead? Bel turned away from the peasant family and wandered around the side of the tower house to the stables where, hidden in the rear behind the other horses, Tempest munched idly at the feed in his box. At Bel's approach, the great horse lifted his head over the gate of the stall so that the prince could pat his nose. His large, dark eyes regarded the prince with a restless energy, as if waiting for a chance to break out and charge across the plain with the force of a lighting strike.

"Soon, my friend," Bel whispered, "Soon."

Beledain had never been one who cared for flattery, even when it was sincerely meant. However, from the common Valendian soldier all the way to Sir Marcus Harding himself, the Silent Prince was regarded as a great leader. But why? Never once had Bel commanded an army, let alone anything larger than the two hundred men of Dermont's light cavalry, yet for some reason, people respected him—even his enemies. Why?

With a heavy sigh, Bel thought of Jarvy and Sir Linton, captured and killed for what seemed little more than Lord Wilmar's vile pleasure at seeing Bel suffer. Why would they have risked trying to reach him? What was it that they wanted from him? Who was he?

He thought back to the journey through the Nivanus when in a fit of rage, he had killed one of Dermont's spies in cold blood, a man whose name he did not even know. It was then that he had asked Jarvy this same question.

You are Prince Beledain of Valendia, who all men know as the Prince of Bells or the Silent Prince. You are a warrior and a knight of great worth, a leader of men, respected by the common folk, soldiers, and enemies alike. More than anything else, however, you are a good man who strives always to do what is right, even when all the world seems wrong.

Bel shook his head and ran a hand through his hair. Suddenly, he felt very weary and the thought of his dead friends threatened to once again tear open the raw wounds of his grief. He rubbed at his eyes and rocked back on his heels as Tempest grunted and nudged his shoulder with his nose.

It was after nightfall when Sir Emory and his men returned to Woodshire. Sir Norton's people were just beginning to set the meal in the hall. It was rather cramped quarters at meals already with the knight, his wife, and now their party of royal guests, but somehow room was made for Emory and the three men who followed at his side. One man was older and bald with a small trimmed mustache, the second was younger with flaxen hair that hung about his shoulders, and the third was a gangly youth of no more than sixteen or seventeen years. Bel veritably leapt from the table at the sight of them and rushed to greet them.

"Armel! Welmsey!" he cried, offering them his hands, "Briden!"

Sir Armel, eldest of the three and known as "the Stone Thistle," smiled beneath the bristles of his mustache, "It's good to see you again, my lord, though, I admit I am uncertain how I should address you. The Tower, the Prince? This boy here claims *his* name is Briden, but of the family Sheradan as opposed to Winfred."

"I suppose 'The Fugitive' might be most apt, given the current circumstances," Bel smiled grimly. Other than poor Sir Linton, he had not seen any man among the Tower's Guard since the day of the battle of Clearpoint when he had bargained with Dermont for their safety, so he was overjoyed to find that in spite of his brother's treacherous nature, they were as yet unharmed.

"Sir Emory here has told us your tale," Armel sighed, "I'm sorry."

The look in the elder knight's eye told Bel that Emory had indeed told them much and more. "Thank you," he said, and turning to the younger knight, "How are you, Welmsey?"

"Envious," Welmsey mused dreamily, looking past Bel as the pair of kings and the princess rose to their feet. Like the Silent Prince, they too were clad in the garb of the servants of Sir Norton's house, but there was no mistaking Marina's fiery hair.

"Welmsey!" Armel whispered harshly, "Have some respect!" Together the two knights strode forward and knelt before their former king and his daughter, leaving Bel to receive the last of the trio.

"It's good to see you, Briden," Bel said, patting the lad on the shoulder, "Though I hoped you'd have been able to remain on with Val."

Briden seemed uncertain as to whether he should kneel or bow, awkwardly shifting his weight back and forth, until finally, Bel grasped him by the arm and steadied him on his feet. "Thank you, my lord," Briden said, "Lady Valerie was made to stay on at court in Reginal and the light cavalry was disbanded."

Bel nodded, and though it pained him, he realized it was simply another consequence of Clearpoint. Dermont would have been a fool to keep an entire company of riders with questionable loyalties.

"As such, my lord," Briden saluted, "I'm here and ready to serve, if you'll have me."

"Of course," Bel smiled, "Though you can see we're few in number."

"It's a good thing then that there's a dozen more outside," Sir Emory broke in, "Most are from the light company, but a few others too. Friends or family members eager to come along."

Briden nodded. "Horn and Wendell rode east to rally some of the others as well."

Bel shook his head in disbelief. "You said you went to scout," he told Sir Emory, "How in all the world did you find them?"

The old knight nodded toward Armel and Welmsey. "Those two lost their lands when your brother started reassigning the Gasparn fiefs and have been errant ever since. Briden and the other two—the big man and the other one. Wendell? They were...about."

"They were 'about'?" Bel smirked, "What does that mean?"

Briden shrugged sheepishly. "Well, sir," he said, "It may have been that Jarvy and that Sir Linton weren't the only ones trying to find a way back to you. Some of us, well, we thought to head back to Tremontane in case you needed us."

Bel's heart felt heavy. "You heard about Jarvy and Sir Linton then."

"Aye, sir," Briden said, "But, if you ask me, they'd done what they were after, eh? They may have lost their lives, but the way I see it, they aided in helping you escape."

Bel nodded and gripped the boy by the shoulder. "I suppose that's one way to look at it," he said kindly.

"Aye, sir," Briden said, "And, if I may, sir..." He paused and dropped his voice to little more than a whisper. "I'm so sorry about Lilia."

Bel gave a nod, doing his best to maintain his composure. "We have a son," he said, forcing a smile, "Did Emory tell you that?"

"He did, sir," Briden said, "Give you joy, my lord."

Bel nodded. "He's asleep upstairs, but you shall have to meet him," he said, "Though for now, why don't you find a seat? I'm sure it's been a long day."

"Thank you, sir," Briden said.

"Thank you," Bel nodded, "You know I borrowed your name for a while in the north?"

"Aye, sir. It made for a bit of confusion when first we met Sir Armel and Sir Welmsey, but it's all straight now," he smiled, "You've been long missed, my lord. It's good to have you back and free."

"You too, Briden," Bel said, "You've no idea how glad I am that you're here."

"Aye, sir," Briden said, "Of course, sir."

Together Bel and Sir Emory watched the young standard bearer make his way through the hall. At length, Sir Emory gave a sigh. "It seems riders have finally been sent from the castle looking for you," he said.

"Yes," Bel nodded, "A few of them came by here this morning."

"Well, as far as I can tell, your name's now on the lips of most of the folk south of the Bloodline and it won't be long before the north knows what we're at as well."

"And what are we at?" Bel asked, folding his arms across his chest, "That I'd still like to know."

Sir Emory raised an eyebrow and leveled his gaze at Beledain. "I think you already do," he said, "You just can't bring yourself to say it aloud."

A pair of servants passed carrying a pot of stew and a stack of trenchers. Bel glanced back over his shoulder as Sir Norton called out orders for more food. King Marius was introducing Armel and Welmsey to King Cedric, and as Bel watched them, Marina caught his eye and smiled.

"Rebellion," Bel said at last, "The renewal of the war."

Emory gripped Bel's shoulder. "You should hear the stories some of them have to tell," the old knight said, "Your brother's been busy this last half a year, but listen to this. The armies are mustering at Whitemane and Roanshead again, and still others are heading west toward the Nivanus Pass."

"Why?" Bel asked.

"Well, they say since Grantis fell the Guardians may have set sights on Baronbrock, and it seems as part of the deal he made with King Kredor, your brother's been called to help."

Bel chewed his lip in thought. With the chaos of the War of the Horses, Montevale had long been absent from participating in the politics of the rest of Termain. Now that the nation was thought to be whole again, Dermont was determined to find a seat at that larger political table.

Sir Emory watched as Bel stood in silent thought. "Not a bad time to strike, should a certain person have a mind to," the old knight observed mildly.

Bel gave a sigh. "For now," he said, "Let's just eat."

Over the course of the meal, the newly arrived knights gave accounts of what had been happening across Montevale in the last few months. Some of it Bel and the others had already heard from Sir Norton, but most of it, particularly the more recent happenings, were new. Whereas during the war, the Bloodline had divided Gasparn and Valendia by north and south, Dermont, in order to better manage the united whole, now organized the land into six separate vassalages each with a designated warden to command it. In addition to Wilmar Danelis, the warden of Tremontane, there were wardens of Whitemane, Roanshead, Reginal, Nivanus, and Pridel. Whitemane and Roanshead, as had been the case in Tremontane, were currently occupied by two of Dermont's other childhood companions, Inen Vilnois and Vaston Delon. Jarrett Harren, a powerful politician among the Valendian nobility was to command the eastern lands around the White Wood from the castle at Pridel, while Giles Pronet, a man who was essentially Harren's Gasparn counterpart, would command the western mountains and the pass that connected Montevale to Baronbrock. Finally, while King Dermont reigned from Reginal, his oldest friend and seneschal, Lord Kurlan Malacco, the Death Knell, served him officially as warden of the king's castle and its surrounding lands.

In each of the six vassalages, the local lords and their knights beneath them now owed fealty to the new warden, and in turn, to the king. Those who refused were stripped of their lands, fined, and often imprisoned with their heirs forced under the charge of their warden-lords. In this way, Dermont and his court could further cement their dominion over the newly united nation, and over the course of the spring, more weddings had occurred among the Montevalen nobles than the past two years combined.

"Thank the Brethren my daughter was already married," Sir Armel smirked, "Else I would have had to match her up with Welmsey just to avoid her being taken into the Death Knell's care."

Bel remembered Kurlan Malacco. He was as strong and as cruel as Dermont was cunning. The mention of the Death Knell's name always conjured up images from Bel's youth of the young Malacco leering over a crippled pigeon. The older boy had knocked it from the sky with a rock and as it lie on its side upon the flagstones of the courtyard, Bel remembered the sadistic delight on the young Malacco's face as he slowly lifted his boot to stomp on the poor creature's head. Even now, such unabashed cruelty made Bel's stomach turn with horror. Armel might speak in jest, but there was a dark truth underlying his words. No father would ever wish to see his child under the supposed protection of the Death Knell.

As for the common folk of both nations, no sooner had they been released from service in the war to return to their homes that many of their lords began summoning them again, sending them off to muster in the highlands along the Nivanus Pass, just as Sir Emory had said. This was most difficult for the farmers of Montevale, for no sooner had they begun sowing their seeds for the spring planting than they were forced to leave them behind once again to be cared for by their wives, young children, and elderly neighbors. For better or for worse, there may at least be some stronger hands to work the fields of Valendia than in the past two generations since Dermont had decided to reinstitute the ban on women serving as soldiers in the armies of Montevale. Bel could only imagine Val's anger and frustration as she sat at court, made to play the noble lady while her Iron Fist was left to rust.

In any case, while Dermont mustered his men in the west to support his Guardian allies in their war upon the Brock, along the southern ports of Valendia, there had been a great influx of other men from Andoch arriving to take their places among the courts of the united Montevale. Most had been church officials—prelates, celebrants, and acolytes—in service to the new provincial hierophant; however, in recent weeks, courtiers and scribes had also arrived in order to wait upon the wardens and assist them in their administrative duties to the Montevalen regent, and in turn, the Guardian-King.

"Your brother is nothing if not organized," Sir Armel said, "I will give him that. He wasted no time in establishing control."

"Oh Dermont has always been very clever," King Cedric observed with a benign smile, "Even as a boy he was always very good at facts and figures, always pouring over maps and books. Few—if any—know this, but when he begged me for command of our armies, he convinced me to hold it as a wager in a game of chess. Unfortunately, I had forgotten how skilled a player he was and it was a veritable rout! Wouldn't you say so, Larius?"

The rest of the table suddenly fell silent. Bel and Sir Emory exchanged a glance. Both seemed unaware of Dermont's little wager. "As you say, father," the prince said, "Though, surely it was not a rout."

"Oh it was," the old man went on pleasantly, "Let me tell you! I kept forgetting how the pieces moved, you see, and he had to keep reminding me! It was dreadful. It was so bad that Dermont even said to me afterwards, 'Father, if you can't command men on a chessboard how can you possibly hope to command them in the field?' And he was right, I suppose."

Sir Emory's jaw tensed with anger and the long white scar along the side of his face looked all the more menacing as his face grew red. Across from King Cedric, King Marius's face went pale and he glanced forlornly at the tabletop. Bel felt his chest tighten at his father's distraught admission, but he could not for the life of him think of an appropriate response and the uncomfortable silence lingered.

"You know, your majesty, I've never been able to understand chess either," Princess Marina said at last, "All those pieces! My brother tried to teach me once, but I was hopeless," she shook her head and smiled, "He decided instead to teach me dice, like the soldiers played. Do you know how to play dice, my lord?"

"Do I?" King Cedric grinned, "We used to call it 'rolling the bones' since most of the dice the soldiers used were actually *made* out of bone."

"Well," Marina said, "Perhaps if we can locate some dice, you would like to join my father and me after dinner and we might all play?"

"Why of course!"

Sir Norton looked quickly to his wife and nodded, "I'm sure we have dice, and made out of something nicer than bone."

"I'm certain we do," said Lady Wherling.

"And you would be welcome to join us as well, Lady Wherling," the princess said.

"Of course. That would be grand!"

"Perhaps we might save the talk of politics until then?" she said.

There was a general buzz of assent and Bel gazed at her with sincere gratitude. For the briefest of moments, she caught his gaze and exchanged with him a sympathetic smile. He found himself wanting to hold her glance just a moment longer when he was interrupted by Sir Welmsey's melodramatic sigh across the table.

Sir Armel coughed and took a drink from his goblet. "So I hear Tempest has returned?" he said, changing the subject, "What luck! There's never been a finer horse!"

Bel cleared his throat. "Yes," he said, "He found us on the road from the castle."

"They truly must be as wise as men," Sir Welmsey said.

"Wiser than some I know," Sir Armel replied, drawing the laughter of the others.

When the meal was over and the princess and the kings had withdrawn with Lady Wherling, the knights were left to discuss the coming days and their course of action. For the most part, Bel remained silent and thoughtful as they spoke. According to Sir Emory, there were three things they would need if they were to mount any sort of armed resistance to Dermont and his wardens. First, some manner of stronghold to act not only as a staging point, but also as a refuge in case of defeat. Second, more fighting men and gear to equip them should they not have their own. And third, enough food and supplies to sustain the army they hoped to build.

Almost at once, Sir Norton offered up Woodshire, at least until a more suitable place might be found. However, Bel refused; for already the knight's hospitality put his home and his peasantry at risk should Dermont discover the Standing Stone had provided the Silent Prince with sanctuary.

Sir Emory suggested a possible return to Castle Tremontane, since Lord Wilmar's remaining guard might still be in disarray, in spite of Sir Eldar. However, again, Bel refused since with the return of the Andochan Provincial, an attempt to take over the castle and the city might also provoke a more militant response from the Guardians, and although Bel was rather certain war with Dermont would inevitably bring war with King Kredor, he hoped to stave off that conflict for as long as possible. Besides, Castle Tremontane had been constructed in such a way as to allow a very small force to defend it.

"If Dermont has created his vassalages, then," Sir Emory said, "Perhaps we should think in the same terms. Ignoring the late Lord Wilmar, which of the remaining wardens seems the mostly likely to brush aside?"

"Pronet is no warrior, I can tell you that," Sir Armel said, "He's naught but a dandy fool."

Bel remembered Pronet from the parley after the Battle of the White Wood. Pronet the Princox, Lilia had called him. He breathed a heavy sigh, conjuring up an image of her in his mind arrayed for battle, black war paint streaked across her skin, shrieking her battle cry as she charged ahead on Banshee. At once he felt both the thrill of fighting beside her, and the intense pain of her loss.

"Though aren't Pronet's lands where the king's armies are mustering," Sir Welmsey mused, invading upon Bel's reverie, "At Ironshod and Valeshade along the pass?

"True," Sir Norton said, "And even if this Pronet might be a fool, there could be plenty of others with the army who are not."

"Still," Armel sighed, "If we were to take the Nivanus, we might ally with the Brock. Their archers manning that line of shell keeps would be a wonder."

"And both of King Cedric's brothers command the farthest keeps north and south," Sir Emory said, "Though, for right now, Sir Norton makes a good point. It might be wisest to wait on the Nivanus. For even if Leon or Talvert supported us, with our numbers as they are right now, we'd have to join one and forsake the other. If we wait until our forces grow, we could divide them at each end and crush the enemy between us."

"Perhaps with the Brock pushing back from the west..." Armel added.

"Yes, perhaps. But, of course, it's all just a flight of fancy for right now," Sir Emory said, "A fine one indeed, but still fancy. I agree that we should definitely send someone to the Lord-Baron, but let's wait until we at least have our foothold. Grantis lost a war to the combined might of Dwerin and Andoch. Add Dermont's forces to the mix and we don't stand a chance against all three. Of course, neither does the Brock."

"Then if not Pronet, then who?" Welmsey asked, "Whitemane and Roanshead are two of the greatest fortresses outside of Reginal and Tremontane. What about Pridel?"

"Harren is more a fop than Pronet," Norton scowled, "But there's not much there. It's primarily forest, farms, and the occasional troop of bandits in the woods. It's no place for cavalry at any rate."

Sir Armel nodded toward Bel, "I seem to recall a conversation with Sir Harding about the benefits of such terrain in confounding the mounted charge, and wasn't it also the Silent Prince who emerged from the cover of the White Wood to rout the Snow Bear and his reserves?"

"It was," Bel said.

"If only there was a keep or something," Sir Norton sighed, "Even a ruin. We could use it as a staging point before attempting to move on the castle."

Tentatively, Briden gave a wave of his hand. "Prince Beledain," he said, "There was that one place along the south edge of the forest. Remember the stone statue shaped like a man screaming? Jarvy said it was a marker pointing the way to the old ruin in the forest. Do you remember? He told a story about it."

"No," Bel said, "I wish I did. It'd be nice to hear one of Jarvy's ghost stories again."

"Well," Briden began, "I can't tell it like him, but I could try…"

"That's…not what I meant, but…"

"Oh."

"But the ruins?"

"Aye. Jarvy said they were old—from back in the time of St. Aiden when the Warlock's folk took over the continent. It was supposed to be the fortress of one of Wrogan's captains, but it was razed after the Fall of the Warlock when the Montevalen Guardians returned home," he paused, "The Shepherd and the Shackle—those were their names, Jarvy said, and the fortress was called Feyhold on account of the local legends saying it was cursed. Still, it's hidden enough and might serve as a place to hold up."

"I vote we should pass on the haunted castle," Sir Welmsey said after a moment, "We have enough enemies among the living without making foes of the dead."

Bel sighed. Between Jarvy, Linton, Igno, Banshee, Larius, Sir Marcus Harding, and Lilia, there were already plenty of ghosts following him around. A few more would make little difference.

"It would only be temporary," Sir Emory mused, "Once we defeated Harren, we could garrison the castle at Pridel, perhaps even recruit the former lord to our cause? Who was it again? The master before Harren?"

"Lord Talevan," Sir Armel said, "He refused to bend the knee before Harren and no one's seen him since."

"Wonder where he's got to?" Sir Norton sighed.

"In any case," Emory asked, "What do you think, Prince Beledain?"

Bel breathed a sigh and considered it. "Pridel is right on a trade road, from what I remember commanding the light cavalry. There would be plenty of opportunity to raid caravans for supplies, though we would have to ensure that any we took belonged to Harren or Dermont and not some poor farmer. It's no longer a matter of black horse or white."

"Thank the Brethren for that," Armel added, "And Pridel has plenty of farmland, as Sir Norton said. Should we assume command of the castle and pledge to protect the peasantry, they would surely provide us with grain."

There were murmurs of assent around the table and at last Bel raised his glance to Sir Emory and gave a nod, "So be it."

"Good."

"Now," Bel sighed, "It's getting late. If it's alright with you all, I'd like to visit the men outside and then return to my son." The others voiced their assent, and together they stood from the table. For a moment, Bel felt lightheaded, and it gave him pause. His heart was heavy with the weight of his grief, but looking around the table at the men assembled, he realized that, for the first time in days, the tightness in his chest had eased.

From the depths of his memory, he somehow recalled the voice of Marcus Harding, speaking to him now from the annals of memory.

A good leader is one who surrounds himself by good men, men of courage and character, who he can trust, not only to do their duty, but to ensure that he does his as well.

These men, Bel knew, were counting on him, believed in him, and were willing to risk all they had in the hope that, like Jarvy had said, he would do what was right—to save Montevale from further tyranny and create a true, lasting peace throughout the land. He could not forsake their faith in him, nor did he believe they would let him.

That, Bel knew, was one of Dermont's greatest flaws. His brother had always seen leadership in terms of command, as a testament to his own superiority, his right to rule and exercise his will. He failed to realize that, in some sense, a true leader was little more than a servant, or, at best, a guide. His duty was not to himself, but to his people, to ensure their wellbeing, to safeguard them from evil, and to create the conditions that would allow them to thrive. Dermont would never understand that.

Enough wavering. He could no longer neglect his oaths or his duties, and he could no longer allow himself to be crippled by grief. If anything, Lilia would never have stood for it, and the longer he wept and bemoaned her loss, the greater dishonor he did her. He would dedicate his future and his fight to her memory and to creating a better world for their son. *Tears will not serve a flower that feeds on blood,* he smiled wanly.

"If I could also add," he said tentatively, as the men halted and gave him their eyes, "I want to thank you all. Truly. It's been...very difficult of late. However, I am with you now—all of you—and though I do not know what is to come, I will do whatever I can to see this through and set our land to rights."

"And we're with you, Lord Tower," Armel said and Welmsey nodded.

"All of us," Emory and Norton agreed, and without a word, Briden fell in at Bel's side, ready to follow as he had a year ago.

"Then, gentlemen," Bel said, remembering Marcus Harding, "The rebellion has begun."

CHAPTER 18: THE BARON OF GALADIN

Brigid rushed down the stairs of the Houndstooth through the third floor hallway to where Geoffrey, Annabel, and the children had been installed among the apartments long kept vacant for visiting household retainers. Through the windows overlooking the bailey below, the sky was slightly overcast, perhaps deciding whether or not to rain. "Annabel," she called as she hurried into the small sitting room, "Are you within?"

"Brigid!" Greta sang from where she sat playing on the floor.

"Hello, little mouse," Brigid grinned and stooped to kiss the little girl on the cheek, "Where's your mum?"

"I'm here," Annabel said passing into the chamber. In her arms she carried a length of cloth for needlework and a few spools of colored thread. Moving into the castle had been a rather awkward transition for the small family from Pyle, at least for the parents. Freddy and Greta seemed to get on well enough, for to suddenly find themselves living in a castle must have been like something out of a fairy story. Without the need to spin thread or prepare meals, though, Annabel often mentioned that she felt idle and struggled to find things to do. She had refused the services of any servants, apart from those whose duties extended to the castle at large, and she had made it a point to hold on to what little possessions they owned in their little Hounton house. Still, she adapted much easier than Geoffrey who seemed, if anything, to feel somewhat guilty about their sudden change in fortune. More guilty, in fact, than he had selling the jewelry. Brigid never quite understood why.

"Where's Geoffrey?" Brigid asked, "And Freddy?"

"That Sir Owain's taken them out to walk the walls," Annabel said, "He wants to show Geoffrey the extent of the fields outside the city and he says they're easier to see from on high." The peasant woman sat down upon a large pillow atop a chair. "Where are you off to?" she asked, raising an eyebrow, "As if I didn't already know…"

Brigid ignored Annabel's tone. "Lughus and I are going to the Market House today," she said, "I just wanted to see if you needed anything."

"Oh, *another* day roaming the town with the young baron, eh?"

Brigid sighed, and for some reason she found herself blushing, "Annabel, do you need anything or not?"

"No, dear," she smiled, "It was nice of you to remember us, though."

"What is that supposed to mean?"

"Nothing. Only we just don't seem to see you as often as we used to."

"Well, we have a whole castle now, before it was just our small house," Brigid said, "And besides, I still see you every day at meals in the hall."

Annabel shrugged, a smile playing at the corners of her lips, "It just seems to me that ever since we came to the castle last week, you suddenly have…other interests."

Brigid felt her shoulders tense with frustration. *This again,* she thought. "Annabel," she said simply, "Lughus is my friend."

"Good. I'm glad. It's good for you to have friends your own age, who are boys. And also handsome. And barons."

"I'm leaving, Annabel. Goodbye, Greta."

"Better hurry; he's probably waiting."

"Annabel, please!"

"Who's waiting, mum?"

"Brigid has a…*friend.*"

"Goodbye, Annabel!" she could still hear the farmer's wife laughing down the hall.

"Have fun, dear!"

Outside of the postern that led down to the grotto, she found Lughus waiting, idly running his finger along the mortar of the curtain wall. Fergus loped around at his side, snapping at a little white butterfly floating above the grass. As she neared them, Brigid took a moment to slow her pace and smoothed down her hair. It was beginning to grow long—too long, for it was now past her waist. She remembered with a shudder how Alan had grabbed hold of it before he stabbed her in the back. If she was to do any more fighting like at the grotto, she would certainly have to cut it. What a change, she thought. A year ago she was but a mouse, yet now she was a falcon in her own right—more than any old falcon. She was *the* Falcon. She was the Blade!

And here was the Baron, the Marshal, the Hound...

"I'm sorry!" she called out when he saw her, "I'm sorry I made you wait."

Lughus smiled and looked away. *He always does that*, she thought, *He always looks away.* It made her feel worried, self-conscious. "You didn't," he said, "I was early."

Fergus hurried over to her, impatiently nudging her with his head as means of encouraging her to ruffle his ears. "Are you ready? Alanday is Market Day. It'll be busy, even with the pilgrims leaving the city."

"After you," he lifted the bar away from the postern and ushered her through.

"Thank you," she waited for him to shut the door and smiled inwardly thinking of all the times she'd wandered the city trying to find a way into the castle to meet the mysterious Marshal. He was not what she expected, but she was glad.

"I have to admit," he said, "I feel kind of foolish."

"Why is that?"

He smiled and shook his head as they began walking down the pathway through the ridge. "You know so much more about the city than I do," he said, "Yet I'm supposed to be the baron."

"You *are* the baron," she smirked, "Whether you like it or not."

"I know," he said, "I just...it's a lot of responsibility. All these people—peasants, burghers, knights—I'm supposed to take care of them, to protect them, to help them live good lives...and I worry I've already mucked everything up."

"How?"

"Harlow and the Provincial for starters."

"Nonsense."

"A baron who's also a Blackguard can't be too reassuring either. I half expect the Guardians to show up any day now to lay siege."

"It's not like we're strangers to sieges, are we?" she smiled, "Not according to the story at any rate."

He shrugged, "I'd just hate for these people to suffer simply on account of me. Who am I to them anyway?"

"Who is any nobleman to the common folk? Born to wealth and privilege, they own the land but don't work it. At least you want to help. That's more than most noblemen I've ever met."

"I want to be a good leader. If I'm to do this, I want to do it right."

"You'll find your way. I know it."

"It's...kind of you to say so."

Brigid sighed. In the week since the Feast of St. Aiden, they had walked down to the town every day to explore. They walked the Trade Quarter on the first day, Hounton the second, the Golden Quarter, the Saints Quarter, even the Lakeside docks. They talked to people—merchants, guards, beggars, children—and as they did so, she watched him. More than anything else, there was one thing about him that struck her as not only unusual, but...she had trouble finding the right word. Charismatic? Admirable? Attractive? The connotation of the last word, suddenly made her blush and she hurried along the path.

"When I lived in Blackstone, I would have to sit sometimes at court with my mother and my uncle," she told him, "They would talk about this party or that feast. The men would fawn over my mother and attempt to outdo one another pledging loyalty to the realm, while the ladies of the court would hang on her every word. Meanwhile the Sheriff, though he was supposed to be overseeing the day to day governance of the realm, spent more time terrorizing the people than leading them." She leapt agilely down the place along the path where the old stone steps had crumbled and waited while he followed behind. "Once in a while," she continued, "An official from the town or another lord would want to ask a question or bring a petition forward—you could always tell by the frightful looks on their faces—yet I cannot remember a time even once when they were allowed to speak. Instead, they would have to talk in private with the Steward, who—if they were lucky, might mention it to my mother over dinner or to my uncle while he sat alone in my father's solar."

"They sound awful," Lughus said.

"They were—*are*, I should say," she corrected herself, "But that's not the point." She smiled at him, and for a moment she held his gaze before he seemed to grow uneasy and turned away. *Why won't he look at me?* she wondered once more. His eyes were strange—not the same as the Falcon's, yet somehow similar in their intensity. As if when he looked at you, he was *really* looking, *really* seeing you in a way that others did not. And they were beautiful as well, deep gray, but with tiny flecks of gold mixed within, like flashes of lightening in a summer storm.

Suddenly, Fergus ran past, bounding ahead along the path, and she remembered that she had been speaking. "The point is," she said, "Never once, did they listen to any voice other than their own. But when I've watched you—in the castle, in the town, even…when it's just you and me like this…you listen."

At long last, he turned his gaze upon her, and for a moment, Brigid felt strangely weak. To her surprise, it was she who looked away this time, though she could still feel his eyes upon her. "It's important," she said quietly, "Listening."

"How can you hear the Song of Wisdom without first knowing how to listen?"

"What?"

"It was just something Rastis—the Loremaster—used to say."

"Oh," she said, "That's very good advice."

He rested his hand on the pommel of his sword. "Anyhow, thank you for saying that," he said, "It means a lot to me to hear that…from you."

For a moment Brigid bit her lip and turned away to hide her face. Her cheeks felt warm and she knew that as fair as her complexion was, there would be no concealing her blushing. Her head felt muddled and her stomach queasy. *What is this awful feeling?* For the past few days, she felt gripped by sudden bouts of this odd illness, usually when she was with him—walking the ground, playing chess, talking about books—but it was getting worse and worse. It made her think of the days after she had just met the Falcon, when she used to imagine the adventures they might have together. However, with Lughus, there was no daydreaming. It was real. She shook her head and hurried on. "We should catch up with Fergus!"

The Market House of Galadin was a wide, high-ceilinged building constructed of wattle and daub upon a foundation of gray stone. Entry from the front was guarded by two large oaken doors, while in the rear, large paddocks allowed for the stabling of livestock and horses brought to the city for sale. Venders of all sorts crowded together based on common trade, competing with one another for the honor of the next sale—leatherworkers, fine smiths, woodcarvers, armorers, sword smiths, bowyers, fletchers, cobblers, haberdashers, tailors, cloth-dyers, tanners, trappers, and half again as many general merchants of no particular specialization. There were farmers from the fields surrounding the city and from each of Galadin's seven fiefdoms selling fresh produce, butter, eggs, and cheese. There were drovers, hunters, and fishermen selling slabs of fresh meat, salted fish, and wild game. A contingent of officers from the weaver's guildhall across the square sold cloth of every grade and level of distinction (though primarily specializing in the Brock's famous wool).

As Lughus and Brigid walked along together, men in the blue and gold tabards of the watch stood taller and tipped their kettle helms in salute, while those merchants or burghers brave enough to overcome their initial fear of Fergus offered greetings and respectful salutations. Like Brigid, Lughus did not seem one for finery or ostentation. His clothing, while well-made, was rather simple and bore little embellishment beyond a single rampant hound emblazoned on his blue surcoat. Beneath it, she noticed, he also wore his ring mail shirt in spite of the summer heat, though it seemed an idiosyncrasy born out of habit rather than any posturing or fear. Still, as mundane as his clothing might be, when the sunlight touched his golden mop of hair, there was no questioning that he was the Baron of Galadin.

For her part, Brigid was content to wear the simple peasant dresses (or so the archduchess used to call them), as opposed to any absurd gowns— something that seemed to vex Jergan, Houndstooth's master of the wardrobe, nearly as much as it had her mother. He found her daggers an added bother as well—not because she was a woman armed, but rather because the gilded hilts seemed such eyesores when contrasted with the simplicity of the rest of her garb. Twice already he had devised fine new baldrics that might allow her to carry the blades in a way that might be more fashionable than where they hung now on her hips. She accepted them graciously, but although beautifully wrought, neither belt seemed very functional. They now remained hanging in the back corner of her wardrobe.

The castle steward, Horus, had also tasked a young woman named Ada to serve as Brigid's handmaid, and according to her, it was likely that Brigid might have to excuse a certain amount of doting from the castle folk. It was a long time since Houndstooth had been home to a young lady—not since Luinelen, Baron Arcis's only daughter. Strangely, it was also a name Brigid recalled spoken of disparagingly from time to time between her mother and Livonia.

As the daughter of the old porter, Ada, too, grew up in the castle, and was only nine or ten years old when the lady died; however, she remembered how people used to say that day or night and in any weather, when Lady Elen drew near, you felt the warmth of the sun. Thus, Brigid, might simply have to endure sixteen years' worth of unspent devotion.

Perhaps, she thought, browsing over an armorer's wares, perhaps tonight she would wear one of Jergan's baldrics to dinner. The folk of Houndstooth were, after all, exceedingly kind, and just as she had advised Lughus when he met with his knights, the refusal of a kindness could sometimes make for an even worse insult. She liked the Brock. It was...*different* than Dwerin. It was simultaneously less reserved, while still maintaining a certain degree of casual decorum and respectability. More than anything else, though, it was...honest, authentic, and while further north, geographically speaking, it exuded a warmth that greatly outmatched the cold stone kingdom of the Ironmen. If one day, through some currently unimaginable series of events, she did in fact return to Dwerin to assume her role as the Falcon's "mountain queen," she would certainly miss the Brock. For, in but a few short months, it seemed more a home to her than Dwerin ever was. In the Brock, in Galadin in particular, she was finally able to live as she pleased, to be herself, with people who cared about her, and people whom she cared about in return. She sighed, and without realizing it, comfortably slipped her arm through that of the young baron.

Immediately, her eyes widened and she felt his shoulder go tense. She let her arm fall limp to her side, wondering what it was that made her do that.

Perhaps the thought of Blackstone had summoned up an old habit from the days when she had been forced to follow Alan's entourage alongside Reid? The thought of both of them still made her skin crawl.

No, it was not that. Not that at all. Her action was far too natural, too comfortable. With Alan, Reid, and the others she had to bend her will to allow them to take her arm, to force herself to ignore her discomfort and disgust. Taking Lughus's arm was something she had done without thinking, out of genuine kindness and friendship. Still, what was she doing? Being so forward? *What is wrong with me?* she thought. What will he think of me now? The last thing she wanted was to be thought of as one of those mindless girls her mother chose to be her companions in the bloody Drove.

"I'm sorry," she said at last, failing in her attempts to keep from blushing, "I just..." she tentatively touched the steel rings of his hauberk. *Ahh! Why are you touching him again?* She cleared her throat. "I...was wondering if this ever gets heavy?" she managed, "I sometimes wonder if I should wear one."

For a moment, he seemed just as flustered as she. "A hauberk?" he stammered, "Would—would you like one?"

"I...I don't know..." *What am I blathering about?*

The merchant, already perched like a great bird of prey ready to fly, leapt at the opportunity to gain the clientage of the baron. "May I be of any assistance, my lord?" he grinned, "It would be my honor to offer protection to the man who protects us all!"

Lughus glanced briefly at Brigid, but she shook her head. "Not now," she smiled and took a deep breath. *What am I doing?* She feigned a sudden interest in Fergus and moved on to inspect what he was sniffing at the next stall.

Lughus hurried after her. "If you'd like," he said, running a hand through his hair, "When we get back to the castle, I can ask Owain or the master-at-arms to gather some things. You can try on whatever you like and see what you find most comfortable?"

"I...I don't know," she said uneasily, "I've just been thinking lately. If there's to be any more fighting, a dress is probably not the best thing to wear. I thought about asking Jergan to fit me for trousers and some real boots. Maybe I'd cut my hair—"

His eyes widened. "Cut your hair? Why?"

She was surprised by the tone of his voice, "You don't want me to cut my hair?"

"No, I...it's your hair. You do as you like. I just...I thought women liked long hair. And yours is...nice."

"It gets in the way sometimes, and it can easily get pulled," she shrugged, "I don't know. Maybe to the shoulder? Nothing more than that probably," she grinned, "If you're worried."

"I'm not worried. I think you would look nice however short it was, or long, or...whatever you like," he cleared his throat and rested his hand on the pommel of his sword—Sentinel—she remembered it was called. He bit his lip and rubbed his eyes. "Though," he said, "Now that you mention it, the thought of you going into battle, and unarmored at that...does make me rather worried. You should have whatever equipment suits you best."

"I'm better at sneaking around anyway—picking locks and things. I don't know how, but I'm actually rather good at it. The clinking of the mail rings would probably make noise and slow me down, which is probably why Gareth didn't wear it, at least not while I knew him. It looks nice on you, though," she said, "Like a proper knight or a hero." *Lady's Grace, stop talking!*

With a deep breath, Brigid shut her mouth and a long silence followed as together they continued to stroll along the market stalls until they paused again where a man was selling furs. Brigid feigned interest in the soft pelt of a winter hare while Lughus stood idly beside her, glancing ahead. "Do they sell books here?" he asked suddenly.

"Not that I've seen," she said, "And I imagine that any they did would cost a great deal of gold."

"I can imagine," Lughus said, "It takes a very long time to copy a whole text."

"Is that what you did in Titanis?"

"Sometimes, though most of the serious copying is reserved for the scribes and scholars. The apprentices mostly copied missives or documents—things requiring less art and embellishment unfortunately."

"I never really thought about that," she said, "That all the books I've ever read—even those ones I borrowed from you—all of them had to copied by hand. It must make the fingers cramp something awful."

"Oh yes," Lughus smiled, "Speaking of books, though, did you get a chance to read any more of *The Wake of the Wave?*"

"A little. Sir Borlan just met the red knight upon the bridge. Actually, that reminds me of something else I wanted to ask you—" she paused abruptly as a young man called out to them from the crowd and bowed his head.

As he approached, Lughus took a step forward to meet him, and Brigid noticed that without even seeming to realize it, his shoulders squared and his feet assumed a natural stance. He had cut two men down in the blink of an eye that night at the grotto. How many more would have fallen to him had Willum Harlow refused to flee? More than she could have dispatched in a pitched battle, she imagined. Hers was the way of the shadows, the quick kill, the Blade in the darkness. Like Gareth, she imagined that she could dispatch an entire castle full of enemies one or two at a time; the young Marshal, however, was built for open conflict—the battlefield or the dueling ground. He possessed the same martial instincts that she inherited when she assumed her title, but augmented by the formal training he had already received. For weeks, Lughus said, Crodane, the formal Marshal, had taught him what he could before passing Sentinel to his hand, and she knew that he often practiced early in the morning with Sir Owain and in the inner ward. Regardless, if this man or any other sought a fight with them, they were more than ready.

To say nothing of the great golden hound that appeared in a flash and fixed the young man with his emerald gaze.

"Um...Pardon me, my lord," the young man said, his eyes never leaving Fergus, "My master sends his regards to you and to the lady. He wishes to offer you this."

Behind the servant, two other men approached carrying a thick roll of cloth—a fine silk brocade of gold and baronial blue. Brigid bit her lip. It was a kingly gift. Such a cloth was both extremely expensive and rare. To give such a quantity away—even to a baron—was a show of spectacular wealth.

Lughus glanced at her uncertainly. She knew that he did not like accepting gifts like this, and was unsure of what to do. "Who is you master?" he asked the servant.

"Adolfo, Master at the Weaver's Guild. He spied you enter the market and bid me bring this and tell you that should you need anything of him, he is your humble servant."

Rarely is a master content to play the servant... Brigid thought, and from what she knew of Adolfo, it seemed unlikely he be the exception to prove the rule.

Lughus leaned toward her, "Do you know him?"

"By reputation," she said, "He owns a great deal of property around the city and handles the contracts for many of the apprentice weavers at the guild. They call him 'Adolfo the Madder' because his hands are always stained red," she smiled at the servant, "With dye of course."

"I see," Lughus mused. She was certain that he caught her meaning; however, a man as wealthy and as influential as Adolfo could not simply be cast aside or treated with scorn, despite how unsavory he might be. She watched Lughus's brow furrow and his eyes harden to adopt the same stern expression he had worn last week when entreating the provincial hierophant. Without realizing it, he had cast aside the soft-spoken youth and assumed the mantle of the young baron.

"You can thank your master for his kindness," Lughus said, "But I cannot accept his gift."

"You...you cannot?" the servant said.

"I'm sorry, but no, for among other things we have no means to carry it," Lughus smiled.

"We could always take it up to the castle for you, if you like?" the young man said hurriedly, "It would be no trouble."

Lughus shook his head, "I'm sorry. You can tell your master that I appreciate his offer, but I'm afraid my tastes in clothing are somewhat unrefined. If he insists on some show of friendship, however, he could sell the cloth and distribute the money among Galadin's poor."

"The poor, sir?"

"I've heard it said that a baron is only as great as his city, but a city is only as great as its people. Thus, if he offers his gift to the people, it is much the same as offering the gift to me."

Brigid suppressed a smile. *Well done,* she thought.

The servant breathed a sigh and offered a deep bow. "I will tell my master what you said, my lord," he said reluctantly, "Good day."

When they had gone, Lughus breathed a great sigh. As he exhaled, the baron seemed to retreat as the kindly youth reemerged. "Adolfo the Madder," he mused, "That was not a gift. It was a bribe to curry favor so I might look the other way on the occasion of his misdeeds."

"Aye, but I think you handled it very well," Brigid grinned, and this time, by her own volition, took his arm and led him onward through the market. *There's nothing wrong with this,* she told herself, *This is perfectly normal. If Reid could take my arm then so can he...*

They walked on, though for a moment, his knees seemed not to bend. "Are there a lot of men like this Adolfo in Galadin?" he asked stiffly.

"Not so many," she said, "Though I expect you'll find them in every city or town."

"You say he's a villain?"

"Such is his reputation. His rates are high, his wages low, and he dabbles in illicit trades."

His whole body seemed to grow tense, like an arrow set to a bow. "Then I shall have to do something about him," he said.

"What do you mean?"

"If he threatens my people, it's my duty."

"Perhaps, but he's also very influential."

"I know, but should I not do something. If he's at the guild hall, I could go talk to him."

"If you want to go after Adolfo, I'm with you, but...right now? Are you sure that's wise? Didn't the Abbot say something about the other barons and the meeting in Stagtide to validate your rights? If Adolfo would so wantonly attempt to curry favor with you, he may very well have the ear of other barons. Few merchants grow wealthy confining their trade to a single city. His reach might very well extend across the Brock."

Lughus chewed his lip. "That's likely true."

"Look," Brigid said, "If you want to go and confront him, like I said, I'm with you, but...now?"

He sighed, "I suppose not right now, but..."

She stopped walking and turned towards him. His face had grown pale and the line of his jaw was set and rigid. His eyes seemed glossy and the storm within them seemed to fade. "Hey?" she said gently, "Are you alright?"

"I'm sorry," he said, and at long last, his arm relaxed around hers. She offered him a smile, but he returned it only briefly, before looking away and rubbing his eyes, "I'm just...I'm very tired."

"Already?" she said as they began to walk again, "It's but midday?"

"I'm sorry. I don't sleep very well these days."

"We can go back, if you'd like?"

"No, no. I like walking," he said, "And it's important. If I'm to be the master of a city, I need to know it. I owe it to these people."

She eyed him curiously, "Very well."

They walked on to the rear of the Market House, and although she remained silent, Brigid could not help but feel a heightening sense of concern. She was just about to say so when Fergus bound on ahead of them, wagging his tail. Suddenly the air was thick with the sickeningly sweet smell of animal dung mixed with hay and straw. In the paddocks, shaggy highland cattle and wooly sheep stood chomping idly at their feed. Chickens, quails, and ducks squabbled from within hutches and somewhere unseen, a rooster crowed.

Fergus poked his head through the wooden slats of a paddock to sniff at a wobbly white lamb. When the tiny creature bleated fearlessly in the great hound's face, Brigid smiled and heard the young baron chuckle softly beside her.

"He's fierce when he needs to be, but he's really just a big pup," Lughus smiled.

"How old is he?" she asked.

"The same age as me. They're not like normal hounds. Everyone knows about their intelligence and their strength, but they also heal quicker, command others of their kind, and live extremely long lives, particularly if they've bonded with someone. My mother found him for Crodane when I was born. I guess you could say he was to be my brother of a sort." He gave a weary smile.

"I was never allowed animals," Brigid said. The sharp memory of an ill-fated litter of puppies flashed momentarily across her mind's eye, but before she had time to focus on any further instances of Josephine's cruelty, Lughus halted and she heard him breathe another of his great, bracing sighs.

"When you became the Blade," he said quietly, "Did you have strange dreams afterwards?"

213

She turned toward him to answer, but was suddenly struck by the look in his eye that seemed to validate her private concerns over him. All of a sudden, he no longer appeared merely tired, but haunted, strained, and, while he spoke of trouble sleeping, it seemed now like he had hardly slept in days. Her chest tightened, "Dreams, you say?"

He nodded, "Or nightmares."

She bit her lip. "Sometimes," she said at last, "Sometimes I would have these dreams where it was as if I was seeing things through the Falc—through Gareth's eyes. Like I was in his mind. Once, I was on a ship somewhere very warm and an enormous seabird was circling overhead. Another time I was in a bell tower overlooking a town, and I felt overwhelmed with impatience, as if I were looking for someone. Hunting, I think. But then once, he was at a tavern and these people were playing music and dancing. I think they were nomads—you know? The Wayfolk?" she grinned, hoping he would too, "I'm pretty sure he was drunk as well because he wasn't dancing, but the room kept spinning."

Lughus nodded, "I see."

"I saw a few battles too," she went on, "Or at least the aftermath. It was…not pretty. And I saw that Harlow man. It wasn't him, but it was a man *like* him—felt like him, chasing me. I had a hard time falling back to sleep after that one," she watched him, hoping he would interject, "Geoffrey believes the dreams to be memories. He used to have them too, but…he doesn't like to talk of it, or much else relating to Regnar."

"I think he's right. I think they are memories."

"Perhaps."

Again, he sighed, and they resumed their walk, "I want to tell you something."

Suddenly, Brigid felt an ache in her chest and her breath grew short, "You do?"

"I told you about Crodane," he said, "How he was my mother's seneschal before she died?"

"I remember."

"I didn't tell you about how she died…or anything else," he said, "They don't speak of it at the castle."

"You don't have to tell me."

"No, I...I want to, if you'd listen," he sighed, and his voice suddenly seemed thick, heavy, "Brigid, I...you're the only one I want to talk to...about...well..." he paused, "I've really appreciated you being here and all the help you've given me—about how to do...any of this."

"Of course," she smiled, "That's what friends do."

"Yes, but..." he paused, "It's been...well, I really like you being here. I really like...you."

That caught her breath altogether, so much so that for some reason she almost felt afraid. Her legs felt wobbly and when she remembered suddenly that they were in the crowded marketplace, she worried she might fall. *What is wrong with me?* Her hand slipped down his arm to take his. "Let's go back to the castle," she said, "We can sit in the solar and you can tell me the rest of the story there."

"It's a long story."

"No matter. We'll play some chess and you can tell me," she smiled, "You can tell me of your mother and Crodane and anything else you want. You can tell me about your dreams too."

"It's all one really," he said softly, "The story, the dreams. It's all the same."

Brigid bit her lip and she lifted his hand in both of hers and gave it a gentle squeeze. "Come on," she whispered, "You can tell me everything, and I'm certain there are things I can tell you too."

CHAPTER 19: MARCHING ORDERS

Loremaster Sabrun, it soon became apparent, was one of the most prolific writers ever to bear his title. Whether it was the result of the man's natural verbosity or the fact that he seemed to have been provided with such significant history to record, Royne was uncertain, but not since the Siege of Three had any individual Guardian (or Guardians) seemed to disrupt the inner workings of the Order as much as its first woman, and Royne was astounded that such an influential figure could have been so completely expunged from their history. For never once in all of his reading, in all of the books, in all the corners of the Loremaster's Tower, had he ever come across the name of Amarthia the Bard mentioned anywhere—ever. Such a degree of thoroughness suggested (or more likely required) a certain depth of hatred, and more and more, Royne found himself wondering just what she had done to draw such deep and seething ire.

In the second year of her tenure as the Bard, Amarthia was admitted, or rather, invited, to sit in as a witness upon the workings of the Council of Five. Technically, she was not a member; however, upon the personal request of the King, she was permitted to attend meetings, speak her mind, and to propose, question, and repudiate the comments of the five Councilors.

The Hierophant, it was clear, found her presence alone to be an insult and a threat to the traditions of the Order. Regularly, Sabrun's reflections upon council meetings reported the holy patriarch's attempts to have her removed. He rarely expressed his desire in such explicit terms though, choosing to speak around the subject in ways that were inclusive in language but exclusive in meaning. In all likelihood, these vague musings contributed to the Council's refusal to exclude her—that, and the fact that King Erolan was clearly so enamored with her.

Truly, Amarthia's beauty must have been spellbinding, for even a bookish man devoted to learning like Loremaster Sabrun was not entirely immune to her charms, as seemed evident by his description.

Her dark, wavy hair shone like a midnight sea, and her eyes blazed with the heat of a summer bonfire.

Her complexion, smooth and flawless, was the color of caramel sweets, and where she walked, one sensed the delightful odor of oranges and cloves.

Her figure was slender as an hourglass, with an ample bodice that she accentuated with exiguous garments of purple and scarlet silk.

It was unclear exactly what realm it was that she hailed from, as she was well versed in the manners and colloquialisms of all, but this ambiguity only added to her mystique granting her the appearance of both the familiar and the exotic.

In addition to the common tongue of Termain, she was fluent in Wrathorn, Sorgund Trade Speech, Kordish, and Tulondis, and could easily translate one into another in either speech or song.

Yet most enticing of all was the sound of her voice—sonorous, smooth, and full of mystery, There was, according to Sabrun, a certain hypnotic quality to it, a magic even that took the Order by storm. For, on the occasions when she would shut her eyes and break into a melancholic ballad or recite the heroic deeds of those Guardians long gone, even the Hierophant could not keep the tears from welling in his eyes such was the power of Amarthia the Bard.

What rubbish! Royne remarked, shaking his head, *Such poetic trash. How many men have been brought to ruin through the ages for the want of a pretty face?* He slipped *The Book of Histories* back into his satchel and sighed. "Conor!" he called, "Where are you, boy?"

The young steward passed through the flap of the tent and offered a salute, "Yes, sir!"

"Help me with this, would you?" he said, clumsily attempting to fasten the wolf's head brooch to the shoulder of his green half-cape. Following the battle at Villa Bruton, the general had issued Royne a new set of clothing, and though reluctant to give up his old habit, it was not a garment very well suited for the heat of the Grantisi summer. Plus, clad as he was now in the trousers, linen shirt, and tunic of a legion officer (complete with the cape and brooch), the larger mass of common soldiers seemed to regard him with more respect than they had before, at least marginally.

And why should they not? he asked himself, *For were it not for me, there's plenty among them who would still be working the Bruton fields.*

When Conor had succeeded in fastening the brooch, Royne offered him a nod of thanks, and passed through the tent to the outside. Spreading before him like a sea of tiny white hills, were the tents of General Navarro's army, a force that—after the surprise attack on St. Aiden's Day—continued to grow as word spread that the Grey Wolf and his pack were once more on the prowl.

Now, a fortnight later, they numbered just over two thousand men, a sizable command, though one that became increasingly harder to conceal from enemy eyes. As a result, many of the soldiers were beginning to wonder when the Fighting Fifth would cease sneaking about and declare themselves in earnest and attempt once again to face the Guardians in the open field.

To Royne, however, such suggestions—though well-meaning—were still laughable. *One would think getting beaten so badly the first time around would have taught them a lesson,* he sighed, *At Bruton we were lucky enough to catch the Plow unawares; had we met him properly, we would not have been so lucky.*

Soldiers, however, were soldiers, and without a war, they were about as useful as an anvil without a hammer. This was particularly true in Grantis where the soldiers of the legions constituted an entire social class. What else would they do—what else *could* they do? At Bruton they had been forced to help take in the harvest, but not one of them knew how to make plants grow (and from what the villagers had told Royne, the Plow had a difficult time as it was trying to train the prisoners as simple laborers). Thus, Royne knew that if he wished to succeed in convincing General Navarro *not* to listen to his instincts as a soldier—*not* to seek open war—he was going to have his work cut out for him.

Still, in no way did Royne consider the Gray Wolf to be a fool, for in truth, he had come to like and respect the man and to understand just why it was that so many others had stayed by his side in spite of the senate's surrender.

Royne had not participated in the actual battle himself; instead, he and Conor had maintained a position in the rear within one of the legion's supply wagons. He had, however, been close enough to observe the general in the act of command, directing his soldiers through messengers and intermediaries, trumpet fanfares and drum cadences. Not a single enemy soldier drew close enough to engage the general and his honor guard in melee, though this was not the result of any fear or cowardice on the part of the Gray Wolf, but rather the result of a brilliant strategy.

While Captain Velius led the mangonels and the light horse in their feigned assault upon the castle, General Navarro and the remainder of the infantry marched upon the granaries and the guarded compounds where the prisoners were held. In spite of their weakened condition—half-starved and ill from drinking dirty water—the legionnaires exhibited the ready discipline for which they had been famous as they marched in groups, shoulder to shoulder with shields at the ready, like great iron tortoises advancing slowly across the fields. Occasionally a man might fall, cut down by an arrow that had somehow been lucky enough to slip through; however, rather than break, the line of shields would simply close around him and another man would step up to assume his place. All the while, Navarro sat benignly upon his horse, impassively watching the battle unfold and issuing instructions whenever necessary. Even when a sudden, desperate counterassault by the kingsman soldiers-turned-gaolers nearly routed the Grantisi left flank, the general remained calm and, to Royne's surprise, rode personally to the point of the breach and through sheer force of will, recalled the men to order so they might turn aside the enemy attack.

"It's not birth but worth that leads the pack," Royne had heard the legionnaires say, and if such was the case, then a man like Navarro was worth his weight in gold.

Outside of the general's tent, the guards on duty offered the young Loremaster a nod, and since the flaps of the pavilion had been drawn back to allow the breeze to pass through, it was but a moment later that the general noticed his approach.

"Ah, Master Royne," Navarro said, "Welcome."

"Good afternoon, sir," Royne said, "I hope all is well."

"Very well," the general said. He paused to scratch out something onto a roll of parchment before passing it off to his valet, "See this gets to Callum, will you Petran?"

"Aye sir," the young man nodded, and with a salute hurried from the tent.

"Umbrio Callum and five hundred men of the Seventh Legion have sent word that they wish to join us," Navarro observed once the valet had gone, "And they are but the most recent addition. Between the men of the First liberated at Bruton and the wandering droves of soldiers cut loose from the Second, Third, and Sixth when they disbanded, that brings our full complement up to…"

"Two thousand men," Royne said simply, "Rather, twenty-five hundred with these new men of the Seventh."

"A sizable pack."

"And one not likely to be ignored for very much longer."

"No," the general conceded, "Though in truth we have never been completely outside of our enemies' notice—even before the battle at Bruton."

"You mean the Guardians know where we are?"

"Of course they do."

"Then why have they not attacked already? It seems uncharacteristically foolish of them to simply allow us to survive—to thrive even."

"True, but whether by chance or by providence, the Order has had much more to occupy its attentions than us."

"Such as?"

"Maintaining control in the cities for one, the coming harvest for another, installing the new viceroy…the list goes on," he shrugged, "The Guardian generals may be fine warriors and gifted leaders, but, like all soldiers, they appear rather ill-suited for peace. This Lord Pryce must be some kind of fool."

"Pryce?" he exclaimed, "The viceroy's name is Pryce?"

"So it is," Navarro said, "And he's tasked the Guardian generals—the Hart, the Stone, and the Spur, I believe they are called—with patrolling the cities and towns under martial law."

220

Royne nearly laughed aloud. *Like father like son*, he grinned bitterly, *What fools!* "I believe I am beginning to understand our good fortune. The generals you mentioned are all justiciars of the Warlord. They're used to commanding armies, not common men. Such tasks are normally meant for the men of the Chancellor's Tower—commissioners, courtiers, and the like."

"From what I understand, many of those men have been sent to Dwerin to maintain the mines, while the others—constables and such—have been tasked with bringing certain fugitives to justice."

"Constables?"

"Yes," Navarro said, raising his eyebrows, "It appears that a certain relic of great import was stolen sometime last year—a book, by all accounts, a record of the history of the Order since its founding."

Royne attempted in vain to mask his sudden anxiety. *I was a fool not to anticipate this*, he thought, *Thank the Brethren for the bloody Wayfolk.* "Tell me, General," he asked after a moment, "How is it that you know this?"

"Captain Velius caught a man—one of the new arrivals—trying to sneak off in the night."

"You mean a spy."

"Yes," The general said, "And not the first, mind you, simply another. I'm afraid it's an occupational hazard when gathering such a large body of men. A sheep in wolf's clothing, you might say."

"So what did this man have to say?"

"As I told you, a book was stolen and the constables were tasked with finding the thief and bringing him back."

"Surely the man was not a constable himself?"

"No, simply in their employ. His task was to fall in with us and keep his eyes and ears open for anything of note."

"I see," Royne said. He breathed a heavy sigh, "In any case, a man cannot be a thief for taking something that is rightfully his."

"It matters little to me one way or the other," the Gray Wolf shrugged, "If it confounds our enemies, then I count it as good fortune. In any case, while our spy meant to gather information on us for his masters, he also happened to yield some rather interesting details relating to them."

"Such as?"

General Navarro motioned toward the entrance of the tent and together he and Royne passed outside. At once, the two guards on duty fell into step behind them as they continued to walk through the beaten path that traversed the camp. Men everywhere paused in whatever they were doing to salute their general, sometimes adding hearty cries of "For the Fifth!"

"As you commented, Master Royne," Navarro began again, "We are no longer small enough to escape our enemy's notice, and as such, I find that soon we will have no choice but to seek shelter in a stronghold of our own."

A shadow fell across Royne's features, "Do you really think us ready?"

"Ready or not," the general said, "We have few alternatives. We cannot run and hide forever—not with such a large force."

Royne halted and folded his arms across his chest. "General," he said, "I do not doubt your mettle or that of your men, but I must admit that I have significant misgivings about any attempt to mount a major offensive against the Guardians. Even as we grow in size, we are significantly outnumbered, for not only do we face the Order and the kingsmen, but also the knights and soldiers sworn to the Andochan nobles and their Dwerin allies."

"And the horsemen of Montevale as well," the General said.

"Montevale has joined with Kredor too?"

"So I hear."

Blast! Royne bit his lip. He recalled the conversation at the first and final meeting of the Council of Five that he attended as Rastis's Steward. With the fall of Grantis and the alliance with Montevale, Kredor now had the support of every major realm across Termain save one.

"What of the Brock?" he asked, "Have you any idea where the barons stand?"

"No," Navarro said simply, "Though our scouts have noted that any of the kingsmen not in the cities have been mustering in the ports and appear to make ready to set sail. Many of the Andochan war galleys have already departed for the north and it seems that the Dwerin fleet is meant to follow. Where else could they be going, then, but the Brock?"

"Wrathorn?"

"The Wrathorn are too savage to pose any serious threat," he said, "They may raid and pillage from time to time, but they're no proper realm. They're disorganized tribals—excellent warriors, mind you—but they lack the virtues of an enlightened society." The General shook his head, "No, I'm afraid the Brock is next."

Royne fell silent and stroked his chin. He knew that what the general said was true; he had only suggested Wrathorn out of vanity, for he did not want to admit the extent of Kredor's successes, to acknowledge just how close the Guardian-King stood to achieving an empire and victory.

Still, the fact that the Guardians and their allies had turned their attentions to Baronbrock in such a warlike manner suggested at least one glimmer of hope: Kredor's attempt to coerce Arcis Galadin into supporting him must have failed. *Which means Lughus must have made it!* Royne thought, squaring his jaw, *He must still be free!*

"General," the young Loremaster said, his blood suddenly growing hot, "I believe now is the time to act!"

"It seems for once we're in agreement then!"

Royne turned to see Captain Velius stride up, a squad of other men behind him. "General, sir," Velius said, "Our friends are quite secure and stand ready to march on the morrow."

"Very good, Denaron," the general said, "See that the men are ready."

"Aye, sir."

Royne's brow knit with consternation. "What do you mean?" he asked, "March where?"

Captain Velius made to speak, but at a look from the general, fell silent.

"See it done, Captain," Navarro said again.

"Yes, sir." With a final nod, Velius saluted and led his men off toward the camp to see to their duties.

Royne glanced around at his surroundings. Somehow over the course of their conversation, he had failed to notice that the general had led him to the far side of the encampment to the woodland area where the army collected water from a small stream. Royne peered into the mishmash of trees and shrubbery aware suddenly that it was from there that the captain and his followers had emerged.

"What is this?" he asked with a touch of annoyance, "Why have you brought me here? And what is this march the captain spoke of?"

The general clasped his hands behind his back and with a slight smile nodded toward the woodlands. "Come," he said.

Royne pursed his lips. His mind was already saturated with half-formed thoughts and stratagems that required further analysis. In the matter of a moment, his focus had shifted beyond Grantis, beyond the plight of a single realm. "General," he said, "We must talk."

"We are talking," the Gray Wolf said, "And we will further, but first, there is something that I thought you would like to see."

"What is it?"

"A show of good faith from General Callum and the Seventh," he said, "Something that very well might help us to find our feet when we inevitably face the Guardians in the open field."

With a sigh, Royne finally nodded, "Yes, sir."

Without another word, General Navarro led the way into the woodlands, following the stream in the direction of its source. Royne stepped carefully, mindful of stray roots and stones. The last thing he needed was to fall. He could only imagine the jibing he would receive once the two men of the general's guard passed on word of such a thing to the jeering captain. However, a sudden noise from the wilderness ahead nearly sent him diving for cover as in a flash of memory he recalled Kredor's hunt and the charging boar.

"Fire and death!" he cried aloud, ignoring the guardsmen's sniggering, "What was that?"

Even General Navarro was smiling. "Have a look," he said.

With some hesitation, Royne hurried to the general's side and together they walked the remaining distance along the stream to a wide clearing surrounded by great, swaying willows. There, watched over by a cadre of grooms, a dozen hulking shapes stood like ancient burial mounds of long-forgotten kings.

"War elephants!" Royne gasped.

"The hallmark of the Second Legion," the general said, "And all that remains of their number I'm afraid after the Second and the Seventh were defeated at Lindonwood."

One of the great beasts slowly lumbered nearer, idly flicking at a flowering shrub with its long, serpentine trunk. Royne thought back to his studies in the tower. Elephants roamed the wilds of the Kordish continent and were often trained for a variety of purposes, for they were significantly stronger than oxen or other beasts of burden and considered significantly more intelligent as well. In war, they were often fitted with large wooden towers and manned by squads of archers to serve as mobile fortresses. When enraged, they were more than capable of causing widespread destruction on their own, impaling enemy soldiers upon their great ivory tusks or trampling them underfoot. *No wonder the captain was so excited*, Royne thought, recognizing even in himself a certain desire born from curiosity to see the beasts in action.

General Navarro strode forward to the nearest elephant and with a nod to one of the Kordish handlers, gently petted the creature's leathery skin. "They will make a world of difference when we attempt to retake the castle at Hedgeford."

"Hedgeford?" Royne started. Suddenly the elephants were but another distraction, another piece on the chessboard. His mind reviewed the geography of Grantis. "You cannot tell me that you intend to try for Lindonwood as well?" he asked, "Surely the Guardians are too strong. A moment ago you mentioned the defeat of both the Second *and* the Seventh. How can you possibly hope to win with but a remnant of the Fifth?"

"The Second and the Seventh faced the full forces of both the Guardian justiciar called the Stone and the armies of Dwerin led by Padraig Reid," Navarro said, "Since then, however, Lord Reid has withdrawn to the Spade while the Stone struggles to keep order in the city. If we take Hedgeford, we will have a fortress of our own from which to begin a concerted attack upon Lindonwood as well as a rallying point for any other men who wish to join us. According to General Callum, there is also a significantly active insurgency that would be more than willing to provide us with support against the Stone when we finally attempt to liberate the city."

Royne folded his arms across his chest. "General, even without the Ironmen, the kingsmen with the Stone cannot be less than ten thousand strong," he said, "And that does not even include the men of the Order, the officers—partisans, cavaliers, and more, some of whom are sure to be of the Anointed." He shook his head, "We were lucky to have caught the Plow by surprise, but to face a justiciar like the Stone? For thirteen hundred years their titles have brought nothing but honor and glory for the Order. They are not to be taken lightly. If you attack them in the open, you will force them to meet you in the field—worse, they might even ride forth to meet you, to hunt you down one by one!"

"Which is why we need a fortress. Which is why we need Hedgeford."

"No, sir," Royne said, "For, even if you should succeed in taking it, what might seem your fortress would soon be under siege. In that case, it would become your prison."

The general's eyes flashed, "Then what do you suggest, Loremaster?"

Royne took a deep breath. "The Brock."

Navarro's gaze narrowed. "What of it?"

Slowly, Royne paused to choose his words carefully. "General, no one can doubt the courage, the honor, or the loyalty of you or your men," he began, "Yet, we must all accept the fact that Grantis is lost and has been for some time."

"There are over two thousand men encamped in the field who would disagree with you."

"I imagine so," Royne said, "And I do not doubt that each man among them would willingly give his life to free his land from Kredor's tyranny. However, at the end of the day, they would still be dead and Grantis still under occupation."

The general gave the elephant one final pat on the flank and clasping his hands behind his back, glanced down at the matted grass underfoot. "And the Brock?" he asked.

"If what your scouts report is true," the young Loremaster continued, "If the Brock is next, they will need all the help they can get. Were you and your men to join them, to offer them your aid, they would be duty-bound to help you in return."

"And just how do you suggest we offer the barons our aid?"

"Go to them."

"Shall we grow wings, or would you prefer that we swim?"

Royne's cheeks reddened with a mixture of embarrassment and irritation. "I'm sure the Gray Wolf can find a way."

"Are you?" General Navarro said coldly, "Strange that you should be so certain of my abilities when with the very same breath you deny them."

"I'm sorry?"

"You ask me to abandon my land, my home, my people to help the Brock?"

"Not to abandon," Royne said, "To retreat. To withdraw so as to return and fight another day—with allies, with friends."

"Yes, and the barons were certainly so willing to help us in our time of need."

"Then surely they will see from your example that now more than ever is a time to band together."

"And in the meantime, we abandon Grantis to Lord Pryce and King Kredor!"

"King Kredor already controls Grantis," Royne said, "You cannot abandon what is no longer yours. It belongs to the Guardians now."

"Then we take it back!"

"You can't!" Royne snapped, "At least not alone, else you would have done so already."

At once, the general's face grew dark with fury and the veins in his temples stood out like great snakes. He whirled on the young Loremaster in rage, yet rather than shout his voice fell to a harsh whisper.

"Blackguard or Guardian, you Andochans are all the same," he said, "You all seem to believe it your divine right to direct the affairs of others as if we were all merely puppets dangling on strings. Let me remind you, boy, that this is Grantis. This is my home, this is my army, and these men take their orders from me."

"General, this war is bigger than just one realm," Royne replied, "It affects the entire continent. If we do not stand together, then rest assured, we will all fall."

"That remains to be seen," Navarro said, "Yet of one thing you can be certain. We march at dawn."

CHAPTER 20: THE SHACKLE

It was another day and a half before Horn and Wendell arrived at Woodshire, though when they did, it was at the head of a small force of thirty-one light cavalry skirmishers. Adding this to the dozen men who had arrived on the first day with Armel, Welmsey, and Briden, as well as another score or so of wanderers who had arrived from the surrounding areas (some of whom, oddly enough, were actually men-at-arms from other lords tasked with capturing the Silent Prince), and Bel suddenly found himself in command of a rather sizable company of men. As such, he knew that they must depart immediately lest Woodshire and the Wherlings become targets of Dermont's retribution for harboring fugitives. So it was that on the following morning, less than two weeks since Bel's son had been born, the Tower and his men set out for the ruins of Feyhold in the White Wood from which they hoped to mount an insurrection against Lord Jarrett Harren.

For five days, they rode eastward though the vales and rolling hills just south of where, for a hundred years, the imaginary Bloodline had separated friend from foe. Now, however, as Bel glanced behind him to see Sir Armel talking with Sir Emory about old battles, or Horn the Half-Wrathorn with his shorn scalp good-naturedly poking fun at Sir Welmsey's flaxen locks, he saw the potential that existed for a truly united Montevalen people. *One land, one blood,* he thought, *No more lines.*

It was not merely the camaraderie among the men of his command that helped Bel to shake off the burden of despair, but to be back in the saddle upon such a fine horse as Tempest did wonders to ease his heart. The horse and the rider are one, King Cedric used to say. They must be in order to survive the dangers of battle. Yet, such a bond often took years to form under the best of circumstances. Therefore, Bel was absolutely amazed to find that he and Tempest took to each other almost at once. As they rode together in the column or on occasion sojourns ahead to scout the forward paths, it seemed as if the great searoan could anticipate Bel's directions by only the slightest shift in his weight. Furthermore, Tempest responded to verbal commands better than any horse Bel had ever known, and he quickly learned that the legendary intelligence of the searoans was not a mere Bard's tale, but truth; they really were as wise as men.

It was truly amazing, and anytime he found himself speaking aloud to the horse (a habit common to most riders), Tempest seemed not only to understand, but in his own particular way, to respond. There was a comfort in that sort of empathy, and before long, the Silent Prince found himself becoming rather garrulous whenever he and Tempest were alone.

With everything that had happened and all of the suffering of the past weeks and months, Bel's mind struggled to make sense of the sudden drastic changes in his day-to-day life. From the great void left by those he lost to the burgeoning rebellion to the beauties, responsibilities, and uncertainties of fatherhood, Bel often felt like a drowning man. As could be expected from the Silent Prince, he found it hard to put his thoughts into words, much less to share them. Being left to ruminate within the chaos of his own mind was enough to drive him mad. Whether unburdening himself to Tempest was further proof of this descent, he could not say, but whenever he saw himself reflected in the searoan's wise and compassionate eyes, he could at least feel that he had a rock to cling to in this raging sea of storms.

Of course, beyond these rather mythical or even legendary qualities of the searoans, even when viewed strictly as a horse, Tempest was nothing short of remarkable. Not only was he strong and surefooted, but he was *fast*—very, very fast, particularly since, as low as they were on equipment and supplies, Bel wore no armor other than a light chain byrnie offered up by Sir Norton upon their departure. Never before had Bel ridden as such speeds—on Igno, on Banshee, or any other horse, and after his first experience of setting Tempest through his paces, his hair whipped back and his eyes watering from the force of the wind, he could not imagine a horse more aptly named.

"I will always love Igno, and may he forgive me for saying this, but I have never seen a finer horse than Tempest," Bel observed one evening as the growing band of horsemen stopped to camp. There was no need to stake the searoan so after removing Tempest's saddle, Bel left him to wander at will without fear. Curiously enough, such was the effect of the great horse lord's presence upon the rest of the riders' mounts that few of them needed to be staked either. It was as if the other horses somehow sensed instinctively the strength of the searoan's presence and instantly deferred to his leadership. Bel had seen this with Banshee at Ironshod, but he still found it remarkable, particularly when observed en masse. "Maybe there is something to the legends about them being gifts of the gods," the Silent Prince added. He sat down in a canvas folding chair, cradling his son.

Beside him, tending to the campfire, Princess Marina smiled and offered him a piece of bread. "In fairness to your Igno," she said as Bel shifted Marcus to his other arm and accepted the food, "A searoan is hardly a normal horse."

"True," he took a bite and gently slipped his finger within the baby's tiny hand. Marcus shifted quietly in Bel's arm and Bel held him closer to his chest. The Prince smiled. "How has he been?" he asked, "In the wagon, that is? I meant to ask Elsa, but after the long day's ride, I try to give her as much relief as possible once we make camp. Has he fussed much?"

"Not that I've noticed," the princess said kindly, "He sleeps most of the time, which, as I understand it, is quite normal."

"You know I meant Marcus, right?" Bel asked, nodding toward King Cedric. Seated upright upon his stool, the old king had fallen asleep with his smoldering pipe hanging precariously from his mouth.

"That's not nice," Marina smirked, "And I like your father. He's very kind."

"He is, and he always has been. Even in the midst of the war. But, I still worry about him," Bel said, "I'm not sure how much he understands about everything that is happening."

"I don't know," the princess said, "He did bring your spear, though, if you recall. So maybe he knows more than you think?"

"True." Were it not for King Cedric, Spire would remain back at Tremontane with the rest of their armor, weapons, and gear, including Bel's beloved saddle with its famous bells. *But does he know that I make war against by brother, his own son?* Bel shook his head, pushing those thoughts from his mind. "How is your father?" he asked, changing the subject, "How is he adjusting to all of...this?"

"I suppose he's fine," Marina replied, "Though I think he feels somewhat...lost, for lack of a better word. Still, he is glad to have Armel and Welmsey nearby to remind him of who he once was."

Bel watched King Marius pacing back and forth beside the knights she had just named. He remembered once again the old man's comments about ghosts without graves. "I wish there was a place you could all be safe so as not to have you all following behind us like this," he said, pressing his lips lightly to Marcus's head, "It can't be good for any of you. Perhaps when we reach this Feyhold."

"It's no matter," Marina shrugged, "To be honest, I rather like it. It's strange, but there's a certain excitement to it, like our days traveling along the Firrinies, but also...different. I don't know exactly why, but it is, or at least it feels that way. Perhaps it's knowing that all these men who were once enemies, have come together as friends, to heal the myriad wounds that for so long have plagued this land and to finally try to put things right."

"One plague in particular."

She blushed. "I'm sorry. It was a poor choice of words."

"No," Bel said, "You're right." He breathed a heavy sigh. "And speaking of Dermont, you should know that in spite of whatever it is that he or the Grand Hierophant or even King Kredor himself might have said, as...as the Tower, and with this whole nonsense of my being named your...your guardian, I want you to know that no matter the cost, I would never grant them any consent for marriage without your approval. Quite frankly, I think the whole notion of guardianship is absurd. As far as I'm concerned, you choose whomever you like. It was only a political diversion to ensure that Dermont couldn't force you—"

"Would you like me to hold Marcus while you eat?" she interrupted with a wan smile, "I'm finished."

Bel paused and glanced over at the campfire, anywhere to avoid looking at her. It was for reasons such as this that he had shunned her throughout all their time at Tremontane, for she was so kind and so beautiful that to see her cast adrift, alone, displaced, stuck with two old men and a man who had rejected her, tore at him with guilt. Since she had awoken him after their escape, he had often felt a sense of comfort in her presence, a solace while he mourned for all and everyone that had been lost. Yet, at the same time, such thoughts also made him feel worse, as if it were a betrayal of his love for Lilia and a disgrace to her memory.

"Thank you," he said at last, and gently passed the baby over into the princess's arms.

"Of course," she nodded, "Eat."

Bel helped himself to more food and returned to his seat by the fire, watching Marina idly rock Marcus at the edge of the firelight. He could just hear the sound of her soft humming and, again, he felt some of the weight in his chest ease. The guilt, of course, remained, heightened by the unconscious pleasure he felt at witnessing the benign tableau.

It brought to mind Lilia's chiding at his refusal to introduce them, and her scornful reprimands that he had not accepted Marina's offer and forsaken her. *You fool! You could have ended the war!* she had said, and though Bel did not believe that it was true, then or now, things might have gone differently. Marcus Harding could still be alive, Marius still a real king, Dermont might still command Valendia, but with Bel at his side, perhaps there could be some check to his ambition...

What madness! He thought, tearing savagely at his bread. He dipped the ragged chunk into his wine, swallowed hard, and nearly choked. No, Dermont was Dermont and always had been. Nothing, no one could have changed that. *Aiden's Flame! How could I have been so blind?*

Abruptly, he left his food and leapt to his feet and strode over to the princess. "I have some things to see to," he said suddenly, ignoring her sudden look of concern, "Would you...would you mind holding Marcus until Elsa returns?"

"I...don't mind," Marina said, "Is something wrong?

"I don't want to burden you," he said, "And I don't want to just pass him off. That's not the type of father that I want to be, but..."

"You're not," she paused, "Prince Bel, are you alright?"

Bel took a deep breath. "I'm fine," he said, "And I'm...sorry. I'm just..." he shook his head, "Anyway, you don't have to call me prince, especially since I no longer bear that title. In fact, you really never needed to call me that..."

"Al—alright," she said.

"I'm sorry," he said again, and leaving her, retrieved the Tower's Spire from among his things and went off alone to train.

For the remainder of the journey, Bel kept his distance from the carriage and the princess. He visited Marcus at odd hours, though told Elsa that Marina was more than welcome to spend time with the baby or help her in seeing to his care. If she wanted to. Or not. It was up to her.

Along the way, they passed through a few small farms and villages, and as Sir Emory, Horn, Wendell, and Sir Armel rode out on occasion to speak to the local guards, peasants, and veterans that had only a year ago returned home, their forces continued to grow.

A handful of men-at-arms and archers who had been with the Tower in the Nivanus had followed after them from Woodshire. For a time they had stayed with Sir Cardolan, another of the Tower's Guard, until Dermont had him executed for his refusal to bend his knee or relinquish his lands. Welmsey took Cardolan's death hard, for they had been friends.

However, Cardolan alone was not the only man to be mourned. Another cadre of veterans of Bel's light cavalry arrived shortly after, bringing with them some of their friends. Originally, they were led by Bel's man Rallo, though unfortunately he too had been killed when they ran into trouble on the road south of Roanshead.

Finally, the evening before reaching the White Wood, another of the light cavalry, a girl named Sparrow, who would sometimes scout in tandem with Lilia, arrived at the head of a group of other women warriors, cut loose when Dermont reintroduced the ban on female soldiers. On their way to meet Bel's forces, the women had taken a caravan headed out of Pridel full of soldiers' gear and stores meant for the army at the Nivanus. They were a welcome addition indeed.

Thus, by the time they reached the eaves of the White Wood on the morning after the Feast of St. Aiden, there were well over two hundred fighting men and women who followed behind Bel in the column, and though it was not a sizable army, morale was high and they were united by their steadfast belief that standing against the Plague King, they were on the side of righteousness.

Nearly a year ago, the Tower had routed Dermont's army in the Battle of the White Wood, and returning there now brought with it a chilling sense of discomfort for Bel. At the time, it was thought that White Wood would be the final nail in the coffin for Gasparn, and an end to the century of war. As he gazed out across the valley where nine thousand common men had died when Dermont abandoned them, Bel wondered how many of their restless spirits would be observed, wandering the killing field and the darkness of the forest at night.

With those thoughts in mind, White Wood now seemed an eerie place, and where once Bel had found the gleaming white trunks of the birch trees so beautiful, they now seemed like enormous bones rising grotesquely from a charnel yard. His memories of Lilia on the morning of the battle did little to calm his nerves either, and from time to time, he could not help but feel as if she were with him, a specter riding alongside him upon Banshee's midnight shade.

Yet, it was not the prospect of any ghostly presence that he feared, for there was, if anything, comfort in that companionship, despite it being from beyond the grave. Rather, it was Bel's fear that all those who now followed behind him would soon join her and all of the others that had met their doom following in his wake.

"Are you alright, my lord?" said a voice, and when Bel turned he noticed Briden upon his mare, Magpie, riding just behind him and to the right.

"It's strange being back here," he replied, "So many dead in but a matter of an hour."

"Not so many of ours, though, sir," the youth said, "At least ours among the light cavalry, I mean."

Bel sighed, "True."

A rider suddenly approached them from ahead, and for a fleeting moment, Bel could have sworn it was Lilia's ghost, outfitted and hungry for war; however, it was only the girl Sparrow, clad in boiled leathers with her hair twisted into a tangle of little braids. "We're coming up on the ruin now, my lord," she said, "It's just through the path up there."

"Very well," he said after a pause.

She nodded and bit her lip, eying him, "You should look through the spoils of the wagons we took. I'm certain there's better armor in there than that rusty hauberk—at least something more fitting for you. Some of the girls I came in with might…might also be able to help you with a shave, perhaps trim up your hair—if it please you, of course."

"Perhaps once we get settled," Bel said with a shrug, "Thank you."

"Aye, sir," she said, exchanging a quick glance with Briden, "Whatever you be needing, sir."

Sparrow fell in alongside Briden, and with a pat to Tempest's flank, Bel urged the great stallion onward, leading his people along the path to the ruins.

From the look of it, Feyhold had once been a mighty stronghold set deep within the forest alongside a rocky outcrop. Like many of the forts built in what would have been considered the wild frontier in the days of Old Calendral, the fortress was constructed in such a way as to make use of the natural features of the landscape until manmade fortifications could be built by imperial slaves or, in the case of the Warlock, prisoners of war. Centuries of abandonment and disrepair coupled with encroachment from the forest had toppled portions of the walls and rendered the small quadrangular keep little more than a large, irregular sheepfold built by the hands of some long departed giant. Great swaths of moss and lichen covered everything, and blankets of ivy clung like raggedy beards to the highest portion of the keep's ruined walls. A murder of crows picked among the old stones for whatever tiny creatures might call the place their home, their cackling calls echoing off of the stones. Still, Bel thought, as he rode through the broken gates into the overgrown interior of the courtyard, for a ragtag group such as theirs, it would do.

"What a place," Sir Armel observed, riding up behind him. He removed his great helm and set it before him on his saddle. "Are those caves?" he said, pointing along the outcrop, "If they're dry, they would at least provide some shelter for the kings and the princess while we stretch canvas or oilcloth over the keep yonder for a roof.

"Aye," Welmsey said, "Though I don't relish exploring them. They look like a breeding ground for bears…or worse."

"What could be worse than a bear?" Sparrow asked.

"Plenty," Welmsey said, "This place was once home to men of the Warlock. We're liable to find all manner of demon or ghost."

"Bollocks," Armel scoffed, "Come now, Welmsey. Show some backbone."

"Laugh if you like," Welmsey said, "But as much death as this place had seen in recent times what with the battle last year and all, I'd not be surprised—and that's saying nothing about whatever in the Abyss it was the Dibhorites did here long ago."

Sparrow's face grew pale and drawn, and from behind him, Bel heard Briden shift awkwardly in his saddle. "Jarvy said the Guardians cleared it out more than a thousand years ago," he said, "I doubt they'd have left any evil behind."

"So we're trusting the Guardians now?" Sparrow asked, "Perhaps King Kredor might be willing to have a look around for us, tell us if it's safe to go in?"

"They weren't the same back then," Briden said, "They used to be good."

"Enough," Bel said. All this talk of ghosts and the Guardians was disquieting, for he had enough restless dead of his own to contend with. "We'll have a look around," he said, "But we'll be cautious, for there are plenty enough dangers in the forest without spirits—loose stones, beasts, bandits, and the Brethren only know what else could—"

Without warning, a trio of arrows flew from somewhere nearby and thumped into the ground at their feet. Briden's horse reared in alarm, and Sir Welmsey, weighed down by his heavy armor, nearly fell from his saddle when he spun around in alarm. Only Tempest remained unperturbed in the face of the sudden danger and the cacophony of strange cries echoing about the old stones of the ruin set the crows to flight. Bel tightened his grip on Spire and held it before him at the ready.

"Who disturbs the dead of Feyhold?" a hollow voice resounded.

"I told you!" Welmsey whispered harshly at Sir Armel, "I told you!"

"Shut up, Welmsey!"

"Silence!" Bel ordered, scanning the keep and the slopes of the rocky crag. *The sun is out,* he thought, *What ghost walks in the light of day?*

"Look there, sir," Briden pointed where upon the outcrop a figure appeared cloaked and cowled all in black; however, among the white tree trunks there were signs of other figures moving and it was from there that Bel expected the arrows had come. *And most likely there are others trained on us even now...*

"Warlock's balls!" Sparrow hissed, "It's a ghost."

Bel shook his head. "Ghosts do not have feet," he whispered. He nudged Tempest forward a pace and with one hand still gripping Spire's haft, he raised his other, empty hand.

"Pardon the intrusion, sir," he shouted, "We mean no harm."

"I find that difficult to believe," the cloaked figure returned, "Clad as you are for war."

Bel breathed a sigh, pausing only a moment to gauge his opponent. From what he could tell at a distance, the man—for he was certain it was a man—was not overly tall, though his posture seemed somewhat stooped or hunched, like one who lives life forever peering ahead. He did not appear to be heavily armed or armored, but from the width of his shoulders and the manner of his stance, he was extremely broad with a muscular build.

"You are correct," Bel said at last, "And more than two hundred arrayed in like manner follow behind us. Yet we do not seek battle with you. We have enemies enough as it is and no desire to make any more."

Now it was the other man's turn to pause and weigh Bel's words—just as he had hoped. For whomever the cloaked man and his companions were, the implicit threat of two hundred soldiers could not be taken lightly.

"Who are you?" the man asked.

"My name is Beledain Tremont, known once by some as the Silent Prince, known now by others as the Tower."

"The Tower? You're a Guardian?"

"I am not," he said, "Or at least, I have sworn no Oath to Andoch. Rather, I find myself at odds with the Guardian-King, allied as he is with men who would hold this land in tyranny."

"And why have you come here?"

"To rest, and to hide—temporarily—while we plan and prepare to wage war in earnest, to set this land free and bring peace."

"Only a fool believes he can buy peace with war."

Behind him, Bel's men muttered at the insult, but he remained unphased. "Perhaps," he said, "But I have no other choice but to try."

The cowled figure shook his head and waved his hand, "We abide no fools in Feyhold. Now, be gone while you have the chance!"

Bel breathed a heavy sigh, "No."

The man stopped short as he turned to depart, "No?"

"We have come far too many miles to be turned away by vagrants or bandits or whatever it is you might be," he said, "Those that follow me do so by choice, by their own accord. Not by levees or for pay, but because they hope for a better realm, and a better world. I owe it to them to see this through, and I'll not have you stand in the way of that. So attack us if you must, but otherwise, stand clear."

The cowled man squared his shoulders, "We could kill you all right now as you stand."

"I sincerely doubt that," Bel said.

In a flash, the man threw back his cowl, nimbly leapt upon the craggy slope, and smoothly slid down to the broken courtyard. As Bel had suspected, he was a strong man, rippling with muscles. Beneath his cloak, he wore a sleeveless tunic pieced together from the tanned hides of various, indiscernible animals. His trousers were of like make, and his boots seemed little more than rough sandals wrapped up to his knees with strips of leather and fur. His face, though patchy and rough with whiskers, bore no beard, and no hair covered his head owing perhaps to a thickly knotted scar that ran the length of his scalp. His jaw was heavy and brutish, his nose flat and crooked, and in his massive hands, he carried the strangest implement of war Bel had ever seen. It was a long length of chain weighted on one end with a heavy iron ball while the other was attached to a sickle in the same manner as a farmer might use. As he held the odd armament at the ready, he scowled menacingly, "I could at least kill you!"

Behind their captain, Bel's men drew their weapons, but remembering the archers, he raised his hand. Tempest's body tightened like a bow string, ready to react at once. Bel patted the great searoan's shoulder. "Wait," he called to his followers before turning back to the forester.

"You know my name," he said, "Tell me. What is yours?"

The man's gaze remained steady. "Folks here call me the Shackle," he said after a pause.

"Another Guardian?"

"A Blackguard."

"I've heard of you, or at least, those that came before you."

"So you know that I'll not yield easily."

Bel nodded, "I know." With a deep breath, he slipped from Tempest's saddle and rested the butt end of Spire upon the ground. "I'd rather not have it come to this," he said, "But for the sake of my people, I can't just turn and go."

The man chewed his lip. "I understand something of that," he said.

"So, if I fight you," he said after a moment, "And I win, you agree to allow us usage of this place in our coming campaign. No harm will come to your people, and as long as they leave us unmolested, they are free to do as they please. However, if you win, my men will withdraw and leave you be forever. Will you agree?"

The Shackle nodded, "I suppose I must."

"So be it," Bel turned away and called to Briden. "Ride to Emory and the others in the column. Tell them what's happened." He tried not to think of Marcus or what might befall him if he fell. *Who would look after him?* he thought, *Who would raise him with both his parents in the grave?* Somehow he suspected he already knew the answer.

"Lord Tower," Sir Armel said. Above on the crag, a trio of archers clad in hide appeared and sat down to watch the duel, "This is all meaningless. Why do we not just brush them aside? They are surely few."

"So are we in Dermont's eyes," Bel said, "Though we expect him to take us seriously."

The older man nodded in concession, though his worries showed clearly in the lines of his face. "May the Brethren keep you," he said.

Bel gave a nod and patted Tempest gently on the flank. The great horse eyed him steadily before nuzzling him with his nose.

Across the courtyard, the Shackle removed his cloak and stretched his thick neck. "I've never faced another Guardian," he said.

"I have," Bel said with an ironic smirk, "He won." He planted his feet and readied his spear, "When you're ready…"

The Shackle gave a nod, and with a flick of his wrist, set the weight of the chain whirling in a wide arc.

Bel held still, poised and ready, though cautious as he watched how the Shackle moved and maneuvered his weapon. It was so unusual. In one sense, it was like a long flail, more than capable of catching around the haft of the spear to wrench it from his hands. However, the end with the sickle could easily act like any other blade, stabbing through his hauberk or slicing into his shoulder or leg. Used together, the chain-sickle could trip him up, tie his hands, or be thrown out to strike at him from reach.

"I've never seen a weapon like that before," Bel told him.

"Nor had I until it was given to me," the Shackle said, and in the blink of an eye, lashed out with the weighted end of the chain. As Bel made to dodge it, the Shackle lunged forward and followed through with the sickle in his other hand, forcing the prince to leap back and whirl the full length of the spear before him. It wasn't an effective attack, but it allowed him the safe distance he needed to defend himself.

Once he regained his footing, Bel took a step backward, lowered his grip along the haft of the lance, and jabbed forward lightly, baiting his opponent to attempt another strike. The Shackle held his attack.

"I've always thought the spear a foolish weapon to fight with afoot," he said, "Or a coward's. It keeps a man's enemies so far away."

Bel's kept his gaze level, "Not always." Quickly, he lunged forth, and anticipating the Shackle's dodge, brought the haft of the weapon around to catch his opponent under the arm. For a moment, it appeared the Shackle might fall, but he nimbly shifted his weight, whirled around with the sickle, and sliced through a length of mail rings on Bel's upper arm. Bel winced with pain, but leapt away before a strike from the weighted end of the chain could catch around his leg.

No more talking, he thought, touching the wound on his arm. It was not deep; the mail and the doublet beneath had reduced it to little more than a scratch, but it was still a misstep. His mind raced, watching the Shackle recover his weapon and reset his stance. If he did not think quickly, he was dead, Marcus would be an orphan, the princess and the kings would be at the mercy of Dermont, and all of the men and women who had only just sought him out would find it all for naught.

On and on they fought, the Shackle whirling his strange weapon and Bel dodging or turning aside blow after blow in a flurry of motion. It was strange. Apart from his recent practices, alone in the early hours before breaking camp, Bel had little experience with the lance or spear when not mounted. Somehow, however, he found Spire fit to his hand as if it had been crafted specifically for him. Each piercing thrust or whirl of the haft was as natural to him as breathing, and he could only imagine how formidable a warrior he might be when fighting in tandem with Tempest.

Yet, for all of his uncanny skill, he found his match in the Shackle with his strange weapon. The forester was a tornado of fury and more than once, Bel nearly found himself caught up in the storm.

Before long, Bel felt his strength beginning to ebb and he found himself more and more on the defensive. Yet, forced as he was on defending himself, Bel soon noticed a certain method behind the Shackle's attacks. For, unlike most opponents, the Shackle did not seem interested in wearing him down through minor strikes or slashes, nor did he seem to be watching for a single, powerful killing blow, and every time the chain lashed out, its intent, Bel realized, was Spire. His heart beat faster in his chest and his hands sweat as they gripped the haft of the spear—and he recalled his battle with Sir Harding upon the field outside of Clearpoint when his shield arm had shattered behind the force of the former Tower's charge whilst his own lance had exploded into splinters.

This time, as the Shackle renewed his whirling barrage, rather than seek to dodge or counter, Bel instead allowed the chain to wind around the lance and hold it fast. Bel gripped the haft tightly between both hands, bracing himself against the Shackle's attempt to disarm him. He smiled inwardly at the forester's grimace, only to realize that the Shackle did not intend to merely disarm him, but was attempting with every ounce of his strength, to snap the wooden shaft of the spear between the links of his steel chain.

It was in this moment of sudden horror when Bel allowed his focus to slip and his uncanny new instincts—the instincts of the Tower—to take over. With a simple shift of his weight, he vaulted the spear upward, and with the butt end, struck the Shackle hard across the face. The Shackle's hands loosened for only but a moment, but it was enough for his strange weapon to slip free and he fell backwards onto the ground, striking his head against a mossy flagstone.

When the forester opened his eyes, Bel was standing above him with the tip of the spear barely an inch from his throat.

"The damned thing's holy oak, isn't it?"

"I suppose it is."

"I should have known. Normal wood would have splintered like a twig," the Shackle sighed and shut his eyes, "Make it quick."

Bel breathed a sigh, "Why? I've already bested you."

The forester's eyes remained steady, placid, already resigned to his fate. "I am your enemy," he said, "You bested me. My life is yours to claim."

"You're not my enemy," Bel said wearily, "You're just a man defending his home, and I don't begrudge you that. If you were truly my enemy, your men up there would have shot me in the back by now." He stepped away, unwound the chain-sickle from the spear, and tossed it to the ground.

With some hesitation, the Shackle got to his feet.

"Now, all I ask is that you allow my men to lodge here," Bel continued, "And honor your part of the agreement. We have our own supplies, and we're willing to share them if you wish—consider it rent or tribute or whatever you like—but only if you swear to do us no harm."

Sir Emory, Horn, and Wendell rode up with Briden, their weapons drawn and ready, their expressions all of alarm. "Prince Beledain," Sir Emory called, "What's happened? You're wounded!"

"A scratch," Bel waved a hand at them, "Stand down, men. All is well." He glanced at the Shackle, "Is that so?"

The Shackle eyed Bel curiously and at last, gave a nod, "Aye, that's so."

CHAPTER 21: RODULF THE CHURL

From Granmouth, *Sigruna* set sail eastward across the Calendral Sea in pursuit of Rodulf and Slink. Magnus drove the crew hard to harness even the slightest of breezes in an effort to close the distance between himself and his old crewmates. His eyes smoldered with the light of vengeance and when the summer sun fell upon his wild red whiskers, he appeared as a man fashioned of living flame. The other seamen feared him, jumping at his commands, terrified that the captain's wrath might spill over and be loosed upon them for not answering quickly enough. Twice they came upon other vessels—a spice merchant from Kord followed by a band of coastal fishermen—and the Wrathorn warrior's talent for violence was put on display, interrogating their captains and crew for information regarding any other Sorgunders seen roaming the waters.

Throughout all of this, Thom remained hidden in the cabin or along the rear rail of the quarterdeck. Like the others, he had no desire to provoke Magnus's ire, but perhaps even more so, because he had his own private thoughts to contend with. The story of the Shield and the Key of Salvation was a puzzle and a half and the fat boy found himself searching the recesses of his mind for anything he might have studied that could in any way make sense of his Wrathorn companion's remarkable story. Why the Keepers would be so interested in discovering the Key of Salvation, Thom did not know, for the men of the Lighthouse were known as scholars of the ancient world, of Old Calendral and the like. Relics of the Guardians and St. Aiden were generally the prerogative of the Loremaster and his men. Why would the Keepers care so much about them? Did they seek to curry favor with the new King? And what did the presence of the Shield mean? Why would a hero of the Order, long believed to be dead, instead be living the life of a hermit on an unknown island off the coast of the southern continent? Could he have turned Blackguard too? There were far too many questions and not nearly enough answers. Not for the first time, Thom found himself in despair, longing for the dusty study rooms of the Loremaster's Tower, the smell of old books, and the laughter of old friends.

"Sail ahoy!"

The shout from the maintop put an end to Thom's private musings as he sat upon the quarterdeck sharpening his quills. His eyes frantically searched the starboard horizon. *Starboard!* he thought absurdly, *What a strange word. Why starboard? Why not just say "right?"* Only then, as he turned around, did he realize that his "right" changed independently of the ship.

Beside the pilot at the wheel, Magnus cried out to the sailor aloft, "Where away?"

"Two points off the port bow!"

Thom watched where the other sailors turned their gaze and peered into the distance. There, barely visible from his vantage point was a small, dark blur.

"She don't seem to be moving much, sir!" the watchmen shouted.

"Mayhap it's just a fisher or the like?" one of the other men grunted.

"Or some hulk in distress," said another.

"Easy pickings, in any case," grumbled a third, "Bout time we see some gain for this venture."

Magnus eyed him viciously. "Another word like that and you'll never see again," he growled, "Set the sails to close with her and be ready for a fight."

Yet as the Sigruna approached the ailing vessel, it became clear that no fight was to be had. For, the carnage littering the deck of the derelict cog was proof enough that the ships' crew had already fought and lost their last battle.

"Dibhor's cock," Thom heard a sailor mutter at the sight. The chubby boy breathed deeply, his eyes searching for anything they might focus on that was free of blood and carrion. Even the waters surrounding the ship were thick with the stuff and carnivorous fish feasted upon the dead flesh. Magnus clambered up upon the port rail.

"Enough gawking and bring her alongside, damn you!" he shouted at the pilot.

As the crewmen rushed to obey, Thom took a deep breath and looked away once more, studying the horizon to the north and east. The clouds hung white and low and the sun shone brightly. Seabirds flew back and forth in the distance and for the briefest of moments he spied a trio of shapes glimmering in the light.

"Oi! Thom Crusher!"

Magnus's cry brought the scribe's attention back to the present, to the ravaged vessel and the slaughtered crew. "Yes?" he asked.

"You're with me," the Wrathorn said.

Thom breathed a heavy sigh.

"Magnus, we be wasting our time with this," one of the sailors said.

"Aye," said another, "It's been picked clean already. There be no need to board."

Thom did not know either of their names; there were far too many to keep track of and they never spoke to him anyway, at least not kindly. Still, to be openly challenging one of Magnus's decisions? Perhaps he had better take note of them. They might be trouble, at least until the Wrathorn captain killed them.

In all the time he had spent with Magnus gallivanting around the Sorgund Isles, Thom had become a reluctant authority on sailors and their ways (nearly as knowledgeable as he had come to be on the subject of brothels and whores). They were a strange lot, part soldier, part laborer, part thief. True, they could vary in regards to individual character; however, in nearly every case, they were creatures driven by passions, plagued by superstition, and as shifting in their loyalties as the tides they sailed. To keep them under control, it took a strong will and a strong hand. Thankfully, Magnus had both. Yet even these could prove useless against the Sorgunder's one true cynosure: greed. And although Ivo had assembled a crew of what Magnus demanded be good lads, the tamest of dogs could still bite.

"We board because I say we board," Magnus growled at last, "If this be the work of Slink and Rodulf, I'll know it! They're the bloody bastards we hunt, not wretched fishermen or fool merchants. Slink and Rodulf have been plundering the coast for near a year and as far I can tell, their holds will be full with far more than some bloody trader. So if you want to waste your time going after minnows, then by all means cast off here because I'm headed after a fucking whale!"

The grumbling ceased with Magnus's words, but Thom wondered for how long. Regardless, the men followed the Wrathorn's orders, and soon enough, Magnus and Thom boarded the launch and crossed over to the derelict merchant vessel.

Up close, the main deck of the cog was even more gruesome than from afar as the bodies of the merchant's sailors lay strewn about in varied reposes of agony and horror. Thom took a deep breath and kept his eyes averted from the worst of it, though he steadily became aware of an uneasy feeling in his stomach as he followed behind Magnus. The handful of other men who had accompanied them searched about for anything of value, and although the big Wrathorn remained silent, it was clear from his expression that he too was searching for something among the dead, glancing from man to man with an expression not of one seeking loot or spoils, but of inquiry. It wasn't until he reached the quarterdeck that he appeared to have discovered what it was he was looking for. At once, his eyes shone with fury.

"What is it?" Thom asked.

"Just look," Magnus said.

Thom braced himself and allowed his eyes to focus on the corpse. A large gaping slash had torn open the man's side and a number of other small cuts marred his shoulder and the outside of his right thigh. Most unusual, though, was the strange wound upon the man's brow. It was by no means mortal, but rather appeared to be some sort of etching, and as Thom looked around, he noticed a number of other bodies nearby bore a similar mark.

"Slink always swore up and down that he could kill more than me," Magnus snorted, "Took to marking his, claiming it kept me from 'stealing' them. Meanwhile that bastard with his little mark was taking credit for mine—at least the ones that still had heads. Slink never could lop a head off in one go like me! Ha! I imagine you'll want to make a note of it for the song."

Thom nodded in numb agreement while his eyes traced the shape of the crude mark, anything to avoid glancing below at the spilled entrails and pooling blood. Bits of it had already clung to his shoes...

"Magnus!" he exclaimed suddenly, "The blood!"

"Aye, what about it?"

"It's still wet!"

"So it is."

"Yes, but not in that sticky, dried out way. It's *wet* wet.

"So?"

Thom's heart gave a flutter. "Don't you know what that means?!" he whined.

The growing realization that dawned upon the big Wrathorn's face filled the fat boy with equal parts excitement and terror. A broad grin stretched across Magnus's lips and his bushy beard shone in the sunlight. In a flash, he hurried aft to the stern rail and shielding his eyes with a meaty hand, scanned the eastern horizon.

Thom thought back to the blurs that he had thought he'd seen while the other men were occupied with the wreck. "Perhaps there's still time?" he said aloud.

"Back to the ship, you bastards!" Magnus thundered.

In a flurry of shouts, blows, and curses, Magnus ordered the crew of *Sigruna* to come about and sail eastward with all haste. Forgotten once more, Thom scurried aft and did his best to stay out of sight and out of mind. Soon, salty spray hissed through the air as the ship crashed through the wine-dark sea. As terrifying as Thom had always found the water, he could not help but admit that there was a certain majesty to the endless blue expanse, a certain sublime beauty that while terrifying, was not without its own charm. As the cog rolled high upon the keel and the wind rushed through his gingery hair, Thom found himself thinking once more of Lughus. Life at sea among pirates and corsairs, a life so ripe with potential for adventure, was exactly the type of thing old Goldimop dreamed of.

A forlorn smile spread across Thom's lips until a hail from the maintop brought his attention back to the present. There, dead ahead on the horizon, he finally saw it, saw what it was that stirred Magnus and his crew into such a frenzy. It was a ship, or rather, *ships*, for there were two or perhaps three separate vessels, and from the look in the big Wrathorn's eye, they were not simple merchants or fishermen, but his brother corsairs. To catch them promised battle and the opportunity for vengeance. More importantly to Thom, though, should Magnus achieve success, it meant a release from forced servitude and the chance to finally return home.

And perhaps, Thom thought, *I might not return empty-handed…*

If it were true that Magnus and his men had attempted to steal the Key of Salvation from the Shield, if it were true that he had no wish to see it in the hands of the Keepers, then perhaps he might allow Thom to return it to the Guardian-King. Such an act would certainly warrant an official pardon for the Wrathorn's earlier misdeeds. True, they would have to remain silent about the manner in which the Shield's death came to pass, and the fate of the Keeper who hired Magnus and his crew in the first place; however, if the Shield did in fact turn Blackguard, then perhaps Magnus was simply doing his duty as one of the Anointed? Perhaps Thom might even convince them that Magnus had turned over a new leaf. Hob was a mercenary once, or so Crodane had said, and he became the Loremaster's steward. Of course, if Magnus simply refused to return to Titanis with him, Thom might still beg the Key as a reward for faithful service in composing the big Wrathorn's song? Certainly the big Wrathorn would not want it. Why would he?

Thom's brow knitted as the idea took shape in his mind. *Yes*, he thought, *Yes, that is what I will do…so long as we survive the battle…*

To the east, the ships had grown steadily larger over the past hours of pursuit. *Sigruna* was near enough now that Thom could clearly make out three vessels, and from the sight of them, they had not simply plundered their way across the Calendral Sea without resistance. Even now *Sigruna* was gaining, for the corsair ships—two fully crewed and a smaller vessel following in their wake (a recent prize, no doubt)—had sustained damages in their previous encounters, as evidenced by their torn sails and broken spars.

By late afternoon, the prize ship had begun to fall behind and before long, *Sigruna* had overtaken her. Rather than stop to sack an empty vessel, Magnus gave the order to ignore her and press on after "the bigger fish." For, as he told the more disgruntled members of the crew, the prize was commanded by a mere skeleton crew, and if indeed she had any plunder worth going after, they could surely catch up with her again later. The real worthwhile booty, Rodulf and Slink would keep for themselves on the flagship, whichever of the remaining two as that might be.

The chase continued. Thom watched in silence and wonder from the stern. He could make out individual men walking and climbing about on deck and aloft. Each ship was manned by a crew comparable in size to that of *Sigruna*, and he found himself wondering why they continued in their flight, for the odds in battle were in their favor—at least in so far as numbers were concerned. Of course, an anointed warrior, Blackguard notwithstanding, could easily make up for any difference. As such, Thom guessed that Magnus's old shipmates were aware of his presence.

Again, Thom marveled at the ways of sailors and the sea, for just as he could always tell Lughus or Royne from a long way off simply by the manner of their walk and their posture, so he imagined it must be with seafarers who know their fellows by the conduct of a vessel rather than any flag or insignia. Magnus himself had never once declared by name that the two ships *Sigruna* pursued were his old mates; it was simply understood.

At length, the sun began to sink below the horizon to the west and in the east the sky was growing darker and darker. Steadily, Sigruna gained on the fleeing vessels until, to Thom's surprise and Magnus's frustration, the enemy sailors scurried aloft and adjusted their sails to change course—divergent courses.

"They're splitting up!" one of the *Sigruna's* crewmen shouted.

Magnus ground his teeth. "Bloody fucking cowards!" he roared at the wind. To Thom's surprise, the big Wrathorn fixed him with his gaze, "Why do they run? Why don't they turn and fight?"

Thom shrugged. "Maybe they recognize you?" he said.

Magnus snorted a laugh, but considered it. "Perhaps you're right," he grinned, "Ha! Bastards know what's coming!"

In a flash, the big man clambered up the rigging and cupping his hands in front of his mouth, shouted at the top of his lungs, "Hear me now, Rodulf and Slink! I am Magnus Bloodbeard and I swear now that I will kill you both!"

Thom wondered privately what the point of such a bold statement could be, particularly when it was clear that the fleeing ships had in all likelihood already surmised the Wrathorn's bloody intentions. However, Magnus was Magnus.

At length, the big man returned to the quarterdeck as the enemy ships were parting ways. "Which way do I go, captain?" the helmsman asked, "Which one do I pursue?"

Magnus breathed a sigh of annoyance. "Rodulf did always fancy himself the leader," Magnus grumbled after a time. He peered into the distance at the enemy ships, studying them closely. At long last, he fixed the helmsman with a piratical glare. "Hard to starboard," he growled, "It'll be Rodulf as has the key, and he's the better sailor. He'll head for open waters while Slink hugs the coast."

At once, the call went around the ship.

"Hard to Starboard!"

Quickly, the sailors hurried to make it so. At once, *Sigruna* lurched forward as the wind filled her sails and brought her careening after her prey like a falcon to a sparrow with a broken wing. Salty spray shot up in great torrents as the bow carved its way through the great undulating waves. Even Thom could not resist a quiet thrill.

"Head straight for them and be ready to board in the crash!" Magnus yelled, his eyes alight with bloody anticipation. He merrily slapped the helmsman on the back and unshouldered his great axe. "Get over here, Thom Crusher. I want you to have a good view so as to record the details of the battle."

Thom breathed a sigh and wiped his sweating palms along his tunic. "Magnus, I would feel considerably safer in the cabin."

"Shut your gob," the Wrathorn said absently, "We'll take Rodulf now as he's trying to flee and then swing north and east to catch Slink!"

"But Magnus—"

"Not another word!"

In dejected terror, the fat boy clung to the rail for the final stretch of the pursuit. The shouted oaths and curses of *Sigruna*'s sailors mingled with the roar of the waves. It rose to a cacophonous din, though Thom could barely hear it above the deafening sound of his own heart beating. Unlike the countless barroom brawls and dockside squabbles Thom had witnessed over the past year, he realized suddenly that this would be his first taste of real battle. How Lughus could ever have found such a subject so fascinating was beyond him. For, as he glanced quickly about him like a frightened rabbit, the men both at his side and across the waves seemed now to take on the guise of savages, beasts, monsters, ready to frenzy at the first sign of blood and the prospect of spoils.

At last, the two ships collided with the sound of thunder. A large wave spilled salt water over the rail and the sudden stop knocked Thom off of his feet. By the time he righted himself, the men of the *Sigruna* had already secured grappling ropes and a pair of gangplanks, locking the two ships together. The battle had begun.

In one great leap, Magnus crossed the narrow chasm between the two hulls, his great axe held high above his head. Before his feet even touched the deck of the enemy vessel, the great bearded blade had already made its mark as the Wrathorn warrior cleaved a man through the shoulder and half his torso, nearly splitting him in twain. A moment later, Magnus wrenched free his weapon and buried it in another man's chest with a torrent of red spray.

Thom, pale and clammy with fear, scurried after him at a distance, across the narrow gangplank, and behind the other men of *Sigruna*, eager to enter the fray.

"Rodulf, you rotten, traitorous bastard!" Magnus thundered over the erupting battle, "Death comes for you!" To punctuate the point, he lurched his great axe up into an enemy sailor's innards, dropping him to the deck in a deluge of gore.

From the rail of the quarterdeck, a raspy voice cried out in reply. "Magnus, my old pig fucker!" A broad, sun-baked man leered at him through wooden teeth. His eyes blazed with fury, though beneath it, Thom sensed a latent fear. "Hardly a way to treat an old shipmate, especially after abandoning us as you did in Galdoran."

Magnus spit a great wad into another man's eye before splitting his skull in twain. "I'll hear none of your lies, Churl!" he growled, "Nor grant you any quarter, but if you give me the key nice and easy, I'll make your end quick!" He paused, swinging his axe to lop off another man's arm at the shoulder, "Or at least, quicker..."

"Alas," Rodulf spat. Drawing a heavy falchion from his side, he strode forward and without pause slew one of Sigruna's sailors, locked in combat with a man of his own. Crimson mist spouted from the gaping wound. "If it's the key you're after, then it appears you chose the wrong ship, my boy!" He nodded to where the second of the corsair vessels was already making sail to speed away, "It's Slink as carries the bloody key!"

251

Justin D. Bello

Thom's eyes grew wide with despair as he watched the sails of Slink's ship billow with the wind. Magnus's lips twisted into a ghastly snarl. "So much for making it quick," he snapped and hurled himself headlong at his old friend.

CHAPTER 22: DEFENDER OF THE SPADE

Of all the things that Geoffrey had seen since he and his family had taken up residency as guests in the Galadin Castle, the table in the baron's solar was one of the most beautiful. Crafted of solid oak, it was not intricately carved or inlaid with gold or pearl like the baron's high seat in the great hall, but it was sturdy, smooth, and the sloping contour of the table legs and crossbeams had been fashioned with uniform precision. It was a fine, if simple, piece of craftsmanship.

"This table, like many of the castle's furnishings, was made for Baron Arcis by Wilbrand the Carpenter, the father of the previous Marshal, Crodane," Horus, the castle steward, observed from his seat across from Geoffrey, "The man could shape holy oak as easily as if it were wax."

"It is very fine indeed."

"So it is," the steward said kindly.

Geoffrey allowed his eye to linger on the grain of the wooden tabletop for a bit longer than necessary. Even after two weeks, he still found it difficult to speak to the castle folk, particularly those of a more refined nature. It was not that they were unkind—quite the contrary, in fact never could he recall a time when he and his family had been treated with such friendly goodwill by complete strangers. However, he could not help but feel somewhat intimidated, and though they may have given him new clothes of soft wool and linen, he was still a farmer's son. His hands were coarse and callused from long years of labor in the fields, which, what with the bandits, wars, and other hazards of nature, often seemed little reward. He was not used to stewards and servants, soldiers and stone walls—let alone leisure time.

Still, for the first time in a long time, he slept soundly through the night knowing that, at least for now, his family was safe and taken care of. They had plenty to eat, soft beds to sleep in, and soldiers to protect them. For that, he was grateful.

He only wished he could do something to feel useful. The idleness of life as a guest in the castle was maddening, and for Geoffrey, each day of leisure and rest brought greater guilt and deeper stress. He remembered again his promise to Regnar, and now that his family was safe, it was time to make good on his word. If only he knew exactly what it was he was supposed to do.

The sound of laughter from the hallway reminded him of another bittersweet facet of life in the Houndstooth, and a moment later Brigid appeared, accompanied by the baron and the great hound. The sentries on either side of the door stood straighter and saluted as they passed, and Geoffrey followed Horus to his feet. The young man, or Lughus as he preferred, waved them back to their ease and led Brigid to her seat at Geoffrey's right, before seating himself just beside her at the head. The great hound sauntered off to the corner and curled up comfortably with his head resting upon his paws.

"Hello, Geoffrey," Brigid grinned, "Horus. How are you both?"

"Very well, thank you, my la—Brigid," the steward said bowing his head.

Geoffrey gave a nod and Brigid winked. "Catches on quicker than you do," she smiled.

"I've always been a slow learner," Geoffrey said kindly.

"That's not what Annabel says, and speaking of, Freddy's come a long way with his reading," Brigid said, "Though I think much of it could have to do with the fact he's finally got some more exciting books. Herbs and poultices can only be so interesting!"

"He's a bright boy," the young baron agreed.

"Thank you, my lord—

"—Lughus—" Brigid feigned a cough.

"—but it's all his mother. Thank the Brethren both he and his sister take after her."

Lughus smiled kindly and glanced down at the tabletop. Geoffrey still did not know what to make of the young man, though truth be told, they had barely spoken since the night of the battle at the grotto and saw little of one another beyond meals in the great hall. He did sense a certain familiarity, even camaraderie, much like he had felt upon meeting Brigid all those months ago in Dwermouth, and the lad seemed genuinely kind enough, and honorable. However, he could not help but also feel a degree of wariness in observing the way the baron interacted with the pretty young maiden, for it was clear that his attention to her went beyond simple politeness—not that it went unreciprocated either. The two had been largely inseparable, particularly so these last few days—walking the town, the grounds, the walls. At meals in the hall one would have thought the two of them dined alone for the attention they paid anyone else, talking about books and chess and whatever else.

In one sense, it made Geoffrey glad. He was fond of Brigid and was glad to see that not only had she found a friend, but one that clearly made her very happy. Just one look at her in the company of the young baron could tell anyone that, for between her smiling and the light in her eyes, she veritably glowed.

Annabel, with significantly less subtlety, was fond of teasing Brigid about this whenever the chance presented itself, and though the young lady swore the baron and she were simply good friends, it was clear that there was at least the potential for something more.

"Let her go," Annabel had said, when Geoffrey, in vague and ambiguous muttering, finally made known his anxieties. "She likes him. Let her go."

"I'm only saying. The baron is a nice lad, and I've no cause to question him," he sighed, "But young men are still young men."

"And Brigid is still Brigid," Annabel laughed, "Believe me, even if did turn out to be a boor—which I sorely doubt—you think she'd hesitate to stick him with one of those blades of hers?"

"Oh now why'd you have to go and say something like that!? As if I didn't already have enough worries!"

"Geoffrey of Pyle—such an old curmudgeon!"

Again, in the solar, Geoffrey breathed a sigh. They were doing it again, chatting in low tones, while Horus and he were left to sit idly as the four of them awaited Sir Owain and the meeting could finally begin. In spite of old steward's presence, the disparity in age between himself and the other two of the Three, made Geoffrey feel as old as Annabel teased, and in truth, he was old enough that either of them could have been his own child. Why they had even asked him to attend the meeting here was also somewhat of a mystery. He was no noble statesman; he was a peasant farmer who had the foolish luck to be shot down with an arrow and subsequently saved by a dying old man. He knew little and cared even less for politics.

Regardless, the old knight arrived a moment later and assumed his seat at the baron's right, offering Geoffrey, Horus and the young pair a nod. Of all the folk in the castle, so far Owain was the one that made Geoffrey feel most at ease. He was older than Geoffrey by about a dozen years or so; yet, there was a pragmatic honesty to the seneschal that was a comfort among all the pomp of the castle. The gruff simplicity of his demeanor and forthright manner made him a welcome acquaintance. In some ways, the old knight put Geoffrey in mind of Captain Barrow, though he could not for the life of him identify why.

"Alright," Sir Owain declared, "What's say we begin?"

There was a murmur of assent. Horus cleared his throat, and with a nod from Owain, he spoke. "In just over a fortnight, the assembly of barons will meet in Highboard for the summer convocation," he began, "It will be a time of great importance, for it will be at that meeting when Lord Lughus will be presented formally as Baron of Galadin to the remaining lords of the Brock. It will also, however, be an opportunity for any detractors to challenge the validity of his claim. Now, the Lord-Baron has already pledged himself as our ally should it come to a vote, and assuming Galadin's traditional allies— Nordren, Brabant, and Derindale—support us, we shall thankfully need only the support of three other barons to carry the consensus."

"Sorry," Brigid interrupted, "But I still do not see how this could even be questioned. Lughus is Arcis Galadin's grandson by direct line of blood. How could his inheritance possibly be challenged?"

"A very good question," Horus said, "And one that might also concern you one day, Lady Dwerin."

"Oh yes. I see," she sighed, "It's because we're Blackguards."

"And not just any Blackguards," Sir Owain added, "*The* Blackguards, and considering the thin line of reasoning King Kredor and the Council used to justify attacking Grantis, a Blackguard Baron could quite easily provoke a war between Andoch and the Brock."

"And I'm sure my treatment of the Hammer and the Provincial did not help much in that regard either," Lughus muttered.

The steward and the seneschal exchanged a glance and Sir Owain looked away, shaking his head and grinding his teeth. "Actually, my lord," Horus said, "A message arrived by bird this morning in regards to that. Both Willum Harlow and Padeen Andresen have taken up residency in the Andochan embassy in Highboard. Apparently, they've been crying havoc to all who will listen and they intend to petition the Assembly to call you out in person."

"Wretched sons of whores, the both of them," the old knight muttered, "Pardon me, my lady."

"No, sir," Brigid scowled, "By all means."

Geoffrey's brow furrowed. Harlow the Hammer, he remembered all too well—from personal experience as well as from the odd flashes of memory that came to him at night as dreams. There was a long history there. Bitter and cold. Perhaps no villain haunted the Three more than those of the line of the Hammer. His strong farmer's hands balled into tight fists.

"Well," Lughus said, breaking the sudden silence, "Our chances of success seem rather low."

"Not necessarily," Horus said, "Challenging? Yes. Difficult? Perhaps. Impossible? Certainly not."

"Aye, not for a Galadin," Sir Owain said with a piratical grin.

"St. Aiden was a farmer," Geoffrey said quietly.

"What was that, Sir Geoffrey?" Sir Owain asked.

Geoffrey's eyes widened with alarm. He hadn't realized that he had spoken the words aloud. Yet now he saw the eyes of all the others at the table upon him.

"Um," he cleared his throat, "Just something my Da used to like saying when times were tough or hard. He'd remind me that St. Aiden—who I suppose now was your great ancestor—St. Aiden was a just farmer and look at all he did."

"Sir Geoffrey speaks the truth," Horus said, "And as I said, you have only to gain the support of three other barons, and while this might seem rather impossible, I do not in any way believe the situation to be so" the steward paused. "Granted," he said with a slight shrug, "I will not pretend that it will not require some…concessions on our part."

"Concessions?" the young baron asked, "What do you mean?"

"Well, let us consider the remaining barons," the steward raised a hand to count on his fingers, "As we've already said, Glendaro, Nordren, Brabant, and Derindale can in all likelihood be counted as allies."

"Leaving us Crofton, Waldron, Helmsted, Agathis, and Igrainne," Sir Owain said.

"But including Highboard and Galadin, that's only eleven," Brigid said, "I thought it was fifteen baronies that made up the Brock."

Horus gave a nod. "Yes," he said, "But as the domain of the Lord-Baron, Highboard is included under the jurisdiction of Baron Glendaro, and as Galadin is the very subject of the vote, we will be obliged to recuse ourselves from the vote as well."

"Right, but that's still only eleven," she said, "What about the other four?"

Sir Owain folded his arms. "They're Marthaine," he said at last.

"Marthaine?"

Lughus sighed, "My father."

"Oh."

Sir Owain ground his teeth and pounded his fist on the table. "Roland Marthaine is more of a threat to us than Harlow, Andresen, and King Kredor himself, and you can count on that!" he declared, "As for his cronies—Edgeforth, Denholm, and Caradon—I'd just as soon entreat a ship of Sorgund Corsairs than I would any of them!"

"I'm sorry," Brigid said, "I should have known."

Horus gave a sigh and the seneschal shook his head. "You've no need to be sorry, lass," he said as his sudden wellspring of anger went dry, "And I should remember my manners."

"What will it take, then," Lughus asked, "What will it take to convince the others to support us?"

Horus raised his eyebrows and touched the tips of his thin fingers together in thought. "Well," he said, "If it's true that Montevale is allied now with Andoch, then Helmstead's greatest concern will be defending the Nivanus

Pass, a route that—for the past hundred years—has not needed defending. Since it shares borders with both Galadin and Nordren, we might both be in a position to aid in the defense against an invasion from the east?"

Sir Owain shook his head, "Nordren will have its hands full defending its southern border with Andoch and its ports along the sea. Their position is precarious enough as it is without committing themselves to the defense of yet another border."

"True," Horus said, "I'll make a note of it."

"In any case," Lughus said, "We at least know Helmstead's concerns. What of the others?"

"Waldron will want support pushing their borders over the River Wyrm into Wrathorn. Agathis will want land, most likely the Wayden or Clomanse fiefdoms along our western border. Igrainne is the prime seat for the Weaver's Guild so you can be assured that whatever they seek will be tied to the wool trade. I've no idea what Crofton might want, though they'll likely be a hard sell since the original line of barons there ended at the hands of a Blackguard, albeit centuries ago. The current Crofton is actually a Lloyan."

The young baron leaned on his arm and his brow furrowed in thought. *What was he?* Geoffrey thought, *Seventeen? Scarcely a few months older than Brigid?* Back in Pyle, Oliver's eldest, Axel, would have just turned eighteen and Nickolas would be sixteen by summer's end. Yet, here were two young people almost of an age with them, seated at a table making decisions that would affect the lives of thousands. *How strange?* he thought, *How maddening?* And it became all the more so when he realized with a shock of fright that he, Geoffrey of Pyle, occupied a seat at that table too. *St. Aiden was a farmer...*

"I am not willing to give up any land," Lughus said at last, "It would not be fair to Sir Herbrand or Sir Gosbert, to say nothing of the people of their fiefs. So if that's what Agathis wants, we may as well not waste our efforts with them."

"I agree," Horus said, "Herbrand and Gosbert each draw at least two dozen mounted men-at-arms from their households alone, and we'll not want them to feel slighted should it come to war."

"They're good men too," Sir Owain added, "and loyal. It wouldn't be right."

Lughus nodded, "I also think it's very important that we gain Helmstead to our side. Again, if it does come to war, it will be they who guard the postern. It would make little sense to leave them unprotected against assault, for if they should fall or agree to a separate peace with Andoch and Montevale, the enemy cavalry will have a significantly easier time staging attacks from Helmstead's plains than they would were they confined to the narrows of the mountain passes."

"In the past," Horus said, "Helmstead and Nordren have forever been at odds over trade agreements with Montevale. As such, any other goods arriving by ship to Nordren's ports from the far reaches of Termain have been forced to pay rather substantial taxes to cross the border by land into Helmstead. Perhaps if we enlist Baron Nordren to aide us in the negotiations—to submit even to minor concessions in the name of the greater security of the realm—it may further entice Baron Helmstead to offer his support, particularly since he will no longer be able to count upon Montevalen trade?"

"Won't require him to sacrifice any soldiers either," Owain added.

"Do you think Nordren would agree to that?" Lughus asked.

"In light of the circumstances? Yes, I do. For if both of them lose trade with Montevale, increased trade *between* themselves will help to make up the difference. Further, if Nordren and Helmstead were on friendlier terms, it would undercut Edgeforth's ports in the north, long Nordren's rival," the steward paused, "Yes…Yes. I believe that may in fact have great potential for success. I will prepare some notes. In all likelihood, Baron Nordren has already departed for Highboard, but there will be time to speak to him before the Assembly officially meets as long as you depart within the next few days as well."

"So that leaves Waldron, Igrainne, and Crofton," the young baron said, "I'd rather not provoke the Wrathorn, particularly if we may already be fighting a war on two fronts. It would be ruin to add a third."

"Then Waldron is out," Sir Owain said simply.

"Igrainne and the weavers then?" Horus asked, "This might well be the easiest to achieve, since for the most part, any agreement will be born out of simple greed. Though, it could have lasting effects on the common folk and the prosperity of the barony for years to come."

"How do you mean?" Lughus asked, shaking his head, "I know very little about trade and accounts. In Andoch, that sort of thing was the business of the Chancellor's Tower."

The old steward shrugged, "For the most part, the weavers will want contracts and reduced rates relating to the purchase and production of wool from each of the seven fiefdoms, and since the customary length of contract is seven years, we will be bound to whatever terms are agreed upon for some time. This will not only have an effect on our coffers here at the castle, but anyone from the knights in command of the fiefs all the way down to the drovers minding the sheep in the field."

"I see."

"There are, however, other ways we can bargain," Horus said, "The wealthiest masters of the weavers guild may have a great deal of money, but they are still common men, and more than anything many of them covet the opportunity to raise themselves or their sons by title."

Sir Owain made a noise of disapproval and folded his arms.

"They would not be warriors, per se," the steward continued, ignoring his counterpart, "But they would still be required to offer service in some form should we have need of them. They may not fight themselves, but they are each wealthy enough in their own right to either hire mercenary soldiers or pay the scutage, which could also then be used to hire more men. Furthermore, you would not have to issue them lands, since many of them already own much of the property in the city."

"But how will helping the weavers in Galadin gain the support of Igrainne?" Brigid asked.

"The weavers are not bound by the borders of the baronies. Therefore, if we elevate the weavers in Galadin, the weavers can then offer incentives of their own to Igrainne. They serve, more or less, as an intermediary."

Lughus nodded, "But you don't agree with this, Owain?"

"I take issue with a knight who has not earned his spurs in the field," the seneschal sighed, "However, it is becoming more commonplace these days, and if it does help us…" he shrugged, "I would simply advise you to be careful who is chosen."

"Aye," Brigid said, raising an eyebrow, "The last thing a man like Adolfo the Madder needs is the legitimacy of a knighthood."

Lughus sighed, "Horus, would you be able to come up with some figures that might be fair, as far as the contracts are concerned?"

"Certainly, my lord. We may even seek to enlist one of the local masters in the city to advise."

Geoffrey felt Brigid's eye, "We rented our house in Hounton from Faden. He seemed a decent sort. He was at least fair, wouldn't you say?"

"I suppose," Geoffrey observed, "He was always kind enough, and he paid my wife a wage for spinning thread."

"Good," Lughus nodded, "We can speak with him then."

"And the knighthoods?" Horus asked.

The young baron sighed, "What if we offered a set number—say, three—to be chosen from among those Galadin masters who prove themselves loyal to the city and to its people. Like you said, the guild knows no boundaries. Therefore, I want men with a vested interest in our lands and our city."

"Three may not do it for that."

"Then five, and if Faden supports us in negotiations with the rest of the guild, he can count himself or one his heirs as guaranteed."

"I will see to it," Horus said, "Now then, that leaves only Crofton."

"Which you say is rather unlikely?" Lughus asked.

"Who's to say?" the steward shrugged, "The word 'Blackguard' alone might set them off. However, the Croftons are also loyal adherents to the Kinship, and you are of the bloodline of the Holy Saint. Who knows what they'll say?" He paused and raised an eyebrow to glance at the seneschal seated beside him. "Do you have any insight as to the minds and motivations of the Croftons, Sir Owain?"

To Geoffrey's surprise, the big man looked somewhat uncomfortable. "Horus," he said at last, "You know very well…"

Lughus and Brigid exchanged a glance, but while neither voiced any questions, their expressions alone made the old knight shift awkwardly in his seat. "My sister is married to a Crofton," Sir Owain said at last, "Not the Baron, but one of his younger brothers—those that still call themselves the Lloyans. Anyway, things are…rather awkward. Years ago, when I was but a landless knight attached to Galadin, they offered me command of my own fiefdom, and…I turned it down."

Horus touched his fingertips together, "Perhaps it might be time you…paid a call."

"Horus, you—" abruptly Sir Owain's shut his mouth and his mustache waggled back and forth like a dog's tail, "Fine. I will call upon her when we arrive in Highboard, though it's going to be damned awkward. Lucia is a frightfully dangerous woman when she gets riled, and there's no promise she'll even receive me, or that our attachment will count for anything. Considering the past, it may well be more liable to harm it."

"Just be your charming self, old friend," the steward smiled.

"Bollocks," the old knight muttered.

"Well, then," Lughus said "It seems we have some measure of a plan, at the very least."

"When you arrive in Highboard, my lord, I would suggest that you speak to Perin Glendaro as well," Horus told him, "His word may also carry some weight in regards to Helmstead and Igrainne—Crofton too perhaps, should Owain's charms fail."

Lughus smiled. "I will."

"Then I suppose that settles it," Sir Owain said, "I'll finish the travel preparations and in two or three days' time, Baron Lughus and, perhaps an honor guard of...say ten men, will ride for Highboard. That should give Horus time to draw up his notes and meet with this Master Faden."

"And don't forget that I'm going too," Brigid added.

The steward and the seneschal exchanged a glance. "We had actually been wondering, Lady Brigid," Horus said, "If perhaps you would mind remaining here to...aid in whatever preparations we might need to make for their return."

"Well..." Brigid began, "Perhaps I might offer an alternative proposal."

Geoffrey suppressed a sigh. *Here we go...* he thought. He knew this tone. It was the same one she used in the past when he tried to deter her from sneaking around the castle or haggling over the price of her old jewelry. It was a pleasant forcefulness, a smile that was actually a smirk, an empty right hand that vehemently waved a greeting only to conceal the dagger poised to strike from the left.

"You...have a different idea, Lady Brigid?" the steward asked.

"Brigid."

"My apologies, Brigid."

"And, I'm sorry, but…" she exchanged a glance with Lughus, "We discussed this yesterday and we agreed that either Geoffrey or I should go along to watch Lughus's back."

"In fairness," Lughus said quietly, "Is it really a discussion if only one person does all of the talking?"

"Quiet, you," Brigid smirked.

Geoffrey could not help but chuckle, "And to be fair, how many times did my name actually come up?"

"You were mentioned," Lughus said, "But it was clear that a choice was already made."

"Hush," Brigid hissed.

Geoffrey grinned.

Horus glanced at Owain and then back at Brigid, "My lady…"

"Horus…"

"Brigid…" the steward sighed, "With the situation as it is, Sir Owain and I simply felt that the safest place for you would be in Houndstooth."

"No one doubts your mettle, lass," Owain said, "But the odds are stacked against us enough as it is with the Hammer fellow—to say nothing of the blasted Marthaines."

"Then why wouldn't we seek to even them?" Brigid asked, "As you said— between Harlow, the Provincial, the Marthaines, or anyone else that might be a threat, we need every advantage we can get. And besides my blades, recall that I grew up in Blackstone, I'm no stranger to politics and courtly niceties. I can help—particularly as a woman. You'd be surprised how much influence a lady of the court can have over the men who surround her. There is an entirely different world of politics that not a one of you will ever have access to. I can help. Believe me."

Sir Owain exchanged a glance with Horace. "She makes a fair point," he muttered.

The steward sighed, "So she does."

Brigid's eyes flashed. "Of course, I do. Besides, I'm not going to stay here and sit idly by if they try to…" she shook her head, "Look, I'm going. That's all there is to it."

"I hadn't planned on going by carriage," Sir Owain said after a moment, "I planned to simply ride a-mount with perhaps a pack horse or two for the baggage and no servants or maids. There will be no luxuries until we reach our lodgings in Highboard."

"Owain, when have I ever wanted luxuries?" Brigid asked, "And as for riding, fine. Gareth knew how to ride, so, I imagine, can I. Ada can stay behind too. I'll have no need for a maid. I think of her more as a friend anyway." She rolled her eyes. "A maid? Really, Owain?"

Geoffrey shook his head and smiled. "You'd best give up now," he said, "There's no winning against her. Even if you forbid it, she'll simply sneak off anyway."

"We could lock her in the dungeon," Sir Owain smirked.

"You could certainly try," Brigid grinned, "But I'll warn you. I've gotten rather adept at picking locks."

"Brigid…" Lughus sighed, "I'm not disagreeing with you, but I can't forget. Harlow killed Crodane—in a manner of speaking. Even one-handed, he's a threat and killer. Perhaps even more so."

"No, Lughus," she said and her blue eyes flashed, "We discussed this. Assume for a minute that all our plans come to naught and the Assembly chooses to hand you over to the Hammer. What then? I'm not letting you walk into danger without someone to watch your back—and I mean you no disrespect, Sir Owain. I just…I'm not staying behind."

Horus sighed, "Then who will mind the city while the baron and the seneschal are gone? I will maintain the affairs of business. However, defense is not my strong suit. It was out hope that you would have seen to it, my lady, for the people have come to know you as," he paused, "As the baron's particular friend."

"Sir Owain may be absent," Brigid grinned, "But my seneschal is right here." She exchanged a glance with Lughus and for some reason, Geoffrey felt the hair on the back of his neck bristle. *What is she at now?*

"And who is that?" Sir Owain asked.

"Why, Sir Geoffrey Pyle, Defender of the Spade!"

"What?!" Geoffrey gasped. His stomach twisted into knots and in an instant his brow was moist with sweat. *She's done it again,* he thought bitterly, *First the grotto, and now this! If I were a wise man, I'd have left her on the docks in Dwermouth for all the trouble she's been!* He breathed a heavy sigh and realized that his heart was racing.

"My lords," he began, "And, my lady—"

"Geoffrey!"

"—Brigid," he said through clenched teeth, "I'm sorry, but you must be joking." He glanced around the table, his arms spread wide, hoping to convey the blatant absurdity of her suggestion. To his horror, however, the other men did not seem at all taken aback, nor did they seem to find the suggestion as inane as he did.

"My lords," he said again, "I'm but a farmer. What could I possibly know about running a barony? Besides, I'm not even from the Brock! Surly one of the knights would be more suited. Or Abbot Woode? Surely the abbot would be a better choice?"

"Woode has already spent more time away from St. Golan's than he is wont to," Sir Owain said. "And you wouldn't have to worry about the whole barony," he said, "The knights take care of their fiefs and Horus minds any other affairs. You'd only have to see to the defense of the city—and even then the master-at-arms and the watch captain take care of the day-to-day affairs. No, Geoffrey, I'm with the lass. I believe you would do rather well."

"Yes," Horus agreed, "Regnar was known to many among the guard by his shield, which you now carry. And as for the matters of command, you've nothing to worry about. As I'm sure you've seen, Sir Owain really does very little at all around the castle other than sit at the lord's table and empty his cellar. It's the steward who actually sees to all the hard work."

"Oh shove off," the old knight snorted.

Geoffrey shook his head, "Still, there must be someone else?"

"Geoffrey," Lughus said, "You could scarcely be less qualified than I am, and I'm supposed to be the baron."

"You *are* the baron," Brigid whispered, shooting him a look.

Lughus suppressed a smile. "Besides," he continued, "Living in Hounton, you already know the city—better than I do probably—and as far as being a foreigner, you forget that I spent nearly all my life in Andoch as a member of the Order itself."

Geoffrey glanced down at the table and noticed thin streaks along the tabletop from his sweaty palms. *Me? The master of a city?* He shook his head and sighed. *Oh father, if you could see the mess your son has got himself into now...*

"Please, Geoffrey," the young baron said, "I would feel so much safer knowing that the city was in the hands of the Vanguard, especially when the

266

man who bears the title is you. You don't give yourself nearly enough credit. Brigid told me the story of what happened in Pyle and how you stood against the bandits when no one else would. Please, Geoffrey. Protect the city."

St. Aiden was a farmer...

Geoffrey breathed a heavy sigh, "Very well."

"Excellent," Brigid grinned, "Sir Geoffrey it is then. We'll see how you like having people call *you* by a title all the time."

Geoffrey glared at her from beneath his eyebrows, but her smile only grew wider.

"You'll be fine," Sir Owain said, "It'll only be for but a few weeks anyway. What's the worst that could happen?"

Horus shrugged, "The Guardians could attack, hoping to take advantage of the baron's absence."

"Lady save us!" Geoffrey winced.

"Oh shut up, Horus!" Owain grunted, "They won't, or at least if they did, we'd hear of it in plenty of time. They'd have to cross a whole other barony before they even got here. It'll be fine."

Geoffrey's chest tightened. "As you say," he sighed.

"Is that everything, then?" the young baron asked, "Is there anything else we need to prepare?"

Horus bit his lip and flipped through his notes. "I don't believe so," he glanced at Sir Owain and the big man shook his head.

Lughus glanced at Brigid and the two of them exchanged a nod. "Then if that's the case," he said, "I suppose we can adjourn—except Geoffrey, if you wouldn't mind."

"Yes, my lord," Geoffrey said miserably. *What now?* he wondered. He knew Brigid was smiling at him, but he refused to meet her eye.

"I will summon this Faden and have my notes for you by the time you depart," Horus told the Baron as he rose to his feet.

"And I'll call on you later, Sir Geoffrey," Sir Owain said, "We can speak then if you have questions about your duties—perhaps over a pint. All this talk creates a powerful thirst."

Horus's lips twisted into a wry grin. "What did I tell you?" he murmured.

Geoffrey forced a smile and gave a nod, "I'd appreciate it."

"I'm going to see to that other…thing," Brigid grinned, "With Annabel and the children." She lowered her voice to the young baron, "Find me when you're done, eh?"

Lughus nodded, and with another flash of a smile, she followed the steward and the seneschal from the room, the great golden hound lagging behind her.

Alone with the baron, Geoffrey bowed his head and fought to remain calm as an uncomfortable silence settled over the room. *Sir Geoffrey!* he sighed, *Wait until Annabel hears about this!* and with a shock of fright, he realized that must have been what Brigid was on her way to inform her of right now. *Perindal's Sword, that girl…*

Beside him, the young baron bit his lip and splayed his fingers on the tabletop. "Geoffrey," he said, "I'm sorry if you felt uncomfortable just now, or if you feel we've treated you unfairly. I do mean it, though, when I say I'm relieved that you've agreed to assume command while we're gone."

"Yes, my lord," Geoffrey said, "Thank you."

"And please don't be upset with Brigid," he said, "She cares for you and your family as her own. She told me so. She's never had anything like that, and you mean a great deal to her."

Geoffrey sighed. Brigid spoke very little of her life in Dwerin, and when she did, it was usually in disparagement. "I know," he said at last, "And she's…come to mean a lot to my family as well, particularly since…we lost my son almost a year ago, come Harvestide."

"Brigid told me," the young man said, "I'm very sorry."

"Thank you," Geoffrey shrugged.

The awkward silence returned as Geoffrey wondered what it was the baron wanted of him, though he felt it was not his place to ask. Luckily, he did not have to wait long before the young man breathed a sigh and stood up from the table. "Will you walk with me?" he asked, "Brigid and I have something for you, and for your family too, though I imagine she's on her way to take it to them now."

Oh what mischief is this now? he thought. "Of course, my lord."

"Please, Geoffrey. Just Lughus. I don't much care for this noble pageantry and I really wan…I want the two of us to be friends."

"Aye, sir. Lughus."

Geoffrey followed the young man out of the solar and down the passage that led alongside the great hall to a staircase leading down to the first floor of the castle. At the end of another passageway, the baron stopped outside of a door.

"If you are going to act as warden while we're away," Lughus said, "We wanted to make sure you looked the part. I know. It's nonsense, but I've learned that there's a certain significance to symbolism that helps people feel safe and secure." He opened the door and inside laid out upon one end of a long table in the center of the room was a full suit of armor—chainmail hauberk, poleyns, gauntlets, greaves, coif, and a kettle helm. On the other end of the table, were a number of other garments, a quilted gambeson, two different baldrics—one of plate and the other of braided leather—and a simple white surcoat bearing a bright red acorn in the center of the breast. Two other sets of fine clothing, also white but for the mark of the acorn, were folded beside it.

"The emblem of the Vanguard is the acorn of the holy oak, correct?" Lughus asked, "I remember it was the device on your shield that night in the grotto."

Geoffrey's breath caught in his throat and as he reached out to touch the links of the mail, rubbing them between his fingers, only to realize that his hands were shaking.

"The clothes are simple," Lughus continued, "In spite of what Jergan wanted. However, Brigid said you'd never wear anything that was too flashy. So, but for the acorns, they're just plain white. We had sets made for your wife and children so that they can wear the arms of your house as well."

Geoffrey swallowed with difficulty and rubbed at his eyes, "The arms of their house?"

"The House of Pyle," the young man said, "She was serious about you being made a knight, Geoffrey."

"My lord—Lughus, I'm no knight. I'm not even from the Brock."

"I know," he said, a slight smile tugging at the corners of his lips, "You're a great lord of Dwerin, seneschal to the Lady Brigid. I told you that you're all very dear to her, and if ever she does return there, she's named you 'Defender of the Spade.' After all, you certainly paid for it in blood and toil."

Geoffrey shook his head. Part of him felt wondrously honored, flabbergasted even with such a turn of fortune from where he was scarcely a year before; however, at the same time, he could not help but also feel somewhat frustrated, angry even, that he should find himself no longer the simple man he was, but now poised—expected even—to rise up in the blink of an eye to become a great lord, particularly when so many others—Karl, Oliver, Cousin Martin—had lost their lives.

Geoffrey breathed a great sigh and put a hand to his brow only to realize that there were tears in his eyes. *St. Aiden,* he thought, *What do you want of me?* So much uncertainty, so much indecision. If only the Lords of the Kinship would speak plain.

"Thank you. Thank you, my lord, but I cannot accept this," he said, "I've done nothing to warrant such generosity. As I keep telling everyone, I'm just a farmer."

"A farmer who fights rather well, I would say. On behalf of his fellows and to uphold the cause of good."

"Luck and desperation, that's all," Geoffrey said, "A man should protect his family and his friends, and his land if he can," he breathed a heavy sigh, "I've failed at all three before. I'll not do it again."

"Good. Then you'll make a fine knight."

"My lord, I will act in Sir Owain's stead, but please," he pleaded, "I'm just a farmer."

"So you keep saying, just as I was a scribbler to the Loremaster," Lughus grinned, "In a sense, I always will be, and I'm glad for it. However, I know now that I have to be more. It took me a long time to realize it, Geoffrey, but if you read the stories like I have, you suddenly see how common it is that many of the greatest heroes were never knights and lords to begin with but simple folk who acted because they saw others were in need. The Wave was a carpenter, the Shadow was a thief, the Quill was a tax collector—even St. Aiden—"

"—was a farmer," Geoffrey finished, "I know. Believe me, I know."

"Like it or not, Geoffrey," Lughus sighed, resting his hand upon the hilt of his sword, "This is the road we walk, and it seems there's no returning."

Geoffrey bit his lip. He examined the white surcoat and his heart leapt at the thought of his children and wife clad in the same. They were very fine, and wasn't this what any man would want? Prosperity? Stability? With a knighthood, his children would never starve, would never find themselves without a home. They would not toil as he and his father had done only to have the fruits of their labors stolen by bandits or soldiers or lords. Wasn't this the very reason he left the Spade in the first place? To answer the call? To fulfill his promise to Regnar? To take his family away from danger and see them safe? A knighthood—Lady's Grace! Oliver would likely have punched him in the nose for his hesitation, his foolish indecision. Perhaps it was finally time to accept things, to move on, and to count his blessings. *If only Karl were here with us...and you, Dad...*

"So be it," he said, "Sir Geoffrey I shall be."

"Good," Lughus said, "I feel much better about heading off to Highboard with you staying behind in command, though to be honest, I wish I didn't have to go at all. I'm afraid I'll have to speak in front of the Assembly and..." he trailed off, "I just thank the Brethren that Brigid's coming with me. Sir Owain too, of course."

"If there's a chance of trouble, there you're likely to find that girl."

Lughus smiled to himself, but remained silent, lost in his own thoughts. Without thinking, Geoffrey heard himself speak, "You fancy her, don't you?"

All of a sudden, the young baron's gray eyes went wide with surprise and his cheeks burned as scarlet as the acorns on Geoffrey's new clothes. "I..." he began, but his voice caught in his throat and after a deep breath, he bowed his head and confessed, "I do. Very much so."

"Well," Sir Geoffrey nodded, "It's good to know that I'm not blind."

"Please don't tell her," Lughus whispered, suddenly looking much more the boy than the baron, "I fear..."

"She won't hear it from he, my lord," he said kindly, "And as far as I can tell, it's rather obvious that she cares for you too."

Lughus's mouth fell open, and for a moment, it seemed as if they young man had been kicked by a mule. *Lady's Grace*, Geoffrey thought, *She's too fool to admit her feelings to herself, and he's too blind to see past his own. Youth!*

"Did—did she say that?" the baron asked.

"No," Geoffrey said, "Though if you tell her that I did, it'll mean the death of me! Both of us probably."

"I won't. I promise, I won't."

"And I'll tell you this too. Remember, I'm her knight, not yours. Any ill comes to her, I'll hear of it." As soon as he finished speaking, he felt a stab of guilt. *By the Brethren, I'm turning into my father...*

"I would never, Geoffrey," Lughus said, his voice unsteady with a blend of joy and anxiety, "You have my word. I promise I'll say nothing to her about this either. Not one word."

"Good," the farmer said, "Then how about you show me how to don this stuff and we'll go show my wife and the Lady Blade what all her meddling has wrought?"

CHAPTER 23: DISASTER

For the first time in a long time, Royne did not feel any sense of smug satisfaction at having been proven right. For, just as he had expected, the Fifth Legion's assault upon the castle at Hedgeford failed and the legionnaires were put to rout. Even with the addition of General Callum's men of the Seventh, when the Guardians occupying the castle rode forth to meet them under the command of the cavalier known as the Wheel, the Grantisi shieldwall crumpled almost immediately and the Gray Wolf was forced to sound a retreat.

Of course, Royne did not actually witness the battle as he had at Bruton. Instead, he remained behind at the Grantisi base camp with those few men left to guard the baggage train and the small contingent of camp followers that gathered like flies as the army's numbers grew. Most were women—cooks, laundresses, and whores (or some combination of the three) who saw an attachment to the army as an easy means of both protection and coin. However, there were plenty of other hangers-on as well—gamblers, beggars, jugglers, and even the odd bard. For the most part, they were invisible to Royne, limiting their interactions to the common soldiers while he maintained the privileged company of the Gray Wolf. Nevertheless, when the attack failed, they would have all been captured or killed had General Navarro not ordered Captain Velius and the skirmishers to return for them.

In any case, for two days now, the army fled southwest across the plain hoping to put enough distance between itself and the kingsmen to lick its wounds and adjust its strategy. In that time, Royne had confined himself to the interior of the supply wagon in which he and Conor had hurriedly sought refuge in the frenzied flight. He had no wish to become the target of the soldiers' wounded pride, for he was certain that his opposition to the attack would be well known among the other officers. He had already sensed their scorn when he last saw them at the meal on the eve of the attack, and even the Gray Wolf had remained cold, so he took it as a certainty that Captain Velius and General Callum would as well.

Callum was a soldier in the same manner of the captain—brash, arrogant, sarcastic—and Royne did not like him at all. A very short man, Callum seemed to feel the need to compensate by treating anyone on the taller side of average with abject scorn. As a result, the lanky young Loremaster could rest easy knowing that his abhorrence for the little general was mutual. Fortunately, Navarro also still outranked Callum, else he might find himself in line for the chopping block simply for having grown too tall.

Unless, of course, the defeat had earned him Navarro's disfavor as well. If that should be the case, Royne knew that his tenuous relationship with the wolf pack could very quickly turn feral.

Royne's disagreement with the general and the subsequent flight had at the very least afforded him plenty of time to read. Though in fairness, his experience of *The Book of Histories* could almost be understood more as *remembering* as opposed to *reading* as he became increasingly acclimated to the ways of the book. Whenever he traced his hand over the empty pages, it was as if he *saw* the story in his mind just as he somehow *understood* the text on the empty page. As such, as he continued to read through the accounts of the Loremasters past, it was as if he saw through their eyes, knew what they knew, and lived what they lived. It was absolutely strange and, if he were being completely honest, strangely wonderful.

Of course, it was not without its own confusions as well.

As he progressed through the pages of Loremaster Sabrun's tale, for some reason that he could not quite explain, he became all the more certain that the sanctity of the Brock was key—not merely for the sake of standing strong against King Kredor's tyranny, but for reasons much more dire, and although Royne was not one to be so easily moved by superstition or folklore, something about the story struck a chord deep within him, resonating with a strange consciousness he did not even know he had.

Five years after the Bard's return to the Order, Amarthia had become a staple of the court in Andoch and had solidified her position as the sixth councilor. Thus, it was the Council of Six that now led the Order, and for all the Hierophant's grumblings, the addition of the Bard's practical, worldly knowledge of Termain and its people helped to usher in numerous reforms that significantly improved the quality of life for the common folk of Andoch and ensured a more enlightened sense of justice in all the lands under the dominion of the Guardian-King.

However, as he recorded the proceedings of the Council at this time, Loremaster Sabrun's accompanying narrative often suggested his private misgivings—not in regards to the influence of the Bard or the Hierophant's occasional attempts to undermine her credibility, but rather his personal reservations about the motives and the machinations of the King, Erolan Drude III.

King Erolan had been a very young man when he assumed the throne, one of the youngest, in fact. For, in his earliest days, long before the appearance of the Bard, Sabrun had often referred him as the "Boy-King." At the age of sixteen, he had made a name for himself defending the city of Galdoran from an invasion by a large fleet of corsairs out of the Sorgund Isles. Over the remainder of his boyhood, he continued to define himself through military successes, from border clashes with the Wrathorn to a pair of failed assassination plots instigated by ambitious Andochan earls.

Not unlike Kredor, Royne thought, *Though it should come as little surprise that those anointed as the King should show such prowess in battle. It is, after all, the duty of the sovereign to safeguard his people. At least in theory...*

Yet even as King Erolan grew older, he seemed in many ways untouched or unhindered by the effects of time, and despite his many battles, he remained unbroken. Amarthia's arrival, or rather, the Bard's return, in Erolan's thirtieth year seemed only to further invigorate the young monarch, who—in spite of his role, title, and popularity, had remained unmarried.

Not that he had not had opportunities. As Guardian-King, the young man could essentially choose from among any of the noblewomen across Termain, which, at times, he had done, though none of these trysts had resulted in an official union. As a warrior king, Erolan had little interest in the matters of court beyond the affairs of the Council and the Order, and it was thought by some that for this reason, he spent the majority of each year away from the Keystone either in the field on campaign or touring the castles and other fortifications his kingsmen garrisoned. Courtly love and intrigue were far too uninteresting a reason for the King to remain at court when he could be out riding, fighting, and seeking adventure.

The return of the Bard, however, put an abrupt end to all of that, and in Amarthia, King Erolan seemed to find something of a kindred spirit. For in a young man so given over to restlessness, what better companion could there be than the unabashed chief of wanderers?

In the songs of the Bard, Erolan found the endless expanse of imagination, a blending of history and geography, fantasy and folklore, truth and wonder. And in her grace and her beauty, he discovered the object of his heart's desire, and the one thing that even as King he could not possess.

Politically, of course, a match between the Guardian-King and a woman of unknown, but in all likelihood common birth, was completely unacceptable. The fact that she was also Anointed with a title only served as further proof of her ineligibility given the Hierophant's ire. However, behind closed doors, these were matters that Erolan could easily cast aside, just as he was also willing to overlook Amarthia's polite refusals.

How exactly it came to pass, Sabrun did not know, for it was some time before he finally discovered the truth. As perhaps the closest of friends to the Bard, the Loremaster seemed little by little to discern a change in her demeanor, a hint of sadness in her songs, and he noticed more and more the ubiquitous presence of the kingsmen accompanying her wherever she went within the confines of Castle Testament. At the same time, Sabrun became conscious of the shifting nature of King Erolan as well, as if age and the authority that accompanied it, had finally begun to set in. He became colder, more aggressive, and at Council meetings, seemed increasingly fond of asserting his sovereign dominance.

Finally, on the 12th of Harvestide in the Bard's sixth year with the Council, a pair of King Erolan's kingsmen woke Loremaster Sabrun just before dawn, summoning him to the Keystone and the King's private quarters high atop the keep. There, his face pale and stricken with the fear of a frightened child, Erolan received the Loremaster in maladroit silence and ushered him through to his bedchamber where Amarthia lay beneath the shadow of some affliction.

As Royne read his long-dead predecessor's account of the incident, the words upon the parchment came to life within his mind's eye. His skin grew cold and prickly, and his breast burned with inner wrath at the sight of the poor woman's shame and despair. His gaze narrowed at the Guardian-King and with a voice that was not his own, Royne spoke.

"What have you done?"

Erolan's eyes widened like a pageboy caught stealing sweets from the larder. "Me?" he gasped, "I've done nothing."

Royne breathed a sigh and drew close to the woman's side. Slowly, he sat down upon the edge of the bed and glanced over her. She lay on her side covered in a thick film of sweat. On the floor just beneath the bed frame a large basin swirled with sick. *Lady save her!* Royne thought, gently pressing a hand to her clammy brow, her dark hair concealing her face like a curtain of silk.

"I know the Hierophants are most skilled in the healing arts," the King mused, "But we feared…and of course, they've never quite been the best of friends…"

Royne ignored him. His throat grew thick and inwardly he struggled to master his anger and sorrow, glancing away at the floor, the ceiling, the tapestries, anywhere but at the woman reclining in the bed. At last, he felt a light touch upon his arm and he glanced down to see Amarthia gazing up at him. The light in her eyes, so notably vibrant, seemed now to have dwindled like the embers of a dying fire. Dying, but not dead, for they flashed briefly in recognition at the sight of the Loremaster, and her lips spread into a wistful smile. *I'm sorry!* he whispered, for in the woman's gaze alone he had read her unsung tale and knew all that he needed to know. *So, so sorry!* The Bard remained silent and shut her eyes once more as she lay back upon the pillow.

"So what's wrong with her?" King Erolan asked brusquely.

Royne took a deep breath. "She is very ill," he said.

"Ill?" Erolan asked, "How can she be ill? She's Anointed."

"The Anointing does not grant complete immunity," Royne said tersely, "It simply offers increased resistance to plague and pestilence. As with wounds, we recover much more quickly and remain much more resilient, but just as a mortal wound might still kill us so might a particularly virulent disease."

The King looked stricken, "Then you're saying she's got plague?"

"In a sense."

"Will I catch it?"

Royne swallowed a sudden surge of wrath, "You will not."

"Are you certain?"

"Absolutely."

"How?"

"Because you're not a woman."

"What do you mean?"

Royne's eyes flashed with latent anger. "She's with child."

All of a sudden, the castle, the Bard, the King, and the bedchamber disappeared and Royne tumbled through the air and slammed his head upon the floor of the wagon. A moment later, Conor came crashing down upon him.

"By the Bloody Brethren, Conor?!" he shouted "What are you doing?!"

"I'm sorry, sir," the small boy said, untangling himself from the young Loremaster, "The wagon—it appears to have stopped."

"I'll say it did," Royne muttered. He shook his head and rubbed thoughtfully at the large bump that was already forming upon his brow. He retrieved *The Book of Histories* from where it had fallen and checked to make sure it was no worse for the wear. However, at the memory of the strange vision, he found himself once more confronted with unexplainable phenomena, and as always, he ignored the sudden upwelling of mental dissonance and stuffed the book under his arm. "Well, I don't hear any sounds of fighting," he said, "So I suppose we should find out what's going on."

At some point in their flight, the baggage train must have rejoined the main force of soldiers, cavalry, and elephants, and as the army drew to a stop, what was once an organized column of rank and file legionnaires was now little more than a jumbled mob.

Royne stepped out of the wagon with Conor in tow, leaping aside as a legion scout thundered past them on horseback. For a moment, Royne considered asking one of the other soldiers or camp followers about the halt, but thought better of it.

"Enough of this foolishness," he told Conor, "We need to find the general."

No sooner had he finished speaking, however, when a second horseman rode up to them, reared in his mount, and offered the Young Loremaster a nod.

"General Navarro requests you join him at the head of the column," the man said.

"Point me in the right direction," Royne replied, "And we'll meet him directly."

With a wave of his hand, the soldier indicated the general's whereabouts and Royne and Conor hurried onward to join the Gray Wolf. All about them, men hustled about here and there while officers on horseback rode around in circles barking orders. At length, the young Loremaster and his steward neared the front of the misshapen column and beneath the dual standards of the Fifth and Seventh Legions, Royne discerned General Navarro, General Callum, Captain Velius, and an assortment of other officers staring in silence out across the plain.

Following their stoic gazes, his eye was drawn to another large mass of people—a veritable army, though while some among them wore the tattered green cloaks of the Grantisi legions, most seemed little more than peasants, wanderers, and refugees.

At the head of the mob, a single man, cloaked, cowled, and leaning upon a long wooden staff, strode forth to meet the Grantisi commanders. A spark of recognition flashed in Royne's mind, and while he had never once seen the man before, somehow he knew him.

"Come along, Conor," Royne muttered, quickening his pace. An odd queasiness settled in the pit of his stomach and his heart felt heavy with a strange sense of nostalgia.

What's wrong with me? he wondered, *First the book and now this? None of it makes any sense...*

"Master Royne," General Navarro said, as the young Loremaster approached, "Allow me to introduce—"

"Salasco the Wall," Royne said, "Yes, I know."

CHAPTER 24: FEYHOLD

The folk of Feyhold were indeed few, though they were far more than Bel, Sir Armel, or anyone else expected. For in addition to the twenty-odd archers and woodsman that lived within the old ruin, there were others still who called the place home—women, children, and the old. All told, they may have been as many as three score in total, camping within the caves, hollows, or rough earthen hovels built from a mixture of mud, dung, and twigs.

"How long have you lived here?" Bel asked the Shackle as the soldiers set to making camp. It was far too late to make any true repairs on the ruined walls or keep so Bel decided to instead use the evening to ingratiate themselves with the denizens of the forest by sharing their food and drink. "I had heard that the Shackle and the Steed came north more than twelve centuries ago," he added.

"Aye, that's true," the Shackle said, "Though it weren't me, of course."

"So I assumed. There are plenty of miracles I've heard attributed to the Guardians, but immortality isn't one."

"No, though barring death in battle, long life is one, for the Shackle before me was well over a hundred when he passed on."

Bel sighed and leaned upon his spear. They stood upon the top of the rocky outcrop watching the soldiers and peasants below. Wendell had been tasked with seeing to the stores, and with the help of a few others, was in the process of setting the cook fires going. "So how long has it been?" Bel asked again.

The Shackle folded his arms and rubbed his heavy jaw. "It's difficult to say. I lose track from one set of memories to the next. From what I can tell there's always been a Shackle in Feyhold, since the day the Warlock's man was expelled. Mostly they lived as hermits, but once the war began among you lords of the plain, folks began turning up in droves. Poor folk mostly, or those left with nothing in the wake of the war—wounded, cripples, orphans, and the like. You know how it is. Men take pains to count the dead after a battle, but the casualties always amount to many more."

Bel gave a heavy sigh. "True," he said. There were those among the light cavalry of the past that met such fates. He had always tried to ensure that they were seen to, but being constantly on the move as the war raged ever on, it was hard to know for certain what became of them. Besides, while he might gift a widow a hefty sum, who knew what became of her once the money was gone?

"At any rate," the Shackle said, "I've had the Gift now for ten, perhaps fifteen years?"

"The Gift?"

"The Gift of the Guardians—the Anointing."

A spark of recognition flashed in Bel's brain. "I see."

"Before that..." the Shackle continued, "I was a thief—a good one too— but I gave it up when I took the title, at least in the usual sense. The forest holds plenty for those just trying to survive, though I'm sure it counts as poaching to one king or another."

"Well," Bel said, "Both of the former kings travel with me, and I'm sure neither would begrudge you and your folk a decent meal."

"That's well and good," the Shackle said, with a crooked grin, "But I wasn't asking pardon or permission."

"I suppose not," Bel smiled, "And, it's not up to either of them to grant it to you anyway. The old war's over. There's a new one about to begin."

"Isn't there always?" the Shackle grimaced.

Bel gave a futile shrug. "It's my hope that this will be the last one—for a lifetime and more, if we're lucky."

The Blackguard snorted. "Well," he said, "It's my hope that when next I decide to take a shit, instead of the usual leavings, I find a pile of gold."

"I know," Bel said, "You could just as soon have a world where horses fly as you could a world without war. But..." he paused, "I can't just let it be. I can't simply accept that war and death and killing are an inevitable part of life. I can't give up on a lasting peace. "

The Shackle gave a low chuckle, "And you really believe you can make that happen, don't you?"

"I have to try," Bel shrugged. "Peace might be a fool's dream, but to be fair, I've never thought of myself as wise."

From his vantage point, Bel watched as Sir Emory, Sir Armel, and a makeshift royal guard led the royal carriage into the courtyard below. When the doors opened, Sir Emory helped the old kings exit through the far side while Sir Armel offered his arm to the Princess. In the light of the setting sun, Marina's scarlet hair shone beautifully, like fire or blood.

"I assume that's the princess," the Shackle chortled, "I hope she's prepared. We've few enough comforts here. I'll tell you right now. Until those caves are cleansed or that keep's mended enough as to keep out the rain, she can turn her nose up as high as she wants, but there's no escaping the stink."

"She's not like that."

"Aye, we'll see."

"She's not," Bel said, "They call her the Winter Rose, the flower that blooms even among the snow."

The Shackle shook his head. "And I thought the Guardians had strange names," he chuckled, "Being in the forest so long, I forgot how you nobles carry on. Silent Princes, Winter Roses, what's next?"

Plague Kings? Bel thought moodily, *Blood Blossoms?*

"Still," the forester added, "In the wilds out here, winter often means only death and cold. It'd be nice to think that among all that there could exist something fair and kind, if she's as you say."

Bel watched her accept Marcus from Elsa while the nursemaid descended from the wagon. The baby fussed about in his wrappings, for Bel knew it was near time he should be fed. Marina simply smiled and gently rocked him in her arms. Again, Bel felt the pangs of guilt mingled with an upwelling of warmth. "She is," he said.

The Shackle gave another laugh. "Well, perhaps I should just take you at your word," he said, "For never in a thousand years would I have ever guessed these ruins would play host to two kings, a princess, and a bloody searoan— all in one day."

"What times we live in," Bel said, and clapping the other Blackguard on the shoulder, began the descent from the slopes of the outcrop to the encampment below.

Over the next few days, the Tower, his captains, and his soldiers rested and planned for the repairs that would be necessary for the defense of the ruin. Already, men had dug trenches and cut posts for a line of palisades, and with the help of the Shackle and his foresters, others mixed mortar and daub to reinforce the crumbling walls. Fortunately, the caves among the base of the outcrop provided additional shelter and storage, and the kings' carriage carried with it the frame for a large canvas pavilion.

Once the men and women were sufficiently rested after the long journey eastward, the construction and repair work began in earnest and continued over the course of the entire next week and beyond into the Month of the Stag. The palisade wall came together quickly and timber was cut to build a new roof over the stone husk of the ruined keep. Construction began on two longhouses; one that might serve as a barracks, and another to function as a stable.

Each morning, Sir Armel and Sir Emory would ride forth with an assortment of volunteers to scout the area beyond the forest, and to make contact with the elders of the few nearby peasant villages. Their hope was to discover what they could about any of the local knights and lords owing fealty to Lord Harren in Pridel—particularly whether any of them might be willing to turn against him. Unfortunately, from what they could tell, it seemed that, like Dermont, Harren had seeded the area with men after his own manner—straw men and politicians, placed not for their quality or knightly virtues, but rather for their wealth and sycophantic support.

There was one knight, though, Sir Umbert Malet, and his son Guy, who joined them readily, while two others—though reluctant to commit to overt militant support just yet, were willing as a show of good faith to offer a cart load of grain, two oxen, a milk cow, and a dozen sheep, as well as certain token luxuries such as wine, pickled fish, and sweet meats. Should the rebellion secure a significant victory in their fight against the Plague King, Sir Armel believed these others would be more than willing to join the cause.

Sparrow, Horn, and Wendell, meanwhile, rode out even farther toward Bel's Uncle Talvert's former castle, the Ebon Keep, in hopes of recruiting more men-at-arms, skirmishers, and any others with a will to fight. Now under the command of yet another pandering nobleman, the folk of the region where unhappy with their new master, and many—peasant and soldier alike—flocked to the banner of their old lord's nephew, the Silent Prince. Soldiering women in particular found a home among the rebels, easily persuaded by Sparrow with tales of Lady Valerie the Iron Fist, Lilia, and others who gained honors and accolades of distinction throughout the years of war. Furthermore, on their return to Feyhold, the three skirmishers and their fellows came upon two supply caravans belonging to the Plague King, which provided a welcome addition as the army of rebels grew and grew.

As such, the full complement of fighting men and women under Bel's command had now surpassed the five hundred mark, with another three or four score of support personnel that included drovers, camp followers, and other hangers-on. Feyhold could in no way host all of them and so a type of shantytown had built up around the rocky outcrop, leading the Shackle to remark that in but a few weeks, he had somehow gone from squatting in a ruin to being the master of a castle.

With such numbers, Bel knew that they could not hide for much longer. By now, Dermont was certain to have heard of Bel's escape, and with the folk of the White Wood vassalage mysteriously heading off to disappear within the forest, it was only a matter of time before he pieced things together. Were this not obvious enough, Bel knew his brother's love of spies and it seemed inevitable that Canton, Dermont's Spymaster, would soon have men placed within his ranks, if he did not already.

Yet was five hundred enough to take Pridel, let alone to hold it? Beyond that, what of the other lords of Valendia and Gasparn? After having just sworn fealty to King Dermont, would they be willing to break those fresh oaths to join now with the rebellion? Even if they were, could he ever really trust men whose loyalties were so fickle?

These were the very reasons Bel had never had any interest in court or politics and why he often counted himself so lucky to be Cedric's youngest son. He admitted as much to Sir Emory as they walked the camp, welcoming new arrivals, and ensuring all was in order.

"Do you think your father or your grandfather trusted all the men beneath them?" the old knight asked, "Bear in mind, these men who support Dermont, once swore loyalty to King Cedric—Marius too."

"So they're not ever to be trusted?"

"Most, no."

Bel sighed, "I hate this."

Sir Emory's lips twisted into a wry smirk. "So did your father," Emory said, "So did Larius, and so does anyone with any sense, even Dermont."

"I don't know. Dermont seems to like these games."

"Maybe, but do you think Dermont has any respect whatsoever for a man like Jarrett Harren or Giles Pronet? Of course not. He offered the important positions to his trusted friends—Whitemane and Roanshead, and the like—but Harren, Pronet, and every other minor lord and knight is little more to him than a pawn upon a chessboard."

"Then what's the use then?" Bel sighed, "If nobles do no good for either the peasants at the bottom or their kings at the top, then why even bother with them at all?"

"You've spent too much time with the common folk," Emory smiled, "Words like that, no wonder they love you."

"Better love by choice than love by force."

"Aye, true, but think of Grantis."

"What of it? They abolished the nobility and created a republic where every man is believed to be an equal. *And*, they choose their own leaders."

"Aye, they choose their own leaders, and they used to like nothing more than to boast of how enlightened and fair-minded they all are. But tell me this: who wins the elections? In fact, who are the only men to get their names on the docket? It's not the fishermen or the swineherds, or some poor farmer—even if he's one of the few who knows how to write his name," Emory shook his head, "No, it's the rich men—the wealthy merchants, the land owners, the masters of the guild. They're the ones who become the senators. Not the poor folk."

"Aye, but it could be. Maybe not the farmer, but if he saves and works hard enough, perhaps it could be his son that becomes the next senator."

"And what would he save? The money he gains from the crops he grows? Those same ones he once had to turn over to his landlord? Sadly, the farmers of Grantis save no more now than they did under the nobles. For, although lords have been replaced by governors, and tribute is replaced by tax, it's all one really."

"But still, the farmer's son—"

"Aye, the farmer who worked so hard to become learnéd, who scrimped and saved so his child might have two coins to rub together instead of just one. In a fair and just world, I would only hope to see his lot improved, his children flourish. But what of the old senator's son? Doesn't he too inherit his father's wealth—already, as it is, substantial? How does the farmer's son with his two coins compete with that come election time?" Sir Emory shook his head and gave a sarcastic chuckle, "They abolished divine right and heredity only to set it up again themselves. Only this time it's not the gods, but gold that marks the favored. For my part, I can't tell which is worse."

Bel could not help but agree, "I suppose you're right, though I find it odd to hear such words from the mouth of a seneschal. I had no idea you had become such a misanthrope."

"Of course, I am. I'm old!" Emory laughed, "No, my prince, if there's one thing I've learned in life, it's that men are men—brutish, selfish, and often stupid. Only once in a while does one come along who is extraordinary in that—somehow—he is none of those things. Those are the men who make great kings, and it's for those reasons that I have devoted my life to serving your father, and why I continue to serve you."

"Emory," Bel laughed, "I have no wish at all to be a king. To be perfectly honest, I was actually rather relieved when Dermont abolished my rights as a prince."

"Strange sentiment from one so surrounded by an army dedicated to rebellion."

"I am not doing this for myself, as you well know," Bel sighed, "I do it for them, and for my son."

The seneschal grinned. "Which is why," he said, "You'd make a rare king."

"Emory, no. For the thousandth time, no."

"Fine," the old knight said, "But if not a rare king, then how about a rare queen?"

"A queen?"

"Surely you must have thought about it at some point," Sir Emory said, "If we are to succeed and dethrone Dermont, *someone* must rule. Your father and King Marius have both decried themselves as unfit, and if you, too, refuse to accept the throne, then that leaves only…"

"Marina."

"But would she accept? Now, that is the question."

Bel's brow creased in thought. "If she believed it would help the people, then I believe she would," he said. For it was hardly a year ago that she first offered herself to Dermont, willingly, in hopes that it might end the war. He had refused her, offering only insult and insolence. That the Plague King had now seemed to have changed his mind in no way suggested a change of heart. Rather, it was simply another means by which to exert his will, solidify his claim, and inflict further shame upon his enemies.

However, on her own, Marina would make a fine queen, for she was kind and wise, and though on the surface, she exemplified the idyllic maiden in temperament and form, Bel knew that she was not simply some simpering lamb, nor could he ever think to describe her as weak-willed. She was thoughtful and brave, intelligent and confident, and while the past year had laid her low with her own share of hardships and sorrows, Bel sensed that the rooted strength of the Winter Rose ran far too deep to be spoiled by the frost.

Sir Emory was right. Between Valendia and Gasparn, there had been a surplus of kings for nearly a hundred years. But queens?

"I think a queen is a fine idea," Bel said aloud.

"Do you now?" Emory smirked.

"And long overdue."

"Well good," the old knight mused. "Of course, whatever man she married would *become* the next king," he shrugged, "But since I could not imagine she'd suffer any other man but you by her side, we're safe enough there as well."

"What?!" Bel stopped short in their pacing and his eyes grew wide with surprise.

"Don't feign surprise with me, lad." Sir Emory raised an eyebrow. "Have you not been down this road before? I believe it runs past Clearpoint?"

Bel sighed, "You're not wrong." They began walking again, and Bel felt his chest grow heavy. With each passing day, the princess was more and more in his thoughts. Sometimes in his dreams, he would be walking with Lilia, and suddenly he would look away only to turn back and find Marina beside him. Seeing her with Marcus only made it worse, for the princess seemed to possess a genuine affection for the babe, the nearest thing, perhaps, to his true mother's love.

"Though...I would be a liar if I did not claim some affection for her either," he said at last, "But...but Lilia. I can't forsake her. I loved her. I still love her, and she's the mother of my child—taken from him, from both of us. It just...I can't help but feel that it...that..."

Sir Emory breathed a heavy sigh. "I know, lad," he said, "I've outlived two wives of my own remember. Good women both, and true."

"I fear I do dishonor to her memory, by even thinking..." Bel rubbed his eyes and shook his head, "I don't know. The wound is still so fresh."

"Well, I did not know Lilia as you did," the old knight said, "But I do know this. She loved you, so much so that when she found out she was the hostage Dermont was using to force you north, she came up with some fool-headed plan to either kill him or die in the attempt. She said that if she couldn't be at your side to guard your life in the field, she would do what she must to guard it at home."

"She did?"

"Thank the gods we learned she was with child shortly thereafter and we convinced her to put it all to rest."

"She always hated Dermont," Bel said, "She'd be happy as a foal in spring to be here with us now."

"I don't doubt you."

"She was convinced we would not last, that I would leave her. She said I was too important. Then, at Clearpoint, I almost..." Bel bit his lip and shook his head, fighting to keep the tears from his eyes, "Fire and Blood, I miss her."

"It's alright, lad," Emory said, gripping him by the shoulder, "It's alright."

Bel shook his head again and sighed, "All of this at once, I just don't know what to do," he nodded toward the camp, "Lilia, Marcus, the escape, the princess, and now all these people! Everyone seems to be looking to me to fix things, and I would do it, if only I knew how..."

"We'll figure it out together," the old knight said, his scar twisting with his smile, "But as far as Lilia is concerned, I would think that for one who fought so hard and so often to safeguard your life, the only way to dishonor her would be to forget to live."

Bel took a deep breath and leaned heavily upon his spear. It was upon the eaves of this very forest that he and Lilia had slain their final enemy together—a Gasparn knight named Raylon Jace, the Snow Bear. The memory of her, splattered with blood and crying in rage, stirred something within his breast. Perhaps that was what he needed to finally allow her to rest. *Only the song of battle could ever serve her as a dirge...*

"In any case," Bel said at last, "Tomorrow we can call all of the captains together and discuss what to do about Pridel. I can't help but feel like we're on borrowed time and we need to act quickly. We're in no position to lay siege so we'll have to be clever and find another way to force Harren's surrender."

"I'll pass the word," Emory said.

They walked on a bit further in silence, and Bel marveled at all of the disparate folk who had come to them, and the many unlikely alliances that the past few weeks had wrought. A Gasparn knight sharing a meal with a Valendian skirmisher. A princess who was guest to a Blackguard thief. A pair of kings who were once the bitterest of enemies sat smoking their pipes together as old friends.

Without the Bloodline," Bel thought, "*What is there to divide us? We're one land, one people, one blood, and, with any luck, one queen.* He paused, and leaning again on his lance, allowed the slightest of smiles. "I think I may have just come up with a plan," he said.

"What do you mean?" Sir Emory asked.

"Listen."

CHAPTER 25: HIGHBOARD

Though it was considered the fifteenth barony of the Brock, Highboard was in fact little more than a single city. Stretching across the entire length of the Brocken Vale that sloped down from the fells of the Firrinies to the shores of Lake Bartund, it was perhaps the largest city in all of Termain in terms of geographical area. In the center of the city, the castle of the Lord-Baron, the Brock itself, overlooked the concentric, walled districts of the capitol, guarded along its perimeter by the fourteen smaller, stone keeps that housed the other barons when the assembly was in session. Still, even in peacetime, clad in the bright blue banners of the Brock and its barons, the sheer size and stonework that comprised the great city made it appear a formidable place indeed.

Yet as much as Brigid longed to take Lughus by the hand and go exploring, she knew that there was too much at stake for her to give in to her passions, for between Harlow the Hammer, Provincial Andresen, and the entire Barony of Marthaine, danger could lie behind any corner. So, since their arrival two days earlier, she had contented herself with remaining safely indoors within the sanctity of the Galadin estate, guarded by Sir Owain's men-at-arms and the great hound Fergus while Lughus and the seneschal quietly paid their calls to the other barons armed with Horus's notes and missives.

Not that they had simply left her behind. In fact it was quite the opposite, for more than once had Lughus invited her to come along, but she had chosen not to. For one thing, a week of riding from Galadin had left her back and legs sore and achy. As she had guessed, she took to riding rather easily, but the intuitive ability *to* ride had not prepared her body for the experience of *actually* riding. Deciding to try out the trousers Jergan had found for her before they left had not helped matters either and she could only marvel at the pain she might have been in had she not been blessed with the Guardians' expedited healing. However, saddle-sores alone were not what kept her from accompanying the young baron as he made his calls. Rather, it was the result of her limited understanding of politics that kept her distant. She had already begun to feel as if she had interfered far more than she should have in the affairs of the Brock, and she worried that her presence in any of these more subtle and private negotiations might cause the young Baron Galadin more harm than good.

Still, it pained her to be apart from him, left as she was to worry about his safety. At least half a dozen times she pleaded with Fergus to follow after him as an added safeguard, but the hound refused to leave her side. Eventually, it dawned on her that her orders could apparently not overrule those previously given to him by his master, and with a mixture of affection and vexation, she eventually gave up.

Thankfully, despite Sir Owain's threats of traveling light, he had indeed made sure that there would be room on their small baggage cart for Brigid's maid so she was at least lucky enough to have Ada's companionship throughout the day. Though they had only just met, the porter's daughter was a lovely girl and Brigid soon understood how the bond between a lady and her maid could become so strong (as in the case of her mother and Livonia). Considering that it was the lady's maid who was to dress her, arrange her hair, help her bathe, and see to any other duties that may crop up, it was nearly impossible not to arrive at some manner of friendship. Since Brigid often preferred to see to her own needs, Ada, who was only a few years her elder, occupied a role not so much as a servant, but rather, as an advisor, instructing her in the practical areas of womanhood that she had never learned.

As in all things, Brigid had no desire to emulate the ways so effortlessly modeled by her mother, and while she had nothing but respect for Annabel, Brigid was neither a mother nor a wife. In either instance, both women were also more than twice her age. Thus, in Ada, Brigid found a person she might trust to instruct her, and yet someone with whom she might also relate. Particularly when, on the eve of their arrival in Highboard, Brigid found herself crippled by sudden, excruciating pains.

The sudden arrival of her monthly, seemed intent on proving itself more an enemy to her than any armed foe. Over the last two years, she had only known it to occur inconsistently, due to—according to Josephine's diagnosis—an "insistence on remaining waifishly thin" combined with the lack of "a man's warming touch." Regardless. she would be forever grateful for Ada's aid and guidance, particularly for sparing her from having to deal with the ignorance and idiocy that such things often evoked in even the most well-meaning of men.

Along those same lines, on the few occasions where Brigid had gathered the nerve to ask, she appreciated that Ada was also willing to speak on matters relating to young men. Unlike the wretched Drove back at Blackstone, Ada was not some giggly, simpering tart eager to play the part of plaything for any man of rank and title. Nor was she some pious handmaid to the Lady, renouncing the world from the sanctity of her cloister. And while she told Brigid from the beginning that it was probably easier to understand the minds of the gods than it was to understand the minds of other people, she still listened and even went so far as to offer her own insights born of experience, and where relevant, her own practical advice.

Of course, it wasn't really young men Brigid really wanted to know about, but rather, a particular young *man*. Yet to admit such a thing was to move it from the realm of vague, undefined feelings and notions, and solidify it into something much more real. So, after two days of talking *around* the issue, Brigid was beginning to get the sense that the maid was becoming somewhat weary of entertaining her questions, just as she herself was with listening to Ada's repeated responses. Thankfully, when Lughus finally returned that evening, and the two of them were dining alone while Sir Owain visited his Crofton sister, she was actually excited when he informed her that the Lord-Baron, Perin Glendaro, had invited her to pay a call upon him, his wife, and his three daughters.

"Why does he want to meet with me?" Brigid asked.

"You are after all the daughter of the Archduke of Dwerin," Lughus smiled wearily, "I think it's a gesture of respect and honor, from the leader of one sovereign realm to the heir of another."

"Oh," she said bashfully, "I suppose that makes sense. Tell me you're coming too?"

He shook his head, "I'm not invited. Besides, Owain and I are to meet with Baron Helmstead again."

"So I'm to go alone?"

"You can take Fergus, in fact, I'd feel much better if you did," he said, "And I'd still like to walk you there myself—not that there's anything to fear, just...I thought that , if you don't mind..."

"Of course," she said, "But it won't make you late for your meeting, will it?"

"The Brock is on the way to the Helmstead keep," he said, rubbing his eyes, "And believe me, there's nothing I want more than to be free to spend at least a little time with you—" he paused, "What I mean is I miss our walks back in Galadin."

Brigid smiled inwardly and glanced down at the tabletop, "I do too."

"At least it shouldn't be much longer. The assembly meets the day after tomorrow," he said, "You will come with me then, won't you?"

"I already told you I would," she smiled, "If you're going to have to look across a room and see the Hammer or the Marthaines or anyone else who might mean you harm, you know I'm going to be right there beside you."

"I know," he smiled, "Thank you."

She watched him for a moment, most of his food left uneaten. "You look exhausted," she finally said, "You're not...having nightmares again, are you?"

"No," he said, "I'm just...I don't know. Things are not going well with Helmstead, even though Nordren agreed to every concession Horus wrote up."

"I thought all that only mattered in the event that someone questioned your rights?"

"Harlow and Andresen have been crying foul to anyone who will listen, and the Ambassador from Andoch—some Commissioner named Corbeil— has been a constant headache for the Lord-Baron on their behalf. Glendaro said to hope for a miracle, but expect a challenge."

"I'm sorry," she reached across the table to give his hand a squeeze, "Still, what's the worst that could happen?"

Lughus shrugged, "They could try to kill us?"

"Oh, they've already tried that, right?" she grinned.

Slowly, he smiled and turned to meet her eye, and for a long time held her gaze. The gray storm clouds softened, though they still shone with electricity. She thought back to how he used to look away, and although she was glad that he no longer did so, when he looked at her like this, it always made her heart beat faster. His hair, too, seemed to shine even brighter in the light of the braziers, curling around his head like a crown or a halo. It made her think of the Wrathorn Sun God from the fairy stories she read as a child, and dressed as he was in the fine blue and gold raiment befitting a baron at court, he looked all the more handsome. Lean and fit as a statue.

Stop being such a fool! she told herself and looked away, willing herself unsuccessfully not to blush. A thin strand of hair had fallen across her eye and hurriedly she brushed it from her face in annoyance. "Do you want to play chess?" she asked suddenly, "If you're not too tired."

"That would be nice," Lughus smiled, "Though you're sure to win this round. I doubt I'll be able to focus."

That makes two of us... she thought. "How are things with Igrainne? Faden seemed helpful, and Horus was rather confident."

He shrugged and returned to picking at his trencher, "I think they're with us."

"You see?" she laughed, "Now that's good!"

"I suppose," he smiled, "I just worry about giving knighthoods to men I don't know. Before Rastis let me begin learning the sword, he made me study treatises and tomes and all sorts of things about what it meant to be a true knight. I'd hate to knight a man who wasn't worth it, for it seems there's far too much of that as there is. Besides, even with Igrainne, we haven't tipped the balance of a vote."

Brigid shook her head, "Oh stop being so dour! You can't give up hope!"

"I won't," he said. *He'll just change the subject,* she smiled to herself, and sure enough, he did, though what he had to tell her caught her a bit by surprise.

"Did you know that Dwerin has an ambassador here too?" he asked, "The Lord-Baron told me today when we met at the Nordren Keep. It's some man named Ingles?"

"I don't think I know him, but I assumed there would be someone from Dwerin," she said, "Though I wasn't exactly sure."

"If you want to pay a call, I'll make time to go with you."

Brigid breathed a sigh. There mere thought of her homeland filled her with conflicting thoughts. On the one hand, she was glad to be free of it, for between her mother, her uncle, her cousin, and all the wretched nobles, Blackstone seemed such a dreadful place in comparison to Galadin and the Brock, which in but a few short months had been more of a home to her than Dwerin had ever been. However, at the same time, she remembered the Falcon and their talks of injustice and the plight of the common folk. She recalled Alan's horrible speeches and his ill-treatment of the servants and of guardsmen like Hodges. Geoffrey, too, had told her a bit about some of the soldiers he had met, in particular about a captain named Barrow, a good man who had been his friend. As the daughter of the Archduke, did she not have some duty to them as well? Gareth had spoken of a Mountain Queen, and though she did not want that by any means, she did at least want to try to help her people. She certainly owed them that much; but displaced and in exile, what could she possibly do against her mother and her uncle?

"I don't know," she said at last, "I'll think on it, and if I do decide to pay a call, I'll tell you," she flashed him another smile, pushing thoughts of Dwerin from her mind, "Now if you're finished, I'll get the chessboard. As weary as you are with political maneuvering, perhaps I can finally outdo your strategy here. I need every advantage I can get to beat you."

"You know that's not true." He grinned.

"No," she teased, "But saying it might make you feel better after you lose!"

The next morning Ada woke Brigid early to prepare her for the visit with the Lord-Baron and his family, and for the first time since leaving Blackstone, she consented to dress not in one of her simple peasant frocks, but an actual gown, periwinkle in color and embroidered with little white doves. For, she had no wish to appear uncouth before the man who presided over the assembly, despite his pledge of friendship to Galadin, and if playing the role of a proper lady and an amiable friend to Lady Glendaro and her daughters could in any way help Lughus, it was the least she could do to help. Still, she would not be "proper" enough to leave Whisper and Shade behind. The fine ladies would simply have to ignore the fact that she was armed.

"Sure didn't Master Jergan outdo himself with this gown," Ada observed with a smile, "You'll be certain to turn some heads in this, my lady—a certain golden one in particular, and I don't mean Fergus."

"I don't what you mean," Brigid lied, "But I suppose it is rather nice."

The maid grinned and draped a thin mantle of white silk around Brigid's narrow shoulders, fastening it with a silver pin. "There!" she said with a nod, "Now that's perfect!"

Brigid bit her lip, "You think so?"

"Of course," she said, "Though if you'd like we could still do something with your hair? Plait it? Or put it up? Show off that fine neck? He'll like that, I'm sure."

"Ada…"

"I'm sorry," Ada smiled, "I'm only teasing. Besides, I remember how worried he was when we cut it."

"Ada, please!" Brigid blushed, "He's my good friend. That's all."

"Fine, fine," Ada chuckled, "Though if you don't mind my saying, there's no rule stating that friendship can't become something more."

When at last, all was in order, Brigid, Ada, and Fergus (still following at her heel like a shadow) made their way through the keep to the hall where Lughus, Sir Owain, and their men-at-arms were gathering. As soon as she met them, Brigid's shoulders went tense and her stomach tied in knots. Her rational mind could not understand why she was suddenly so nervous. Perhaps it was the look in the young baron's eyes when he saw her—stricken, stunned, his face drained of all color. He rose quickly to his feet, as if by reflex, followed by Sir Owain and any of the other men who happened to be seated.

"Good morning," she said, fighting to keep her voice steady.

The men returned her greeting in unison, though they remained standing. Hesitantly, Lughus stepped toward her like one in a daze, his eyes wide and his voice little more than a whisper. "You look lovely."

Beside her, Ada feigned a cough to cover her grinning, and Brigid felt her cheeks grow warm and red. "I haven't made you late or anything, have I?"

she mumbled, somewhat unaware of anything she was saying, "I know you have the meeting with Helmstead."

"It's not for a while," Lughus told her, "We have plenty of time to walk you to the Brock." He cast the seneschal a quick glance, "Owain, are we ready?"

"Aye, sir, four men walk in front, then myself, yourself and the lady, and four to guard the rear." The old knight turned to Brigid and smiled, "I'm afraid you'll have to indulge us in referring to you as 'Lady Brigid' for today. Appearing as you do, one might well confuse you with the Lady of Light."

"The Lady of Light is always depicted as fair-haired." Brigid mumbled, "Like the sun."

"Holy Brethren," Ada smiled, shaking her head. She took Brigid by the hands and adjusted the baldric around her waist. "Now go on, my lady," she said, "You'd best see these men on their way. It seems they've all taken leave of their senses."

I should have just worn my trousers... Brigid thought, though she could not help but feel some measure of glee at the attention, particularly when Lughus offered her his arm with an almost ceremonious gesture and she discovered that she was not the only one blushing.

The city streets outside of the Galadin Keep were crowded with burghers from every corner of the Brock. Most were merchants and tradesman, for just as the capitol was the meeting place for the fourteen barons, those who wished to trade beyond the borders of their home barony found a much easier time brokering trade deals in Highboard. Furthermore, the capitol boasted embassies from a few of the other realms—Andoch, Dwerin, and Grantis—as well as great meeting halls for the major craftsmen's guilds. While the powerful weaver's guild certainly boasted the most grand, the stonecutters, shipwrights, goldsmiths, barristers, and physicians guilds were certainly well represented. Beyond these institutional buildings, there were inns and taverns named for beasts and birds of every color (though most were blue), barracks for both the city watch and the larger mercenary companies based in the Brock, no less than ten churches dedicated to each of the great gods of the Kinship as well as to various minor saints, and unlike Galadin, Blackstone, or anyplace else that Brigid had ever been, Highboard also boasted a theater where one might see both new, contemporary plays, but also well-known classics from the days of Old Calendral.

"We could spend the rest of the summer here and still only scratch the surface of all there is to see." Brigid observed with a smile as their procession passed a small crowd of people gathered around a puppet show.

"Assuming we're not all fleeing for our lives tomorrow," Lughus said, "Perhaps we can finally go exploring. Theo Nordren told me that there's a master blacksmith here who imports steel from Dwerin."

"Theo? He's Baron Nordren's son?"

"Aye, you'll probably meet him at the Assembly," Lughus said. He glanced at her quickly and smiled, "You really do look wonderful."

"And all it took was a gown?" She laughed to hide her nerves. "I must look absolutely horrid in those trousers."

"Of course not," he said, shaking his head, "You look lovely all the time, I just meant..." suddenly he fell silent and his face turned bright scarlet, "It's very warm today."

For a moment, she thought to tease him, but the flutter of affection she felt in her breast caught her tongue and she remained silent.

"Annabel said your birthday was this month," he said, once the coloring of his face had begun to fade.

"It was the third. We passed it on the road."

"If it's all the same. I'd like to get you something."

"Lughus," she said, "I've lived off of your hospitality for a month. You've given me more gifts than I could ever repay."

"Those aren't proper gifts," he said, "I meant something real."

"You're not going to give me jewelry, are you?" She raised an eyebrow. "Don't let the bloody gown fool you. It's still me."

"No, I...I know that." He gave a heavy sigh. "Do you remember that day in the market, the day we...talked about the dreams and everything?"

"Of course."

"Well, you mentioned armor. Then, when we found that suit of mail for Geoffrey you mentioned something about it again," he paused, "And with the Hammer here and everything else, I just...if it comes to battle, I would feel much better about it if you were...somehow armored."

"You want to get me armor?" She grinned.

"You tried on the byrnie. You said it wasn't that heavy—the shirt at least, and it won't make that much noise. Besides, if not mail, then there's always leather. It's lighter and even less restrictive."

Somehow without realizing it, they had reached the barbican that guarded the entry into the great citadel of the Brock. Sir Owain brought the soldiers to a halt and stepped forth to speak to the porter at the gate.

"I'll think about it," Brigid said quickly, glancing up at the immensity of the castle, "My, that's enormous. Have you been inside yet?"

"Not yet, but it's where the Assembly meets, so we'll be back tomorrow."

"It's amazing." She watched the seneschal conversing with the Lord-Baron's guards. "How did Owain's dinner with the Croftons go, by the way?"

Lughus sighed. "Don't ask him."

"I'm sorry."

"It's alright, but he was rather upset when he returned last night."

Sir Owain hurried down from the steps of the barbican to their side. "The Lord-Baron awaits, my lady." He grinned. "They're expecting you."

Lughus looked somewhat uncomfortable. "Why don't we leave some men?" he asked, "For the walk back?"

"Baron Glendaro will see to it," Owain told the young baron, "And she'll have Fergus."

Lughus bit his lip with uncertainty, and Brigid could not help but smile. "It's alright," she said, slipping her arm free to give his hand a squeeze, "I'll be back. You'd think I was going off to Dwerin again, for the look in your eyes!"

"I'm sorry," he said, resting his free hand on the pommel of his sword, "It's just...the Hammer and all. It has me on edge. At any rate, you probably shouldn't keep the Lord-Baron waiting."

Brigid's smile faded, but suddenly it seemed there was a hammer of a different sort pounding in her chest. In the mid-morning sunlight, his hair shone brightly, while his brow furrowed with concern, half-concealing the pair of storm clouds raging just below. It seemed her wrists were trembling and her hand that held his felt numb. Her mind raced back to a similar moment with the Falcon a long time ago. *How foolish I had been,* she thought, *How remarkably stupid.* Yet, whereas she remembered questioning in that moment whether or not she was *supposed* to kiss the Falcon, she was certain that right now, more than anything, she *wanted* to kiss Lughus, even in front of Owain, the soldiers, and half the city.

But, she did not. For just as she knew somehow that the Falcon would have refused her, she knew that Lughus would not, and that brought with it

300

an entirely new world of anxiety. *You're still just a fool!* she thought miserably, *You might have grown wings, but you're still just the same old mouse!*

"I'll keep thinking about that armor," she said at last, offering his hand one final squeeze before releasing it. She took a deep breath and walked with Fergus past Sir Owain to the gate. "Good luck with your meeting!" she smiled quickly and hurried away across the ward, fearful that, for some absurd reason, she might cry. *Aiden's Flame! What is wrong with me?* She shook her head and wiped a stray bit of hair from her face, *I am such a fool!*

By the time she reached the center of the ward and the great, ironbound doors to the keep, Brigid's anxiety had settled into a general malaise of self-loathing, though when a pair of the Lord-Baron's guardsman ran past her to open the portal, she was mortified to realize that they were among those speaking with Owain at the barbican. They had followed her as escort all the time she had been walking, and in all likelihood heard her muttering aloud to herself. *They'll think I'm going bloody mad!* Fergus sniffed at her hand sympathetically, but it did not do much to help, for in her preoccupation, she had forgot his presence as well. *Lady's Grace!* she thought, *Perhaps I have already...*

"The Lord-Baron awaits, my lady," one of the men said.

"Thank you," she said quickly, and scurried past avoiding their eyes.

A short while later, after being escorted by a porter, a steward, and finally the Lord-Baron's seneschal—a tall, brown-skinned knight named Sir Dalton Griegg—she was led out into a large room, splendidly lit by four enormous windows of colored glass. There, she was received at last by Perin Glendaro, his wife Lady Imanie, and his three daughters, Millicent, Rosamon, and Alyson.

"It is so good to finally meet you, Lady Brigid," the Lord-Baron said with a smile, "And I see the Golden Hound of Galadin has provided you with an escort."

"This is Fergus, my lord," Brigid said.

"He's beautiful!" Lady Imanie observed.

"He is," Brigid grinned, nervously ruffling the hound's ears, "And a great warrior to boot. He's saved my life more than once already. I hope you don't mind that he's followed me?"

"We would never dream of turning away one of the great hounds of Perindal! Doing so would constitute some horrific sacrilege or another, though luckily we Glendaros also happen to like dogs." The Lord-Baron laughed and offered his hand for Fergus to sniff. "The Glendaro symbol is the harp. It may not be as rare or as handsome as Good Fergus here, but perhaps later you'll allow us to indulge you with a bit of music. All three of my daughters are quite skilled. Of course, I admit to being a bit biased."

"That would be very nice," Brigid said.

Lady Imanie's maid departed to see to the serving of tea and cakes, and a pair of serving men appeared carrying a large cushioned chair so that Brigid might join the other women in comfort. The baron himself remained standing, leaning against the mantle over the empty hearth. He was not a particularly tall man, nor did he seem possessed of a soldier's broad build, but he carried himself with the polite dignity of a man of intellect and honor, if not war.

"Thank you," Brigid said when she had been seated, adding, "Your city is marvelous, though I regret that I have not yet had much opportunity to explore."

"It is quite impressive," the baron said, "But though the elected Lord-Baron, I am little more than Highboard's steward. The city—and the castle, in truth—belong to all the Brock."

Brigid gave a polite nod. She was nervous. Despite how often she had found herself in situations just such as this at Blackstone, her role back then was limited to serving as further ornamentation to the radiance of her mother. Now, suddenly finding herself the center of attention among such fine folk, and already flustered with her earlier private thoughts, she was uncertain exactly what to say or do.

"We so rarely have visitors from Dwerin anymore," Lady Imanie said pleasantly, breaking the sudden silence, "Apart from Lord Ingles, of course."

"The ambassador," Glendaro said at Brigid's look of uncertainty.

"I see," she said.

"Yes," the lady said. She was an august woman, middle-aged and elegant, with the same caramel complexion and dark brown hair as her daughters. Though, while their hair fell in plaits, hers was gathered in a bejeweled netting at the nape of her neck. "We invited him to join us, but unfortunately he had to refuse on account of some such business." She sighed. "Men and their politics. It's no wonder that the girls and I so rarely make the journey here from Glendaro. We much prefer the quiet of the country and the moors."

"Perhaps *you* do, mother," said Alyson, the youngest of the daughters. She was of an age with Brigid, perhaps a year older on the outside. "Personally, I love the city," she said pleasantly.

Millicent, the eldest girl, breathed a sigh, "You love the jugglers and their absurd plays."

"No, I love the *theater*."

"What's the difference?" Rosamon, the middle girl, smirked.

"Plenty," Alyson said. "Have you had the chance to see it yet?" she asked Brigid, "The theater?"

"No, not yet," Brigid said.

"You're not missing much," Millicent told her, "A bunch of fools weeping and running about like children at pretending."

"Or lewd women dancing on stage like some filthy sailors' tavern," Rosamon added.

"Don't listen to them," Alyson said, "It's wonderful. They put on all sorts of stories—Bard's Tales and legends, tragedies from Old Calendral. You'd like it, and perhaps the young baron would too. Father said he was an Apprentice to our Uncle Rastis."

"He was," Brigid confirmed, though she was reluctant to speak of him any further. It was not that they were being unkind or overly invasive, but for some reason she felt a touch defensive.

"We still have yet to meet him," Rosamon said, "Tell us. What is he like? Father is just dreadful about such things."

"I told you," the Lord-Baron said, "He has golden hair, gray eyes, and a noble bearing. What more could you possibly want to know?"

"Darling," Lady Glendaro said pleasantly, "Allow our guest to speak."

Thankfully, before Brigid could even begin to think of how to reply, the maids returned with the tea and cakes and Baron Glendaro stepped away from his place at the mantle to use their arrival as a means to make his escape. "Unfortunately, I have a matter of some import to attend to before tomorrow's assembly so I will leave you all to your conversing," he smiled pleasantly, "Though I admit that it pains me, for never has there been a lovelier bunch of ladies!"

"More politics," Lady Imanie told Brigid with a roll of her eyes.

"It is the times we live in," he said with a sigh, "However, if it's alright with you, Lady Brigid, I would very much like to speak with you again before you depart."

Brigid sat up straighter in her chair. "Yes, of course," she said, though part of her wished she might leave the pleasantries for another time and follow the baron now. Politics and stratagems, she knew that she could handle. Polite discourse, she did not.

Baron Glendaro inclined his head, "Enjoy your day, ladies."

For the remainder of the morning and on into the afternoon, Brigid sat with the four Glendaro women, chatting, smiling, and doing whatever she could to control her nerves. It was not that it was unpleasant, quite the contrary. They treated her very kindly, and before long, she found herself wondering how her life might have been different if the women at the court of Blackstone had been similar to these fine women of the Brock. In particular, she enjoyed the conversation with the baron's youngest daughter, Alyson, for in many ways Brigid recognized in her a certain kinship, as far as their interests and attitudes were concerned. She was a smart girl, educated and thoughtful, and Brigid hoped that perhaps they could someday count each other as friends.

However, in spite of the pleasantries, her curiosity regarding the Lord-Baron's "matter of some import" gnawed at her mind almost as much as her generalized anxieties relating to her relationship with Lughus. Was it something related to the assembly, or did it have to do with her role as a Blackguard? The Provincial had mentioned something about her being kidnapped from Dwerin. Perhaps word had finally reached her mother, her uncle, or the ambassador about where she had been. In any case, she was not expecting good news.

When at last, the afternoon was drawing to a close, the Glendaro ladies said their goodbyes. Alyson led Brigid and Fergus to her father's solar promising that they would speak again tomorrow. It was customary after the assembly meeting for the Lord-Baron to hold a great feast to honor the other lords and their retainers.

"It was very nice to meet you," the youngest Glendaro said, "It's not often I can say such a thing."

"I understand," Brigid said, "My mother chose all of my companions at Blackstone."

Alyson rolled her eyes. "Thank the Kinship mine had not tried that—not that she wouldn't love the chance. She's just far more preoccupied arranging matches for my sisters. Better them than me, though!"

Brigid gave a nod. "I narrowly escaped that once myself."

"You'll have to tell me how you did it so when the time comes, I'll know what to do."

Brigid smiled, though she doubted the young noblewoman would much enjoy the story of Sir Reid and his ignoble demise.

"Well," Alyson said, "Father's men will show you inside. Goodbye!"

CHAPTER 26: THE ASSEMBLY

Lughus awoke before dawn on the morning of the Assembly, and dressed himself in his formal baronial raiment—a surcoat of deep blue-of-the-Brock emblazoned with the mark of the rampant hound, a linen shirt and woolen trousers of gold, soft leather boots, a thin blue mantle with a hood, and as had become his habit, his light chain hauberk beneath it. Nothing in his outfit was as decorative as many of the other barons might have liked, but he did not find he had much in common with them anyhow.

In the dim light of his chamber, he paced for a while in thought, drew Sentinel, and practiced his stances and guards. When he was finished, he whetted the blade to hone its edge, and polished it with an oiled cloth before returning it to the scabbard. *The sword is an extension of the will*, Crodane had said. Perhaps if his blade was sharp, so might his mind be too, or else after today it was very likely that he would no longer be a baron.

It was strange. In one sense, he was glad for that, for he had never really wanted to be a nobleman. Rather, it was thrust upon him when he would have been much happier to remain simply the Marshal (*simply* the Marshal—as if being labeled an outlaw and a brigand could ever be simple). Yet, in the weeks since his grandfather's death, he had to admit a certain reluctant satisfaction from being the Master of Houndstooth and Baron of Galadin. It was a strange sort of feeling that, for once, the things that he did and the choices that he made truly mattered, and though that brought with it an eradicable feeling of angst, it provided him with the opportunity to have a positive impact on the larger world.

For that reason, if for no other, the prospect that he might lose the title wracked him with remorse for what would be his abject failure.

From beneath the collar of his shirt, he drew out his mother's ring, securely fastened on the strip of rawhide upon which Crodane had worn it for fifteen years. It astounded him to imagine such a period of time roaming the continent as the Marshal, a Blackguard and hunted man, weighed down by his grief. Yet, Lughus knew that should he lose the barony today, he too would wander, just as Crodane had done, beneath the burden of defeat. He too would be crippled by the shame of knowing that he had failed to fulfill his promise to not just the swordsman, but also his grandfather, and in some sense, his mother as well. In all cases, they had expected him to do his duty, to rule justly and wisely, and to safeguard not only the Brock, but all Termain. Even Rastis, he now realized, had anticipated such responsibilities, grooming him as a boy through his required reading and through their many discussions on the nature of virtue and justice, law and order, and the qualities that made a great man. To think that it all might now be for naught was a prospect he did not wish to entertain.

However, he knew that he must be prepared for the worst. For as the Lord-Baron said, by clear right of heredity, there should be no question of his standing as Arcis Galadin's rightful heir. However, his status as a Blackguard—and not just any Blackguard, but one of the fabled Three—was cause enough to challenge his ascension, particularly for the Marthaines, the original targets of the storied Siege. The uproar Harlow and Andresen had caused, as well as the ease with which Andoch had achieved victory over Grantis in the recent war, also offered plenty of reason to give the other barons pause.

Despite any of the plans they had made in Galadin for securing the support of the other barons, the matter still looked bleak. Although Igrainne had pledged to back the Galadins in the case of a vote (thanks to the intercession of the Weavers' Guild), Helmstead refused to commit to anything that might provoke the ire of the Guardians, for already it was said a great force of horsemen were mustering on the Montevalen side of the

Nivanus Mountains. Crofton too had proved a forlorn hope, as Sir Owain's call upon his sister, her husband, and her brother-in-law the baron served only as an opportunity to subtly vent their resentment toward the seneschal for his refusal to accept their once offered command. In exasperation, Lughus and Owain attempted to pay late calls last night upon Waldron and Agathis; however, in both cases, they were refused at the door.

"If it comes to it," Sir Owain had said, and not for the first time, as they walked back from the Agathis keep, "You can count on Horus and me to stand by you through and through. The Houndstooth is a mighty castle, and it wouldn't be the first time Galadin's withstood a siege."

"Thank you, Owain," Lughus told him, "But I don't think it would be wise for me to stay. I'd just as soon take to the road like Crodane."

"Well, you can't go alone," the old knight said, "And without a Galadin, there is *no* Galadin, so I'd have no reason to stay. Rest assured that any as might come for you will have to taste my blade."

"It they do come, it won't just be for me."

That thought alone was enough to set his blood on fire, gazing out his chamber window as the first rays of the sun brightened the edge of the horizon in the east. *Do not hesitate,* Crodane had said as they stood side by side in Lenard's Crossing, *For you can be certain they will not.* Lughus felt his jaw tense and his hand tightened around the hilt of his sword, Crodane's sword, the Marshal's sword. He would not hesitate, and woe be to any man who tried to harm her.

With a sigh, he turned away from the window, paced across the length of his chamber a few times, and without thinking, passed from his room out into the hallway up the small staircase to the battlement of the small keep. The braziers still glowed faintly above and below him, the watchmen on guard standing vigilantly in the light of the predawn. Lughus wiped his palms upon the hem of his surcoat and breathed in the cool morning air to calm himself when he suddenly realized his hands were shaking. As if the politics of Galadin and the Brock were not enough to trouble him, there was also Brigid.

With each passing day, he felt himself drawn to her more and more, and he would be lying to himself if he did not admit that she was in his thoughts throughout the meetings with the other barons—a distraction, he knew, but one he continually chose not to ignore. She was so beautiful—her eyes, her fair skin, her smile—and yesterday in the gown! Aiden's Flame, one would have thought her the Lady of Light herself were it not for her dark hair (but what hair it was, smooth like silk!). Rather, she was like some maiden descended from the stars, a mythical goddess of the moon!

Yet her beauty was but one of the things about her that tore at his heart, inflicting both the greatest pain and pleasure all at once. For, she was kind, she was clever, and she was so spirited. She said what she thought when she thought it and never seemed afraid to do what she thought was right, particularly when it came to how she treated other people. As hard as he had been trying to learn the names of his soldiers, servants, and the folk of the city around the castle, she already seemed to know them all, and to remember them without any effort.

More than anything else, however, she was his friend. From the day they had sat together in the solar and talked, just the two of them, when he told her about his nightmares, and his mother and father, and anything and everything else that came to mind, he no longer felt alone, and if what Geoffrey had told him was true, then he must have meant something more to her as well. For, she too had told him things, with more detail than she had told him earlier, or than she had ever admitted to Geoffrey and Annabel. She told him all about Blackstone, about her mother, her uncles, and their plot against her father. She told him of her daydreams confined to the castle and about her meetings with Gareth in the Tower. She told him of the man who was to be her betrothed and how she'd killed him defending herself, about all of the terrible things her cousin said or did, and the scar she now bore from him beneath her back.

Truly, of all things, her friendship was what he valued most, and though he knew that through that affection he had also come to love her, he refrained from telling her so. For, he feared that if she did not feel the same, it might drive her away, and to be without her was to be worse than alone.

But as far the Assembly was concerned, or Harlow the Hammer, the Provincial, King Kredor, or the entire bloody Order of the Guardians—if any or all of them intended her harm simply for bearing the title of the Blade, they would have the Marshal to contend with first.

He lingered on the battlement until the sun had fully risen, and only then, descended the stairs into the keep to await the others before the fateful hour when they would process together through the city to the Brock and the assembly chamber. The hall below was vacant when he entered, cleared even of the long dining tables, so he sat down on the servant's bench along the side wall. Before long, the keep's year-round chamberlain (a squat little man named Gleids) appeared and asked if he might like anything to break his fast. Lughus refused.

I might try, he thought, *But most like I'd just bring it back up again faster than old Thom Fatty aboard the barge.*

The memory alone brought a slight smile to his face, and he wondered how his old friends fared, hoping that whatever might have befallen Rastis, the two of them had been spared from any harm.

"What's so funny?"

He looked up to see Brigid and Fergus standing nearby. He was not surprised that he had not heard her approach. She was good at keeping quiet; he had noticed as much very early on in their acquaintance while they walked together around the Houndstooth. Rarely did her footsteps make any sound.

"I was just thinking," he shrugged. "Remembering my old friend Thom."

She smiled kindly and sat down beside him. All of the sudden he noticed how short the bench was and how closely that forced her to sit.

"You look nice," he told her. She was dressed all in black, from shirt to surcoat to trousers, though in places they were embroidered with a pattern of little anvils stitched in gold.

"Not lovely?" she teased, "Isn't that what you said yesterday?"

He blushed, but his smile spread wider. "That wasn't all I said," he managed at last.

"You said 'wonderful,' I think too," she grinned, "I guess trousers are no match for a gown."

Lughus breathed a sigh and looked away to playfully ruffle Fergus's ears. *More than a match,* he thought, avoiding the way the cut of the hosiery fit her slim form, the way the hilts of her daggers rested upon her slender hips. "Did Jergan make that for you too?" he asked.

"He did," she said, "Though, truthfully, if you think it inappropriate for the Assembly, I'll go change into a dress. I don't want to embarrass you or cause a scandal. I only thought, with all your talk of fighting and the Hammer and all…"

"I think I'm enough of a scandal myself that even if anyone had a problem with you, it wouldn't matter," he said, "And besides, I think you look very nice."

"Ooh, *very* nice now?" she grinned, "Well, so do you."

He nodded silently and gave a wan smile. "Listen," he said, "If there is fighting..."

"If there is, I doubt it would happen right away," she said, "They wouldn't want a fight in the assembly chamber, and besides, the Lord-Baron likes you, or so I get the feeling. He wouldn't simply give you over to Harlow right there—though that doesn't mean the Hammer won't try something."

"True," he said, "But just in case—"

"We stand together. Side by side."

"No, that's not what I was going to say," he sighed. *What was I going to say?* "If there's fighting, I would rather you try to get away—"

"No."

"Brigid—"

"Nope."

"I'm serious—"

"You should just stop talking." She smirked and gave his shoulder a playful shove. "Geoffrey said the same stupid thing at the grotto. I wouldn't leave him, and for damned certain, I'm not leaving you."

"Brigid..."

"Lughus..."

He sighed; there was no arguing with her. He had learned that too very early on. Besides, it was nice to see her in high spirits again. When he returned last night, she seemed a bit out of sorts. She had claimed nothing was wrong, of course, but he had come to know her well enough to see beyond the façade. "So be it," he said at last, "Come what may."

"Come what may," she grinned. However, a moment later, her smile faded and Lughus watched her brow crease. "Speaking of," she began, "The Lord-Baron told me something yesterday that's...somewhat complicated, and I fear I've caused even more trouble."

A loose strand of hair slipped down over her face and he fought the desperate urge to gently brush it away. "What is it?" he asked.

"You know that my mother and my uncle were betrothed. Well, they plan to marry come Harvestide. They even invited the Lord-Baron. That's not it, though—the problem I mean," she took a deep breath, "The problem is that, since word reached them that I was alive *and* a Blackguard, they're claiming that it was Gareth and I together who conspired to murder my uncles, and that we would have killed the Sheriff and my mother too were it not for Alan stopping us. They've also...argued that, as such, I'm to be denied any rights I may try to claim."

Lughus's hand closed on his hilt and his jaw went rigid, but he remained silent for a long time. *The day I meet Alan Beinn will be his last!* He shook his head and scowled, "How did word reach them so fast?"

"By bird, I assume," she said, "It's really not that far from the Brock to Titanis as the crow flies, and it's even closer from Titanis to Blackstone. Plus, if the ambassador from Andoch has one of those bloody great birds the Guardian-King uses..."

"The Calendral kites," Lughus sighed bitterly. He remembered Thom crying hysterically when he thought one of the great birds bit his finger off. From then on, anytime they heard an eagle or a falcon's cry, the fat boy would freeze up and hide his hands in his underarms.

Regardless, Brigid was right. It had been more than a month since he allowed the Hammer to flee. A kite could have easily flown from Highboard to Titanis to Blackstone and back again half a dozen times. "I was a fool to let Harlow go," he muttered, "Showing him mercy has rewarded us with nothing but trouble."

"No," Brigid said, patting his arm. "Showing him mercy is what marks you as a good man and the Hammer as a villain."

"Still," he said, "I'm sorry."

"It's not your fault," she said, "You're not the author of the lies. Anyhow, I wanted you to know in case our...friendship, or simply my presence, causes any trouble."

Lughus shook his head. "We stand together. Side by side," he said kindly, "Isn't that what you just said?"

Brigid flashed him a smile and glanced down at the ground. Her face was hidden from him behind her hair, but for a moment, before she looked away, he thought she might have been blushing. *Why do you not just tell her?* he thought as the dull ache in his chest resumed, *Hesitation means death in battle, but is this not simply another type of duel?* He shook his head, quietly willing himself to shut up.

A short time later, their guard arrived led by Sir Owain. The old knight was outfitted from coif to sabaton in his full array of heavy plate. His great two-handed sword hung across his back, and under his arm, he carried his great helm plumed with horsehair dyed bright blue.

"My, Owain," Brigid said, suppressing a smile, "Perhaps I did not realize things were so dire."

Sir Owain's thick mustache bristled, "My lady, as the baron's seneschal, his safety is my responsibility, and in accordance with that task, my office requires that I appear as such."

"My apologies, then," she said.

"Believe me," the old knight smirked, "You think I'd wear all this if I didn't have to? It's bloody heavy..."

Lughus smiled at the seneschal's joke, but knew better. The old knight had complained more than once that they had not yet found time to fit him for anything more than his hauberk. Owain's fears about Lughus entering battle so lightly armored nearly rivaled his own concerns over Brigid. *An oversight I will see to immediately, should we get through this day,* Lughus thought. Thus far, with the exception of outfitting Geoffrey and his family, he had been reluctant to spend any more than a pittance of the Galadin treasury and left all money matters safely in the hands of the Steward and Seneschal. However, if Glendaro's miracle should occur and his ascension to baron be confirmed, perhaps he would allow himself some small indulgences, for armor was not in the least impractical.

But that would have to wait. It was time.

Brigid leapt to her feet. "Are you ready?" she asked him.

No hesitation. Without a word, Lughus stood up, offered her his arm, and gently took her by the hand. Owain called the men-at-arms to order and the soldiers hurried to form their ranks.

"I'm glad you're with me," Lughus whispered.

"All will be well," she smiled, offering his hand a squeeze, "One way or the other."

"Alright, Owain," the young baron called out, "Let's go!"

The assembly chamber was a large circular room situated behind the Lord-Baron's great hall. In its center a series of thirteen ornately carved tables were

313

arranged into a ring with a slightly larger, higher table to serve as the head from which the Lord-Baron would preside. Only the barons and their close advisors were admitted to the closed-door sessions; however, a small line of long, low tables were also kept along the rear of the room for the foreign ambassadors and those with petitions that might affect the Brock at large.

The Barons of the Brock were known across Termain as a somewhat fickle bunch with a tendency for squabbling and feuding, and accordingly, the atmosphere before the meeting was one ranging from polite jocularity to mitigated hostility. Only Perin Glendaro's guardsmen were admitted to remain on watch while the honor guards of the other barons remained outside in the ward. According to Sir Owain, more than once over the years had fights erupted between the barons' men-at-arms as they often took it upon themselves to stand up for the honor of their respective lords. Thankfully, Naden and Pike, two of the Galadin guardsmen who had not only accompanied them to Highboard, but had also been present at the grotto, were left in charge, and both seemed well aware of the troubles such brawling could only have upon their young lord. *If I'm still baron tomorrow, they'll both be made sergeants.*

Sir Owain led the way through the crowded chamber to the Galadin table. To their right, at the table marked by the emblem of the White Ram, Baron Lorick of Igrainne sat with his seneschal and an advisor from the Weavers' Guild. He offered a courteous nod, and Lughus could not help but wonder what type of windfall the baron was enjoying in exchange for the five Galadin knighthoods.

To their left, Lughus recognized the emblem of Denholm, the Gray Gauntlet, one of the allies of the Marthaines. He felt Baron Denholm and his attendants peering over at him with interest, but they offered neither word nor greeting and Lughus chose to ignore them, scanning the rest of the tables for friendlier faces. Baron Brabant and Baron Derindale, who with Nordren comprised the other longtime allies of Galadin, had already arrived and were deep in conversation, though they paused to wave to him in greeting. He had only had the opportunity to meet them briefly on the day of his arrival in Highboard, but both spoke of the respect with which they had esteemed Arcis and renewed their bonds of friendship. Tampanis Brabant, the elder of the two, was middle-aged, dark-haired, and as prickly as the trio of Sable Caltrops that were the symbol of his house. Orilus Derindale, whose emblem was the

Sanguine Drum, was younger at about thirty. Fair-haired and friendly, if somewhat dour, he, too, had recently been elevated to baron after his father fell in combat with bandits two years ago. According to Owain, both were stout fighters, steadfast and loyal, and though neither barony was very large, they could still hold their own in battle against any other.

Of all the other barons, however, it was the Marthaines that Lughus most dreaded and most desired to see. The house of his father, Gaston, and led by Arcis Galadin's lifelong nemesis, Roland, the table of House Marthaine, designated by the symbol of the Argent Eagle, remained empty. According to the other barons, the Marthaines' arrival had been delayed by the flooding of the River Rockfall that flowed down from the Firriny Mountains to feed into Lake Bartund on the opposite shore from Galadin. It was strange, Lughus thought, that the stronghold of Galadin's perennial enemies should lie so near the Houndstooth on the far side of the lake—almost as strange as it was to consider that the man who led them, Roland Marthaine, the Argent Eagle himself, was also his grandfather.

That thought alone filled him with worry and he was glad that Brigid still held his arm in hers or else he was certain it would have been visibly shaking. Again, he was thankful she was with him, for she was the only one to whom he had confided his fears regarding the Marthaines. Sir Owain, Horus, anyone else of the Galadin court were so staunchly embroiled in generations of hatred and feuding that they could not even speak of the Marthaines without their fists clenching or their teeth gnashing in anger, particularly those whose service began before the death of Lughus's mother. Lughus did not excuse or forgive his father's action in any way; however, he had difficulty coming to terms with the havoc that had resulted after his birth and his subsequent entrustment to the Loremaster. He had grown up believing himself to have no family beyond his few friends and master, only to suddenly learn of so many other relations, half of which he was to love and the other half he was to hate.

Only Brigid understood the turmoil that could result from such ignominious family affairs, and though she had no answers for him, she still listened and told him all about her situation in Blackstone. *If not for her, surely I would have gone mad long ago*, he thought, calmed by the mere presence of her at his side. *Perhaps I should tell her…*

315

Thankfully, she spared him any further rumination when she nodded at two men approaching. Both were rather tall and skinny with close-cropped auburn hair. Upon their surcoats, a pair of embroidered salmon circled one another.

"Lord Leoric," Sir Owain said as Baron Nordren and his son greeted them.

"Well, here we are then," the elder observed. "It would be nice for the Lady of Light to smile upon Galadin once again. Perhaps this time, she might strike dumb any who would call the ascension into question."

"One can only hope," the old knight replied.

And not much more, Lughus thought. His senses steadily grew more muddled with anxiety, and when Theobold Norden slapped him on the shoulder, he nearly fell over.

"Oi, Young Lughus. You ready?"

"I suppose."

"Well," Theo grinned, "In the stories, don't they say that the knight with the favor of the prettiest lady always carries the day?"

"What?" Lughus asked. Beside him, he heard Brigid give a sigh of impatience.

"Maybe I should find me a great hound like Fergus there too" Theo said pleasantly, "We don't see him all week and when he finally turns up, it's at the heel of such a beauty," he grinned, "How about an introduction?"

"Oh," Lughus felt Brigid's grip tighten on his hand, bringing him back to his senses. "Lady Brigid," he said, clearing his throat, "This is Theobold Nordren and his father Leoric, the baron."

"Just Brigid," she said.

"Just Theo then. It's a pleasure to finally meet you," the young Nordren said, adding to Fergus, "Good to see you too, old boy!"

The hound gave a snort and Brigid suppressed a laugh. "Lughus told me you've been a friend to him since he arrived in the Brock," she said.

Theo shrugged. "Nordren and Galadin have always been friends, and any friend of his is a friend of mine." He cast Lughus a conspiratorial wink. "You know, Brigid, I'll never forgive myself for doubting your man's word. Spoke of nothing but your beauty these past days and more. The Lady of Light made flesh, he said."

"He did?" Brigid asked as Lughus's jaw tightened and his hands went numb. He cast Theo a stare of abject horror and betrayal. *What are you saying, you bastard?*

"No, he didn't." Theo smirked. "But when I asked after you, he avoided the question, which of course told me just as much."

Brigid's face turned steadily redder as the young Nordren's grin grew wider. Lughus feigned interest in Sir Owain's conversation with Theo's father to avoid catching either of their eyes.

"Well, we should sit down probably," Brigid said at last, "It looks like the Lord-Baron's just arrived."

"Aye," Theo said, patting Lughus's shoulder, "And honestly, mate, don't be cross. I was only fooling. I'm afraid I'm at my most disquieting when I try to be helpful."

Helpful how, you ass? Lughus thought, though all he said was, "It's good to see you."

"Good luck today, friend."

"Thanks."

"What a peculiar man," Brigid said as Lughus helped her to her chair.

"I'm sorry," he said.

"For what?" she grinned and once Lughus had sat down beside her, flashed him a smile. "At any rate, here we are."

"Here we are," he repeated.

As the Lord-Baron assumed his seat at the high table, the remainder of the barons and their attendants hurried to find their own places. At Glendaro's side were his seneschal and his steward, though a handful of other clerks and servants were also on hand should they be needed. Acting as moderator, the seneschal sounded a bell to indicate the session would be coming to order soon. Sir Owain sat down on the opposite side of Lughus from Brigid and placed his helm upon the table. A servant hurried by depositing rolls of parchment, quills, and inkpots, and Lughus breathed a sigh, thinking back to his days as an apprentice.

All of a sudden, however, a chill ran through his bones, as if a great pitcher of ice water had suddenly been poured down his back. It was the same sensation he had felt at the grotto, and moments later, he felt Brigid's grip tightening on his arm. For, the Andochan ambassador had just been shown into the room followed closely by none other than Provincial Padeen

Andresen and Chief Constable Willum Harlow. Lughus's hand touched Sentinel's pommel and beside him Sir Owain muttered curses under his breath. From the floor at Brigid's feet, Fergus began uttering a low, steady growl. When Harlow's eyes found them from all the way across the Chamber, Brigid's jaw tightened as she audibly ground her teeth. Lughus remained stoic, meeting the Hammer's hate-filled glare with stoic defiance.

"I can't help but feel afraid the nearer he is," she whispered, "It makes me angry."

"It's alright," Lughus told her, "He's no match for us both."

"No, that's not what I mean," she paused, "I told you I had that dream once about a man not him but like him? I think he—the Hammer, I should say—came very close to killing the Blade once and for all. It was the same at the grotto before you showed up."

"He won't get another chance."

For the second time, the Lord-Baron's seneschal sounded the bell, and this time, Perin Glendaro rose to his feet followed by the rest of the barons and their attendants.

"Be welcome, one and all," the Lord-Baron said, "It has been some time since last we met in the spring session, and it grieves me to report that one of our number has fallen."

Sir Owain breathed a heavy sigh.

"As you may all have surmised," Glendaro continued. He motioned toward the Galadin contingent. "Lord Arcis, Baron of Galadin, finally succumbed to his illness, and though it has been many years since he personally met with us in Assembly, I would ask that we all pause a moment to honor his passing."

The assembly stood in silence for a long moment, and most, Lughus noted glancing about the room, bowed their heads. One man, however, did not. Instead of examining the flagstones, a somber expression stretched across his features, Lughus felt the man's eyes boring into him, as if he were a some rogue specter back from the dead. At first, he attempted to ignore it, but when the man showed no sign of turning away, Lughus returned the gaze and held it.

He was an old man, perhaps somewhere in his sixties, though in no way did he seem frail. His shoulders were broad and his back was straight as he stood confidently, clad in fine, but sober raiment of silver and blue. His hair, though as a dark as Brigid's down the center had gone steely gray around his temples, and his ruddy, weather-beaten face was deeply lined and scarred, as if it had been carved out of granite with a blunt mace. What struck him most about the old man were his eyes—gray like storm clouds seeded with lightning—just like Lughus's own.

The young baron's heart thundered in his chest. In all the excitement of the Hammer's arrival, he had failed to notice the Marthaines. There were three of them standing now behind the emblem of the Argent Eagle—Lord Roland, his seneschal Sir Ulfric Gond, a cadaverous man with an ill-favored look, and finally, another man, tall and muscular, that, standing beside the other two, some might have even have called handsome. He, too, had gray eyes, though they lacked the electric brilliance of the patriarch.

The moment of silence passed. Still, Roland Marthaine did not turn away, but held his focus intently upon his grandson, and, if anything, seemed only to narrow his penetrating gaze. Even when the Lord-Baron resumed his speech, it did little to alleviate Lughus's sense of disquiet or distract the Argent Eagle's scrutiny.

"Succeeding Lord Arcis," Glendaro announced, "it is my pleasure to introduce his grandson, Lord Lughus, known hereafter as Baron Galadin, named as his heir by Arcis's word and will, and signed by witnesses including myself." He finished quickly, "So welcome, Baron Galadin, and let us continue with the meeting at hand."

There was the sound of muttering and shuffling among the Andochans, and a few of the other barons and their advisors whispered among themselves. However, the Lord-Baron's seneschal rang the bell and the murmur soon died down.

"They'll wait until Andoch speaks to call us out," Sir Owain told him, "Perin knows it's likely to cause uproar so he'd rather get other matters sorted first."

Lughus gave a silent nod.

At his high table, the Lord-Baron resumed his seat, and the rest of the assembled folk did as well.

At long last, Baron Marthaine turned his eye from Lughus and sat back in his seat with a look of respectful interest while Perin Glendaro made a few announcements and opened the discussions of matters relating to trade. He called upon a few members of the various guilds, and a number of the barons raised questions or made comments. Lughus seemed not to hear much of it, for as much as he tried to pay attention, he was far too consumed by the anticipation of what was to come. His shoulders and his back began to ache from sitting so rigidly upright and his palms sweat as he continually touched the pommel of his sword. Owain seemed no better, for the sound of his teeth grinding against one another could be heard over any moment of stillness, and the vein in his forehead seemed fit to burst. Only Brigid remained calm, and although Lughus knew that she too was nervous, when she gently took hold of his hand beneath the table and cast him a furtive smile, he felt his heart glow.

Finally, after what seemed half a day, though it could only have been but an hour, the moment had come. After a few words of introduction from the Lord-Baron, the Andochan Ambassador, Commissioner Corbeil nodded to Willum Harlow with exaggerated gravity and the Hammer stood to address the crowd.

"Good barons," he intoned, "It is with a heavy heart that I, Willum Harlow, Chief Constable and Anointed Guardian of the Order under the title of 'the Hammer,' come before you today. Since the days of St. Aiden and King Halford Drude I, our two nations have been as brothers, and in the fine tradition of friendship begun by the Saint and King, never once has there been even the slightest of disagreements between us."

Lughus breathed a sigh. He knew Royne would have had something to say about all of this. The lanky Apprentice liked nothing more than to point out discrepancies in other men's rhetoric.

"However," Harlow went on with a sigh, "It has unfortunately come to pass that the actions of a few—nay, of one—have threatened the peace between us that for so long has been a testament to those two great men and our two great nations."

"Here we go," Owain muttered.

"On the very eve of St. Aiden's Feast, in the city of Galadin, on the most holy grounds of St. Elisa's Grotto," he raised a finger to point at the Galadin contingent, "This boy who would be baron, aided by his nefarious accomplices, attacked a Constable of the Order of the Guardians and profaned the holy grounds of St. Elisa's Grotto with blood!"

Lughus's eyes flashed and his heart burned with resentment and rage, but he willed himself to keep his hand away from his sword. Sir Owain's knuckles gleamed white as he gripped the edge of the table, and from the floor beside them, Fergus bared his teeth and sustained another low growl. Harlow continued undeterred.

"Here before you in the flesh stand two of those figures, those traitorous dogs, cursed for their villainy with the brand of the Blackguard—and not just any Blackguards, but two of the infamous Three, who for a thousand years have haunted the lands of Termain, vaunting their disrespect for the virtues of my Order, of Justice, and of Peace!" the Hammer cried, "Yet even before their unlawful anointing—or perhaps in accordance with—both were already poised to follow on the paths of the Dark Brother. One, an apprentice to the greatest traitor in the history of the Order, and the other a conspirator and a kinslayer who sought to murder her entire family! And now, as the Marshal and the Blade, the darkness of their souls only increases tenfold!"

Without thinking, Lughus nearly leapt to his feet; however, Brigid's hold tightened on his arm and she held him back. "Lughus, no!" she whispered, and though her face remained calm, her blue eyes smoldered like flames, "He forgets himself to speak ill of the Lord-Baron's uncle." True enough, at the High Table, Perin Glendaro's brow knit with anger. "Let him spout his lies," she added, "You and I and others know the truth."

Lughus gave a slight nod, and in place of his hilt, took her hand. Yet as his attention returned to Harlow, who was now offering a disdainful review of the Three and their crimes, he paused and again found himself the object of Roland Marthaine's scrutiny, caught within the thunderstorm of the old man's eyes. This time, though, rather than look away or falter, he returned the gaze—but not with malice or contempt, but simple honesty, with authentic truth. To Lughus's surprise, it was the other baron who turned away first.

"And so, my good barons, I beseech you!" Harlow breathed a sigh and wiped a bead of sweat from his brow, "If you are indeed allies of the Order— if you still hold dear the long tradition of friendship between the Guardian-King and the Barons of the Brock—release unto me these fugitives, these Blackguards, that after a thousand years, they might finally face the justice they deserve! Let the will of King Kredor and all the Drudish Kings before him finally be done!"

When at last, the Hammer finished, the room fell silent, and for a long time, no one, not even the Lord-Baron, spoke. Harlow returned to his seat and the provincial and the commissioner offered him smug looks of congratulations, but the constable merely nodded and sat rigidly in his seat, a guest of honor at a banquet impatiently waiting to be served.

Lughus's eyes fell to the tabletop like a man upon the block awaiting the fall of the executioner's axe. *I may lose the barony, but I will not let them take us. Even if the whole city should rise against us, I will not see my friends harmed.* He turned to Brigid and without a word, caught her eye. His heart warmed in anticipation of whatever was to come, and for the first time perhaps ever, he felt no uncertainty, and he was not afraid. *Come what may,* he thought, *I love you.*

At last, the silence was broken by a long, drawn out sigh, and as all the Assembly turned to the source, Roland Marthaine slowly stood up from his seat and with a gesture to his followers, appeared to be making ready to depart. The other barons eyed one another in confusion, and at the Andochan table, the Provincial beamed and offered Harlow a hearty pat on the shoulder. Finally, from his high table, the Lord-Baron cleared his throat.

"Baron Marthaine," he asked, "Where are you going?"

The old man sighed. "This meeting is a waste of time," he said simply.

A low murmuring settled over the room, ranging in tone from weary agreement to quiet disapproval. Perin Glendaro glanced at Lughus and his brow furrowed. "My Lord Roland," he said, "I admit I do not understand. We have yet to even begin discussing the matter, let alone decide upon anything."

"My mind is already made up," he said simply, "And I doubt anything you or anyone else can say will change it." He turned away from the Lord-Baron and once again, Lughus felt himself caught in the Argent Eagle's steely gaze. "Baron Galadin!" he called out across the assembly, "Will you join me?"

Silence reigned as not a soul moved or spoke. At length, Roland Marthaine continued.

"I believe we have a war to prepare for."

What?

Lughus's head felt thick with confusion and his lungs felt suddenly like they were made of lead. He watched Brigid's eyes grow wide and Sir Owain's mouth fall open in shock. For a long moment, he watched the great Baron Marthaine, weighing the truth of his words. *Why is he doing this?* he wondered, *Why would he ever offer his enemy his support?* Still, Lughus knew he would have few other options should he refuse. Hesitantly, he offered the old man a nod and with his friends at his side, led the way along the side of the chamber toward where the Marthaines were slowly filing toward the door.

From his place at the Andochan table, Willum Harlow's features twisted in rage. "Baron Marthaine!" he cried, "Are you truly choosing to side with this boy? This boy who is not only a Galadin, but the Marshal? One of the very Three who murdered your noble ancestor? Surely, you do not forget—"

"No, Constable, *you* forget!" Roland Marthaine roared in a voice like a boulder sliding down a mountain, "*You* are a guest in Baronbrock and your presence and your tongue are tolerated solely due to that same fine friendship between our two realms that you went on about just now." The old man's jaw grew rigid and his voice teemed with malice, "*You* are not in Andoch, Constable. *You* have no authority here!"

"The authority of the faithful knows no bounds!" the Provincial intoned weakly.

Baron Marthaine rounded on the both of them, "You assaulted the person of a *Baron of the Brock!* What you have done is nothing short of an act of *war!*"

The two Andochan men shrank back to their table, but the old man was not yet finished.

"Now, Constable, I suggest that while you still can, you run back to your King Kredor and find yourself a new hammer, or at least a bigger sword. For when next we meet, I can promise you, that you'll have need of it!" he paused to glance around the room, from the Guardians through to his fellow barons, and back again, "And the same can be said for anyone else who chooses to stand with you."

At the doors leading out from the Chamber, the Marthaines met the Galadins, and with a nod of fierce determination, Baron Roland walked side-by-side with Lughus from the solemn confines of the assembly room. As soon as they had crossed the threshold, the assembly erupted into chaos and disbelief. *Is it over then?* Lughus wondered, crossing the Lord-Baron's great hall in silence, *What does all this mean?* They had nearly reached the entryway leading out of the castle to the inner ward before he was finally able to speak.

"Why?" he stammered, breathlessly, "Why are you doing this?"

Slowly, Roland Marthaine came to a halt and turned toward him. "You look just like her—your mother—and Arcis, and all the Galadins, for that matter. Hair of burnished gold, lean build, regal bearing—a proper Hound with the blood of a Saint, even down to the shape of your eyes. However, their color..." he paused, "Their *color*..."

Lughus breathed a sigh and much to his surprise, he saw that suddenly the old man's gaze had become remarkably soft and rimmed with red.

"You have the eyes of the Eagle," Baron Marthaine said, "Like those of your father. Like *mine*."

Lughus remained silent and felt the old man reach out and grip his shoulder. "You are my grandson," Roland said earnestly, "And for nearly your entire life, I've thought you were dead. The Lord of Darkness himself could not come between us now." He turned quickly to his two attendants, his seneschal and the other man of his house. With a dismissive nod, the pair of them went off to gather the men of their guard.

"I will call upon you soon," he told Lughus, and with a glance at Sir Owain added, "Alone, if need be, or at the very least, with your grandmother. I know she'll also wish to see you. In any case, we will put ourselves at your mercy if that's what it takes to gain your trust. It will come to war, and there will be much to discuss, though, if you'll forgive us...there is much too that we would like to know...about you..."

"Yes, sir," Lughus said. "Of course."

"Then until next we meet, be well," Baron Roland said, and with one final squeeze of Lughus's shoulder, departed with his men.

As soon as he had gone, Sir Owain shook his head and watched the Marthaine men and their guard as they formed their ranks and departed. "Never in my life would I ever have expected that," he said, "The Argent Eagle coming to our aid. I cannot believe it."

"Am I still the baron?" Lughus asked wearily.

"I doubt there's few in there who'd be willing to risk voting against you now," Owain said, "Between the barons already on our side and those that simply follow behind Marthaine's lead—Denholm and the like—we're sure to carry any vote. Still, you'll have to pardon me, but I'll not trust a man among them so easily, and I'd advise you be cautious too. I call the whole thing unbelievable for a reason, and the memory of…your mother…makes it very difficult for me to regard the Marthaines with anything short of disdain."

"I understand," Lughus said, and although inwardly, he desired to believe in the verity of the old man's claim, he knew that Owain was right to preach caution.

Still, in siding with Lughus, the old man had in all likelihood drawn the entire Brock into a desperate war. Why else would he have done that? Why else would he have risked it all? He felt a touch upon his arm and knew it to be Brigid. More than anything in the world, he wanted to embrace her, to hold her near. However, voices carried across the hall from the Assembly Chamber and it seemed the Lord-Baron was bringing the matter, and the entire meeting, to a close.

"We should return to the keep," Sir Owain said, "Before the Hammer and any others have a chance to sow more mischief. I'll gather the guard."

"Thanks," Lughus said. He offered Brigid his arm, forcing away thoughts of anything more.

"Of course," the seneschal said, and with a wink added, "Baron."

Lughus smiled in spite of himself and watched Owain go when suddenly he felt something soft and warm alight upon his cheek. It took some time before he realized what had happened and when he turned toward Brigid, her blue eyes sparkled warmly from the heat of her blushing. "Congratulations," she smiled gently and gave his arm a squeeze, "On your victory."

"Our victory," he said, "We stand together. Side by side."

"I suppose," she said.

His heart beat faster and he found his gaze wandering from her eyes to her lips, glistening with moisture from where she'd kissed him. "What was it Theo said?" he asked her. "The knight with the prettiest lady at his side always wins?"

Her blush deepened and she tightened her hold on his hand. "In stories," she whispered.

No hesitation. He breathed a heavy sigh, "Brigid…"

She bit her lip and her eyes grew wide. "Yes?" she said.

It was becoming increasingly difficult to think straight and, as always seemed to happen, his head once again felt as if it were a block of wood. *Just tell her, you ass!* He took another deep breath and realized suddenly that she was trembling, and even more disquieting was the fact that he was too. *What a fool I am…*

Then all at once, there was the sound of a great commotion, and the men of the Assembly began flooding out. *Damn it!* Lughus bit his lip and cursed himself, *I am a bloody fool!* He exchanged another glance with Brigid, and she smiled at him, but he wondered if it was with relief or if she also shared his disappointment. *Bloody coward!* He nearly grimaced as the ache in his chest grew. *Such a fool!*

"Is that Owain?" she asked softly, as the first of the departing barons and their attendants passed them, "Just there, leading the men?"

"Aye," Lughus nodded, his heart heavy, "We should join them."

"After you, *my baron*."

"Keep it up, and I'll start calling you 'my lady.'"

"Fair enough," she grinned.

He hesitated only a moment, wondering what she meant, when suddenly a man hurried up to them in a tizzy. Lughus's hand reflexively went to his hilt and he took a step forward in front of Brigid. until suddenly he recognized the insignia on the man's surcoat. He was Dorgan, Baron of Agathis.

"Baron Galadin," he said quickly, "I'm so glad you're still here. I need to speak to you immediately!"

Without warning, Lughus's frustrations with himself suddenly gave vent upon the other man. "When I paid you a call the other day," he said, narrowing his gaze, "your men refused me at the door. Why should I pay you any heed now?" Out of the corner of his eye, he noticed Brigid suddenly fold her arms across her chest, furtively sliding her hands over the hilts of her daggers. A moment later, he felt it too. Harlow was on his way.

"We should go," she whispered in his ear, "Now."

Lughus nodded, and he turned toward Dorgan Agathis in dismissal. "Good day."

Agathis shook his head urgently. "Please," he pleaded, "you have my apologies. Believe me! I am trying to make amends!"

"No," Brigid said, "You just fear Roland Marthaine."

"Perhaps that is so," the baron said, "But I have information that is of vital importance to you, my lord."

"Then speak quickly," Lughus said, taking Brigid's hand, "As we walk."

"Fine," Baron Agathis grunted, following after them. "Before I left for the assembly, a contingent of kingsmen arrived in Agathis sent from Stonebridge Castle that guards the mountain pass between Andoch and the Brock." He paused, "I may have…granted them passage through my lands on their way to Lake Bartund…where they…might have disguised themselves as fishermen and traders so as to pass into Galadin by way of the lake…"

Both Lughus and Brigid froze in midstride.

"For what purpose are they going to Galadin?" she asked.

"I am sure you can guess as much…" the baron muttered.

"I'd rather you say it."

Dorgan Agathis sighed, weary and pained by the forced admission of his guilt. "To attempt to infiltrate—if not take—the castle whilst you were away…" he said, "I'm sorry.

"You bastard!" Brigid snapped and made to fly at him, but Lughus held her to his side.

"Please! I only seek to warn you!"

In a flash, Baron Agathis's seneschal hurried to his side and Lughus held up a hand to allow the baron to back away just as Sir Owain and the rest of the Galadin guard rushed forth.

"Calm down everyone!" Lughus commanded, for Harlow had just reached the far door. All he needed to fan the fires of unrest would be an incident such as this. "How many kingsmen did you say?" Lughus asked Dorgan Agathis.

"Four score? Perhaps five?" he said, "I do not know. I was busy making ready to journey here."

Lughus sighed, Galadin commanded roughly a hundred men-at-arms. Some he had brought with him to Highboard, and still some roamed the nearby villages and farms outside of the city. The remainder made up the city watch. A hundred men was not a large force, by any means, but it was enough.

"Harlow," Lughus muttered to Brigid, "He was so confident in his victory that he sent those men to capture Geoffrey!"

Brigid gasped in a mixture of anger and alarm. "Lady save them!" she cried, "We need to return!"

"We will. Immediately," Lughus nodded while Sir Owain looked on, still unsure as to what exactly was happening, but ready to receive his lord's command. "You had best hope that I find my folk at Houndstooth as I left them, Lord Dorgan," Lughus said, "Else I will see that you answer any harm inflicted upon them tenfold."

"We should hurry!" Brigid said.

Lughus cast a glance back over his shoulder and for a moment, his eyes met those of the Hammer. *Would that we had more time, for never again will I suffer you to put my friends in danger!* he swore inwardly, *So until next we meet, you wretched bastard, savor every breath!*

CHAPTER 27: THE ACORN KNIGHT

"Alright," Geoffrey said, "Now the surcoat."

"Here you are, dad."

Freddy held out the garment, and with a slightly puzzled look, Geoffrey flipped it over his head only to realize that once again, he had somehow got it backwards. "Damn," he muttered, spinning the long white cloth around his neck so the mark of the red acorn sat squarely in the center of his chest. As if the time it took to don the chainmail were not enough, now it seemed even the simplest of garments took forever just to put on. *No wonder these nobles need servants and maids just to help them dress. You need a bloody map just to find the right hole to put your arm through!* Still, he was not ungrateful, and truth be told, he could not help but feel a certain enthusiasm each time he saw himself in the glass clad in his full regalia. However, that excitement paled in comparison to the pride he felt at the sight of Freddy and Greta in their finery, or the joy at seeing Annabel in hers. The thought of it alone was enough to bring a warm feeling to his breast, for one of the other amenities of life in the castle was that since the children had their own quarters, he and Annabel were more often free to enjoy their nights together alone.

"The belt now, Freddy."

"Dad, it's not just a belt. It's a baldric."

"Fine," Geoffrey smirked, "The baldric then."

"Here," the boy said, and while Geoffrey gathered the surcoat and bound it around his waist, he watched as with an odd type of reverence, Freddy lifted Oakheart and held it out in his hands.

Geoffrey gave a loud sniff, but remained silent. He attached the club by its leather strap to the baldric, while his son turned back to fetch the shield. *He's just a boy*, Geoffrey reminded himself, *Head full of adventures from all those books, no doubt. Living in the castle, he probably thinks he's in one.* With a slight sigh, he slung the oaken targe across his back. *Then again, maybe he is...*

"Well," he said aloud, taking up his kettle hat from the table, "How do I look?"

"Splendid," Freddy said.

Geoffrey could not help but grin. *Sir Geoffrey Pyle!* he thought, *Father, if you could see me now! What a laugh you'd have!*

"Dad," Freddy said, "Mom said you're to walk the grounds outside the city today with Master Flann."

"Who?"

"Denan Flann, the master-at-arms."

"Oh, right," Geoffrey thought. There were too many names to remember. How he would ever keep them all straight, he did not know. From the looks of things, there would only be more to come too. For, although Sir Owain had already shown him the lay of the land from atop of the battlements, today he was to go down in person to the small villages of peasants who made their homes near the fields beyond the city walls. Having been in their position but a year ago, Geoffrey knew the importance of making a good impression on a farmer. As a man of the castle, they would already see him as something of a thief, reaping the benefits of the harvests without doing any of the work (the same sort of thing that drove men to risk working the Spade). However, for a lord to meet a man in person, to know his name, and to show in any small way his appreciation—simply by acknowledging his existence— meant much and more to those who so often seemed doomed to have so little.

"Aye, we're visiting the farms," Geoffrey told his son, "I'd like to have a better look at how they do things up here, and Steward Horus said it's good to let the people know we're guarding them while Baron Galadin is away."

"Lughus."

"What?"

"He just likes to be called 'Lughus,'" Freddy said, "Like Brigid."

"Oi! How many times you going to contradict me today, eh?" Geoffrey laughed, ruffling the boy's hair, "Baldrics, barons, and masters-at-arms? What's next?"

"Just trying to help," Freddy shrugged.

"And I appreciate it," Geoffrey smiled, "Come on. We'll go say goodbye to your mother, assuming we can find her." He hurried out into the hallway past a Galadin guardsman who greeted Geoffrey with a smart salute. "As you were," Geoffrey muttered, pausing to return it.

Freddy followed along. "She said she and Greta were to meet with Jergan and his wife," he said.

"The warder?" Geoffrey asked, "Or master of the wardrobe, I should say?"

"Aye," Freddy said, "But listen, Dad..."

At the end of the hall, Geoffrey reached the stairs and paused.

"Down the stairs, out through the hall and across the ward," Freddy told him, "Jergan lives in the south tower of the middle bailey."

"How do you remember all this?" Geoffrey asked, shaking his head.

Freddy simply shrugged, and together they hurried on.

"Sir Geoffrey." Another pair of guards greeted them as they passed through the entryway of the keep out into the inner ward.

"Good morning," Geoffrey said politely as he passed.

"So Dad?" Freddy began again.

"Aye, son?" he paused, glancing up at the towers. "South tower of the middle bailey..."

"Dad?"

"What?"

"How's about I go with you and Master Flann today?"

Geoffrey paused, and his brow furrowed, "What?"

"How's about I go with you and Master Flann when you go about the country today?"

He eyed the boy carefully and suddenly realized that he had dressed in his finest set of clothing, complete with his small table dagger on his belt. *Or baldric too, no doubt...* "Son, we're just riding about the farms," Geoffrey said, "I can't say it'll be that exciting."

"Well, you need a squire, don't you?" Freddy said, "If you're a knight then you just have to have one. Plus, I like Master Flann. He said he'd teach me how to fight."

"He said what?"

"When I'm older."

"Oh," Geoffrey sighed, "I don't know. I think we're to be riding and you don't know how to sit a horse. To be honest, I barely know myself." It was true, though once again, he found himself taking to it quite easily. No doubt owing to his legacy as the Vanguard.

"I know how to ride!"

"What? Since when?"

"The lads and I used to see who could stay on Oscar's pigs the longest back in Pyle."

"Son, that's not at all the same thing."

"I know, but it still helped," Freddy said, "Then, while Lughus and Horus were meeting with Faden and all that, Brigid taught me."

"Of course she did," Geoffrey chuckled.

"Aye, on a pony. She wanted to see if she knew how to ride too so she let Fergus and I go along with her."

"And I suppose she taught the hound to ride as well?"

"No. Just me. Although she said Greta was probably small enough she could learn to ride on Fergus. He didn't seem too keen on that, though."

Geoffrey shook his head in exasperation. *That girl...* he thought, *At least with the young baron around there's someone else for her to drive mad with her mischief.* He thought back to his conversation with Lughus in the armory and smiled inwardly, *Something tells me, he don't mind it much though.*

Freddy sighed with impatience, "So, can I go with you or what?"

Geoffrey chewed his lip. He could see no harm in it. Plus, a ride around the farms might remind the boy of Pyle, and though their fortunes may have turned, he believed it was important for his children to know their roots. *Besides, if all goes awry in Highboard, who knows what's to come of us next,* he thought, *It could be back to the farm, to the wilds, or worse. Make hay while the sun shines, as the farmers used to say.*

"Alright, I'll tell you what," Geoffrey said at last, "You lead me to your mother and wherever else I need to get to, and you're welcome to come along."

"Huzzah!" Freddy exclaimed, punching the air in triumph.

Geoffrey couldn't help but feel his heart warm at the sight, for he could not remember the last time he saw his son so excited. *It's a shame, that,* he said to himself, *He deserves such happiness, both he and his sister. Much and more.* With a flood of affection, he reached out and as they were walking, embraced the boy in a one-armed bear hug.

"You know, you're a good lad," he said, "I'm proud of you. Always."

"Alright, dad," Freddy said bashfully, though his grin stretched from ear to ear, "It's this way."

Jergan, the master of the wardrobe, was one of what could easily be described as Horus's lieutenants in the army of household officers and servants under his command. Though not a warrior, the Master of the Wardrobe was a well-respected member of the castle community. He was a tall, thin man with a neatly trimmed beard, and, as befitted his position, an impeccable sense of fashion and finery, which made him an interesting contrast with his wife, Willa, who was short, rather plump, and though not shy, very easily seemed so when accompanied by her pleasantly effusive husband. They were both very good people, however, and had been particularly kind to Annabel in recent days while Geoffrey was busy with Horus and the management of the estate. The farmer, too, had taken to the couple, for although Jergan and his wife had lived in the castle for twenty-five years and seemed to fit seamlessly amongst the finery of high society, the warder had learned his trade from his father, a simple tailor whose skill with a needle had earned him his position by catching the eye of Baron Lughus's mother.

It was that same great lady they alluded to then, when Freddy led Geoffrey up the stairs of the tower to the door to their rooms. Peering around the doorframe, he could see the three adults, Jergan, Willa, and Annabel seated with cups of tea while in the center of the room Greta smiled sweetly and turned about in circles, cheerfully admiring herself in yet another new frock. *I really am in trouble when she gets older,* Geoffrey sighed, and not for the first time.

"You have no idea, Annabel, what a joy it is to have such pretty young ladies about the castle again," Jergan said, "With the Weavers' Guildhall so nearby, it broke my heart to see such fine clothes and know that I would never have an opportunity to put them to use. Baron Arcis never had the taste for such things himself, and I'm sure you've noticed the disheveled nightmare that is Sir Owain. Between the pair of them, it was all baronial blue and gold—no embellishment, little embroidery, and say nothing about silk brocade! Only Steward Horus would permit any such thing from time to time, and even then, it was only for the celebration of a holiday."

At his side, his wife rolled her eyes. "He even tried to get me to wear such things."

"But she'd refuse!"

"I'm too old and too fat!"

"Oh you most certainly are not!"

"Darling, I've told you time and again. Fashion is fine, but it will always come second to comfort, at least in my book."

"My dear, one does not prevent the other."

Geoffrey watched Annabel smile at the other couple's banter, and he was glad she had yet to notice him waiting at the door. He had indeed found the baron's gifts of new clothes much easier to accept after seeing his wife look so fine and so happy. It made him feel twenty years younger. Besides, what was all his hard work for if not to bring his family joy? They had already suffered so much. *Poor Karl...if only you were here with us...*

Greta curtsied to no one in particular and took another turn, lost in her own daydreams. Once more, Geoffrey felt his heart glow.

"It's so nice to use different shades of color as well," Jergan went on, "I thought to try a tawny or perhaps a sage for Lady Brigid, but alas! With those eyes of hers, the only color for her is blue. Still, you should have seen the gown we put together for Highboard!"

"I thought she looked quite fine in the black," Willa mused.

"In the trousers?" Jergan said, pulling a face, "And the doublet? It made my stomach sick just to fit her for them!"

"Nonsense, Jergan. She looked simply beautiful, though I doubt there's much she doesn't look fine in."

"Yes, exactly! Which is why it is so sad that she refuses to wear gowns! I just hope these trousers do not last, for I would take those drab frocks any day over the trousers! We have enough trousers and hosiery with all the men." Jergan sighed, turning toward the little girl. "Greta, promise me you'll always wear gowns. In fact, only wear gowns. Lady Brigid alone is enough to drive me mad!"

"Aye, she's good at that," Geoffrey said, stepping into the room.

"Well, who is this handsome knight?" Jergan's wife said merrily, as her husband called out, "Ah! Sir Geoffrey!"

"Daddy, do you like my new dress?" Greta beamed, "Isn't it splendid?"

"That it is, my lovely," Geoffrey nodded, ignoring Annabel's smirking glance, "Like the queen of the fairies herself!"

The little girl beamed and went back to her twirling. "You look all set to go," Annabel observed.

"We are," Geoffrey said, "Freddy's coming along too."

"Alright," Annabel smiled as Geoffrey hurried over to kiss her brow. "Then, my brave knights, we shall see you when you return."

Geoffrey nodded to Jergan and Willa and patted Greta on the head before quickly exchanging one last kiss with his wife before ushering his son out of the room.

"Be careful, darling," Annabel called after them.

"We will!" the farmer answered.

"If Greta keeps getting all of these clothes," Freddy said, leading his father toward the guardhouse and the stables, "I believe I should have a sword."

"Aye," Geoffrey muttered, "And she gets any more spoiled, you can stick me with it."

"Really?"

Geoffrey tussled the boy's hair. "No, not really."

"But it's not fair!"

"Nor is life," he said, then added, "But perhaps we'll see. You wouldn't be allowed to carry it around though. It'd just be for learning."

"Deal!"

They met Denan Flann outside the stables where he waited with three other men of the Galadin guard. Flann was a man of middling age, probably near enough to Geoffrey's own. He was thin, strong, and rather rugged in appearance, though not unkind. When Geoffrey apologized for their late arrival, mentioning their brief stop to see Jergan, Flann held up a mailed hand. "Say no more," he grinned, "Talking to Jergan is like pissing off a bear. Once it starts after you, it's next to impossible to get away. Thank the bloody Brethren we've Willa to handle him, but onward. We can talk as we ride.."

The fields outside of the city of Galadin proper were arranged at intervals as to appear, when viewed from the heights of the Houndstooth, like the squares upon a chessboard or like patches sewn together in a quilt. At the center of each grouping of fields—to the north, the south, the southeast and the northwest—small clusters of houses formed little villages where the tenant farmers resided. In most ways, the villages appeared to be the very image of Pyle, though with the added addition of large circular sheepfolds built of stone.

As the Month of the Stag was underway, many of the farmers were plowing their fields and sewing wheat and rye for Harvestide, while others set about shearing the great flocks of sheep that drove the Brock's famous wool industry. As he watched them work, Geoffrey could not help but feel a mixture of envy and relief. On the one hand, there was something deeply satisfying about working the soil, a certain intimacy with the land that could only come from being covered in sweat and dirt. On the other hand, when he remembered the pain and the seemingly endless toil, only to be robbed blind by bandits, he could not help but take some measure of happiness knowing that his family was being cared for inside the keep.

Still, the Barons of Galadin had a reputation to uphold as nobles of good character and bearers of the blood of the Saint. As such, its farmers, both around the city and in each of the seven fiefdoms, enjoyed a standard of living that in many ways was unmatched, not only by the other baronies, but all across Termain. For instance, as Master Flann told Geoffrey, the Galadin Barons had made it a rule generations ago that for every twelve lambs born to a given flock, the shepherd who cared for them was allowed to mark one as his own personal stock. As Galadin grew even more prosperous under Baron Arcis, the ratio was changed to one for every ten, a policy the Baron Lughus had pledged early on to Horus that he would not change. Thus, in Galadin, it was possible that a simple shepherd could one day raise a full flock of his own.

"I've never heard of such a thing," Geoffrey said as they stopped to watch a team of men working a field.

"Aye, and the tax the farmers pay for the use of the Galadin mills is lower than any other barony in the Brock," said Flann with a grin, "Funny thing how people seem to work harder when they're treated fair."

"Imagine," Geoffrey said.

"Not that we don't have problems too, mind you," the master-at-arms added a little later, "Any time the fighting starts up again with the Marthaines, the poor folk suffer the worst of it with the raids and such. Back before the..." he paused, "Way back then, things were particularly bad."

Geoffrey nodded. He had only heard bits and pieces about these times of trouble at the castle, the times that resulted in the young baron being sent away as a babe from Galadin. However, every city, every village, and every family had its troubles. It was not his place to pry in the affairs of folks who had treated him with such kindness and respect.

"Anyway," Flann shrugged, "There are always men willing to take advantage, or to cheat, or to lie. About a year ago, Sir Burnel as oversees the Wrendale fief had a problem with brigands waylaying folk along the road to the mill out that ways, but he sorted it out right quick. In the city, the watch captain, Ross, finds a gambling den or a brothel every now and again that are exploiting the poor. And of course you still get the odd murders, beatings, drunken brawls, and the like. The fairs bring problems with them too, St. Aiden's Day and the like, with all the pilgrims. Although I expect you know plenty about that."

"Aye," Geoffrey said, "We lived in Hounton before coming to the castle."

"Ah, that's right. I'd forgotten."

"It wasn't what I'd call bad, but occasionally you'd have brutes and such trying to take advantage of people. Paying for protection. That sort of thing. Thieves as well, though I suppose you'll find both anywhere."

"From what I understand, Baron Lughus and Sir Owain have had Ross double the patrols through there."

"Dad?" Freddy called, "There's a man riding towards us."

Geoffrey turned and shielded his eyes from the sun, "Where?"

"Look. He's really riding hard."

Flann wheeled his horse around, "We had best go meet him."

Geoffrey nodded and the small party quickly turned and rode for the oncoming rider. It was another soldier dressed in the tabard of the Galadin guard. "Sir Geoffrey," he saluted, "Steward Horus begs you and Master

Flann return at once. We've had a report of trouble brewing at the docks along Lake Bartund. Captain Ross is headed there now with some of his men."

"What kind of trouble?" Flann asked. "Adolfo the Madder toss another debtor in the lake?"

"Adolfo the Madder's the one who *sent word* to Sir Geoffrey."

Adolfo the Madder? Geoffrey wondered, *What's he warning us for?* He had little enough idea that Adolfo the Madder even knew who he was, let alone knew enough to send him word. Something was not right. Geoffrey nodded toward the rider. "Lead the way."

It was a short ride from the fields back to the city; however, as they drew nearer, a cold uncertainty sat festering like a sore in the pit of Geoffrey's stomach. He glanced over his shoulder at Freddy and slowed the pace of his horse to match the soldiers following behind him.

"Um, you two," he said uncertainly, for it was his first attempt at giving a real command, "Can I ask you to return my son to the Houndstooth once we're inside the gates?"

"Aye, sir." The soldiers nodded.

"Thanks," Geoffrey said, "Did you hear that Freddy? You're to go with—" he paused, "What are your names, lads?"

"Tonkin and Grimes, sir."

"Freddy, you're to go with Tonkin and Grimes—"

"I know, dad, I heard."

Geoffrey nodded, "Right." He spurred his horse, and before long, they reached the gate to Hounton. It was immediately clear that something was wrong, for it was but the middle of the afternoon the streets were bare.

"Why are there no guards?" Flann asked the soldier who had come to fetch them.

"I don't know, sir. They were here when I rode out."

Geoffrey readied the Acorn and loosened Oakheart from his belt. Somewhere far off in the direction of the docks was the sound of a great commotion. His eyes scanned the rooftops and he sniffed at the air. *What in the bloody Abyss is going on?*

"Is that smoke?" Freddy asked.

"We need to go," Geoffrey said, "Now."

"I'm with you," the master-at-arms said.

"Freddy…"

"I know, dad," the boy said, "I'll stay with the soldiers. Just be careful."

Geoffrey breathed a sigh and offered his son a quizzical smile. *He's not even phased by this,* he thought, *What in the world has he been reading?* "I'll be back soon," he said, and casting the soldiers a meaningful glance, rode off with Master Flann and the remaining men of the guard in tow.

In a flash, they passed through Hounton and into the Trade Quarter, the horses' hooves clattering upon the cobblestones of the barren streets. Entire cartloads of goods had been left out in the open, and at the produce stalls, vegetables rolled wantonly about on the ground as if knocked over by a frenzied mob. In the buildings along either side of the road, doors normally left open for trade, were shut up tight, and every window with a shutter had drawn it closed. Even the great market house was empty, the animals up for auction simply abandoned in their stalls. Geoffrey glanced again in the direction of the lakeside docks. The odor of smoke could be discerned now much more clearly and a thin, gray column suddenly caught his eye.

"Aiden's Flame!" Flann cried, "We're under attack!"

Geoffrey wheeled his horse around and shouted to the last pair of soldiers. "Ride to the castle and the garrison house in the Golden Quarter! Gather every man you can and tell them to rally at the docks! Now!" and with the master-at-arms at his side, he charged off toward the smoke.

As the cobblestone streets gave way to boardwalks built upon the shores of Lake Bartund, the cries of battle echoed off of the walls of the warehouses and dockside taverns of the wharf. Geoffrey and the master-at-arms dismounted and with a light slap sent their horses off back the way they had come, for the wooden planks made for unsteady footing, and in battle, Geoffrey preferred the certainty of his own two feet.

"This way!" Flann cried, drawing his sword. "Ross should be here somewhere, and if he's not, he'd better be dead for neglecting his duty!"

Geoffrey held the Acorn before him and tried to steady his breathing. Beneath his feet, lengths of rope, splinters of wood, and overturned trade goods were everywhere, though they soon gave way to bodies—some in the garb of the Galadin watch, others clad like simple sailors, and still more in the roughspun garb of peasants. However, when he saw the first of the bodies wrapped in the bloody red-cloaks of the kingsmen, his grip tightened on

Oakheart, his jaw locked in place, and tremors of battle frenzy flooded like a monsoon through his veins.

Onward ran Master Flann. Geoffrey hurried to keep pace, until all at once, the smoke cleared and they found themselves charging straight into the center of a raging battle as the remnants of the watchmen fought to push the attacking red-cloaks back into the trio of keelboats from which they had sprung forth.

"Galadin! Galadin!" the master-at-arms cried, and with a great swipe of his sword cleaved a kingsman in twain.

"Pyle and the Spade!" Geoffrey shouted, and joined him, knocking one man clear into the water with his shield and shattering another's arm at the shoulder with his club.

"Galadin!" the men of the watch rallied alongside them. With renewed vigor, they pushed forward once more, hacking, slashing, and bashing with their weapons. Geoffrey could see now that not all of the kingsmen wore their customary red cloaks, but were disguised like common sailors, mercenaries, and merchants' guards.

Still, uniform or not, there were a bloody great many of them, and from the decks of the keelboats, even more men swarmed—as well as something else, something dreadful.

"Perindal's Sword!" Geoffrey roared, "Watch out!"

A ballista bolt the size of a palisade post shot forth toppling an entire squad of blue and gold guards. One or two of them died instantly—the lucky ones—while the remaining wounded roiled about on the dock in agony as blood poured from the terrible wounds gouged from their sides. Geoffrey's stomach turned. With the other remaining men of the watch, he dove now for cover in a boardwalk alleyway next to nameless lakeside tavern. Mere moments later, a second bolt shot forth, cutting down even more men in its horrific flight. Among them, Geoffrey realized with a cry, was Master Flann.

"No!"

The scattered guardsmen huddled together behind the shallow cover of the alley, and Geoffrey hurriedly took off his helm to wipe the sweat from his brow. The gambeson beneath his mail felt heavier than ever, and his shoulders suddenly noticed the weight of his mail.

"What do we do, sir?" one of guardsmen asked him.

"Aye, if we don't act now, we'll be overrun!" said another.

340

Think, Geoffrey, think! He ground his teeth together, and his eyes grew wide with a mixture of rage, confusion, and alarm.

"Alright," he said at last, "Alright, where's Captain Ross?"

"Dead," came an answer, "He was one of the first to fall when they came at us.

Damn it! Geoffrey scowled, *What do I do?* He glanced around and did a quick count. There were eight men with him, though surely more had sought refuge in other alleys, and some, perhaps, in the mud below the docks. He had no idea as to how many kingsmen were out there, but he had counted only two ballista, one on each of the far keelboats. Of course, two was more than enough.

He thought vaguely about the men he sent to rally the castle and the garrison, but if they were not here now, then it was likely they would be too late—assuming there were even men left to be found.

"They're forming up again, sir!" a soldier shouted from the corner of the alley, "What do we do?"

"Alright," Geoffrey said all at once, "Form up back here and we'll let them come to us! They have to pass by if they plan on making it through to the city, and they won't risk firing the ballistas through their own men! That should give us a chance to hold them back until help arrives!"

A moment later, a cluster of Kingsmen attacked; however, the narrowness of the alleyway forced them to stand closer together, allowing Geoffrey and his men to have to engage them only a few at a time. Again, the men of Galadin beat back the Andochans, though this time they were quick to withdraw to the safety of the alley again before the ballistas let fly.

"There are still so many of them," said a man at Geoffrey's side. Only six remained of the previous eight, for one lay dead and another wounded and bleeding.

Where are the rest of those bloody men? Inwardly, he grimaced, yet to the soldier who spoke he said, "Fewer than before, though, lad. Fewer than before!" He took another deep breath. "Alright, men, form up again," he said, thinking suddenly of his old friend, Captain Barrow, "We owe it to the fine folk of this city to do our duty and to stand our ground—even if it takes me all day. Now, are you with me?

"Aye, sir," the guards replied, but as they formed up alongside him, he could sense that they were tired and their nerve was beginning to fail. *Well, whatever happens,* Geoffrey thought to himself, *I'll hold them here, for the sake of the good folk of Galadin, and for the sake of my family.* He took a deep breath and tightened his grip on Oakheart and Acorn, steeling himself for the coming assault.

The hollow tread of innumerable footsteps clattered along the wooden planks of the of the docks, and from where the alley joined the cobbled streets of the wharf, a rallying cry rang out.

Thank the Brethren! Geoffrey sighed, and with his men, rushed from the alley to join the fray. His relief turned to uncertainty, for they were not the men he had hoped they were. Instead of the tabards of the Galadin guards, they wore a miscellany of armor—from chain to bits of plate to leather, and they were armed with anything from mauls and axes to crude clubs and rusted scimitars.

Blast it all! he thought, *Kingsmen on one side, bandits on the other!*

Yet rather than attack, a man appeared at the head of the mob, and suddenly brought them to a halt with a wave of his hand. Unlike his followers, he wore no armor at all, only a sable doublet beneath which he wore a shirt and breeches of burgundy linen. His head was shorn smooth from brow to pate, but upon his upper lip and chin, dark hair sprang forth in three tiny arrowheads, granting him a somewhat villainous air. He was armed with a crossbow, finely crafted, intricately carved, and inlayed with gold, and in his baldric, a bright red ruby glimmered from the hilt of a silver stiletto. What caught Geoffrey's attention most, however, were his gloves—soft, calf-skin dyed bright scarlet. "Sir Geoffrey of Pyle," he said in a slow drawl, "I am Adolfo the Madder."

Aiden's Flame, he thought, but all he could manage to say was, "Yes?"

"I'm pleased to see that you received my message," Adolfo said, "Though since you seem a bit hard pressed at the moment, I thought I might offer my men to help you."

"Might?" Geoffrey grunted.

"I misspoke," Adolfo said with a slight smile, "I *do* offer them—these twenty and another dozen more in an alley farther on along the dock. They're with a few more of your soldiers."

"And why would you do that?" Geoffrey asked, his eyes on Adolfo's gloves.

"The same reason I sent word before. The Brock is my home—Galadin in particular—and I have no wish to see it harmed."

Geoffrey bit his lip. It was only a matter of time before the kingsmen renewed their assault, yet, he had heard more than enough rumors about Adolfo the Madder to trust him outright. "Forgive me," he said at last, "I am very grateful, but I have a hard time taking you at your word."

Adolfo shrugged. "I don't doubt it," he said, "I know I have something of a reputation. In fact, I've worked rather hard for it, but as I said, my men are yours."

"And you want nothing in return?"

"I did not say that," Adolfo said, "Though what I want is not something you can grant. I would hope, though, that you might perhaps bear my wishes to the one who can."

Geoffrey gave a snort, "I think I know what it is you seek."

"I'm certain you do, and though I doubt you will believe me, I truly am a man of Galadin through and through. For among many other things, I was born here, which—and I mean this without offense—is more than I can say for you."

"Then your aid is welcome," Geoffrey said, "But as you said, payment, rewards, or whatever it is you wish are not my responsibility. Protecting the city in the baron's absence is."

"A sentiment I believe we both share," Adolfo observed, "But come. All this talk matters little if we're both dead. Let us instead drive these fools back to Andoch or the Abyss. I care not which."

CHAPTER 28: THE WALL

Following the meeting with Salasco upon the plane, General Navarro decided that after two days' flight, enough distance now lay between the broken legions and the Guardians to warrant the construction of a proper camp. Orders went around the disheveled column at once, and soon enough, a sea of tents and pavilions dotted the tall grasses of the southern fields.

Though at first glance, Salasco's mob of followers appeared to be little more than destitute refugees—the flotsam and jetsam of half the settlements of the southern coasts—this was only partially true. Among them there were numerous men and women trained in the arts of herbs and healing, trained by the Wall himself, and for the ragged pack of wolves licking their wounds, they were certainly well-met and welcome, working tirelessly throughout the afternoon to ease the pains of those soldiers that would survive to fight another day, and to offer a final moment of peace to those who would not.

As for the Wall himself, among the wounded soldiers of the Fighting Fifth, Salasco had quickly established himself as a veritable miracle-worker. His skill as a surgeon saved many and more brought down by blade or bow, while his remedies and salves brought comfort to those in agony and helped to prevent further infection. Yet somehow, such aid did not appear to come without a cost; for, as the day wore on, the Wall seemed increasingly burdened by numerous wounds of his own, wounds that seemed to intensify for every patient he attended.

Though he had not witnessed these deeds first hand, Royne had an idea as to what was really happening. After all, he had experienced as much himself upon his first meeting with General Navarro. This was not to suggest that there was anything magical about it; Royne was still not willing to deal with those matters right now. There were far more pressing issues to consider, issues that required him to focus solely on logic, strategy, and observable truth. These were, of course, the Young Loremaster's areas of expertise, and it was for these reasons, Royne believed, he had been restored to the general's inner circle without discussion or delay (and without apology, he might add).

So it was that at sundown Royne found himself seated in silence at the foot of the Gray Wolf's table alongside the pack's remaining leaders, men that only that morning would have been more than willing to tear out his throat—Callum, Velius, and a handful of others whose names the Young Loremaster had not even bothered to learn. Only one vacant seat remained, directly across from Royne, and it was reserved for Salasco the Wall.

As the Grantisi soldiers and their leader awaited the Wall's arrival, Royne listened while they lapsed into muttered talk of wines and weather, horses and old acquaintances, anything to avoid a concerted reflection upon the disastrous defeat. Despite their differences of opinion, Royne could not help but pity them, for they were proud men and honorable (at least in the warrior-sense), and over the past year, the legions' reputation had been continually shamed in a manner few could have thought possible.

Royne breathed a heavy sigh. True, such maddened loyalty bordered on base stupidity, but there was something strangely enviable about such a thing. From general to captain to the lowest legionnaire, the men of the wolf pack had something Royne lacked, something he wondered if he would ever possess: belief. Belief in something greater than himself, even greater than in his friends. A belief in something that defied his senses, that defied logic, and defied truth.

The Young Loremaster shook his head and bit his lip. It was this same blind idealism, blind romanticism, that had defined Lughus, and although in nearly every case these qualities drove men to ruin, there were those rare occasions that they also made men great.

At long last, the flap of the general's pavilion rustled and a sentry appeared to announce the arrival of Salasco the Wall. The men rose to greet him, but the sight of the Blackguard as he stepped forth to take his place at the table brought utterances of surprise from even the veteran soldiers, for in likeness Salasco appeared more the patient than the healer. From head to two, he was wrapped in strips of cloth bandages, marred here and there with splotches of blood, and rather than a simple walking stick, he leaned upon his staff like a crippled man with a crutch.

"Good evening," he said simply, peering out at them from beneath the shadow of a long, winding bandage that covered half of his skull.

The officers exchanged wide-eyed looks of uncertainty, their grim faces creased with skepticism. General Navarro alone remained unmoved, and with only the slightest of glances to the young Loremaster, inclined his head cordially to the bandaged man. "Good evening, good sir," he said, "And be welcome."

The Wall smiled briefly and assumed his seat. "Thank you, General."

For a long moment, the table fell silent. Callum, Velius, and the others examined the tablecloth before them and Royne began to sense the discomfort shifting toward a certain resentment at the Healer's lack of decorum. *Foolish soldiers,* he thought, *How bizarre that they should so wantonly stand upon courtesy in one moment and abandon it the very next?*

General Navarro nodded to one of the attendants standing in wait along the wall of the pavilion and at once the servants spurred to action. Wine was poured and platters with what few niceties the army could muster were set forth upon the table. A youth with a basin of water and a clean cloth passed from man to man, inviting them to wash their hands. When he stopped to aid Salasco, the water in the basin immediately turned a vivid red.

"Tell me, Salasco," the Gray Wolf said, "Your hands bear the mark of great industriousness. I trust you have been of great comfort to our wounded?"

Salasco dried his hands upon the cloth. "As best as I was able, General," he said, "And though I regret that I could not save them all, it is my sincere hope that some shall survive who may not have otherwise."

"In either case, you have my thanks," Navarro said, raising his goblet, "For your efforts and for those of them who follow you."

"Again, thank you."

At the Gray Wolf's right, General Callum shifted in his seat and exchanged a glance with Captain Velius. A moment later, the captain took a sip from his glass. "I say," Velius began, "It was certainly our good fortune to find you on the plane such as this—and with an army of healers at your back, particularly when we had such a difficult time finding you in the past."

"There's no accounting for the whims of Fortune," Salasco observed, "Or so the Sorgunders say."

"So I have heard," the captain said pleasantly, "And am I right in recognizing one or two of them among those following you?"

"Sorgunders?" Salasco mused, "In all likelihood. I believe we discovered a few men washed ashore when the war began last autumn. They may have decided to stay with us through the winter and spring." The Wall shrugged, "Many of them come and go as they please so it is hard to say. However, I imagine you may very well find folk from every land across Termain, though of course most will be of Grantis."

"Most?" Velius repeated.

General Navarro cleared his throat and cast the captain a glance. General Callum, straightening in his chair, would not be silenced so easily. "Every land?" he asked, "Do you mean to say that there are those among your mob that hail from Dwerin or Andoch?"

"More from Dwerin then Andoch, I would imagine," Salasco said blithely, "Though I'm not certain of it."

Royne could not help but betray a slight smirk of amusement as half the soldiers at the table went white, stricken with shock and indignation. Captain Velius's brow knit with consternation while General Callum's lips twisted into a sneer. "Am I to understand," he said, "That you have welcomed enemies into our midst? Granted them solace and shelter?"

"If by solace and shelter you mean to ask if I tended their wounds, then by all means, yes. I did."

"Why in all the world you ever do that?!" Callum growled.

Salasco took a sip from his goblet and as he did so, Royne felt for a moment the Blackguard's eye catch his own. "I realize, sir, that with the exception of the young Loremaster, every man seated at this table has the honor of being a soldier, and for the sake of duty, the land of a man's birth and the object of his loyalties are of significant import," he paused, "Yet, as a man who studies the arts of healing, I must admit that the requirements of my duty are less complex. For my part, I ask only if a man is suffering, and if the answer to that question is yes, then I am honor-bound to provide him with aid. You see, while a soldier defines his enemy as Dwerin or Andochan or Grantisi, to a healer, there is but one enemy—Death."

"That may be," Callum said, "But what of those who follow you? Were they not soldiers as well?"

"Perhaps," Salasco said, "Though I imagine if they still viewed the world as such, they would not have worked so tirelessly these many hours to see to the aid of your wounded."

Royne fought to contain a sudden flash of mirth. *Well-played*, he thought, and glancing down the table, his eyes met those of the Gray Wolf. Navarro too seemed impressed with the Wall's candor, though his visage remained that of the gracious host. "Come now," General Navarro said pleasantly, "Enough of this hot talk." He nodded once more to an attendant and a servant was sent to prepare more wine. "I'm afraid you must excuse us, Good Salasco. These past days have been rather trying, and such a sound beating at the hands of our enemies has left us soldiers with a bad taste in our mouths that it seems wine alone cannot wash away."

The remainder of the meal passed uneventfully, pleasantly in fact (though not without an undercurrent of hostility). Royne was glad for the addition of the Wall's presence among the sea of soldiers, and, strangely, he could not help but recognize a degree of subtle familiarity between himself and the old healer. What it was, he could not tell, but as the meal went on, he longed more and more for the opportunity to speak to the Blackguard alone, for he had many questions to which he suspected Salasco might hold the answers.

It was not until the meal was over that the chance for any private discussion finally occurred. Weary from wine and the long march, General Navarro dismissed the party to their private quarters with the promise of resuming the talk of strategy the following morning. As they departed the pavilion, Royne fell in step beside the elder Blackguard as he strode in the direction of that portion of the camp given over as an infirmary. Behind them, the ribald laughter of Captain Velius and the other officers echoed in the dark, in response, no doubt, to yet another one of their tiresome soldiers' jokes. Royne breathed a sigh and shook his head.

"So am I to understand," Salasco said, "That Old Rastis has finally met his end?"

Royne's eyes went wide and he felt suddenly as if he had just been punched in the gut. "I don't know," he said quietly. "He was alive when last I saw him, but…" The memory of the old man instantly grown even older—ancient—filled him with dread. His skin was so pale, wrinkly…like egg shell or old paper…like death…

Salasco gave a somber nod. "So he passed the title to you by blood oath, rather than by sacrifice."

It was a statement. Not a question. Though, not one Royne understood. "I'm afraid that I'm not quite sure what that means," he said.

"It means that passing the title on to you did not require his death."

Royne's heart fluttered. "So he may yet live?"

"Impossible to say." Salasco shrugged. "The Gift of the Guardians—the blessing that accompanies the transfer of the title, or 'the Anointing,' as the Order calls it—it can sustain him, see him through trials and hardships that would break a normal man. However, without it…" The Wall paused, "Rastis is an old man, very old, and without the Gift to sustain him…"

Royne bit his lip. "Kredor held him prisoner," he said, "Locked away atop the Tower of the Judge."

Salasco shook his head sadly, pausing momentarily to lean upon his staff. "Regrettable," he said, "Though clearly it was something he anticipated, for here you are. I take it you have the book as well?"

"I do."

"Then in spite of his imprisonment, Rastis may claim victory yet."

"What do you mean?" Royne asked.

Salasco shook his head.

"Please," Royne began again, "For months now I have been wandering around in the dark trying to discover just what it is that Rastis was doing and what he intended me to see through. When last we spoke, he made mention of the Dibhorites and something about Callah's Key—something called the Bard's Heresy. He claimed *The Book of Histories* would show me the way, but as much as I have read, there are many things that I still do not understand. I had hoped that in Commonwealth, you might be able to offer me the truth."

The healer's eyes gleamed. "Truth," he said softly, "Slippery subject, that. Like the surface of a lake. We gaze into its waters hoping to see what lies beneath, yet more often it merely reflects the image of the beholder." Salasco shook his head, "In any case, I may at least be able to offer you some insight, some meaning, some explanation that might guide you through the long night."

"Please," Royne said.

"Very well," Salasco said. He breathed a heavy sigh and stood straight, gazing out across the sleeping camp with the quiet resolution of a rustic shepherd. "The Bard's Heresy," he began at last, "Is perhaps the most closely guarded of all of the Order's secrets, more even than the Rites of Initiation, the Anointing, and the Gift. For, the Bard's Heresy—or prophecy as some call it—speaks of the End of Days, the end of the Order, and the return of Dibhor's Beast."

"Prophecy?" Royne remarked, "I'm sorry, but I do not believe in such things. It smacks too much of magic and other such nonsense."

"And yet you read from a book with blank pages."

Royne's breath caught in his throat, though he tried not to show it, turning his gaze away from the healer. Salasco did not press the issue further. Instead, he cleared his throat and in a soft, low voice, began to intone:

When all the lands of Calendral are bound by Callah's Key,
The Bard shall sing a doleful dirge for Wisdom's unheard plea,
For the Testament unto the Light will seek to snuff the Flame,
When the slumbering Beast of Dibhor wakes, who shall bear the blame?
The Armies of the Dead shall march whilst all the Children weep,
And the Scions of the Brother Dark shall rise from their long sleep,
If the last of Aiden's Blood is spilled to profane the Lady's Grace,
Will any man be left alive to rise up in his place?
So heed the words of Wisdom and mark well the strains of Song,
The Pariah whose heart remains still pure will be welcome erelong,
For all that Guard must take up arms to hold the night at bay,
Else who will rise to bring the Dawn and drive the Dark away?

For a long moment afterward, Royne remained silent, for somehow, the words were not unfamiliar to him, and for a fleeting moment, an image passed before his mind's eye. It was a woman clad all in scarlet and sable. She stood before the gates of the Keystone, her dark hair streaming out behind her while her bright eyes blazed with grief and wrath, as beautiful and terrible as a thunderstorm, an avalanche, a typhoon. Royne's stomach twisted into a great tangle of knots. He knew at once who she was.

"Assuming there is some truth to this business," he said, swallowing a sudden surge of feeling, "Why is it heresy? It sounds more like a warning than anything else. Why should the Order not take it seriously?"

"Because of the source."

"The Bard?"

"*The* Bard, you might say."

Royne took a breath. "Amarthia," he said, "Yes, I was just reading about her. The King...he took her into his bed."

"And the child...?" Salasco said.

"The child..." Royne's gaze narrowed as he stared up at the night sky, at the stars, and somehow he remembered, "King Erolan had Amarthia confined, imprisoned. Only Loremaster Sabrun and a select few others were permitted to see her." He paused; all at once the memories began flooding back to him, "The Shield was to guard her, the Wall was to ensure her health. No others were to know, no others could know..."

"But..."

"But Erolan..." Royne thought, "Erolan was wounded...struck by a spear in battle against Wrathorn rebels...struck in the genitals, a wound that even one with the blessing of the Anointed could not heal..."

"There is no simple cure for the loss of an arm or a leg...or anything else of the sort," Salasco said, "And so it seemed that the line of Drudish kings was finally at an end."

"At least," Royne said, "To those who did not know Amarthia was with child."

"Yes," the Wall mused, "And with the threat of his line's end, Erolan soon forgot any fears of sin and indiscretion that he might have had. Rather than consult the wisdom of the Loremaster, he chose to consult the politics of the Chancellor and the absolution of the Hierophant."

"Yet both were vengeful, and though they agreed to offer Erolan their support, it was not without cost. As soon as the child was born—a boy, as fate would have it—he was taken into the church's custody and his mother denied contact with him."

Royne stared up into the darkness of the night sky, his eyes unfocused regarding the tiny pinpoints of light from the stars. Sabrun was incensed, for the birthing was not easy and were it not for the skill of the Wall, the mother would have surely died.

Royne shuddered with anxiety, recalling how the Shield broke beneath the indignity of dishonor. His role transformed from loyal defender to simple turnkey, left to guard one so unjustly imprisoned.

Yet, his wrath paled in comparison to that of the Loremaster.

Sabrun was furious and in more than one occasion, he spoke out openly in defiance of the King and the rest of the Council. Amarthia was his friend, and, in a certain fashion, Royne knew that the man had come to love her. To see her so ill-treated by those held in such high regard—the paragons of the entire Order—he soon began plotting, strategizing, so that he might discover a way to grant the Bard her freedom. That she might return to the hidden paths and villages of the wilds where she and her forbearers had roamed for generations following the days of the Blessed Saint.

And so it was, whether through wisdom, compassion, or resentment, that Sabrun sought help from others who had fallen out of favor with the Order, with those who—like the Bard—had kept to the "old ways" before the Oath of Fealty. He sought out the Wandering Guardians. He sought out Blackguards.

He found the Three.

Or rather, they found him. For over the generations of their wanderings, the Marshal, the Blade, and the Vanguard had often crossed paths with the Bard as they traversed the roads and the wilds from the frozen wastes of Wrathorn in the north to the fertile plains of Grantis in the south. They had known of the Bard's intentions in returning to the Order, had heard the ballads of dark foreboding that Amarthia and those before her sang beneath the cover of stars, strange premonitions about the fall of the Guardians and the return of the Dibhorites. How ironic, Royne thought now, that in seeking to save the Order, Amarthia should be the tragic object of its corruption and the harbinger of its fall. *Yet still she tried. She bought us time…*

"That song," Royne said, "The Bard's Heresy…"

"She sang it just before she made her escape on the eve of her child's first birthday," Salasco said, "She was forced to leave him behind, of course. She chose to, in fact, for even she believed that the Order needed a Drudish King.

Yet, just as Erolan had taken what was most precious to her, upon her departure she took with her what was most precious to him."

The Young Loremaster's eyes grew wide. "The Key of Salvation!" he exclaimed, "Callah's bloody Key!"

"Aye," the Wall nodded, "For, if the King and the Council were so easily felled by the seeds of Dibhor's corruption—pride, envy, greed, lust—then they could hardly be trusted to safeguard the very key that binds the Dark Brother's Beast."

Royne fought to suppress an involuntary snort of derision. Still, nonsense and monsters aside, the Key was the symbol of the realm and the Order. Forged by a goddess or not, its symbolic meaning was more than enough to make it the very stuff of magic, and somehow this key was wrapped up in whatever it was that concerned Rastis and Natharis Tainne.

"So the Key wasn't lost in war against Tulondis after all?"

"No, that was simply a convenient explanation for its disappearance until the true Key could be recovered or a passable replacement forged."

Royne considered this and gave a nod. It had been Sabrun's idea, he suddenly remembered, part of the larger plan to cover his subversive activities and consorting with Blackguards. It was amazing how willingly people would believe anything in order to maintain tradition.

"Yet," Royne mused, "There is still one thing I do not understand. Amarthia returned to the Order for fear that it might fall. However, in stealing the Key, did she not in some way also threaten its destruction? Truly, the loss of such an important symbol could only suggest to the rest of Termain—nay, the rest of Lann—that the Order was in decline."

The Key's importance far exceeds that of any mere symbol, young Loremaster."

"Aye, but it's been missing for hundreds of years now and surely no disaster has befallen the Order in that time."

"No, it was missing, or rather, it was *believed* to be missing. However, it has at last been found, and if the rumors are to be believed, it has fallen into most dangerous hands."

Royne thought back to Rastis's crumpled form locked in his cell atop the Judge's Tower, "Then you too believe that the Dibhorites have returned?"

Salasco's eyes twinkled with the light of mystery. "Returned?" he said, "No, not returned. They never left. Rather, they have finally chosen to act."

"But were they not killed long ago? Hunted down and hanged for their crimes?"

"Those who committed crimes worthy of such punishments, certainly. However, you cannot simply run around executing people for believing in something you do not agree with, for that was the problem with Kalius Wrogan in the first place and to do so is but another step along the path of tyranny," Salasco said, "No, the Dibhorites still exist, though mostly in secret, and for many long years, they were watched—not by members of the Order, perhaps, but by others. It is a task, I assure you, that has grown increasingly difficult as they gain in their number while ours seem to fade. Like a poison, their influence has spread to infect many of the wealthiest and most influential noble families in Andoch to every corner across Termain. Still, for hundreds of years they have behaved, safely confined within the walls of the Lighthouse of Castone. It is only recently that they seem to have awakened from their slumber. Clearly they were not idle."

"The Lighthouse?" Royne asked, "Then the Keepers are Dibhorites?"

"Not all, but many, more now than in the past. Remember, the Lighthouse predates the Order by hundreds of years—back to the days of Old Calendral when the Dark Brother was still worshiped as one of the Brethren." Salasco breathed a heavy sigh and leaned upon his stave, "There were some who would have seen them all put to the sword, but to do so would have been nothing short of murder. The Keepers are scholars, not warriors. Of course, I am certain I do not have to tell the Loremaster that knowledge is no less formidable a weapon in a time of war."

Royne paused to think and gazed up at the night sky. Somehow the stars seemed to shine less brightly and in his mind he envisioned the unnatural eyes of Natharis Tainne. "But this is all madness," he said after a moment, "Magic keys and Bard's heresies? Should we not be more concerned with the political consequences of Kredor's conquest, his call for the Protectorate?"

"Of course we should," Salasco said, "For, it is the first part of the prophecy. The Guardian-King, the one man tasked with safeguarding the Key of Salvation, seeks to bind the lands of Termain into a single empire…"

Royne shook his head bitterly. "Coincidence," he said, though he could not help but recall the Council meeting long ago when Rastis spoke in defiance of the King's wishes only to be ignored. *Wisdom's unheard plea…*

"Still," he said aloud, "I see nothing regarding St. Aiden and his bloody flame."

"Do you not?" Salasco said with a grim smile, "You knew him quite well from what I understand."

"What do you mean?"

"The Galadins of the Brock are the heirs of St. Aiden," the Wall said, "The fire that burns through all the ages. They guide the folk of Termain through the darkness by shining their golden light."

Royne's fists clenched and his heart felt like a battering ram beating against a castle wall. "Lughus!" he cried, "Then he made it! He's alive!"

"If the rumors are true."

"Ha! Good Ol' Goldimop! I knew it!" his breast swelled with renewed vigor, "Aiden's Bloody Flame!"

"Indeed."

"But you say he's still in danger?"

"Testament," Salasco said, "True, it's the name of the Guardian-King's castle, but is it not also the name of his heirloom sword?"

Royne bit his lip. The Drudes have always viewed the Galadins as rivals to their power, and how could they not? Had St. Aiden not fallen against the Warlock, who is to say that the next war would not have been between the two leaders of the rebellion?"

"Regardless of whether or not you believe in the Beast or the Prophesy or even the Brethren themselves," Salasco said, "It is clear that the Guardian-King has set his aim against the Brock, for with Grantis defeated and Montevale and Dwerin as allies, the Barons are all that remain in the way of Kredor's conquest. Yet, even as the King comes closer to reaching his goal, he is but a puppet in the larger scheme of the Dibhorites."

"And what might that be?" Royne asked tersely.

"The end of the line of Galadin, the destruction of the Order, and the resurrection of the Dark Brother's Beast."

"I mean you no offense, Salasco," Royne sighed, "But I have a hard time believing in any of that."

"So did Rastis, I imagine," Salasco said, "Though in time, he too came to believe. The preponderance of evidence supports it, for the Bard's visions are seldom wrong, least of all in the case of Old Sigmund."

"Sigmund?"

"The current man to bear the title of the Bard. He lives among the Wrathorn far to the north. He is the one that the third apprentice was meant to replace."

Royne's gaze narrowed. *Thom and his bloody songs...* He shook his head. *Rastis, why did you not just tell them the truth? Mystery upon mystery.* "Well," he said at last, "If Rastis was willing to suspend his disbelief, then so shall I."

"Good," Salasco said, "'For all that Guard must take up arms to hold the night at bay, else who will rise to bring the Dawn and drive the Dark away?'"

CHAPTER 29: PRIDEL

The large walled castle town of Pridel stood in the center of a rolling, green plane north and west of the White Wood. During the war, it remained consistently in the hands of the Gasparns, though it was not without the occasional Valendian siege or assault. The crofters who tended the land around the city were primarily farmers of vetches, potatoes, leeks, and other such crops, while herders tended droves of cattle and goats to produce milk and various cheeses for trade at the Pridel markets.

Approaching the city from the southern road, travelers often marked their journey's end by the sight of two ruins that stood but an hour's ride from the gates. The first was the low stone ring of a broken watch tower, toppled some thirty years ago, while the second was the empty husk of a dilapidated monastery long left vacant when the Grand Hierophant withdrew his clergy in protest at the outbreak of the fratricidal war.

It was in the shadow of these ruins where the Sirs Malet, both the Elder and the Younger, met Lord Harren's sentry as they led the royal carriage north toward Pridel. With them, guarded by a small cadre of men-at-arms, the father and son escorted the Princess Marina, recovered from the perilous clutches of the Silent Prince as he was attempting passage through the Malet lands. Their intentions now were to present her to the Warden of White

Wood so that he might hold her in his protection until such time as King Dermont could find time to reclaim his bride-to-be. At once, the sentry mounted his horse and rode hard for the town to inform Lord Harren of their impending arrival.

After a brief pause to rest and to provide the castle folk with a bit more time to prepare an appropriate welcome, the carriage continued on until it reached Pridel's main gates. Waiting to meet them were a sergeant and six guardsmen clad in glimmering mail and tabards bearing the symbol of the white gannet upon a field of light rose, the emblem of Lord Harren's household. With a nod to the knights, the sergeant commanded his men to open the gates, and together, the entire party began a slow procession through the town to the castle. As they passed, a few of the common folk stopped and stared in confusion on their way to and from the market stalls, shops, and places of employ, wondering vacantly what new personage had come to join the oft rumored indolence that marked the daily activities of Lord Harren's court.

At each of the castle gates—the first at the main barbican, the second at the portcullis separating the inner from the outer wards—the carriage was forced to stop and wait while, with exaggerated ceremony, the gannet guards greeted them and cleared the way for the carriage to proceed. Finally, at the main entry to the keep, Lord Harren's seneschal, a proud, fresh-faced man in gilded plate armor, received the Malets with a peremptory bow. He introduced himself as the Lord's nephew, and with an overabundance of zeal, offered the princess his arm so that he might personally present her to the Warden.

Clad in a simple, yet elegant gown of forest green (the best the Malet's master of wardrobe could put together at such short notice), Princess Marina appeared to Lord Harren's court as the very image of the flower by which she was known, for her fair skin shone like newly fallen snow and her red hair, plaited and arranged beneath a thin circlet of gold, were as the petals of a budding rose. A cascade of polite applause greeted her as the seneschal led her to the court. Behind her, at a respectful distance came the knights Malet, and following them still, four of the six men-at-arms, the other two having been left behind to mind the carriage.

When the seneschal reached the edge of the elevated dais upon which Lord Harren sat enthroned, the Warden stood, received the princess from his nephew and offered her the kiss of friendship upon the back of her hand. Arranged among the periphery of the hall, the lords, knights, ladies, and officers of Pridel's court renewed their applause with greater vigor, and with a courteous bow and wave of his hand, Lord Harren encouraged them to fall silent.

"My, my!" the lord exclaimed, "What a beautiful rose the Malets have plucked from the brambles of my garden, and what a wonderful victory we have to celebrate today!" To emphasize the magnitude of his victory, Harren had dressed for the occasion in his own immaculate armor, its silver and gold tracery shimmering alongside his embroidered surcoat and mantle of cloth-of-gold. "My dear Princess Marina," he beamed holding both of her hands in his, "Be welcome in Pridel!"

The court offered another brief flurry of applause as the princess offered a polite nod. "Thank you, Lord Harren," she replied, her green eyes wide with a slight reticence. As she glanced around the great hall at the smiling noble faces, her cheeks suddenly reflected the crimson shade of her hair. "You are most kind," she added.

Harren basked in the glow of a princess's gratitude. "Be not afraid here, my noble lady," he declared, "We have delivered you from danger, and though, as I hear it, the traitorous Prince Beledain—or should I say, the Blackguard Prince Beledain—escaped, rest assured that you have my pledge that I will personally root him out and serve him what's for!"

The princess's blush deepened as the applause again resumed. "I should warn you to be careful, my lord," Marina said, "For the prince—the Tower, as they call him now—is very clever and a great warrior."

"Rumor and hearsay! Rumor and hearsay!" Harren said, "Fear not, lady, for I know him personally! In truth, he is neither clever nor great! He is but a pup who scrambles for scraps at his brother's table, envious of his elder and more noble king. He is no true knight, my lady, but a master of cutthroats, traitors, and thieves! He attacks my caravans and wagon trains stealing stores, trinkets, and trifles meant for the good men of King Dermont gathering in the west! He slew his brother's own best friend, kidnapped his own father, and attempted to abscond with you, my dear! Why, the Tower is naught but a brigand and a beast!" He turned to address the court and raised a hand to invite their applause. "And we will soon sort him out, will we not? Huzzah!"

359

"Huzzah!" the court shouted in answer, "Huzzah!"

"My lady," Lord Harren continued, "My only wish is that he were here right now so that I might serve him here in my very hall! To serve him the swift, blinding justice he deserves!"

"My lord," the princess said with a touch of amusement, "You should be careful what you wish for."

In a flash, the knights Malet drew their swords, and behind them, the four men-at-arms readied their weapons. A collective gasp sounded from among the noble gallery and one elder noblewoman cried out in alarm. The quartet of guards on duty in the hall readied their halberds and eyed their lord and seneschal uncertainly, awaiting a command. Their hesitation, however, cost them dearly as one of the Malet men-at-arms hurled a strange chain-like weapon and caught hold of a guard's halberd, pulling it from his hands. Before he even had a chance to look surprised, the man sent the whirling chain around again to tie around another's legs and knock him to the floor. Two more men-at-arms wielding swords rushed forth and subdued the guardsmen flanking the lord's high seat, while the final one, a lancer, removed his kettle hat and raised his weapon to the throat of Lord Harren himself.

"Greetings, Lord Harren," Bel said. "It has been some time."

Harren's face twisted with rage, but he ignored the disguised prince. "Stegan, you're the seneschal," he snapped. "Do something."

The lord's nephew, furious with a blending of shame and rage, sneered. "What is it you would have me do, uncle?"

"Kill them, you fool."

"I would not advise trying," Bel said sternly.

"There are six of you, at best," Harren scoffed, "You'll never leave here alive. I'd advise you to surrender now while you have the chance."

"Bold words for a man with a blade at his throat."

"You wouldn't kill me. You're not *that* stupid. No sooner would you strike than Stegan would cut you down."

"Do you wish to try it?" Bel asked the nephew, "Are you quick enough to draw and get to me before I dispatch your uncle and turn to you?"

The seneschal glared at Bel with hatred, but remained still. In the galleries, other men sat armed too, yet unarmored. Beneath the naked blades of the father and son Malet, not one of them made any move.

360

"Best hurry on with it, Tower," the Shackle called from the rear of the room.

Bel glanced at the princess and offered her a reassuring nod. He knew from her posture and the way she held her hands clasped together across her slender waist that she was nervous; however, to anyone else she was the picture of confidence and haughty poise.

"Get on your knees, Harren," Bel said.

The Warden's eyes went wide. "Why?" he sputtered, "I'll not kneel to the likes of you."

Bel shook his head. "I'm not asking you to kneel before me, you fool. I'm ordering you to kneel before your queen."

"What? What queen?""

Bel nodded at Horn holding a guardsman at bay beside the throne. In a flash, the skirmisher lashed out and kicked Harren behind the knee, knocking him to the floor. "On your knees, you dandy shite."

Sir Armel cast Bel an impatient gaze. "We haven't much time…"

Bel nodded and breathed a heavy sigh. "My name is Beledain Tremont," he began, "Third son to King Cedric of Valendia, known as the Silent Prince, and now called the Tower." He paused. Fops like Harren may enjoy their speeches, their worthless words and prattle, but unless rallying his men before a battle, Bel did not. "I have come to inform you that as we speak, an army marches to Pridel's gates with the intent of laying siege."

More gasps and cries of concern sounded from among the members of the court, though Lord Harren and his nephew remained silent.

"However," Bel continued, "It is our sincere hope that it will not come to battle and that you, lords and ladies, knights and officers of the court, will hear us now, and in the interest of peace, stand *with* us rather than *against* us in support of a united Montevalen queen.

"What queen?" Harren said again, "There is no queen!"

"Queen Marina," Bel said, "Daughter of King Marius of Gasparn, and rightful heir to the throne of Montevale."

The murmuring of the gallery grew louder and Bel offered Marina another furtive glance. Suddenly, to Bel's surprise, Lord Harren shook his head and grunted a sardonic laugh.

"So that's your game, boy," he leered, "You coerce the meek, doe-eyed maiden into playing the pretty puppet whilst you usurp your brother's crown? You've seen to deflowering his bride, now you hope to see him dethroned!"

Without warning, Marina's brow creased with fury and she struck Harren full in the face. The lord's nose ruptured in a torrent of blood and beneath the weight of his absurd armor, he collapsed upon the floor. His nephew made to draw his sword, but before he could fully free the blade, Bel whirled Spire around and drove its point between the links of mail separating the seneschal's pauldron and breastplate. The wound was not mortal, but it was very painful, particularly for one who had never before felt the sting of any wound.

"You would be wise to mind your discourteous tongue, Lord Harren," the princess said, "Or I shall allow my friend, Prince Beledain, to separate it from your unctuous mouth." For the briefest of moments, her eyes met those of the Silent Prince. Gone were the subtle hints of uncertainty, replaced now with a fervor that made his heart glow. He returned her glance and offered her a bow of his head.

From the floor, Harren made a gurgling noise, matched in tone by his nephew's whimpering, but Marina ignored them. Gracefully, she climbed Harren's dais, and stood with regal poise to address the rest of the hall.

"The Tower speaks the truth," she said over the sudden murmurings of the castle folk, "Our army advances as we speak, and I say *our* army not to mean mine or his or any *one* person's, but rather *ours*—all of us, *all* of Montevale. For, no longer are we Gasparns or Valendians. No longer do we fight a war between a Black Horse and a White Horse. Rather, we stand united together—one land, one blood, one people—to heal the wounds of one hundred years of senseless, bloody war."

"Now," she continued, "King Dermont in Reginal may believe that his victory upon the Nivanus Highlands brought an end to the war already, and that Prince Beledain, myself, my father, and his own father, are naught but rebels preaching insurrection and breeding malcontent. He would accuse us of being enemies to peace and harbingers of destruction. Yet, all of us know better than to believe the word of a man known as the King of Plague, a man who surrounds himself with Death Knells and Sundering Hands, who gathers to him men known as plague-bearers, and fights wars not with arms and honor, but with terror and disease. As King Cedric once said, 'All men earn their titles,' and surely each one of us has heard the stories—some of us may have even seen firsthand what the Plague King is capable of.

"Can we really expect peace, then, from such a man? Can he truly heal the strife bred from a century of war? Will he restore the pride of our people in the wake of so much shame and death? If such is the case, then why do our armies gather along the border to the west to do the bidding of the Guardian-King? Why are our friends and relations stripped of their lands in the name of peace? And how is it that men of two lands—in spite of a hundred years of war—can come together under one banner as friends, as brothers once again, to oppose such a man in hopes that pride, honor, and dignity may be restored?"

Marina paused to breathe, but when she spoke again, her voice was clear and strong. "Prince Beledain, though by Dermont's decree be prince no longer," she said, "Has asked that I step forward to serve as queen. I will do so—not because I lust for power like the Plague King, but for the *love* my lands and out of *duty* to my people, and though Dermont would lay claim to me, I am as yet unwed, and I refuse, now and forever, to accept his hand. For, only a man who is true and bold and just will serve me, for such a man would be the next Montevalen king, and what truly is a king—or a queen—but a servant to all?

"So I ask you, all of you, people not of Gasparn or Valendia or even Pridel, but as men and women of Montevale," she paused, "I ask you to stand with us—all of us. One land, one blood, one people."

When she finished speaking, a heavy silence fell upon the hall and not a person moved. Bel held Spire steady over Lord Harren and his seneschal, but his eyes shone with warmth upon the fair princess—no, the queen—for the strength of her words had proven her mettle and the strength of the spell they wove kindled within his breast a zeal that he had never felt before, and though much of what she said they had discussed together when he had first proposed the idea of sovereignty to her at Feyhold, to hear them uttered forth now with such eloquence and such conviction made him believe.

For some time the silence lingered, until a heavyset lord clad in a sable surcoat marked with a pair of white trefoils got to his feet. Under the watchful eyes of Malet the Elder, strode to the center of the hall, drew his sword, and laid it on the floor at Marina's feet.

"My name is Lord Balvane Grimbol of Dromlan," he said, slowly bending his knee, "I was once a Lord of Valendia, but I'd rather be a man of Montevale."

"Thank you, Lord Grimbol," Marina said, and from the other side of the hall, another man, a knight, stood and did the same.

"Sir Kedgen Dastone of Gasparn," he said, "Now of Montevale."

"Sir Lorgan Bregor of Valendia, now Montevale."

"Lord Ioun Kindel of Gasparn. I fought with your brother at Whitemane. He would have made a good king, but I'm certain you'll make a finer queen!"

And so the nobles followed, one after another, until finally, to a man, they pledged their support to Marina. Lord Harren and his seneschal were led away to have their wounds seen to, and the men of the Pridel watch, commanded now by the nobles of the court, had no choice but to stand down and submit their arms.

When Bel's forces arrived soon after, holding steady as they were by the ruins, they found that Pridel's gates were open to them. They paraded forth through the city in a grand column of horse and foot. The men of Harren's guard were allowed the option to leave peaceably with their lord or to join in the army of Queen Marina and the Tower, a choice many accepted. The former Warden and a few other minor officials whose loyalty he had long since bought were allowed, by order of the Queen, to go free. However, their assets were seized in the name of Montevale and by day's end distributed to the bewildered common folk and burghers of the city.

Once again, heartened by her earlier victory, and with the Tower at her side, Queen Marina gave a formal address to the masses, recapitulating the same notions and principles with which she had enamored the gentry. In the wake of Harren's indolence and self-indulgence as their leader, they were more than happy to accept the sovereignty of two such ardent friends of the common folk as the Silent Prince and the Winter Rose. As Sir Emory pointed out whilst planning the ruse in Feyhold, the people love nothing more than a hero—particularly one with a reputation for fighting at their side rather than at their back. A common man was expected to fight at the command of his lord, but a noble always had the choice, not only whether to take the field or pay the scutage, but whether to toe the line of battle or hide behind the shield wall of his levees. Bel could not help but think of Lilia and how she loved mocking Dermont under his pavilion while his army took the field of battle.

By nightfall, a feast had been hastily prepared in the great hall for the nobles, officers, and other important personages attached to the fledgling royal court, as well as many of the notable burghers of influence among the common folk. Messengers were sent to the surrounding fiefdoms as far as the Ebon Keep informing the other knights and lords of what had transpired, and requesting that they declare themselves friend or foe. By the end of the meal, Bel was exhausted. No less, he imagined, than if the bloodless coup had come to a pitched battle. He had lost his taste for diplomacy and politics long ago in the Highlands of the Nivanus, and such a thing wore upon him like a millstone.

"If I were you," the Shackle told Bel that night as they stood sharing a drink in the corner of the castle hall, "I'd not trust a single one of these fine folk just yet—if ever. They might be with us while the sun shines today, but what happens if there's a turn in the weather? Will they stand by us in the wind and rain, or will they run for shelter at the first sound of thunder?"

"Indeed," Bel said. They watched as a couple dressed in silk brocade reverently approached Kings Cedric and Marius seated beside one another at the queen's table. With practiced synchronicity, they offered the former sovereigns a low bow and, what Bel knew without hearing, was a grandiose complement of some sort. Again, the Shackle gave a snort.

"Look at them, smiling and pandering. Bloody nobles. It makes me sick."

"Why do you think I'm standing over here with you?" Bel smiled, "Though I have to admit, I was a bit surprised when you offered to come with us—not that I'm ungrateful. I just didn't expect you to leave your forest."

The Shackle shrugged and drained his cup. "What can I say?" he shrugged, "You fixed my house. I figure I can help you fix yours."

Bel laughed, surprising himself, for it had been some time since he had done so freely. It felt good and for the first time in what seemed weeks, his wine did not carry with it the same bitter aftertaste of despair.

"Plus," the Shackle continued, "You keep pissing in the eye of the Guardians, you'll need the help of any Blackguard you can get."

"Much appreciated," Bel said, "Lord Shackle of Feyhold."

"Let's not start that now," the Blackguard said, "At any rate, I'll watch your back, since of course, I expect you'll be busy watching hers."

Bel paused, "The queen?"

"Aye, there'll be many as will be competing for her favors now after that bit she said about her one-day-husband-king," the Shackle winked, "They're like to turn hostile once they notice she's only got eyes for you."

Bel shook his head, "She's a queen now, and I'm nothing."

"Ha! Don't be fucking daft, man," the Shackle scoffed, "You're hardly nothing; you're a Blackguard, an outlaw, a hunted man."

"Just like Harren said, eh? A scoundrel and a brigand."

"Exactly! What's more appealing to a cloistered maiden than a man with a bit of danger around him?" he chuckled, "Besides, two peas in a pod, you two. You both actually seem to believe all that rot about fairness and honor and whatnot. At the very least I think I'll stick around long enough to see how it all turns out."

Bel gazed across the hall to the where the queen sat at her table beside his empty chair at her right hand. She was smiling as she spoke to Sir Armel and the younger Malet, and without realizing, Bel found himself staring, unabashedly, a fond smile playing upon the corners of his lips. "We have to try," Bel told the Shackle, "What else can we do?"

"Aye," the Blackguard laughed, "So I've heard you say before."

"It's the truth. What else *can* we do?"

"You can stand and fight, you can run and hide, or you can die. Though, I suppose either of the first two could just as easily result in the third."

"Well," Bel said, "I already ran from Tremontane, I hid in Feyhold, and I've seen more than enough death. So, I guess the way is clear. We stand and fight."

"Good. You chose the fun one."

CHAPTER 30: MUTINY

Before Rodulf's corpse had even grown cold, Magnus—in a frenzy of cursing, threats, and blows—ordered his men back to *Sigruna*, leaving but two behind to guard the captured ship and its spoils. It was clear to Thom that the crew was not happy. For most of the day they had driven the ship hard in pursuit before engaging in one of the most brutally bloody fights that Thom had ever seen. Most bore wounds of one make or another and a few would not live to see the sunrise. Yet now, here was Magnus ordering them under threat of death to continue their hasty pursuit into the dead of night. Their resentful discontent hung like a fog upon the night air. Yet despite their grumbling, not a man among them was willing to defy their captain, for the recent display of his martial prowess was more than enough to deter any of that—for now.

"Five men dead of wounds, two more with the heads clean off, and Rodulf himself," Thom muttered quietly, adding the tally to his journal, "That makes fourteen all told, seeing as the headless ones count for two and Rodulf counts for five."

Magnus gave a nod, but kept his eyes level upon the darkening horizon. "Only fourteen," he said, "I must be slipping."

Thom remained silent, regarding the great Wrathorn from head to toe. Blood ran in rivulets down his shins and forearms while above his waist, red speckles stood out on his chest and shoulders like a bloody pox. Yet, for the first time ever, Thom noticed an alarming change in Magnus's demeanor. It was quite subtle, buried as it were beneath the overwhelming brashness and anger, and though he could not quite identify exactly what it was, it was still there. *Is it doubt he feels? Or worse, fear?* Regardless, the young scribe held his tongue, and Sigruna continued her pursuit.

The moon shone high above, casting a ghostly reflection upon the shifting surface of the sea below. The howls of a dying sailor brought a chill to the night air and Thom, wrapped in an old piece of sailcloth in his corner of the great cabin, tried his best to sleep.

In the following days, Magnus drove *Sigruna* even further north and east across the Calendral Sea along the coast of Andoch to Baronbrock and Montevale. It was a mighty risk, for the navies of the proper realms were on the hunt, playing their part in whatever mad war the lords of the continent were engaged in, and should the corsairs happen to stumble upon a war galley out of Dwerin or Galdoran, they would find no quarter. A pirate was an enemy of all lands.

And like as not, I'd be hanged as one of them, Thom thought miserably, *Oh Lady let us find Slink soon so I can go home…*

Thankfully, there was little doubt as to where the last of Magnus's old shipmates was headed. This far out from the Sorgund Isles, the only safe harbor Slink might hope to find was with the Keepers at Castone, should they still prove amenable after such a long delay.

Such as it was, *Sigruna* sailed onward over the coming days until at long last a cry from the maintop brought all eyes to the horizon. There, only just visible in the light of the setting sun, Thom could make out the form of a tall, white tower. Surrounding it along the rocky shore was a small city overlooking a wide harbor accessible by a narrow inlet. At once, a hush fell over the crew and a palpable wave of cold resentment washed over the main deck of the ship.

"Castone."

It was impossible to know which of the sailors had spoken, but the utterance was a death knell. Thom could smell the men's fear and anger on the wind, nearly as pungent as his own. If Magnus sensed it as well, he did not care.

"There she is, boys. Journey's end," he called out as the ship's speed slackened. He pointed across the waves. "The selfsame ship as fled from us. Slink may think he's safe at harbor beneath the cover of the great bloody lighthouse, but he's a thing or two to learn, eh? We'll sink that bugger, sack the town, and live like kings until the end of our days!" His lips split into a broad grin, "What say we attack at midnight?"

The men eyed each other uneasily. Finally, one man muttered, "That's the Lighthouse of Castone."

"So it is," Magnus replied.

"Castone is cursed," said another.

"Aye," said a third, "And any who enter that harbor be damned!"

Magnus chuckled with defiance. "Shite," he spat.

"It's true," said the first again. "Any ship I know to set sail for these shores never returned to the Isles. They disappear without a trace."

"Aye. Clearly," Magnus said, motioning towards Slink's vessel idling far off in the harbor, "She looks ready to burst into flames at any time now."

"It's unwise to challenge fate, sir," the third man said coldly, "Every true Sorgunder knows that."

"Aye, we bless the ship with your heathen Wrathorn ways!" said the second sailor, his anger boiling over, "And you've the gall to call us fools?"

Thom's heart fluttered. He readied himself for blood. Magnus's eyes smoldered with mounting rage, yet to Thom's surprise, he remained silent.

"We signed on to this bloody venture with the promise of riches unlike we'd ever seen," another man cried, "And in so many weeks, we've caught naught but a few bloody cogs—all of which we've left in our wake in the madness of this bloody pursuit!"

"No wonder those buggers marooned you!" came another shout.

Lady save us! Thom muttered fervently, *Kin keep me safe and send me home!* He scurried back along the quarterdeck, hoping to be out of harm's way once the violence began. Yet, to his surprise, there was no sudden eruption of fighting, no bursting fonts of blood and gore. Instead, he glanced up and noticed the eyes of the Wrathorn warrior upon him. No longer angry, the big man offered him a reassuring nod. Thom eyed him back, attempting to discern what it was he sensed in Magnus's eyes. It wasn't fear. Certainly not. Perhaps weariness? A profound weariness?

At length, Magnus breathed a heavy sigh and climbed up onto the gunwale to address the mutinous crew.

"So this is to be the way of it?" he said, "Fine. So be it, then. If you're all in agreement, I'll honor your rights as a crew. Despite what you say, the Sorgund ways are my ways too, and as crew, you've your rights. Yet, first and foremost, I'm Wrathorn, and I've my ways to honor as well. So while I'll step down as captain, I've still my own matters to see to. I'll turn over the ship and my share of the other spoils, but in exchange, I'll have the launch and a stock of food enough for myself and the boy."

"There'll be nothing left for us then!" a man jeered, echoed by a chorus of laughter.

Magnus ignored it. "What say you?" he asked again.

The crew fell to muttering until one man called out, "What's to stop us just killing the both of you?"

"You're welcome to try," the Wrathorn grinned maliciously, "All of you at once may succeed, but I can promise that I'll take at least half of you with me."

The men eyed one another and the most vocal of the crew once more conversed in hushed tones. Thom watched them with suspicion, straining his ears to make out what they were saying.

Magnus stood still at his place upon the gunwale gripping the stays with one hand while the other lightly felt for the haft of his great axe. Should it come to a fight, Thom wondered who the victor would be, for in spite of Magnus's brutish ignorance and brash impulsiveness, when it came to combat, the big man appeared to have no equal. *Still*, the fat boy thought, *I would not see him killed. In spite of everything, I suppose he has become my friend.*

That realization puzzled him, but before he could consider it further, Magnus called out to the assemblage of sailors, interrupting Thom's private musing.

"Come now. What's it to be?"

The sailors exchanged one final glance and their spokesman stepped forward. "Fine," he said, "The launch is yours and we'll offer a bit in the way of water and stores for you and your fat scribbler."

"Aye, take them and be done with you," another man chimed in.

"Fine," Magnus said, "The sooner you men make ready, the sooner I'll be on my way." As the men hurried to carry out these final orders, he turned to Thom, "Fetch your things from the cabin and be quick about it."

"Yes, Magnus," Thom said, happy that there should be no blood, "I won't be a moment." He scurried down from his place upon the quarterdeck past the mutinous crew. With the big Wrathorn's departure eminent, however, they no longer hid their brash contempt for Thom. As quickly as he could manage, he hurried to collect his things—his pack, ink, quills, and his old journal—the only possessions in all the world that he could claim as his own. He paused only a moment to wonder what Old Rastis would say to the strange tale he had recorded: the odd, bloody tale of the barbarian called Magnus.

Like as not, he'll ask me what I learned, Thom thought, *How will I answer?*

A shout and a loud splash recalled his attention. The launch was ready; it was time to go. He secured his things in his pack and hurried back out to the main deck. Magnus remained as he stood before, leaning upon the rail. Most of the sailors had returned to their posts, ready to make sail as soon as their old captain was off, though a few—those most vocal in instigating the mutiny, remained on deck to bid him good riddance. Thom approached them hesitantly, wary that they might wish to inflict some parting evil, and wondering why Magnus did not.

"Hurry along now, Thom Crusher," Magnus called, "We're wasting daylight."

"Aye, sweetheart, make haste," one of the more bold sailors mocked. "Bad luck to bring a woman aboard!"

"No wonder the whole bloody venture's been a curse," said another.

Thom ignored them and made his way to Magnus's side. "Here you go, lad," the big man said, offering him a hand as he clambered over the rail to descend the rope ladder to the launch, "I'll be along shortly."

So struck was he by the Wrathorn's uncharacteristic show of kindness, that he nearly capsized the small boat. A large swell of salt water splashed over the side, soaking his habit and inviting a hearty round of jeering from the crew as he struggled to right himself. Once more, however, he noticed that

Magnus was not among those laughing. Instead, the Wrathorn stood tall and stern, his great arms folded across his chest.

"Laugh as you will, you bloody fucks!" he called out, "But that boy's more man than any one of you, you motherless pack of cowards!"

Thom could hardly believe his ears. A strange sensation kindled in his breast, an odd warmth that set his limbs tingling, for in all of his life, not a single person had ever seemed to acknowledge him in such a way. Not even by his own reckoning did he consider himself more than a silly, fat coward with a knack for bumbling foolery. To suddenly hear himself spoken of with such casual regard—indeed by one such as Magnus—filled him with a new type of pride. He gazed up at the great Wrathorn, flabbergasted, only to be surprised even further when the big man offered him a reassuring nod. It was nearly too much for him to bear.

"Alright, Magnus," one of the mutineers growled, "You've got the launch."

"Aye, shove off before we change our minds."

"So be it," Magnus declared. He turned as if to go, but in a flash drew Pavlos's falchion from his baldric and hurled it through the air. Men dove for safety as the blade struck home, shattering the lantern that hung beside the conn. At once, flaming oil littered the quarterdeck and to the sailors' horror, set the ship ablaze.

"Gods curse you all!" Magnus roared, and swung down the ladder to the boat below. Thom gazed up aghast at the burning ship while voices bellowed orders to put the fire out—too many voices, for no clear successor had yet been chosen among the mutineers to assume the mantle of captain. Thom's eyes widened as the fire spread and another lantern exploded. Magnus chuckled grimly and took up the oars, calmly paddling the boat toward Castone's stony shore. Before long, Sigruna was a towering inferno.

"Farewell, my darling," Magnus observed, "She was a good ship while she lasted."

Thom nodded. "She was. It's a shame to see her go like this."

"Aye, but better to burn than to see her in the hands of those wretched bastards."

"I suppose so," Thom said.

"Anyhow," Magnus grunted and spit into the swirling waves, "We're still alive, we're still afloat, and we've still got you and me."

The scribe nodded, "And we've still got a story to finish."

Magnus grinned in the light of the dying vessel. "Aye, so we do, Thom Crusher," he said, "So we do."

CHAPTER 31: ADOLFO THE MADDER

Lughus stood with his arms outstretched and his legs shoulder width apart. His hauberk clung to him as he stood sweating in the center of the great hall, for the day was hot and donning and doffing the full assortment of armor pieces the smith and his assistants brought with them from Highboard made the heat seem even worse. Seated across from him in a pair of canvas folding chairs, Brigid and Freddy watched the craftsman circling the young baron, winding lengths of string around his chest, his shoulders, his waist, his thighs, and all other places, taking measurements to adjust and refit the armor. Brigid could not help but smile at Lughus's clear discomfort and had to look away, stroking Fergus's ears to keep from laughing. She knew well how awful this sort of thing could be, and she was thankful that she seldom wore anything but breeches and hose now. Jergan was not happy, but he wasn't the one who had to wear the frilly gowns and endure the tedious fittings.

The Dwerin smith had only just arrived that morning, sent from Highboard at the behest of Baron Marthaine to fit Lughus for a suit of his finest armor. Not only was plate more protective than Lughus's old hauberk, but when fitted properly, a full suit from the Mountain Kingdom felt lighter than mail alone and offered more mobility. It was expensive, considerably, even without additional embellishments such as enameling or gold tracery, though how much it was to cost, neither Brigid nor Lughus were to know. According to the smith, the fee was to be paid by the personal fortune of Baron Roland.

"Alright, my lord, we're almost finished," the smith said, "I just want to check the breastplate one more time."

Lughus gave a silent nod while the smith's attendants buckled the armor piece upon his chest, and exchanged a private look of impatience with Brigid. She returned it with a friendly smile, and gave the young boy seated next to her a playful shove.

"What do you think, Freddy?" she asked.

"About what?" Freddy asked. Lughus had allowed him to hold onto his sword during the fitting and the boy's eyes had not left Sentinel's pommel for half an hour or more.

"About what? About the armor." She tussled his hair. "Doesn't he look fine?"

Freddy paused. "That's only one piece," he said, "And they're only checking his sizes so that's probably not even going to be the real one. When it's finished and he's got it all on, then I'll give you an answer."

Brigid smiled and shook her head, "What a strange one you are."

"The boy's right, my lady," the smith grinned, "Though from these measurements we should have it all completed within a week or two since, of course, work for the Baron of Galadin takes priority above all others."

Brigid eyed Lughus; she knew he did not like that sort of thing, but he remained silent. He knew he would need the armor for the coming war.

"Generally speaking," the smith continued, pleased at having found an opportunity to describe his work, "We craft the armor in various states of completion and adjust them accordingly. For the base pieces, though, we try to fit them to the dimensions of icons and statues depicting the saints and heroes—tall, lean, strong. It makes them look all the finer when on display for prospective customers." He gave a quiet laugh. "Men who are too fat or too short rarely purchase armor they think will make them look that way."

Brigid gave a nod. It was the same with the ladies at Blackstone, she remembered. Even her mother had the tendency to commission gowns that were far too small.

"Lucky for you, my lord," the smith told Lughus, "The blood of the Saint flows strong in you. Sure enough I could find masterpieces among those already in my possession that could fit you as is, though unfortunately, most of them are already embossed with other symbols and arms. If only I'd had foresight enough to design one bearing the mark of the Golden Hound! We could craft one for you, if you like? It would take some time, but we could have it for you in a month or so."

"I appreciate the offer," Lughus said, "But no, thank you."

"Then perhaps something else? These are but a few samples, and as I said, there are many and more packed away in our wagons. I have a whole set ready to go—a masterwork in craftsmanship and design! I call it 'the Flower of Knighthood' with a pattern of roses running the length of the plate from the sabatons to the spaulders, and down the arm through the vambraces. The knuckles of the gauntlets are fashioned like thorns and the helm bears a wreath of blooms like a crown! All of it engraved! All of it enameled green and red! You'd swear the flowers were real!" he paused, "Except for the thorns, of course, which are fashioned out of gold."

"It sounds very impressive, but no."

Brigid suppressed a smile. She knew he would never, ever wear a thing like that. It was far too flashy for the young baron's tastes. *Still, it would be fine to see him in it,* she said to herself, *He certainly has the look of the hero, like a statue, just as the man said...*

Quickly, she folded her arms across her chest and tried to push those thoughts from her mind, for they seemed only to bring her anxiety and frustration. She was certain he would have kissed her back in Highboard, after she had—much to her own surprise—kissed him first on the cheek. However, with Baron Agathis's confession and the mad dash to return to Galadin, whatever feelings he might have had for her, or she for him, had to be ignored in the advance of the kingsmen and the coming war. It was not easy, though, for as much time as they spent together, she feared that to have left the moment so unresolved, had created an awkwardness between them.

How foolish I am, Brigid thought once more. She often worried now that she was turning into one of those idiotic girls at Blackstone, fawning, giggly, and stupid. They threw themselves at Alan and the other young men like pretty baubles to be toyed with for their pleasure. The memory alone filled her with loathing. *No, I am not one of those girls*, she swore, *And he is not a scoundrel like Sir Reid...*

"Brigid?"

She looked up in surprise, awakened from her private musings, "Yes?"

"Are you alright?" Lughus asked with a look of amusement. The smith had finished measuring him and Freddy was helping him with his surcoat and baldric.

"Of course," she grinned, fighting the urge to blush, "You're done then?"

"I am," he said, "But I thought to ask him about something for you, since he's here and all."

This again, she thought fondly. "Lughus," she said, "You really don't have to."

"Please, it'll make me feel better with everything that's to come," he turned back to the smith and Brigid stood mutely by as they conversed. Fergus had gone off to sniff the pungent odor of a freshly oiled leather breastplate, while the two attendants carefully packed their remaining wares, careful not to draw too close to the great hound. At her side, Freddy, grinning from ear to ear, folded his arms.

"What are you smiling at?" Brigid asked, raising an eyebrow.

"He bought me a buckler," the boy told her.

"Lughus?"

He nodded, "Said I could pick any one I wanted before they go."

Brigid shook her head and tussled his hair again, ignoring his muffled protests, but paused once more at the sound of her own name.

"Of course! It would be my pleasure to outfit Lady Brigid!" the smith exclaimed suddenly, "First the Baron of Galadin, and now the daughter of my own Archduke! By the Brethren, I'll never return to Dwerin!"

"You might not be allowed to," Brigid said quickly, "Supplying, as you are, folk my mother and my uncle count as enemies."

"My lady, I am a merchant. My only enemies are the customer who turns me away or the thief who would steal my goods! Beyond that, I sell only protection, and there's no harm there. Armor saves lives; it doesn't take them," the smith said, "Besides, according to many of the other merchants out of Dwerin, it's a good thing to be gone these days. Many saw their entire stock seized in the name of the war effort against Grantis this last year without any compensation at all."

"I see," Brigid said, though she was not surprised given the rapacious appetites so common among the Dwerin elite; though it did make her think, "If the smiths are unhappy in Dwerin, I can't imagine the miners are much better?"

"Oh no, my lady. Unrest abounds all over, especially without your uncles in place to manage things. Things worked fine under the old ways with your noble uncles sharing power; however, I'm afraid it's all a bit too much for your lady mother and the Lord Sheriff. The Guardian Chancellor had to send men of his own to set it all to rights, the way I hear it. Surely, my lady, if you wanted to wreak havoc at home you knew what you were doing when—" he paused, for Lughus's eyes flashed with anger, and she felt the color draining from her face.

"Those are lies," the young baron said simply, though in a tone that would not allow discussion or dispute.

"Yes, my lord," the smith said hesitantly, "I'm sorry, I—"

"Lies," he said again.

"Yes, my lord."

"Tell me about this armor," Brigid said hurriedly. She left her chair, and with a pleasant smile at the smith, walked over to Lughus's side and furtively touched his arm. "I'd need something that won't make any noise," she said, "And it needs to be lightweight."

The smith glanced quickly at the baron, took a deep breath, and folded his arms. "I...I believe I may have just the thing," he said, and feeling about on his person, drew forth a small square patch from a pouch along his middle and handed it to Brigid, "It's mail, but the rings are so small, one might think it was cloth."

Brigid gave a nod, turning it over in her hands, and held it out for Lughus to see. The rings were indeed very small, no larger around than her littlest fingernail. "What do you think?" she asked, catching his eye.

"Very fine," he said at last.

"It might not look it, since it's so supple and light," the smith interjected, "But it's still strong enough to stop a slash from a blade, though like all mail, it won't do much against an arrow or a direct thrust. However, I'll throw in a quilted vest for that at no charge."

"Won't it make noise when I move around?"

"Not really. The quilting will muffle the sound and help keep the links from making any noise. However, if I may be so bold as to conjecture..." he quickly glanced over at Lughus again and after a moment's hesitation continued, "If you're hoping for something to protect you while trying at the same time to...avoid attention, Lady Blade. You might find the greater concern with metal armor, as opposed to leather, is its tendency to reflect light. If that's the case, I have some habergeons that I had been intending to add color to, which remain unpolished and would be less likely to catch the light?"

"That sounds fine," Brigid said, turning to Lughus, "Don't you think?"

"It does," he said with a wan smile, "We'd like one."

"Do you care to discuss the price?"

"No. Whatever it is, I'll pay it. Does she need to have it fitted?"

The smith shook his head, "I have some already that are sized for squires and pages. I'm sure among those there is one that will fit my lady. I can send one of my men tomorrow so that she might peruse the stock."

"Very well," the young baron said shortly, "Until tomorrow then."

When the smith had gone, Brigid sat watching as Freddy ran about the hall punching the air with his buckler and deflecting imaginary blows. Fergus loped after him, barking at his heels.

"I would have loved something like that when I was his age," Lughus said, seating himself in Freddy's vacant chair at her side, "When I was about his age, I can remember getting into trouble once at the Tower for trying to pull this gilded shield down off the wall."

"Well, you certainly made his day," Brigid smiled.

"It's the least I owe Geoffrey for saving the city," he sighed, "If I only knew now what to do about Adolfo the Madder."

"He's coming tonight?"

"Aye, as if there wasn't already enough to worry over."

Word of Geoffrey's victory over the kingsmen had reached them on the road half a day away from Galadin. In the end, nearly a hundred Andochan soldiers lay dead or captured in their attempt to take the Houndstooth, and if any doubt remained among the other baronies that Andoch was poised to go to war, it was gone now. Thus, as Roland Marthaine argued to the remaining barons on the morning after Lughus's abrupt departure, an attack on a single barony by a foreign power was as good as an attack on the entire Brock. So it was with little argument that the assembly drafted an ultimatum to King Kredor, demanding that he cease hostilities and withdraw his men lest he face the consequences. At once, the Andochan ambassador sent the assembly's demands to Titanis by way of Calendral kite.

Before the week's end, the bird returned bearing the Guardian-King's formal declaration of war.

Now, the barons of all fourteen baronies were busy assembling their knights and men-at-arms, increasing the patrols along the borders, and gathering any men they could from among the peasantry and the burghers. For, although the sword was the weapon of the professional soldier, in the Brock, even the humblest of shepherds learned from a very young age how to wield a bow, if only as a safeguard against wild creatures that might prey upon their flocks. As a result, the archers of Baronbrock were second to none, and they would be sorely needed against the combined might of the kingsmen of Andoch, the ironmen of Dwerin, and the cavalry of Montevale.

Still, in spite of their many enemies, the Barons of the Brock remained undaunted, and the surprise assault on Galadin's city served as a rallying cry around which the common folk could unite. Day by day, Roland Marthaine proved himself an even stronger (if unexpected) ally. Not only had he sent the Dwerin smith to Galadin, but on the very day the kite returned with Kredor's declaration or war, Baron Marthaine himself led a force of men to storm the Andochan ambassador's keep in Highboard and expel the Hammer and his allies from the city. According to the Nordrens, who had stopped to spend the night in Galadin on their way home, the Lord-Baron was not particularly pleased at the manner in which it happened, but he conceded that it needed to be done.

And so, for the first time in generations, the united barons endeavored to raise their armies and reinforce key positions around the Brock—Nordren on the border with its port, Helmstead to guard the Nivanus pass, and a smaller reserve force along the border between Waldron and Edgeforth in the case of an attack by sea in the far north. Interestingly enough, it was the two ancient enemies, Galadin and Marthaine, which would serve as the Brock's key strongholds. For although Highboard was a mighty fortress, without farmlands, it lacked the resources for a prolonged siege, and if the enemy brought the war far enough to reach the capitol's walls, it would mean that the majority of the baronies had already been lost.

Further, between the two of them, Houndstooth and Harrier's Keep (the castle of the Marthaines) were near enough to reach any of the other baronies within a week, and positioned as they were on opposite sides of Lake Bartund, allowed for easy communication and transportation between one another.

Of course, most of the Galadin folk still found it difficult to believe the Argent Eagle's pledge of friendship, which would make for quite a clamor when he arrived for his promised visit. Yet, he was not the only unlikely ally. For in spite of the bravery and the sacrifices of the Galadin guard, Geoffrey freely admitted that he could never have succeeded in turning back the kingsmen without the aid of Adolfo the Madder.

According to Sir Owain, the entire force of Galadin when fully mobilized for war numbered over five thousand men, which included peasant infantry as well as professional soldiers. But, in times of peace, Houndstooth's garrison and the city watch combined amounted to little over one hundred, with perhaps only a third of that on duty at any one time. Thus, when the kingsmen attacked, the men of the guard were not only surprised, but outnumbered roughly three to one. The deaths of the watch captain and the master-at-arms added further confusion, limiting the leadership of the Galadin defenses, particularly after the ballistas had left the men scattered. Adolfo's band of mercenaries, though little more than petty thugs and cutthroats, were a welcome addition, and rallying behind Geoffrey, they were able to charge the keelboats and crush the invaders.

Now, with the success, Geoffrey admitted unhappily that he was in Adolfo's debt, a debt Lughus knew the Madder hoped to be paid with one of the five promised knighthoods. For even if the assembly had not called a vote to contest his rights, a deal was a deal, and the Weavers' Guild still expected it to be honored—a sentiment they had politely reminded him once already in writing. To deny Adolfo a commission after he so readily offered his aid to the city would appear ungrateful and unseemly in the eyes of the guild, the city, and the Baron of Igrainne—despite the Madder's unsavory reputation.

Brigid knew that the very idea of authoring "Sir Adolfo's" rise to nobility weighed heavily on Lughus's mind; however, it was only one of a number of matters plaguing him. Soon Galadin would play host to soldiers, knights, and barons from across the Brock, many of whom would look to the Golden Hound for direction in the war. His actions and decisions would be judged and weighed, and were he to make a mistake, he would quickly earn their disdain. For, not only was he the youngest of the Barons, by far, but he also lacked any true experience of command.

Sir Owain, ever-faithful, cast these fears aside, claiming that more than once had Lughus already tested his mettle—in battle and in the assembly chamber, which was much more than career politicians like Agathis and Igrainne had ever done. Even the Lord-Baron, Perin Glendaro, readily admitted that his strengths did not lie on the field of battle. Yet, Brigid knew that the seneschal's reassurances did little to assuage the young baron's doubts. For on more than one occasion, even before their journey to Highboard, Lughus had confided to her that if a Baron he was to be, he would strive to act as he believed one should—to be fair, just, and good, and to strive always to act in accordance to the principles he had learned apprentice to the Loremaster.

In short, he sought an ideal, and although Brigid believed in him with all her heart, she also feared for him. For men of such quality seemed only to reside in Bard's Tales or tragedies. Even St. Aiden's quality did not save his life, but rather demanded he give it, and she prayed that as his descendent, Lughus would not be required do the same.

That last thought brought a feeling of emptiness to her chest, and she shook her head as if to drive it away. Out on the floor, Fergus had somehow grabbed hold of Freddy's buckler and now loped back and forth taunting the boy as he gave chase. Lughus caught her eye and they shared a quiet laugh together watching the boy and the hound at play.

"I'm sorry about just now," the young baron said after a moment, "With the armorer. I didn't mean to get angry. It was stupid of me. I owe the man an apology."

"It's no matter, but when he returns you shall have your chance," she said, "To be honest, I found it a bit strange that he seemed so enthusiastic to believe the tales about Gareth and me."

"Well, you said that your mother and the sheriff cared little for the common folk," he shrugged, "Perhaps your other uncles were the same way? In any case, I'm sorry for that, and for forcing the armor on you. I know you weren't very interested in the whole thing."

"That's not true," she said, "Not at all. I'm just very grateful for everything else you've given us—your home, your food, clothing, to say nothing of saving us from the Hammer that day."

"I just want to make sure that you're protected," he said hesitantly, "I don't know what I would do if…if anything were to happen to you."

"Don't worry about me," she said, "Look after yourself and the people."

"I will, or at least I hope to," he said, glancing down at the flagstones, "But you mean a great deal to me too, Brigid."

"Me too," she blushed, "I mean—you mean a lot to me as well."

She watched his cheeks redden and he offered her a soft smile. His hair shone like a candle's flame and his eyes flashed at hers. *Eyes of the Eagle*, she recalled, *Keener than the eyes of the Falcon.* Her heart quickened and she felt the strong compulsion to lean over and kiss him, not on the cheek this time, but the lips. Yet, once more, unbidden, her mind returned to Blackstone and the foolish giggling of the girls of the Drove, the licentious young noblemen, and her mother's horrid sermons on the nature of love. *It is not the same*, she told herself, *It is not!* Still, the memories suppressed all thoughts she had of kissing him and instead she simply reached out and took his hand, delighting in the feel of it and the gentle firmness of his grip.

Later that evening, in the hour before they were to dine in the great hall, Brigid and Lughus met in the solar with Geoffrey, Horus, and Sir Owain to receive Adolfo the Madder. The Galadin seneschal was clearly not looking forward to it, and though he tried to be pleasant as they awaited the weaver's arrival, hunger and weariness darkened his mood. Eighteen men-at-arms had died in the battle at the docks and another nine were seriously wounded. Losing the master-at-arms and the watch captain as well, not only weighed Sir Owain down with grief, but since they were both his direct subordinates, added to his personal duties until such time as their positions could be filled. Geoffrey strived to aid him as he could and between the pair of them the city was safe and under guard; however, many of the remaining guardsmen were working longer shifts, and while they understood the need and not one had complained, they could not do so forever. More men would have to be recruited and trained. Quickly.

Horus too had been busy these days with his accounts. The spring harvest and the seasonal sheep shearing had all been completed, and so the steward had been hard at work allocating funds and organizing the treasury.

Thankfully Galadin was prosperous, for the impending war required a great deal of coin outfitting soldiers, stockpiling stores, and preparing for the arrival of so many other honored knights, nobles, and their attendants at the Houndstooth.

Thus, the leaders of Galadin found their energies, and thereby their patience, to be in short supply when the sergeant on duty announced that Adolfo had arrived. He was not met with a very warm welcome. However, it did not seem to Brigid that the weaver minded much.

"My Lord Galadin," the Madder said, bowing low, "I am honored by your invitation. Rarely does one receive such an intimate audience with a baron, let alone find himself in the presence of the fabled Three."

Brigid regarded him carefully, for though she had often heard Adolfo's name, she had never seen him in person. Though she knew it was rather foolish, she had assumed him to appear before them like a villain in a story— brutish, boorish, and uncouth—as one might expect from a man with the reputation for being a thug and a crook. Adolfo seemed none of those things, though. He was thin (slight even), well-dressed, and seemed at once to be rather clever. Of course, these qualities did nothing to assuage her beliefs that he was very dangerous, and if anything only strengthened them.

"You're welcome," Lughus said politely, "And particularly well-informed."

"I am," Adolfo said. "Though with the stir Constable Harlow has caused across the Brock, there are few who do not know of Sir Geoffrey the Vanguard, Lady Brigid the Blade, or Baron Lughus the Marshal."

Sir Owain breathed an impatient sigh and folded his hands on the table in front of him. The young baron continued.

"From what Sir Geoffrey has told me, you and your men offered significant aid to the men of the watch during the recent raid," he said, "And for that, you have my thanks."

Just 'aid,' Brigid thought, though she kept her face stoic, 'Significant aid' will simply embolden him.

"As I told Sir Geoffrey," Adolfo said, "Galadin is my home. It is important to me. I have no wish to see it suffer."

Only its people when they cross you.

"You may also be happy to know that I took your advice," the Madder continued. "Regarding the brocade—the gift I offered to you and to Lady Brigid. Should you wish to look into it, you will see that each of my tenants in Hounton has received a rate reduction in their monthly rents for the next six months. I have also taken the liberty of purchasing the deed to the tavern that caught fire during the battle with the kingsmen, if only to ensure that its previous owner does not suffer too harshly as a result."

He really wants this knighthood, Brigid thought, *But why?* If it was simply to lend a sense of legitimacy to his business dealings, any of the other less scrupulous barons might have offered him one already. Dorgan Agathis, for instance, allowed the kingsman to cross his lands in order to assault his neighbors. Surely a man like that could have easily been bought.

Perhaps it was the Galadin name? Agathis's judgment might be questioned, but not Galadin. It was the whole reason why the knighthoods were such an important bargaining piece in the first place.

"I see," Lughus said, "Again, you have my thanks."

An uncomfortable silence spread over the room like a heavy fog. Sir Owain's eyelids drooped and Geoffrey continued to stare at the tabletop as he had from the moment he first sat down. Horus coughed politely into his fist, and sat up straighter in his chair. Brigid glanced from Lughus to Adolfo in consideration, though neither one returned her stare. Something had to be done, she knew, for Adolfo was too influential a man to treat with open scorn, particularly in light of the coming war. Treating him unkindly now might drive him to deal with the enemy or confound their own defensive efforts. Yet, she knew that Lughus would never honor a man he believed to be a villain any more than she would.

Then perhaps, if he really is such a bad man, she thought, *He should simply die.* She glanced over at the weaver again; he was unarmed and unarmored. True, he had influence with the guild, but surely there were other, less nefarious men just waiting for the chance to take Adolfo's place. Few would probably miss him and there might be a sense of justice in his body being tossed into the lake…

No! she shook her head and folded her hands upon her lap. That would not be justice, especially after he had just helped them. It would be wrong. Just as she believed allowing the Hammer and the Provincial to go free was a testament to Lughus's quality, to advocate murdering Adolfo in cold blood was to paint herself with shame.

It was not the first time that her thoughts had so quickly turned bloody either. At Blackstone, before she had even inherited the title of the Blade, she had felt the impulsive pull of violence, of expedient, willful death. After all, was it not her intention that night when she first approached the Falcon to free him so he might exact a bloody vengeance upon the entire Dwerin court?

She noticed it happening more and more frequently and in some sense, it frightened her. Numerous men had fallen to her blades, without her even giving it a second thought, and although she knew that in every case she was acting in self-defense, the ease with which she had not only killed, but then promptly relegated it to the past and forgotten it, was somewhat unnerving.

When did I become so bloody minded? she wondered. An image flashed before her mind's eye of the Blackstone passage and the soldiers dragging away the corpses of her uncles. *Is that who I am? Is my legacy one of blood?*

All of a sudden, she felt Lughus's eyes upon her and she knew that he sensed her disquiet, just as she had learned in recent weeks to sense it in him. She pretended not to notice and avoided his gaze.

At length, it was Adolfo, who broke the silence. "If it pleases you, my baron," he asked in his slow drawl, "Might I speak plainly?"

Brigid felt Lughus glance at her again, though he quickly returned his attention to the Madder, "Please do."

Adolfo gave a curt nod and pressed the tips of his fingers together, encased as they were within their scarlet gloves. "I do not have a reputation for being a good man," he said, "I know that, my lord, and I understand if it should give you pause."

"It does," Lughus said, "Particularly when I know what you seek, if we are indeed speaking plainly, is my word elevating you to knighthood."

Sir Owain opened his eyes and his brow creased as he exchanged a look with Horace.

"You are correct," Adolfo said, "And though you have no reason to believe me, my desires are not born from vice or deceit, but in this, if in nothing else, I am driven by honest intent."

Lughus sighed. "According to the stories, honesty is a thing unknown to Adolfo the Madder. A wealthy master of the guild though one not known to have ever created a masterpiece, a shrewd moneylender with the highest rates of interest in the city, a landlord more than willing to turn his tenants out into the streets for a single late payment, a proprietor of illicit goods right under the nose of the watch—these are not the qualities of an honest man, let alone a man who seeks to become a knight."

"You forgot to mention what they say about the lake," Adolfo mused, "That those who become my enemies are soon rewarded with a watery grave."

Brigid's eyes flashed at the Madder and beside her, Geoffrey looked up, his jaw set in anger. "Was that a threat?" Brigid asked.

"No, my lady," Adolfo sighed, "It was not. It was merely to illustrate the sensational nature of stories. Have I killed men? Yes, of course. However, with the exception perhaps of my lord steward there, so have all of us in this room, perhaps not at the lake, but on the sacred grounds of St. Elisa's Grotto—and if we are to trust every story we hear, believe me, that one is perhaps the least damning currently on the lips of the noble folk of Andoch."

"Tread carefully," Sir Owain growled in warning.

"Believe me, Lord Seneschal, I intend to," the Madder said, "But I would advise all of you to do the same—not because you have reason to fear me, but rather because of what I know. These are dangerous times, as I am sure you are aware; however, this war that seems suddenly so inevitable with the Guardians has been so for some time. The kingsmen who attacked us here in Galadin were but a small detachment of the larger contingent of men gathering at Stonebridge Castle, just over the mountains bordering Agathis— men not only of the Guardian-King's standing army, but also of the most influential Andochan lords. The fleets of both Dwerin and the Guardians currently refit at Galdoran, though any day now they will sail north to blockade Nordren, around which, they already patrol. If that were not enough, for weeks now, King Dermont in Montevale has been gathering his forces along the highlands below the Nivanus Mountains. Surely, these recent disagreements with Constable Harlow and Provincial Andresen were merely the excuse Kredor needed to justify what he was already intending."

"And how would you know that?" Lughus asked.

"Oh, I know many things," Adolfo said, "Things I will gladly share with you freely when time allows, regardless of whether you see fit to grant me the reward I seek. For, as I said, Galadin is important to me. I was born here, I made my fortune here, and though I doubt you will ever believe me, I have always acted with the best interests of the barony and its people at heart."

Brigid's eyes narrowed. Something about him suddenly struck her as familiar—the particular tone of voice and cocksure manner with which he spoke about the extent of his knowledge.

Horus raised an eyebrow, "I fail to see how such things as gambling and prostitution, or such high rates of interest serve our best interests."

"Of all the Baronies of the Brock, only Galadin attempts to curtail many of these illicit trades. Even Andoch and their Holy Guardians allow the sale of vice—perhaps not publicly, but they turn a blind eye to anything short of slavery. But, when it was deemed unseemly to allow such things in the city that marked not only the birthplace, but also the tomb of the Holy Saint, what do you think that did for the market of such goods and services in the city?"

Adolfo paused and shrugged, "Now, if I knew anything about those bodies in the lake, I might wonder if they were not the remains of enterprising men who perhaps saw the City of the Saint as a place to make their fortune in defiance of such decrees, particularly whilst Baron Arcis took ill—first with grief and later with disease. Perhaps—knowing that the denial of something only serves to make men want it more—another man might seek to control such trades himself—to regulate them, and to ensure certain standards of conduct. He might even consider it the least of possible evils. He might soil his hands so that others' might remain clean."

"Is that how you sleep at night?" Sir Owain muttered bitterly.

"Ask anyone in my employ. They will tell you. I am loyal to them and I *always* treat them fairly. Poverty can be especially cruel to women, with few options for employ open to them beyond the street. Certain…establishments provide them with refuge and protection from the dangers they could easily face alone."

"Any man who was a knight of mine," Lughus said, though Brigid could see his discomfort with such topics, "Would have to cease such activities."

Adolfo gave a shrug, "I have heard of only two such places that exist within the city. However, what of the women who work there? Are they to be turned out into the street?"

"Surely a weaver has need of women who can work a wheel?" the baron said, "Perhaps the owner of such a place might see it to his advantage to allow you to convert the use of his building from one to the other—as a place of support or education, where they might be taught a trade, or at least provided with the opportunity?"

"I suppose such a thing could be possible," Adolfo said, "Though I am not certain that such a practice would...erase the market for such services, services that—at least currently—can be overseen."

"True," Lughus said, "And believe me, I am not ignorant to the practical realities of human nature or of business, and in terms of chosen profession, I am certain that there are those who are content in their profession and who may...value the one who employs them. Where I take issue, is in the denial of choice. How many among those employed in such an establishment were pressed into service without the natural right of choice? Even among the nobility, a woman's fate can be bought and sold without any regard for her consent. Can you pretend for even a moment that the very poor fare any better?"

"I cannot," Adolfo said.

"Women in Montevale at least may serve as soldiers in the military, as officers even, and have done for generations. I would welcome the same in the Brock."

"With the Lady Blade as an example, I imagine you will find many willing to enlist."

"But I would not stop there," Lughus said, "You would have us knight you as an unconventional choice. As a master of the Weavers' Guild, with both great wealth and greater influence, should we be willing to trust you in the defiance of convention, would it not be reasonable to expect that you might also do the same?"

"In what manner, my lord?"

"There are many women who do the work necessary for the prosperity of the Weavers' Guild—Sir Geoffrey's wife once among them. Yet, as I understand it, women are denied membership in the guild. I would have that change."

Adolfo considered the matter, and Brigid was surprised not to see even a hint of defensiveness or distress at the undoing of such longstanding tradition. "I suppose that may be," the Madder said.

Lughus sighed. "I am not a fool," he said, "I understand the benefits of a wolf half-tamed, over one that is allowed to simply roam free. However, I insist that those who are fed to the beast at least have the choice of whether to do so willingly, and it is my belief that any man who calls himself a Knight of Galadin—who truly sees it as his duty to safeguard the people of this city—

provide opportunities for those who would choose otherwise, rather than exploit them in the name of antiquated convention and fragile masculinity."

"Agreed," Adolfo said.

"And what of the interest rates and rents?" Brigid broke in, "While we speak of knightly conduct and exploitation."

"You will find, my lady," Adolfo said, "That my rates are dependent upon the wealth of the borrower. I would be a fool to loan money that I would never see returned to me. And as for this foolishness of debtors being drowned in the lake—correct me if I'm wrong—but while a live man may one day repay what he owes, a dead man never does."

"Still, generosity is a knightly virtue, is it not?" she asked, "Perhaps a display of such quality to the people is warranted."

"I have already offered much in concessions these recent weeks," Adolfo said, "Though I...suppose those who fortune has favored can always be persuaded to give a bit more."

How peculiar? she thought. Between the loss of his brothels and the reduction of his rates, the Madder stood to lose a substantial amount of coin. Something was not as it seemed, and she would have to find out. She bit her lip and when Lughus caught her eye, she could only shrug.

"In a short while," Lughus said at last, "The other men of your guild will join us in the hall for a feast celebrating their knighthood. If you please, Adolfo, you may wait with them and join us then for an answer, for I believe we must discuss the matter further in private."

"Very well," the Madder said, "I thank you for receiving me, my lord, and I will await your word." With a final bow, he turned and departed from the solar.

"What a shite," Sir Owain grunted as soon as the weaver had gone, "I say we simply hang him. He admitted as much to give us cause."

"I do not believe that would be wise," Horus said, "Particularly at this time. Not only does his word carry a great deal of weight with the guild, but his aid in the attack has granted him at least some degree of good faith among the people—at least for the moment. It would look terribly unseemly to do him harm."

"What do you think, Geoffrey?" Lughus asked.

"I don't know," Geoffrey shrugged, "His aid was welcome, but...I just don't know. If he's a villain, I'd not see him knighted, nor would I want to be known as the one who put his name forth for honor should he continue to do wrong. Still, there's something…something that inclines me to believe him. I don't know."

Lughus nodded. "Brigid?"

Brigid bit her lip and folded her arms, aware suddenly of the golden hilts of her daggers resting so lightly at her sides. "I don't know either," she said softly, "You decide." She glanced down at the tabletop, attempting to adopt an heir of impartiality, though she knew from the weight of his gaze that the young baron saw right through her.

"It's true that, as Owain said, he admitted much. However, he also pledged to curtail his activities, which I can only imagine would cost him dearly."

"All the more reason not to trust him," Owain said shaking his head, "Besides, I feel as if he threatens us. His words seem to slither like a bloody serpent. Given the right opportunity, I'm certain he would do any of us harm."

"Yet, again, he claims the opposite," Horus said, "And, he pledged his aid—his knowledge—regardless of the decision. His wealth too will be welcome, I imagine, as well as his word in guild matters, particularly should we or our allies need to borrow any gold. Furthermore, if he stands for Galadin among the weavers, it could help our people prosper in future trade negotiations as it has Igrainne."

"So you're willing to take him at his word?" the seneschal grunted, "Surely not."

Horus sighed, "Owain, there are many worse men who bear the rank of knight, let alone baron or king. In fact, it often seems to me that the word 'knight' is more synonymous with 'villain' than 'hero.' Consider the behavior of men in war or on a raid. Consider the ease with which they change loyalties or mistreat the common folk. At least, in the case of Adolfo we might exercise some control over him, and his ties to the word of crime and vice might also aid us in that end. Every city has its wolves, if I might continue Baron Lughus's comparison. Would it not be beneficial to us if the leader of the pack was one we, ourselves, kept tethered?"

Owain shook his head in disbelief, "First, we trust the Marthaines, and now we trust a rogue like Adolfo? This is madness! Men so long our enemies are now expected to be our friends? I know Baron Roland helped us in

Highboard and that the Madder also aided us in our time of need, but…let us still be cautious. Knighting Adolfo? Inviting the Marthaines for a visit? Trusting too quickly can only lead to betrayal."

"Yes," Horus said, "But trusting no one leaves us all alone."

Lughus gave a sigh.

Brigid leaned toward him and offered him a sympathetic glance. *He hates this,* she thought, *For either way he feels it might leave his hands dirty.* He would not bear the weight of it alone, though. Dirty or not, she would gladly hold those hands. "Whatever you decide," she said, "Remember, we're with you."

When the meal was served, five new knights stood now as peers to the seven of the fiefdoms, and though each of the newly risen men held no parcel of land to command, each owned considerable portions of the property within and just without the city walls. In addition to Faden's eldest son (for he considered himself far too old for knighthood), there were two brothers by the surname name of Petran, a large, bearded man named Kradoc, and finally, Adolfo the Madder.

"What a pity it would be if the sword slipped," Sir Owain whispered to Brigid as they watched Lughus touch the Madder's shoulder with the Marshal's blade.

Brigid sighed, "You know he doesn't like this."

"I know," the seneschal said, "And Horus was right—the wolf you know and all—but with the Marthaines too?" he paused, "Promise me this, my lady. When the Argent Asshole and his wife come calling a few days hence, promise you'll watch his back," he said.

"Where will you be?"

"I'll be here, though Horus has already suggested I limit my exposure to the Marthaines. I've killed men of theirs; they've killed men of mine. It's hard to sit at table together under such circumstances."

"I would imagine so."

"I'll have plenty to do anyway, training new men and outfitting them with arms now that poor Master Flann is gone," he shook his head, "Anyway, I expect he'll keep you at his side for as long as you're willing to stand by him."

"Owain, I'm in exile." She smirked. "Where else would I possibly go?"

"Were it up to me, my lady." The old knight smiled kindly. "I would see the two of you were never parted for the rest of your lives."

"At any rate," Brigid said hurriedly, ignoring the rush of warmth that burned her cheeks, "I'll be sure to watch his back…for as long as he'll have me there."

"Then I hope you find your quarters comfortable."

Lughus did not remain long at the feast after the brief ceremony. The hall was filled with men of the Weavers' Guild, personal friends of the new knights, and their families. Still, to Brigid, seated at his left hand, it somehow felt rather empty, for there were far fewer blue and gold tabards than usual with all that had fallen against the kingsmen. Though she had not known Master Flann or Captain Ross very well either, the absence of their faces was apparent in the expressions of every man among the household guard.

"If it's alright with you," Lughus told her, "I think I'll retire."

"To the solar?" she asked, "Do you want company?"

He shook his head, "No, I think I'll to bed. I've had too much wine, and the ham didn't agree with me either." He offered her a faint smile, "I'm sure Fergus will stay to keep you company though."

Brigid gave a nod. She knew that the true cause of his distress had little to do with meat or wine, but she decided not to press him. "Can he sit in your chair too?"

"If he likes," he grinned, "At any rate, if you don't have other plans, perhaps I'll find you tomorrow? Owain is drilling the men and I thought that perhaps you'd like to spar."

"Certainly," she said and gently patted his arm, "Feel better."

"Goodnight."

"Goodnight."

Once he had gone, Horus assumed command of the feast, and Sir Owain withdrew to the company of his sergeants seated together at the table along the far wall. Geoffrey and Annabel chatted pleasantly with Faden and his newly-knighted son while Freddy and Greta ran about playing with the other children of the castle community. Surrounded by so many masters of the cloth trade, Jergan was in his glory, and more than once Brigid heard his playful jests bemoaning a certain young lady's recent choices in clothing. Alone at the lord's table with Fergus at her side, Brigid ruffled the great hounds ears and smiled at the old fop's teasing.

"Maybe one day he'll try wearing one of his own gowns," she told the dog, "Then he'll know what it's like."

Fergus gave a loud sniff and rested his head upon her knee, gazing up at her with his great watery hound eyes. It made her smile and after a sip of wine, she breathed a heavy sigh. Unlike at Blackstone, she did not feel lost or disregarded with her present solitude, but rather a sense of quiet contentment. Though in truth she did miss having Lughus to talk to, she still felt rather happy, particularly when she remembered Sir Owain's candid remarks from earlier. *I am comfortable here,* she thought with an inward smile, *Perhaps more so than I've ever been anywhere. It feels like a real home ought to.* However, the moment soon faded when Fergus lifted his head from her knee and his ears sharpened in alarm.

"It seems, my lady, you've found a way to hide in plain sight, though I doubt such a thing is difficult for the Blade."

"Sir Adolfo," Brigid said simply, somewhat surprised that he would approach her so freely considering the circumstances of his earlier meeting, "I congratulate you."

"Thank you," the Madder said, "Though I realize knighting me was not an easy thing for our young baron."

"It was not," she said, "He is a good man and he fears that as one of his knights, you might try to use his name to bring legitimacy to your corrupt dealings. The Guardians already name all of us Blackguards and as you said earlier, rumors of all manner of horrid things accompany our names thanks to Constable Harlow and the rest."

"My lady," Adolfo breathed a heavy sigh, "I assure you that I have no wish to bring any ill down upon him, precisely the opposite in fact. Galadin is dear to me, and it would not be the same without a man of the Saint's bloodline as Baron."

"You keep saying that," Brigid said, narrowing her gaze, "But why? Why is Galadin so dear to you? Is it all simply because of your wealth? Surely, you could have prospered elsewhere, for if you do indeed hold to what is required of you in exchange for the title, you stand to lose a great deal."

"True," Adolfo said, leaning against the lord's table, "But I believe the long term benefits are far greater."

"So it is money, then, that drives you."

"No," he said, "But it is self-interest. For, I have been to other cities, in the Brock and beyond, but never have I found one such as this. It is a good place, not perfect, but good, and I want it to stay that way."

"Why?"

"You think because I am a bad man that I do not want what is good?" Adolfo asked, "I admit. I am a bad man. However, all men—be they good or bad—want the same things: peace, prosperity, contentment—not only for themselves, but for the things that they care about. It just so happens that I care about Galadin. In any other realm, I would be your enemy in a heartbeat. However, in Galadin, I seek to be your greatest friend. For, I believe that your young baron, like all the Galadins, is cut from a different cloth. I have watched him closely since he arrived—even before Baron Arcis was dead. He *is*, like you said, a good man, and he truly wants what is best for the city."

"Yet," Sir Adolfo continued, "Good men are seldom willing to do what is necessary to achieve *all* of their ends. Bad men will, and believe me, my lady, the men who count our young baron as their enemy are nothing if not very bad men. Surely you have not forgotten your uncle and his ways? Or your cousin? Do not look surprised, for I told you. I know much and more. Add to them men like the Hammer and this Plague King of Montevale, add their followers and their faithful, and you will soon realize—though I expect you already do from the look in your eyes—just how extraordinary it is to meet a good man like the young baron," he grinned, "Nearly as extraordinary as it is to meet a young woman like you."

Brigid's eyes narrowed, "If I were you, I would mind what you say. This is precisely what he feared, and if you dare bring shame upon him through working some evil, even if you think it good, I will not hesitate to cut your throat!"

"I do not doubt your nerve any less than I doubt your ability, Lady Blade," he said, "For I knew well the extent of your predecessor's skill. I saw it firsthand when those daggers that shine so prettily on your hips were awash with other men's blood."

"You knew Gareth?"

"I did, and he knew that sometimes bad men required bad things be done to them in order to achieve a greater good. Knowing the rumors spreading now about you and your uncles, I assume you know this too."

"I did not kill them," she said sternly, "Nor did Gareth." Fergus gave a low growl.

"No," Adolfo said, "But Gareth nurtured the seed of evil growing in the Sheriff's mind—not that it took much tending. Still, he might just as well have wielded the knife."

"Gareth was a good man, or so I believe," Brigid said, "He gave his life to save mine, and besides that, if he were truly evil, there were plenty of times he could have harmed me."

The Madder paused and breathed a sigh, "True, for I expect that he saw helping you as proof to himself that in spite of all, he still served the side of good. Can saving one life, however, make up for all the others that he had taken?"

"Gareth served Galadin, alongside Regnar the Vanguard and the former Marshal, Crodane," her eyes flashed, "He worked with Baron Arcis to protect the people of Termain.

"So he did, just as I have sworn to serve Baron Lughus. Yet clearly, such a promise does not wipe the slate clean."

Brigid stood up from the table. Her breath came very quickly alongside her anger, and her blue eyes blazed like flames. Yet, she did not wish to cause a scene or to call Adolfo out after Lughus had so recently honored him. Instead, she forced a smile and gave a polite nod.

"You must excuse me, Sir Adolfo, but I have no more time to speak with you," she said, "For, I find I am suddenly very tired." At the tables below, Sir Owain, Geoffrey, and many others suddenly paused in their conversations and bent their gaze upon Sir Adolfo and her.

"Very well, my lady," Adolfo said at last, "And if I have upset you, I apologize, for that was not at all my intention. I simply beg you to remember that whatever you may think of me, I am not your enemy—and as for your friend Gareth, do not think I seek to insult his memory, but to honor him by following in his wake. For, while to you, he was the Blade, to me, he was and will always be my little brother. Goodnight."

CHAPTER 32: VULGAR SEEDS

In the weeks following Queen Marina's ascension, the mood in Pridel was one of watchful apprehension as Bel and the other members of the new court awaited word from the nobles of the lands surrounding White Wood as to whether they would stand in support of the Plague King or the Winter Rose. Thus far, the fiefdoms were split, as those nearest the borders of Roanshead and Reginal, reluctant to draw Dermont's ire, mostly remained with him, while those nearest Pridel, whether out of true belief in the cause of peace or for fear of the Tower and his men knocking on their doors, were far more willing to support Marina. Yet while the nobles continued to weigh their allegiance out of self-interest, it was fair to say that the common folk, at least, overwhelmingly cast their support behind the new queen.

So it was that by the midpoint of Stagtide, the queen's forces under the command of the Tower swelled to an impressive forty-eight hundred men and women that included heavy horse, light horse, professional infantry, and peasant militia, as well as control of the fortresses at Pridel, Feyhold, and Bel's Uncle Talvert's former stronghold, the Ebon Keep. It was not a moment too soon either, for at long last, after more than a month since their escape from Tremontane Castle, King Dermont had finally sent word.

Bel had been out riding with Tempest, reacquainting both of them with the feel and the weight of armor. He still refused to don the plate of the former Tower's guard, disliking its weight and limited mobility; however, as Lord-General of Marina's forces, should he be required to lead a heavy charge himself, the old leather lamellar of the light cavalry would not provide adequate protection. As a compromise, he had decided upon a simple suit of chainmail for himself with an open-faced bascinet, and for Tempest, barding of similar make that protected his neck, breast, flanks, and hindquarters as well as a spiked chanfron to protect his head.

Since the Battle of Clearpoint, Dermont had reclaimed the old arms of Montevale—the searoan upon a field of green—as his own; however, if the Black Horse and the White truly were no more, neither Bel nor Marina could in good faith fly either emblem alone. Instead, it was suggested by Sir Welmsey (to no one's great surprise), that in honor of the new queen, the banner of the rebellion should be a field of purest white bearing the mark of a single red rosette. As such, it was this symbol that now adorned Bel's shield, surcoat, and Tempest's caparison.

Thusly clad, when Briden rode to fetch him at the behest of the queen, he returned to the great hall in haste to receive his brother's long awaited messenger.

Marina sat in what had once been Lord Harren's high seat. At her side Sir Armel, acting as her seneschal in Bel's stead, stood red-faced and stern before a squad of guardsmen and the gentlefolk of Pridel's court. Sir Emory had recently returned to his former role as King Cedric's seneschal (assuming that duty for King Marius as well), and was now seldom seen at court, but he was there now.

As Beledain crossed the threshold from the antechamber into the hall, he removed his helm and stowed it under his arm. His jaw set in anticipation of what was certain to be unpleasant news, for although no one else in the hall would have noticed, his casual acquaintance with the young queen allowed him to see past the regal façade to her true feelings beneath. She was upset, that much was clear, yet it would have been foolish to believe Dermont would have offered them cordial words in the face of their direct challenge to his authority, and Marina was no fool. It was something else, for she was not so much sad as she was angry. Bel ground his teeth, *What has he done now?*

"Lord Tower," the queen said, "Dermont sends word."

"King Dermont," the messenger corrected her, and when he turned around, Bel's blood turned to fire.

"Canton!" he sneered, "I should kill you where you stand."

"Aye, but you won't, not this time at least." The spymaster grinned. "And it's *Sir* Canton now—while we're all making sure of our titles here, Tower."

Only once before had Bel met his brother's master of spies, on the field of the tourney when he had gone north to infiltrate the ranks of Sir Marcus Harding's elite guard. Since that time, as Bel reflected upon the tales of his brother's nefarious deeds that for so long he had listened to with deaf ears, he suspected that although it was Dermont whose mind first conceived the evil, it was most often Canton and his army of rats that carried out the orders.

Canton's clothing was finer than when last they met and he wore a thick golden chain with a medallion. Little else about him had changed—his crooked nose, beady eyes, and the odor of stale drink (though cheap wine now as opposed to cheap ale). Yet, Bel knew better than to simply cast him off as some stupid thug, for he was not without a certain cleverness, a wicked intelligence honed to a fine edge for the sole purpose of committing ills. If men like Dermont and Lord Harren represented the worst that the noble class had to offer, surely Canton was alike to those born poor.

"What does my brother say?" Bel asked, circumventing the use of any titles.

The spymaster snorted a laugh and tossed a roll of parchment on the ground at Bel's feet. "Read it," he said.

Sir Emory breathed a heavy sigh of disapproval while beside Marina's throne, Sir Armel's face turned purple. As Bel bent to retrieve the missive, he was thankful that Horn, Sparrow, and the others of the light cavalry had taken the Shackle and gone ranging for the afternoon. Their loyalty often excited their tempers, before their self-control, when confronted with an insult to their chosen commander.

"What does it say?" Marina asked softly.

Bel began to read:

My dear little brother—what a shame it has come to this! When you stood against me upon the field before Clearpoint, you broke my heart, but to find you now actively opposing what our ancestors fought for a hundred years to achieve, I cannot possibly express in words. I do not know what it was that transpired between you and the Tower in his final moments, though the result seems to have left some dark taint in your blood. For no longer are you a Tremont, yet neither are you a Guardian either. So now I ask myself, what are you? Since word reached me of the tragic events that took place in our father's house, I have grappled with this question. What are you? What have you become?

My Guardian allies speak of traitors and turncoats who bear the brand of 'Blackguard.' They are men without honor and without loyalty who blight the lands they once swore to defend. It is with a heavy heart that I must conclude that you have become one of these monsters. Who but a monster would murder a friend like Wilmar Danelis? Who but a monster would hold his own father hostage? Who but a monster would kidnap the lawfully betrothed of his brother and make her his puppet with his corrupt and vile ways? Only one with a heart of darkness. Only the blackest of Blackguards.

I'm afraid you leave me no choice, brother. As the legends and the stories teach us, for a monster, there can only be but one fate. You must be stopped. You must be purged—you, those you have corrupted, and your vulgar seed.

When Bel finished reading he let the parchment slip through his fingers to the floor. In the wake of his great anger, he was unable to move or even speak. Marina gave a sharp intake of breath and she stood up from her seat. "Marcus," she whispered, and the hall, which had long ago fallen silent, now seemed as hollow as a tomb. Only Canton appeared to be free of the spell, and clasping his hands behind his back, he paced slowly past Bel toward the door.

"It should only be but a week before your brother's army arrives," he leered, "I think he's sending Lord Malacco. What do they call him, the Death Knell? Best hope you're prepared."

"Lord Tower," Sir Armel said, his voice echoing in the silence of the hall, "Grant me leave and that man will hang before he reaches the city gates."

"You can't kill a messenger so wantonly," Sir Emory said, shaking his head, "As much as he deserves it, his blood would only dishonor your blade."

Bel barely heard them, for he felt as if he had taken leave of his senses as he stood staring vacantly at the parchment on the ground.

"What are your orders then, my lord?" Sir Armel asked.

When he did not answer, Sir Emory got to his feet. "Prince Beledain," he said softly, eying the mute members of the court seated in the gallery, "What say you?"

Yet still, Bel could not bring himself to answer, for his brother's words had been like a hot coal pressed against his bare skin. *Vulgar seed!* he thought, over and over again, *Vulgar seed!* In his mind's eye, he saw Lilia painted for war, screaming her battle cry and flailing her weapons as she charged into battle upon Banshee. *Vulgar seed!*

"Bel?"

Bel glanced up at the sound of the voice and saw the face of the young queen staring at him with regal visage, but behind the mask, he could sense her fear—fear for him and for his son. *If you fall to pieces again,* he told himself, *Then Dermont has already won.*

Slowly, Bel took a deep breath and with the slightest of nods to the queen, he turned to Sir Armel. "We make ready," he said, his blood like liquid fire, "For too long our men and women have been without a battle and today my brother has offered us one. We should not see this messenger as a threat, but rather a gift, for our blades are thirsty and the Plague King offers us a feast of blood. Let the Death Knell be but the first note to sound in the tyrant's dirge!"

The guards posted at the doors and the few fighting men in the gallery offered a cheer of support. Soon after, Marina whispered quickly to Sir Armel and the court was declared adjourned. While the knights, nobles, guards and others present erupted into frenzied talk of what they had just observed, Marina withdrew through the rear door of the hall to her solar and Sir Emory made his way to Bel.

"Curse your brother," the old knight said, "There's a vulgar seed if ever I've seen one."

"I don't want to talk about it," Bel whispered.

"I'm sorry," Emory said, shaking his head in disarray, "I'm angry."

"So am I."

"Lord Tower," Sir Armel said, hurrying over to them, "The queen wishes to see you."

Bel nodded, but said nothing. His stomach churned with bile and he suddenly became conscious of the pain in his jaw from clenching his teeth.

Armel leveled his gaze, "You know we are with you."

"I know," Bel said, "And we'll be ready."

"Good."

Alone in her solar, Marina was more agitated than Bel had ever seen her, pacing back and forth and shaking her red head like a watch fire caught in a wind storm. "What a disgusting little man!" she said, "The very sight of him made my skin crawl!"

"As it should," Bel said, "He is dangerous, and his presence here only confirms what I have long suspected—that surely Dermont has eyes within our ranks and within our city, and most likely within our court as well."

"You think one of those who has pledged to us is false?"

"At the very least one."

"Perhaps Armel was right then—that you should have simply killed him. Perhaps it would have flushed the rest of the traitors out?"

Bel shook his head, "I don't believe so, just as I do not believe that our false friends are any more loyal to Dermont than to us. They are simply politicians who hope to save their skin in the event we fail. Had I sought to kill Canton, they would never have come to his aid. They would have merely watched it happen rather than betray themselves. Such are the ways of those we deem 'noble,' for though they claim friendship, they are not at all our friends."

Marina folded her arms across her chest and turned her back to him. "With each passing day, it seems the blight upon our land grows worse and worse," she said at last, "How do we even begin to heal it?"

"I don't know," Bel said, "But a victory in battle against Kurlan Malacco will be a start. Things have gone far too easily for us to this point and we've seen a remarkable degree of success for spilling so little blood. If we defeat Dermont in the field, it may strengthen the loyalty of our wavering 'friends' and inspire others to our cause as well."

Marina considered his words and nodded, "I see."

"Still, it won't be easy. Malacco is ruthless, as one might expect from my brother's closest friend. Dermont writes of monsters, but in truth the greatest monsters are the men who stand at his side. But I do believe we have a good chance of defeating him, for although we may question the resolve of our nobles, the common folk who follow us do so by their own volition and not simply out of conscription and fear as is the case for the Death Knell."

"But without knights and nobles can we really hope to win?" she asked, "What of the heavy horse? What of the charge?"

Bel gave a slight smile. "If my days in command of the light cavalry taught me anything," Bel said, "It's to not underestimate the common man—or woman. They're made of sterner stuff than we give them credit for, though who's to wonder for the rough lives we of so called 'higher birth' force them to lead." He sighed, "Fear not, your highness, for fear is the meat that my brother most thrives upon."

For a long moment Marina was silent, until at last, she took a deep breath and wearily blinked her eyes. "I know I agreed when you asked me to be queen," she said, "But really, for all my ignorance in matters of war, Bel, it is you who should be king."

Bel shook his head. "I think kings and their wars have caused us enough trouble these past hundred years," he said, "And if we truly seek peace, then we need a monarch who can command a court rather than an army, who knows how to inspire *all* people, rather than simply soldiers."

"I'll do what I can," Marina said, "But I'm not sure I'm the best suited for what you ask of me."

"I think you're better suited than you're willing to admit," Bel said, "And you know it. For although your brother Gislain and Sir Marcus Harding may have once commanded your father's armies in his stead, someone else must have assisted him in managing the rest of the realm."

"Perhaps I did help him," she said, "But to be a queen? I cannot recall a time ever that a queen reigned without a king—not just in Montevale, but in any realm. Ours is a man's world. How could a woman possibly hope to survive?"

"I don't know," Bel said, "But they do. I've seen it, even on the battlefield. Look at my cousin Valerie, for instance, or Sparrow and the other women who follow us," he paused, "Or Lilia."

"They are all remarkable women," Marina said, "But I am not a warrior."

"Perhaps not," Bel told her, "But never have I ever found you to be any less remarkable, your majesty."

The young queen breathed a heavy sigh. "Please stop calling me that," she said.

"What?"

"Your majesty, your highness, or any of that," she said, "To you, I'd rather remain simply Marina."

Bel took a deep breath. "Alright," he said, "Marina."

Marina turned away for a moment and paced along the perimeter of the solar's far wall. Bel could not help but watch her from the corner of his eye. She was beautiful, and good, and kind. "I'm very sorry to hear what Dermont said of Marcus," she said at last, "His own nephew. His own blood."

"I'm sorry as well, though I cannot say I'm surprised," Bel said, ignoring a flash of his latent anger.

"But to say such things…"

"You know as well as I that Dermont's indecency is often intentional, for he is fully capable of fine speech when it suits his purposes, as it did when he accepted your father's throne in Reginal. However, more often his true nature shows through when he offers barbs and insults designed to shame or wound. It is no less a tactic than his plague-bearers and assassins."

"So I remember from when I first offered him my hand."

Bel agreed, "He sought to hurt you and goad your father into committing some rash action out of anger." He paused, realizing suddenly how easily he too had been affected by Dermont's message. "Forget all this talk of vulgar seeds and monsters," he said at last, "For the longer we let his words linger inside of us, the greater chance we have of falling victim to his plague."

Marina gave a nod, "I will."

Bel eyed her carefully. "Don't let it bother you," he said earnestly, "Please, Marina."

"I won't."

"Good," he said, "Now, I should see to rallying our forces. It may take time to gather the levees from the surrounding fiefs and farms."

"Will you return to sup with us tonight?" she asked.

"If I can, I should like to," Bel said, "Though just in case, I believe I shall check in on Marcus now. I worry that all these weeks of travel and uncertainty have been too much for a child scarcely a month old."

"From what I can tell, he seems to be thriving," Marina smiled, "He's a sweet boy."

"I hope so," he said, regarding her once more. "Marina, I…" he paused, "I want you to know how much I appreciate your concern for him, in the absence of his mother. If he cannot know her then, I'm glad that he has you."

The young queen smiled, "You have always done everything you can to see to our welfare. I will do anything and everything to see to his."

Bel shook his head, ignoring the unsolicited surge of passion he felt when he happened to catch her eye. "I appreciate the praise," he said, "But save it until the battle against the Death Knell is decided."

"Then let it be so," said the young queen, "And may our victory pay Dermont out for his indecency."

"I'll see it done," Bel nodded, and without another word, withdrew.

CHAPTER 33: INSUBORDINATION

"Enough!"

Royne's eyes smoldered beneath his thin brows, glaring with as much courage as he could muster beneath the iron gaze of the Gray Wolf.

"General," he said, "There is no other option. Grantis is lost, but the Brock remains."

General Navarro paused, settled into his chair, and straightened his posture. When he spoke, his voice was soft, but not without a touch of latent anger. "We have discussed this before, Young Loremaster," he said, "And my answer to you now is the same as it was then."

"But General—"

"I will not abandon my home and my people in their time of need for fear of some archaic superstition."

Royne breathed a sigh of frustration. "I know that it sounds preposterous, and believe me, I'm not going to profess my own faith in a bit of ancient verse—a Bard's Tale, no less..." He cast an apologetic glance in Salasco's direction, but the Wall simply gazed silently at the ground underfoot. "However," Royne continued, "I do believe that the Brock is the key to any defense against the Guardian-King—not only for their military might, which we all know is considerable, but also—and perhaps more importantly—for the weight of the Galadin name."

"I hardly see how one bloody nobleman can turn the tide," Captain Velius griped.

"The Gray Wolf is but one man and you expect the world of him," Royne snapped.

Velius's lips twisted into a sneer.

"The Galadins are the heirs of St. Aiden, the warrior saint and hero of the Order and the Church of the Kinship," Royne continued, returning his attention to Navarro, "Were the Galadins to stand with us against the Guardian-King, men in every country from Grantis to Dwerin to Montevale would begin to question Kredor and his motives."

"Yes, because they were so willing to aid us in our time of need before," Velius remarked.

"You men are quick to say that the rest of Termain abandoned you," Royne said, "But did you ever actually request it? From what I recall, Grantis has forever remained apart from the other nations by its own choosing. I find it strange you wolves might expect the hand of friendship without offering one." He paused, "Yet now you have the chance. Offer your hand and the Brock will stand at your side to drive the men of Andoch from your lands. I am certain of it."

"How?" Velius snapped, "How can you be so sure?"

"Because the Heir of Galadin is a personal friend of mine and I would trust his honor above all others," Royne declared, "Stand with him and he will stand with all of you."

At length, General Navarro breathed a sigh. "You place a great deal of faith in this friend of yours," the Gray Wolf said, "But even should I decide to do as you ask, the Brock is half the continent away with Andoch in between."

"Hardly a leisurely stroll," the captain said, "It would be utter madness to expect to get their by foot."

"Agreed," Royne said, "Which is why you shall be travelling by sea." He nodded toward Salasco, "According to Salasco's people, a contingent of the Dwerin fleet lies at anchor in Granmouth awaiting companies of kingsmen marching from the nearby forts to join in the assault of the Brock. If we can take the port before they arrive, we can assume control of the fleet, and be on our way north before the week's end."

"Abandoning our countrymen to greater tyranny," Velius said snidely, "Why! What a plan!"

"Do you have a better one?" the Young Loremaster snapped.

The captain's gaze narrowed, "We renew the assault on Hedgeford."

Royne's eyes went wide with disbelief. "You must be joking?"

General Navarro's face remained impassive. "It is one possibility that General Callum, Captain Velius, and I have discussed," he said simply.

The Young Loremaster nearly laughed. "Never have I heard of something so foolish!"

"Easy, lad," Salasco whispered, though Royne could scarcely hear him. He was weary, exhausted from what seemed an endless parade of fools. "No wonder Dibhor thought to destroy mankind," he muttered bitterly, "At least the Keepers value knowledge."

"There's quite a difference between knowledge and wisdom, Young Loremaster," Salasco said.

Royne took a deep breath, "General, renewing the attack on Hedgeford would be nothing short of suicide."

"They won't expect us to return so soon," Velius said, "We will catch them with their breeches around their ankles."

Royne shook his head. "You aimed to catch them by surprise last time and they put you to rout!"

"This time shall be different."

"And if it's not?"

"Then we stand our ground and fight like men."

"Because clearly that too has served so well in the past," Royne said bitterly, "I do not understand—"

"I would not expect you to understand, boy," the captain said, rising from the table.

"Captain…" the Gray Wolf said.

Royne shot the captain a quick glance before returning his gaze to Navarro. "General, please, I implore you. You have seen firsthand the might of the Guardians. You cannot stand alone!"

"The Wolfpack never stands alone," Velius growled, "Where you find one wolf, you shall always find others".

"So you can all die together!"

"If we must!"

"Madness! You're all bloody mad!'"

"Mind your tongue!" the captain spat.

Royne's fists clenched in exacerbation and without thinking, he lashed out at Velius, striking him across the face with a lanky arm. "Oh kiss my ass, you wretched boor!" he shouted.

The sting of the captain's counterblow nearly knocked him off of his feet, but rather than falter or fall to silence out of shame or fear, Royne felt something within him break. He was angry, he was exhausted, and most of all, he wholeheartedly believed that he was right. Before he realized what he was doing, he leapt at Velius, flailing his fists in rage.

"Stop this! Now!" he could hear the general shouting as the captain rejoined his assault, "Both of you! Stop this at once! Guards!"

At once, the armored sentries of the general's personal guard rushed in to separate Royne and Captain Velius as they shouted curses and threats of retribution. The Young Loremaster was incoherent with anger, fighting to free himself from the restraining grip of the guardsmen to vent the past year's frustrations upon the ruddy, leering face of the captain. At long last, he finally felt as if he knew what it was he was to do, what Rastis had intended for him, and with the discovery of such purpose, he had finally discovered that he had indeed found something worth fighting for. "Curse you! Curse you all!" he cried in a frenzy of bitter anguish, "I offer you the chance at life, but you will all go to your deaths!"

"Enough of this!" General Navarro shouted, "Take him outside and place him under guard!"

"Your choice is simple, general!" the young Loremaster seethed, "The Brock and life, or Grantis and death!"

"Master Royne," the Gray Wolf replied, "I shall always owe you a debt for your service; however, it appears that for all of your talk of life, you seem rather willing to throw yours away. For in striking an officer of the legion, you have committed a crime that in the very least carries a sentence of a flogging and at the most demands your death."

CHAPTER 34: EYES OF THE EAGLE

When the cog bearing Roland Marthaine and his wife Lady Morgana arrived at the Galadin pier after its journey across Lake Bartund, it was met with a reception few would have expected from a city that for a thousand years had so often been its bitterest enemy. For as he stood to welcomed them, the young Baron of Galadin was accompanied by a column of two dozen men-at-arms, five knights, and his seneschal, all of whom were outfitted in the full regalia of their armor, his intentions (if not those of his men) were peaceful, and as such, he intended to greet his unexpected ally with every possible honor.

Clad in his finest clothing and his old hauberk, Lughus rested his hands upon Sentinel's hilt took a deep breath as he felt a bead of sweat slip down his spine. He was keenly aware of a low growling sound, though it did not come from Fergus, who sat regally at his left, but rather, from Sir Owain, who stood sweating in his great armor upon his right. The seneschal's mustache bristled in the heat of the noonday sun.

"Are you alright, Owain?" Lughus whispered. Given the seneschal's age, the fine weather, and the weight of the plate, he feared the old man might faint.

Sir Owain pursed his lips. "I'm fine," he said shortly, "Considering."

The young baron nodded, but remained silent and quickly cast his eye at the remaining men who had accompanied him. Outfitted in armor ranging from leather cuirass, to scale mail, chain mail, and full plate, five knights—three from the fiefdoms and two of Weavers' Guild—stood behind him in a line before the double rank of men-at-arms commanded by Sergeants Naden and Pike. Whether or not any of them shared Owain's antipathy was unclear, but if they did, they were doing a much better job of hiding it. That was at least some small comfort, Lughus thought, for not only was he extremely nervous, but distracted. Instead of accompanying him down to the docks, Brigid had chosen to remain at the castle.

I wish you'd come with me, he thought, conscious of her absence from the moment the procession departed for the docks. She had claimed that her presence would be an intrusion; it was their grandson that Roland and Morgana Marthaine wished to see, not the displaced Daughter of Dwerin. But while there was probably some truth to that, it still bothered him. Something had been out of sorts with her lately, and though she might try to hide it, he had come to know her too well to be fooled.

It was on the morning after the Weavers' Feast that he had first noticed it. They had joined Sir Owain in drilling with the guardsmen and new recruits. He and Brigid had stood apart from the others to spar as they had done on occasion, and he could see immediately from the way that she went through the motions of her footwork and the imprecision of her stances that she struggled to focus. Eventually, fearing her lack of attention might lead to some hurt, he suggested they instead take a walk around the battlements or through the postern to the Grotto, and although she agreed, her mind was clearly elsewhere.

Perhaps she was growing tired of Houndstooth and the affairs of the Brock. Perhaps she was longing to return to Dwerin, particularly now that it was denied her by the lies her wretched mother had sown. He knew that she hoped to go back someday, to free her people from the oppression of the Sheriff and his cronies, and he understood the anxiety such truly noble desires could bring—the constant feelings of inadequacy in trying to discover the best possible way to serve one's fellow man. Being exiled could only serve to make it worse.

Whatever it was, though, he wished she would confide in him, for the longer she did not, the greater his worry that what troubled her was somehow related to him, a concern her absence now only encouraged. Still, after the initial greeting here at the docks, she would of course be waiting for him at Houndstooth with Geoffrey, Annabel, and the rest of the castle community, and from then on, she would join him for whatever he required.

Required… He didn't like her use of that word. It sounded coerced. *Is that how she feels? Aiden's Flame, I hope not.* Hopefully, it was just an expression, a common idiom in formal speech. Regardless, the chronic ache in his chest grew worse just as the Marthaine sailors affixed the gangplank to the dock and the baron and his wife disembarked.

"Baron Galadin," Roland Marthaine observed with what might have passed for a smile in his scarred, stony face, "It's very good to see you again."

"Baron Marthaine," Lughus said, trying in vain to force all anxieties related to Brigid from his mind, "Be welcome."

"Thank you." Lord Roland was dressed in shades of sable and silver highlighted in parts with Baronial Blue. A longsword with quillions fashioned in the shape of wings hung beside a matching dagger upon his belt. They were beautiful, but solely ornamental, for according to Sir Owain, the eagle preferred the raw power of a heavy mace, capable of caving in men's skulls. Thunderclap, as it was known.

The lady at his right appeared similarly garbed in a gown of black and silver with a circlet upon her brow. Despite her closeness in age to her husband, her hair had not yet lost its dark brown color, and although the features of the face it framed seemed somewhat plain and severe, her brown eyes shone with genuine affection now upon her grandson.

"Lady's Grace, let me look at you!" she gasped, and without pause, placed her hands alongside Lughus's face and kissed him on the brow.

"May I present your grandmother," Lord Roland observed with a touch of amusement, "Lady Morgana."

Lughus's eyes went wide, uncertain as to what he should properly say or do, for although they were his relations, the Marthaines were still strangers to him, just as Arcis had been. "My lady," was all he could think to say when she finally released him.

"Oh please," Morgana said, "The last time I saw you, you were not yet old enough to speak and I've waited far too long to hear you call me 'gran' or 'grandmother' or the like."

"Gran, then," Lughus said, wishing again that Brigid was there with him. She was so much better at this sort of thing—graceful, gracious, regal... Thankfully, however, in her absence, his grandfather came to his aid.

"Leave him be for now," Lord Roland said, "You'll embarrass him before his men."

The lady sighed, "Fine. But my dear boy, it is so, so good to see you. Your grandfather was right. You're the image of the Galadins all over, but for the gray in your eyes—the Eyes of the Eagle!"

"Thank you," Lughus said, though he was not exactly sure if that was the right response. He had no idea how to react. He had never known any maternal affection before, or at least any that he could remember, and he wondered what to say or to do in order to be polite. "We should return to the castle," he said at last, conscious of his nerves twisting up again, "Sir Owain will guide us."

"Ah yes, Sir Owain Rook," Baron Marthaine nodded to the seneschal, "I owe you much and more for aiding my grandson these months. Please, take my hand."

Lughus exchanged a furtive glance of encouragement with the old knight, for he knew Owain's aversion to the Marthaines was stronger than any other man of Galadin. However, despite his reluctance, the seneschal accepted Lord Roland's gesture, muttering, "You are welcome, Baron."

Though it was not a long walk from the lakeside docks to the Houndstooth, Lughus was conscious of a certain lag brought by the awkwardness of the situation. It had been a long time since the Marthaines had walked the streets of Galadin, Lady Morgana observed. For, after their wedding, Gaston and Luinelen chose to make their home at Houndstooth, though they did from time to time make the short voyage across the lake to Harrier's Keep.

"Your father felt she might be more comfortable with the arrangement if she remained a part of her father's household," Lughus's grandmother said, "And though I understood, I regretted her absence, for she was an absolute delight to be around."

"Yes," Baron Roland agreed, "Your mother was a terrifically beautiful person."

Justin D. Bello

Lughus nodded, but could not think of anything to say. He found it somewhat disquieting to hear his parents spoken of so openly, for the mere mention of them, his father in particular, seemed taboo at Houndstooth.

At long last, they reached the castle barbican and were there received by the remaining men of the Galadin guard, all splendidly outfitted for war—a detail Lughus could not help but sense had been chosen by Sir Owain to serve more than just a ceremonial purpose. The wall of polished shields bearing the mark of the rampant hound were particularly striking as Fergus, in a golden flash, loped on ahead of the arriving column to where the household staff stood waiting by the entrance to the keep. Horus, in a fine doublet quartered blue and gold, stood at the head of his own command— the officers, servants, and maids that comprised the steward's domestic army. He bowed graciously at the Marthaines' approach, welcoming them and assuring that every need they might have would be met. Lughus barely heard a word he said, however, as behind him awaiting their introductions were Geoffrey and his family in their acorn garb, and of course Brigid.

She was beautiful, dressed in a gown of soft yellow with a delicate pattern of blue embroidery that was no doubt the source of Jergan's smug grinning. The fact that she insisted on retaining her daggers in spite of her formal attire made the flood of affection he felt for her swell all the more.

Lughus forced himself to look away from her. "Please allow me to introduce Sir Geoffrey of Pyle, the Vanguard, as well as his wife, Lady Annabel, and his children Freddy and Greta."

Lord Roland took Geoffrey's hand. "The Acorn Knight," Lord Roland said as Lady Morgana exchanged pleasantries with Annabel and the children. "You've a strong hand there, Sir Geoffrey. Strong enough to toss a hundred kingsmen back into the lake, as I hear it."

"I had plenty of good men to help me," Geoffrey said, "I only wish more of them had survived."

The old baron sighed. "Isn't that always the way of it?" he agreed, "It's good to know you, Sir Geoffrey."

"And you, sir."

Lughus smiled at his friend the Vanguard and, with a sudden intake of breath, motioned toward Brigid. "And this..." he announced, "This is Lady Brigid Beinn, the Blade, daughter of the late Archduke of Dwerin, and my particular friend."

Brigid offered the Marthaines a demure smile, for her cheeks glowed softly at the last part of his introduction. "It's very nice to meet you, Baron and Lady Marthaine," she said, offering her hand.

"And you, young lady," Lord Roland said, "Please forgive me for not introducing myself after the Assembly in Highboard. After Constable Harlow's tirade, my temper was up and with it I lapsed into my old soldier's ways. Regretfully, I forgot my manners."

"No need to apologize, my lord," Brigid grinned, "The Hammer seems to have that effect on people."

Lady Morgana took Brigid's hand, but then stepped closer and offered her a kiss on both cheeks. "We were just speaking of Lady Luinelen," Morgana said, "I had believed her the most beautiful young woman ever to walk these halls, but now I'm not so sure. Any particular friend of my grandson is a particular friend of mine."

Lughus blushed to hear his words repeated back to him, and he avoided Brigid's eye. *Why did I say that?* "Perhaps we should go inside," he said at last, "Horace had Boyce, our chief cook, prepare something special for the midday meal. You must be hungry after the morning's journey across the lake?" *I am such an idiot!*

At this cue, the party continued onward into the great hall and while they assumed their seats at table, Horus and his folk spurred into action. Lughus had insisted that Baron Roland be seated at his right to share the center place of honor at the lord's high table, with Lady Morgana at her husband's other side followed by Geoffrey, Annabel, and Sir Burnel of the Wrendale fiefdom. On Lughus's left sat Brigid, Sir Owain, Sir Balric of Parth, and Sir Gosbert of Clomanse, while at the lower tables, the benches were filled by the young Sir Faden and Sir Kradoc of the Weavers' Guild, Galoes Lot, the new master-at-arms, and Ibert Fressen, the new captain of the watch, Jergan and Willa, Freddy, Greta, Brigid's maid Ada, and the remaining sergeants, soldiers, and staff not needed to serve the meal. Already the hall was quite crowded, but would only grow more so as the day wore on, for by the evening meal many other men would be arriving—Sir Emont of the Glennbrook fief and Sir Forgan of Shorefold, Sir Adolfo the Madder, the brothers Petran, and more sergeants from the army camp that now grew daily outside the city walls. Randal Wood and a few of the cousins would be visiting the city as early as tomorrow from St. Golan's, Perin Glendaro and Theo Nordren in half a week, the Brabants, the Derindales, the Igrainnes, and who could say what other barons might arrive once the grand army of the Brock had finally assembled.

It would not be long now. As Sir Adolfo had said, the longships and galleys of the Andochan and Dwerin fleets would arrive any day to begin their blockade of Nordren's port. Baron Leoric and the majority of the Nordren knights had gathered any ships they could muster, and spent a tidy sum of the Brock's collective wealth employing as many Sorgund and Wrathorn mercenary sailors as possible to defend the coasts. In Helmstead, the Barons of Edgeforth and Crofton gathered their men to guard the Nivanus pass; however, since word reached the Brock of Montevale's continued domestic troubles, the Baron of Denholm would now join Waldron, Caradon, and the bulk of the Marthaines in guarding the western boarders from the Guardians in the south and the Wrathorn Clans Kronwall and Dreadworg in the north.

Lughus regarded the newly dubbed Sir Adolfo with caution, but in fairness, the Madder was not lying when he claimed to know "much and more." Apparently, his network of trade contacts ranged well beyond the Brock to other lands, and accordingly, put him in communication with many wealthy merchants and court officials willing to share what they knew. Not only had Adolfo been able to learn of the movements of the Guardian-King's forces, but bits and pieces of other rather intriguing news. Dandon Rood, for instance, the Warlord in the Order of the Guardians, had apparently fallen out of King Kredor's favor, and while he had not yet fallen so far as to disappear in the same manner as Loremaster Rastis, he had been virtually cut out of all decision-making related to the war. The men of his tower were now being treated as an extension of King Kredor's command of the kingsmen.

Lughus had not known Dandon Rood well, but the Warlord was known to be a friend of Rastis, and unlike the Hierophant and the Chancellor, was kind enough to remember Lughus's name, particularly after he defeated Pryce in the tourney so long ago. He remembered that the big man used to call him "the squire-scribe" whenever he would see him sparring with Sir Marcus Harding.

The Tower too figured into the Madder's news, though not happily. For apparently, while attempting to put an end to the War of the Horses, Sir Harding fell. A new man, a former prince, now bore his title. The details surrounding the elevation of the new Tower were still somewhat unclear, though it was said that in defiance of the Order, he supported the rebel queen, which of course, would paint him as another Blackguard. The idea of a man of such high honor as the Tower reduced to an outlawed brigand was for Lughus very strange, almost sad. However, considering what he had come to know now of the Order and the Guardian-King (to say nothing of his own status as the Marshal), he wondered if some day he might possibly find an ally in this Silent Prince. The Brock could certainly use a friend, and whether intentional or not, diverting the Plague King's attention from the Nivanus Pass and Helmstead was already a blessing.

The final piece of information Adolfo had offered was one that was of particular interest to Brigid. Apparently, there were great problems plaguing Dwerin in the wake of her uncles' murders. Neither Darren Beinn nor Brigid's mother Josephine could adequately command the realm, the armies, the navy, and the mines all at once. As a result, King Kredor and Rordan Baird, the Guardian Chancellor, had all but assumed control of the navy and much of the trade. Padraig Reid, the father of the brute Brigid had killed, commanded the armies in control of the Spade; however, a large force of Dwerin knights had recently arrived in Andoch at the court of Lord Hanson Fowler. They were said to be under the command of the Young Sheriff, Alan Beinn, though in all likelihood, they were truly led by his new tutor, Sir Vernon Wissant, a Guardian Anointed under the title of the Miller. What Brigid would do once he told her of this, Lughus did not know; for, Fowler's lands were not far from the borders of the Brock. However, a great part of him hoped that he might have the chance to face Alan himself.

The very thought of Alan Beinn or his crony, the Young Reid, set the storms in Lughus's eyes raging. He had thought a lot recently about Horus's comment that so often the word "knight" seemed synonymous with "villain." After much thought, Lughus could only conclude that it was true. Even worse, it seemed that the more powerful the noble and more weighty the title, the greater the capacity for evil. It was one of the things that frightened him most about being a baron, and made him all the more thankful for Rastis's tutelage. Between Pryce, Alan, Young Reid, King Kredor, Emperor Veirne, and his own father, history was full of privileged men more than willing to exploit others through their own power and positions. Perhaps that was the reason Rastis, Crodane, and Arcis had all been so ardent that he oppose Kredor, even if meant war. Perhaps that was ultimately what they wanted him to do—to lead, to guide, to safeguard the people, to create the conditions that would provide them the chance to live good lives free of darkness and fear.

"Lughus?"

The soft sound of Brigid's voice in his ear startled him, and when he turned toward her she was smiling. "What is it?" he asked, gazing into the depths of her eyes. The corners of her mouth curled upwards in amusement and her lips glistened from her last sip of wine.

"Your grandfather asked you a question," she whispered.

"Oh," he started, and turning toward Lord Roland added, "I'm sorry. I was just…thinking of the war."

"It weighs on us all," Baron Marthaine said, "Believe me."

"He asked about your armor," Brigid said, nudging his shoulder with hers. "I told him the smith had you all fitted."

"Aye," Lughus nodded, the lingering traces of his reverie still pawing at him with awkward fingers, "He said it should not take long to adjust."

"Good," Roland said, "There are no finer smiths than those of Dwerin. They do you and your realm great honor, Lady Brigid."

"It is I who feel honored by their work and skill," she said, "And if you don't mind, my lord, it's just Brigid."

"Very well, Brigid."

"Roland too dislikes the pomp and decorum so common at court," Lady Morgana piped in, "Too many years in the field to appreciate the finer things in the hall."

"Well," Brigid said, raising an eyebrow at Lughus, "It's not just your eyes that you have in common then. I thought the smith was going to cry as many times as Lughus turned down his offers of tracery and gilding."

"War is never pretty," Baron Marthaine said mildly, "Why pretend it is?"

"Indeed," Lughus said.

"Still," Lord Roland continued, "I once had the opportunity to visit the workshop of a master craftsman of the Blacksmiths' Guild in Dwerin and saw men there shape metal as if it were clay. They may hire engravers and finesmiths to embellish the final pieces, but after watching the armorers at work, I believe that steel is no less suitable a medium for art than is silver or gold."

"You've been to Dwerin?"

"Twice," Lady Morgana, "Once not long after we were married, and the second time for your mother and father's wedding."

At his side, Lughus could feel Brigid suddenly tense. "You knew them?" she asked.

"Not very well," the lady said, "However, your mother's mother was a cousin of Baron Caradon, and we knew her."

"My mother's mother? My grandmother?"

"Yes. So, you see, dear, you too have ties to the Brock."

"My mother told me very little of our family," Brigid said, "And my father was not often at Blackstone for very long before departing again for the Spade. Can you tell me anything about him, my lord?"

"Not much, I'm sorry to say. It was often said that he possessed a very keen mind, particularly as a strategist in battle, but that's all I know," Baron Marthaine told her, though Lughus had begun to sense a certain discomfort in him discussing the Beinns of Dwerin.

He must have heard the stories too, Lughus thought, *And he knows what it is like to be scandalized.* Thus, he was not surprised then, when Lord Roland cleared his throat and changed the subject.

"You know," Lord Roland said, "I have always envied Arcis's view from the top of the Houndstooth. The Firrinies block out the beauty of the sunset over Harrier's Keep, though we are lucky in the dawn. Still, if there's time, perhaps before we return home, you wouldn't mind indulging your grandparents with a look?"

"Of course," Lughus said, "And afterwards, when darkness falls, there's no better place to view the stars."

"That would be lovely, dear," Lady Morgana said.

Lughus offered his grandmother a smile, though he noticed that Brigid had gone back to thoughtfully picking at her plate.

When the midday meal came to a close, the Marthaines were shown to their chambers where they might rest before a second round of feasting. Lughus joined Sir Owain, Geoffrey, and the other knights for a ride around the army camp. Brigid had intended to accompany them; however, encumbered by her gown, she claimed that she could not ride. Instead, she chose to remain at the keep with Annabel, Ada, and the children. Again, her absence left Lughus full of concern and wondering what it was that weighed upon her.

Something was not right, but of course, the circumstances of the moment would not allow him to go to her. Again, he attempted put it out of mind, as Owain and the others led him around the camp, but, as before, that simply proved impossible. For although, he tried to pay attention to Sir Balric's tales of Wolfram of Parth, or to the good-natured arguing of Sir Gosbert and Sir Herbrand over which of their wives was the prettier (a running joke, Sir Owain informed him, since their wives were actually twin sisters), he could not keep thoughts of Brigid from his mind.

Thankfully, Sir Geoffrey had come along too, and of all the knights gathered around him, he was most at ease with the Vanguard by his side. For, although the others were his sworn men, he did not know them like Sir Owain. They were much older and had the benefit of experience, serving under Arcis and alongside Wolfram or Crodane. He couldn't help feeling like a child again, an apprentice once more surrounded by scholars.

Geoffrey, like Lughus, seemed to be equally out of place, for not only was he not native to the Brock, but his roots were among the soil as opposed to among the privileged. And while the farmer had, according to Freddy, seen plenty of battle in his brief tenure as the Vanguard, he seldom spoke of it and never in any great detail. Thus, while Owain and the others lapsed into stories of old skirmishes with the other baronies (Marthaine in particular), Lughus matched his horse's pace with Geoffrey's so they two might ride side by side in comradely silence or occasionally speak of the third.

"I hope you don't mind that I bought Freddy that buckler," the young baron said.

"Better a shield than a sword," Geoffrey smiled, "Though you've been more than kind enough to us already, my lord."

Lughus gave a shrug and ignored the use of the title. He didn't feel comfortable teasing Geoffrey for his insistence on formality like Brigid did. "I'm not so sure, Geoffrey," he said, "Since you saved the city, I'd argue my debt to you outweighs yours by considerably more."

"Though I also indebted you to the Madder."

"He's proven to have his skills," Lughus shrugged, "And though he has a somewhat...questionable reputation, he hasn't yet shown himself to be anything but loyal."

"True enough," Geoffrey said, "And to be fair, I probably owe him my life."

"All the more reason to give him a chance," Lughus said, and after a pause asked, "By the way, have you noticed anything unusual about Brigid these past few days? As if she doesn't seem herself?"

"Apart from the gown?" Geoffrey chuckled.

Lughus smiled wanly, "Yes. Does she seem...I don't know? Less excitable?"

Geoffrey chewed his lip. "She has her moods, just as any of us. Though with the war and everything they say about her mum and all that, I don't blame her. Still, since the moment we left Dwerin for the Brock she's run about like a hummingbird on fire, especially since the business with the Hammer. Perhaps she's finally just taking time to land before we're all forced to take flight again."

"Perhaps you're right."

"It's a hard thing," he said, "This much change. I can tell you from my own experience. This last year has seen so much of it that there are times I wake up in the morning and have no idea who I am, who I was, or who I'm supposed to be. Bloody madness."

"I understand you there," Lughus said.

"Aye, I'm sure you do," the farmer said, "Perhaps it's just her turn."

"True," Lughus said.

"Of course, the best thing to do would just be to ask her," Geoffrey smirked, "Beats the two of us just guessing."

Lughus gave a nod, and would have said more, but at a call from Sir Owain, he was drawn away to hear the day's report on how the gathering army fared.

Thus far, the Galadin forces numbered roughly one hundred and eighty heavy horsemen comprised of the Galadin knights and mounted men-at-arms, another eighty light horsemen, five hundred men-at-arms afoot, eight hundred bowmen, and another thousand or so of peasant militia gathered from among the city, villages, and farms. To see them all encamped in and around the city walls was impressive, but also, at least to Lughus, somewhat unbelievable, as if he had somehow stepped into the pages of one of the adventure books he had read. He still had a difficult time accepting the soldiers' cheers or calls when he passed them, and riding beside his knights, he suddenly felt very small and lost. His youth was also no help, for it seemed many of the men—whether mounted soldier, archer, or militia farmer—were significantly older than him, and although at seventeen, he was considered a man, he wondered how many might scoff at his leadership.

These doubts still plagued him later once they returned to the castle, and while, for a time, they suppressed his concerns over Brigid, as he awaited Horus's summons to begin gathering for the meal in the hall, he withdrew to the privacy of his solar. In a slight frenzy of study, began pouring over Arcis's maps, old books, and anything else relating to war. It was very frustrating, for despite the almost obsessive devotion he had applied to such matters throughout his studies with the Loremaster, it seemed now that when he needed it most, all the facts, figures, and historical accounts had all gone clear out of his head.

Perhaps once the real fighting began, Sir Owain or the Lord-Baron would assume command and he could simply follow their orders, for it was one thing to draw his sword and fight an enemy alone, but to be responsible for the lives of thousands where the only guarantee was that some of them, surely, would die, was a heavy burden and not one he looked forward to have to bear.

"How am I possibly going to do this?" he asked Fergus, lounging at his feet, "It's absolute madness!"

"Of course it is. It's war."

Lughus looked up to see Baron Marthaine standing with his hands clasped behind his back in the doorway to the solar. It gave Lughus pause, for not only had he exposed his lack of confidence in his own leadership, but he had still not determined how to address the old man: Baron? Lord Roland? Grandfather? At length he simply sighed, "I hope everything in your chambers is to your liking?"

"Very fine," Lord Roland replied, "In fact, they are the same rooms that we stayed in for the wedding of your mother and father."

Lughus nodded. "Horus said something about that." He shuffled together some of the maps to clear a space at the table. "Would you like to sit down?"

The baron paced slowly across the room and with a slight smile lifted a small, leather-bound book. "*The Battle of Thedwyn Fen*," he read aloud.

"Have you read it?"

Lord Roland shook his head and sat down. "I don't read books about war," he said, "I prefer poetry, philosophy—things that represent the pinnacle of man's creation, rather than the depths of his depravity."

Lughus sighed. "I understand," he said, "But in light of everything, I need to learn."

"It'll come to you with experience. You've got a good man in Sir Owain Rook too. The Saint knows he's beaten back plenty of my men in the past."

It was strange to hear such a complement, and Lughus wondered to hear it given. "Do you find it hard to be here," he asked, "In this place with the folk who were for so long your enemies?"

Baron Marthaine shrugged, "Yes and no."

"What do you mean?"

"I did not hate Baron Arcis," he said, "Despite what many assume, and though we often fought and I mourn the loss of many friends killed in battle with Galadin, I always respected him. For in all things, he acted with honor and in accordance with his duties to his people."

"But does it not make you angry to think about the men who died in the fighting between you?" Lughus asked.

"Of course, but just as I lost friends, so did he. We all have our duties to perform."

"Why war at all then?"

"Foolishness? Pride? Duty? There are many reasons men go to war and few of them, if any, are ever good."

"I worry about this coming war," Lughus said, "I worry that it's all my fault."

"I very much doubt that, considering the fate of Grantis," Roland said. "If Kredor seeks to build an empire through this Protectorate nonsense, the Brock was simply next in line."

"But did it have to come to war?" Lughus said, "If I would have simply given myself up to the Hammer, could all of this have been avoided."

"I sincerely doubt it. Besides, you are not the only one he sought. Would you have encouraged good Sir Geoffrey or Lady Brigid to surrender as well?"

"Of course not."

"Then don't be so quick to play the martyr," Lord Roland said, "You may have the blood of the Saint, but your name is not Aiden and I see no dead army marching."

Lughus gave a weak smile.

"Besides," Baron Marthaine said, "You may think you caused a war, but your presence alone has already healed a lot of old wounds. For never in my lifetime has the Brock stood so united. Not only that, you've offered both Galadin and Marthaine a future after such horrible losses in the past. Arcis was not the only one left without an heir, remember."

Lughus gave a nod, but his eyes fell to the tabletop at the awkward allusion to his parents. It did not go unnoticed.

"I realize that you may feel...uncomfortable, knowing what happened with your mother and father," the old man said softly, "I'll not deny what he did, or try to justify it, for it was evil."

"So he did do it then," Lughus said, "It wasn't just a nightmare."

"Oh, it was. Believe me."

"But why did he do it? How could any man do such a thing?"

Lord Roland breathed a heavy sigh. "I've spent years asking myself that very question, and I still don't know. I'm not sure it really matters anymore." He paused. "However, he was still my son, and I love him—as much as I hate what he did."

For a long moment, Lughus was silent. He had somehow always hoped that what had happened between his parents was simply a story. To hear his grandfather confirm it made him suddenly feel very cold and ill in the pit of his stomach. "I don't know," he finally said, "I'm still trying to find ways to...accept any of it..."

"That's fine too," Baron Marthaine said, "It's no easy thing."

For a while they sat there in silence, though, strangely, Lughus did not find it disquieting. Rather, to have the tragedies of the past acknowledged so plainly and laid bare felt somewhat calming. It was indeed an ugly truth, and rather than simply avoid it or attempt to forget that it ever happened, as so many of the castle folk did, Lord Roland looked it in the eye, confronted it, and carried it with him so he might carry on. And while Lughus still had many questions, for the moment at least, he was content to accept the reality, however tragic, and for the time being, let it simply be.

At length, the stillness was broken when, from the hallway, Brigid peered around the corner into the room.

"Excuse me, Baron Marthaine," she said, "Lughus? Geoffrey said you were asking after me?"

Something about the look in her eye made Lughus feel somehow frightened. She seemed nervous, wary. *Why?* he thought in frustration, *What is the matter?*

"Lady Brigid, good afternoon," Lord Roland smiled, and stood up from the table.

"Oh you don't have to go," she said hurriedly, "I didn't mean to interrupt."

"No, no," the baron said, "We were simply talking. Besides, I had best return to Lady Morgana before we're called to the hall." He turned back to Lughus, "Any time you wish to talk—about anything—don't hesitate to pay a call."

"I won't," Lughus said, rising to his feet.

"Good." Lord Roland nodded. "Perhaps when the war is over—if we all make it through—you can visit us in Harrier's Keep. Both of you. We can go falconing. Have you ever tried it?"

"I haven't," Brigid said.

"Lughus?"

"No," Lughus said, nervous now that Brigid had drawn near. "The only time I've been hunting, I was with Fergus, and he did all the work."

"Then bring the hound too. We can see who sights prey first, the golden hound or the silver eagle."

Fergus rose from where he lay and gave a snort.

"I'd call that a challenge," Brigid said kindly. "Your eagles had best be swift."

"Oh they are," Baron Marthaine said, "Have you ever seen a silver eagle? The symbol of our house? They're a sight to behold," he smiled, "Slightly smaller in build than a Calendral kite, but with broader wings and greater speed, though only over short distances. Lughus's father was the greatest falconer I've ever seen. With any luck some of that skill passed on to you too."

"Perhaps," Lughus said.

"At any rate," Baron Marthaine said, "I will see you both at table."

When the sound of Lord Roland's footsteps had receded down the hallway, Brigid spoke. "I'm sorry I couldn't go with you before. I would have liked to, but…" She shook her head and motioned at the extensive folds of her dress. "Bloody gown."

Lughus gave a nod and paced back to the table, still littered with its maps and books. "You do look beautiful," he told her, glancing down at the tabletop, "Very much so."

"Thank you," she reddened, "And you look very handsome."

All of a sudden, he felt very strange, foolish even. Maybe there's nothing wrong after all. Maybe it was all simply in his own head. *Why do I feel this way when I'm near her?* he thought, *Foolish! Foolish! Foolish!* He shook his head in frustration and noticed she was watching him. "Would you like to take a walk or sit here?" he asked.

"Whatever you like," she said, and a moment later asked, "What were all the maps for? Were you and you grandfather planning for the war?"

"No, I was just..." He rubbed his eyes and shook his head before offering her a weak smile. "It's funny. I don't remember."

Brigid's brow creased with concern. "You're not having the dreams again, are you?"

"No, no. Not really."

"Then what is it? Lughus, are you alright?"

Lughus gave a sigh. *Am I? I don't know?* "To be honest," he said after a moment, "I was about to ask you the same question."

She gave a wistful smile and ruffled Fergus's ears, but seemed to avoid catching the young baron's eye. "Why don't we sit then?" she said tentatively.

"Alright." Quickly, he made room at the table, gathering together even more of the old documents, irrationally embarrassed by what seemed suddenly to be a mess. Once he had finished and helped her to her chair, he sat down and took a deep breath. "You know that you can tell me anything," he began.

"Of course I do."

"Then," he paused, "Brigid, these past few days..." He shook his head again. "Are you upset with me?"

"What?" Her eyes went wide and an incredulous smile spread across her lips. "Of course not. Why would you think that?"

He shrugged. "I don't know, but..." He sighed. "I know something weighs on you. Just...after everything..." He eyed her beseechingly. "You know that you can confide in me."

"Lughus," she said, "Of course I do, but really, it's nothing."

"Brigid..."

"Lughus..."

"Don't mock me." He smiled. "I'm serious. I...worry about you."

Brigid heaved a heavy sigh. "You have plenty to worry about with the war. I'm not going to add to your cares with my absurdity."

"So there is something?"

"I—" A smile tugged at the corners of her lips through she tried to suppress it. "You're infuriating sometimes."

"Brigid, please." He reached across the table and took her hand, halting but an instant to appreciate its softness. "Fine. You're right. There's the war and all of that, and I do worry about it, and it does weigh on me. However, in spite of all of that, I can't think of anything else but you."

Her eyes went wide. "Me?"

"I mean," he could feel his cheeks burning scarlet, "I mean, what's bothering you? Is it your mother? Is it the war? Is it Houndstooth? Is it the armor I bought you? Is it me? Am I bothering you? Are you tired of my company?"

"Lughus!" she said, "Of course not! I just told you so! Don't be foolish!"

"Then what is it?"

"Lughus…" she sighed in exasperation. "Fine, I'll tell you, but like I said, it's nothing. It's stupid."

"Then prove it," he said.

"Alright," she began. "I know it's foolish and I hate to admit it with the war and everything else that's going on, but lately I've been worried about…well, about myself."

"Do you think that your uncle or your mother might try to harm you? You know that I would never let that happen." He smiled. "Not that you would need it, Lady Blade, but still…"

"No, it's not that," she said, "And thank you, but it's not that." She took a deep breath, "Lady's Grace, I'm such a fool."

"No, you're not."

"Oh if you only knew." She made a sound of disgust and rubbed her eyes. "Alright, since you want to know so badly, I'll tell you. I'm worried that I'm losing my mind. I'm worried that I'm going mad—or at least if I'm not now, that I might soon."

"What?" He smiled. "You really must be if you think that's true."

"I told you it was absurd, but I mean it," she said. "There are times when I have these thoughts—bloody thoughts, and I think about the men I've killed. Reid, the kingsmen in the grotto—both times—and all the others I might have killed or wanted to kill."

"You were defending yourself."

"Aye, but how much should that really matter? To take a man's life?"

"Brigid," Lughus said, "I'd kill Reid a thousand times over for what he tried to do to you. As I said, you were defending yourself—against the kingsmen too. They were the artificers of their own deaths—not you."

"I don't know…" she shook her head, "Besides there are other times. The other night with the weavers, for example—the whole time we met with Adolfo, all I could think of was how easy it would be to kill him, just to end him right here in this room in cold blood."

"Did you?"

"No, but I wanted to."

"But you didn't."

"But I could have."

"Brigid…" Lughus sighed.

"There's more," she said. "At the feast—after you left—Adolfo spoke to me. He tried to reassure me that he was loyal to you, tried to explain why." She paused. "Anyway, he started talking about the Blade and all the…the blood Gareth spilled over the years, and I admit, none of it surprised me. You know how the dreams are. The visions. The mere mention of it and I remembered some of them."

Lughus shook his head, "How would Adolfo know anything about Gareth?"

"He was his brother."

"What? No."

"I believe him. It was in the way he said it," she sighed, "And there's more. Since then…It was like, simply by him admitting it, it triggered something in my mind. I've had dreams, new dreams."

"And you saw Adolfo?"

"I think so, or someone who could be him, but much younger. It was somewhat hard to understand. I saw through Gareth's eyes and he couldn't have been much older than Freddy while Adolfo was perhaps..our age? Give or take a year? In any case, it was some manner of trial in the hall. Here at Houndstooth, and I think…I think I saw your grandfather—"

"Arcis?"

"Yes, and a man dressed as a hierophant. A young Andresen perhaps? Gareth didn't really understand what was going on, but I could tell he was...scared. Worried. His brother was in trouble for something..."

She paused to scatter the memory from her mind's eye. There was more, but it did not matter right now. "In any case," she continued, "I'm just...I'm worried. Killing should not be easy, though I find that for me, it is. I remember Gareth saying something about how he walked so often in Darkness that he forgot the ways of the Light."

Lughus's eyes fell to the tabletop. "And now you're worried that you're going to end up the same?"

Brigid replied with a resigned shrug. "I want to fight in this war. I want to stand at your side, and I'm going to—no matter what," she paused a moment, bit her lip, and looked away. "I just...I worry what doing so might do to me. If men seek to harm you, or Geoffrey's family, or the good people of Galadin, I will not hesitate to kill them. I will slaughter an entire battalion of kingsmen if I have to, to say nothing of the Hammer, the provincial, or King Kredor himself. I would have done it in Highboard had it come to it, every last one of them. It frightens me."

"Each time you draw a blade, you make a choice to take life or to give it," Lughus told her, thinking suddenly of the currach on the river and Crodane. "You might slay an enemy, but you save a friend."

"But are the kingsman all really evil? All of them? Surely not. You lived in Titanis and saw them up close. They're not monsters; they're men. Some good, some bad, like all soldiers."

"So we seek not to attack them, but rather to defend our own borders. Nothing more. Do you think that I want to face the men of the Order? I grew up admiring them, reading about their great deeds, dreaming of their battles. Now, I find myself playing the part of a villain in one of those same stories." His eyes flashed. "Yet, I will do I must in order to do what is right. It's King Kredor who threatens war and lusts for dominion over the Brock and all Termain. It's the Hammer who demands we forfeit our lives, even after all our shows of mercy towards him and his. So, let's have no more talk of slaughter or murder. For, we fight only to give life, not to take it. We fight to defend our people and to stand against tyranny."

"Yes," she said, "We do, we do that, but..."

"But what?"

"Lughus, look at my family. Look at their crimes—murder, rape, tyranny, and the Lady only knows what else. That is my heritage. That is my blood."

"Brigid," Lughus implored her, tightening his grip on her hand, "You are *not* like them."

"I'm not so sure."

"Brigid, look at me," he waited until she fixed him with her gaze, steeling himself against the sudden jolt of sympathy he felt to see her blue eyes turning to glass, "*You* are not like *them*. Do you think any of them—your mother, your uncle, your bloody cousin—do you think any one of them ever stopped to worry about whether *anything* they did was wrong? Your own mother looked you in the eyes and told you that she hated you!"

"In fairness, I said it first."

"Aye, but you told me that you regret it. Do you think she does? Especially considering how easily she brands you a murderer now?"

Brigid breathed a heavy sigh and looked away, but as she did, a single tear fell from her eye and left a glistening trail down her cheek. "I know," she said softly, "I know."

Lughus's brow creased. "Do you think my family's any better? People speak of the Blood of the Saint and how kind and beautiful my mother was, but don't forget how she lost her life," he said. "Do you want to my grandfather and I were talking about before? He so much as told me that the story about them is true—not that I didn't already know it. I saw it. However, to hear it—to hear that he killed her…"

Brigid shook her head. "I'm so sorry."

"You've no reason to be sorry. I just…" He cleared his throat and shook his head. Seeing her upset and thinking of his own parents' end was affecting him too. *Enough is enough.* Acting purely on impulse, he stood up from the table, and led her by the hand to her feet. Her eyes were wide with uncertainty as she gazed into his, but when he gently drew her into his arms and held her close she returned the embrace.

"Listen to me," he whispered. "I am not my father any more than you are your mother, or your cousin, or any of your uncles. We are who we are, Brigid. We are not Gareth or Crodane or anyone else to have borne our titles, even if we have their memories or their skills or anything else. We are *us*. I am me, and you are you." He paused. His heart was pounding in his chest like a battering ram against a castle wall. *No hesitation.* Gently, he reached up and turned her chin so that once more he could lose himself in the depths of her bright blue eyes. "I want you to know this—" he said, ignoring the warmth of his blushing and the rush of excitement he felt standing so close to her, "I want you to know this so that when I tell you that I love you, you know that *I* love *you*."

As soon as the words left his mouth, it was as if a great weight had been lifted from his shoulders, and when she replied with a soft whisper of "I love you too," he feared that he might faint, so moved was he by her admission of reciprocated love. As his senses returned, he drew her ever closer, noticing the way that she gazed up at him in earnestness, inclining her head ever so slightly toward his, a silent invitation to kiss her and to know the truth of her words.

Never before had Lughus kissed a girl in such a way, though many times these past weeks, he had often privately envisioned—or rather hoped—that with Brigid, such a moment might finally occur, and although he could not fully ignore the sudden swell of self-consciousness, his heartfelt feelings for her overpowered any concerns.

So it was that very gently, his lips parted and he pressed them to hers. Graciously, she received him, and while he savored the sweet flavor of her and the soft, moist touch of her tongue, she too drank deeply from his lips like one lost in a dessert and on the brink of dying from thirst.

At last, for want of air, they were forced to part, though as soon as he was able, Lughus bent to kiss her again only to discover that she was smiling. Her white teeth gleamed with the light of her joy, and unwilling as he was to stifle such a show of delight, he instead pressed his lips to her brow, her cheek, and halting but a moment to breathe in the scent of her hair, he kissed the soft flesh of her neck.

"Oh Lughus," she whispered beneath the onslaught of his kisses, "I love you too. I do. Oh, I do. I love you." Again, her thin frame fell weak in his arms and as he held her closer, her head lolled softly against his and her lips gasped for air as they gently sought to join with his once more. When again they were forced to part for want of breath, with faces flushed and lips swollen from the sudden torrent of kissing, Brigid let her head fall limp against his shoulder and Lughus breathed a sigh of contentment unlike any he had ever known.

"I swore an oath to Crodane that as Baron and Marshal, I would protect this land and lead well, but I feel I've stood on the edge of failure since ever I first began in earnest to do so," he told her, "Between the Hammer, the Assembly, and now the war, so often all seemed lost, and I believe it would have been were you not standing beside me."

"Lughus..."

"So let's have no more talk of madness or Darkness or anything of the sort," he said, "Because as much fear or uncertainty as you may have about yourself and your place in all of this, you inspire me. Brigid, you make me believe that I can do this. Aiden's flame, you make me *want* to do this—to help lead Galadin, the Brock, and all Termain on to a golden age!" he shook his head, conscious of his own babbling, "I'd march to Dwerin tomorrow were Andoch not knocking at our doors. I'd help you free your people and set you up as a Mountain Queen!"

"I don't want to be a Mountain Queen," she smiled and gently kissed his lips, "I just want to be with you."

Lughus pressed his brow to hers, closed his eyes, and breathed deeply, comfortably. For some time they stood together, happy and free in the unfettered affection of the other's embrace, and as he held her, Lughus became aware an uncanny sense of completeness, as if the great gaping chasm, the great void within him, had suddenly been filled. At length, he kissed her again and drew his arms around her as if it were possible to hold her even closer.

"I've been wanting to tell you that for some time."

"That's funny," she grinned, "Because I've been wanting you to tell me that for some time."

"Then hear it again. I love you."

Brigid breathed another sigh and softly kissed his neck, "I love you too."

Lughus gave a slow nod. His breast swelled thinking of the secret wish that had lodged like a bodkin point within his heart since the moment he first looked into her eyes at St. Elisa's Grotto, that same absurd desire that with each passing day became harder and harder to keep buried within him. *Why hesitate now?* he thought, *She already confessed her love for you; what could you possibly have to fear?*

"You know," he said at last, his voice scarcely a whisper, "I meant it when I said I would help you free Dwerin. I know it's important to you."

"So it is," she said. "I want to help the common folk of Dwerin, to end the tyranny of the nobles. But, as for myself," she shrugged, "I've been happy here in the Brock—happier than I've ever been, and even after such a short time, Galadin seems more of a home to me than Blackstone ever was."

"Well," Lughus said, pausing to take a deep breath, "What if it was your home? Always?"

"What do you mean?"

"I mean…" he said softly, "That the Baron of Galadin might make a fine match for the daughter of the Archduke of Dwerin—if she'd have him."

"What?"

As soon as the words left his mouth, Lughus felt her back straighten and she pulled away to look him in the eye. "You want to get married?" she asked, her eyes wide with surprise.

Lughus bit his lip as his shoulders slumped beneath the weight of his returning inhibition. "It would be a very good match…politically," he mumbled, "The Brock and Dwerin…united…"

Brigid's brow knitted as she seemed to consider it. "That may be," she finally said, "But I swore a long time ago that I would never marry for politics."

"Oh…"

"Nor for money," she added, "Nor for power, nor for any other such nonsense."

"I see," he said miserably, "Then, what would you marry for?"

Brigid's eyes alighted with merriment and she smiled at him coquettishly. "Only for love," she said with a kiss to his cheek, "So it's a good thing I love you."

Lughus's eyes narrowed in confusion. "Then…" he stammered, "You *do* want to get married? To me?"

"Of course I do, you fool!" she laughed, "I'd run down to the cathedral right now if you hadn't banished the bloody Hierophant from the city!"

"I wouldn't want a man like Andresen to marry us anyway," he grinned, "Abbot Woode will be here soon. He can do it then."

"Do you think he will?"

"Why wouldn't he?"

"Don't we need some sort of formal betrothal, or at least my mother's consent?"

"A formal betrothal's never legally required," he said, happy to make use of the hours he spent studying the judicial codes at the Loremaster's Tower, memorizing the marriage laws while Royne stood by poking fun at him. "And as for your mother, she denied herself any and all rights she had over you the very moment she chose to disown you."

"She did?"

"She did," Lughus smiled, "Besides, even if we did need her word, I wouldn't let that stop us. She's caused you enough unhappiness already. If you love me and want to marry me, Brigid, that's enough."

"I do!" she said merrily, planting little kisses all across his face, "Oh Lughus, I do!"

"I just…" he whispered, "I want you to be happy. You make me so happy; I want you to be happy too."

"You *do* make me happy," she grinned, and he could see her eyes beginning to gloss over again with tears, though of a different nature than before. "So, so happy," she echoed, kissing him again, "I just wish this wretched war wasn't looming over us. I do so love you. I love you so, so much, my dear."

He sobered momentarily by her mention of the war. In all the excitement of their joint admissions, he had nearly forgotten. *The war! It always comes back to the bloody war!* He did not relish the idea of marrying her only to see the two of them charge off into battle. "If you'd rather wait until afterwards," he told her, "We can."

"Of course not!" she said, continuing to plant little kisses upon his chin, his cheeks, and around his lips, "Lady's Grace, Lughus! I'll not let the Hammer or any other wretched Guardians try to confound this for us too."

"What was it we said in Highboard," he smiled, "Side by side. Come what may?"

"Aye, come what may," she laughed and hugged him even closer, "Let Old Harlow just try to stop us now!"

"Though, to be fair," he teased, "The Hammer could probably claim credit for bringing us together."

"Does that mean we have to invite him to the wedding?" she grinned, and stifled his laughter by pressing her lips to his.

No sooner had she done this, however, when they heard the sound of heavy footsteps hurrying down the corridor and scarcely had time to slip from the other's embrace before Sir Owain, Sir Burnel, and many of the other knights appeared in the doorway of the solar. For a split second, Lughus was stricken with an irrational fear, as if in their intimate moment of kissing he and Brigid had been caught guilty of breeching some taboo. However, not one of the knights seemed to notice in the least how close they stood to one another or the blissful shine of their flushed faces, for their own countenances were marred by a heavy shadow. Something was clearly wrong.

"My lord!" Sir Owain exclaimed, "Sir Deryk of Lomedan has sent a messenger from his fief along the southwest border with Agathis!"

"Agathis!" Lughus's jaw set in sudden anger. "What is it?"

"A great host of kingsmen crossed the border into the Brock and took Dorgan and his men by surprise. Now, they head north toward Galadin burning and pillaging everything before them as they go."

"What?" Lughus asked, "Andoch has begun their attack? How did we not hear of this sooner?"

"Agathis is no warrior. It seems he failed to send messengers before the kingsmen had him besieged. It was fleeing peasants who informed our border guards of the attack," Sir Owain said, his expression grim. "Now, the farmers and peasants south of St. Golan's are swarming to the abbey in droves seeking shelter. Sir Deryk and his men are doing their best to protect them from Andochan raiding parties, but the rest of the forces are already making the slow march north from Agathis to the abbey itself. I fear if we don't leave soon to provide aid, they're sure to be routed and St. Golan's razed."

"They wouldn't do that, would they?" Brigid said, "Attacking an abbey? For knights who claim to do the will of the Kinship, they seem quite fond of sacrilege."

"Woode's got a history," Sir Owain said, "If they take St. Golan's, it's certain they'll hang him as a heretic for naming you his friend."

"No!" Brigid said, "Lughus, we have to help him!"

Lughus gazed over at her and his eyes flashed with determination. For staring at her, his love, his bride, he felt his chest swell. *Let the whole bloody Order stand against us—for nothing can stop us now!* With one hand he clenched the hilt of his sword and with the other, he took her arm. "We will," he said with a resolute nod, and turning to Owain added, "Make ready. We'll leave within the hour."

"Aye, my lord," the seneschal said.

"They failed once already to trespass on our lands and catch us unaware." Lughus said. "And now they want to try again? To bully peasants and attack our friends? I say it's time enough we show them the wrath of the Golden Hounds!"

"Aye! Release the hounds!" the other knights cried. In assent, Fergus let loose a mighty howl.

"Then let's make for St. Golan's to protect our people, defend out lands, and send the red cloaks back to Andoch!" Lughus said with a nod to Brigid, "And afterwards, when the abbot is safe, he's wanted for a wedding."

CHAPTER 35: THE RELIEF OF THE RAM

"On your feet, boys! On your feet and form ranks!"

Geoffrey stood watching the sergeant call his men to order—archers clad in quilted gambesons, already sweating beneath the early light of dawn.

"Sir Geoffrey," the sergeant said, "I'll have this lot ready to march directly, sir."

"Very well, sergeant," Geoffrey replied, loud enough for the men to hear, "And remind them if you will, that should we reach St. Golan's by day's end, they can all look forward to a pint of The Ram's Reward!"

"Aye!" the men cheered, "For St. Golan's!"

Geoffrey gave a slight grin and continued his walk down the gathering column toward where his horse was being seen to by one of the Galadin grooms. A small squad of men-at-arms in the tabards of the Golden Hound saluted him as he passed and he returned their greeting with a nod. Two of them he recognized from the skirmish at the lake, though the others were unknown to him—a matter he would have to remember to remedy. Strange, he thought, how his life seemed determined to change so completely. For, it was only this time last year that he had departed from Pyle for the markets of Granmouth as a simple farmer, only to return the Vanguard, and where once he and his family struggled day by day in the field and slept each night in their little peasant hovel, they now enjoyed the comforts of a knighthood and the hospitality of a legendary baron's castle.

Oliver had told him once to count his blessings, to accept the gifts the Brethren had bestowed upon him, and to take solace in the knowledge that they were watching. For too long Geoffrey knew he had resisted, had found himself too unworthy, and as a result of his wavering many he cared for had suffered—his eldest son Karl, Cousin Martin, and Oliver himself. Yet in the past few weeks he had finally arrived at the conclusion that his friend was right. Humility was indeed a virtue and pride the worst of sins; however, insisting that his own low birth required that he and his family continue to live in squalor seemed now not only a lapse in his duties as a provider for his children, but also its own form of vanity. To require that Freddy and Greta grow up as poor peasants simply because their parents had was the height of injustice, for what was the purpose of being a parent if not to provide one's children with the opportunity for a better life? No wonder Old Amos had been so insistent that Geoffrey take his family and go. No wonder St. Aiden had waged an impossible war against the Warlock to build a better world for his son.

Still, he knew that he was not a knight in the same way as Sir Owain, Sir Balric, and all the others of the Galadin fiefs. Nor was he a knight like Young Faden or Adolfo of the Weavers' Guild. For, although they were kind to him and seemed decent sorts, they were men of the cities and the castles, and though they owned farmlands and flocks in the country, they were at their core men of iron and stonewalls. Geoffrey, as a peasant of the Spade, was a man of the soil and the wood, a difference also made manifest in the rustic nature of his device and arms. His cudgel and targe, Oakheart and Acorn, were hardly the traditional armament of a nobleman with their steel swords and embossed shields. However, they were his, and just as he had grown from farmer into knight, so the red acorn became the holy oak.

When he reached the groom minding his horse at the front of the column, the young man saluted, and at Geoffrey's nod went off to see to his other duties. Seeing to the horse while Geoffrey volunteered to take a turn at watch, was a duty that would normally have been assigned to a squire or a page, yet since Geoffrey had required that Freddy remain at Houndstooth (to protect his mother and sister and to aid Horus, or so he had told him), Sir Owain had offered him one of the other young men of the court. For a moment, Geoffrey sucked his teeth, struggling to remember the lad's name, but to no avail. He was always horrible when it came to names.

One by one, the knights appeared, garbed in their chainmail or plate with their squires, grooms, and trusted sergeants at their sides. There were but five present and thusly armed (in addition to Sir Owain), for of the men of the Weavers' Guild, four of the five had chosen to pay the scutage and enlist, in their stead, hired professional mercenaries to supplement the ranks of the men-at-arms sworn to the court.

With one exception. The remaining weaver knight, Sir Adolfo, accompanied them in person leading his own men. As was the case at the battle with the kingsmen at the lake, the Madder wore no armor himself apart from a studded leather jerkin, and while armed with a thin bladed dueling sword, it seemed more decorative than functional. Apparently, the Madder's men had been busy reconnoitering all throughout the previous night's march, riding on ahead in secret while the bulk of the forces were forced to take their pace from the men afoot or when they paused briefly to make camp and have a few hours' sleep.

St. Golan's was a three day journey from the city, but since haste was of the essence, Sir Owain and the young baron hoped to make it even sooner for fear of what might become of Abbot Woode and Sir Deryk of Lomedan. Thus, they marched swiftly for many miles long into the night; however, the seneschal knew well the dangers of leading a weary army into battle and made certain to ensure that the men had adequate rest.

Geoffrey did not envy Lughus. To be thrust in such a position at such a young age was, at least to Geoffrey, a cruel fate. Still, he was impressed by the young man's handling of it in that he neither shrank from his obligations in fear nor did he petulantly demand that other men bend to his will. Just as he had at their meetings in the Houndstooth solar, he listened to what others had to say and then accepted the responsibility for making the ultimate decision, and though Sir Owain was in many ways sharing the burden of leadership, it was clear that he did so as a means of grooming the young baron for ultimate command.

439

May the Brothers grant him a victory then, Geoffrey thought, for he had taken a liking to the young Marshal, and he knew that, for all their shows of fealty, the rest of the soldiers would regard him as little more than an untested boy. *A boy who's soon to take a wife,* he added with an inward chuckle at the sight of the young couple walking hand in hand behind Sir Owain, the great hound Fergus, as always, following at their side. They nodded greetings to the men nearby and while Owain in his heavy armor, directed the knights and sergeants to call their ranks to order, Lughus and Brigid found their horses.

"Good morning, Sir Geoffrey," Brigid smiled as Lughus helped her up into her saddle. She was clad in the black trousers Jergan had bemoaned designing, though now with the addition of a light shirt of mail, and she had tucked her dark hair up underneath a small steel cap.

"Lady Brigid," Geoffrey smiled.

"Vanguard," Lughus nodded, mounting his horse beside hers. He paused to thank the grooms and then turned back to Geoffrey, "Owain thinks we should reach St. Golan's by late this afternoon."

"We'll get there in time," Geoffrey said optimistically, "I'm sure of it."

Lughus bobbed his head in agreement, though Geoffrey could tell from the look in his eye that he was not so sure. Unfortunately, the fine suit of armor that the young baron had been fitted for had not yet been completed and as a result, he wore the chainmail and quilted gambeson of a common man-at-arms; however, between the embroidered hound upon his surcoat and the golden mop upon his head, there was no mistaking the young Baron Galadin.

While they stood waiting for the remainder of the column to muster, Geoffrey soon found himself forgotten by the two young people who only had eyes for each other, and though he tried not to, he could not help but overhear their conversation.

"Did you sleep well?" Brigid whispered, furtively reaching out to squeeze the young baron's hand, "No dreams?"

"Well enough," Lughus said, "You?"

Brigid gave a nod and smiled, "Although it was very warm with Fergus curled up next to me. No matter what I said, though, he wouldn't leave my side." She batted her eyes, "I wonder why that is?"

440

"He wanted to make sure you were safe, I suppose," the young man said, "But it does explain all the snoring I heard coming from your tent. I just assumed it was you."

"Oh shut up," she laughed.

Geoffrey breathed a sigh and suppressed a smile. With some regret, he recalled the early reservations that he had voiced in private to Annabel so long ago. He was happy to have been proven wrong as he had watched their relationship bloom. They did care for one another, deeply, and with the circumstances of each of their lives—their class, their duties, and their enemies (to say nothing about their characters)—he doubted that either one could ever hope to find a truer partner. Most importantly, however, was the abject happiness they brought one another. Never before had he seen Brigid so happy as when she informed Annabel and him of the impending wedding. Almost at once, Annabel erupted into tears of joy, and for a moment, Geoffrey worried that he too might lose control and shame himself by weeping. Still, it was good; there was a rightness to them, and in the face of war, it was something to offer hope.

He sighed, and naturally, his mind recalled his own wedding to Annabel. They were not much older than Lughus and Brigid, though perhaps by a year or two, and the Cousin who had performed the ceremony was a man named Dugan...or was it Dolan... It was hard to remember now—as it was most of the details apart from his visions of Annabel. She was lovely, the prettiest girl in the village. Her father was a farmer like his (and everyone else's practically), though like her mother and her sister, he had died shortly after the wedding from the red plague. He was a good man, though, and made sure that the wedding was accompanied by a feast to rival that of Harvestide.

How old I've become. Geoffrey shook his head and replaced his helm, remembering the gray hairs Annabel had discovered sprouting at his temples. *Soon I'll be as gray as Old Regnar.* He breathed a sigh and noticed another horse trotting up beside him in the column. Seated on its back, however, fully outfitted for war was a man significantly older and grayer that he was.

"Good morning, Sir Geoffrey," Roland Marthaine said, his voice, even at a normal speaking volume, always sounded to Geoffrey like a harsh whisper.

"Good morning, my lord."

Marthaine paused, shifted in his saddle, and offered a ghastly grimace at the sound of a loud pop when he stretched his back.

After the arrival of the messenger where it was announced that the kingsmen had crossed the border, rather than return to Harrier's Keep, Baron Marthaine, who made it his habit to bring his accoutrements of war with him wherever he went, determined to accompany his grandson. His wife, Lady Morgana, would return home with dispatches providing orders to Marthaine's seneschal and other leading men. Some of the Galadins were still uncomfortable with his presence, particularly Sir Owain, but as he was only one man and the patriarch of the rival barony, his willingness to place himself at their mercy convinced most that he meant them no harm, at least for now.

Another father taking risks for a son, Geoffrey thought, *Interesting.*

When at last the army of Galadin was assembled, Lughus nodded to Sir Owain, and with a shout and a strike of a drum, the march began. According to Sir Deryk's messenger and the reports that fleeing common folk gave to Sir Adolfo's scouts, the force of kingsmen en route to St. Golan's was considerable, numbering between four and five thousand. However, it was but a small detachment from the larger force besieging Agathis. Messengers had been sent to Nordren, Brabant, Glendaro, and Derindale—all of whom should have already been en route to the Houndstooth as it was; however, it was still unlikely that any of them would arrive in time to join in the assault.

The journey across the fields and pastures toward St. Golan's was slow going beneath the heat of the Falcontide sun. Geoffrey was thankful for the horse that bore him, for it wasn't long before his brow was wet with perspiration and he could sense patches of sweat already soaking various areas of his gambeson. He was surprised, however, to find himself so calm in the face of what he knew would be a hard fight against unfavorable odds. Then again, when he reflected upon his past experiences in battle, he realized that such had always been the case—at Ashfort, at the grotto, at the docks. In every case, he had been forced to combat a superior foe, and though he could not claim to be completely without fear, he did not feel as burdened by uncertainty as before.

As the birthplace of the Blessed Saint, it was in Galadin thirteen hundred years ago that Aiden began his rebellion against the Warlock, against tyranny and oppression, so that men might live free of fear. As such, the folk of Galadin, Geoffrey had learned long ago, were a proud and willful people, and in the wake of Andoch's attempts at forcing the Brock into submission, they intended to face the challenges ahead with the steadfast tenacity and determined resolve that the barony's namesake had displayed so long ago. They may not yet know if their new boy baron was worth fighting for, but they would not simply sit by idly while the Guardian-King and his cronies gathered at their walls. Again, Geoffrey remembered the words of Sir Adolfo the Madder—that Galadin was precious to him and something he had no wish to see come to harm. If that was the sentiment of the barony's greatest villain, then woe be to the kingsman who first encountered one of its heroes.

At midday, the army encountered its first fleeing peasants, commonfolk and rustics hoping to head north beyond the reach of Andochan swords. By mid-afternoon, the bands of refugees turned up in droves—on foot, some leading carts, some leading herds, and the occasional man on a plow horse. Most claimed they were on their way to the capital, seeking safety beneath the protective shadow of the Houndstooth. Baron Lughus and Sir Owain halted briefly on occasion to question a few of the folk regarding their pursuers. Most had simply abandoned their cottages and fled at the first sight of smoke on the horizon and had little to say regarding the true nature of their foes. Geoffrey did not blame them. He remembered well from the past wars along the Spade the abject terror that such a sight could evoke. His thoughts and prayers went out not only to the Galadin peasants, but also to Oliver's sons and the other folk of Pyle, including Old Amos, should he still be alive.

As the sun neared the western horizon, the soldiers paused briefly to rest and take their evening meal. According to Sir Owain, St. Golan's was scarcely an hour's march away and more than once had the army of Galadin passed the ruins of a farmstead or the bodies of peasants and occasional livestock butchered by Andochan patrols.

While the men ate what was sure to be their last meal before the battle, watches were set and a small contingent of light horsemen, some sworn to Sir Herbrand and others to Sir Adolfo, were sent to scout the area around the monastery in hopes of discovering more about the position and relative strength of the enemy. The mood among the soldiers—peasant, professional, and noble—was light, and as they supped upon a snack of hard bread, dried fruit, and jerky, Geoffrey found it strange to think that in but a short while so many of these men might die. *What a thing it is to be a soldier...* he thought, his mind returning once more to the Spade, Captain Barrow, Mason, the sergeants, and the slowwitted cook who was the first to fall at Ashfort with an arrow to the eye. *What was his name? Arnold? Ernalt?*

He was still trying to remember when he spied Baron Lughus and his bride-to-be with their great golden hound in tow, wandering together among the soldiers. Those they knew (and whom Geoffrey, for the most part, at least recognized from the Houndstooth) they addressed by name, and those they did not they attempted introductions. It was clear that such a thing was unusual, for rarely, if ever, did nobles seem to offer their social lessers anything more than contempt. To receive a kind word or even a handshake from a baron, and one with the blood of a saint, for that matter, was something else altogether. As he watched the humble nods and smiles the men offered their young lord and lady, Geoffrey was glad once again not to have been born a nobleman. *I can scarcely remember the name of the old cook!* he shook his head with admiration, *Imagine trying to recall a whole bloody army!* He breathed a sigh and took another bite of his bread. "Ernald! That was it! Poor Ernald and his stew!"

"Sounds like a song," said a voice, and reddening with embarrassment, Geoffrey turned toward the speaker and discovered that once more he was in the company of the one other person who among all the sons of Galadin was without place—Roland Marthaine.

"Would that it was, my lord," Geoffrey muttered by way of reply, "But as it is, it was just the name of a man I knew who died."

All through the long ride, the old man remained silent beside Geoffrey, regally poised upon his borrowed warhorse and encased in the somber austerity of his plate armor. His eyes gleamed with determination and focus, anticipating the coming battle, a battle in which he was to fight side by side with men who until but a few weeks prior he had counted as his enemies. Still, Geoffrey did not find the Argent Eagle altogether unsettling, like so many others appeared to. Rather, he found the old man's silence a strange sort of comfort, for he was not a man of many words himself, particularly when it came to small talk, and preferred the quiet camaraderie of men employed on common tasks—such as in Pyle with a team of farmers at work in the field or building a barn or some such. In fact, Geoffrey found that the measure of a man could often be accounted for by what he did not say as opposed to what he did.

Lord Roland dug around inside his saddlebag, drew forth a short stemmed pipe, and paused to light it. When he had it going, the old man took a heavy pull and after a long, wheezing cough, sauntered over to Geoffrey's side. "I have to admit," he said mildly, "That worries me."

Geoffrey raised his eyebrows and glanced out where the old man pointed with his pipe stem toward where Lughus and Brigid were speaking to a cadre of archers. "Those two?" he asked without thinking, "Why?"

Marthaine shrugged. "Don't misunderstand me," he said, "They make each other happy—that much was clear the moment he introduced her at the castle. However, between their births, their titles, and the responsibilities required of them, I doubt very much that life for them will ever be easy."

"Is it for anyone?" Geoffrey asked, somewhat surprised at his own candor toward the old baron, "But at least those two have each other."

"True," Lord Roland observed, "And thank the Brethren for that, for it will be some comfort in the days ahead."

"You fear some ill will befall them?"

"Don't you?"

Geoffrey breathed a sigh. "The hardest of all hardships to endure are those that affect the young," he said, "I lost a son not a year ago. I would hate to lose one who I've come to know in his absence as a..." he paused, "As kin."

The baron nodded. "I too have lost a son," he said, "And one I had hoped I might know as a daughter." He took another pull from his pipe and offered it to Geoffrey. "I'll not let it happen again."

Graciously, Geoffrey accepted the old man's proffered pipe, tried it, and gave it back with a quiet, "Thank you." As he breathed in the lingering heady aroma, he discerned a sudden amity that calmed his nerves in the face of the coming battle, and though the men of Galadin might still suspect the Marthaine patriarch or doubt the sincerity of his commitment to his grandson and the cause, Geoffrey decided that, at least for his part, he was glad the Argent Eagle had insisted in riding along.

As the meal came to an end, the scouts returned from their reconnoitering and Geoffrey and the old baron followed along as the other knights and a few of the veteran sergeants gathered around Sir Owain, Sir Adolfo, and the young baron. For a short while, the three of them spoke together in hushed tones as they waited for the men to assemble, and to Geoffrey's surprise, he glanced over his shoulder to find Brigid and Fergus had somehow fallen in at his and Baron Marthaine's side.

"Fancy seeing you here," Geoffrey told her, "I'd have expected you to be up there with Owain and Adolfo."

The young lady shrugged. "He's the baron," she said, "It's him the men follow, not me."

"Lady Brigid," Lord Roland said, only to catch himself, "I'm sorry. 'Just Brigid.'"

Brigid smiled, "Hello, Lord Roland. It's nice to have you with us."

"Likewise," the old man said.

According to the scouts, the kingsman had surrounded the monastery walls but had not yet begun an assault in earnest, content as they were to await the arrival of the main force laying siege to Agathis. There was no way of telling as yet whether Dorgan's castle at Cragbarrow had fallen, and so haste was of the utmost importance if the Galadin soldiers hoped to avoid the untimely arrival of the remaining Andochan army.

Geoffrey listened as the other men went over the plan of battle, nodded when they asked him to, and tried his best to follow along. Since he was not in any particular command, he would simply be responsible for defending himself, and—as Baron Lughus quietly reminded him with a look of urgency—Lady Brigid. He was her seneschal after all.

When at last all was in order, the knights dispersed and rejoined the column to steel themselves and rally their men before the march resumed. The sun was but a sliver on the western horizon when St. Golan's came into view, and almost immediately the sentries posted around the Andochan camp sounded the alarm. In the dying light the white key of the Guardian-King blazed like a heart of flame on their long red pennants, flanked by the emblems of two dozen noble houses of the northern Andochan fiefdoms.

As if in answer to the kingsmen's trumpeters, the Galadin heralds sounded their calls and the column broke ranks to form the line of battle. *So it begins...* Geoffrey thought to himself. His breath came quicker now as the excitement of battle stirred his blood. He swung lightly down from his horse as a squire took his borrowed mount by the bit and led it away.

At his side, Roland Marthaine lowered the visor on his helm and offered Geoffrey a nod. "May the Brethren protect you, my friend," he said, his gruff voice soft but steady.

Geoffrey raised Oakheart in front of his face in what he knew from Regnar's memories was the traditional warrior's salute. "And you, my lord," he said.

Marthaine drew his heavy iron mace, Thunderclap, and wheeling his horse about, trotted off down the line while Geoffrey hurried ahead to join Brigid, Lughus, and Sir Owain.

"Alright, my lady?" Geoffrey asked Brigid as she slipped from her horse.

The young woman bit her lip, wiped her hands along her trousers and touched the hilts of her daggers. "I think so." Around them, a contingent of the other knights and men-at-arms dismounted and shouldered their lances. "You?"

"I'm fine," Geoffrey said, surprised suddenly by the truth of his words. For the first time in his short tenure as a warrior, he felt less out of place than ever in the past. Whereas previously, he felt a fool, a farmer masquerading as a fighter, he now felt...different, as if he were somehow—much to his surprise—exactly where he was supposed to be, doing exactly what he was supposed to do. He really *was* Sir Geoffrey Pyle, Defender of the Spade, anointed the Vanguard, and a Guardian in the name of St. Aiden.

Sir Owain Rook unsheathed his massive great sword, and shouted orders down the line. Beside him, the young baron took a deep breath, readied his own blade, and ran a hand along Fergus's shoulder. Somewhat tentatively, Brigid stepped to his side and, her cheeks flushed with color, hurriedly offered him a quick, furtive kiss—or would have, had the young man not gently held her fast so as to prolong the moment. Some private words passed between them, lost in the clatter and clang of the other soldiers readying their arms. *Lady save them,* Geoffrey sighed, *Brethren keep them safe.* When they finally drew apart, he stepped nearer. "Marshal."

"Vanguard," Baron Lughus said, though Geoffrey could discern a certain depth in the young man's eyes, a yearning, a concern, almost a plea. However, all he said was, "I have to stand with the front rank, to lead them."

"Then we'll stand with you." Brigid smiled.

"No," the young man said hurriedly, too hurriedly, "I would rather you guard our flank." His gray eyes flashed, "Or better still, the rear."

At once, Geoffrey understood. "Aye, my lord," he said.

"What?" Brigid said, "You must be joking. I'm not leaving your side."

"Brigid, please..." Lughus said.

447

Brigid's blue eyes flashed with cold fire. "The Three stand together!" she said. "As it always has been, it must be."

Geoffrey could feel the young baron's eyes upon him, but he feigned interest in the archers nearby forming their ranks.

"Alright," Lughus sighed at last, "As you say."

Together, the Three made their way along the line to the center of the front rank of infantry. There, Sir Owain was directing the sergeants to place their men-at-arms carefully within the larger mass of archers. Each man had been armed with a spear, a pike, a javelin, or any other type of improvised polearm. For as the strength of the Brock lie in their archers, it was the prerogative of the knights and other footmen to protect them should any horsemen be lucky enough to pass unscathed through the storm of arrows unleashed by each Galadin volley. Brigid took the place at Lughus's right, opposite Sir Owain, and Geoffrey, beside her, tightened his grip on his cudgel and targe.

"You're sure you wouldn't rather guard the flank?" the young baron whispered once more to his bride-to-be.

"I'm exactly where I want to be," she replied. "Stop worrying. I'm as much a warrior as you."

"I know you are. I wasn't doubting you."

"Then shut your mouth." She grinned. "Side by side, remember? Come what may."

"I know," he said. "I'm sorry. I won't ask again." He took a deep, bracing breath. "We're strongest together," he said, and nodded to Geoffrey. "All of us. The Three."

Fergus gave a terse bark.

Geoffrey smiled. "I think that means 'Four.'"

Across the field, the Andochan soldiers had formed their lines and were slowly advancing across the field to join the battle. The heavy plate of the mounted knights glimmered in the setting sun and the red cloaks flailing behind them made them seem, to Geoffrey at least, like men made of flame. Out of the corner of his eye, he glanced at Brigid, her jaw set and gaze narrowed, and he wondered once more at her. She was such a waifish, mousey thing it was easy to forget that she was more than capable when it came to killing.

"They're almost within range," Sir Owain observed, breaking the silence.

Baron Lughus nodded, and with Fergus in tow, paced forth ahead of the battle line and raised his voice.

"King Kredor and the Guardians believe that they can simply march across the Brock and attack our cities? Do they forget that it was here in Galadin where the Order began? With men such as all of you fighting for their lands, their homes, and their families?" He paused, "Archers! Ho!"

Among the rank and file, there was the sound of shuffling as bowmen stepped out and prepped their arrows, pinning them into the ground at their feet like goose-feathered palisades. Many of them had removed their boots and shoes so as to maintain better footing while firing their longbows. Across the plain, the Andochan battle line continued to advance. Geoffrey's heart beat faster in his chest and his grip tightened around the wooden haft of Oakheart. The young baron raised his sword and behind him, the Andochan knights and mounted kingsmen spurred their horses to charge.

"Let's remind them of how we in Galadin deal with tyrants!" he shouted, "Let fly!"

By the time the first volley met the oncoming riders, the third was being released, and the front ranks of man and horse crumpled in a dark cloud of ruin. Long, thin arrow shafts pierced through metal plate and barding, sinking down deep into the soft flesh beneath. As the first riders fell, those behind were thrown into confusion, their progress slowed as they attempted to maneuver around their fallen comrades to continue the charge, easy pickings for the next round of volleys loosed by the Galadin archers.

Two entire companies of heavy horse, or as near as Geoffrey could tell, had fallen before the Andochan commander called off the mounted charge. A cheer rang out from the Galadin host as the remaining horsemen rode back into place behind the infantry, advancing slowly now with their shields held before them in a tight defensive formation.

"Another round to soften them up, and then we run to meet them!" Sir Owain cried merrily.

"As you say," Lughus said, though without the old knight's mirth.

"This time we fight as Three," Brigid grinned, and remembering, added, "Four. I mean four."

When the final flight of arrows hit home, Sir Owain thrust his massive sword into the air and shouted, "Galadin! Galadin! Go!"

Like two charging bulls, the armies met in the center of the field with a resounding clash. Geoffrey's heart beat faster and faster and his lungs sucked in great torrents of air as battle frenzy took hold of him. The first man he met wore a domed, steel nasal helm that crumpled like a nutshell beneath Oakheart's first hammer-blow. The second, he knocked to his knees with a blow from the Acorn, stunning him long enough for Fergus to leap forth and find the man's throat. Hot blood streamed forth from the wound, coating the hound's jaws with gore. Nearby, Geoffrey glanced over to see Brigid fighting in tandem beside Lughus. The young man's sword was a whirlwind of death, shining like a torch in the low light, raining down blows like bolts of lightning in a summer storm. And at his side, beneath the shadow of those storm clouds, Brigid was more than earning her title. For, while Lughus would draw their enemies to him, engaging three or four men at once, Brigid would slip in quickly beside or behind and dispatch them while they were focused on the young baron, sinking her daggers between the seams of their armor, only to leap away again like a deadly ghost.

When the initial clash of the armies passed and the fighting settled in, Geoffrey turned around to stand back-to-back with the young couple and together the Three waded deeper into the oncoming horde of Guardian soldiers, carving a path of blood and gore through rank after rank of the enemy army. Man after man fell before the combined might of the Three; so many that Geoffrey soon lost count. Before long, the blue and gold tabards of the Galadin Hounds outnumbered the red cloaks of the kingsmen and the assorted emblems of the Andochan nobles. The dead lay in heaps across the field, black lumps beneath a darkening sky, and the ground was slick with blood.

Yet suddenly, from the Andochan siege camp, a cheer rang out and Geoffrey felt his chest tighten in alarm. All about him, the warriors of both armies froze, their ears ringing with the sound of thunder, and as Geoffrey peered into the gloom, he saw them—the remaining force of heavy horse, having regrouped from their first failed charge, had reformed their lines and now drove on once more, heedless of whether they rode down friend or foe.

A slight pain in his upper arm drew Geoffrey's attention away from the riders and he recalled with annoyance the kingsman he was engaged with upon the field. Quickly, he knocked the man's sword aside with the Acorn, caved in his ribcage with Oakheart, and cried out to his companions.

450

A few yards away, a man swung his bearded axe in desperation at Brigid, but she easily dodged the blow and countered, slicing the man across the shoulder and throat. Beside her, Lughus swept his sword down from on high, splitting another soldier from shoulder to navel. As he wrenched the blade free from the man's innards, Brigid touched his shoulder, and the two paused briefly to meet Geoffrey's gaze.

"Riders!" the farmer shouted.

"Blast!" the young baron cursed and turned to assess the new threat.

Suddenly, Brigid sheathed her daggers and from among the fallen soldiers at their feet lifted the haft of a long pike. "Look here!" she cried, "There are more of them!"

The young baron called out over his shoulder to the nearest squad of Galadin men-at-arms while Geoffrey dug among the corpses for any other pikes, spears, or fallen lances that might help to repel the charge.

"Hurry!" Brigid called, as Lughus, Geoffrey and the other men scrambled to form a tight cluster of sharpened polearms alongside her.

"Brace yourselves!"

With a loud crash, the lead horseman drove forward into the wall of spears hoping to break through. Geoffrey grunted against the force of the enemy's charge and with all his strength, fought to maintain his footing. The agonizing squeal of the rider's horse impaling itself upon the pike shook him to the bone, but he held fast to the haft of his weapon and dug his heels even deeper into the choppy dirt. At last, the poor creature fell silent and dropped backwards onto the ground, crushing its rider to death beneath its own weight.

"Lady save us!" He winced at the sight.

"Alright, Geoffrey?" Brigid gasped.

The farmer nodded and readied his targe and cudgel again, "You two?"

Brigid gave a weary smile. "It's not over yet."

"Far from it." Lughus pointed, as the knights lucky enough to break through the Galadin line reigned in their mounts to fight at close quarters.

"We're with you, my lord!" one of the men-at-arms exclaimed.

Lughus dropped his pike and drew his sword. "For Galadin!" he shouted, "Release the hounds!"

"Release the hounds!" the men of Galadin echoed.

Suddenly from nearby, the low rumble of a second charge shook the ground underfoot. *Not again!* Geoffrey gasped in exacerbation, scrambling to ready his pike. However, to his shock and surprise, the riders that rolled in across the plane were not kingsmen, but the remainder of the Galadin horse kept in reserve, and at the head of the charging line was none other than the Argent Eagle, Roland Marthaine, whirling his great mace overhead like a wheel.

"For the Brock!" the old man roared, driving his horse headlong into the thickest mass of Andochan horsemen.

"By the gods!" one of the man-at-arms muttered at Geoffrey's side, "I'm glad he's on our side—at least for today."

"Aye," Geoffrey replied, "Me too."

Brigid's lips spread into a wide grin and she nudged Lughus gently with her shoulder, "Back to it, eh?"

"Aye," the young baron said, his eyes ablaze with the selfsame lightning as the old baron. Fergus let loose a savage howl as together the Three shouted, "For the Brock!"

Before long, the kingsmen had been driven back, past their encampments outside of the monastery's walls. Steadily, the common levees and infantrymen from among the Andochan army began to scatter, turn tail, and flee while the honor guard of knights and nobles in command formed a small, defensive column and rode off hastily to the southwest.

"Holy St. Aiden," Geoffrey breathed in exhaustion, dropping heavily to one knee. He removed his kettle helm and wiped the thick coating of sweat and blood splatter from his brow. At his side, Brigid's shoulder slumped with weariness and she wiped her daggers clean upon the backs of her trousers. "Alright?" she asked.

Lughus gave a nod and sheathed his sword, "You?"

Brigid slipped her daggers back into her Baldric and gave the young baron a quick kiss. "Just wonderful," she grinned.

At long last, in the dim light of the besiegers' bonfires, the army of Galadin gathered at the gates of St. Golan's in victory to be received by Abbot Woode and Sir Deryk of Lomedan. Only then could they begin to account for their wounded and dead.

Sir Owain, thankfully, was among the former as opposed to the latter. In the fury of the battle, he became separated from the young baron and found himself and a small squad of guards surrounded by kingsmen. Whirling his great two-handed sword, the seneschal carved a pathway back to the main body of the Galadin host, but in the process took a wound from a kingsman's pike beneath the arm and snapped the blade of his own mighty weapon in twain. Still, he and all of the men who had been lost with him were alive, and the old knight himself was on his feet to stand beside his baron and claim the victory.

"Saints alive!" Abbot Woode chuckled and grasped Lughus's hand. "Surely the blood of Aiden is strong in you, my boy."

"I'm only glad we were able to get here in time," the young man said.

"Indeed you did," Woode nodded, "With all the common folk who arrived seeking refuge, we were in no way prepared to withstand a prolonged siege." He paused to offer his hands to the others at Lughus's side. "Lady Brigid! Sir Geoffrey! How good it is to find you here too."

"Aye, sir," Geoffrey said, conscious suddenly of the blood and filth that coated his body from head to toe. His snowy, white tabard was speckled with bright teardrops of vivid crimson, yet the abbot seemed not to mind as they shook.

Brigid, at least, remembered to remove her gloves, before taking the abbot's hand, but as she did so, her face reddened, burning with impatience of her personal request. Not to Geoffrey's surprise, the young baron's coloring changed to match hers.

"Alright, Woode. Enough with the niceties." Sir Owain smirked. "It was the beer we were really here to save, not you!"

"Then to the victors go the spoils," said the abbot, "You and your men have earned it."

"My lord, I would not claim victory just yet," said a voice, and with a heavy sigh Geoffrey recognized it as belonging to Sir Adolfo the Madder. The weaver knight's quiver was significantly lighter and his boots were splattered with mud; however, apart from that, he was unsullied and unscathed.

"My scouts and I have learned that the remaining force of kingsmen are to arrive here at any moment," the Madder said, pressing the fingertips of his gloves together, "These men were sent ahead to gain a foothold in Galadin whilst the rest remained behind to complete the siege of Agathis. They were but a third of the main army."

"He's right," said a young man clad in chainmail standing among the abbot's attendants. "The men you fought were but a fraction of Kredor's kingsmen sent to supplement the Andochan nobles under the command of Lord Deglan Tensley. The Guardians—the partisans and the main battalions of red-cloaks—are under the command of Sir Brennan Bercilan."

"Anointed the Chough," Lughus said. "A justiciar of the Warlord."

"Aye, that's what they called him, my lord," said the young knight who Geoffrey could only assume was Sir Deryk. "They demanded we surrender this afternoon, claiming they'd just received word that Agathis had fallen. Whether or not that's true, I cannot say. In any case, we refused them."

"Good man." Sir Owain nodded.

"But if they were telling the truth," one of the other knights said, "The Chough or whatever-they-call-him could arrive at any moment."

"With ten thousand men at his back," said another.

"We should waste no more time then," the first rejoined, "Form up the army and the folk of the monastery and ride with all haste back to Galadin. Surely the other barons and their men might have made it to Houndstooth by now?"

"Or we could ride out to meet the Andochans head on. They won't expect to find us so soon, will they? Perhaps we might take them by surprise."

"Don't be fools," Roland Marthaine growled. "Your men are weary and wounded. They need rest."

"Baron Marthaine." Abbot Woode bowed to mask the sudden flood of resentment from the Galadin knights, "I apologize. It is good to see you again, my lord."

The old man grunted a laugh, "I doubt that, Woode."

"Alright, alright," Sir Owain said, wincing against his wound. "Though I hate to admit it, I agree with Baron Marthaine. The men need rest, and the longer we stand here, the more time we waste. Sir Adolfo, how long until the Guardians arrive?"

The Madder pursed his lips, "A few of the prisoners claim that their return was imminent; however, I am not certain. I plan to speak with them again once we are finished here. Then, perhaps, I will know more."

Brigid's eyes flashed, "I suppose these prisoners offered that information freely? Or under duress?"

"My lady," Adolfo sighed, "It is customary to award prisoners of noble birth the privilege of ransom. You may rest assured that they will not be harmed."

"And the common men?"

"I'm afraid custom is not quite clear on their behalf."

"Enough. Everyone, be calm," Baron Lughus said. He breathed a sigh and shook his head, "First, Sir Adolfo, any and all prisoners are to be turned over to Sir Owain immediately. You may question them, but under his supervision."

"Yes, my lord."

"As for the rest of us, we shall stay here and fortify the monastery. We are far too few to meet the Kingsmen head on and too weary to return to Galadin. I will send word to Horus and the others back at Houndstooth with messages for any of our allies that may have arrived. Sir Emont and Sir Forgan at the least should have made it by now, and if we're lucky, Brabant, Derindale, or Igrainne. Hopefully, they can relieve us should the Chough appear and besiege us." He paused, "For now, though, we should have the men eat and rest in shifts while those who are able can begin digging wolftraps and setting palisades. Balric, Gosbert, perhaps you can oversee that?"

"Aye, sir."

"And Sir Deryk, you've defended St. Golan's thus far, I would welcome your opinions as to maintaining its defenses."

"My honor, sir," said Sir Deryk, "And if you would like, my lord, my men know the lands between here and Agathis well. They could ride out to see what our enemies are up to."

"That would be welcome. Thank you," Lughus continued, "Perhaps your men, Sir Adolfo, would be willing to assist since they seem so skilled in this regard."

"Of course, my lord."

The young baron breathed another heavy sigh, "Alright then. We can speak again once these matters are settled."

"There is space within the walls for the wounded, my lord," the abbot said, "And my Cousins stand by to assist. I will also see that quarters are prepared for you, Lady Brigid, and your captains as well."

"Thank you," Lughus said, "But see to the wounded first."

"Of course, my lord."

"Then let's make haste. There's no telling how much time we have."

With grunts of assent, the men of Galadin hurried to perform their duties leaving only Geoffrey, Brigid, and Baron Roland alone with the young baron and his golden hound. Geoffrey took off his gloves and rubbed the weariness out of his eyes. He was tired and dirty and longed to lie down somewhere with a pint of the Ram's Reward. Though he bore no grievous wounds, he had plenty of bumps, bruises, and scratches, and his shoulders ached from the weight of his chainmail. Beside him, Brigid too looked weary, staring off into the middle distance, her eyes half-closed.

"Wake up." Geoffrey winked. "It's not over yet."

Wearily, she smiled and did her best to fight the effects of fatigue.

Only Roland Marthaine seemed unaffected. Though no less stained by the marks of battle, the old man was like a gnarled, old tree that, though leafless and battered by wind and storm, refused to fall. Once the men of Galadin were out of earshot, the old baron took off his helm and rested it on his hip. "You did well," he told his grandson, "A fine first victory."

"Thank you," Lughus said, idly ruffling Fergus's ears, "Let's hope it's not the last."

"So dour." Brigid smirked and turned to the Argent Eagle. "I'm beginning to believe that's another thing he gets from you."

The old man's stony features cracked. "Perhaps."

The young baron gave a weak smile. "I have to meet Sir Deryk and oversee things," he said, "But if you should walk the fortifications and have any advice, I'd be glad to hear it."

"Certainly," the old man said.

"What do you need from Geoffrey and me?" Brigid asked.

Lughus bit his lip. "I'd like you to rest, really," he said lowly, "But since I know you'll refuse, perhaps you might speak to the common folk, the peasants who came to St. Golan's seeking shelter. You both have a way of speaking to them that they appreciate, and that's important, especially now. Take Fergus with you too. Let them know the Golden Hound of Galadin has not forsaken them."

"Aye, sir," Geoffrey said, "As you say."

"Then we should get to it," Lughus said, "The Chough is a seasoned commander and there are plenty of legends about him in his own right. We'll not brush him aside as easily as we did Lord Tensley."

Lord Roland nodded in agreement, and motioning for Geoffrey to follow, began pacing away toward the remainder of the army.

"It's nice to have a reason to fight again," the old man sighed.

"For the Brock?" Geoffrey asked.

"Aye, for the Brock," Marthaine said, "But more importantly, for a family, for a future."

Geoffrey glanced behind them and saw that Brigid had lingered at the young baron's side, the great hound loping about them merrily. Once more his thoughts returned to Annabel and the children, blessedly safe in the Houndstooth. "Aye, my lord," he told the old man, "It can lead a man to do incredible things."

"So long as it doesn't ruin him."

Geoffrey paused. "Surely, she must be right then," he smirked, "You are the source of his grim spirit."

Again, Marthaine smiled, "Sure enough, then. He's mine."

CHAPTER 36: THE DEATH KNELL

By the time the armies of the Winter Rose had mustered upon the field outside of Pridel, news of the Death Knell's bloody approach from the north spread like wildfire, faster even than the flight of the peasants who fled before him. Since their lords had declared for the rebel queen, the towns and villages that lie between Reginal and the White Wood were now subject to the raiding and pillaging that was a customary part of war. It mattered little that the poor farmers and craftsmen, women and children, old and infirm who called such places home had not had any say in the decisions of their social superiors to join with the queen and the Tower, but Kurlan Malacco was a man for whom blood and slaughter were their own reward, and any unfortunate whose home happened to lie upon the lands of a rebel lord was to be treated as a rebel himself.

When those few survivors began arriving in Pridel in the days after Canton's visit, their faces masks of horror and dumb despair from witnessing the rapine destruction of their lands and the wanton murdering of their neighbors, Beledain's fists clenched in wrath just as his heart grew heavier with guilt. For a time he considered sending the light cavalry to provide escort for the fleeing refugees and to confound the Death Knell's approach. However, he knew that to do so would deprive the mustering army of the bulk of their horsemen, for many of the nobles were slow to heed the call to arms, and should Malacco arrive earlier than expected, Bel wanted his most trusted men and women close at hand.

Still, it was not an easy choice, and despite his rank and title, Bel found himself unable to meet the despondent gazes of the peasants as they told him their tales of dead husbands, sullied wives, and slaughtered babes.

"You must have expected this," Sir Emory told him following one of the more terrible accounts of Malacco's depravity. "You know your brother for what he truly is now, and the Death Knell is no better."

"That does not make it any easier," Bel said. His jaw ached from clenching his teeth and his stomach churned with bile and rancor.

"Perhaps the sound of the Death Knell will hasten the nobles and their levees to our side."

"Aye, we can hope."

However, by the time the scouts returned with reports that Malacco's forces were encamped within a day's march of Pridel in the ruins of the small farming village of Glennhoof, only but two-thirds of the sworn noblemen had arrived with their soldiers in support of the new queen. A few of the absent lords had sent token forces of yeoman militia or ill-equipped mobs of peasant rabble under the command of a sergeant or a minor knight. In any case, they claimed their lords were needed to maintain the defenses of their own castles and would, unfortunately, not be able to heed the queen's call. It was disappointing, for though Bel's army had continued to swell in size, his heavy horse would find itself significantly outnumbered by Malacco's knights and mounted men-at-arms. Like in a fist fight, the light cavalry could pepper the opponent with jab after jab, but it was nice to have the heavy horse when you wanted to deliver a good, solid punch.

It matters little now, Bel thought as Briden helped him don his armor. Like his lord, the young man had replaced the Black Horse upon his tabard with the Winter Rose. Sir Emory stood with them, leaning against the window frame, gazing out at the encamped army as it broke and formed ranks.

"The weather should be clear," the old knight said without turning, "And the land between here and Glennhoof is fine and flat. Your light riders will have an advantage in that."

459

"Aye," Bel nodded, "Easier to maneuver." He paused, "Are you certain that you won't ride out with us?"

Sir Emory shook his head, "As much as I'd like, my place is at your father's side. Besides," he gave a snort, "I'm too old."

Bel shrugged. "I'm not so sure of that," he said, "Though it'll be a comfort to know that you will be here alongside Marcus and Marina. Since Armel is to take the field, I wanted someone in command here that I trusted in the event that I should fall."

"I'll guard them with my life," Emory said, "No matter what should come to pass."

"Thank you."

"If it's all right with you, sir," Briden said, "I'll go tend to Tempest and Maggie?"

Bel nodded. "I'll be along in a moment," he said, "I'll see my son before I go."

"Aye, the queen wishes to see you too," Emory added.

"Alright," Bel said, though part of him hoped he might escape without a final audience, for in light of the coming battle, he feared the manner in which her affection for him might make itself manifest—almost as much as he feared his own feelings for her. However, to ignore her at a time such as this would be the height of discourtesy.

Once Bel was armed and armored, he and Emory parted with young Briden and together made their way to castle's private apartments. The men of Marina's household guard saluted them as they passed, each man chosen personally by Emory, Armel, or Bel himself, and though they too would not fight in the coming battle, Bel trusted that each man among them would freely give his life in defense of the queen, the old kings, and the new Tower's infant son.

At length, when they arrived in Bel's quarters, they were met by the soft hum of feminine voices, and inside discovered not only Elsa the nursemaid, but also the queen's handmaid, Lourdes, as well as Marina herself. At once, the two maids bowed their heads and Marina's emerald eyes went wide as if suddenly caught unawares. She held Marcus gently to her, the tufts of his soft, dark hair against her fair cheek. "Lord Tower!" she said.

"My lady," Bel said, faltering beneath her gaze. She wore a light dress of sage green, simple but finely cut, and framed by the curling tendrils of her bright hair, she appeared yet again the very image of a winter rose.

"I hope you will pardon the intrusion," she continued, "But I wished to see you before you took the field and I suspected that you would not depart without first visiting Marcus."

"You were correct," Bel said, "Though I'm afraid I cannot offer you pardon, for the castle is yours, my lady, and it is not my place or any others' to prevent you walking where you will."

Marina gave a weak smile, but remained silent.

A long moment passed in silence until suddenly, Sir Emory cleared his throat. "Your majesty," he said, "If you'll excuse me, I must see to your fathers."

"Oh yes," Marina smiled vacantly.

The old knight gave a nod and touched Bel's shoulder. "Gods be with you today, my friend," he said and withdrew, the two maids, unasked and unbidden, following after him.

Fire and Death, Bel thought, a tremor of anxiety creeping down his spine, *Not now...*

The young queen too seemed to grow more flustered and her fair cheeks blossomed with a soft, rosy glow. "I expect you wish to see your son," she said hurriedly.

Bel took a deep breath and removed his gauntlets, "I would."

Marina nodded, "Would you like to sit?"

"Only after you, your majesty—" he paused, remembering, "My apologies. Marina."

The queen smiled nervously, but said nothing as she sat down in one of the soft chairs alongside Marcus's cradle. Bel waited until she was seated before assuming the other chair himself, aware suddenly that his knees and elbows seemed to have somehow joined with the tempered steel of his poleyns and vambraces.

"Your son," Marina said at last, offering the child, and for instant, his heart stopped. For, seated across from him, all at once, he saw not only Marina, but Lilia as well, looking just as she had on the morning of Marcus's birth. Without warning, a great rush of emotion struck him in the chest like the hammer blow of a great maul.

461

"Bel?" the queen called gently, still holding the baby, "Bel, are you unwell?"

Beledain's head fell to his hands and his breath came slow and thick. He lurched back to his feet and turned his back to her. "Sir Emory Knott will command the city's defenses during the battle," he said stiffly, absurdly. "Should I fall, he will defend it and you with his life, if need be. He is a good man and a seasoned warrior. You can trust him."

"I have long trusted Sir Emory," Marina said.

Bel nodded absently. His head felt strange, wooden, and he felt the color draining from his face. It was becoming increasingly difficult to think straight, yet for some reason he could not stop himself from talking, the thoughts spilling from his lips as suddenly as they formed.

"Kurlan Malacco is more monster than man, and should he succeed in sacking the city, he will not hesitate to lay it to waste. No matter what happens, you cannot let him catch you. He knows no nobility nor has he any sense of honor."

"Bel..."

"There will be no negotiating or diplomacy, so do not for a moment think of entreating him by sacrificing yourself for the good of the city or the people. You must think only of yourself and your escape," he shook his head and rubbed his eyes, "If you can escape the city, make your way west to Sir Norton and from there..."

"Bel..."

"From there, head southwest to my Uncle Leon at Shoulderidge—No, not Shoulderidge. Dermont might use Val to subdue Leon. Head north to Hoarfrost and Uncle Talvert. He has friends in Baronbrock. Perhaps they might offer refuge. In any case, you cannot let them get you. You cannot!"

"Bel!"

Bel's vision clouded with images of the past, Dermont, Malacco, and the others beating him as a boy, Larius's cold corpse being placed in its tomb beside his wife and child, Marcus Harding saluting him before their duel upon the Nivanus, Lilia painted and cackling like a madwoman riding beside him in battle. Jarvy, Sir Linton, Igno, Banshee, silver bells, golden bells, silent bells, ringing from the belfry of a single stone tower, its tall, steel spire stained with blood. "You cannot let them take you, either of you," he gasped, "You cannot! Promise me, that you will not!"

"Beledain, please!" the queen called gently, "Calm yourself! Please!"

"Promise me," he said earnestly, "I need you to promise!"

"Hush, Bel! Hush!" she shushed him, and holding the baby in one arm, touched the other to his side. "Be calm." Her arm slipped around his surcoat, and gently drew him closer. Even clad all in his armor, he sensed a certain warmth radiating from her. Mindful of the child, Bel wrapped his arms around the both of them, and as she continued to whisper softly to him, held her closer.

"Far too many have already fallen," he said at last.

"And many more will join them before this is all over," she told him.

Slowly his vision began to clear, and he discerned the sleeping visage of his son, safe and content in the young queen's arms. "I cannot bear the thought of either of you being among them," he said at last.

Marina sighed and tentatively let her head fall to his shoulder. "You are the greatest warrior I have ever known, my Tower," she said, "But even you cannot save everyone."

Bel's shoulders slumped in anguish. "I know," he said softly, "But I can try."

She smiled, "As you always have done, and always will do."

At length, Bel nodded and with a great sigh, let the queen slip free from his embrace. "I should take the field," he said, "I plan to meet Malacco before ever he reaches the walls of the city."

The young queen's red lips spread into a forlorn smile, "I will await your return then."

Bel gave a nod, and lifting his son into his arms, kissed the child on the brow. "I'm...sorry," he said a moment later as he returned the baby to the queen, "Forgive me."

"For what?" she asked, cradling the child.

"For just now," he told her, "It unmans me."

Marina shook her crimson locks and her green eyes flashed, "Men may clad themselves in iron and steel, my lord, but the heart beneath is meant to be soft and warm, else the gods would not have made us this way."

"I suppose," Bel said.

Once more, Marina offered him a gentle smile, and very slowly, drew near to him once more to plant a kiss upon his lips. "In any case, Lord Tower," she said, "It's your heart that makes me love you."

For a long moment afterward, Bel stood frozen, unable to move or to speak until at last, with a deep bow, he departed to assume command of the army.

Outside of the castle walls, Bel was met by his captains and those nobles who had appeared in person to join in the battle. Armel, Welmsey, and the Malets wore their heavy plate alongside the painted captains of the light company, Horn, Wendell, and Sparrow. The Shackle, for now at least, rode upon a borrowed mare, though, as he reminded them at regular intervals, once the battle was met, he would take to his own two feet rather than trust in some beast, however noble it might be. Also present were Lords Grimbol and Kindel, Sirs Lorgan and Kedgen, as well as a few other men of rank and high birth, though it was clear from their faces and their posture that they were uncomfortable with the motley crew of captains and the camaraderie they displayed in defiance of social convention.

Bel accepted Tempest's bridle from Briden with a nod of thanks before swinging up into the saddle. "Raise the colors, Briden," Bel nodded.

"Aye, sir!"

Bel steeled himself, forcing all thoughts of death and failure from his mind. Marina might value the heart beneath the armored shell, but on the battlefield, it was the iron exterior that often saved a man's life. That, and a fine horse. He removed his gauntlet and patted Tempest's flank. The searoan knickered and shook his head, and by some uncanny bond, Bel felt suddenly strengthened by the great stallion's charismatic presence. He took a deep breath and forced a grin. "Do you hear that, gentlemen?" he asked, recalling Marcus Harding's tone, "The Death Knell sounds his call. Little does he know it tolls for him."

The gathered men raised their gauntlets in a rallying cry as Briden held the standard aloft. "Let's ride!"

Together, the horsemen rode from the castle gates through the cobblestone streets of the castle town to where the remainder of the army awaited outside of the city walls. The sunlight shone brightly upon the steel blades of the infantrymen's pikes and the great helms of the heavy horsemen as the soldiers marched in formation like the mechanisms of some strange machine. Bel replaced his own helm and rode alone at the head of the column, Armel and the Shackle behind him to the left and right.

He concentrated on breathing, forcing his mind to be quiet as he led the way toward Glennhoof. In one sense, he welcomed the coming fight. There was a certain purity in battle, when the rest of the world seemed to fade away and one could act purely in terms of duality—friend and foe, alive or dead, victory or defeat. It was simpler, easier.

Bel took a deep breath and, again, reached out to pat the barding armor alongside Tempest's flank. The summer breeze was cool and carried with it the scent of the meadow flowers. He recalled another battle, last summer or perhaps the spring before, part of the long campaign that was to culminate in the Battle of the White Wood. The light cavalry had been tasked with hunting down a band of skirmishers like themselves, deserters from both sides of the Bloodline hoping to carve out their own fortunes through waylaying any folk unlucky enough to be caught unawares upon the road. There was a type of justice to it, hunting down bandits and criminals. The waters were much less muddy than in a real battle.

Bel sighed. His actions upon the Nivanus were meant to end the war, not begin it anew. *Blood and Death!* he wondered to himself, *Will there never be peace?*

No, at least not for the moment, he realized, for on the horizon, he suddenly spied a lone horseman. The Death Knell could scarcely be an hour away. He murmured for Tempest to halt, and before long, the rest of the army did as well.

A few of the White Wood nobles broke from the column and rode toward him, but a threatening glare from the Shackle kept them from drawing too close. "What is it?" one of them asked.

"A scout," Sir Armel muttered.

Horn and Sparrow rode up alongside him. "Should we go after him?" the girl asked.

Bel took a deep breath and shook his head. "No," he said, "The Death Knell can't be too far off now. We'll wait here and let him come to us." He nodded toward Armel and the others, ignoring the perturbation of the noblemen, "Have the heavy horse form ranks in front of the infantry and have the light cavalry divide into two so as to guard the flanks."

"Heavy horse before the infantry?" Lord Grimbol asked, "Should not the infantry stand first?"

465

The Shackle made a noise of impatience. Bel ignored him, but his reply to the nobleman was marked with no less brevity, for he knew it was not a question of tactics that gave Lord Grimbol pause.

"No."

Silence lingered on the air for a moment longer than Bel would have liked, but it soon passed as Sir Armel spoke. "We have our orders," he said to the others, "Make it so."

Quickly, the men spurred their horses into action, passing word to the sergeants who in turn shouted commands to the remaining men and women of the queen's army. The Shackle and a handful of his woodsman took position along the right flank beside the contingent of light cavalry commanded by Wendel and Horn. Sparrow had the remaining group on the left flank beside the infantry under the command of Malet the Elder. Armel, Welmsey, Malet the Younger, and the remaining knights and mounted men-at-arms that comprised the heavy cavalry formed their ranks as commanded, but no sooner had they done so than Lord Grimbol and Lord Kindel left the line of battle to assert their rank and influence by joining their Lord-General and his standard-bearer as they watched the military exercise.

Though he knew they might find it unseemly, Bel did not join the two noblemen in their idle conversation, relying instead upon his former title to explain his silence, for his mood had grown black in anticipation of the coming battle and as the sun climbed higher in the eastern sky, so grew his appetite for blood and carnage. *Kurlan Malacco, the Death Knell, Dermont's best friend and seneschal, Warden of Reginal and a monster of a man,* Bel thought. *For the sake of the queen, for the sake of my son, for the sake of the people of Montevale, he cannot survive this day.*

And as if by some unnatural summons, a fanfare sounded. Spreading across the plane to the north like the shadow of some great carrion bird, the enemy army appeared in view. A moment later, Sir Armel rode to Bel's side.

"The men are in position, my lord," he said.

Bel gave a nod. "Good." He took a swig of water from the leather skin in his saddlebag and spit. "It will be a moment before they are in position."

Lord Kindel lifted the visor of his helm with a metallic squeak. "My lord," he said, "I believe they send another rider."

Lord Grimbol pointed along the plane. "Yes, just there," he said, "Shall we meet him?"

Sir Armel's mustache bristled and he raised an eyebrow at his commander. Bel recalled the last time he entreated one of Dermont's messengers. It was doubtful that the Death Knell would be any more cordial. "Very well," he said at last. "We shall see what he has to say."

The messenger was a young knight in his early twenties with full plate armor polished to a mirror-like sheen. Upon his surcoat, a sable tern raised its head just as haughtily as its wearer.

"Gilgoyne," Armel whispered to Bel. "Father's scutage bought half a legion of mercenaries for Marius."

"Yet now he sends his sons to fight with Malacco," Bel replied as the young man reached him.

"After the sacking of Delfoal, Prince Gislain took exception to Gilgoyne's notion of 'spoils' and had four of the Tern's men hanged."

Bel set his jaw and nudged Tempest forward to greet the messenger. Briden gave the haft of the standard a shake to catch the wind; the red rosette flickered in the light of the sun.

"I am Sir Rogden Gilgoyne," the young man announced. "I come on behalf of my lord Kurlan Malacco, the Death Knell!"

"Remove your helmet, boy," Sir Armel sneered. "You address a Prince of Montevale and the personal representative of a queen!"

"I do not remove my helmet for rebels and brigands," the messenger said.

For a moment, Sir Armel's face contorted with rage, but at a wave of Bel's hand, he held his tongue. "What would your lord have of us then?" Bel asked. "The Death Knell does not offer terms any more than he does mercy."

"He does not," the young man agreed, "At least not to those who count themselves his enemies, or rather, the enemies of our rightful king."

"What do you mean?" Lord Grimbol asked.

The messenger pursed his lips, "King Dermont was most displeased with Lord Harren's show of abject cowardice and accordingly, he holds no malice to those lords who may have been coerced into revolt. Thus, should you at once remove yourselves from the field, the king himself has promised to count you as friends."

Bel's lips twisted into a sardonic sneer as he sensed the pair of lords wavering at his side. *Clearly they have no understanding of Dermont's friendship*, he thought. Though they might keep their lives, they would lose all else, including, perhaps, a finger, a hand, a daughter, or whatever else Dermont's whims required.

The young man continued, "Those who do not, in other words, those who insist on standing in rebellion will be dealt with accordingly." He allowed a moment of dramatic silence to punctuate his threat before adding, "Farewell."

"Well, that parley was a waste of time," the Shackle said as the messenger rode away. Bel's eyes widened with surprise, for he had not heard the woodsman creep up.

"As they often are," Armel said.

Bel kept his gaze diverted from the other two lords as he nudged Tempest closer to the Shackle. "What is it?" he asked lowly.

The woodsman spit and rubbed his hands together. "There's a band of riders skulked past to the east using the brush for cover," he said without turning, "They were trying to keep out of sight, but I seen them."

Bel clenched his teeth.

"What was that rat bastard's name as brought word last week? Cunt-face?"

"Canton."

The Shackle bit his lip. "As much as I hate to miss all this…" he said, waving across the plane to where the Death Knell's forces were breaking into ranks, "Want I should have a look? See what mischief they're about?"

"Go," Bel said, "But take care. Canton is not to be trifled with."

The Shackle's lips spread to reveal a ghastly grin, "Neither am I."

As the woodsman hurried off, Bel and the others returned to join the rest of the army.

"Shall we rally the men, sir?" Briden asked, as they neared the line of horsemen, "Like old times?"

The Tower could not help but smile. "Of course."

Together, Bel and Briden spurred their mounts and rode forth along the line of soldiers, the Banner of the Winter Rose held aloft. As they passed, the men raised their spears or clashed their swords and shields together in a great clamor to stir their blood. For the common soldier, Bel knew, this could mean the difference between success and failure, for if the will of the men held strong, if their collective strength could be maintained, even a force much larger could not oppose them. Yet, if they faltered, if they recognized the precarious nature of their situation, they might easily give in to fear. The lines would break, the men flee, and all would be lost in the chaos.

Fortunately, and to Bel's surprise, the men seemed hungry, particularly those whom had been with him since the first long ride east from Sir Norton's keep. Their enthusiasm was contagious, and he discerned within his own breast a hearty fire, a mounting anger, a cold wrath. Even young Briden was smiling with malicious glee. For this truly was the moment they had all been waiting for, the opportunity to prove to themselves the truth of the promises that had for so long resided solely in the young queen's soft words and their blind faith in him, their commander. For far too long, they had ridden upon hope like a wild stallion; now was the time to pull back on the reins, tilt the lance, and charge.

So be it, Bel declared, patting Tempest again gently on the armored flank. He thought once more of all those who had died in the past weeks, months, and years of pointless war, though this time, it was without despair. *Today we begin collecting our debts*, he thought. *Today shall truly mark the beginning of the war's end, once and for all.*

Together, Bel and Briden rode back to their position in the line of battle beside Sir Armel. The knight tilted his lance in salute to his commander, and with a grin, flipped the visor down on his helmet. Down the line, the Lords of the White Wood were dispersed among their men, speaking to them, Bel hoped, in order to prepare them to withstand the shock of the enemy's initial mounted charge. For, as Bel well knew, Kurlan Malacco believed the solution to any problem lie in hitting it as hard as possible. Thus, as he had in nearly every battle against Gasparn, he would lead with the mounted charge of his heavy cavalry, counting on the strength of his men and the fear they invoked to ride right over their opposing forces like new-fallen snow.

Expecting this, however, Bel led his own force of heavy horsemen right out to meet them full on, halting their progress long enough for the light cavalry to circle around and flank them, raining down arrows from their short bows. From there, the infantry with their pikes and spears could engage on foot without fear of being ridden down by the enemy knights in the ensuing melee.

True, such tactics meant that, at least in the initial attack, the noblemen would bear the brunt of the risk. However, to those whom much is given, much and more is expected, as Bel's father used to say, and a man in full plate mounted upon a great armored destrier stood a much better chance than a farmer wearing little more than a quilted shirt.

Yet, for all the iron and steel a man might wear, it was nerve that made him a warrior, as King Cedric also said, a truth proven yet again when, to Bel's great disappointment, nearly two thirds of his heavy horsemen spurred their mounts and, as one, followed Lords Grimbol and Kindel from the battlefield in a clattering of hooves.

Sir Armel tore his helmet off, his eyes ablaze with abject rage. Beads of sweat seemed to boil upon his bald forehead like an egg as he shouted threats and barked commands at the fleeing riders. Briden's face was a mask of horror and in his surprise, he nearly dropped the standard.

To Bel, however, time appeared to have stopped with the beating of his heart. Across the field, the Death Knell's heavy cavalry were forming up, clearly preparing to begin their charge, while at his back, the infantry, slack-jawed and confounded by their social superiors' sudden flight, muttered to one another in apprehension and disorder. He knew at once that if he did not act, they would break, and all would be lost. Even Briden's fear was palpable, staring at him with mounting anxiety, pleading for direction.

"Dibhor take you, you bastards!" Armel cried in rage.

Bel glanced down the line, in addition to Armel, there was now only Welmsey, the Malets, Sir Lorgan, and the few mounted men-at-arms loyal to them. All the rest had gone.

"Red Death and Black Abyss!" Armel continued to shout. "I'll have Grimbol's head on a pike, that fat bastard! Kindel too, you wretched coward!"

Briden tightened his grip on Maggie's reins. "What do we do, my lord?" he asked.

Bel took a deep breath. "Let them go," he said, and calling to Armel as well, added, "Divide the rest of the horsemen and join the light cavalry in guarding the flanks."

"Do you want us to reform the lines?" Armel asked, struggling to contain his anger.

"There's no time," Bel said, and without another word, he spurred Tempest around and approached the long line of infantry, leaving the horsemen to join their lighter brethren.

Far off across the field, the Death Knell's army was in position and Bel knew his time was running short. With a deep breath, he rode to the center of the line of infantrymen—farmers, shepherds, peasants mostly, some with true spears, others with what seemed only sharpened sticks. He raised his voice.

"I will not lie to you," he said, "The lords have fled, the lords and the majority of the knights as well, and I would not blame you if you felt compelled right now to flee too."

There was a sudden swell of murmuring and as Bel scanned the lines of men and women before him, he sensed their rising terror, saw them shifting their weight, eying one another in anticipation of following the first of his or her fellows to run. He took a deep breath.

"But…" he began again, "*I* will not flee, that I promise. That, I swear." He paused. "Never once since the beginning have I or Queen Marina demanded your presence, your allegiance, your faith, and so I can only assume that your willingness to follow us this long was not through coercion or under duress, but freely given, and for that, *I* will not abandon you. For *that*, I will not flee. For *that*, I will fight." Swiftly, he swung down from Tempest's saddle and raised Spire aloft before him.

"In a matter of moments, Kurlan Malacco, the Death Knell, will send his heavy horse against us believing that they can shatter our line just as for the past hundred years, this endless war and strife have shattered our lives. His hope—and my brother Dermont's hope—is that in doing so, they can crush the fragile dreams upon which you and I and Queen Marina have rested our futures—a dream of peace. A dream of a land united not in tyranny and corruption where the privileged and the wealthy oppress the weak and the poor, but a land of justice, of truth, where those born noble fulfill their duties to protect those they lead, to defend them, to provide for them the opportunities they seek and they deserve for their children and their children's children, now and forever!"

Slowly, Bel paced his way to the front rank of soldiers and joined their line. "Noble or common! Valendian or Gasparn!" he shouted, raising his spear, "I fight for Montevale! One land, one blood, one people!"

With one voice, the masses of infantry raised their weapons, a forest of tall, sharpened shafts, and cheered, the sound echoing across the plane like thunder. In answer, the light cavalry too raised their voices, challenging the Death Knell and his army to do their worst. No more men would flee; they would fight or they would die.

Bel took a deep breath and fought to keep his arms from shaking, so shocked and relieved he was by the success of his words. He had never feared an enemy so much as he had feared giving speeches. Yet when the trumpets sounded across the field ordering Malacco's heavy horse to charge, the energy of those around him, crackling like lightning in a storm, erupted once more into a defiant cheer.

"Hold together!" Bel shouted down the line. He set the butt of his spear against the ground, anchored it with his heel, and braced himself for the impact of the enemy charge.

When it came, the clash of the opposing forces resounded across the plane in a frenzy of blood and ruin. Spire shuddered beneath the sudden impact of a great ironclad warhorse as it attempted to rush the line, and as the beast stopped short, pierced through upon the shafts of myriad spears, its rider, carried by his forward momentum, flew from the saddle onto the ground where he was promptly dispatched with a quick, sharp blow to the helm. All along the line that stretched to Bel's right and left, the death cries of dying knights and warhorses told similar tales, and as he pulled the crimson shaft of his lance free from the dead horse's innards, Bel gasped in a blend of surprise and relief. For, to his great amazement, the line had held, Malacco's charge had been halted, and the remaining horsemen stood now stymied in the center of the plane unable to continue their ride through the mountain of dead men and horses littering the field.

Thank the gods! Bel raised Spire aloft, rallying those nearest him in another great cheer, and, waving the heirloom spear forward, led his men onward to engage their mounted enemies head on. From the backs of their mounts, the enemy knights had the advantage of speed and height; however, without room to maneuver, they became easily surrounded by the agile infantrymen who used the considerable reach of their weapons to strike at their armored enemies from afar. Inevitably, the cornered knight would be knocked from the saddle (or thrown by a frenzied horse as it attempted to flee), and the warriors afoot would swarm upon him, beating at him with their blunt shafts or, if he was lucky, kill him quickly with a blow to the head or a knife to the throat.

Gripping his spear, Bel swung Spire with both hands, clearing a path through the enemy that sent men and horses scattering in all directions. Even wielding their lances, not a single horseman could get near enough to reach him, so furious and so fast were his blows. Soon enough, the sound alone of Spire cutting through the air like a highland gale was enough to send men running.

Still, the horsemen were well-armored and many, and as their confidence waned at the failed charge, they fought harder, fueled by desperation. Hard pressed as they were, the Death Knell's heralds quickly touted another blast, ordering his own footmen to join their social betters in the fray. The sound of their trumpets was maddening, panicked even, for Kurlan Malacco was not accustomed to entertaining thoughts that his army might lose. Yet somehow, Bel's common men had done the impossible; they had endured the full force of a Montevalen heavy cavalry charge, and what had suddenly seemed an opportunity for the noblemen of the Death Knell's army to glut themselves on blood and slaughter would require the intercession of their own impressed yeomen.

However, as Malacco's infantry ran forward into the thick of the fighting on a mission to sacrifice themselves to save their lords, it was here that the Bel's light cavalry finally engaged, riding forth along either side of the melee to attack the new threat on either flank. Their whoops and cries of bloodlust and fury carried clear upon the air as the arrows fired from their short bows showered the plain.

"The Winter Rose!"

"The Silent Prince!"

"One land, one blood, one people!"

Bel's heart sang as it had on the morning of the Battle of the White Wood, and as he whirled his spear, he thought of Lilia and their victory against Raylon Jace. He heard her laughter ringing in his ears and his lips spread wide into a grim smile as he watched the light cavalry converge upon the enemy lines, wreaking havoc upon their disciplined advance, and running down any who attempted to flee.

Suddenly, his gaze travelled beyond the fray to the wind-swept banners of the enemy commander's honor guard preparing to withdrawal. For, what had at first seemed an easy victory with the departure of Lord Grimbol and Lord Kindel could only end in shame and defeat for the Death Knell. Without a second thought, Bel's heart burned with vengeance. His blood boiled in the afternoon heat. "Tempest!" he shouted at the top of his lungs, "Tempest! Lord of Horses! Hear me!"

From the southern edge of the battlefield came a horse's high-pitched whinny and as Bel turned, he spied the great searoan galloping toward him, answering his call. With barely a moment's pause, he leapt into the saddle, and together, horse and rider charged off to engage the enemy commander as one. To best Malacco not only in the field, but in personal combat, would secure the victory and establish the legitimacy of the rebellion across Termain.

Leveling Spire before him, Bel urged Tempest onward after his brother's fleeing seneschal. With every stomp of the horse's foot, Bel's blood grew ever hotter. He recalled Malacco's history of violence, the countless atrocities the Death Knell committed over the course of the previous era of war that, like his brother's, Bel had tacitly ignored. To slay him would not erase the legacy of horror, but it might in some small way bring justice to the poor souls of his victims.

However, the Death Knell had not risen to his position through political squabbling and flattery like Dermont's other sycophantic lords. Malacco earned his spurs with blood and battle, if not honor, and of all the Plague King's captains, he was unmatched in his skill at arms.

Before long, Bel reached the far side of the field, having passed through the carnage of the bloody fray. Somehow, as he looked behind him, he noticed another rider following in his wake and was surprised to see that the young standard-bearer had made his way to his commander's side. The Banner of the Winter Rose, the white pennant now flecked with blood, still shone brightly as the wind from the speeding horse set it dancing.

At the sight of the standard, the Death Knell and his band of officers cut their pace, reined in their horses, and turned. Bel slung his shield across his back and tightened his grip upon the haft of his lance. Two of Malacco's knights rode out to meet him, their swords drawn and ready, but in one swift motion, Bel whirled Spire's shaft in a wide arc from one side to the other, unseating one man with a blow from the butt to the shoulder, before driving the spearhead beneath the second man's visor. They fell heavily to the ground with cries of pain and terror, scurrying away on hands and knees from the threat of their horses stomping hooves. Without a word, Bel readjusted his hold on his weapon and leveled his gaze at the line of riders, their full plate shining with intricate tracery and enameling.

"I've come for you, Kurlan," Bel shouted.

From the center of the rank, the Death Knell drew forward mounted upon an enormous black steed. His armor was forged of darkened steel and decorated with tiny golden skulls. From either side of his great helm protruded a long, curling spike fashioned like the horn of a ram, or a demon. From within the depths of his metal skin, a man's voice resonated.

"You've come for me? You've come for *me*, boy?"

Bel kept his gaze steady, meeting Malacco's enraged stare. "I come to bring justice for all those whom you have wronged," he said.

"Your brother wanted you brought back alive so he could kill you personally," the Death Knell said at last, "But I'd rather beg his forgiveness for denying him that pleasure than lose the opportunity myself." With a wave of his hand, the knights at his side—a full half-dozen—urged their horses along into a wide semicircle and drew their swords. Bel's heart beat faster in his chest as he tightened his grip on Spire. From behind him, he discerned the sound of Briden drawing his sword. "I'm with you, my lord," the young man said.

Kurlan Malacco drew a heavy battle axe from along his saddle. "I remember King Cedric telling stories about the skill of the Guardians," he said, "At least, before he went and lost his bloody mind."

"Perhaps you should have listened to him," Bel said, his body tense and waiting for whichever of the horsemen would be the first to come forth, "Else you would know when to surrender."

"Ha!" The Death Knell spat. "When I'm done with you, I'm going to cleave your bastard in two upon my axe, and fuck your cunt of a queen in every hole—so long as Canton hasn't done it first!"

"Never!"

To Bel's surprise, it was Briden who shouted, spurring Maggie forth to charge. *Briden, you bloody fool!* he thought as Malacco's knights rode to engage. He touched his heel to Tempest's flank and the great horse shot forth like a bolt of lightning, crashing into two of the converging knights like a battering ram. Bel's spear pieced one man through the gorget while Briden used his sword to deflect the second's blow. Bel freed Spire from the dying man's throat and whirled the haft around as two more riders engaged. Tempest sidestepped nearer to Maggie and shifted his weight while Bel braced his weapon against the new charge. He squeezed his legs as tightly together as he could, straining his ankles in the stirrups, and allowed the nearer of the oncoming riders to impale himself upon the readied spear. When the man fell backward from his saddle, Bel had just enough time to swing the butt of the haft around and unseat the second man with a swift, hard blow to the helm.

Briden, meanwhile, had withstood the assault of his man, wounding the knight along the shoulder. However, as he struggled to maintain his hold on the standard, his parrying blows were growing progressively weaker. At last, with a final desperate blow, Briden swung his sword high, stabbing his opponent beneath the arm. Yet, in doing so, he unsteadied himself and fell from his saddle into the mud. Maggie, suddenly free of her rider's weight, gave a scream, lashed out, and ran. In her fear, she drove headlong into one of the remaining knight's palfreys knocking both horse and rider to the ground.

Now, only Bel, the Death Knell, and one of his knights remained still standing and ready to fight. As one, Malacco and his remaining man charged. Bel directed Tempest straight toward them, and knowing full well that the Death Knell would expect Bel's counterblow to be aimed at him, instead shifted his weight in the saddle and turned his lance to unseat the final knight. In doing so, however, he allowed the Death Knell to score a glancing blow against him on his upper arm.

Grinding his teeth, Bel ignored the flash of pain and allowed Tempest to nimbly step to the side and whirl around to give chase, denying the Death Knell a second change to levy a charge. Together, the two horses—the black and the gray—galloped down the stretch of the battlefield. However, no normal horse, no matter how well-bred, could match the speed and surefootedness of the searoans and before long, Tempest had overtaken the black destrier. With every ounce of his remaining strength, Bel lunged forth with Spire and drove the point home between the seams of the Malacco's fine armor. The Death Knell cried out in rage and pain before slipping sideways from his saddle. He fell like a boulder with a resounding thud. In an instant, Tempest checked his pace, reared up onto his hind legs, and turned to trot slowly toward the defeated enemy commander.

"You are beaten," Bel said raising Spire's point to the Death Knell's throat, "Surrender."

Grunting against the pain, Malacco removed his helm and fell back heavily into the mud. "You'll get no such thing," he said, "You forget. I know you, you bastard. You're no killer."

Bel's blood turned to fire. "I wasn't," he said, struggling to keep his voice steady, "Until Dermont forced me to become one."

The Death Knell's face twisted in horror just as the point of Bel's spear pierced his throat.

When the dead man's body had stopped twitching, Bel slumped forward in his saddle, withdrew Spire from the corpse, and rested it across his lap. He could hear the cries of victory from out upon the field, could hear the soldiers calling his name, but he ignored it all. He was weary and, though he had borne only antipathy for Malacco, he was shaken at having authored the death of yet another man whom he had known since childhood. Further, his own words had unnerved him. *Was it true?* he wondered, *Has Dermont corrupted me too?* He was still wondering this when Briden hurried up to him, limping from the fall from his horse.

"Prince Beledain!" he shouted, "Are you unharmed?"

"I am," Bel said, "Unharmed, that is.".

Briden breathed a heavy sigh. "Thank the gods," he said, "My lord, I believe we've won."

Bel took a deep breath. "No," he said, "Not yet."

Briden's eyes went wide. "What do you mean?"

However, instead of answering, Bel checked the wound upon his arm and wiped the smear of blood upon his tabard. "What you did, Briden—charging the Death Knell—was both foolish and stupid, and I never want to see you do anything like that ever again."

The young man bowed his head, crestfallen, and his voice fell to a whisper. "I'm sorry, my lord," he said. "I won't. I promise."

"No, you won't." Bel said, "Find Maggie and gather Armel and Horn and any of the other captains you can, Sir Knight. The battle's not through yet."

"Yes, sir," Briden nodded, and suddenly paused, "Sir Knight?"

"I'd say it's long overdue you've earned it," Bel told him. "Now make haste, Sir Briden. The queen might be in danger. We must go!"

CHAPTER 37: THE BLADE IN THE DARKNESS

The moon that revealed itself in the night sky above St. Golan's after the battle was not the soft, eggshell-white pearl whose light guided travelers through the paths of darkness to the dawning of the next day. Rather, it hung instead like the great red eye of an angry god, as if Dibhor himself had come forth from the Abyss and peered out across the grounds of the monastery with a malicious glow, happy for the gift of blood and battle, and promising more to come. It was as ill an omen as men might wish for, and all the folk of Galadin could do now was to wait.

From the northern end of the courtyard, Brigid gazed out across the ward toward the southern gate upon which she could still make out the forms of the young Baron of Galadin and his seneschal overseeing the completion of the impromptu defenses below. For hours now, those men still able worked to construct a perimeter of palisade beyond the high stone walls of the monastery, or dug long, low trenches that might serve to confound an enemy cavalry charge. The young baron himself had even taken a turn at digging, working right alongside his retainers as they prepared for what promised to be yet another battle against a vastly superior force. Even at this distance, as

Brigid watched him, she could sense the grim determination with which he scanned the horizon line, quietly anticipating the enemy that was sure to come. More than anything, she longed to climb the battlements and stand beside him, to take his hand, to be with him in silence and in sympathy, and to enjoy these last few moments of calm before the coming storm. Yet, just as he had his duty so she had hers, and the thick, furry head of the golden hound nuzzling at her side reminded her that she had better get back to it.

"Alright, Fergus," she whispered, scratching the dog behind the ears. "Alright."

Fergus gave a loud sniff and yawned at her touch, then stretched and licked at a small gash upon his flank. Already, after but a few short hours, it seemed as if the wound had already begun to heal, and she wondered if there was something of the Gift of the Guardians common to Perindal's Hounds. For her own part, Brigid had barely a scratch upon her from the previous battle, due, she well knew, to Lughus's insistence on goading their enemies into focusing their attacks upon him, providing both of them with cover from his long sword. She was not at all pleased with him putting himself at greater risk for her; however, she knew that she would have done the same were the tables turned. Besides, she thought with an inward smile, they had fought so well together, for his focus on the defensive had allowed her greater liberty to act offensively and there was no telling how many enemies had fallen before them. Once more, she paused and glanced back at the barbican, her blue eyes searching the darkness for the young baron's lean form, but with a sigh of disappointment, she saw that he had gone.

Again, the hound nuzzled her leg, gently rocking her back onto her boot heels. "I know, Fergus. I know," she said, "Okay. Come on."

As Sir Deryk's messengers had informed them at the Houndstooth, any folk lucky enough to escape the advancing Andochan forces had sought sanctuary with the cousins at St. Golan's. As such, in addition to the many knights, men-at-arms, and yeomen militia fortifying the walls of the monastery and its keep, dozens of peasant men, women, and children huddled together like sheep in the chapel, the cloister, the chapter house, and the dormitory as well. It was these people to whom Brigid and Geoffrey had intended to speak, but while Geoffrey spoke to the men lodged in the stables, most of them farmers and rustics like he himself had once been, encouraging them to take up arms and fight, so she intended to address the others—the mothers, the children, the elderly, and the infirm. *After all,* she told herself, *If I'm to marry Lughus, these are to be my people too. It's important, now more than ever perhaps, that I come to know them and they to know me.*

That thought alone was enough these past few days to bring a flutter to her heart and a blush to her cheeks, and despite her distaste for fawning and blubbery, as it reminded her too much of the Drove back in Blackstone, she could not help but betray some overt overflow of emotion at the prospect. The memory of those moments together in the solar when he had held her so close and looked at her so earnestly, and the way the lightning flashed in his eyes when he confessed his love! Again, she felt a smile tugging at the corners of her lips and she shook her head to force herself back down from the clouds.

Lady's Grace, she grinned, *What a wonderful thing it is to be in love!* With a sigh, she turned and began to follow along with the golden hound.

Love! She recalled when last she had heard the subject spoken of at length, in Blackstone only days before the Betrothal Feast and her subsequent flight. She remembered the girls of the Drove sitting like ornamental poodles around the elder ladies of the court, her mother the Archduchess enshrined above them on her divan. It was a memory that at once filled her with loathing and regret, for it was the first time in her life that she had ever made her own voice known within the repressive environs of her childhood home, the first time that she had ever taken a stand to declare herself as something more than Josephine's taciturn daughter. However, in the argument that ensued, the occasion also marked the last time that Brigid and her mother spoke, when the façade of filial devotion was torn down and their mutual disgust for one another finally and viciously exposed. As she reached the dimly lit pathway of the cloister and spied the rustic families huddled together in the inner courtyard beyond, she could not help but feel a sense of isolation, of solitude, at the sight of a peasant mother pressing her children to her breast in consolation.

But I'm not alone any longer, she reminded herself, ruffling the golden hound's floppy ears. *For, in place of a mother, I've gained a husband, a love, a home.*

Be sure to offer him my deepest sympathies! Josephine's voice mocked her from the depths of memory, *Lady's Mercy! What a horrible wife you would make!*

"Good evening, Lady Brigid," said a welcome voice, banishing the Archduchess to the past. Brigid rubbed the weariness from her eyes and glanced up to see Abbot Woode standing beside her, having just crossed the ward from where the wounded soldiers were being seen to in the monk's dormitory. His brown habit was stained in places with dark splotches of dried blood, though in the wake of the battle, his appearance was significantly less ghastly than her own. The blood on his clothing came from a desire to heal while hers had come from a desire to harm. In one hand he carried a heavy iron lantern and across his shoulders he bore a large leather satchel trailing lengths of white bandages from its side. Woode's brow creased with care, though his sharp eyes pierced the red twilight with his customary intensity and determination.

"The Scrolls of the Hierophants claim that those with hearts of Darkness remain forever restless. Yet surely your presence here would prove them all false," he remarked, "I asked the handmaids who tend the Lady's Shrine that they prepare a place for you. I pray that they have not been remiss in their duties."

"I doubt that they have been, Abbot," Brigid said, "However, I do not think it would be right for me to rest while so many others are so hard at work preparing for the Chough. Besides," she sighed, "Lughus asked that I see to the common folk, to raise their spirits, and to remind them that their lord will not forsake them."

"When the Darkness deepens, so much brighter the Light of the Lady shines," the Abbot sighed, "Yet I do not like this red moon. Even I cannot help but think it an ill omen, and though I may be a man of faith, I have never been a man of superstition. Little wonder that the common folk find it cause enough to cry out in despair."

"It is those cries, then, that I shall seek to silence."

"Then may the Lady light your path, or, if you will permit me to walk a while with you," he said, raising his lantern, "Allow me."

Together, Brigid, Fergus, and Abbot Woode entered the vaulted pathway and traversed the colonnade toward the courtyard. Thick, waxy tendrils of ivy encircled the stone columns on either side of the walk, flanked by flowering shrubbery and clumps of heather. As she passed them by, Brigid glanced around the grounds of the monastery at the old stone buildings—the keep, the chapel, the brewery, and all the others—and imagined that in times of peace, St. Golan's would be an ideal location for those seeking the serenity of a life lived in quiet meditation. It struck her that Galadin seemed so full of delightful places such as this, from St. Elisa's Grotto with its little pool to the lofty heights atop the Houndstooth with its view of Lake Bartund. Lughus had once told her of an old ruined tower that marked the border between Galadin and Nordren. According to Crodane, it was a place that Lady Luinelen had been fond of riding, for on a clear day, the view commanded the entire southeastern reaches of the barony all the way to the castle. Surely, such amenable sites were but one more reason why the sovereignty of the barony, and by extension all the Brock, must be defended from the encroachment of the Andochan King, for as Brigid had long since noticed in her interactions with the folk of the Brock, particularly after making the journey to Highboard, whether great or small, common or noble, every man, woman, and child seemed to demonstrate a profound and very personal relationship with their land and people. She could not help but wonder if the same could be said for Dwerin.

Brigid breathed a heavy sigh, as it seemed had now become her custom whenever her thoughts turned toward her homeland, a land she felt obligated to care for, though one she had barely known. She recalled her conversations with Gareth in his tower cell, his pronouncement that hers was a land that was plagued by injustice, and his fanciful prattle about a Mountain-Queen. She could not help but fear that in her flight and in her exile, she had abandoned them to the mercy of her mother and her uncle and the nefarious passions of her cousin. However, more than anything else, when she thought of her homeland, she feared that in marrying Lughus, she was sacrificing the welfare of those she felt a duty to protect in exchange for her own happiness. *But why should I care for a land from which I am forbidden? Is Houndstooth not more of a home to me than Blackstone had ever been?*

Again Brigid heaved a sigh and winced against a sudden surge of agony, as if Alan had magically appeared out of thin air to stab her a second time in the back. She did not wish to simply forsake the folk of Dwerin, but in her heart, she knew that she could never leave Lughus. He had become her life, just as she had become his. She could not be parted from him and live any more than she could part from her breath, her heart, or her soul. They were no longer hers alone, but his as well, just as all that he was and all that was his had become hers too. She sighed.

482

"That's three times now in a matter of moments that I have heard you breathe as such, my lady," the abbot observed, "I must admit, such symptoms often connote an infirmity of the body," he paused, raising an eyebrow, "Or the mind."

Brigid offered the abbot a weak smile. "Forgive me," she said, "The events of the day have left me very weary and I find myself more burdened than usual by certain thoughts."

"Then perhaps I should prepare for an outbreak of plague, for Baron Lughus too seems to be suffering from similar symptoms."

"Then you've spoken to him?" she asked quickly.

The abbot shook his head. "No," he said, "At least not at length, though he too seemed to have more on his mind than simply the impending battle."

"Yes," Brigid said, "Though I wonder if I should speak of it in his absence, for we had wished to speak to you about a matter of great importance concerning us both."

"Ah, I see," Woode nodded, and from the sudden glimmer in his eyes, she knew that he understood more than she had said, "Then I suppose it best if we forestall that conversation until the young baron is free to join us, though if you'll permit it, allow me to say that since we last met upon the Feast of St. Aiden, the possibility of such a discussion has more than once been the subject of my thoughts these past weeks. Even then I sensed a certain…connection." He smiled. "May the Brethren give you joy, my lady."

"Thank you," she murmured, a bashful smile slowly spreading upon her lips, "I…I will look forward to such a conversation after the battle."

"Yet," Abbot Woode said, "I find it rather strange that the promise of such a happy future should lead to such fretful breathing."

"I should think the battle alone enough cause for consternation."

"And so it is, for most. However, for one of the Three?" he shook his head, "There is nary a time I can recall seeing the Marshal, the Vanguard, or the Blade weighed down beneath the burden of fear."

Suddenly, she stopped and turned toward the abbot, "You knew them?"

"Of course," Woode said, "For, as Blackguards they were forbidden from visiting the holy sites overseen by the Order and thus, they occasionally sought my advice concerning matters of the faith. More importantly, though, they were my friends."

"I see," Brigid nodded. "I must admit that it is not necessarily fear that concerns me." She paused, "I mean, I fear for Lughus, of course, and Geoffrey, and Owain, and everyone else. However, I must have faith in their strength and the strength of our friendship as well, for if the story is to be believed, it was the Three alone who brought an entire barony to its knees. With an army at our backs, even a small one, that flies the banner of the Golden Hound of Galadin, I think we have more than enough cause to have faith."

"Perhaps you may impart some of that selfsame optimism to the peasantry when you speak to them."

"Such is my hope," she said. "As for my own cares, it is not the Brock, but rather Dwerin that so concerns me at the present, for as much as I love Galadin, I was born in Blackstone, the daughter of the Archduke. Does that not require that I seek their prosperity as well? If I bind myself to the Brock, do I forsake the Mountain Kingdom?" she sighed, "When I first met Gareth, he spoke to me of injustice, of tyranny, afflicting the lands of my birth like a great plague. He spoke of how one day, together, we might heal it. Yet now he is dead and I am in exile, disowned and disgraced."

Abbot Woode's brow narrowed. "There I must disagree with you, my lady," he said sternly, "For if anything, I see in you enough grace to turn the cold barren stones of the mountain into a garden paradise. No, you are neither disgraced any more than are your claims negated. It was, after all, your father—not your mother—who carried the title. Kredor and his people simply find it more convenient to treat with your mother and your uncle. No, your claim is still intact, my lady. Rest assured."

"Then all the more reason for despair!"

"Whatever for?" Woode asked, shaking his head, "My lady, do you know why it is that the Three have never bent the knee to take the Oath of Fealty?"

Brigid shrugged. From somewhere in the recesses of her memory, of the Blade's memories, she recalled the answer, "Because they insisted on keeping to what they called 'the Old Ways,' the principles upon which the Order was founded."

The abbot nodded. "Regnar used to speak of the Old Ways from time to time. 'The Ways of the Road, the Ways of the Hills and Dales,'" he paused and gave a snort, "The old codger had all sorts of names for it, as Gareth was fond of mocking. Regardless, as far as Regnar was concerned, the true purpose of the Order was to do exactly as the name implied: *to guard*. To safeguard the roads, to safeguard the hills, to safeguard all the lands and all the people regardless of boundary, border, or birth. To swear the Oath was to swear not to serve all, but rather to serve one: Andoch and its Guardian-King. We cousins are much the same, for recall that I was once an Acolyte of the Order myself. However, as a cousin, I serve not the will of the Hierophant and the institution, but rather the needs of the people—faithful or faithless."

"But Lughus and I—will we not simply be trading Andoch for the Brock? The Guardian-King for the Baron of Galadin?"

"Only if you lose sight of your duties," Woode said, "Such was my fear once in accepting the elevation to Abbot of St. Golan's. However, if anything, I have seen my promotion as a means to do greater good, to meet the needs of even more people than I might have done before. For the Golden Hounds, it has been the same. Since the time of the Blessed Saint, the Galadins have continued to bend their efforts toward safeguarding all Termain. Why else would Arcis have sheltered Gareth and Regnar or commissioned special ships and crew for the sole purpose of carrying them to Dwerin and the Spade? Wolfram of Parth, the Marshal before Crodane, was Arcis's seneschal, and though he was sworn to protect the baron, he was just as often abroad, fighting bandits in the Firrinies, protecting merchant ships from pirates out of the Sorgund Isles, and all manner of things. Lady's Grace! Less than a year after his own daughter's death and his grandson was whisked away in secret, Arcis was back at it, working with the Three to hunt bands of slavers kidnapping Wayfolk. Such is the duty of the Galadins. For, remember that it was close on a hundred years before the Galadin heirs agreed to accept the command of the barony named in their ancestor's honor, yet even afterwards—with the exception of the unfortunate feuding with the Marthaines—they're duties did not end at the edge of their fiefs."

"No," the abbot continued, "I am certain that you will make a fine Lady Galadin—the finest, in fact—and rest assured, my lady, that Baron Lughus will make you a fine Archduke."

Brigid's eyes flashed in surprise, "What do you mean?"

Woode raised his eyebrows, "Is it not true that as the rightful heir of Dwerin, the man you marry will be the next Archduke? Considering the Galadins are duty-bound as it is to protect all Termain, you certainly chose wisely in selecting the baron himself—and a Guardian at that." The abbot smiled and once more began to walk toward the cloister, "Have no fear, Lady Brigid. You have not been remiss in your duties to your people. On the contrary, I believe that in pursuit of your duty, you have secured the greatest of all possible allies, not only for yourself, but for all Dwerin. But come! The Mountain Kingdom will have to wait for the time being. Let us return our attentions now to the folk of the Brock."

In spite of the late hour, many of the common folk encamped within the courtyard were wide-awake, quietly muttering to one another in hushed tones. The majority of them were women and children, though here and there a gray-bearded old man sat gazing, wild-eyed, upwards at the red moon. For most, it seemed their flight from the kingsmen had been sudden and hard. Few had anything in the way of possessions other than the clothes on their backs and whatever trinkets or tools they managed to carry along with them as they ran. Many of the children went about barefoot with filthy faces smeared with dirt and ash. However, what struck Brigid even more than their haggard appearances were their dull, vacant expressions, for these, she knew, were the lucky ones, the ones who had made it to the monastery in time, yet though they may have survived, not one among them did so unscathed. The physical wounds they suffered would eventually heal, but the mental scars would likely last forever. That thought alone was enough to make her sick to her stomach with apprehension and remorse. She had heard plenty from Annabel regarding life in the Spade and the plight of the common farmer, about the deaths of her eldest son Karl, Geoffrey's friend, Oliver, and the Cousin who tended Pyle's chapel.

What could I possibly say to these people? Brigid wondered, *How could I possibly hope to alleviate any fragment of their suffering with mere words?* For a moment, she felt a cold emptiness in the pit of her stomach and she could sense herself losing her nerve; however, the light of Woode's lantern soon attracted the peasants' notice and as soon as they spied the abbot, the hound, and the young lady approaching, all eyes turned toward them. Those nearest rose to their feet and bowed their heads.

"Good evening," the abbot's deep voice resounded clearly across the courtyard.

"Good evening, my lord," came the muffled reply.

486

"I hope that the evening finds you all well," the abbot continued, "Particularly since the arrival of the good baron and his companions was able to lift the siege at sundown."

There were some mutterings of assent, though more of confusion, for surely they realized that if the siege were truly lifted, they would be free to depart and to discover what was left of their homes. However, Abbot Woode continued undeterred. "This is Lady Brigid Beinn," he said, motioning toward her with the lantern, "Lady Brigid was among those who fought in the battle, and one who continues to fight with Baron Galadin now. She has come to ensure that you are comfortable and to assure you that you are safe."

Brigid felt her heart quicken in her chest; she was nervous, and in spite of all her adventures over the past months, she felt once again like a mouse. Many times and more while living with Geoffrey and Annabel in Hounton, she had walked the streets, mingling with the townsfolk, learning their manners, and discovering their pursuits and aversions—a practice she had continued in her walks with Lughus. However, these folk were different, not because they belonged to the country over the city; rather, it was the circumstances of their meeting that caused her such alarm. She suddenly wished that Woode would be silent, that he would have allowed her to forego the formal introductions and simply speak for herself. It was too late now though.

In any case, she turned to the abbot, and with a nod, said, "Thank you for walking with me, my lord abbot, and for your kind words."

"I shall look forward to our next conversation," he said kindly, "Unless of course you wish me to remain here with you."

"I'm sure you are weary from tending to the wounded," she said, "And besides, Fergus is a fine enough escort as it is."

"As if the Blade should have need of one besides," Woode smirked. He offered her the lantern, "At the very least, let me offer you this. I know these grounds well enough without it."

"Thank you."

"Then until next we meet," the abbot declared, "May the Lady of Light watch over you."

"May she watch over us all," Brigid said.

When Abbot Woode's footsteps had faded to silence, Brigid returned her attention to the courtyard and the clusters of peasants seated, resting, or trying in vain to sleep beneath the expansive vault of the red nightfall. Fergus nudged against her with his long snout, and, ruffling the dog's ears in response, she took a deep breath. *Aiden's Flame! I've just come through blood and battle! What have I to fear from these folk?* Her thoughts conjured up an image of Lughus in the solar, the feel of his arms around her, the sweet taste of his lips. *No hesitation*, she told herself, and strode forth.

"Good evening," she said kindly, ignoring the sudden tremor of anxiety she felt in her chest. Before her were a pair of country wives and an assortment of small children, the eldest of which was no older than Geoffrey's daughter Greta.

"Good evening, lady," the women said with a nod of deference. One of them adjusted her hold on a squirming infant and breathed a weary sigh.

For what seemed an eternity, Brigid stood awkwardly, struggling now to think of what to say. She could feel her cheeks reddening with embarrassment. All around the courtyard, she could feel eyes upon her, eyes that simply stared without emotion, regarding her in the same manner as one might examine a tree or a stone. *Perhaps this was a mistake*, she thought as Fergus sat down mildly at her side and licked the palm of her hand. She continued to stand unmoving for a moment longer, until finally, rousing herself from her mortification, she prepared to depart when suddenly an embittered voice sounded in the darkness.

"What manner of woman goes about in arms and armor?"

With a flash of anger, Brigid's eyes searched the darkness for the speaker. It was an old man, knobby-kneed and gnarly as an alder tree, leaning on a cane. White clumps of hair sprouted from his nose and his ears and his beady, little rat-eyes glimmered with resentment and sardonic glee.

Without thinking, Brigid's hands slid to her hilts. "What manner of man does not?" she snapped.

All she had wanted was to be kind, to be helpful, to reassure these people that she and Lughus and all the others would do their best to ensure that they all made it through the battle unharmed, yet here was this old man, mocking her. A heavy silence spread across the courtyard and eyes once vacant began to widen with interest. A few even drew nearer so as to better hear the exchange. She had always understood class distinctions and class snobbery to be a particular type of cruelty reserved for those of the upper classes in relating to the lower. However, as she sensed a mounting anticipation among the other peasants at the prospect of seeing a noble lady brought low by one of their own, she realized that the poor were just as capable of condescension as the rich. *Why should I be so surprised?* she thought, *Rich or poor, people are still people. Same capacity for beauty as well as ugliness.*

Sensing now his audience, the old man's lips twisted obscenely revealing a row of broken teeth. "So you fought in the battle, did you, Lady Brigid?" he leered, "They say that a women who chooses to take up arms, does so because she has no other charms."

From somewhere beyond the glow of her lantern, Brigid could hear the sounds of stifled laughter. Her fist clenched in fury and she thought back to Blackstone and to Alan and his absurd wordplay, his sing-song aphorisms, and alliterative insults. A tutor had admonished him for it once stating that such things were the basest form of wit, practiced only among low-born rogues who wished to set themselves up as clever. Needless to say, the man's tenure as their instructor did not last much longer, though Alan made certain to provide him with a taste of his tongue as a parting gift. In any case, Brigid had always remained silent as her cousin spouted his filth, mocking the servants and the soldiers of the guard.

But she was a mouse no longer. She was a woman grown—and she realized suddenly, gazing about the courtyard, that there was at least one aspect in which she belonged not to the minority, but to the majority of the mob.

"Better a woman with a will to fight," she said, narrowing her gaze, "Than a doddering old man worth nothing but spite!"

Once more, the other peasants voiced utterances of amusement and eyed one another in mild anticipation while still others gathered round to hear the old man trade barbs with the young lady. Brigid might have been embarrassed if she were not suddenly so annoyed.

"Why was it you came here, my lady? Seeking new recruits?" the old man laughed, "Can't say I would advise it, for a woman with a sword is like a fish that seeks to fly, and such a soldier as that can do naught but wail and cry?"

A few of the other old men voiced airy laughs accompanied by the high-pitched giggling of one of the older boys. Brigid ignored them. "Perhaps I came not seeking soldiers, but rather to ask advice," she said, "For, as a woman ages, they say that she grows wise, but as a man grows older, they wonder how long until he dies?"

At that, a number of women laughed aloud, and Brigid allowed herself a satisfied smirk. Somewhere among the small crowd, a voice called out, "I've been wondering that myself for years!"

The old man's lip curled in anger in the direction of the speaker and his knuckles turned white gripping the crook of his cane. With a loud cough, he cleared his throat and spit upon the ground. "A woman is meant to be mild and meek, do as she's told and never speak! And if she cannot learn her rightful place, the only cure is a slap to the rump or the face!"

"Yet while I—a woman—fought in this night's battle," Brigid said coldly, here blue eyes alight with fire, "You've done nothing but weary us with your prattle."

Immediately, the crowd erupted into laughter and the old man's fist shook with fury. "Shut your mouths, you pack of bloody hens!" he whirled on Brigid and cried out, "The only women who belong in a war are trollops, strumpets, and soldiers' whores!"

"And the man who offers only spite and bitter talk, sure enough does so because he's lost the use of his—" She let the last word remain unsaid, but by the sudden roar of laughter, it was clear that the crowd could anticipate the final rhyme.

The old man's eyes went wild with rage, and in his wrath, he hobbled forward and raised his cane. At once, Fergus leapt up from his haunches and snarled, and the man fell backwards in terror. All the while, the crowd laughed louder and louder, and though she was glad for the sudden good will, Brigid could not help but feel some sense of guilt.

"Let him be now, Fergus," she said quietly as the laughter began to die down, "Let him be."

On command, the hound returned to her side leaving the old man in the dirt. Without a word, Brigid caught the eye of two of the older boys and motioned in the direction of her dishonored foe. With nods of assent, the boys hurried to the man's side, helped him to his feet, and followed along as he shuffled away muttering bitterly.

"You certainly showed him, my lady," said one of the country wives, wiping tears of laughter from her eyes. "How's that for a woman's wit?"

"I suppose," Brigid said, "Though I hope I did not wound his pride too much."

"Him?" said another woman, "Of course not! He's had it coming for years. Why, went through three wives, he did. Beat the snot out of them mornings *and* evenings with that stick of his. The most recent—much younger than him, poor thing—he made stay behind while he fled north here. Figured it would buy him time to get to safety if he left her behind to 'entertain' the Andochan soldiers. I only hope she had the good sense to flee as soon as he was out of sight. Horrid old coward!"

"That's terrible!" Brigid said, feeling that perhaps she should not have called Fergus off after all.

"Aye, so it is," the first woman said soberly, "But anyhow…" she paused momentarily to pick up a small child, a little boy, chubby with flaxen hair and a smear of dirt across his left cheek. The boy eyed Brigid with sudden wonder as his mother paused to wipe a thick stream of snot from under his nose with the hem of her shawl.

"I like your dog," the boy said, "He's big."

"So he is," Brigid smiled, "His name's Fergus."

The boy erupted into giggles, "That's funny."

"Why is that funny?" Brigid grinned.

"'Cause it's funny," the boy said again.

For some time after, Brigid spoke with the women and children—their initial reserve broken down by such a trivial thing as her war of words with the wicked old man. At first, they did not speak of the battle or of the struggles they might have endured in their flight to St. Golan's, but rather of mundane things—the weather, the children, and the big golden hound. However, little by little, the women became more forthright, and so they told her of soldiers on horseback, raiders and looters, dead husbands and lost sons. Yet again, Brigid felt herself growing angry, furious at the atrocities men seemed so willing to inflict upon their fellow men. She thought once more of what Abbot Woode said about the "Old Ways," and her heart swelled with pride. *Let the Guardians have their city and their Order. Let them keep their Council and their Guardian-King,* she thought. *I shall be proud to bear the name of Blackguard—nearly as proud as I shall be to be a Galadin.*

Yet, as she neared the far end of the courtyard along the edge of the chapter house, she saw by the light of her lantern, a small pavilion illuminated by the light of a single candle. Laid out upon rough woolen blankets within was an assortment of restless forms watched over by a weary old woman dressed in the habit of a handmaid. At Brigid's approach, the old woman stirred from her dozing and gazed up at her with rheumy eyes.

"Might I help you?" the old nun asked in an airy whisper.

Brigid's eyes peered beyond the light of her lantern at the floor. "Who are these people?" she asked.

The old woman rubbed at her eyes with a shaky hand and stifled a yawn, "When the Andochan vanguard crossed the border from Agathis into the Lomedan fief, the first village they came across was Bromsted. These folk are the survivors."

"I see."

"Most of the menfolk died from wounds taken in the fighting. These others are but the women and children as yet remain."

Sure enough, as the old woman claimed, many of those lying prone upon the ground were of smaller stature, there slight bodies stretched out at awkward angles or wrapped in strips of sullied linen and wool.

"What happened to them?" Brigid asked.

"All manner of things, though none of them good. There is a girl who was run down by a mule. Over there is a woman burned when her roof was put alight. Back there is a boy who was flogged."

"Flogged? Why?"

"Many horrible things and more happen when a village is raided. It matters little enough afterwards as to why. It just seems something men do."

Brigid shook her head, biting back an intense swell of anger. "Will they recover?"

"Some will," the handmaid claimed, "Though there's little enough we can do for them now. Abbot Woode saw to them himself as best he was able. They're in the hands of the Brethren now."

With a deep breath, Brigid carefully tiptoed into the pavilion, leaving Fergus beside the old woman at the entrance. One by one she stepped past the wounded peasants, some half-covered with blankets and others stretched out on their backs like corpses. Most lacked boots or shoes and wore clothing that was either worn or torn, spotted in places with blood and smears of mud.

"Why are their feet all bloody?" Brigid whispered to the old woman.

"When the kingsmen attacked them in the night, there was little enough time to don their boots before fleeing," she said, "They were forced to make the journey through the woodlands on foot."

Once more, Brigid shook her head as she regarded the rows of small bodies lying prone. She could sense her throat growing thicker, and whether through weariness or compassion, her eyes began to burn. *One might almost sympathize with the Dibhorites for believing mankind too wicked to live,* she thought bitterly, for she knew that for each of the folk that suffered still in the pavilion, many had suffered worse before finally succumbing to death. Her hands slipped to the blades on her belt, and as she tightened her grip on their hilts, her arms shook with vengeful wrath. She glanced down at the child lying at her feet and with a shock of fear saw that her eyes were open.

"Hello," Brigid whispered.

The girl's eyes grew wider, but she remained silent, simply staring.

Slowly, Brigid knelt down at the little girl's side and smiled. As she drew nearer, she noticed scrapes and raw scratches along the girl's arm and a moist brown poultice wrapped with bandages around her leg. Absurdly, she thought back to Freddy's book of herbs and remedies, wondering what manner of treatment the Abbot applied.

"Does your leg hurt?" Brigid asked.

For a long moment the girl continued to stare wide-eyed with uncertainty before answering with a slow, silent nod.

With a gentle touch, Brigid smoothed away a lock of brown hair from the girl's brow. Her heart felt heavy with compassion, not only for the grievous wound, but for the experiences, the memories that would remain—written upon the annals of her memory forever—of a village burned and neighbors, friends, and perhaps even family cut down. In an instant, Brigid envisioned the rest of the girl's life (assuming, of course, that they all lived past the arrival of the main force of the Andochan army), and she recalled with sadness the phlegmatic acceptance with which so many seemed to regard the misery of war—the cold indifference to wanton murder, rape, and pillaging, as if such horrors were not abnormal, but simply the way things were.

Brigid's chest grew even tighter and she sensed her eyes welling up with tears. Her mind returned once more to Blackstone after Sir Reid's death when the Falcon flew to her chambers. He had shown her sympathy without desire, kindness free of any expectation; he had healed her.

The Gift of the Guardians… Brigid remembered, *The power to heal…*

With a deep breath, Brigid whispered softly to the little girl. "I'm going to try to help you," she said. "Don't be afraid."

For a moment, the child remained silent, until at length, she nodded her head.

"Close your eyes," Brigid said.

When the girl had done as instructed, Brigid gently took hold of her hand, offering it a light squeeze for reassurance. Then, with another slow, bracing inhale, she placed her other hand upon the child's wounded leg just below her knee.

When Gareth had healed her arm those many months ago, Brigid remembered the soft, cool touch of the mending sprain as if she were simply washing the wound in a clear mountain stream. However, now, as she focused her will upon comforting the little girl, she understood why to some, the Gift was more of a curse. All at once, her skin tingled as if set afire, centered in the space on her own leg. She felt the sting of thorns and brambles digging into her arms and shoulders and a great rending pain in her own knee. For a moment, she felt as if she would collapse beneath the intensity of such agony as she assumed the burden of the girl's suffering, but in an instant, it was over, reduced to a dull ache.

I've done it! she thought, and as she opened her eyes, the sight of the child's body unmarred by hurt or wound confirmed her hopes as much as the stiffness in her leg and the small red stains spreading now in various places, staining her own clothes.

At the entrance to the pavilion, Fergus stood rigid and sniffed aloud with concern, discerning the scent of her blood upon the wind. The old nun's eyes shone in wonder and she sat forward on the edge of her chair. "Lady of Light, bless us!" she gasped.

Wincing against the pain, Brigid struggled back to her feet, regretting that she had not thought to doff her shirt of chain beforehand. The little girl scurried to her feet in amazement and stood as still as a stone staring up at her.

"All better?" Brigid asked.

Again, the girl nodded, and with one final squeeze, Brigid released her hand. The great golden hound loped forth and nuzzled her side, agitated by the sudden appearance of her wounds.

"It's alright, Fergus," Brigid whispered, patting his head, "It's alright." She turned to the old handmaid. "I'd like to see to as many of the children as I can," she said. "Will you help me?"

"Of course, my lady," the old woman said reverently, "Of course."

CHAPTER 38: THE MARSHAL COMMANDS

"I've never quite understood why a monastery should be built like a fortress," Sir Owain observed, "What could bandits possibly hope to gain from attacking folks sworn to lives of poverty and service?"

"Quite a lot, I'm afraid," Lughus said. He gazed over the side of the battlement atop the gatehouse at the defenses below. In addition to St. Golan's high curtain wall, the Galadin soldiers had constructed a double-perimeter of palisade fencing and pockmarked the field with wolftraps—long low ditches designed to impede a heavy cavalry charge. Truly, for a place dedicated to religious devotion and the ministration of alms, the monastery did indeed seem just as capable of withstanding a siege as any nobleman's castle. "The cousins might not flaunt their wealth as the hierophants do with cloth-of-gold vestments and silver candlesticks encrusted with precious jewels," he continued, "But seeing to the needs of those who have nothing still requires something. The sale of ale alone provides St. Golan's with considerable wealth. Granted, all of it goes to aiding the poor, but it is still quite a sum. If that alone were not enough of a temptation, there are also the relics. St. Golan was one of the very first Guardians to join Aiden against the

Warlock and the only man ever to bear the title of "the Ram." Summons, the great maul he carried into battle, is probably worth far more by itself than the entire holdings of a wealthy earl—including the cost of his estate."

"So I guess there's no use in me asking Woode to borrow it, eh?" the old knight said, "Be a nice replacement for my bloody sword."

"You never know. The situation gets any more dire and he might offer it to you," he grinned. "How is your wound?"

"I've had worse," Owain shrugged, "And as for things here, I wouldn't call it dire just yet. We've got two thousand men survived the first fight unscathed, we've got the walls and the battlements, and we've got allies on the way—Kin willing! We might not have the stores to survive a lengthy siege, but we're fine for the time being, and if worse comes to worse, we can always bake the ale into bread. Of course, I'm hoping it doesn't come to that," he smirked, "What's more, we've got something else that the Guardians don't."

"What's that?"

"We've got you Three."

"The Chough's anointed too," Lughus said, ignoring the seneschal's bravado, "And he's bound to have others with him as well—Guardians, that is. Not just kingsmen. Partisans, gallants, perhaps even a few cavaliers, and some of them are sure to be anointed as well. And Brethren only know where the Hammer's gotten himself to these days too."

"Aiden's Flame," Sir Owain smirked, "Sure enough that young lady knows you! Dour and dread, doom and gloom!"

"You heard that, did you?" The young baron blushed.

"Hopefully as Lady Galadin she can do something to change all that. Wash some of the Marthaine stink off of you."

"I don't know. I've always preferred it to the smell of dog."

Both Lughus and Sir Owain looked up in surprise to see Roland Marthaine had suddenly joined them. "Still, apart from the odor, you Galadins know your business when it comes to mounting a defense." He smirked. "For I would not relish the thought of attacking St. Golan's myself. Your men do you credit."

"I suppose that's high praise," Owain said stiffly, "Coming from you."

Lord Roland inclined his head. "You might also like to know that your Sir Adolfo's scouts have returned," he said, "Though from what I gather they report only to him."

"Bloody Madder…" Owain grumbled, "We should have just hanged him when we had the chance."

"Such men have their uses," Baron Marthaine said, "And from what I gather, he's loyal. He's even had a man shadowing me since we left Houndstooth—much more adeptly, I might add, than your man, Rook."

Lughus cast the seneschal a glance.

"It's my duty to see to your protection." The old knight shrugged. "It was only a precaution."

"What about Sir Deryk's men?" Lughus asked the elder baron, "Have they returned as well?"

"Not to my knowledge."

"Then perhaps we should pay Sir Adolfo a visit," Sir Owain said.

Together, the two barons and the seneschal descended the stairs of the gatehouse to the courtyard below, pausing only once for Sir Owain to summon the men he'd chosen for Lughus's guard. *Naden, Pike, Tonkin, Grimes, Kender, and Sedge,* Lughus noted, reciting their names to himself, *They've sworn to defend my name; the least I can do is remember theirs.*

The Madder and his mercenaries had set up camp outside the eastern wall of the monastery beside a small postern. Unlike the soldiers sworn to Houndstooth or its fiefs, the mercenaries saw no uniformity among their arms and armor, and those few displaying badges or insignias wore not the golden hound of Galadin, but rather the emblems of their companies or guilds. Most were under the direct employ of Sir Adolfo, though others still had been bought and paid for by the scutage of the absent weaver knights. Man to man, they were a rakish bunch, and as he passed through their camp toward the Madder's small pavilion, Lughus could not help but think back to Lenard's Crossing and the duel with the mercenary Stokes. *They gather like flies at the first sign of blood,* he thought, *I just hope they fear Adolfo more than they do our enemies, for no doubt we'll need them.*

On guard outside of Adolfo's tent, a large tattooed Wrathorn stood stripped to the waist but for a broad, leather bandoleer upon which hung a heavy maul. On his head he wore a helm fashioned from the skull of some beast and his beard, twisted into a tangle of braids, reached well past his middle. For a moment, he eyed the baronial contingent menacingly, but with a nod motioned for them to pass on.

With a quick word to Naden and Pike, Lughus ordered the Galadin men-at-arms to wait outside, and with Sir Owain and Baron Roland behind him, approached the entryway to the pavilion. As he drew back the flap, a gruff voice snarled from within.

"Lady's teats, Adolfo," the voice said, "Ten thousand men is more than we bargained for. I'll not throw my life away for so little."

"You've been paid amply, Wyrglen," came Adolfo's slow drawl, "Five-to-one simply makes your fees seem more fair. Besides, I would never have sought your services in the first place if I'd known you and your men gave in so easily to fear."

"We more than proved our mettle outnumbered two-to-one in the first fight," said another voice, "And earned our fees for that matter."

"Yes, and now you seek to spend it," the Madder said, "Though I wonder where you will do so, for I assure you that if you abandon its lord now, Galadin will most certainly be closed to you. Agathis has fallen, Marthaine's lord is also here..." he sighed, "And I can't imagine that Andoch will treat you very friendly in light of the recent gallantry as you claim to have displayed against them. Gold tarnishes quickly when you've no place to spend it."

For a long moment there was silence. Lughus sided his way into the tent to see Adolfo seated at a small writing desk, while beside him two more mercenaries clad in an array of plate and chain armor pieces sat in canvas folding chairs. A single servant stood in the rear holding a ewer of wine, though neither of the hired soldiers had been served. As the Young Baron and his followers entered, the two men exchanged a glance of quiet alarm before rising to their feet.

"Baron Galadin," Adolfo observed. He paused a moment to finish whatever it was he was writing and rose to his feet.

"I understand your scouts have returned," Lughus said, "I had hoped to speak with you regarding their discoveries."

"Certainly," the Madder said with a slight bow, "These men were just making ready to depart."

"The pavilion," one of them said hurriedly.

"Aye," said the other, "To make ready. For the battle."

Adolfo fixed the two men with a penetrating stare, and with a nod, hurried them on their way. When they had gone, the servant hurried to set up another chair for Sir Owain, but the old knight refused it with a wave of his hand, content instead to stand at his lord's right, while Baron Marthaine assumed the seat at his grandson's left.

"I would have sent word sooner regarding the return of the scouts," Adolfo said mildly, "Mercenaries are useful beasts, but like most animals they are easily subject to their passions and not noted for their discretion. No sooner had the rider returned than he began blathering to the fellows of his company. Hence, my former company."

"I cannot imagine it was good news then," Lughus said, "For I expect mercenaries are not often willing to show fear."

"No," Adolfo said, "But they are more than willing to voice their discontent if they believe doing so might compound their fees, particularly when their employers find themselves in a spot of bother."

"An army of ten thousand men sounds like slightly more than a spot of bother," Owain muttered.

"Perhaps," the Madder said, "Though my experiences over the years have taught me to place little faith in laying odds, for very rarely is it chance alone that determines the outcome of a dice roll."

The seneschal clicked his tongue in disapproval; however, Baron Marthaine gave a quiet snort of assent. "True enough," he said.

"So what did your man discover?" Lughus asked.

Adolfo inclined his head. "As you may already have surmised, in but a short while we are to be met by a force of at least ten thousand men. I say 'at least' because this is simply a projection and one that does not include any of the scattered forces that fled the field after the previous battle. The majority of the force is comprised of kingsmen—mounted and afoot—though they are supported by still smaller contingents of men sworn to the northern Andochan lords, mercenaries, and some peasant levees. Yet, as you might expect, the greatest threat is from the Order. In addition to the Chough, the army is commanded by fifty partisans, twenty gallants, and three cavaliers. Among them are the anointed Guardians known as the Jay, the Chase, the Cockerel, the Swift, and the Willow."

Lughus drew a long, slow breath. Each one was known to him; each one the subject of his own legend. "What of the Hammer?" he asked, "Is Willum Harlow with them?"

The Madder shook his head, "The Hammer and the Breath were recalled to Titanis with the Andochan ambassador after Baron Marthaine drove them from Highboard."

Lughus's brow furrowed. "I cannot believe that the Hammer would give up his chase so easily."

"I do not believe he was offered the choice," Adolfo said.

"Shame," Sir Owain said, "Would have been nice to finally face him toe-to-toe."

Lughus remained silent, though his hands rested once more upon his hilt. In spite of everything, he wondered what would happen if he were to meet Harlow in the field, for as much as he hated the man, as much pain and fear as the Hammer had caused—the near scandal in Highboard, his pursuit of Brigid and Geoffrey in St. Elisa's Grotto, Crodane's death—Harlow was only acting in accordance with the principles of the Order, principles that Lughus himself once held to be true. *Had Rastis not sent me away,* he wondered, *Had I not become the Marshal, would I still think the same? Would I still believe a Blackguard to be little more than a villain? Had things turned out differently, what of Brigid or Geoffrey? Would I—could I—count them among my enemies?* That thought brought with it a stab of self-loathing, and he bit his lip in disgust.

"For a simple mercenary, your scout seems to have learned a great deal," Roland Marthaine observed, bringing an end to the sudden stillness, "I cannot help but feel rather astonished at his level of detail."

The Madder breathed a sigh. Lughus eyed him carefully, for though subtle, the old baron's speculation was clearly a challenge. "I will admit that the scout's report was but the final thread in a tapestry that I have been weaving for some time," Adolfo finally said, "However, it seemed unimportant in light of the first battle. Having now survived that ordeal, I set to work once more. I meant no offense in failing to share this knowledge earlier, but I did not wish to offer my baron a tapestry that had hitherto remained threadbare."

A sudden sound turned their attention around to where Adolfo's Wrathorn guard stood waiting in silence beside the flap of the pavilion.

"What is it, Bursa?" the Madder asked.

The Wrathorn lifted the flap wider to reveal Abbot Woode waiting behind him, his hands folded beneath the sleeves of his habit. "Pardon my intrusion," Woode said, "Baron Galadin, I must have a word."

Something about the abbot's demeanor filled Lughus with concern. *Something is wrong*, he thought, *Else he would have simply sent a messenger*. However, the young baron betrayed none of his private thoughts. He simply nodded and rose to his feet. "How long did you said until the Chough arrives?" he asked Sir Adolfo.

"An hour. Perhaps less."

"Then it seems we were right to remain here rather than attempting to return to Houndstooth." He turned to Sir Owain and Baron Marthaine. "Pass the word among the rest of the knights to complete their preparations and to ensure that the men are at their posts."

"One final thread, my lord," Sir Adolfo said quickly. "My man also reports that the kingsmen bring with them great engines for laying siege—trebuchets—fresh from laying waste to Agathis. It is said they smashed the walls of the city with great barrels of St. Aiden's Flame."

"Perindal's bloody sword!" Owain cursed.

Lughus bit his lip. "Have men place barrels of water at intervals around the monastery and douse anything likely to burn—the stables and any other buildings constructed of wood and thatching," he said quickly, "And have the poor folk sheltered indoors within the chapel or anywhere else we can find room. I'll not have them camped in the courtyard to be burned alive once fire starts raining down from the sky, and..." he hesitated, for a sudden premonition gave him pause, "If you should see Brigid and Geoffrey before I do, send them to me at once."

"Aye, sir." The seneschal, the Madder, and the elder baron nodded in agreement, and without another word, Lughus joined the abbot outside.

"I apologize for the interruption and I do not wish to add to your burdens with the enemy so near," Woode said, "But I felt I must inform you at once."

"Inform me of what, Lord Abbot?" Lughus asked.

The abbot breathed a heavy sigh. "Lady Brigid," he said, "She's been...injured."

At once, Lughus felt a pain like fire flash in his chest, as if the wound he suffered at the hands of the Hammer's arbalest—long since healed with

Crodane's sacrifice—had suddenly been torn open anew. "What do you mean?" he asked, "Injured how?"

Woode held out his hands in supplication, though it did little to stay the sudden tide of panic the Young Baron felt rising within him.

"She is alive," the abbot said, "And I do not believe she is in any danger of…becoming otherwise. However, she is very weak and she is in a great deal of pain."

Lughus's breath caught in his chest and his knuckles whitened around Sentinel's hilt. "Where is she?" he said quickly, "You must take me to her."

"My lord, I have already betrayed her wishes in informing you of this in the first place," he said, "She did not want to distract you from the battle."

"Did she think I would not notice her absence?"

"Believe me, my lord, she was not in any position to think straight. She was…sorely wounded."

"Wounded!" Lughus growled, "By whom?"

"By…by her own hand it seems."

Lughus felt the color drain from his face, for by some preternatural sense, he knew. He remembered sitting with her that afternoon in the solar, when he told her the truth of his mother and father, of his dreams and his fears. It was then that she told him of the young scoundrel Reid, of his attempt to harm her, and her desperate defense that left her with bloodstained hands and a broken arm. *The Gift of the Guardian*, he thought bitterly. *Oh Brigid, what have you done?* He took a deep breath, willing himself to calm down, and swallowed the lump in his throat. "Please," he said, "I must see her."

At length, the abbot nodded. "Follow me."

Fergus stood guard in front of the door to the handmaidens' dormitory. Clearly, the great hound was agitated, pacing back and forth and pawing at the oaken door. His tail wagged to and fro like the mast of a ship lost in a storm, and from his throat there issued a soft, high-pitched whimpering. A great crowd of peasant folk were gathered at a distance—women, children, and the occasional old man—gazing with mingling wonder and fear at the distressed hound.

"Fergus!" Lughus called.

At once, the great hound bounded over to the young baron's side. The crowd of peasants drew back at once and even Abbot Woode gave pause.

Justin D. Bello

"It's alright," Lughus whispered, as much for his own reassurance as the hound, "She's alright." He nodded to Woode to carry on and with a nod, the abbot continued to the dormitory.

"She barely made it to the door before she swooned, leaning on an old handmaid for support." The abbot shook his head. "There were at least a dozen children lying wounded in the pavilion, and by the Brethren, she healed every last one of them. I knew Gareth or Crodane to cure one or perhaps two in a moment of great need. Regnar could sometimes manage up to four, but twelve! Father, forgive me, but I thank the Lady she swooned after seeing to the children, else she might have killed herself trying to cure the grown women."

"What happened to them?" Lughus asked.

"They were commonfolk wounded when the Andochan raiders pushed northward from Agathis."

"Yes," Lughus said, "But I mean their wounds. What was the extent of their wounds?"

"Most could scarcely walk from sores to their feet—the results of fleeing through countryside without shoes. Some had suffered a few blows from clubs or riding crops," Woode paused, "One lad was flogged."

"Flogged?"

Reluctantly, Woode nodded. "According to Dame Heloise, he was the last that Lady Brigid saw to."

Inside the dormitory, the nuns stood in the entry hall to receive the abbot. There were but four of them present, and although Lughus could sense their discomfort at two men intruding upon their private quarters (to say nothing of the golden hound), he did not care. "Where is she?" he asked.

"This way." The abbot led him down the central corridor away from the hall to the nuns' private cells. Two more handmaids awaited their arrival, their faces pale with a mixture of concern and confusion. When he spied the russet stains upon the drab white cloth of their habits, Lughus felt his blood turn to bile and his limbs go numb.

"They had some...difficulty relieving her of the byrnie due to the...damage from the flogging," Woode said, "But they have cleaned the wounds and applied plasters and poultices. I mixed something to help her sleep, though it seems to have had little effect."

504

"No," Lughus said softly, "It would not." He had noticed long ago how little wine or ale affected him anymore. *No wonder Hob could drink so much,* he thought absurdly, *It's as the stories say: 'Neither poison nor plague does the Guardian fear, while the Lady of Light yet holds him dear.'* He breathed a great sigh. *She will feel every stroke for days. Oh Brigid! Lady, ease her pain!*

"I wish to see her," Lughus said at last.

The handmaids raised their eyes to the abbot, and for a long moment Woode kept silent. "She...asked not to admit you," he said.

"What?" Lughus felt his throat thicken, "Why?"

"She was afraid."

"Afraid?! Of what?"

Woode glanced from one handmaid to the other. "What you see may alarm you," he said at last, "She is...she carries wounds enough for a dozen people."

"I assure you, Lord Abbot, what I do not see will alarm me even more," the young baron said, "I will be left to imagine."

"Yes, but..." Woode's voice dropped to a whisper, "The sight of such suffering in one we love can often inflict deeper wounds than any sword."

"Or serve as a whetstone for our wrath!"

"Lord Lughus..."

Lughus's eyes flashed with anger. "I am the Baron of Galadin! You will stand aside."

Reluctantly, the abbot nodded. "So be it," he said.

A single candle cast its soft light over the interior of the room. Quietly, Lughus crept in, just as Fergus hurried by past his legs. Before the abbot or either of the old nuns could follow, the young baron shut the door. *The Lady only knows what may come of me in the battle,* he thought bitterly, *If I am to fall, let us have these last moments together in peace and in private.*

When the door was secure, Lughus took a deep breath and gazed into the soft candlelight. He could sense the vague outline of a reclining form on the small bed, but beneath the shroud of linen he could discern no more.

"Brigid?" he whispered, "Brigid, are you there?"

A long moment passed in silence and as his eyes adjusted to the dimness, he could see Fergus had sat down at the side of the bed, his head held high—

alert, regal, and ever-faithful. From beneath the linen coverlet he spied a slender, white hand come to rest upon the great hound's furry pate.

"Lughus?"

Lughus breathed a great sigh and choked down his gall. "Oh, Brigid," he whispered, "What did you do?"

"I'm...I'm sorry. I just..." Her voice trailed off and in the low light, he heard the sound of her sobbing. "I couldn't let them suffer."

"You used the Gift?"

"I had to."

Lughus shook his head, "You could have been killed."

"They were just children."

"I know," he said sorrowfully, "I know."

"I'm sorry," she sobbed again, "I just...please don't be angry."

"Brigid," he heaved a great sigh and in a sudden swell of emotion, drew near the bedside. "I'm not angry," he whispered, and kneeling down, slipped his hand into hers and lifted it to his lips. "I'm...terrified," he told her as his eyes began to burn, "Were I to lose you, I would not..." he shook his head again, "I would be lost."

"I know," she whispered, "I know, but..."

"But they were children," he finished, "And you knew you could help them. And for that I..." he paused to kiss her hand again, "For that, I understand. For that, I'm proud of you. For that...I love you all the more."

Brigid's hand closed tightly around his own, and though she remained silent, he could hear her labored breathing. His eyes searched the low light to better discern her slight form. She lay on her side facing him so as to avoid aggravating the wounds he knew must line her back, and though it seemed she was attempting to keep still, from time to time a spasm of pain passed through her like a leafless tree in a strong breeze.

"There must be something I can do to help you," Lughus whispered.

"The abbot and the handmaids have done what they can," she said, "Though I think time shall be the best healer. I witnessed Gareth suffer deeper wounds in Blackstone."

"Though surely not so many."

"Do not underestimate my uncle," she said, "Or my cousin."

"Yes, but this is far more than you should have to bear by yourself. Gareth was alone and there are two of us. Tell me how to use the Gift and surely I can bear some of this for you."

"No."

"Brigid, please."

"No!" At once, she snatched her hand away from him and concealed it beneath the linens. "I'll not send you to battle against the Guardians wounded. I've enough on my conscience as it is for being unable to stand at your side."

"Brigid…"

"No."

Lughus breathed a heavy sigh, for he knew there would be no arguing with her. Besides, she spoke the truth. The coming battle promised to be hard. To wade into the fray already wounded would only stack the odds further against them. *And if I fall, if they sack the monastery, it will not only mean my death, but also hers, Geoffrey's and who knew how many others?* He breathed another sigh, "I just wish I could help you."

"You are," she whispered and returned her hand.

"I thought you did not wish to see me," he teased, "Or so Abbot Woode said."

A sudden spasm of pain took her and her fingers tightened around his. "I'm sorry," she said when the agony had subsided. "I was…I was worried you would be upset."

"You were right, though not at you."

Another moment passed in silence before Fergus sauntered around to the foot of the bed and leapt up to lie in the space by Brigid's feet. In the low light, Lughus heard a quiet laugh.

"I assume that was Fergus?"

"I'll leave him here to keep you company when I go," he said, "Should the worst come to pass—"

"Let's not speak of it."

"But if it does, I—"

"Lughus, please. Let's just enjoy the moment now," she whispered and gave his hand another gentle squeeze, "If…if this is the only happiness we're to know, I'd rather not see it spoiled with thoughts of fear and despair."

"True enough," he said at last, and with a deep breath, leaned closer to the mattress until he could smell the straw sewn within it. Upon the pillow, her face was concealed beneath the cascade of her soft dark hair, though from behind it, he could make out the glimmering light of her eyes. Yet, as he drew closer, she appeared to hesitate.

"What is it?" he asked.

"I..." she paused, "I don't want you to see me."

"Why ever not?"

"I'm...I must be a fright to look at."

"I very much doubt that."

"You..." she sighed, "It's strange. When you heal a person with the Gift, not only do you feel the pain of the wound as it happen, but...it's like I can remember it too."

"The memory of pain is part of the burden, I suppose."

"I suppose," she agreed, "In any case, one boy—one I healed—he was beaten about the face with a gauntlet."

"Why?"

"I don't know..." she sighed, "I don't think any of those I healed suffered their wounds for any real reason—other than not being able to outrun our enemies."

Fire and Blood! Lughus cursed inwardly. *The Kingsmen have much to answer for!*

"In any case, I'm...I'm afraid of what you'll see when...if you should look upon me."

"Brigid," Lughus sighed, "You'll heal. Lady's Grace, even the scars from the flogging will heal. It's part of the Gift. The only mark of battle you'll bear is the wound you suffered in the Anointing. Believe me, I suffered plenty sparring with men in the yard before I met you. Or even then, the wound you took in the leg at the Grotto—is there any trace left of a scar?"

"No, but—" she wept, "But what if this is different? What if it never heals? What if...what if you no longer find me pretty?"

Lughus shook his head and gently slipped his hand free from hers and laid it softly alongside her cheek. By touch alone he could sense the swelling from the boy's beating, the scrapes from the metal rivets, yet he swept aside her thick, dark locks and without hesitation, kissed her lips. When he drew away to breathe, his eyes discerned only hers. "How many times do I have to tell you?" he said kindly. "Brigid, I love you. Not just your eyes, or your lips, or your hair. Not just your voice, or your sweetness, or your wit. I love *you*, Brigid. *You.* Scars, bruises, and whatever else may come." He laughed aloud. "Come what may, remember? I love *you.*"

The light in her eyes grew glossy with tears and with a light touch upon his wrist, silently bid him kiss her again. "I...I know, my love," she whispered, "I just...Lady's Grace, I'm such a fool."

With a smile, Lughus bent close and kissed her again. "If that's true, then so am I," he said, "Because my heart, my life, I bind to you." From around his neck, he drew out his mother's signet ring, hanging still upon Crodane's leather string, and pressed it firmly into her hand, "Let this seal it."

Brigid's voice was somber as she examined the ring in the candlelight. "Lughus, this is your mother's ring."

"It's Lady Galadin's ring," he said, "It's your ring."

"Lughus..."

"Don't tell me you refuse."

"But," she whispered, "I've nothing to give to you."

"You already have," he smiled, and kissed her once more, "You've given me a reason to fight. You always have—here, in Highboard, in Houndstooth. You are what drives me Brigid. I'm so proud of you. You are what makes me want to make this a better world."

Suddenly a sharp knock upon the chamber door shattered the moment of quiet peace. Brigid lurched to one side in fright and reeled in agony. At once, Lughus leapt to his feet and his hand went to Sentinel's hilt. *Aiden's Flame! Every damn time! We can never seem to get a moment!* "Who calls?" he shouted in anger, and returning to the bedside, glanced down to see Brigid wracked with pain. Already dark patches were appearing on the white linen from where in her fright she must have reopened her wounds. *Lady save her!* His breath caught in his throat as he glanced around the cell for something to staunch the flow of blood.

"Lord Lughus," the abbot's voice called out, "My lord, my apologies, but your men send word. The enemy comes!"

"Go!" Brigid whispered, grinding her teeth in pain, "Lughus, you must go!"

The young baron's eyes went wide with fright, though not at the prospect of the battle. "Will you be alright?" he gasped.

"Fine, love," she whispered, "I'll be fine." She reached out to take his hand and with a weak tug, pulled him close to kiss her. "Now go," she said, "And know all my thoughts and all my prayers are with you."

With a bitter reluctance, Lughus let her hand slip free and unbarred the cell door. "I love you," he said again, "No matter what comes, know that."

"I do," she said, "And you know it too."

Lughus cleared his throat and quickly wiped his eyes before he addressed the abbot waiting in the doorway. "Take care of her," he whispered, "Please."

"Of course," Woode said, but as Lughus made to pass by, the older man caught him by the arm. "Mind yourself," he said softly, "And remember she awaits your safe return, as do we all."

"I will." The young baron gave a nod, "And...I'm sorry for how I spoke to you before. You are my friend and you didn't deserve that."

"There is no need," the abbot said, "I understand."

"But still," Lughus said, "I apologize."

"Then, I accept," Woode told him. "Now, go."

Outside of the handmaid's dormitory, Lord Roland stood waiting in silence beside Sir Geoffrey. The farmer gripped the brim of his kettle helm between his mitts as if he meant to break it off. Beyond them in the yard, the poor folk stood in silence like pilgrims at their vigils on St. Aiden's Feast. Lughus could not help but wonder which of the children standing with them were among those Brigid had saved.

"How is she?" Geoffrey asked.

"She's fine." Lughus smiled weakly. "She'll live."

Geoffrey shook his head. "I'd say here she was being reckless, but if what those folks say is true..." He sighed, nodding toward the peasants. "I can't say I blame her."

Lughus nodded and his jaw set with fury. "Bastard Kingsmen," he cursed, "Raiding villages like bloody bandits! Turning out women and children with fire and sword! I'll kill every last man among them!"

"Will you?" Roland Marthaine said.

"They're monsters."

"Aye," the old baron said, "They're men. They're soldiers."

"True soldiers fight with honor," Lughus said, "They don't sack peasant homes for no reason or turn to theft and rapine looting, and they certainly don't harm children or flog small boys like Sorgund sailors."

"Don't they?" the Argent Eagle snorted.

"Not in Galadin."

"Oh yes, they do," Marthaine said, "Believe me. I can show you the ruins in my lands to prove it. Graves too. Plenty of times through the years have the peasantry of my lands turned to their heels and fled at the baying of the Golden Hounds—led by some of the very knights who fight beside us here. For, just as your men count me and mine to be villains, so too do mine judge them. You Hounds might claim the blood of Saints, but your men are still men and there's no accounting for what a man might do when armored, armed, and emboldened with battle fury." He shook his head. "Now, I won't begrudge them that or even name them, for I know my men were guilty of such wrongs too. It was bloody and it was wrong, but it happened. Why else do you think the Lord-Baron sought to end the strife between us with your parents' union?"

Lughus ground his teeth in bitterness, though he remained silent. He knew that his grandfather spoke the truth.

"Men are men. No matter the arms they wear or the banner they unfurl. Men are men. Good, bad, and sometimes both."

"So we are to just let them be, then?" Lughus snapped, "To accept the suffering and the horror?"

"Of course not," Baron Marthaine said. "*We* lead. It falls to *us* to live lives of honor in hopes that other men might follow. Why else would they call us nobles?" The old baron sighed. "I told you when we first met that though your grandfather was my enemy, he always had my respect, for unlike most of our ilk, I knew that he strove always to be a good man—despite what his men might have done or the demands of his duty. I only hope I did the same, and that you will too. So let's have no more talk of wanton slaughter, for whether Galadin or Marthaine, it is unseemly."

Slowly, Lughus took a deep breath and gave a nod, "I'm sorry."

"Don't apologize. Not to me," the Argent Eagle said evenly, "Let's go join your men. We will defend this place and these people, and in doing so, we shall win. You're right. The kingsmen must be stopped, for I believe that if Kredor wins not just these folk alone will suffer, but all the Brock."

No sooner had Baron Marthaine finished speaking when a slight, leather-clad man appeared before them. With a flourish, he doffed his hood revealing a pockmarked face and a thin, ratty mustache. "Begging your pardon, my lord," he said, "But my master, Sir Adolfo, sent me to ask after the Lady Blade."

Lughus's jaw tensed. "You may tell him that she is well," he said, "Or that she will be soon enough."

The man nodded. "Thank you, lord," he said, "Pardon, then, but as my master was assuming that to be the case, he asked if—with your permission— he might have a word with Sir Geoffrey."

Geoffrey's brow furrowed and he shifted his weight. "In what regard?" he asked.

"That I don't know for sure, my lord," the man said, "I only do as my master commands."

Lughus exchanged a look with the Vanguard. "Sir Geoffrey doesn't need my permission," the young baron said, "He's his own free man."

The big farmer rubbed his jaw in thought. "You tell Adolfo I'll be along in a minute," he said at last.

The messenger offered a final bow and scurried off.

"I'll see what he wants and find you," Geoffrey said. "Adolfo is a crafty sort. Perhaps with the odds we face, a bit of craftiness is what we need right now."

"Be safe, Geoffrey," Lughus said. Baron Marthaine offered the Vanguard a stoic nod.

"We should return to Owain and your men," the old baron said, "It won't be long now."

Lughus gave a nod of agreement, and though he couldn't help but notice the absence of his comrades, he tightened his grip on Sentinel's hilt. *Be steadfast*, he resolved himself, *Steadfast and resolute*.

When the sentries first sighted the approaching Andochan horde, it was not an oncoming army they believed approached St. Golan's, rather an enormous wild fire. For, as they made their approach beneath the eerie glow of the red moon, so numerous were they that, as each man carried with him a torch or flaming brand, it appeared that the fields themselves were ablaze, threatening to engulf the monastery in a fervently self-righteous burn. It was only after the first staccato notes of the marching drums reached them that the men of Galadin knew that the Guardians had come.

Atop the walls or assembled in the field before the monastery gates, the soldiers stood in utter silence watching the slow approach of the enemy host.

Before them, Lughus stood waiting, his hand resting casually upon his hilt. At his back, stood Owain, Woode, his knights and retainers, and his grandfather, Roland Marthaine. Neither Geoffrey nor Adolfo had rejoined them yet, as the Madder had sent word that together they were attempting to enact a plan that, should it succeed, might help level the field, or at least, confound the Andochan siege.

Together, they watched the approaching horde until at last, they could discern individual soldiers and horsemen from among the great conflagration. Leading them was a single horseman clad in ebon plate armor and from his great helm flared a red and white striped plume.

At a wave of his hand, the army came to an abrupt halt, the drums fell silent, and with a touch of his spurs, he rode out to meet the monastery's defenders and offer terms.

And so it falls to me, Lughus thought, sensing the eyes of those under his command, *May the Brethren make me worthy of the faith these people place in me, and may I not bring them to greater ruin.* He took a deep breath and paced forward to meet the Guardian general alone.

When they were within a dozen paces of each other, the enemy commander removed his helmet. He was a sharp-featured man, with dark eyes and a pointed beard. "Are you Lughus, Baron of Galadin, anointed under the name of the Marshal?" he asked.

Lughus rested his hands upon his hilt and met the other man's gaze unwaveringly. "I am."

"My name is Sir Brennan Bercilan," the Guardian replied, "Justiciar of the Warlord, anointed under the name of the Chough."

"I know who you are," Lughus said, "I remember reading stories about you and those others to bear your name."

"Then you know that when I give my word," the Chough said, "I mean it."

Lughus nodded. "I do."

"Then hear this," the Justiciar declared, "You and your men are outnumbered by more than five to one. You have with you women and children, cousins and handmaids, the very old and the wounded. St. Golan's is a monastery that, at best, houses enough stores to last a few hundred. In no way can it withstand a prolonged siege."

"That is so," Lughus said.

"Now," the Chough began again, "I dislike attacking an enemy under such circumstances, and I would not see innocents suffer needlessly."

"Is that why your men laid waste to my villages?" Lughus sneered, "Slaughtering women and children as they fled in fear?"

"Those were *not* my men," the justiciar said, "Those men belonged to Lord Tensley. I was at Agathis maintaining the siege."

"They were men of Andoch, and as you stand in supreme command, regardless of Lord Tensley, they are still *your* men!" Lughus shouted, "You cannot so simply wash your hands of their misdeeds."

The Chough took a deep breath. "No, I cannot," he said solemnly, "And for that, you have my apologies. Perhaps in the spirit of contrition, I come to offer you a means by which we might prevent any further hostilities."

"I'm listening."

"My orders," Sir Brennan told him, "Are to see that you are taken *alive*. Surrender yourself and my army will stand down. Your people may return to their homes and you have my word of honor that I will appeal to the King and his council to cease any further violence and renew attempts at diplomacy."

Alive? Why Alive? Lughus's brow furrowed, "I am a Blackguard, one of *the* Blackguards. Why would King Kredor want me alive? So he can execute me himself?"

"I do not know. I was told that you were not to come to harm," the Chough shook his head. "But consider for a moment this: How many will die if it comes to battle? How many will suffer needlessly? Even if you are to face execution, your single death would save how many lives?"

"What makes you think a Blackguard would care?"

"He would not. Yet a ward to the Loremaster—to Rastis Glendaro..." The Chough raised an eyebrow. "Let us just say that I do not believe the old man's lessons could so easily be un-learned."

Lughus breathed a heavy sigh and glanced behind him at the soldiers of the Galadin army gathered in ranks before and upon the walls of St. Golan's, ready to defend those who sought shelter within. *All those people...* he thought, *Brigid nearly gave her life to save but a handful. If I offer mine, I can save all of them.*

The thought of her brought a sudden tightness to his chest and his heart reached out to her, lying in agony in the handmaids' dormitory. To surrender himself now would be to part with her perhaps forever. He might never hear her voice, stare into her eyes, or hold her close ever again.

"Wait," he said suddenly, "You did not specify as to the fates of my fellows. If I surrender to you, does our accord extend to guarantee the safety of the Blade and the Vanguard?"

The Chough hesitated. "My orders did not specify any such mercy towards them," he said, "Nor did they have the luxury of your illustrious education."

"Lady Brigid is the daughter of the Archduke of Dwerin!"

"And a kinslayer."

"That's a lie!"

The King believes otherwise," said the justiciar, "And this Geoffrey Pyle is an outlaw from the Spade."

Lughus's knuckles went white around the hilt of his sword and the muscles in his jaw tensed and set. "I'm afraid that I cannot accept your offer," he said.

"So you would risk the lives of all of these people?"

"Yes," he said, "I alone am not the object of Kredor's war with Brock, for I am but one of fourteen barons, and though you claim your men will stand down today, you will most assuredly return tomorrow. Your King seeks an empire and the Brock is all that stands between him and his goal."

The Chough shook his head. "Young man," he said sternly, "Come now. Don't be a fool! If you insist on fighting, you and every man who stands with you will certainly die."

"Perhaps," Lughus said, "But it is a chance we will have to take."

"So be it," the Guardian general said, "I will give you until dawn to reconsider; however, if you do not, I can promise you no quarter, and by nightfall tomorrow, St. Golan's will be but a ruin." Without another word, he replaced his helmet and spurred his horse to return to his men.

Lughus took a deep breath, and paced back to his awaiting captains, steeling himself for the horrors yet to come.

CHAPTER 39: THE LIGHTHOUSE

From its place atop the coastal cliffs, the Lighthouse stood like a large white bone above the thatched roofs of the wattle and daub buildings of the surrounding town, and from its very top, in the swirling mists of the midnight darkness, the great watch fire, normally a comfort to sailors and wayfarers, adopted an eerie glow. Thom wiped his damp palms upon his habit in a futile attempt to keep them dry. However, he was satisfied that this was the only outward sign of the fear he struggled to bury deep within his breast, for having so recently been recognized by Magnus as a "real man," he had no desire to prove the Wrathorn otherwise, despite how utterly disquieting a locale the Lighthouse might be.

Such a strange place, Thom said to himself, *So quiet. So calm*. He crouched low beside Magnus under the cover of a twisted old alder just outside of the town. *Not even an animal or a bird to make any sound*. "Magnus..." Thom began at last, "I can't help but feel as if there's something...*unnatural* about this place."

To his surprise, the big man grunted in agreement. "You and me both, mate," he said, "You and me both. It may not mean much now, but I can't say I blame the men for not wanting to come ashore." He laughed grimly. "Ah well. Live and learn."

Thom took a deep breath and gazed down toward the docks where the masts of Slink's ship could just be seen against the deeper darkness of the sea. Not a single lantern had been lit aboard the ship nor could any silhouettes be seen aloft climbing about the rigging. To his sudden surprise, he realized that every one of the windows in the town was dark too. Indeed, the tower's pallid beacon was the only source of light. Thom took a deep breath.

"Do you think they know we're here?" he whispered, "I mean, they must have seen the fire from *Sigruna* burning."

Magnus sucked his teeth. "I don't know," he said at last, unshouldering his great axe. "Slink certainly knew we was after him. No doubt he'd have told the Keepers to expect company."

"You're certain that's his ship in the harbor?"

"Course it is. You can tell by the rigging—fore-and-aft like instead of square. Slimy bastard swore it was faster no matter how often we proved him wrong. It's another reason I had us chase down Rodulf once they split."

"Right." Thom nodded, though he understood none of what Magnus had said. "So in any case, we should assume Slink and the Keepers know we're coming for them?"

"I'd say so."

"Alright," Thom said calmly, "What's the plan, then?"

Magnus's gaze narrowed. "What plan?"

"The plan."

Magnus tugged at his beard. "Same as it's always been," he said, "Kill Slink, take the Key, and get back to the bloody launch."

Thom's stomach suddenly twisted into knots, though he struggled to ignore it. "Magnus," he said slowly, "That's not a plan."

"Well, I don't know what else you had in mind, but that's what I'd planned on doing."

Thom dried his palms again and took a deep breath. "Magnus," he sighed, "You don't even know where Slink is, or if he's still got the Key with him. Furthermore, if these Keepers are as dangerous as you seemed to think they are—"

"What? When did I say that?"

"Well, you killed the one who hired you."

"Only because I didn't like the bastard."

517

"Well, the other sailors seemed to think Castone dangerous enough to stay away."

"Cowards, the lot of them. Pay it no mind."

Thom rubbed his eyes, "Only just now you agreed with me that this place felt unnatural!"

"Well, of course it feels unnatural. What did you expect? Why else would people think it's cursed?"

"All I'm saying," Thom said at last, his frustration rising with every word, "Is that I think it would be wise to stop for a moment and simply think— think about where Slink might be, think about where the Key might be, think about how we can get back to the launch. So unless you want me to have to rename 'The Song of Magnus Bloodbeard' as 'The Song of Magnus the Dead Fool,' I think that we should *think*!"

In the stillness of the night, Thom's unintended outburst seemed the sounding of a war horn, and having so recently being recognized as worthy by the great Wrathorn, he prepared himself for the consequences his hasty words must have earned him. He was surprised, however, that rather than answering with a curse or a blow, Magnus instead offered a wry grin.

"Now, I may not be a bloody great man of learning like your Loremaster," he began, "But it stands to reason that with the whole place dark as Dibhor's bloody arsehole, there's but one place in all this town we're likely to find Slink, the Key, or anything else for that matter."

Thom breathed a sigh. "The Lighthouse."

"Aye, the Lighthouse," Magnus said, and without another word, he charged off toward the town, skulking quickly through the shadows cast by the great watch fire, his axe gleaming in his hands. Thom was left with no choice but to follow, stumbling as best he was able, struggling to keep quiet and keep up.

For all of Thom's worry, they met not a soul along the way. Not a single guard or town watchman was on patrol, nor even any stray dogs or cats wandering the night. No livestock grunted in paddocks behind the houses, and no chickens sat roosting in any of the coops. It was as if the entire town had been built and then subsequently abandoned in one mass exodus.

Yet, as empty as it appeared, Thom could not escape the sudden feeling that every move he made was being watched. He was about to mention this to Magnus, when suddenly the big man stopped at the corner of a large stone building and held up his hand; across a small courtyard and a long staircase, the Lighthouse loomed high above them upon the sheer cliffs overlooking the great eastern ocean.

Up close, Thom could see that it stood wider and taller than any of the towers in Titanis, constructed of smooth, white marble that shone brightly in the light of the beacon. Its gates, ironbound and intricately carved, stood open and unguarded revealing a vast, illuminated entry hall culminating in a grand staircase that marked the beginning of the tower's ascent.

Thom shook his head and breathed another sigh. The mists had thickened as they had traversed the town and every once in a while he felt a raindrop strike his cheek. "Magnus..." he whispered, surprised at the harshness of his voice in the stillness, "I was thinking now of sheep."

The big man chuckled. "Aye, you would."

Thom shook his head. "No," he said, "We're the sheep. It's as if we're being led here, being *allowed* to reach this place. I mean, surely you feel the eyes? It's like they're all around us, watching us, marking every move we make. If I can sense it, then surely you can too."

"Let them think me a sheep," Magnus said, raising his axe, "I'll show them what it's like to herd a bear." At once, the Wrathorn warrior rushed the Lighthouse gates. With a sigh, Thom followed, left with no choice now but to see "The Song of Magnus" through to its conclusion. *Lady grant us a happy ending*, he thought miserably.

Onward Magnus ran, through the Lighthouse entry hall and up the grand staircase, taking the steps two at a time. Thom struggled to keep up; for although Magnus may have thrown all caution to the wind, trusting his tenacious desire for vengeance to protect him, every step Thom climbed filled him with greater certainty that they were being drawn deeper and deeper into the Abyss. Still they saw not a soul, though the invisible eyes Thom felt watching them seemed to multiply the higher they climbed. The hair on the back of his head stood on end and his palms were as clammy as a tide pool after a winter squall. However, he could not allow himself to be consumed by fear, not when they were so close to the end, not when he was so close to going home.

He tried to focus on that idea as he choked down his fear: Home, the Tower of the Loremaster. From the first moment he sighted the Lighthouse, he had expected it to be much the same—both were known across the land as centers of learning, havens for scholars, and monuments to history. However, as he looked around him, chasing after Magnus, he realized with a shock that while in structure the two buildings were much the same, in spirit they could not be more different.

In form and in function, the Loremaster's Tower was an enormous library. With its tall, overflowing bookshelves and ascetic cells open for study. It contained some private chambers and dormitories, as well as a restricted storeroom where many of the most ancient tomes and relics of the Order were kept. However, overwhelmingly, it was characterized by an inviting atmosphere, as if any with the desire for knowledge would be welcome, encouraged even, to bask in the ideas, truths, and arguments that lie within.

The Lighthouse, however, was quite different. For, though perhaps more impressive and a bit taller with its great beacon, it seemed to hide its reputed stores of learning behind closed doors. No bookshelves lined the walls, nor did it seem there were very many books. In their place, intricately embroidered tapestries shone brightly in the light of the gilded wall sconces while great glass cabinets displayed treasures of bygone ages--pottery, plate, assorted objects of art and master craftsmanship, here and there an illuminated scroll or tome—many, many more than Thom had ever seen at home and the majority bearing the symbols of Old Calendral or the Church of the Kinship before the founding of the Order. It was all very beautiful, but also very cold. There may well have been study rooms and dormitories as well, for Thom passed many heavy, oak doors as he climbed the stairs; however, they were all shut, closed. Though like the Loremaster's men, the Keepers were often sent across Termain, taking positions as tutors and advisors at the courts of the nobility, he expected that at least some must remain behind in residence. A community of learning was no community without any people.

For a moment, a hollow feeling filled Thom's chest as his mind's eye conjured up an image of his home. He smelled the sweet odor of Rastis's pipe smoke, heard Hob's mighty laugh, and saw himself being silly with Lughus and Royne.

Soon… he thought, *Very soon…and in triumph with the Key!*

At the summit of the staircase, a large, ironbound door barred their passage any further. Magnus took a moment to check his axe and prepare

himself for what lay beyond. Thom, huffing and puffing with exertion, fell
to his knees, clutching a stitch in his side. He was grateful for the delay; he
would need to be ready to dodge and hide while Magnus wrought his
customary destruction—if indeed there was to be a fight, for they still had yet
to see a living soul. However, someone had to keep the beacon lit, Thom
knew, and whomever it was, the person or persons would most likely be
found behind this door.

Carefully, he boy pressed his ear against the wood and discerned the low
hum of voices. "There's someone there," he whispered, "I can just hear
them."

"Let's hope it's Slink, his crew, and the whole bloody town," Magnus
grimaced, his eyes alight with bloodlust. "I'd hate for our last battle together
to have the lowest count!"

Thom gave a nod, and as he gazed up at the grinning Wrathorn, he was
surprised to find his heart growing heavy. For over a year he had followed
this man on what often seemed the most absurd of journeys, from Galdoran
to the Sorgund Isles, to Grantis and the open sea, and finally to Castone, all
the while recording the most ridiculous and often horrific stories of
nonsensical violence, carousing, and debauchery. He could not count the
number of times he thought his death was certain (though he could count a
great number of other men who had lost their lives), and he had little
memory of moments when he was not consumed by terror. However, while
he was excited and relieved that it would all soon be over, he could not escape
a certain sadness that not long from now, he would be saying farewell to his
Wrathorn guide. The thought caused his eyes to burn.

"Magnus…"

"Quiet."

"But Magnus…"

"No."

"Please Magnus," Thom said again, his voice airy and weak, "Listen, I just
want to say…" he paused, "I just…" He heaved a great sigh and fell silent.

"Oh shut up, Thom Fatty," the Wrathorn grunted, though not unkindly.
With pommel of his axe, he pounded on the door. In the stillness, the echo
resounded throughout the interior of the tower, and to Thom's surprise, it
was open. The warrior and the apprentice exchanged a glance as light
streamed out through the small seem where the door came ajar. Then,

tightening his grip on his axe, Magnus gave a mighty kick and flung the door wide open. Bright light flashed from the room beyond and it was a moment before Thom's eyes adjusted.

Inside, a short set of stairs led up to a broad chamber that spanned the entire diameter of the Lighthouse. In its center, a great, roaring bonfire crackled madly upon an elevated dais. A strange network of crystal lenses reflected and directed the firelight through eight enormous archways that stretched from the vaulted ceilings down to the cold, stone floor and gazed out into the darkness of the night. A large marble pedestal, intricately carved with ancient runes, stood beneath each arch, laden with what must have been the greatest of the Keepers' treasures--a dagger with a twisted blade, a heavy, flanged mace, a strange iron mask, an illuminated scroll, a gilded censer, an aspergillum carved from ivory or bone, a tarnished, brass cup, and finally, on the far side of the room, a large, silver key.

"There it is!" Thom gasped, he made to run for it, but Magnus held him back with a rough shove. Only then did Thom notice the group of figures gathered at the base of the bonfire, only then did he notice the body splayed open upon the marble table, and only then could he discern their low chanting and sense the odor of blood.

"Lady save us!" he cried. Magnus made ready to charge, but to Thom's surprise, he hesitated as the chanting ceased and a voice addressed him by name.

"Magnus of Clan Bloodbeard," the voice said, hollow and low, "We have long been expecting you." The speaker was a tall man, gray-bearded and, like the half dozen other men surrounding him, dressed in fine robes of a deep purple hue. "It is a shame Keeper Caprice did not complete the journey as well," he continued, "Though as you can see, we have recovered the Key and have you to thank for it."

Magnus had no time for pleasantries. "Where's Slink?"

"He is here." The bearded man motioned toward the body stretched out upon the table. It was indeed the form of a lanky seaman, naked but for his sailcloth pants and a pair of gleaming scimitars that hung from a thick leather baldric girdling his waist. His face, dirty and unshaven, was a frozen mask of agony and terror, for in the center of his chest, gaped a great cavernous wound.

Thom's stomach churned, and to his surprise, even Magnus looked slightly taken aback.

"Is he dead?" the Wrathorn asked.

"In one sense, yes," the old man said, "And in another, no. He stands upon the threshold of eternity, and it is in this manner that we seek to reward him." He nodded to one of the other men at his side, "Keeper Levard, I believe we are ready to proceed."

"Yes, Grand Keeper," the man said, bowing his head.

Deep within the flames, a small, shriveled lump smoldered in an iron brazier. Spellbound, Thom and Magnus watched as Keeper Levard drew forth a pair of long, metal tongs and withdrew the blackened object from the brazier and placed it, fuming, within the cavity of Slink's chest. "In the name of Lord Dibhor, the one true god," he canted, "I bind you in life and in death to the bosom of his truth, now and forever."

"Now and forever!" the remaining keepers intoned.

Thom felt the blood drain from his face. He could not breathe. *The Dibhorites!* his mind screamed, *The Dibhorites have returned!* Wild-eyed with terror, he gazed at Magnus beseechingly, but the warrior remained still. *Why does he hesitate? Kill them! Kill them now!*

The ritual complete, the grand keeper calmly returned his attention to the intruders. "Now, Magnus, called the Reaver," he said, "Your arrival is an auspicious one, for we have long desired to meet you, and not simply for your victory over the Shield and retrieval of the Key."

Slowly, Magnus seemed to shake himself awake. His lips twisted into a scowl and while it was clear that he still seethed with rage, Thom sensed the Wrathorn's nerve had given way. "I did not come here to listen to your shite," he muttered, "I came here for Slink and for the fucking Key. You've robbed me of one; now hand over the other or I'll throw you from this fucking tower."

"Magnus, please," the grand keeper said with the tone of a parent to a petulant child, "We have no wish to harm you, for in spite of your…disagreement with Keeper Caprice, we welcome you here as a friend." He nodded to his fellows and smiled in a way that sent a shiver down Thom's back. "We seek to offer you the greatest of all rewards."

"Like you rewarded Slink, eh?"

The grand keeper's smiled widened. "For you, no," he said, "The reward we offered Captain Slink and his crew was one that we felt was more befitting of their character, just as is the case with the reward we would offer you."

Magnus's jaw tightened. "Unless your reward is the bloody Key and Slink's head on a plate," he said, "I can promise you the reward of my fucking axe."

"Really, Magnus," the grand keeper sighed, "What purpose would the Key serve for you? You owe no allegiance to the Guardians or their King. You are not bound by any vow or oath. It is the very reason Keeper Caprice sought you out. It is the very reason that even after murdering him and deceiving us, we seek but to reward you."

"Oh yes," the old man continued, sensing the Wrathorn's sudden interest, "It was you and you alone who we sought. You, a man with the Gift of the Guardians, a man bearing a title of strong lineage with the martial prowess to defeat the Shield, a man who might serve as the Champion of our Lord when he returns! Magnus, my boy, I do not offer you gold or jewels, or even a trinket such as the Key; I offer you the very world!"

Until now, Thom had hung back, struck dumb with disbelief and fear, but from somewhere within him, a spark of courage flared and without thinking, he stepped forward. "Don't listen to him, Magnus," he shouted, "They're disciples of the Warlock! They're servants of evil!"

The grand keeper turned his gaze upon Thom and the scribe felt his courage wilt beneath the old man's eyes—strange eyes, pale eyes, eyes as cold as death. "Who is this?" he asked.

"My name is Thom!" he shouted, struggling to keep his voice strong, "Apprentice to Loremaster Rastis Glendaro of the Order of the Guardians of Light!"

"Well, Thom the Apprentice," the grand keeper hissed, "I am certain we can find a use for you as well." He returned his attention to the Wrathorn. "In a year's time the Guardians will have crumbled, the realms of Termain will have fallen, and in the wake of their destruction—by the power of this Key—our Lord Dibhor will rise to restore order to the chaos. Yet to do so, he will need a champion to serve as the executer of his will. Today, you are a Blackguard, but in a year's time, you will be a god! The world will tremble at your approach! All men and women will leap at your command! You will have wealth and power beyond your wildest imagination! The Guardians may have destroyed Clan Bloodbeard, but give yourself to Lord Dibhor and your clan—your legacy—will live forever!"

Magnus's eyes smoldered, reflecting the light of the beacon, and Thom noticed his grip relax on the haft of his axe.

"No!" Thom cried, "Don't listen to him, Magnus! Dibhor is evil!"

"You have tracked your old shipmates across the continent to claim vengeance for their betrayal," the grand keeper continued, ignoring Thom, "But what of your family? What of your father who died at the hands of your Guardian foes? What of your vanquished Clan? Do they not deserve retribution as well? Honor demands it! The Wrathorn demand it! The last man standing fights for all who fell before him! Is that not the Wrathorn way? Give yourself to Lord Dibhor and it shall be done!"

"Magnus, no!" Thom's eyes burned with indignation. His mind raced over the lines of his prose, the strange tales that together comprised Magnus's bizarre song. They had set out together in search of revenge, to punish Magnus's false friends for betraying the bonds of the clan (for what was a crew but a clan at sea?). He thought of Magnus's childhood and near-death by his father's hand. He thought of the bloody raids and the fratricidal deaths of Magnus's brothers. He thought of *Sigruna*, a ship named for Magnus's mother. And all of a sudden, to his great surprise, he suddenly felt he understood the great warrior, understood his purpose in binding Thom to him as his scribe and scholar, and through him, understood all the Wrathorn. It was precisely the task that Rastis has assigned him to learn. His voice fell to a whisper, "Is this truly the ending you would have for your song? Binding yourself as a slave to someone else's god?"

Magnus's brow furrowed and once more his knuckles whitened upon the haft of his axe. "No," he said, "It's not." His beard bristled like fire in the light of the beacon and he shouted at the grand keeper in his rage. "How dare you speak of a Wrathorn's honor! How dare you speak the name of my clan! My father took up arms against the Guardians. He fought hard, but he failed, and paid for it with an honorable death! The Shield was the greatest warrior I've ever faced, and when I came for him, he fought me like a man and died an honorable death. Your man Caprice may have promised the others their reward, but it was my axe that won that Key! By right of combat and by honor, it's mine and I will have it now!"

"Submit to my Lord Dibhor," the grand keeper said with growing impatience, "And the Key and more shall be yours. Refuse, and death shall be your only prize!"

"Then fuck your god," Magnus cried, raising his axe, "And *fuck you!*"

With that, he charged the line of keepers and cleanly felled the nearest with one swift stroke. At once, they scattered, terrified of the enraged Wrathorn warrior—all save the Grand Keeper. Without any show of panic, the old man raised his arms before the great flame of the beacon and cried out in a voice of thunder.

"Dibhor, Lord of Darkness, I, Riggilo Huskarn, Grand Keeper of the Lighthouse and Warlock of the Blood, do beseech you! Send forth your servants to smite these blasphemers who defy your justice and your will!"

In answer, the bonfire flared brightly, and to his horror, Thom saw a vision of a strange, serpentine creature dancing in the flames. He threw himself to the floor behind one of the marble pedestals, frozen with fear. Outside of the tower, a war horn sounded from the direction of the town answered by another and finally a third. *Lady save us!* he prayed, *Brothers defend us from the Darkness!* Whether or not Magnus, too, spied the vision in the flames or heard the call of the horns, Thom did not know, so set was he upon the path of violence.

Two more fell to the frenzy of the whirling axe, great lakes of their blood glistening in the firelight, before the remaining keepers made it to the safety of the tower stair. For, Magnus's rage was directed upon their leader, still as a statue before the roaring flame. It was he who robbed the Wrathorn of his revenge; it was he who would next face death upon the axe.

Thom watched as Magnus drew ever-nearer to his prey and slowly raised his weapon on high as if to cleave the grand keeper in two. Yet just as the axe began to fall, there was the flash of a blade and the clang of steel upon steel, and to the boy's horror and the Wrathorn's surprise, there stood the corpse of Slink, his twin scimitars raised high to turn aside the killing blow.

"Behold the power of Dibhor!" the grand keeper shouted.

Thom stood still, frozen with fear and disbelief as there before him he saw a creature that had forever been bound to the realm of legend or nightmare. In a matter of but a few moments, the skin of Slink's corpse had taken on an ashen pallor and within the charred cavern at the center of his chest, his blackened heart smoldered like a burning coal. Once more, the war horns called, but this time they were much closer, perhaps as near as the base of the tower.

"The Army of the Dead!" Thom gasped, "Dibhor's Darkness has returned!"

Magnus remained silent, his eyes alight with wonder, his face grim.

"If you will not serve Dibhor in life," the Grandkeeper sneered, "Then you shall serve him in death!"

Slink's corpse pressed forward, forcing the Wrathorn to disengage and take a step backwards, bracing the haft of his axe before him in a defensive posture. The dead man's scimitars whirled, preparing to attack. Thom scurried for cover behind one of the marble pedestals, terrified at the dull, empty glow emanating from the corsair's eyes.

If Magnus was afraid, he made no show of it. Rather, his lips drew back in a broad, fey grin. "I'll grant your god good for one thing," he growled, his eyes alight with battle lust, "At least now I can claim my revenge!"

With the force of a great northern bear, Magnus let loose a cry of rage and hurled himself at his foe. The mighty bearded axe flashed like lightning in the light of the bonfire, and blow after blow fell like summer rain. How the dead man managed to counter each attack, Thom could only wonder. Still, Magnus drove the dead man back across the floor to the very edge of the tower, invigorated by the battle song of steel upon steel.

"Good thing death taught you something, you slippery bastard," the Wrathorn smiled at the mute corpse, "Be a shame to come all this way for it to be over too quickly!"

The dead man made no reply, but the eerie light of its eyes grew bright with a dark hunger as it renewed its assault.

All of this Thom watched from behind his pedestal, wide-eyed with wonder and despair, until from the corner of his eye, he saw a flash of movement. It was the grand keeper, his face a mask of self-righteous determination, certain of victory and secure in his dark fervor. He knelt beside the bodies of his slain brethren, whispering in a strange tongue.

The apprentice's heart thundered in his chest. He could not begin to imagine what new evil the old man was working, and he had no more wish to find out than he had to learn the source of the war horns.

Blast it all! he cursed inwardly. *What am I to do?*

527

A loud crash sent him ducking for cover as nearby as one of the other marble pedestals toppled over, knocked down, no doubt, by the Wrathorn and his dead foe. Thom pressed his hands to his forehead, grinding his teeth in bitterness. He cursed his impotent uncertainty, his perpetual lack of courage.

And then, suddenly, not far before him on the floor, his eyes fell upon a large silver key, gleaming in the firelight.

Callah's key! Thom thought, *It must have fallen when the pillar overturned!*

He glanced once more over the edge of his sheltering pedestal; the old keeper continued his whispering while Magnus and the dead man continued to wage war. Outside of the great vaulted windows of the tower, the wind seemed to be increasing, while from below, he discerned the low rumble of thunder and the heavy tread of marching boots.

And somehow, in the rising chaos, his own presence—as always—seemed suddenly forgotten, even ignored, and he knew that his time had come.

Lady Callah, guide me! Thom whispered, and throwing caution to the wind, he rolled from his place of cover and scampered across the floor. In one fluid motion, he swept up the great key and hugged it to his chest.

At once there came a flash of lightening and an echo of thunder that sent him tumbling to the ground again in fear; however, the Key was his, clenched tightly against his chest with both hands, like a mother defending her newborn.

"Magnus! I have it!" he cried out in wonder at his own success, "I have the Key! "

A heavy slash from a scimitar sent Magnus reeling as he hurriedly turned to parry a second blow. A vivid gash opened along his shoulder, but the Wrathorn ignored it, grinding his teeth in rage as he staged his counterattack.

"Hurry, Magnus!" Thom shouted again, "We must go! I have--"

A sharp tug at the back of his habit stopped him midsentence. It was the grand keeper. In his sudden surge of triumph Thom had lost sight of the dangers surrounding him.

"Give me the key!" the old man snapped.

"No!" Thom shouted in defiance. He attempted to pull backwards, away from the grand keeper's grasp, but the old man held him fast.

"Give me the Key!" the keeper hissed once more.

"Never!"

The old man's eyes blazed. "You cannot possibly believe that you can escape here alive," he sneered, "Your battle is lost. Your resistance simply prolongs the inevitable. You, your barbarian friend, and your blasted Order will be cleansed from this land by Darkness and Flame! Now, give me the Key!"

From somewhere deep within him, Thom felt a burst of righteous fury. Again, the lightning flashed and the thunder roared. With all of his might, with all of his weight, he drove himself headlong into the old man's midsection and sent him sprawling like a rag doll across the floor.

The grand keeper was very slow in righting himself, and from the side of his temple blood oozed from a nasty gash. His expression twitched with an almost inhuman viciousness and when he spoke, his voice was as cold as a serpent's hiss. "As you wish."

At once a dozen dead soldiers flooded the room from the tower stairs, followed by the clatter of arms and the stomping of boots that promised dozens, if not hundreds, more.

"Great Lady of Light!" Thom shouted, "Magnus! There are more of them!"

"Stone's Bollocks, Thom Crusher! Would you leave off with the bloody shouting!" Magnus cried. He had climbed atop one of the last remaining pedestals and from here defended himself against Slink's corpse. Two more gashes, one across his left thigh and another along his right wrist, joined the one on his shoulder; however, not one of the wounds seemed to slow the great warrior down. Slink's corpse, meanwhile, though seemingly tireless, had lost the use of its left arm, which hung flaccidly by but a few strands of sinew at the shoulder.

"You know the price of treachery is death, you bloody bastard," Magnus shouted at his shipmate's corpse. He leapt high into the air, dodging a slash at his feet from the only remaining scimitar, and landed lightly behind the dead man's back. "Looks like you'll have to pay it twice!" he cried, and brought down the axe with all of his might, splitting Slink's skull like a melon.

Thom watched the corpse fall to the floor. A short flash of emotion spread across the Wrathorn's face, but he allowed himself no more time for ceremony. For, with the continued arrival of the dead army, it seemed the battle had only just begun.

"Got the Key?" Magnus said as Thom hurried to his side. The pair of them withdrew to one of the vaulted windows on the far side of the room, as far away as they could get from the advancing soldiers. Outside, the storm gathered even thicker in the night sky and the waves raged in the waters far below.

"Yes," Thom said, "I have it."

The Wrathorn nodded. "Can't say I'm certain we'll make it out of this alive," he said, "Not that I mind dying in battle. Prefer it, actually. But, I can't say I fancy the idea of being turned into one of them."

Thom breathed a heavy sigh and gazed down at the silver key. Clenched tightly in his hands, it had grown warm. *I won't let them have it*, he thought, *I'll throw it in the sea before I see it in their hands again.* Callah's Key. How he wished he could have told Lughus about this, or Royne, or had time to at least finish writing of his adventures with the great Magnus Bloodbeard.

"Kill them!" the Grand Keeper cried, "Kill them both!"

The first rank of dead men advanced, packed shoulder to shoulder in neat ranks of five. In life, they were men and women who appeared to have come from lives as diverse from one another as the scribe and the barbarian— farmers, fishwives, sailors, and soldiers from across the realms. However, in death, or rather, un-death, they had found common cause.

No, Thom thought, they had found nothing, for the person who once occupied the deceased flesh had long since departed, whether for the Realms of the Blessed or the Blackness of the Abyss. All that remained now was an empty husk, discarded like old clothing to be repurposed by the devotees of the Dark Brother.

Living or dead, though, it mattered little to Magnus, for at the onrush of attackers, he raised his axe and met the enemy without fear. With his first strike alone, two of the dead returned to the grave, their heads severed cleanly from their necks. A third corpse fell cloven from shoulder to hip, and a fourth crumpled, its skull caved in with a blow from the axe's pommel. When Magnus turned to engage the fifth, however, four more had already advanced to replace the fallen while still more flooded in from the tower stairs.

Still, the great warrior fought on undeterred. Another great swing opened a dead sailor's stomach, spilling his rotting innards upon the floor. The corpse of an old woman raked at Magnus's shoulder with gnarly hands, until a blow from a the haft of the axe crumpled her broken form. At once, though, a dead mercenary replaced her and turned aside the Wrathorn's next attack with his shield. In life he must have had some skill at arms, for he succeeded in scoring a quick slash to Magnus's right side before the big man knocked him to the ground and stomped his skull flat with his boot.

"I hope you're keeping the count, mate." The Wrathorn smiled grimly, taking a step back to reposition his footing, "Did you see the first two? Two heads clean with one blow? That should be at least five!"

Thom tried to return the big man's grin, but the din of steel, the clash of thunder, and the roar of the great flame silenced any stirrings of warlike mirth. He turned his eyes through the archway, away from the tower. His gaze stretched out over the dark expanse, the swirling mists, the tumultuous eastern seas. For a fleeting moment, he thought of jumping, wondering if by some miracle he could leap far enough to clear the edge of the cliff at the tower's foundation, but no. Even if he actually had the courage to try, it was way too far a distance, too high a drop. At his back, Magnus had rejoined the battle, smiling still in the face of death, ready to sound the final notes of his song.

This really is the end, he thought. Strangely, he did not feel overly sad, nor did he feel any inclination to weep. He simply bowed his head in resignation. Face death with a smile, the Wrathorn way, Magnus's way. At least it would be an ending worthy of song, tragic perhaps, but still worthy. Worthier than he had ever imagined. Besides, it would not be a complete loss. He could still deprive his enemies of the Key. He could hurl it with every ounce of strength he had left and it would sink straight to the bottom like a stone.

Thus, some good might come of his absurd adventure, his comically meaningless existence. What a shame that only in the end should he finally accomplish anything worthwhile. He breathed a heavy sigh and his gaze fell.

And suddenly, something caught his eye that kindled in him a forlorn hope.

While from below the sides of the Lighthouse tower appeared completely smooth and sheer, as if it were one continuous shaft of white marble rising high into the sky, from his current vantage point, he could see that this was not so. For, below him at regular intervals, he could discern breaks in the stone, revealing a series of balconies, half-hidden behind low, sloping walls— like a long, narrow pine cone that had just begun to open.

Thom bit his lip. He had little faith in his ability to climb, and even less in his ability to jump; however, if he could manage to simply *fall* with any sense of accuracy, then perhaps—perhaps—escape was not as impossible as he had hitherto thought.

He turned back to Magnus and the battle raging at his back. The Wrathorn had been busy, committing himself fully to his work. A mounding semicircle of corpses had built up around him and Thom counted over a dozen bodies that the big man had granted a second death. Yet evermore they filed in from the tower stairs, rank after rank, flooding the chamber, their chests aglow with the unholy fire of the beacon. There was no sign of the Grand Keeper. Content that the dead would take care of the living, the old man had disappeared.

"Magnus!" Thom called, "The window!"

The big Wrathorn smashed a dead man's jaw clean from his face and sunk the axe head deep into another's smoldering heart. "The what, now?"

"The window! If we jump, there's a chance we can escape!"

"Aye and die smashed to bits in the courtyard below."

"No the courtyard's on the other side. Below us it's the cliff's edge and the sea!

"Aye, even better," Magnus snorted. He lashed out with a mighty kick and snapped a dead man's leg with a loud crack and caved in his skull with Death's pommel.

"No," Thom shouted, "There's a ledge—a balcony—right below us. And more, all the way down! Look!"

The big man gave a grunt and holding his axe before him pushed the front rank of dead soldiers backwards, toppling them over and buying himself enough time to throw a quick glance over the side.

"If we move swiftly, we may be able to get to the base of the tower before they can regroup," Thom waved his hand at the dead soldiers as they clambered back to their feet, "They're quick enough at fighting and marching, but most of them look like they lack real skill, especially without the Keeper shouting orders."

"Aye, true enough. Slink was a warrior, a shit one, but he knew his way around a sword. Most of these folk look like townsmen or merchant sailors. Farmers even. They're puppets. Sheep."

"Magnus," Thom said, his eyes ablaze with fervor, "We have to try. How else will I finish the song?"

Magnus's brow furrowed in thought. The first of the dead to find its footing rushed forth and Magnus easily knocked it flat and opened its skull with his axe. "Aye, then, Crusher," he said, stepping back to the fat boy's side, "I suppose it's the best chance we've got."

"And the only one," Thom muttered.

The big man gave a nod, "You first. I'll hold them off."

Thom nodded. "Be quick! They may not all be warriors, but some are, and once we jump, it won't take them long to figure out what we're about and regroup." He was surprised at the sudden authority with which he spoke, and even more so at the big man's nod of camaraderie. It stoked the tiny ember of courage he felt kindling in his chest.

"Look at you! Finally grown a pair, eh?" Magnus laughed, "Go on! I'll follow right behind."

Quickly, Thom stuffed Callah's Key into the belt of his habit, taking care to ensure that it was completely secure and would not slip loose in the descent. Then, with a deep breath, he clambered up over the edge of the window and prepared to hang-drop to the balcony below. The wind whipped through his hair and at a sudden crash of thunder, he let go. His heart caught in his throat and his blood turned to ice for the split second in which he fell, and when he hit the stone ledge of the balcony below, his ankle twisted painfully beneath him, but he made it. He was alive, for now.

That's one, he thought as he collected himself and attempted to find his bearings. A heavy wooden door separated the balcony from the tower's interior and below him he could make out the next balcony a floor below and a few feet to the south. His ankle was stiff and quavered beneath him, but he had no other option than to jump, no way to but down.

Another flash of lightning and a body fell hurtling past him from above and exploded on the edge of the cliff below. At once, Thom cried out in terror, "Magnus! No!"

To his relief, the big man dropped down beside him a moment later.

"What are you still doing here?" he growled, "Move! Don't stop!" Without waiting, the big Wrathorn climbed up onto the edge of the balcony and leapt easily to the next one below. Thom hurried after him, leapt unsteadily over the void, and fell hard upon the stones once more. Pain coursed through him as if he had been struck by lightning, but still he made it.

"Come on, you slug," Magnus urged him, but when Thom tried to stand, his ankle gave way and he fell once more to the floor.

"It's over," the chubby boy said, but there was no fear behind it, no despair; simply acknowledgement. He raised his eyes to the Wrathorn warrior and for a moment, they shared a meaningful gaze. Thom couldn't quite explain it, but somehow in that moment, he felt brave—that even in the face of certain doom, he had attempted something extraordinary, and though his ankle may be broken and he could not rise again, he had at least tried.

Something in Magnus's eyes told him that the big man understood that, and shouldering his axe, he grabbed hold of Thom's arm and lifted him—like a fallen comrade—to his feet.

"Hold fast, Thom Crusher," the Wrathorn said. He led Thom to the edge of the balcony. "Get on my back," he said, "And I'll take care of the rest."

For a moment, Thom made to protest, but at the resolute look in the Wrathorn's eye, he held his tongue. "Alright," he said.

"You don't get to die today," Magnus said, clambering awkwardly over the side, "Least of all to these fucking bastards. Now, mind my axe and hold on to that fucking key."

CHAPTER 40: BLOOD & FIRE

In the fallow fields outside of St. Golan's, away from the assembled armies, six figures crept like shadows beneath the eerie light of the bloody red moon. Adolfo the Madder led the way, and at his side strode Sir Geoffrey of Pyle.

Geoffrey had not realized just how comfortable he had become within the steel skin of his armor until he was suddenly without it. Yet, even before Adolfo mentioned it, Geoffrey knew that it would only inhibit him in this errand—an errand for which silence and swiftness would be of the utmost importance. True, it was a task for which the Blade may have been better suited, but with Brigid indisposed, the Vanguard was more than up for the task, and sure enough, Geoffrey had plenty of latent memories—of Regnar and even a few others before him—to prove it.

Now, as he rolled his shoulders and stretched his legs, he almost felt as if he were floating, free as he was of the heavy burden of the mail. An almost youthful spring had come into his step, though he could not say that the doffing of his armor was entirely to blame. Surely the impending battle, which promised to be the largest in which he had ever participated, was certainly a contributing factor, and he could not resist a certain frenzied anticipation.

Let's just hope that what we do here helps to even the odds a little, he thought.

From the tiny postern along the eastern side of the monastery wall, the Madder led the small party, which consisted of Geoffrey and four of Adolfo's mercenary cutthroats. They skulked across the fields, making their way to the rear of the Andochan army's position, to the small encampment where men clad in the red garb of the kingsmen were busily at work assembling a trio of trebuchets.

"Sweet Lady's Teats!" one of the cutthroats murmured, "Those bloody things could raze the whole fucking Houndstooth to the ground, to say nothing of the monastery." He was the same rat-faced man who came to fetch Geoffrey earlier. Like the other men in Adolfo's employ, Geoffrey had not learned his name nor did the man seem in any hurry to share it.

"Aye," another man added, "The Baron of Agathis learned the hard way, so I hear."

"And with the way those bastards raced out here to meet us, I'll bet there's plenty of plunder to be had among the ruins they left behind," said the first, "Makes you wonder why in all the Black Abyss we're out here and not hightailing it there to help ourselves…"

"Enough," the Madder snapped, "You'll have your chance once this job's done and I'll tolerate no more talk to the contrary." He turned to Geoffrey, "Do you see those barrels assembled around the oxcarts?"

Geoffrey gave a nod.

"They're filled with St. Aiden's Fire," the Madder said, "It's a substance—somewhat like honey in appearance—but when ignited, it burns like a forge fire and is extremely difficult to put out."

Geoffrey chewed his lip and peered out across the plane at the Guardian siege encampment, illuminated as it was by the numerous cook fires where the Andochan soldiers sat about enjoying what, for some, would be their last meal. In addition to the red-clad workmen, armored sentries stood watch while a tall, lanky nobleman in a plumed beret paced back and forth inspecting the assembly of the great machines. Every so often, he stepped forward to issue a command or peer across the field through a brass spyglass. By some preternatural sense, Geoffrey knew the man to be one of the Anointed.

"That, I believe," Adolfo said, following the farmer's gaze, "Is the Guardian known as the Cockerel."

"I suppose I should have known him by the feather," Geoffrey observed. He released a sigh and rubbed his chin in thought. "It's quite well defended," he said.

"Aye," one of the cutthroats muttered, "But if that shit burns so easy, why not just shoot it with a flamin' arrow and be done with it?"

Geoffrey shook his head. "If we stop now to kindle a flame, they'll surely see us and raise an alarm."

"Then what do you expect we should do?" the rat-faced man asked.

Adolfo's gaze narrowed as he peered across the plain. "We circle around further and approach from the rear," he said, "And while the barrels of fire should be dealt with, the true threat is from the trebuchets."

Geoffrey eyed the site ahead. Clearly, the men were still in the process of setting up the engines and arranging their ammunition. Even the oxcarts remained partially unloaded with the barrels of fire sitting in idle clusters awaiting the workmen to place them in convenient reach of the trebuchets. "What if there's a way to kill two birds with one stone?" he finally said, "Perhaps even three, if the Cockerel should get caught in the middle of it."

"I'm listening," Adolfo said.

A short while later, Geoffrey made his way silently over to the oxcarts and with a bumbling type of casualness, leaned idly against one of the barrels. Before parting ways with Adolfo, he had entrusted the Madder with Oakheart and Acorn, and while their absence made him feel even more exposed than his lack of armor, the simple peasant tunic and hose that he wore beneath it made him appear all the more nondescript.

Geoffrey crouched beside one of the half-emptied oxcarts. The ground underneath was soft and moist where the wheels of the cart had worn furrows. The pungent odor of the soil was a small comfort, a reminder of something he knew in a sea of uncertainty. He breathed in the scent of the soft mud and instantly recalled his days in the Spade. What a thing it was like to live the life of a poor country peasant—the automatic deference, the near-constant fear. He tried to assume the persona of his former self while at the same time—perhaps for the *first* time, understanding just how far he had come in the world.

Sir Geoffrey of Pyle, he thought, *Defender of the Spade.* He would go back there someday and earn that title, Kin willing. He would show the common folk—farmers, peasants, and the like—how far a man might climb in the world if he simply had the will to follow through. For, in spite of his anointing as the Vanguard, he did not believe himself to be anything special—just a man like any other with a will to do right by his fellows and his family.

And a desire to stand as a force for Good.

St. Aiden was a farmer...

A gruff call broke in on his musings, as one of the red-cloaked sentries approached, knocking the butt of his pike against the side of the oxcart.

"Oi! What in the bloody Abyss are you doing down there?"

Geoffrey scurried to his feet, slumped his shoulders, and hung his head. "I'm sorry, sir," he mumbled, "Begging your pardon."

The sentry eyed him closely, and at once, Geoffrey squirmed sheepishly to maintain the ruse. "Where are you from?" the man asked, "Somewhere in the south?"

Geoffrey's heart quickened, but he fought to appear contrite. With brown skin like his, it was unlikely he was born to lands this far north. Perhaps, as Adolfo suggested, he should mingle a bit of truth in with the deception.

"Dwerin, sir, or near enough," he said, "The southern tip, close to the border with Grantis."

"Grantis, eh?" the sentry scoffed, "Land of the bloody garlic-eaters and Kordish half-breeds."

For the sake of the ruse, Geoffrey suppressed a flash of indignation at the man's bigotry. "Aye, sir," he said, "When Andoch and the Ironmen smashed the Republic, I felt I owed it to the Guardians to join them wherever I could. Of course, with the fighting all done down south, I was forced to come north in hopes of helping with the war effort. I may not be much of a fighter, but I got a strong back. Plenty strong enough to move some barrels."

From beneath the shade of his kettle helm, the sentry continued to hold Geoffrey in his skeptical stare, and as Geoffrey watched the wheels turning in the man's mind, the farmer began to steel himself for violence.

At last, the sentry gave a grunt and spit a great wad of phlegm across the field. "Well," he said, "Best get your ass moving then. Dawn will be here before you know it and these barrels had best be in position for the attack so no more bloody loafing!"

"Aye, sir," Geoffrey said, "Right away, sir." He turned a barrel onto its side and began to roll it along the grass. He felt the weight of the sentries glare linger a moment longer, but in the end, the man walked off to continue his rounds.

Bastard! Geoffrey thought, *Well, he'll be in for quite the flogging should the plan work out...*

By now, the teams of workmen had just completed the assembly of the trebuchets and had broken up to eat or get what rest they could before the battle. As such, there were few around to pay any notice as, one by one, Geoffrey rolled barrel after barrel from the oxcarts and placed them alongside the great siege engines. Close enough to seem a plausible place to store excess ammunition, and near enough to spread to the wooden frameworks should St. Aiden's Fire somehow ignite prematurely.

This, of course, was ultimately the plan, though it would be up to Adolfo and his men to finish the job.

The ease with which Geoffrey found that he could hide in plain sight was remarkable, and he could scarcely believe how easily he had not only infiltrated the enemy camp, but actively worked to sabotage them under their very noses. Simply by acting in accordance with the expectations of social class and rank, and by adopting a façade of quiet confidence (or at least, surety of purpose), he had been able to successfully place four barrels of Aiden's Fire at the base of each of the first two trebuchets. In all that time, apart from the sentry who initially challenged him, he had encountered no further questioning, rather, in numerous instances was met instead with the occasional nod of camaraderie.

As he was placing a third barrel alongside the final trebuchet, however, his luck seemed to run out. Behind him, he heard a weary voice sigh with irritation.

"No, no, no. The fire barrels are too close here. They need to be placed over *there*."

Suddenly, Geoffrey stopped short and turned only to find himself face to face with the Guardian in the feathered beret, the Cockerel.

At once, the Guardian's eyes went wide with shock and Geoffrey felt the vague sensation of familiarity wash over him. This near, Geoffrey could see that dressed as he was in the finery of a nobleman or a wealthy burgher, the man was no warrior.

"The…the Vanguard," the Cockerel stammered breathlessly, "A b-bloody Blackguard!"

Time stood still as in an instant, Geoffrey's mind worked through numerous courses of action. He was unarmed and unarmored, and while he believed that he could quickly overpower the Guardian, the resulting scuffle was sure to attract attention. From there, the men of Andoch would surely swarm him and he would be overwhelmed.

Otherwise, he could attempt to run; however, he had no idea where Adolfo and his men were hidden or if they had even succeeded in their part of the plan. Thus, the entire endeavor stood upon the brink of failure, and so it seemed now to Geoffrey that he stood between a rock and a hard place.

Yet, as he steeled himself for violence and made ready to spring, a dull thump gave him pause. For all of a sudden, the shaft of a crossbow bolt seemed to spring suddenly from out of the Cockerel's chest. The Guardian's eyes went wide with horror and he collapsed heavily upon the ground breathing in great, raggedy gasps. For a moment, Geoffrey felt the automatic compulsion to help the man, as he would have in a time before he knew so intimately the ways of warfare, but at a harsh call of "Vanguard!" he turned to see the Madder and his cutthroats materialize beside one of the nearby cook fires.

"We move," Adolfo said, tossing Oakheart and Acorn at Geoffrey's feet. He paused only long enough to reload his crossbow and grab a burning brand from the fire.

"Now!"

At once, the men sprang into action. The cutthroats, armed with flaming branches, rushed to ignite the barrels around the trebuchets. At the sight of the obvious and imminent danger, the men of Andoch leapt to their feet and launched themselves with reckless abandon at Adolfo's men.

A soldier in an arming jacket tried to charge past Geoffrey in pursuit, only to be thrown from his feet when the farmer plowed into him with the force of a battering ram. Another two men followed, but with the Acorn braced before him, Geoffrey scattered them like chaff across the grounds of the camp.

A sudden explosion and a flash of light announced that the first of the trebuchets had caught fire. At once, the entire Andochan camp began to rise for fear that the Galadins had attempted a preemptive strike, and while in some sense that was true, the resulting confusion allowed two more of the cutthroats to make their move. Geoffrey watched their mad dash for the second of the three trebuchets, only to see the first man beaten to the ground. Moments later, he was swarmed and bludgeoned to death by a mob of workmen wielding whatever blunt tools were nearest at hand.

Yet, while it might not have been his intention, the cutthroat's sacrifice allowed his partner to slip through, igniting the barrel with his flaming brand. The sudden torrent of flame that burst forth scattered the swarming soldiers, and they fled before the threat of another explosion while the frame and counterweight of the trebuchet burned.

The thud of Adolfo's crossbow brought Geoffrey's attention back around, and he turned just in time to see a man topple over in a heap of agony.

"Now, Vanguard!" the Madder cried. He tossed his flaming brand lightly at the base of the final trio of fire barrels. "We run!"

Geoffrey tightened his grip on Oakheart and Acorn and hurried to follow, noting as the final barrels began to blaze that the Cockerel had somehow dragged himself to safety and disappeared.

"This way!" Adolfo called, pausing only to smash an oncoming soldier's face with the butt of his crossbow. "Behind you!"

Geoffrey turned as another Andochan ran at him from the side. He raised the Acorn just in time to turn aside the enemy's slash, and a quick counterblow from Oakheart knocked the man flat. The Madder continued his flight toward the line of carts and barrels, waving Geoffrey on.

A scream from the encampment checked Geoffrey's pace, and through the growing clouds of smoke, he watched in horror as the rat-faced cutthroat was lifted into the air, impaled upon a sentry's pike. If the Madder even recognized his former employee's fate, he gave no indication. Without pause, he began to kick over any additional fire barrels wherever he passed them. Geoffrey joined him in the arbitrary destruction, even slapping a pair of oxen on the flank to set them trundling out into the open field, spilling the unsecured barrels out of the carts behind them.

More men scrambled to intercept them. Adolfo dispatched one man with a bolt through the throat, while Geoffrey caved in the skulls of another two who attempted to engage him in tandem. At length, content with these final acts of chaos, Adolfo leapt from the back of another cart. "Vanguard, Hurry!" he shouted before plunging into the darkness of the field. Again, Geoffrey made to follow, but a sudden war cry announced the arrival of the bigoted sentry from earlier.

"You Kordish fuck!" The man spat at him, charging with his pike. Geoffrey sidestepped just in time to knock the polearm aside with the Acorn. It smashed into the side of an oxcart and stuck fast between the remaining barrels.

Wasting no time, the farmer whirled Oakheart around and brought it down on the pike's haft, splintering it like straw. The sentry barely had time to register his surprise before a second blow from the cudgel crushed his kettle helm. At once, Geoffrey took off running again after Adolfo.

The burning siege camp was but a twinkle on the horizon before either man stopped running.

"We're the only ones to make it out," Geoffrey observed, breathing hard. He took a moment to check the few scratches, bumps, and bruises he had sustained in the course of the skirmish and the frenzied flight across the field.

"The others were expendable," the Madder said, "And were paid accordingly."

Geoffrey took a deep breath, his senses alive with the scent of the fields and the lingering rush of battle. Far off in the distance, it appeared as if the Andochans had finally gained control of the fires—or at least—found a way to contain them, though the trebuchets were no more. "Do you think the Cockerel is dead?" he asked.

"You know as well as I that it takes a lot more than a single arrow to kill a Guardian," Adolfo said, "Though I doubt he'll be well enough to take the field at first light."

"Three birds with one stone."

The Madder gave a silent nod.

"Well," Geoffrey said, "We should get back. There's still much and more to be done."

"Indeed," Adolfo said, "And in spite of our actions here, the enemy still outnumbers us five to one."

CHAPTER 41: FOR THE QUEEN

With all possible haste, Beledain, Sir Armel, and the newly dubbed Sir Briden raced over the fields northwest of Pridel to return to the city and the queen, for in his final moments, Kurlan Malacco had all but confirmed what the Shackle had suspected. Canton and his vermin were out for royal blood, and just as the Death Knell was meant to raze the Tower in the field, so the Rat King was to pluck the Winter Rose.

Bel's fury knew no bounds as he urged Tempest onward. By some unnatural sense, the great horse understood that time was of the essence, and before long, he outpaced Maggie and Armel's destrier, Anvil, leaving the pair of knights far behind. Bel was glad for it; he needed the time to focus, to think—or rather, to *not* think, to clear his mind so that he might remain steadfast and resolute. There were already too many invasive thoughts, too many distractions and fears. *No more can die*, he swore, his eyes watering as he stared into the rushing wind, *I have to save them.*

Without the slow march of the army at his back and Tempest's great speed, it was but a short while before Pridel's keep appeared on the horizon. Yet, from what he could tell, there were no signs of battle, of war. No smoke flittered about on the horizon to mark a burning city district. No bells rang out in warning or alarm. The city simply carried on as usual, waiting for the army's return, but it was this quiet that, to Bel, was all the more frightening.

"Fly, Tempest!" Bel hurried, "Fly!"

At the main gates to the city, the watchmen on duty spied his approach from a long ways off. They stood waiting when he reached them, no doubt hoping for news of the battle; however, Bel did not stop nor even check Tempest's pace as he stormed past them, up the cobbled thoroughfare toward the castle barbican.

As he galloped ahead through the city streets, he was increasingly alarmed by prevailing the sense of calm. While he knew that the majority of the townsfolk would have barricaded themselves in their homes as a precaution against a possible sacking, he had at least expected some measure of carnage wrought by Canton and his band of assassins. A fire, a body, the odd pool of blood—anything to mark some show of armed conflict, particularly if the Shackle had caught up with them. Yet, there was nothing, at least, until he passed through the open gates of the barbican into the inner ward of the castle.

Cautiously, Bel slipped from his saddle and gently ran a hand down Tempest's muzzle. "Where is everyone?" he asked the horse.

Tempest replied with a snort, pressing his great head against Bel's shoulder.

"I know," Bel said, "It's too quiet, but I don't see any signs of battle."

The searoan said nothing, but Bel could sense an undercurrent of anxiety in the horse lord's demeanor.

Bel patted the horse on the flank. "I know. I feel it too." He readied Spire, "Stay here and wait for Armel and Briden. I'm heading inside to have a look."

Without another word, Bel passed through the main doors of the castle and onward into the great hall. Still, he met no one—not a guard nor a servant—and he could hear nothing beyond the faint sound of Tempest pacing the courtyard. At the far end of the hall, he passed through a small archway that led deeper into the keep. It was here that for the first time he saw signs of a struggle, or rather, the evidence of murder.

Three men, one, a hulking mountain of a man clad from head to foot in chainmail, was slumped against the wall beside two dead servants, their throats red and gaping, cut from ear to ear.

They're here! Bel's mind screamed. *The rats are loose in the castle!*

At once, he ran for the stairs leading upward to the queen's and his own private quarters. All at once, the marks of battle revealed themselves: bodies of guards, servants, and others unknown to him lie in various states of death upon the floor, throughout the hallways, and along the spiraling stone stair. Steaks of blood marred the walls, trickling down to fill the furrows between the stones underfoot, or emanated from the corpses, shimmering in wide, crimson pools.

Bel's breath came so quickly that he feared he might faint for lack of air, and his hands gripped the haft of his spear so tightly that they began to ache with the effort. *It was foolish not to suspect something like this,* he cursed himself, *Bloody Canton and his rats! I should have killed him when I had the chance!*

As he neared the top of the staircase, the stillness of the empty castle was finally broken by the sound of men shouting and the clash of metal upon metal. Bel ran even faster towards the clamor, and as he did so, the mass of dead grew thicker and thicker. In place of Sir Emory's men, however, many of these new dead were clad in the garb of common folk, though a few still wore light shirts of mail or leather armor. Many of these bore deep gashes to the face or the throat, though here and there some bore the telltale signs of a sword thrust or deep, cleaving slashes that split from the shoulder down through to the heart.

The sound of fighting was even louder now from the direction of King Marius's apartment, and as Bel ran to join the fray, he saw the Shackle surrounded by half a dozen attackers. At his feet lay Sir Emory Knott, and behind him, wounded and leaning upon his sword, was Bel's own father, King Cedric Tremont.

Bel's approach caught the Shackle's attackers by surprise, and as they turned to acknowledge the new threat, the Blackguard lashed out with his sickle and hooked one man by the collarbone. With a rough tug, the Shackle pulled him down to the floor and King Cedric hurried forth to open the man's throat. From the doorway, Bel swung Spire in a wide arc and scattered the remaining men backwards, allowing the Shackle to strike out and dispatch another.

Caught now between the wrath of the two Blackguards, the remaining men panicked and made a desperate charge. The Shackle tripped the first with his length of chain, turned aside the second's blow with his sickle, and with a flick of his wrist, cut the man's throat before finishing the man on the floor. Bel broke a man's nose with the haft of his spear, whirled Spire around, and impaled another. With the immediate threat over, King Cedric collapsed heavily into the arms of a wooden chair, exhausted from the effort.

"What happened?" Bel asked. He wrenched his spear free from the dead man's innards and wiped it clean on his tunic, "How did they get in?"

The Shackle let his chain fall limp upon the floor and leaned forward onto his knees, struggling to breathe. His muscular arms were scored by numerous gashes and scrapes, and a few red punctures marred the side of his tunic, though none appeared to be mortal. "I don't know," he said quickly, "I followed the others from the field, but the bloody horse threw a shoe and I couldn't catch up with them in time. Once I finally got here, they'd already gotten inside. Someone let them in, I'd wager—a spy, no doubt—and there were others joined 'em as well. More than a score all told." He shook his head and motioned toward the fallen seneschal. "The old knight's dead," he said sadly and nodded to another body on the far side of the room, "Marius too. He was one of the first to fall when they forced the door."

"Blood and Fire!" Bel shouted, "Where is the queen? Where is Marcus?"

"Emory sent them to the nursery," King Cedric said, "The queen, the nurse, your son...He told me to go with them but..." the old man shook his head.

"Damn it, father!" Bel growled, "Are you mad?" He noticed a blotch of red staining the king's left side, "You're wounded!"

"It matters little now," Cedric coughed, "Go! Find the queen! Find your son!"

"Canton's still around," the Shackle said, "I saw him, but I couldn't get to him."

"Go, Beledain!" King Cedric said, "Go, my son! Go!"

Without further hesitation, Bel ran out into the hallway toward the nursery. Two more bodies lie dead upon the floor, and to his horror, Bel recognized one as a woman. It was Lourdes, Marina's maid. Blood stained the white cloth of her frock, and Bel felt his stomach turn. *This is my fault!* He winced, grinding his teeth, *I should have anticipated this!*

The shrill scream of a woman roused him from his bitter self-loathing and he hurried onward, struggling to ignore the weight of both his armor and his grief. *No one else can die!* he swore, *No one else!*

The door to the nursery was shut when he reached it, though it was unbarred and gave way instantly beneath his charge. Inside, Canton stood over the twisted corpse of Elsa, Marcus's nursemaid, while in the corner of the room Marina knelt upon the floor rocking back and forth. Her lips worked furiously mouthing silent words, and in her arms, she clutched Marcus to her, as if to shield him whatever harm Dermont's master of spies might seek to inflict upon them next.

"You bastard!" Bel shouted, and before the spy master had time to even react, Bel leveled his spear, charged, and ran Spire through Canton's innards halfway down the oaken shaft.

Canton opened his mouth as if to speak, but Bel would not suffer any more of his poisoned words. He forced Spire even deeper, until he was within an arm's reach. Then, with one hand braced upon the haft, he drove his mailed fist over and over into Canton's face before tearing the spear free and forcing the spymaster's body over the window ledge. With a horrifying sound, it crumpled upon the cobblestones of the courtyard far below, as twisted and broken as the man's soul.

At once, Bel threw off his helm and his gauntlets and rushed to the young queen's side. "Marina!" he whispered, and mindful of the child, pulled her into an embrace, "By the gods, are you hurt?"

"He killed her," she shuddered, staring into the middle distance, "He...he held her down and...and cut her throat."

Bel's blood boiled with wrath and fire, and his eyes burned with tears of fury. Never had he been one for words, and even if he had been, he knew nothing he might say could ease the torment of such an ordeal. Instead, he simply held her, hoping that in doing so, he might at least help her to feel safe once more.

"You were right," she whispered, "So many dead. My father...I saw...I think he's dead too...They're all dead..."

"Not everyone," Bel said, "Not you. Not Marcus."

"No," she managed. A pair of great tears welled in her eyes and spilled over down her pallid cheeks, "Not us. And not you."

"As long as I live, I will always return to you," he said, "No matter what." He held her ever tighter, losing himself in the emerald depths of her eyes.

"I know," she said. "I know you will."

A white hot flash gripped Bel's heart, and with a gentle touch to Marcus's brow, he breathed a great shuddering sigh. "I love you," he choked, his voice heavy with emotion, "I love you both."

Marina swallowed a great lump in her throat and with no hesitation, pressed her lips to his. "I know that, my Tower," she said softly, as her tears began to flow, "I know that too."

CHAPTER 42: THE STRENGTH OF THE PACK

For three days Royne sat imprisoned within a large iron cage mounted upon the back of a wagon, a makeshift prison for kingsmen spies and other prisoners of war. At the current time, he was its sole occupant, which allowed him plenty of time for uninterrupted brooding as the wagon trundled along at the rear of the marching column.

He was consumed with the certainty of failure, for on the morning after his attempt to persuade the general to change course for the Brock, the legions assembled, and by dawn's first light, they were on the move, ready to renew their foolish, impossible assault on Hedgeford.

Strangely, the prospect of a flogging or his own execution for striking Captain Velius meant very little to him at the present moment, for such a thing would only be carried out, it appeared, after the battle was decided, and in the meantime, he could simply ruminate and be miserable.

Black fire and red death… he cursed bitterly, hiding his face beneath his cowl. For a moment he felt a stab of panic at the absence of *The Book of Histories* and hoped dearly that Conor or Salasco had thought to take care of it. Anything, to save it from being torn up and used by some bestial soldier to wipe his bum.

Though I suppose it matters very little now, he thought. *All is lost. It is over.*

At noon on the following day, the battle began.

From his prison, he could not see it, but he could hear it in the distance—the shouts, the clash of arms, the blare of horns, and the cadence of drums. All around him, the guards sat restlessly, whispering in hushed tones. At regular intervals one might wander off to have a look, reporting back to his companions with a face lined deeply with consternation. Wallowing in his bitterness, Royne tried to ignore them, but as the afternoon wore on and the battle continued, he considered asking for news. However, when he discerned pugnacious glares with which the men regarded him—even more hostile than usual—he decided not to bother. *They'll die too before this is all over,* he thought, *At the first sign of defeat, they'll flee and I'll be left for the enemy like a rabbit in a snare.*

The prospect of his own capture allowed for further cynical brooding and while he awaited his fate, he imagined numerous possibilities in which he might meet his end. He would be paraded northward to Andoch to be brought before the court of the Guardian-King. There would be a great public spectacle as they announced the treachery of the Loremasters. The Chancellor and the Hierophant would rally behind the King's lies, and Natharis Tainne, by some strange path, would arise as the savior of the kingdom and the Order. In the absence of the Loremaster's Wisdom, perhaps the Keepers would be invited to return to the capitol, heightening their influence and clearing the way for the execution of whatever dark plot they had in mind—the destruction of the Order, the end of the Galadins, even the fanciful resurrection of the bloody Beast.

Regardless, in the end, he, himself, would be put to death, one way or another. He had caused too much trouble to be worth keeping around, as had all the Loremasters to come before him. They would be pronounced Blackguards and their legacy would be one not of wisdom and learning as the foremost scholars of Termain, but rather, of conniving treachery, villainy, and deceit. At least if Rastis were still alive, there was a chance they might share that spot at the block after all. It would be nice to have company in the end, and if he was to die, it would be a great honor to do so at the side of the man he respected most of all in his short life. His teacher, his father, his friend.

In all likelihood, however, he would simply be executed on the spot, a victim of the wanton slaughter characteristic of a victorious army as they sacked an enemy camp. Some drunken buffoon of a kingsmen would simply stab him with a sword or shoot him with an arrow without ever even knowing the prize he had won. Thus would end of the line of the Loremaster!

Such were Royne's thoughts as he sat in his cage beneath the shadow of the setting sun when finally, shielded from the eyes of his guards by the cover of darkness, he gave in to his despair, hung his head, and wept.

When dawn broke the next morning, Royne was awakened by the sound of the rusty iron bars of his cage squealing open and the gruff muttering of his guards ordering him to his feet. With as much dignity as he could muster, he wiped the drool from his lip, ran a hand through his hair, and disembarked. "Where are you taking me?" he asked.

"The general wishes to see you," the guardsmen said brusquely.

Royne breathed a heavy sigh. The air was clear and crisp, he noted, as he turned to follow behind the guards. That was at least some solace.

And suddenly, at the edge of the trees, the cry of a certain bird soaring high above his head brought him to an abrupt stop. *No...* he thought, *Was that...?*

"Wait," he asked, "The battle. We should all be dead. What has happened with the battle?"

The guards exchanged an impatient look. "See for yourself," one of them said, motioning ahead.

Royne followed after them and to his great surprise, it was not Hedgeford that he saw looming before him, but rather a small seaside port town. At least a dozen warships lie to in the rising sun, the sun's rays illuminating their mastheads like pillars of fire.

"Aiden's Bloody Flame!" he shouted as once more the gull cried out in mockery overhead.

A moment later, the guardsmen ushered him along again over the grassy commons outside of the town and into the narrow streets leading to the docks. Before long, the odor of salt and fish reached him, and here and there men were hard at work loading great crates of stores into the hulls of the captured ships. The small shingled houses of the port were not without damage from the battle; however, Royne could discern the overwhelming pride of victory emanating from the soldiers who milled about the dockside taverns to the bevies of elated locals, happy, at least for the moment, to be free of occupation.

It's a shame that in all likelihood they'll be back under the yoke of the kingsmen before the week's end, Royne thought, *But as long as the Brock holds strong, there's hope that it won't be forever.*

A small stone battlement defended by a line of ballista stood watch overlooking the harbor. It was here that the pair of guardsmen finally led him, and it was here where, gazing out over the line of war galleys, they found General Navarro.

"Well, Master Royne," the Gray Wolf said without turning, "What do you have to say for yourself?"

At once Royne's blood turned cold and his insides felt as if they had been bundled up and cast into the sea. "I'm not quite sure what you mean, sir," he said at last.

With a sigh, General Navarro dismissed the two guardsmen and turned to face the Young Loremaster. "In spite of your ignoble behavior these days past, I have chosen to listen to your advice—and then some." He motioned toward the war galleys and the squads of soldiers hard at work preparing for the journey north and east by sea. "Though it pains me to leave my land— my home—in its time of need, I have come to wonder if my services and those of my men might be better put to use elsewhere. For, as you have insisted many times these past weeks, the war is over in Grantis, and has been for some time—at least in so far as my skills might serve. It is time to acknowledge defeat."

Royne folded his arms across his chest and bowed his head. "I would not say you have been defeated, general. Rather, shall we say, that victory has been…delayed?"

Navarro's lips twisted into a hint of a smile. "Is there a difference?" he muttered.

Royne gave a shrug. "You carried the day here and deprived the Ironmen of a rather sizable fleet," he said, "That seems quite a victory to me."

"And now we flee to foreign shores."

"Consider it a tactical withdrawal so as to live to fight another day—and with allies."

"Sailors on land fight about as effectively as soldiers upon the water," Navarro said. He gazed out once more over the captured vessels, "I do not believe we wolves were meant to swim. Should it come to battle upon the waves, I am not certain we shall ever even reach the Brock."

"Nothing is ever certain, General," Royne said.

"A sentiment that carries equal parts hope and despair."

"So it does."

Royne breathed a sigh and regarded the galleys. Standing nearest at hand, Captain Velius oversaw the loading of the remaining war elephants onto what was the largest of the vessels and clearly intended as the flagship. The sight of the captain brought memories of his outburst in the general's pavilion and he could not help but feel the shadow of shame fall upon him for such irrationality. "I apologize for lashing out at Captain Velius," he said at last, "And I fully intend to accept the consequences of my actions, whatever they might be."

Navarro raised an eyebrow. "Denaron is a good soldier and a good friend," he said, "For what's more, he's loyal and he likes to fight. However..." The general paused, "By devoting himself to the elimination of his enemies, he may have sacrificed many of the skills necessary for maintaining allies."

"Well," Royne said, "As you pointed out, it was ignoble of me and you have my apologies...as does he."

The Gray Wolf's sardonic smile grew more pronounced. "We all act ignobly at one time or another," he said, "And as for the captain, well...a good soldier is one who fights for what he believes in—whatever that might be. He will not begrudge another for doing the same."

"Ha!" the Young Loremaster laughed with relief, "I'm hardly a soldier."

"Perhaps not in the traditional sense," Navarro said, "But here you are, caught up in the tide of war by your own volition, your own will."

Royne breathed a sigh. "Well, in any case, it's a relief to know I will not be flogged."

"I imagine it is, and I doubt the young Baron Galadin would welcome a man who freshly flogged his friend. Hardly a show of good faith."

"True enough." Royne grinned. "When do we set sail?"

"As soon as we finish loading the stores, we will be off. Your boy Conor has already prepared quarters for you in the flagship. We've dubbed her, the *Seawolf.*"

"Good," he said, "And I take it Salasco will journey with us as well?"

"Unfortunately, no."

Royne whirled around to find the Wall himself standing behind him, leaning upon his stave. He exchanged a nod with the general and returned his attention to the Young Loremaster. "I will not be joining you in the Brock just yet," he said, "For, even with the addition of the general and his legions, the Brock will be hard-pressed to defeat King Kredor and his allies all at once," he sighed, "I believe that there are others who may help us, others like us, others who keep to the old ways. Pariahs. Blackguards. I will seek out who I can and rally them to join the Brock in the north. I also intend to seek an audience with the University."

Royne's eyes went wide. "The University?" he said, "With the Alchemists? The Kordishmen who follow the Sign of Four?"

"Even now, the walls of their complex inside of Commonwealth have yet to be breeched by any of the kingsmen," Salasco said, "They remain an island unto themselves within a sea of enemies. Yet, not a man among them is a warrior and their gates remain forever undefended."

"The Alchemists are dangerous men," General Navarro said, "And powerful, but when the senate sought their aid in against the kingsmen, they refused. They claimed their knowledge was too important to waste in the banality of war."

Salasco nodded, "So I recall, though I hope to fare better in my negotiations. I, too, am overall, a man of peace."

"Then may luck be with you, Good Salasco," the Gray Wolf said, offering his hand, "And may you stay safe until next we meet."

"And you, sir."

The two men shook and Navarro made to depart, "Master Royne, worry not. We shall make sail soon."

"Aye, sir," Royne said, "I will be along shortly."

Once the general had departed, the two Blackguards stood in silence for a long moment, watching as the Gray Wolf joined Captain Velius and his men at the *Seawolf.* Royne's mind felt heavy, yet strangely clear, for after so many long months of stumbling around southward in the dark, he was finally heading north to the Brock, to his best friend, his brother. For what was more, at long last he understood his own greater purpose in the larger machinations of the Order and its never-ending tide of history. There were still many pages left in *The Book of Histories* to be read; however, he felt now a certain familiarity with their contents, as if the memories of the previous Loremasters were even nearer to the surface of his mind's eye than before, and to read the records of his predecessors was akin to remembering what he ate for his last meal or the nature of the weather on the previous morning. Soon enough, he would finish, and at long last he would begin recording his own thoughts and his own adventures. He would write the history of the Order's Fall and the Bard's Prophecy, when the Dibhorites returned and the Guardian-King sought to subjugate those he was sworn to protect. Never had he felt so honored and so unimaginably afraid.

"I wish you luck in your journey, friend," Salasco said at last, "May the Brother Galdorn safeguard and protect you."

"Thank you," Royne nodded vacantly. He sighed. "You believe there are other Blackguards in Grantis?"

"I know it," the Wall said, "Though I am not certain all can be trusted, for there is, of course, truth to some of the tales of Blackguard villainy. Not all men who refuse to take the Oath are like you and me." He paused. "Still, I have heard of some who might help. Old titles. Powerful titles. The Archer, the Fox, the Tiller, and more. Their aid would be quite welcome, as would the learning of the University and this philosophy of theirs they call the Sign of Four."

"The Sign of Four," Royne mused. He recalled his first meeting as Rastis's Steward and how Natharis Tainne and Hagan Shawn seemed to regard the alchemists with such disdain. *Could the enemy of our enemies be our friend?*

"Do you believe they will help us?" he finally asked.

"I do not know," said Salasco, "But until the war broke out between the Republic and the Guardians, they were held in very high regard by the Grantisi Senate."

"Enough to gift them a veritable fortress within the heart of their own city."

"True," Salasco added, "Although, let's not assume that they are wholly innocent. For, what I told you was true. Any man to set a hand upon the gates of their complex has been cooked alive in his armor while whole squads of kingsmen have been burned by falling snow—in midst of the summer heat."

Royne's brow furrowed with skepticism, "Surely you do not believe in such things?"

"I shall reserve my judgment until I know more," the Wall said meaningfully, "But you know as well as I that there are many mysteries in this world that defy logical reasoning."

"'Man is but a single eye gazing out upon eternity,'" Royne muttered.

"Aye," Salasco said, "And not all of the Hierophants were fools, you know."

"I suppose," Royne sighed, gazing forlornly at the masthead of the *Seawolf*, "And I suppose that if a man sets himself up as a seeker of truth, then it best that he never deny himself the opportunity to have a better look."

"So," Salasco said, "Why not have one?"

Royne's eyes went wide, "You mean...stay here? In Grantis? After all I've done to convince the general to aid the Brock?"

The Wall shrugged. "The battle for the Brock is a war waged with swords," he said, "It's the war the general and his wolves were made for. You and I, however....while we might face the same enemy as our martial friends, our way of fighting is quite different. It might do that we should arm ourselves with whatever might provide us an advantage."

The young Loremaster sighed, "I can't abandon Lughus. He's my brother."

"Nor should you," Salasco said, "And I'm not suggesting that you do. I only mean that we men of learning might find a better use for ourselves than idly awaiting the outcomes of battles."

"At the University?"

"Aye, at the University."

Royne frowned. Again, he gazed out at the *Seawolf* and the raucous company of soldiers. He did not relish being stuck below decks in such close quarters with them, though he could not deny that they had their uses. He sighed, "If we divide our purposes—you rally the other Blackguards, while I attempt to make contact with the alchemists—then perhaps we can afford to delay the journey northward a little while, if only so as to better help the Brock."

"So be it then," Salasco said, his face twisting into a broken grin, "I'll speak to the general. You should get to writing. When the men of the Brock find a fleet full of wolves seeking safe harbor upon their shores, it'll help if they should bear the Loremaster's letter of introduction."

"I just hope they get there in time," Royne said.

"It'll make little difference whether you sail with them on that account," the Wall said, "Though for the sake of the Brock, I sincerely hope so too."

CHAPTER 43: THE BATTLE OF ST. GOLAN'S

When news of the fires in the Andochan camp reached the leaders of the Galadin forces, gathered as they were to discuss strategy for the looming battle, Sir Owain Rook, wounded and grim, allowed a broad smile to spread across his lips.

"I still don't trust that bastard, Adolfo," the seneschal said, "But damned if he doesn't get the job done."

Lughus breathed a sigh of relief, but could not escape a flash of anxiety. "I just hope Geoffrey's safe. He left his armor behind in the name of stealth and caution. Hopefully he had no need of it."

"Sir Geoffrey's a brave man," Roland Marthaine said, "And a lot wiser than I think he himself even knows. I trust that we'll see both of them back with us before the dawn."

The other men nodded in agreement and began to talk quietly among themselves. Lughus turned his thoughts to the matter at hand.

While it was true that St. Golan's was surrounded by walls and his men had worked tirelessly these last hours to secure it with the addition of palisades and wolftraps, it was still a monastery and not a fortress. Thus, while it was certainly secure enough to protect those within, it could not claim the defensive amenities of a castle like Houndstooth—especially in size. Even while the forces of Galadin remained considerably outnumbered, the army was far too large to fit within the monastery walls, nor did the supplies the Cousins kept in storage come anywhere close to those that would be required to withstand a lengthy siege. Thus, while it would serve as a fine place to fall back to in the event of a rout, doing so would mean that the battle had already been lost.

And so we're left with only two options, Lughus thought, *Fight against overwhelming odds, or run, abandoning the monastery to the mercy of Andoch.*

Unless, of course, he chose the third option and agreed to surrender himself to the Chough.

Sacrifice.

The young baron sighed. He had no intention, of course, of turning over either Brigid or Geoffrey to the Guardians; however, perhaps with the prospect of the battle drawing ever-nearer, he wondered if he might still find a way to sacrifice himself—in some grandiose show of pomp and ceremony—that would not only appease the Guardians enough to spare the lives of the good people of the Brock, but create enough of a distraction to allow Brigid and Geoffrey to escape. Surely someone like Adolfo could assist with that.

He paused to recognize how useful, and more importantly, how loyal the Madder had turned out to be. Truly, if he were to end up surviving this whole ordeal, he would be certain to adjust his judgment of the man and grant him the honor and respect he was due.

If he survived. If *any* of them survived.

Lughus breathed another heavy sigh and sat back in his chair. His thoughts turned to Brigid and he felt a deep, aching chasm grow within him. Even in her wounded state, Geoffrey and Adolfo could get her out and keep her safe. Fergus too. From there, they could hurry to Houndstooth to retrieve the rest of Geoffrey's family and flee. By then, Brigid's wounds might well have healed, and wherever they chose to go and whatever they might choose to do, there would be no stopping her.

Thus, while he might die or be imprisoned at the hands of the Guardian-King, his friends, his retainers, his people would all live.

"No."

Lughus raised his eyes to the speaker and found himself locked within the gray-eyed gaze of the Argent Eagle.

"No," the Eagle said again. "I know what it is you're thinking," he said, "And you're wrong."

The other men gathered at the table—Sir Owain, Abbot Woode, Sir Deryk, and more watched in wide-eyed silence. Lughus's brow furrowed. "There's no other way," he said.

"Of course there is," his grandfather said, "We *fight*."

Lughus, gazing at the tabletop, sensed the nods of agreement from the men gathered round. "I can't expect these men to risk their lives—to lose their lives—when mine alone could save everyone," he said, "As baron, it is my duty to serve them."

"And they have a duty to serve you," Marthaine said, "But forget duty for now, for when you stare death in the face, you find out very quickly how little duty matters. It's not duty that holds these men here at your side. It's honor, it's trust, it's *love*."

Lughus felt a tightness in his chest and he could sense the weight of the gazes of his gathered retainers, but, still, he kept his eyes leveled and unfocused.

Yet Roland Marthaine was not finished.

"Any one among them would knowingly follow you into the bloody Abyss," he said, his voice like a boulder rolling down a mountain, "Not because of *duty*, but because of their bonds with you and with your grandfather before you, because they know, without even having to think it, that you would do the same for any of them. It's the Galadin way, and it's something that I always truly admired about Arcis, and something that I, myself, tried my damnedest to emulate."

All around him the men began to nod in agreement, their eyes smoldering with stern resolution that drove away any sense of fear.

The Argent Eagle breathed a sigh. "Besides, five to one?" he said, "Tell me. Would you trade any single man among yours for any five Andochans?"

Lightning flashed in the young baron's eyes. "Absolutely not."

"Then the battle hardly looks bleak to me," Marthaine observed, and casting his gaze about him at those men who until so recently had been his enemies, he asked, "What say you, men of Galadin? Is it true? Is each man among you worth five of those Andochan bastards?"

"You're bloody right, we are!" Sir Owain shouted as the other men cheered.

"Then let me hear you," the old man growled, "For Galadin!"

"For Galadin!"

"For the Brock!"

"For the Brock!"

"Then release the hounds!"

At once, the assembly erupted in to wild cheers of excitement. Men clapped each other on the backs, swore oaths, and called down curses on their red-cloaked opponents. Even Lughus felt his blood stir with battle lust and his sword arm tingled with anticipation.

"I told you," Roland Marthaine said quietly beneath the rallying cries of the men, "I lost you once already. I'd fight Dibhor's Beast itself before I lose you again…and so would they."

Lughus returned the old baron's nod and with a deep breath, stood up from the table.

"Thank you, my friends," he said, his eyes ablaze with inner light, "Let's show these bastards what happens when you take arms against the Brock."

With renewed vigor, the wheels of his mind began to turn, recalling the countless hours spent studying famous battles at the Loremaster's Tower, as well as the practical, almost intuitive knowledge that came with the title of the Marshal. He thought about the layout of the fields surrounding the monastery and the advantages and disadvantages of his forces. Beyond simply the numbers and outfitting of his troops—both likely at a disadvantage in comparison to the mighty war machine of Andoch—he considered Galadin's intangible advantages: loyalty, pride, fellowship, love—concepts that alone could have the power to make one man fight like ten. All at once, he began to see a way forward.

Dawn's first light revealed the armies assembled upon the plain. Arranged in ranks outside of the walls of St. Golan's, the men of Galadin prepared to make their stand. The armored footmen stood together in five companies armed with shields and polearms of various types—spears, pikes, halberds, and whatever else they could find. Each company would form a line of defense, a bulwark, to protect the even larger companies of archers assembled behind them. These men, a blending of deadly professional marksman to simple peasant militia, made up the bulk of the Galadin forces. Beyond the ranks of men afoot, a small company of lightly mounted skirmishers and another, larger contingent of mounted men-at-arms would be positioned along the northern flank of the army and led by Sir Deryk.

Across the plain, the Army of Andoch assembled in massive blocks of professional soldiers, those sworn to the various nobles houses and the red-cloaked Kingsmen of the Guardians. These were then supplemented by a smaller, though still formidable contingent of conscripted peasantry. Together, they formed a line that stood nearly six thousand strong with the professional fighting men outnumbering the conscripts two to one.

Yet in spite of the massive horde of footmen, it was the heavy cavalry that inspired the most fear. From the cavaliers of the Warlord's Tower, to the great and powerful Andochan lords, to the lowliest of mounted man-at-arms, they formed a line of steel and horseflesh that in number equaled the entirety of the Galadin forces. When the Chough issued the order to charge, as Lughus knew that he would surely do, the cavalry could strike like a blacksmith's hammer shattering a crystal shard.

And yet, regardless of this, among the outnumbered Hounds of Galadin, spirits ran high, and as their leaders took up position and prepared to fight at their sides—as was their custom—the rallying cries rose to a deafening roar.

Standing before the front rank of men at the center of the Galadin line, Lughus felt his heart glow. In spite of everything, he couldn't keep the smile from stretching across his face, and his eyes flashed with the breaking light of the dawn.

"This is it," Roland Marthaine observed. The corners of his mouth turned up slightly as he regarded his grandson, an unaccustomed warmth discernible in the cold granite of his stony features. "In spite of it all," he said, nodding in the direction of the rallying Galadin force, "It feels pretty good, eh?"

Lughus tightened his grip on Sentinel's hilt. "Yes, it does," he said.

Sir Owain strode toward them from his final inspection of the Galadin lines. "Everything's ready," he said, "And the men are hungry—as I'm sure you can hear."

"For the first time in my life, I actually appreciate the baying of your hounds, Rook," Marthaine said.

Owain smiled, and in spite of himself, removed his gauntlet, and offered his hand to the Argent Eagle. "If you'll permit it, Baron," he said, "I'll regret it if either of us should fall before properly making amends."

Without pause, Roland Marthaine took the old knight's hand. "A new day dawns in more ways than one," he said, "The Brock stands together, friend."

"Aye, it does."

From within the ranks of soldiers at their backs, Abbot Woode appeared. He had donned a chainmail byrnie over his brown habit and carried a longsword and a heater shield. Behind him, two other cousins, similarly armed and armored, also carried between them a large, two-handed hammer.

"Morning, Woode," Sir Owain grinned, "Here to offer us a blessing before the battle?"

Woode pursed his lips. "Oh Blessed Brethren, keep us safe from harm," he said, "And grant us the strength to send these fucking bastards back where they belong."

The old knight burst into laughter and even the Argent Eagle smiled. "Can't say that I recognize that from the Hierophants," Marthaine said, "But I approve."

"It's what St. Golan said to Aiden the day they first fought the Army of the Dead," Woode joked, "Or so I've always liked imagining. But speaking of the Ram, my friend, Baron Lughus and I decided that without your sword, you're even more useless than usual. So in light of the auspiciousness of the occasion, and because, quite frankly, we've little left to lose, we decided to offer you the use—temporarily—of Summons, St. Golan's hammer."

Owain's eyes went wide and he blushed. "You know I was only joking," he said to Lughus.

Lughus gave a smirk, but remained silent.

"Use it well," the abbot said, "But don't bloody lose it."

Sir Owain laughed. "I don't know what to say, Woody."

"Say you won't lose it," the abbot needled, "Still, better to see it in your hands than to leave it sitting idle in the chapel waiting to be looted."

"I won't lose it," Owain said. He held the maul up in the early morning light and admired the image of the charging ram carved into the steel head. "And thank you," he said, "Both of you."

Woode gave a nod. "Baron Lughus," he said, "Sir Geoffrey and Sir Adolfo have returned. Adolfo is taking command of his men further down the line, and the Vanguard will be along as soon as he dons his armor."

"Good," Lughus said, "I take it you'll be joining us too, Abbot?"

"I'm no stranger to the ways of war, my lord," Woode said, "We've all got our histories."

"Indeed," Roland Marthaine said. He peered across the plain. "It looks like the Guardians have sent a rider."

Lughus gave a nod, "I'll see what he wants." He paced forward away from the line of battle and out into the field. The horseman, a Guardian Partisan, reared up before him and to Lughus's surprise, it was someone he knew.

"Lane?" he said. He recalled their last meeting and the fight in the tower with Pryce. It seemed ages ago.

"Baron Galadin," the young man said, and Lughus noticed the effort with which the young man refused to meet his eye. *Or perhaps he's just trying to remember the message? Lane never was the brightest…*

"My Lord, the Chough, sends to offer you one final chance at mercy," Lane continued, "Surrender yourself and the other two Blackguards as well as the monastery, and those seeking refuge within shall be spared. Refuse, and none of you shall survive to see the sunset."

Lughus took a deep breath and glanced thoughtfully at the boisterous army behind him. A smile tugged at the corners of his lips and a sudden flash drew his eye to the top of the monastery gatehouse. There, wrapped in bandages and a woolen shawl, Brigid stood with Fergus. Even at this distance, she locked eyes with him and raised her palm. Beside her, Fergus eased back on his haunches and released a long, sonorous howl. When he finished, the Army of Galadin erupted in a cacophony of cheers and rallying calls.

Lughus grinned. "There's your answer," he told Lane, and turned away to rejoin the rest of the hounds, leaving the messenger alone in the field.

Geoffrey was awaiting him when he returned, standing alongside Baron Marthaine, Sir Owain, Abbot Woode, and the others of the Galadin guard.

"Quite a night you had, Vanguard." Lughus grinned.

"It seemed a bit cold." Geoffrey beamed. "Sir Adolfo and I thought the men of Andoch could use a bit of fire."

"Looks like the messenger's giving the Chough your reply," Owain said.

"We had better get ready then," Lughus said. He watched as Lane gave his report. The Chough shook his head back and forth with a great show of disappointment. For a long moment, Lughus felt the general's gaze from across the plain. *There's no going back now*, he thought, but aloud he said, "It's time."

"Archers, ho!" Sir Owain cried.

The men of Galadin fell silent. It had now come to it. The archers readied their longbows and stuck their reserves of arrows in the ground around them. At the same time, the front ranks of infantry adjusted their shields and set their polearms against the inevitable charge.

As Lughus anticipated, the Andochan heavy horse formed their lines. Their horses pawed at the turf and the bright scarlet trappings of the kingsmen and the myriad color of the noble household guards shone gloriously in the morning light. Secure in their armor and privilege, they directed their mounts at the Galadin lines, and at a signal from the Chough, spurred their horses to charge.

"On my command" Lughus shouted.

The pounding of hooves echoed with the sound of thunder as the riders screamed with battle lust and anticipation.

"Hold!" Lughus called.

The riders drew nearer.

"Lady save us," a pikeman gasped nearby.

"Steady, men. Steady," Sir Owain hissed.

Abbot Woode called out, "May the Brother Perindal guide us!"

The pounding of hoof beats felt like it was inside Lughus's chest. "Hold!" He shouted again.

Together, the Andochan riders lowered their lances.

"Holy St. Golan!" an archer whispered.

"Courage, men!" Owain said, "Courage now!"

"Together as one!" Lughus shouted, "Let fly!"

"Let fly!" echoed the command, up and down the line. "Let fly!"

As one, the archers of Galadin loosed their bows in a great torrent of piercing death. Men and horses screamed in agony as together they fell, stung in a thousand places by the massive swarm of iron wasps. At such a short range, the archers of the Brock, known to practice their marksmanship since childhood, could not fail to hit their targets, and with the power and strength of their longbows, even heavy plate armor was no match for the bodkins of the Brock.

Still, in spite of the hale of arrows, a few riders were able to make it through, and here the stalwart footmen—inspired by the archers' show of skill—endeavored to show their mettle as well, standing strong in the face of the charge and turning aside horsemen with their polearms.

And so it was that after the disastrous charge of the front rank of cavalry, a trumpet sounded from the Andochan commander, and Lughus watched as the second rank of horsemen, turned their mounts off and away, returning in a wide arc to the safety of their lines; however, more than a few fell to an arrow sent by one of the Galadin marksmen.

At once, the sight of the riders in flight, drew another raucous cheer from the Galadin ranks and Lughus raised Sentinel high above his head, whirling it around to rally his men. For, while they may have withstood the assault of the heavy horse, they would still have to fight toe to toe with the massive Andochan host.

Across the field, the Chough looked furious. Red-faced and angry, he bellowed the order for his infantry to begin their assault. Shouts of the Andochan sergeants relaying orders mixed with the kingsmen's cries for King and country, and like a monstrous beast awakening from slumber, the Andochan horde began to march.

At the order from the young baron, the archers of Galadin continued to fire. Volley after volley, shot after shot, hoping to cut down as many enemy soldiers as possible before the inevitable clash. Truly, the bows of the Brock had more than proven their worth, dealing death from on high like a rainstorm of steel. Adolfo's arbalesters in particular wreaked havoc among the enemy with mortal effect, cutting down sergeants and standard bearers with lethal precision.

After the second round of firing proved particularly brutal to the Andochan first rank, the slow moving advance became a sprinted charge. The Galadin archers continued to fire, while the footmen readied themselves to engage the enemy in the long anticipated melee.

When it came, the resounding clash of steel upon steel echoed throughout the countryside surrounding St. Golan's. The soldiers of the Galadin guard stood like a wall against the oncoming horde, sheltering the archers as they continued to fire as best they could, no longer in unified volleys, but at will.

Sir Owain Rook wielded Summons, the Ram's great maul, with a strength that defied both his age and his wound, carving great swaths through the enemy lines and crumpling armor and helmets like eggshell. The men of the Galadin guard rallied behind him. Inspired by the old knight's fury, they fought together as one, and before long, their glorious tabards of blue and gold were splattered with innumerable flecks of red.

Abbot Woode and his brother clergymen, too, showed that for men of peace, they could certainly hold their own in war, bashing with their heavy shields and hammering away with their swords, and from the trail of defeated foes he left behind him, one might have wondered if the dour abbot had missed his true calling.

Roland Marthaine crushed all who stood before him. His mace, Thunderclap, was only slightly more terrifying than his cold, gray stare. A veteran of more battles than even Sir Owain, the old man proved that experience was more than a match for youth, and before long, the kingsmen scattered like chaff before him, terrified to meet his flashing eyes.

Outfitted once more in the full regalia of honored knighthood, Sir Geoffrey of Pyle, with his farmer's strength, stood like a beacon of hope wielding his shield and cudgel. Oakheart and Acorn, the tools of the Vanguard, performed their bloody work, carving paths through the Guardian forces as befitted the legendary Blackguard.

And at the head of the Golden Hounds, Baron Lughus Galadin, the Marshal, heir of the Saint, and one-time apprentice to the Loremaster, led the desperate forces of the Brock. Where once he dreamed of fighting alongside the red-cloaked heroes of the Order of the Guardians, he now stood against the tyranny that they had come to represent. All fled before his wrath and Sentinel sang across the plain as he cut them down in droves.

Yet for all their gallant bravery, the men of Galadin could not hold out forever against the sheer numbers of the Andochan horde, and with the few short hours between the previous day's skirmish to the battle that began with the rising sun, they were utterly exhausted, and it was beginning to show.

Little by little, the Guardians began to hedge in the Galadin flanks, forcing them into a tighter and tighter defensive posture, like a hedgehog curling into itself for protection. In desperation, Sir Deryk attempted to lead a charge of the Galadin cavalry and mounted skirmishers, but was he intercepted by the remnants of the Andochan heavy horsemen, who yet remained a formidable force. Their battle now raged just to the north of the massive melee.

The fighting continued, more intense and more desperate with the full light of day. Beside Lughus, Naden, one of the men of his personal guard, fell to the blade of a red-cloaked kingsman, and while the Marshal was quick to avenge him, the death of one of his trusted men stung. This pain, however, increased tenfold when Sit Owain Rook, wounded once already, collapsed in the field beneath a flurry of red wounds. At once, Geoffrey and the Galadin sergeant Pike, dragged the old knight from the thick of battle, and while the seneschal's hand never once loosened its grip around the haft of St. Golan's maul, his survival remained uncertain.

Casting his gaze around him, Lughus exchanged a grim glance with Roland Marthaine. The old man returned it with a resolute nod before together, they rejoined the fray. It was hard and desperate work against an enemy that seemed to have no end, for in spite of the countless men Lughus cut down, there were always more ready to take their place. For hours, it seemed, the battle raged, and even with improved heartiness granted through the title of the Marshal, Lughus felt his body, and his mind, beginning to wear down.

He dispatched one armored enemy, only to turn just in time to partially deflect another kingsman's thrust. The blade almost seemed to burn as it sliced along his underarm, scattering a cluster of mail rings. A small trickle of blood ran down from his forearm to his wrist, but he ignored it, countered, and opened the offending kingsman's throat.

"You alright?" Roland Marthaine shouted across the chaos.

Lughus nodded. "Just a scratch," he said, and readied himself for more. For a moment, the barons, old and young, held one another in a silent gaze. Then, without a word, returned their attention to the battle and the endless waves of enemies.

When all of a sudden, a wild cheer erupted from the north that gave the barons pause.

"The Eagles!" men shouted, "The Eagles are coming! The Eagles! The Eagles are here!"

As if on cue, the thunder of hooves and a resounding clash announced the arrival of Marthaine knights and mounted men-at-arms. Joining with Sir Deryk, they smashed into the Andochan flank like a flash of lightning before a heavy rain. Battle cries of "Soar!" and "Take flight!" echoed those shouting "Release the Hounds!" and to the shock and awe of all assembled, Galadin and Marthaine now fought side by side against the Guardians of Andoch.

Lughus's gray eyes shone with disbelief.

"That would be your cousins," Roland Marthaine told him, "And they took their damn time getting here too," He smirked.

"You'll hear no complaints from me," Lughus said, "They're here now and that's all that counts. For that I'd forgive them a hundred times, but there's nothing to forgive."

"And I suppose loading horses onto keelboats to sail across the lake *is* a huge pain in the ass," the old baron grinned, "But like you say, better late than never."

With the addition of the Marthaine forces, the Galadin army rallied, and the fresh fighting men of the Argent Eagles gave pause to the advancing Guardian host. Still, the fighting raged on. The blood of the wounded and the stamping of hooves steadily turned the field to mud, and the wails of the dying mingling with the clashing of arms rose to a deafening roar.

At length, while the Guardians still outnumbered the forces of the Brock, they had suffered far greater losses, obliging the Chough to sound the call for his reserve forces, with the general himself to lead them.

Lughus, though weary and wounded in places, spied the Guardian commander, and raising Sentinel high above him, strode forth to meet him.

"You should have accepted the mercy I offered you, boy," the Chough said when the two leaders finally met blade to blade, "You would have at least kept your life and some semblance of your honor."

"My honor is intact," Lughus cried, parrying his enemy's slash, "I have a duty to keep these people and these lands free from tyranny—and I intend to do so."

"Ha! What does a Blackguard know of duty!" the Chough cried.

Again their swords met, and Lughus felt a painful tremor travel down the blade of his swordarm. The Chough was strong and skilled, but more importantly, he had the advantage of experience, while Lughus was—at least by comparison—untested. With a determined step forward, the Guardian brought his sword down in a quick succession of blows from on high and Lughus was forced to scramble backwards, bracing himself as best he could to turn the blows aside.

By the time he was able to leap back and recover his footing, he was breathing hard and Sentinel felt heavy in his hands. With the muscles of his arms half-numb and aching, he readied his guard and attacked, striking hard from below, trying as best he could to close the distance between himself and his opponent to catch him off balance. However, the Chough parried each blow with grace and an unnatural sense of anticipation.

"You may bear the title of the Marshal and the litany of violence that it carries with it," the Guardian said, "But that alone will not save you."

He struck again, and this time, Lughus stepped to the side, faster than the older man had expected, and with what force he could muster, he struck from the Guard of the Dragon, the same form, he recalled absurdly, that Crodane had used when fighting Stokes those many months ago. The blade bit into the unprotected area below the Chough's arm, and with a grunt, the Guardian stepped backwards, pressing his gauntlet to the wound.

Lughus took the opportunity to regain his footing and recover. He knew that although he had scored a hit, it was little more than a scratch, and as much as he had hoped to wear the older man down, the unnatural endurance of the Guardians kept the enemy commander fresh and strong. At the same time, the hours of near constant battle against overwhelming odds coupled with his own exhaustion and multitude of incidental wounds, had left the young baron struggling to keep his feet.

"This ends now," the Chough sneered. He raised his blade and leapt forward, bringing his sword down like a hammer blow from on high. Lughus gripped Sentinel with both hands, raising his blade in a desperate act of defense—

But the blades never met, as with the force of a falling tree, Sir Geoffrey of Pyle charged in from the side, sending the Guardian commander flying with a blow from the Acorn shield.

With a silent nod, the Vanguard offered the Marshal his arm and pulled him to his feet just as a great golden flash appeared at Lughus's other side.

Fergus uttered a deep growl and his green eyes glowed like some primordial creature out of a Wrathorn legend. In the morning light, his luminous coat shone like a second sun.

"You're right about one thing, Guardian," Brigid's voice cried. In one hand, she gripped one her daggers while with the other, she leaned heavily on the arm of Adolfo the Madder, "This ends now."

The Chough ground his teeth in rage. His eyes blazed with fury and his seething anger was palpable. "Curse you!" he snarled, "Dibhor take the Three!" He lunged forth, hacking with his blade in desperation.

Lughus whirled Sentinel around to counter the stroke just as Fergus leapt and caught the Guardian's steel vambrace in his slavering maw. At once, Geoffrey drove forth and swung Oakheart like a battering ram, crumpling the steel of the Chough's breastplate like eggshell and knocking him backwards to the ground. However, before Fergus could leap in again for the kill, the commander withdrew behind the safety of his men and their shield wall. "Kill them!" he shouted, his voice heavy with shock and desperation. "Death to the enemies of Andoch!"

At once, Adolfo shouted a command and a cadre of his mercenaries ran ahead to engage the Andochan line, while his cutthroats slipped past in pursuit. Lughus paused to catch his breath, and with a gracious nod, Adolfo transferred Brigid to Geoffrey's arm. Fergus barked merrily, his tongue lolling out of the side of his mouth.

"You couldn't expect me to just stand there," the Blade smirked.

The Marshal smiled and shook his head, then leaned forward to plant a soft kiss upon her brow.

The Vanguard breathed a sigh. "So back to it then?" he shrugged.

"Just a moment," Brigid said, "It wasn't just to face the Chough that I came to join you., but when I when spied them from the battlements, I wanted to be the first to tell you myself."

"What do you mean?" Lughus asked. "Who?"

As if on cue, a clarion call of horns heralded the arrival of yet another force. The men of both Andoch and the Brock looked on in confusion and disbelief as they gazed at the disciplined rank and file of Grantisi legionnaires entering the field. They marched by the hundreds to the rhythm of drums, their tall, rectangular shields in tight formations, their deep voices raised in rhythmic song. And behind them, to the wonder of all, marched a dozen great war elephants outfitted for battle.

From the heights of the foremost elephant, a standard unfurled proclaiming them to be the Fifth Legion—the Fighting Fifth—and accompanying them, rode dozens of other horsemen carrying banners with designs they all knew. At once, the spirits of the Brock soared as those of the Guardians fell.

571

"It's Nordren!" voices cried, "Nordren and the other barons!"

"And they brought a bloody wolf pack!" proclaimed another.

"By the Brethren! Even the wolves answer when the Hound sounds the call!"

Lughus was quick to seize the moment. There was no time to hesitate. "For the Brock!" he shouted as loud as his voice would carry, with Brigid and Geoffrey at his side. Fergus let loose a resounding howl. "Soar with the Eagles and release the Hounds!"

"For the Brock!" came the resounding answer, "For the Brock!"

By the time the sun reached its zenith, the Battle of St. Golan's had ended. Hundreds, if not thousands of men and horses lay wounded, dead, or dying upon the fields in a terrible red harvest. What began as a forlorn hope for the young baron of Galadin and his men, concluded as a great victory and a rallying point for all the Baronies of the Brock. For the Guardians, however, with their leaders defeated and their forces put to rout, it was the greatest loss in over a century, if not more, sending a clear message to King Kredor and all the Guardian Order. The Brock would not go quietly, and the Three, it seemed, had returned.

CHAPTER 44: THE REAVER

The sun had long since risen when Thom finally awoke from his swoon. He could hear the sound of the coastal waters lapping against the side of the rowboat and the smooth swish of the oars cutting through the waves. His clothes were half-soaked with bilge and his stomach churned with the pains of hunger. Yet, he was alive, and when he recognized the warm metal object gripped tightly in his chubby fists as the Key of Salvation, a tremor of excitement rocked his body. The Dibhorites, the dead—somehow he had survived them all! At once, he lurched upright, setting the small boat rocking from side to side.

"We did it, Magnus!" he cried, "We did it!"

"Aye, so we did, Thom Crusher," the big man nodded, "But quit your flopping about before you knock us both in the drink."

Thom breathed in deeply, and again gazed down at the glimmering relic in his hands. The Key—truly, if only Lughus and Royne were here to see it! He nearly smiled, when a sudden flash of intense pain caused him to grimace. His eyes snapped to his ankle and his breath caught at the sight of it— blotchy, purple, and swollen to nearly twice the size. "Lady's save us!" he said.

The corner of Magnus's lips twitched. "Aye, you fucked it up good," he said, "But now that you're awake, we can handle it."

Justin D. Bello

Thom winced against the pain and cast his gaze about. The sun had risen, but it was still relatively early. A light breeze danced upon the surface of the sea and the occasional gull flew past overhead. "Where are we?" he asked.

Magnus turned the boat toward the shore. "Down the coast a-ways," he said, "Out of sight of that fucking Lighthouse, that's for sure."

Thom's eyes widened at the memory. "The Lighthouse!" he said, "Lady save us, Magnus! We've got to tell the Guardians right away!"

Magnus's jaw set, and with the same rhythmic pace, he continued to row for the shore. "Why in the name of the Great Bear's Bollocks would I tell those bastards anything?" he asked.

Thom leaned forward onto his knees and he gripped the Key even tighter. "Magus," he said, "We're talking about the Dibhorites. This is important."

"Aye, and last I checked," Magnus said, "Your precious Guardians were looking to take my head—lest you forget the manner of our first meeting."

Thom sighed. "Surely the Key of Salvation is enough to buy your freedom!" he said, "You return it to them and I'm certain anything you've done in the past would be stricken from the scroll of your misdeeds."

Magnus fixed him with a glare, his great beard smoldering like fire in the light of the morning sun. "What makes you think that for even one moment, I would want a single word stricken from my story, eh?" he growled, "You—who for this many months—has been the scribbler of my fucking song?"

Thom's gaze fell. "I'm sorry," he said, and meant it, "But in truth, Magnus, this business with the Dibhorites goes far beyond you or me."

With a sudden jolt, the boat scraped ashore and Thom was thrown forward, falling face first into bilge water at the bottom of the hull. "Ah!" he cried, "Magnus!"

The Wrathorn stood, tossed the oars aside, and leapt to the shore. "Get out," he commanded.

Against the pain of his swollen ankle and the dirty water in his face, Thom righted himself. "Where are we going?" he asked.

"Get. Out," Magnus said, each word biting like a gale wind from the frozen north. "Get out of the fucking boat," he said again.

Thom's heart fluttered and he felt his skin tighten with fear, though he did as he was commanded. In silence, he began to follow the Wrathorn warrior inland to where the pebbly coast began to give way to grassy fields.

Something was different, Thom couldn't help but sense. Something was wrong. There was no mirth in Magnus's demeanor. The swagger seemed to have gone out of his step. As Thom watched him, he saw the big man's gaze narrowed and his eye seemed to be constantly darting around—at the sea, at the shore, at the sky. His breaths were slow and deep and his movements, so often chaotic and impulsive, had become steady and full of purpose.

At length, in a grassy hillock upon which stood a lone pine, the Wrathorn halted. He stood in silence, gazing out across the waters at the far horizon and listening to the gentle whisper of the waves. "This'll do," he said aloud, though more to himself than to Thom, so it seemed.

In spite of the agony of his ankle, Thom ambled up beside Magnus and, huffing and puffing, matched the big man's gaze. Again, the sense of dark foreboding gripped him, but he tried to ignore it.

"Right then," he asked, "What are we looking at?"

With a movement so casual as to avoid notice, Magnus drew his axe. "The end of the song," he said, and without warning, whirled Death around and sunk it deep into the flesh of Thom's belly.

"Lady's Grace!" Thom cried as he toppled over onto his back. At once, a pain unlike any he had ever known tore through his body. So intense and overwhelming was it that he did not even feel the impact of his heavy body slamming backwards upon the ground. Blood flowed freely in great waves, soaking his clothing and spreading out beneath him upon the plain. His breath came only in short, sputtering gasps, and a metallic tang filled his mouth.

Yet in spite of it all, he kept his fingers clenched tightly around Callah's Key, and his gaze stared fixedly upwards at the clear, coastal sky. He could still sense the slight warmth that seemed to radiate from the ancient artifact, just as the rest of him turned steadily more heavy and cold.

With a slow, measured pace, Magnus stepped into his field of vision. "I'd tell you that I'm sorry," he said, "But I'm not."

Thom, struggling just to breathe, remained silent. Even if he were able to speak, he was not quite sure he could think of anything to say. A small part of him wanted to cry, but not for the pain, not even for the betrayal, rather, for the sense of loss, of grief. Not for himself, but for his friend.

The shape that he recognized as Magnus was beginning to blur, yet still it continued to speak. With another slow breath, the big man knelt down beside him and gripped him roughly by the shoulders.

"I want you to feel this pain," he said, "To feel it, to know it, and to think of it always."

Thom's vision grew even dimmer and his mouth was bitter with the taste of his own blood.

"Know this pain," Magnus said again, "Know what it's like to stare Death in the face, and know that as loud as that bastard may be calling for you, know that you still live."

Thom's vision cleared for only a second, yet in that moment, he saw the Wrathorn's face gazing down at him, though it was not anger or resentment or pity that blazed within the big man's eyes. It was resolve and respect.

"Swear it to me," Magnus said, "There's some bloody rhyme or the like, but I can't remember it. Besides, in the end, I don't think it fucking matters so long as you swear."

With every effort he could muster, Thom whispered his oath.

"I swear it," he said.

"There's a storm coming, Crusher. A storm that's beyond the likes of one like me. Bur you, you—why! That soft, lumpy clay of yours has only begun to bake, and this thing coming is just the fire to form you, to make you strong. You'll need that strength, Crusher. You'll need it to see it all through and do what must be done. And one day, when it's all over, who knows? Maybe you'll get to scribble your own song?"

Thom wanted to speak, to voice the goodbye that he somehow knew was coming, but he lacked the breath.

"Bury me facing the sea," Magnus said. And with that, Thom's vision went black and he knew no more.

DRAMATIS PERSONAE

The Nation of Andoch and The Order of the Guardians

- Guardian-King Kredor Drude, Lord of Titanis, Protector of Andoch
- Rordan Baird, the Chancellor
  - His followers in order of rank: Commissioners, Constables, Counselors, Courtiers, Pages
  - Willum Harlow, Chief Constable, bearer of the Guardian Title of "the Hammer"
  - Commissioner Wilks Porthen
  - Constable Kedge Unwin
  - Constable Ortho
- Hagan Shawn, the Grand Hierophant
  - His followers in order of rank: Hierophants (Provincial), Prelates, Ministers, Celebrants, Acolytes
  - Provincial Padeen Andresen, Provincial Hierophant of Baronbrock, High Cleric of the Cathedral of St. Aiden, bearer of the Guardian Title of "the Breath."
- Dandon Rood, the Warlord
  - His followers in order of rank: Justiciars, Cavaliers, Gallants, Partisans, Cadets
  - Justiciar Sir Richard Cormier, bearer of the Guardian Title of "the Hart"

- o Justiciar Sir Angus Calderon, bearer of the Guardian Title of "The Stone"
- o Justiciar Sir Viktor Gaines, bearer of the Guardian Title of "The Spur"
- o Justiciar Sir Brennan Bercilan, bearer of the Guardian Title of "The Cough"
- o Cavalier Sir Lornis Ulban, bearer of the Guardian Title of "The Plow"
- o Partisan Galen Pine, his steward
- Lord Natharis Tainne, the Loremaster, boyhood companion to King Kredor, Keeper of the Lighthouse of Castone in the First Degree
  - o His followers in order of rank: Sage, Seer, Scholar, Scribe, Apprentice

- Lord Marcel Pryce, Viceroy of Grantis in the Name of the Guardian-King
  - o Marcel Pryce the Younger, his son
- Alvin Bemis, Earl of Dunfathom, Speaker of the Council of Lords, and Commander of the Lords' Private Levies
- Lord Deglan Tensley
- Lord Hanson Fowler
- Lord Basilar Gendrik
- Lord and Lady Lunette

The Nation of Dwerin and the Castle Blackstone
- Archduke Darren Beinn, formerly the Lord Sheriff of Dwerin
  - o His wife, Archduchess Josephine Beinn
    - ▪ Her maid, Livonia
  - o His son, Alan Beinn, called the Young Sheriff
  - o Lord Padraig Reid
    - ▪ Wilfred Barrow, captain of Lord Reid's scouts

- Assorted Members of the Court in Blackstone

The Nation of Montevale

- King Dermont Tremont, Lord-General of the Armies of Valendia, called the Plague King
  - Kurlan Malacco, his seneschal, Warden of Reginal, called the Death Knell
  - Inen Vilnois, Warden of Whitemane, called the Golden Garron
  - Vaston Delon, Warden of Roanshead, called the Boiling Sea
  - Wilmar Danelis, called the Sundering Hand, Warden of Tremontane Castle
  - Lord Giles Pronet, Warden of the Nivanus Mountains
  - Lord Jarrett Harren, Warden of the White Wood
  - Canton, Dermont's chief of spies
- King Cedric Tremont, called the Laughing King or the Black Horse
  - His wife, Queen Eloise (deceased)
  - Prince Larius Tremont (deceased)
  - His Seneschal, Sir Emory Knott
  - Prince Beledain Tremont, called the Silent Prince or the Prince of Bells, bearer of the Guardian Title of "the Tower"
    - Lilia, his lover, called the Blood Blossom
    - Marcus Tremont, his son to Lilia
  - Lord Leon Tremont, Cedric's younger brother, called the Black Lion
    - His daughter, Lady Valerie Tremont, called the Iron Fist, second-in-command of Prince Dermont's light cavalry
  - Lord Talvert Tremont, Cedric's youngest brother, called the Summer Storm
- King Marius Tremont, called the White Horse
  - His wife, Queen Annalisa (deceased)
  - Prince Gislain Tremont, called the Snow Prince (deceased)

- o   Princess Marina Tremont, called the Winter Rose
- Men and Women of the Light Cavalry under the command of Beledain Tremont
  - o   Jarvy
  - o   Horn (Harold Half-Wrathorn)
  - o   Briden Sheradan, Beledain's standard-bearer
  - o   Wendell
  - o   Rallo
  - o   Sparrow
- Other assorted knights and nobles
  - o   Sir Raylon Jace, called the Snow Bear (deceased)
  - o   Lord Talondaire, called the Young Talon, kinsman of King Marius on his mother's side
  - o   Sir Linton Traver, called the Steady Arm
  - o   Sir Gurney, called the Knight of the Rooster
  - o   Sir Trenton, called the Knight of Lilies
  - o   Sir Welmsey, called the Knight of Verse
  - o   Sir Cardolan, called the Ruddy Spear
  - o   Sir Armel, called the Stone Thistle
  - o   Sir Norton Wherling, called the Standing Stone
  - o   Sir Umbert Malet and his son Sir Guy

The Baronies of Baronbrock

- Lord-Baron Perin Glendaro, son of Harlan Glendaro and nephew to Loremaster Rastis Glendaro
  - o   Imanie, his wife
  - o   Millicent, Rosamon, and Alyson, his three daughters
  - o   Sir Dalton Griegg, his seneschal

The Barony of Galadin

- Baron Arcis Galadin
  - o   Luinelen Galadin, his daughter and mother of Lughus (deceased)

- - Crodane, formerly the Marshal after Wolfram of Parth, her seneschal, swordsmaster who trained Lughus (deceased)
  - Sir Wolfram of Parth, formerly the Marshal (deceased)
  - Sir Owain Rook, Seneschal to Arcis Galadin
    - Denan Flann, the master-at-arms
    - Walder Ross, the watch captain
  - Horus Denier, his steward
    - Jergan, the master of the wardrobe, and his wife, Willa
    - Brennan, the butler
    - Kelan, the pantler
    - Boyce, the chief of cooks
    - Ada, a maid
  - His knight retainers in command of the seven fiefdoms
  - Assorted soldiers: Naden, Pike, Tonkin, Grimes, Kender, Sedge
- Lughus Galadin, Heir to Arcis Galadin, former Apprentice of Loremaster Rastis Glendaro, bearer of the Guardian Title of "the Marshal"
- Fergus, a spirit hound of Perindal
- Randal Woode, Abbot of the Monastery of St. Golan the Ram
- Brigid Beinn, daughter of the late Archduke Danford Beinn and the current Archduchess Josephine, bearer of the Guardian Title of "the Blade"
- Geoffrey of Pyle, former farmer in the village of Pyle on the Spade, bearer of the Guardian Title of "the Vanguard"
  - His wife, Annabel
  - His eldest son, Karl (deceased)
  - His youngest son, Frederick
  - His daughter, Greta
  - His father, Amos
- Faden the Weaver
- Adolfo the Madder
- Gareth the Blade (deceased)

- Regnar the Vanguard (deceased)
- Grendel the Butcher (deceased)

The Barony of Marthaine
- Baron Roland Marthaine
  - His wife, Morgana
  - His son, Gaston Marthaine, father of Lughus (deceased)
  - Sir Ulfric Gond, his seneschal

The Barony of Nordren
- Baron Leoric Nordren
  - Sir Theobold Nordren, his son

The Republic of Grantis
- Royne, bearer of the Guardian Title of "the Loremaster"
  - Conor Vendik, his steward
- General Cornelius Navarro, the Gray Wolf, Commander of the Fifth Legion
  - Captain Denaron Velius, Navarro's Second-in-Command
  - Petran Gigas, Navarro's valet
- Salasco the Wall, a Blackguard

The Sorgund Isles
- Magnus Bloodbeard, Chieftain and last of the Bloodbeard Clan of the Wrathorn, bearer of the Guardian Title of "the Reaver"
- Thom the Apprentice
- Ivo, proprietor of the Sea Dragon tavern
- Pavlos, a cutthroat
- Slink
- Rodolf the Churl
- Dochet, Gened, Faleen, Nantes, Kradoc, Fleice

ACKNOWLEDGEMENTS

This book would not have been possible without the love and support of my family and friends. I appreciate you all and I am thankful to have you all in my life. Specifically, in the case of *The Blackguard's Bond*, I wanted to mention a few people in particular.

To Lorraine Hudson, thank you for being my first and most comprehensive beta reader. I appreciate all of your feedback and your thoughtful consideration of my characters and the world they inhabit. I can't wait to hear your thoughts on Book III.

To Joan Washburn, thank you for your support and encouragement. I hope you're enjoying the adventure and having a chance at a glimpse of the weird things that have gone on inside of your nephew's head over the last few decades.

To my parents, thanks for the support, especially to my dad, who, though not a reader, has made every effort with these books to try and to help in any way he can.

Finally, to my wife, Dominique, and to George, Heidi, and Bastian. No adventure is complete without you all and I hope you've enjoyed this one even more than the first. I love you always and forever.

ABOUT THE AUTHOR

For as long as he can remember, Justin Bello has always been a lover of adventure stories. As a writer, he likes to create morally ambiguous worlds full of characters who struggle to fight for good even when faced with seemingly insurmountable evil. He enjoys reading, writing, drawing, tabletop role-playing games, and more hobbies than he realistically has time for. A full-time English teacher, he lives in Pittsburgh with his wife, Dominique, and three children. Visit his official website at justindbello.com or follow him on Instagram @justidbello_author

Made in United States
North Haven, CT
20 November 2024

60351915R00357